DEMON IN WHITE

Christopher Ruocchio

DEMON IN WHITE

THE SUN EATER: BOOK THREE

DAW BOOKS, INC.
DONALD A. WOLLHEIM, FOUNDER
1745 Broadway, New York, NY 10019
ELIZABETH R. WOLLHEIM
SHEILA E. GILBERT
PUBLISHERS
www.dawbooks.com

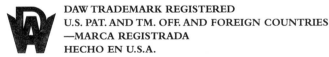

For my wife,

Jenna.

From our first year,

to all the years to come.

CHAPTER 1

BEHOLD A PALE HORSE

SILENCE.

The silence about the Solar Throne filled the great hall like water, like the deep dark of the sea. Not a soul stirred. From my place amongst the courtiers, I watched the two common soldiers where they knelt on the mosaic. They had crawled the length of the hall, proceeding down the central aisle flanked by members of the Martian Guard like scarabs in their formal blacks. How long had it been since two persons of so low a station had come to that exalted place? The white vaults had stood like Olympos atop the clouds of Forum for more than ten thousand years, and save for the artisans who had crafted them—creatures whom the nobile people about me would have spurned like insects despite the beauty they had wrought—I was prepared to wager my good right hand that fewer than a hundred serfs had knelt before our Radiant Emperor in all that time.

That they were in that place at all was a signal—clear as the changing of bells—that the world had changed. That they would *speak* in that place of gold and carnelian, that hall of ivory and jet, was a sign that the change was terrifying.

Both soldiers knelt at attention, eyes carefully fixed at the base of the dais where fifty-four steps rose toward the gleaming throne flanked by the Knights Excubitor in armor of mirrored white.

By the stars at her shoulders I saw that one of the soldiers was a ship's captain, but it was the other who spoke, rough tones betraying him for a common legionnaire. He had been prompted, coached on what to say by logothetes and by the eunuch homunculi who served the Imperial presence. But fear floated off the man in waves, and for a tenth and unnecessary time he bowed and pressed his forehead to the tile. "Your Radiance," he said, voice breaking. "Holy Emperor. I abase myself before you. I am

Carax of Aramis. I have been your faithful servant for nearly eight hundred years." His tongue tripped over the words, and I could tell that he'd tried to rehearse them. "I were at Hermonassa, Radiance. Were on the *Inviolate* when it fell." From the reports I'd seen of the battle, I knew the *Inviolate* had been the flagship of the defense fleet at Hermonassa. It had died nameless, for once violated it was the *Inviolate* no more. The woman beside Carax had been its captain. By rights, she should have ended her life after so devastating a defeat. Perhaps she intended to do just that when this audience was ended.

Carax spoke, describing the Cielcin attack on the flagship. "The Pale come aboard. Cut through the hull and swarm in. Ship's leaking air. Life support's compromised. I don't know a thing about the battle outside, but the captain's ordered retreat and we're pulling back to decouple the bridge section when—"

"Get to the point!" snapped the slippered eunuch at the soldier's side. At a gesture from the androgyn, one of the Martians advanced to chastise the legionnaire with the haft of his energy lance.

"Let the man tell his story in his own way," came the voice Imperial, halting the androgyn and the Martian in their tracks. Carax and the captain at once pressed their faces to the floor as a child hides from the thunderbolt. Caesar's words resounded from the throne, amplified by speakers hidden in the filigreed vaults above so that he spoke God-like from every corner of the hall. When he spoke again, it was not unkindly. "He has traveled far and seen much that interests us. We would not have his tale hurried."

Spluttering thanks, Carax straightened, still on his knees.

"But you wanted to hear about *it*." Almost I thought I could hear Carax swallow. "About the Pale King." I guessed the man had given his official report when the survivors from Hermonassa had arrived on Forum, and from that report had been selected to come before the Emperor.

I glanced sidelong at Pallino where he stood beside me, but my old friend and bodyguard did not so much as blink.

I felt a shadow stir in my mind, but listened carefully as Carax continued. "My decade were left to guard the airlock. Last line of defense. On the *Inviolate* the bridge section's got to by this long hall, and Thailles—he was my decurion—Thailles had sealed the door. A foot and a half of solid titanium, only they got *through*." His voice shook on the last word, and he hunched where he knelt, eyes downcast. "Cut its way in with a sword like those our knights use. Highmatter. Cut through the bulkhead like it weren't nothing, Radiance. Lords and ladies. Only it weren't like no sword I'd seen. It were too big. And all . . . twisted. Cut through the bulkhead like it weren't there." He seemed to realize that he'd repeated himself, and his face darkened. "Cut through the men, too. I never seen one of the Pale so big. Had to stoop in the corridor as it came at us. All black and silver it was. And when it see us standing at the end of the hall behind the prudence shield it bares its fangs at us. Smiling, like.

"'Surrender!' it says, and Honorable Caesar I swear by Holy Mother Earth it spoke our words." He rubbed his arms. "Said our lives were forfeit. That they'd taken the shipyards. Broken the fleet. We fired on him, but they had shields. Never seen that before, neither. Pale with shields. They just laughed at us, and their king, he said he was . . ." The man struggled with the name.

I hardly heard him.

I knew the name.

Syriani Dorayaica.

The Scourge of Earth.

The soldier's words seized in me, and once again I beheld a vision I had twice seen. First in the darkness beneath Calagah, and again in the cold clutches of the Brethren of Vorgossos. I saw the Cielcin arrayed across the stars, rank upon rank, file upon file, ship and soldier and swords uplifted, scratching at the sky. And at their head there came one taller and more terrible than the rest. Black its raiment and black its cloak, and its horns and its silver crown were terrible as the glass fangs in its lipless mouth.

"Did it wear a crown?"

Silence again.

I realized a moment later that it was I who had spoken, I who had disturbed the air and perfect order about the Solar Throne. The courtiers about me drew away, leaving Pallino and me alone on a little island beneath pillars tall as towers. Someone giggled nervously, and I felt the eyes of the Martians pick me out through their suit optics, their faceless masks dispassionate.

Carax turned, and our eyes met. His eyes widened. Did he know me? I did not know him.

"We will have order!" cried a sergeant-at-arms.

Because it was expected of me, I went to one knee and bowed my head. I did not press it to the floor as the soldiers had. I was palatine, and distantly a cousin of our Emperor. Caesar's eyes were on me, twin emeralds in that alabaster sculpt he called a face. Was it my imagination, or had one corner of his mouth turned upward in ironic amusement? Whispers burbled around me.

"That's Marlowe, isn't it?"

"Hadrian Marlowe?"

"That's *Sir* Hadrian Marlowe, the Knight Victorian."

"That's the Halfmortal?"

"Is it true he can't be killed?"

The sergeant-at-arms slammed his fasces against the tiled floor, brass tip ringing against the stone. "Order! We will have order!"

The Emperor raised a hand, and order was restored. A moment later, His Imperial Radiance, William XXIII of the House Avent, spoke in a voice that brought to mind the touch of fire and the scent of old wood. "Answer our servant's question, soldier."

Attention returned steadily to Carax and his captain. His eyes stayed fixed on me as he answered, ignoring Caesar where he sat amidst gold and velvet. "A crown?" The words seemed alien to the man, and he mouthed them stupidly. "A crown? Yes. It were silver."

Alone, this revelation proved nothing. Prince Aranata had worn a coronet of silver. The Cielcin had dozens of princes, perhaps hundreds, each the master of a nation fleet that plied the waterless seas of space. I had no reason to believe that Syriani Dorayaica, whom the Chantry called the Scourge of Earth, was the creature from my visions.

And yet, I knew.

But Carax was not finished. "He called himself a king," he said, and turning broke the inviolable protocol of the throne room by looking up upon the face of the Emperor. "He said he was coming for your crown, Honorable Caesar." On seeing His Radiance enthroned atop the mighty dais, the soldier's voice broke, and he prostrated himself once again, lying almost flat against the tile. No longer the center of attention, I stood again, peering over the shoulders of the richly dressed personages before me. "Your Radiance, he let me live. Killed everyone else in my decade."

The smell of incense burning in golden thuribles above filled the air, but I smelled the smoke of fires and burning men. I saw the corridor in Carax's tale as he spoke. The Cielcin king—if king it was—striding relentless, pale sword flashing. I imagined plasma fire and bullets breaking against its shield as its sword fell like rain. How bright the flashing of that blade! How terrible its glass-toothed smile! And when its work was done it seized Carax by his throat and plucked him one-handed from a floor slick with blood and strewn with the limbs of dead men. How clearly I saw that moment then: Carax alone against the enemy. I pressed my lips together in pity. I had a vision of boots dangling useless above the floor, and of the Cielcin lord holding this man calmly in its grip.

"Tell your master I am coming," it said, and Carax shuddered to repeat the words. Then it threw the man down like a child's doll and turned, vanishing into the wreck it had made, and was gone.

"I don't like this one bit, Had," Pallino said when the audience was over.

"I know, Pal." I rubbed my chin, leaned my head back against the pillar behind me. The Martians had chivied the courtiers from the Sun King's Hall after the Emperor made his departure, his massive throne carried on the shoulders of a hundred men and flanked by the Knights Excubitor. The vestibule outside the throne room was larger than many palaces, so high one could confuse the vaulted ceiling fifty stories above for the sky. Indeed, I'd heard it said there were mechanisms in the ceiling designed to suck all the moisture from the air, lest clouds form within and rain fall upon the nobility.

My lictor crossed his arms. "The bastards are getting smarter. Or this one is."

"Dorayaica."

"That's the one," Pallino said, then said again, "I don't like this one bit. The Pale are animals. They've always attacked without warning or order, burned cities and carried off people for food. In and out. But this bastard . . . Hermonassa was a military target. He didn't even raid the planet, just torched the shipyards and crippled the fleet. I bet it was him that did for the Legion base on Gran Kor, too."

Still rubbing my pointed chin, I added, "And Arae." Pallino had been at Arae with me, had seen the unholy mixture of Cielcin and machine the Extrasolarians had bred beneath the mountains on that arid and airless world.

"Could be. You think he's allied with the Extras, too?"

"It," I corrected. The Cielcin were not male and female. "And I hope not." An alliance between the Cielcin and the barbarians who dwelt between the stars would be a hideous thing. I shivered. Even after nearly a hundred years of waking life, the memory of my imprisonment in the dungeons of Vorgossos lay on me like a film. "It's bad enough facing the prospect of a Cielcin chieftain who understands our warfare without dragging Kharn Sagara and his ilk back into the mix."

Pallino grunted, and at last I lowered my gaze to look at the man who had come with me out of the fighting pits of Emesh, one of a mere handful of people who remembered me as Had, as only *Hadrian,* and not as Sir Hadrian, the youngest man not of the Imperial family ever to be named a member of the Royal Knights Victorian; nor as the *Halfmortal.*

My friend.

When I had first met Pallino, he'd been an old man. Hoary, white-haired, and one-eyed. He'd lost the eye fighting the Cielcin at Argissa a lifetime before. Old as he was, he'd been strong after the way of old soldiers, and when I had asked him to enlist with me, to leave the life of a coliseum myrmidon for life as a mercenary, he had not blinked the one eye remaining him.

He had two eyes now, and the hair on his head was black again, though not so black as mine, and the skin of his face and hands—which once had been spotted and leathered with age and use—was smooth again and youthful, though shot through with a tracery of fine scars like silver wire, the mark of the surgeon's knife and fingerprint of the gene tonics that had remade his body and elevated him to the patrician class. He'd received a new lease on life, and a second youth, all because I had asked it, all because I had named him my armsman and a member of my house when the Emperor knighted me.

He narrowed those eyes then, and made a warding gesture at the sound of Kharn's name. "You think they'll send us out again?"

"We'll know soon enough . . ." I said darkly, watching the brightly clad nobiles flock in the shadows of those impossibly high columns. I felt shabby by comparison in my black tunic and high boots, the tall collar of my greatcoat close about my jaw. I leaned back against the pillar, hands behind my back.

"Lord Marlowe?" a low voice interrupted.

I looked round, expecting to see a servant in the Imperial livery. But the man who spoke was not suited in the servants' white, but in blacks more worn than my own.

It was the soldier, Carax.

Before I could answer, the man took a halting step back, mouth half-open. "It is you. God and Earth and Emperor . . ." He sketched the sign of the sun disc then, touching forehead, chest, and lips in rapid succession. "It is you." His hand lingered on his chest, touching some amulet through the front of his uniform jacket. "I thought it were you in there. When you spoke to me, I . . . I almost didn't believe you were real." He glanced round at the nobility flowing around us. At the logothetes in their black and gray suits, at the guards in white and Martian scarlet. He had the air of a man who yearned to be invisible, which was impossible in the Eternal City. Ten thousand eyes were watching us, and ten times ten thousand. Cameras and microphones, hoverdrones and spydust and sensors of all descriptions kept their ceaseless vigil, spying on and protecting the Emperor and the cream of the Sollan Empire from treachery and death.

No one was invisible. Not even a lowly legionnaire.

"I'm real enough," I said, stepping away from the pillar.

Unheard by all but myself, Pallino muttered, "Enough to be a real pain in the ass."

I threw the old soldier a glance, and he flashed a rueful grin. "You spoke well today. I've seen many a great lord do worse." We stood opposite one another a long moment, neither speaking. The legionnaire was bald as any enlisted man, and I could see his identification tattoos standing out black against the dark skin of his neck. More than once he seemed on the verge of saying something, but he kept stopping himself. I had grown familiar with his affliction in the years since I'd risen to knighthood. Offering the fellow my best, most crooked smile, I said, "They said your name was . . . Carax, wasn't it?"

"Yes, sir! I . . . lordship." He stood a little straighter, leaped almost to attention. "Carax of Aramis, sir. Triaster. Second Cohort of the 319th Centaurine Legion, sir. Lordship. Sir." Only then did the fellow remember his salute and press a fist to his chest.

Returning the gesture I said, "Just *sir* will do, Carax. We are both soldiers."

When had that happened? When had I become a soldier? I hadn't set out to be one. I'd left home to study languages—to become a scholiast. Not to fight. Certainly not to kill.

To die.

"Is it true?" he asked. I knew what he wanted to know, but I let him ask it anyway. "They say you can't be killed."

Mindful of the cameras all around us, I knew I couldn't tell him the truth. Even if I could, whatever I said would not be believed. If I said yes, he would think me a fraud, and if no—a liar.

"That is what they say."

Carax nodded as if I'd answered his question. "They say you killed one of their kings with your bare hands."

"Princes," I said, raising two fingers. "Two of them. Though I had a sword." I caught myself toying with the ring on my left thumb, the ring I had taken from Prince Aranata's hand after I killed it. I clenched my fists to stop them fidgeting. I had taken the prince's head *after* it had taken mine. I could remember the sight of my own headless body toppling before the darkness took me. Before I came back. I felt Pallino stir beside me. He had seen it all. He knew the truth.

"Will the war end soon, sir?" Carax asked, eyes downcast, as if he feared to look at me. "Only . . . I've been on the Emperor's dole since before the war began. So much time on the ice, you know? Not been home in . . . I don't know how long anymore. Seven hundred years? Reckon I'm a grandfather a hundred times over. Family won't even know me when I get back. Lot of lads like me in the service. Lads never going home. Lads got no home. Just want the fighting done." His hand tightened on whatever it was he wore beneath his shirt.

Something in me broke for the poor soldier. Just how long had he spent in cryonic fugue, slumbering between the stars? His was the fate of many soldiers: to be locked away in an icebox to await their day, to serve their tenure piecemeal. A month—two months every decade. It wasn't just, but then, the universe is not just.

"I don't know," I said, and took a step nearer the other man.

He stepped back, as if afraid I might burn him. "But they say you can see the future."

"They say a lot of things," I said. I couldn't. I had only been shown the future. I had no power in myself. They say a man should never meet his heroes, and I feared I was letting this poor soldier down, but I could not tell him the truth. I stood in the Emperor's favor, and that offered me some protection, but to talk too freely in that place was to court disaster. "But the war will end, Carax. One day. And perhaps we will meet again when that happens, eh?"

I had expected the man to slump, defeated by my lack of a proper response, but he brightened and stood a little straighter. "Wanted to give you something, sir. If you'll let me." He spoke as if the thought had just occurred to him, and at once he drew a slim chain from around his neck and offered me the little silver medal on his outstretched hand. "I were at Aptucca, sir. Fifty years back. I only wish it were something better, but I don't have much."

It was prayer medal with an icon of Fortitude embossed on its front. I took it and held it in my palm, trying to keep my feelings from my face. I did not and do not believe in the Chantry religion. But I smiled. "Thank you, soldier. I'm glad you were at Aptucca, I—"

"How did you do it?" The words came spilling out of him. "How did you get the Pale to retreat without firing a single shot?"

"I . . ." My words trailed off as I turned the medal over. It was a small thing, no larger than the end of my thumb and round as a coin. On its back side was the Imperial sunburst, twelve rays twisting. But over it—carved as with the point of a knife—was a crude trident, a pitchfork such as a devil might carry. Such as the pitchfork embroidered on my greatcoat in crimson thread. Its shaft passed directly through the heart of the Imperial sun precisely as the one on my chest pierced a pentacle. I shut my fist and hid the thing at my side. "I killed their prince, too." I smiled, though it was not the whole truth. They had taken me aboard their vessel when I challenged Prince Ulurani, and the Prince had accepted, that it might avenge the death of its fellow prince, Aranata. While I'd distracted them with the duel, Pallino and Lieutenant Commander Garone had managed to place charges throughout the interior of their ship. We had held them to ransom, and they had fled.

The Cielcin were not human. They could not be reasoned with like humans. I'd learned that on Vorgossos with Aranata nearly three centuries before.

I realized that Carax was looking at me, hoping for a story. I shrugged, trying not to think about the treasonous, blasphemous amulet he had given me. "The Cielcin don't have laws exactly. They have rulers—and if you kill one, they don't know what to do. When I defeated their prince at Aptucca, they retreated to choose a new leader."

"A bloodless victory," the soldier said, grinning ear to ear.

"Nearly bloodless," I said, but it was Aranata I thought of, black blood staining the pale grass in the gardens of Kharn Sagara.

"Would you bless me, sir?" Carax stammered. "Lordship? I thank Earth every day she sent you to us. I'd have died at Aptucca, I know it. I had dreams about it for weeks. But you saved me. Saved all of us." And then he went to one knee, head bowed as one about to receive knighthood, hands clasped above his head.

"Oh, get up," Pallino mumbled, but Carax did not hear.

"Halfmortal Son of Earth, protect us."

The edges of the medallion pinched against my hand. I had known for a long time that there were those in the legions who thought of me this way, but none had come to me before. My own men knew me well enough to know that I was a man, though many of them had seen my death with their own eyes. But the legend of me had gone beyond me, traveled with Bassander Lin and his soldiers back amongst the wider legions.

There were always cults among the soldiers, though worship of any gods save Mother Earth and the God Emperor was forbidden. As in Rome so long ago, when the soldiers worshiped Mithras and the Unconquered Sun, so our soldiers worshiped the Cid Arthur and—like my friend, Edouard, and the Romans before him—the ancient Christ.

This lonely soldier worshiped me, and I had no power to bestow blessings, and no hope to give.

I felt at once very, very tired.

So I took his hands in mine. They seized me with a fervor I had not expected, nor felt in any person save Valka for more years than I could recall. "Get up," I said, and pressed the medallion back into his hands, imagining that to him it gained some special significance because I had held it.

It was a relic now.

There were tears in the soldier's eyes when he stood. "They say it's hopeless, master. The war."

Master. The word echoed in my ears.

"They say a lot of things," I said again, and drew back. "There is always hope." And I clapped the man on the shoulder and sent him on his way. He looked back the whole while, bumping into court logothetes and women dressed in bright gowns, until at last he was lost in the throng of people and swallowed up.

I never saw him again.

CHAPTER 2

THE FIRSTBORN
SON OF EARTH

A FULL TWO DECADES of the Knights Excubitor marched around
me, ten to either side, such that I walked at the center of their column. I
must have looked out of place amongst their mirrored armor and red capes,
a grim shadow amidst all that bright finery. As was their custom, they
marched with highmatter swords active and held in both hands before
their faces, ready to kill me if I made any sudden moves. I was acutely
aware that I had no weapon myself. My sword had remained on my ship,
and they had not even permitted Pallino to accompany me, and no wonder.

We marched down corridor after gilded corridor, over patterned carpets thick as the centuries, beneath Rococo scrollwork and baroque images
old perhaps as Earth herself. Golden light streamed through crystal windows, revealing in narrow slices the shining towers and the infinite, bottomless sky beyond.

Perhaps you've seen it, if only in a dream? The Eternal City: her fair
towers gleaming in the sun. Her halls great as cities rearing their mighty
faces through banks of rosy cloud. Colossal statues looming like shadowy
giants over windy streets and airy plazas. Hanging gardens as in Babylon
of old flowering from terraces above a sky ten thousand miles deep. The
Eternal City: old and venerable as sages, proud and beautiful as any queen.
She was the heart and eye of the galaxy. The axis about which all our
worlds turned.

We passed beneath an arched window, and far below I saw the knife-
edged shape of wings where lighter craft patrolled the skies below. They
sailed beneath the arched shadows of a white aqueduct that carried water
from one floating isle to the next.

I would have stopped if the Excubitors would allow it.

They would not allow it.

The Emperor was waiting.

The approach to the Imperial apartments in the Peronine Palace brought us in time to the Cloud Gardens, where silver fountains played beneath misty boughs lit even in daylight by glowspheres like distant stars. I had walked there but once before, on the day of my investiture, when His Imperial Radiance had made me a knight and restored me to the nobility. Before I had been *outcaste,* disowned by my father, without title or name.

The memory of that other day dogged my steps as I went. It had been right after I'd first arrived on Forum, fresh from my confrontation with Prince Aranata aboard the *Demiurge.* Nearly three hundred years had passed—eighty for me. So long ago, and yet still I heard the ringing of His Radiance's voice beneath the dome of the Georgian Chapel.

"In the name of Holy Mother Earth and in the light of her sun, I, the Sollan Emperor William of the Aventine House, the Twenty-Third of that Name; Firstborn Son of Earth; King of Avalon; Lord Sovereign of the Kingdom of Windsor-in-Exile; Prince Imperator of the Arms of Orion, of Perseus, of Sagittarius, and Centaurus; Magnarch of Orion; Conqueror of Norma; Grand Strategos of the Legions of the Sun; Supreme Lord of the Cities of Forum; North Star of the Constellations of the Blood Palatine; Defender of the Children of Men; and Servant of the Servants of Earth, call upon you to kneel."

I sank to my knees as I was ordered before the steps of the altar. Incense burned and votive candles, and in the niche above the altar fey shadows danced against a statue of the God Emperor triumphant, one foot crushing a marble cube. His living descendant stood over me, holding in his hands an ancient sword. Not highmatter, but common steel and so black with age that at first I thought it raw iron. The pompous grandeur of his titles still ringing in the air, Caesar stood a moment, and behind him a panegyrist in robes of sable and cloth of gold sang out in Classical English, saying, "In the name of Holy Mother Earth and in the light of Her Sun we pray! May the Mother bless her servant."

The soldiers and courtiers at my back—my friends and enemies together—murmured the benediction, "O Mother, bless us all."

Then Caesar spoke. "Do you, Hadrian Marlowe, pledge yourself now and forever to our service? To the service of your Emperor and of the Empire which he serves?"

Knowing what was expected of me, I said, "I do."

"Do you believe in our Creator, the Holy Mother Earth? Do you believe in the God Emperor, Her firstborn son and heir—our ancestor? Him who crushed the Mericanii and the machines and delivered the universe once more into the hands of men?"

"I do," I said, but I did not believe it.

"Do you pledge your sword, your possessions, your powers and faculties—your very life—to the defense of our Empire?"

"I do."

"Do you swear to forgo reward, to seek justice for its own sake?" I kept my head bowed all the while, hiding my face, afraid something of my uncertainty or disquiet might show there and be read by His Radiance.

"I do."

"To live with temperance through feast and famine?"

"I do."

"To act with prudence in matters great and small?"

"I do."

"To show fortitude in the face of tribulation?"

"I do."

"To safeguard the honor of your fellows?"

If they have any, I thought, but said only, "I do."

"And of your betters?"

I hesitated only an instant, thinking of my lord father, of Balian Mataro, and the lords I had met in the vestibule of Vorgossos. Then I thought of Valka, of Pallino and the rest. My friends. My family. And so it was not a lie when I answered, saying: "I do."

"Do you swear to respect the honor of any person: man, woman, or child?"

"I do."

"And to defend it?"

"I do."

"To never refuse the challenge of an equal?"

There were so many oaths. Too many, and I confess that I have had to find a book on the shelves here to get them all down correctly. But I answered, "I do."

"Do you swear to despise cruelty, deceit, and injustice?"

"I do!"

"Do you swear to see to its end any course begun?"

I have rued that oath more than all the others, though I thought little of it as I answered, "I do."

"And do you swear to keep faith with your oath, from this day, until your dying day, in the name of the Emperor, and of the God Emperor, and of the Earth who is Mother and Victim of us all?" And here His Radiance made the sign of the sun disc, holding his saber vertical before him as he touched forehead and heart and lips, and I sensed that everyone behind me moved with me as I mirrored the gesture, moving in a silence deepened somehow by the clink of jewelry and the rustle of human action that disturbed it.

As I made the gesture, I said, "I do."

The Emperor lowered his sword and—laying it first against my left shoulder, then my right—dubbed me, saying, "Then rise a knight, *Sir* Hadrian, and Lord Marlowe in your own right." He offered me his left hand then, and I kissed the ring upon his thumb, the one which bore the twelve-rayed sun that was the emblem of his house.

There is a strength in ceremonies, a power in ritual that *is* whether or not we believe in the principalities upon which those rituals are founded. So despite my cynicism, I could not help but feel a warm flowering of love in my chest as I stood and the swell of pride. I was a knight, and no mere knight, but a knight of the Royal Victorian Order, one of the Emperor's own.

There are not many people in the galaxy who can claim to have visited the Peronine Palace, that palace within the greater palace of the Eternal City where the Royal Family makes its home. There are even fewer who can claim to have visited more than once.

On that second visit, the great doors swung open soundlessly, and within, the mechanisms of a great clock chimed. Upon crossing the threshold, the pace of the Excubitors changed, flowing seamlessly from a brisk march to a slow and steady goosestep. The ringing of their boots on the tile aligned with the ticking of the clock whose pendulum swung free and mighty above the pointed arches ahead.

We came at last by many turnings to a water garden built of the whitest marble. Bright fountains played on waters thick with pale lotus blossoms and the azure blooms of nenuphars. Two women sat in one corner softly plucking at harpstrings while His Radiance sat in a humble seat beside a small table. Four of his Excubitors stood near at hand, watching me through mirrored masks. I bowed as my guard saluted, right hand over my heart, the left thrown wide. "Your Radiance," I said, "I am honored to have been summoned."

Caesar William rose from his seat—setting aside a small, black book he'd been reading—and approached me with a jovial wave and a warm smile. "Sir Hadrian! It is good to see you again."

I looked down at my feet. "I wanted to apologize, Radiance, for speaking out of turn at the soldiers' audience earlier."

"It is forgotten already, cousin! Please! Stand upright that we may see you." The Emperor smiled as I stood and gestured to dismiss my escort. The Excubitors retreated backward, folding away between painted columns, leaving me with the impression that they were not truly gone, but waiting invisibly amongst the pillars. "We have not yet had occasion to thank you for your service at Aptucca. That is two of these Cielcin princes you've put an end to."

Bowing my head, I said, "Again, you honor me, Radiance."

"The honor is yours." The Emperor waved one velvet-gloved hand, rings glittering, indicating that I should walk with him. "Would that all our servants were so effective."

I had no response to that and so said nothing, but walked in step with His Radiance around the pools, our shadows leading the way. The Emperor was taller than I, and though I knew him to be more than four times my hundred years, there was no silver in the red of his hair. But for the red velvet of his long gloves and slippers, his suit was of the most brilliant white silk, chased with gold. If I had felt underdressed outside the Sun King's Court, I felt insignificant in Caesar's presence. His rings alone might have fetched the price of a planet—not for their gems or their craftsmanship, such things could be manufactured cheaply enough—but for their age. I did not doubt that each of them had come out of Old Earth before the fall.

"They are singing your praises throughout the Empire, you know? Defeating the Pale at Aptucca without spilling a drop of human blood."

"Would that it were so," I said soberly.

The Emperor stopped his steady pace. I could feel his eyes upon me, burning a hole in my cheek. "It is so. We have decreed it so, and you would do well to stand by the official tale."

"As you say, Radiance." I dared not turn and meet his gaze, risked only a sidelong glance. His Imperial Radiance William XXIII was frowning, a slight furrow slashed between his eyes. Then it was gone, expression returned to one of pharaonic calm. Recalling that expression makes me hesitate even to this day. Aptucca was a stunning victory, but the lies the propagandists in the Ministry of Public Enlightenment piled atop the truth made it shine out all the more.

"You're certain the prince is dead?" Caesar asked, resuming his orbit of the pool.

I glimpsed one of the Excubitors between the pillars, watching through the hollow eyes of his mask. "Quite certain, Your Radiance. I killed Ulurani myself."

His Imperial Radiance nodded, traced the line of his jaw with one velvet-wrapped finger. Something plainly was weighing on the Imperial mind, but we walked on in silence a moment, passing delicate frescoes on the walls of the quadrangle depicting fantastic tableaus of nymphs and angels.

"Tell me something, Hadrian," the Emperor said. Something in his tone caught my attention, and I turned to look at him. "Are you my man?" He had abandoned the royal *we,* and in doing so revealed himself—though it is blasphemy for me to record these words—as only a man, and one exhausted by the crown and station he bore upon too-narrow shoulders.

I did not know how to answer him. "Your Radiance?"

"Enough of that. Answer me. Whom do you serve?"

Had he seen that treasonous medallion Carax had tried to give me? Did he believe I plotted against his throne and family? I felt my knees begin to bend and cursed myself for it. To kneel would be to appear contrite and so guilty. So I did not kneel, though I sensed a great many things hung upon my answer, my life not least of all. "I am a soldier of the Empire," I said. What else could I say? I had not wanted to be, but few is the number who live the lives they wish for.

His Radiance huffed through his nose. "The Empire . . . very good. In that case, I have a job for you." His irritation fading to amusement, he turned his back on me and examined the nearest fresco. It depicted an icon of Beauty rising from the sea, high-breasted and golden-haired. "Have you heard about this business on Gododdin?"

"Gododdin?" I echoed, not sure I'd heard the name correctly.

It was the first time in my life I'd heard the name. The name of the planet I would one day destroy. How insignificant it seemed to me in that moment! A meaningless word, a meaningless world.

"It's a primary Legion base between the Sagittarius and Centaurus Arms of the galaxy. We've been using it to stage troop deployments across

Centaurus as the Cielcin advance. Intelligence dispatched a Legion to Nemavand in Ramannu Province, but it never arrived."

Something cold turned over in my stomach. "Another lost legion?" More than a dozen had vanished in the last century, convoys hit while traveling at warp, the soldiers taken or slain in their icy sleep. I had been sent to locate the 378th Legion on Arae decades earlier, and but for a few survivors, I had failed. "The Cielcin?" It had not been the xenobites on Arae, but the Extrasolarians.

"Quite possibly. Ramannu Province is badly in need of supplies and reinforcements, and the loss of the caravan may cost them dearly. We do not wish to lose another province, cousin. We require that you make all possible speed for Gododdin, ascertain what has happened to our legion, and return them if possible."

I felt the jaws of the trap close around me. It was an impossible task. On Arae, at least, there had been a planet nearby, a place worth searching. Though our chances had been slim, we'd had a trail to follow. They may have been singing my praises throughout the Empire, but they sang too loudly. I had flown too close to the sun—and standing so near the Emperor, the Firstborn Son of Earth—that thought nearly brought a smile to my grim face.

The sun, indeed.

I was meant to fail, that I might return humbled and be made to abase myself before the Solar Throne, to crawl the length of that interminably long hall beneath the eyes and nervous laughter of the high lords and ladies of half a billion worlds.

But something was missing. The Emperor would not have called for a private audience to tell me what any of his servants and logothetes might have done. I looked again around the garden, at the lotus blossoms and nenuphars and the icon of Beauty reclining upon her shell. At the Excubitors and the eunuch functionaries lurking in the shadows, always waiting for the Imperial order to approach and be useful.

I looked at the Emperor again, and because it was expected of me, said, "As you command, Honorable Caesar."

His Imperial Radiance did not reply at once, but remained standing with his back to me. "For more than seven hundred years now we've been at war. Too long." He raised a hand, two ringed fingers extended, like a priest issuing a benediction. "We are going to tell you something, Sir Hadrian. Something that is not to leave this garden." And here he turned, hand still raised, eyes narrowed. "Assuming, of course, that you *are* truly our man." I knew better than to say anything, to interrupt that most exalted personage. Still His Radiance waited as if in expectation of a reply. But I had stood before the throne of the Undying in Vorgossos, where the hours fell like seconds and were lost. I had learned to out-sit Kharn Sagara. I could out-sit the Emperor. His placid face twitched in the smallest smile I have ever seen. "Very good." He let his hand drop and, without preamble, said, "I am old, cousin. I would see this war end before my reign does." The royal *we* was gone again, but he amended the breach as he continued. "You are thinking that we do not look old, but you are palatine. You know how quickly the end comes for us when it does. We must think to the world we wish to leave our children—and to the children we wish to leave our subjects. And so we have a request—one we will not require of you." I did not believe that for a second, as the barest request of the Emperor was ever the gravest command. "In your travels to Gododdin, you will take our son, Alexander. He is an admirer of yours and in need of seasoning."

You will take our son, I thought. *A request indeed.*

"As you wish, Radiant Majesty."

"Nemavand lies on the border between Centaurus and the Norman Expanse. We are not willing to lose this province, Sir Hadrian, or to risk the Cielcin spilling from the frontier into the mass of our Empire," the Emperor said, looking back over his shoulder. He clasped his hands behind his back, the red of the long gloves standing out bright against the white of his coattails. "We trust the Halfmortal-Hero-of-Aptucca will not fail us."

"Of course not, Radiant Majesty," I said, shutting the trap about myself. To fail now was to lie to the Emperor. And to lie to the Emperor was death. I bowed my head, hoping the angle and my fringe of ink-dark hair would hide my face. Was the Emperor threatening me? Or only mocking?

The Emperor waved one hand glittering with gold. "Then go. Our logothetes will inform you as to the particulars of the Gododdin mission, and a messenger will be sent to find you when you must collect Alexander. You are to be careful with him, but to treat him as you would any squire."

"As you wish, Radiant Majesty." Aware of the Excubitors, I dared, "May I ask His Imperial Radiance a question?"

The Holy Sollan Emperor replied, "But of course, cousin."

I inhaled sharply. "I have had a request for access to the Imperial Library on Colchis pending for the last fifty years." Fifty-three, in point of fact, but that was not the moment for pedantry. "I would very much like access to the archives."

His Imperial Radiance frowned slightly. "The archives? Whatever for?" Access to the Imperial Library at Nov Belgaer was limited to the scholiasts who staffed it. Not even my position as a Knight Victorian could open the doors; only a writ of approval from the Imperial Office could do that.

How could I answer the Emperor? I could not tell him the truth, that I sought answers about what had happened to me aboard the *Demiurge*. About the howling Dark beyond death. About the Quiet. Kharn Sagara had told me the Mericanii machines believed the God Emperor of old had been aided by the same forces that had delivered me from death. It stood to reason that somewhere, buried in some forgotten corner of that most ancient library, there yet remained some clue, some scrap of evidence to further my quest. But to acknowledge there were alien forces in the universe older and perhaps greater than man was a heresy punishable by death. Even to admit my knowledge of the Quiet would have been enough to invite disaster—and not only for myself, but for Valka, for Pallino and Crim and all the others who knew the stories of Hadrian Halfmortal were not stories at all.

But the Emperor's eyebrows were rising with each passing microsecond, and I had to say something. "On Vorgossos, the Undying said the Cielcin have been raiding our worlds for far longer than we believe. That this war is only the full-scale invasion following centuries of smaller attacks like the first battle at Cressgard. The Colchis library is meant to keep a copy of every text in the Imperium. It is possible some account of these earlier raids exists, but lacking reference to the Pale directly has been overlooked. I am not only a knight, Radiance, but a scholar. If there is something in these accounts which might aid the current war effort, I think it worth the cost of a few years of my time to uncover it."

"Do you?" the Emperor asked, and clasped his hands behind his back again. "It is for us to decide what the years of your life are worth, Sir Hadrian." He bit the words off sharply, and it seemed that some shadow passed behind his mask-like face. "But perhaps . . . This request of yours is new to us! It had not been brought to our attention these past years," he said. That, I thought, was a lie. A request from one of his Knight Victorians—particularly his youngest and most well-used—would have crossed his desk at once. He had ignored it. "We will consider it upon your return."

CHAPTER 3

THE EMPIRE OF
THE CLOUDS

"WITH RESPECT, MINISTERS, THIS isn't much to go on," I said, steepling my hands before me, elbows on the polished, black glass table. I surveyed the eclectic mixture of military and ministerial personnel gathered for the briefing, high palatines and upjumped peasants alike.

In snide aristocratic tones, Sir Lorcan Breathnach replied, "I am quite confident the great Devil of Meidua will prove equal to the task." This elicited titters from the older men on the bench, among whom I was disheartened but unsurprised to find Lord Augustin Bourbon, the Minister of War himself. "We all sleep more soundly at night, Sir Hadrian, knowing that you are guarding the door."

As well you should, I thought, but only offered my tightest smile. Breathnach had been Director of Legion Intelligence for more than three hundred years, and despite the scars still visible on his neck and hands, his patrician life extension was running out. There was gray in the brown of his hair, a rime of frost at temples and forelock, and the craggy lines of his face seemed worn, as by countless winds. He was—or so I guessed—the sort of self-made man who despises such as I, we sons of ancient houses accorded positions which he believed we did not deserve.

"I am glad, sir, that despite the many labors crying for your attention you still find time to sleep at night," I said. It was unbecoming of one in my position, but as a Knight Victorian I did not answer to Sir Lorcan.

Breathnach's jaw tightened, but before he could reply, one of his junior aides interrupted. "The caravan's beacon data hasn't hit the datanet yet. Once it does we'll be able to narrow our area of search."

"Assuming the beacon transmitted at all," said Otavia Corvo from her place at my right hand. My Norman captain gestured at the starmap holographed above the conference table, indicating the crimson line that stretched from Gododdin system toward Nemavand on the Norman frontier. "We'll have to retrace their flight path exactly and just hope we catch something on our sensors." She pressed the fingertips of one hand against the desktop to underscore her next thought. "I'm sorry, but why are we doing this? This is a job for interstellar patrol, not a special company."

Before Breathnach or one of the others could answer, I said, "Because the Emperor ordered it, captain."

"And you will do your duty!" snapped Lord Bourbon.

"As you say," I said, trying to take the council's ire from my officer onto myself. "But gentlemen, you must understand. You've given us little by way of intelligence. Peace." I held up a hand for calm, studied the map once again. For more than sixteen thousand years the Sollan Empire had been expanding, its influence spreading across an ever-widening and lengthening wedge of the galaxy, spreading along the spiral arms until at last some brave pioneers made the leap across the gulfs that separated one arm from the next. Perseus at the outer rim; then Orion, where Earth lay in smoking ruins and mankind was born; then Sagittarius; Centaurus; and at last to the source of the Norma Arm so near the core where we had first encountered the Cielcin. Gododdin glowed brightly red, a lonely mote in the midst of the emptiness between the mighty shoals of Sagittarius and Centaurus. I followed the lost legion's progress: a blazing thread woven across the gulf into Centaurus and across it, moving almost straight toward the core and galactic north. Their destination, Nemavand, lay on the far edge of the Centaurus Arm near the core, near the frontier and the free-holds of the Norman Expanse wherein I had spent so much of my youth. Somewhere in that distant country—nearly twenty thousand light-years from Forum—was Emesh at the very edge of Imperial dominion. And beyond that were Pharos and Rustam and Nagramma. Even with the *Tamerlane,* which was by design among the fastest ships in the Empire, we would be gone for decades, perhaps even a century.

Even if I succeeded at this dreadful task, I would have been removed from court life and the attentions of the Imperium for so long that to return would be like being born again. A lot could change in a hundred years, especially when one slept the frozen sleep of the sailor and did not change oneself. Whatever friends I had at court and whatever momentum my celebrity had won for me at Aptucca would be gone. I would never gain access to the Imperial Library, and all my efforts in the Imperial service would be for naught.

It was a kind of death sentence, and I did not doubt that one or more of these fine gentlemen had suggested it to the Emperor. Bourbon, perhaps? I could see the old minister's full moon face whispering at His Radiance's side. How Bourbon could manage to be so exalted a palatine and yet so corpulent was a mystery, yet corpulent he was: as round of body as he was of face, with thick sideburns and a thicker mustache that recalled some species of walrus or manatee such as swam in the royal aquaria. He was a man of evil reputation, treacherous and venal. I'd heard it said that Augustin had sold out his own father, Philippe, when House Bourbon turned against itself centuries ago, backing his uncle—Prince Charles LIV—for the throne. He whispered then, muttering some comment or other to the gaunt man at his side—a senior logothete I could not name.

Sir Friedrich Oberlin, the junior logothete who had intervened with Breathnach moments before, cleared his throat. "Nemavand is crucial to the defense of the Centaurine border. Until Hermonassa, the Cielcin had not crossed the gulf in force for nearly four centuries, when they raided as far south as the Sagittarius." He indicated a belt of systems far closer to Forum and the heart of the Empire. I remembered those raids. They had come when I was just a boy on Delos. One of those attacks had destroyed Cai Shen, a Consortium mining colony, and made my father far wealthier than he had already been. "Since then the bulk of their efforts have been concentrated in the Norman Expanse, we *think* because they have territory there."

I nodded. That had been the consensus, though in seven centuries of fighting we had not found a single Cielcin colony. The xenobites did not establish colonies. They lived in migratory starship clusters, plying the dark and waterless seas between the stars, falling into solar systems long enough to suck of the stars for fuel and of our worlds for meat. And then they were gone, vanishing into the Dark like wolves in the misty forests of night.

"I know all this," I said. It was possible the Cielcin had planetbound colonies somewhere in the Norman Expanse or the Veil of Marinus, or perhaps it was in those regions of space the greater part of the nomadic hordes sailed between the stars.

"There is more," Breathnach said, tone almost grudging. "Give him the rest, Friedrich."

The young officer cleared his throat. "Yes, sir." He called up a set of schematics depicting half a dozen vessels, two troop carriers and four smaller battleships, each graceful and pointed as an arrowhead. "The convoy we sent to Nemavand was fifty thousand strong. Two legions: the 116th and the 337th Sagittarine. But they're not the first we've lost in that region." Two more red lines flowed out of Gododdin on the map, crossing the gulf into Centaurus before diverging to disparate points in the farther arm. The man Friedrich pressed on. "As you can see, we've lost two others in the last century. One forty years ago and the other about ninety. Their paths diverge rather dramatically once they reach Centaurus, after they refuel here, at Dion Station."

"So you think they're being hit somewhere between Gododdin and Dion," I said, finishing the man's train of thought.

"The Cielcin would have destroyed the fuel depot if they'd found it," Corvo said, meaning the station.

"Bloody likely," said one of the legion brass, a woman nearly so tall as Corvo.

"Unless they know exactly where Dion is," I said, staring at a spot on the table before me. "Unless they like us sending our convoys straight toward it time and again. Why would you keep sending them if you'd lost four legions this way?"

I saw the answer a moment before Bourbon gave it to me, "Because there's not another road into Centaurus for a thousand light-years east or west. Look at the map, boy!"

Not for the first time, I was glad my hands were in my lap. I twisted Prince Aranata's ring on my thumb and scowled at the fat man. "Nevertheless . . ." I let the word drag across the air between us before continuing. "So you think the odds are good our convoy vanished somewhere in the gulf between Gododdin and Dion." I studied the map of the galaxy hanging above us. "That does narrow things down a bit. But even still by the time we get there I rather doubt there'll be anything left. It'll take years just to reach Gododdin, to say nothing of how long it will take to sweep the gulf. Gentlemen, I'm afraid those men are already dead."

"Very likely," Breathnach agreed. "But you're just the man for the job, Marlowe."

Beside him, Augustin Bourbon made a low, wet sound that passed for laughter. "Just do try and bring them back alive this time, if at all possible. We were so disappointed after the Arae affair . . . So few survivors. And the barbarians escaped as well. Such a pity."

Unbidden, my fists clenched in my lap. The soldiers we had been sent to rescue on Arae had been dead when we arrived, converted into mechanical puppets by the Extrasolarians. *Rage is blindness,* that part of me that yet spoke in Gibson's voice whispered. When I spoke, my tone was calm. Steady. I did not argue. Lord Bourbon and the Director were not the sorts of men one argued with. "I'm confused, honorable gentlemen," I said, and paused to allow Breathnach or Bourbon the opportunity to insult me again. To my surprise, neither man did, but I supposed the bait was too obvious. "On Arae, we discovered intelligence that the Cielcin have part-nered with certain agencies among the Extrasolarians. Was something about this discovery unsatisfying to you? Or would you have preferred to learn about it only when the enemy was at our gates?" Having found enough forward momentum, I stood, palms pressed flat against the table. "With respect, none of you was at Arae. None of you saw what was left of those men, and none of you wishes more than I that they were still alive. So don't insult me."

Despite Bourbon's hand on his arm, Breathnach stood to match me. "Are you quite done, Marlowe?" The fat minister had been right to try to restrain the craggy Director. The question would have been more com-manding if he hadn't lost his composure to ask it.

Not quite, I thought. Still in the same even tone, I said, "The Emperor has ordered me to Gododdin, so I will go. And with your leave, I will go now." I extended one hand in salute before plucking the storage crystal from the table before me.

I did not wait for permission to leave.

"They mean for us to fail," I said to my companions once we regained the relative security of our shuttle. I looked from Pallino to Otavia and back again, never minding the pilot officer and the four Red Company soldiers who'd accompanied us as something of an honor guard. "What we did at Aptucca's frightened the politicians. They're afraid of *me.*" I twisted Ara-nata's ring again. Through the small portholes on the shuttle the Legion Intelligence offices fell away, white columns and painted capitals and domes glittering in the sun. I watched the Eternal City roll beneath us. Forum was astonishingly temperate for a gas giant, the winds milder than they had any right or reason to be—and their worst excesses were curbed by the weather satellites that kept the storms at bay.

From our height, the Eternal City blossomed from the clouds like the palace of some fairy queen, like Olympos of old. Here among the clouds, humanity had worn the trappings of godhood for so long they had almost forgotten they were animals, though still they snarled and bit.

"Would it really be so bad?" Pallino asked. "Maybe they'd let you go."

I almost laughed at that. "Let me go? Go where, Pal?"

"Wherever you like," he said, and crossed his arms. "Back to the Veil, back to mercenary life. Hell, you could slip off and be a scholiast if that's what you really want. You and Valka."

Valka. There was a thought. Valka had not left the *Tamerlane* since we'd returned to Forum two years before, fresh off our latest mission. She was Tavrosi, and the machine implanted in her head—though it was a secret known only to a few of our company—put her in danger. The Chantry's Inquisition would not have looked kindly on someone carrying the dreaded machines into the heart of the Sollan Empire. I was not sure her diplomatic status could protect her here, where security mattered more than justice.

From the perversion of the flesh, O Mother deliver us.

But if I was dismissed from the Imperial court in disgrace, we might go anywhere, might see the Marching Towers on Sadal Suud, climb the mountain to the Temple of Athten Var, visit all the ruins the Quiet left littered across the galaxy. Might forget the war. It was tempting.

"You know we can't do that," I said. I could still see the blood and the way Raine Smythe and her soldier had been torn apart by the Cielcin, could remember clearly the way one held her severed arm aloft before feasting on it. And the visions I had seen . . . the Cielcin burning across the stars, billions dead and dying or enslaved.

I squeezed my left hand with my right, feeling the faint ridges on the artificial bone. I had lost the arm when I lost my life aboard the *Demiurge,* and even after almost a hundred years, the arm did not feel truly mine. It had been a gift from the Undying King of Vorgossos, from Kharn Sagara himself. I had saved his life—both his lives, for he had splintered, his consciousness transferred into both the clones he kept near at hand to protect his immortality. It was a permanent reminder of what I had lost, what I had given to the fight.

"But it will be good to get the hell out of this place," Captain Corvo said, staring down at the city through hooded eyes. I wondered what she saw when she looked down on the gilt spires and soaring domes, the cataracts pouring from the clouds and vanishing only to fall upon some terraced garden suspended far below. There was nothing like it in all the universe. No city so fair . . . or so terrible.

We banked round the ivory finger of the great clock tower that overshadowed the Campus Raphael. Despite myself, I felt a longing for my own home, for the black fortress of Devil's Rest on its acropolis overlooking the sea. For all its faults—and they are numberless—I felt a sudden affection for the Empire of my home, for Delos where I was born, and even for the Eternal City. How much worse the world would become if that beautiful city fell! How much poorer. And though the men who ruled her were terrible and venal and cruel, no city or empire was made great by its rulers. Or by merely its rulers. Rome of old was not loved for its greatness, so the poet wrote. Rome was great because men loved her, as I loved my Empire in that moment.

"When do you pick up this prince we're taking with us?" Pallino asked.

I forced myself to stop fidgeting with my hands and look Pallino in the eyes. It was still strange seeing him like this: his youth and eye restored. I leaned back in my seat. "Not for three days. He's being prepared, as I understand it. Medical exams and the like. RNA indoctrination."

"So he'll at least know how to lace up his boots, then," Corvo put in, brushing floating, bleached curls from her dark face.

"Or buckle them, at least," Pallino said with a snort. "Strange they're saddling us with a princeling for a punishment detail like this. Isn't it?"

"Not at all," I replied. "This way he won't be in any danger."

"You'll forgive me if I don't complain about that either," Otavia said, the trace of a frown touching her lips. "Be nice to not be fighting for our lives for once."

Pallino leaned forward, hands still tucked into the crooks of his arms. "I take it you didn't get access to the archives like you wanted, eh?"

"No." I turned away to look out the porthole and propped my chin against my fist. "I asked the Emperor, but . . ." I made a vague gesture with the other hand. That thought did not need finishing. We flew on in silence a while after that. I watched the city marching on and the play of aircraft threading the towers.

"If we fail, the Emperor may dissolve the Red Company," I said, still not looking at any of the others. I wet my lips. "You're sure this shuttle's not bugged?"

Corvo nodded. "Ilex went over it personally. Even had the doctor give it a once over."

Valka, I thought. Well, if Valka had cleared it. "I think that either the Emperor or someone very near him thinks I've grown popular enough to pose some kind of threat." I thought about Carax asking me to bless him and the medallion he had offered me. "Maybe they think I'm going to make a play for one of the ministries. War, maybe. Maybe that's why Bourbon hates me—thinks I want his job—or maybe it's more than that.

They can't possibly think I want the throne. The Emperor has . . . a hundred ten children? A hundred twenty? I couldn't get close if I wanted to. Even if this whole city fell out of the sky today, half that brood's offworld. Besides, I'm not another Boniface the Pretender."

"You really think someone's out to get you?" Corvo asked.

"I think they've got me," I said coldly, fixing Otavia with my sharpest glare. "How long will it take us to reach Gododdin?"

The captain shrugged, shaking off the force of my evil eye. "Twelve years at full warp to cross the Sagittarius Arm."

"That's twenty-four years *minimum* I'm away from this place. By the time we get back, I'll be irrelevant, especially if we return empty-handed— which we are intended to do."

Now it was Corvo's turn to cross her arms, an impressive gesture with her physique. "You're sure we're meant to fail?"

My eyebrows shot up. "We're being set up. I'm sure of it. I can't blame them. I'd do the same . . . The only question is: who's behind it? Was this mission the Emperor's idea or has someone been whispering in his ear?" Augustin Bourbon came to mind. The Minister of War sat on the Imperial council. He had the Emperor's ear. It would have been no difficulty to suggest that the troubling upstart Hadrian Marlowe be sent on a fruitless expedition to the edge of forever *just until things settle down.*

"Does it matter?" Pallino asked.

"Of course it matters," I said, a little too sharply. I sat up straight, extending one hand, palm up. "It's bad enough if it's Bourbon or some other minister behind this, but if it's the Emperor himself . . ." That was another thought that didn't need to be finished.

I squeezed my fist shut.

CHAPTER 4

CHILDREN OF THE SUN

THE GRILLED GATE OF the tramcar rolled back and allowed me to disembark. I followed the androgyn servant in silence, hands behind my back. So vast is that baroque pile of metal and stone that it has its own tramways—like the largest legionary dreadnoughts—to ferry the servants and soldiers and members of the nobility from place to place. Intricately wrought iron bristled all around, imitating the flowering vines with which it wove. I was struck by just how much plant life there was in the palace, so that it seemed as much a garden as a castle. So much beauty and design had been lavished on the palace that it staggered the heart.

The ironwork and the ivy gave way to stone walls, and beyond an arched portal rich wooden panels drank the warm light of sconces. The round-vaulted ceiling above showed images of the sky—not the rosy color of Forum's heavens, but jewel-blue as Earth's was said to be, the clouds white and golden.

The homunculus stopped outside a door and knocked to announce us. The door sprang open almost at once, and I was astonished to find an attendant had opened it. No mechanism, unless one counted the tinkling of silver bells to announce the door had moved.

"Sir Hadrian Marlowe, Lord Commandant of the Red Company, Your Majesty," the androgyn said in high, angelic tones.

"Majesty?" I echoed the word dumbly, then went to one knee at once as I understood.

The woman seated in the chair before me was perhaps the loveliest I had ever seen. Cold and terrible as a winter storm was she, but warm and rich as autumn. Her hair was red as the Emperor's—for they were cousins—and fell in a braid thick as my arm, bound with golden cords. She might have been cast from ivory, from marble. Her gown was pale as she and slashed with crimson to match her hair, and gold was her belt and gold the bangles that dripped from ears and throat and arms. All the art that the geneticists of the High College could contrive was in her body, and the strength of empires was in her eyes.

"Your Majesty," I said, "it is an honor. Forgive me, I was not expecting to meet you."

The Empress Maria Agrippina raised a hand in greeting, and remembering that I should not stare, I looked down at the thick carpet that covered the floor. "Please stand," she said. "We wished to meet you before you take our son from us." She smiled, but the light of it did not reach her emerald eyes. She offered a hand glittering with rings.

Formal protocol would have had me approach that hand on my knees, but the Empress had commanded me to stand. It may have been a kind of test, but I despised kneeling, and so stood to take her hand and stooped to kiss it.

"Alexander will be with us shortly, but I wanted to see the Hero of Aptucca for myself. Sit, please!" She indicated a chair opposite her. "Tea?"

I did not care for the stuff, but would not refuse the Empress. "Please."

She gestured, and another of the androgyns emerged from an arras to pour the drink into a cobalt teacup. I accepted it graciously and took a sip before setting it down, knowing that that had likely been enough to satisfy courtesy.

"Do you have children, Lord Marlowe?"

I blinked, surprised by the question, because I felt certain the Empress must have known perfectly well that I did not. "No, Majesty. My . . . paramour is Tavrosi." I could have said more. That Valka did not want children, that Valka did not wish even to be married, that I suspected the High College would not approve of such a union anyway, pairing one of the Imperial Peerage with a foreigner.

"I had heard that," the Empress said with the sort of interest that suggested what I said was some species of terrible scandal. "I didn't think it was *true*. A Tavrosi witch? And you keep company with homunculi and other degenerates. Fascinating."

"I'm afraid that what they say of me is more true than not, Majesty."

"I see . . ." Her voice trailed off. "That makes you something of a rarity. Most men are smaller than the stories told about them. You should be careful. Grow too tall and someone will take an ax to you." Warning? Or threat? Maria Agrippina leaned back in her chair, and I was struck by how perfect her posture was: every line and motion precise as a dancer's, as some elf queen of antique fable. I think she frightened me more than the Emperor himself. "But this is interesting!" she said, and smiled another smile that did not touch her eyes. "You must be careful with my boy, sir."

"Of course, Your Majesty."

"If something were to happen to him," she said, lifting her own teacup from its saucer, "I would be obliged to see that something happened to you. Are we clear?"

I took up my teacup again to give my hands something to do. "Perfectly," I said. "Although where we're going should be quite safe. It's only search and rescue."

Her Majesty set her cup back on its saucer. "All the same. He is a prince of the Empire. A child of the Sun, and my son, and you will look after him."

"I will," I agreed, and smiled despite the visions of torture and torment in the dungeons that I felt certain must lurk beneath this holy city in the sky. Nervous, I spared a glance for the androgyn servant standing now beside an antique-looking red figure vase on a stone table. It was trying its best to appear a part of the furniture, bright eyes fixed on the ground. The palace servants were all identical, or nearly so. Intelligent but not creative, they were perfectly loyal and obedient, rapier-thin and long-faced. They frightened me, but I pitied them. They had not chosen to be born as they were.

The Empress's tea table stood beneath the apex of a glass dome overlooking part of the Cloud Gardens. Leaves so green they were almost black brushed against the glass and the ironwork.

"I cannot remember the last time a mere knight drew such a following," she began, and I sensed she was working toward some pronouncement or point. "To have fallen so far . . . to be *outcaste* and to rise again . . . I mean, you're practically *patrician*." She said this last word in a tone that suggested patricians were little better than goats. I held my face still in a rare moment of near-scholiast blankness. The Empress was the product of the finest genetic tailoring in the universe: a living icon. Had I shown her image to some Achaean shepherd, he would have fallen to his knees in worship, mistaking her for Demeter. Small wonder she held those of lesser blood in contempt! What else could a goddess feel for a goat? "Nevertheless," she continued, "you've found yourself quite the following. You're a true hero."

Was she mocking me? Like her Imperial husband she had too fine a control of her face, and nothing of her emotions that she did not expressly allow showed in her expression.

"Mother!"

The voice came from behind me, so I had to set the tea down again and turn to see the young man standing in the door of the solarium.

He looked precisely as I imagined. A boy of perhaps thirty standard years. Red-haired like his parents and green-eyed, with high cheekbones and a strong jaw. I'd expected more of the Imperial white, but the only white he wore was a collared half-cape over his left shoulder. His tunic and trousers were black as my own.

"Alexander! Come in!" The Empress rose in a swishing of skirts. "Come meet Lord Marlowe! He's been waiting for you!"

"Not very long, I hope," the prince said, stepping into the room, and it was only when he did so that I saw he was not alone. A woman followed him, and so like was she in form and color to the Empress that I knew she must be one of the woman's own daughters.

I was not certain whether or not I'd seen the prince before. The Imperial princes and princesses were all of so strong an archetype that I could not have told one from another without careful study. I did not kneel, which ordinarily would have been appropriate, my being only a knight and a petty lord without holdings before two of the Imperial children. But I was also, by Imperial decree, *the* knight appointed to train this young prince, and so I confined my salutation to a simple nod, shifting my posture to stand at attention. I fixed my eyes on a spot on the wall and said, "Sir Hadrian Anaxander Marlowe, at your service."

The prince smiled nervously, teeth flashing. "Yes, you are!" And to my astonishment, he bowed. "It is a pleasure to meet you, Sir Hadrian, sir."

"Your father has requested and required that I train you," I said formally. "With your royal mother's permission, we plan to leave Forum at fifteen hundred standard." Directing my question at the servant standing behind the prince, I asked, "I trust the prince's effects are already aboard my ship?"

"The *Tamerlane*?" Alexander asked. "Father said we're going to Gododdin. I've never been offworld. Have you? Been to Gododdin, I mean." He looked down at his boots and seemed to chew his tongue.

I shook my head. "I've come in along the old core routes more often than not, returning from the Veil. This'll be a new adventure for both of us."

To my surprise then, the young prince took a step forward, jaw gravely set. Solemn-faced, he did something I have never seen a member of the Imperium do before. He thrust out his hand for me to shake in the peasant fashion. So surprised was I that I took it unthinking. In a voice grave as his expression, Prince Alexander said, "I have heard stories about you since I was a boy."

What could I say to something like that? In its way, it was almost as incredible a line of conversation as my encounter with Carax in the great hall. Unable to help myself, I felt the crooked Marlowe smile bleed across my face as I said, "I hope you did not believe all of them."

Alexander gave a short, hollow laugh and released my hand. "Oh! I should introduce you!" He stepped aside. "Sir Hadrian, this is my sister, Selene."

The princess offered me a hand, and as she wore no ring upon her slim, white fingers, I kissed my thumb instead as I took those fingers in mine. "Highness," I said, looking up at her. I found I had no other words.

For I had seen Selene Avent once before. In a vision given to me by the daimon Brethren in the dark waters below Vorgossos. The vision the Quiet had left with them for me to find. A vision of my future, or one of many futures. In that vision I sat on the Solar Throne with a circlet on my brow, and this princess sat at my feet in a gown of living flowers. Other visions I had seen of a life we two might share, and though we had not met, I remembered the perfume of her hair and the taste of her lips and the way she moved beneath me. Struggling with all this, I kept my eyes downcast in what I hoped was a respectful manner. I could still feel where her hand had touched mine, and thinking of Valka, I made a fist at my side. I did not like to think about that future, or any future without Valka in it.

"My brother speaks most highly of you, sir knight," the princess said, and the sound of her voice was like a half-remembered melody playing in a distant room. "We are fortunate to have men like yourself defending us." Her smile was like the first blast of sunlight around the limn of a planet from orbit, and again I averted my eyes.

Haltingly, I answered, "That is kind of you to say, Highness."

"Will we be leaving now, Sir Hadrian?" Alexander asked. "Directly, I mean?"

"That is my intention."

"Good, good." He looked round at the solarium as if he'd never really seen it before. I knew the look well. It was a look more closely kin to fear than people really believe. A fear born of the fact that though we may come back to a place at the end of our journeys, we never really return, for we are not the same person who departed.

Watching this, I could not blame the prince, I who have survived several such transformations myself. So I smiled instead. "We'll spend a year or two awake on the journey. See what you know, what you can do. See to your training." The prince brightened visibly at the news, though I sensed the shadow of distaste from the Empress at my brusque tone.

"Please take care of my brother, sir," Selene said, and clasped her hands before herself.

"I will, Highness," I said, and I did bow then. "You may depend on it."

"Should we go now?" the prince asked, eyes still wandering around the old solarium.

I told him we didn't have much time to linger, and stepped aside as young Alexander said his goodbyes. He knelt before his mother and took her hand in both of his and swore he would return. I remember smiling at this gallant display, thinking that in that moment he seemed everything a prince of the Sollan Empire should be. How little I perceived the weight hanging on his shoulders, or the desire to prove himself. He was one of the latter-born, the one-hundred-seventh child of the Emperor's impossible brood. A living spare, destined to live out his days in the Peronine Palace, studying statecraft and diplomacy to sit a throne that would be never his, that would go to Crown Prince Aurelian or to Princess Irene, the second-born. He would be denied marriage and children by the High College and his own father to keep the Imperial clan from swelling to too unmanageable a size. The Kin Wars had taught their bloody lesson and left their mark burning across a million worlds so long ago, when the days of the palatine were counted in years and not in centuries.

Alexander needed desperately to *become* something. To become *someone*. To matter. Thus it is for all men. We are nothing until we have accomplished something. Even for the young prince it was so, though his rank gave some identity. Recalling the Hadrian ignored and belittled by his lordly father, I felt a pang of sympathy for the boy.

A thought occurred to me, and I asked, "You're traveling alone? You're not bringing servants or guardians?"

"Is your sword not guard enough, Sir Hadrian?" the Empress asked, arching one perfect eyebrow. I felt an echo of Bourbon's tone in her question. *Surely the great Devil of Meidua can keep one little boy safe?*

I matched the ice in the Empress's eyes with flint. "You may depend on it, Majesty."

"We will," she said tartly, and I noted the royal style of that reply.

What was said as we departed I do not now recall. I remember the princess's nervous smile and the Empress's hard-eyed gaze. So similar were they in appearance and dress. So different in substance. And the boy beside me? The man? There was little of the warrior in his step, little of the commander in his bearing.

How little I guessed of what he would become.

Our shadows raced ahead of us as we descended the steps of the palace, my coat and his cape fluttering in the wind. The Martians saluted as the prince descended, and I turned my collar up to shield my face. As we passed the fountain, he stopped, and I went on for three paces alone before turning back.

The prince leaned against the rim of the fountain, one hand flat against the marble.

"Sir Hadrian, I know my father did not offer you a choice in taking me, but . . . I am grateful." The boy would not look me in the face. "I won't fail you."

I crossed my arms. "Good."

What did he see when he looked at me? The Hero of Aptucca? The man who had slain not one but two princes of the Cielcin? The man who they said could not be killed? To the boy I was like a character from a storybook—not a man at all. He looked at me as I might have looked at a dragon had one crawled off the page and curled itself around the Galath Tree.

"I want to be a knight. Like you."

"This isn't a field trip, you know." I did not wait for a reply, but turned and continued onward, moving back toward the strand where my shuttle waited to carry us to orbit and the *Tamerlane*. I did not hear footsteps on the path behind, and after a moment I stopped, turning back. Prince Alexander still stood there, hands balled at his sides. How small he seemed! How narrow those shoulders bred to wear the mantle of empire. Strange to think of him as that young man again, after all these years, after Gododdin.

After he ordered my execution.

"Are you coming?" I called.

The prince stirred. "I . . . yes!"

"Right then," I turned away, "let's be off." But I stopped short, for something just off the path had caught my eye, white as snow on the mossy stones. I knelt. It was a Galath blossom, so bright it glowed. The wind must have tugged it free of those sacred branches, for it was said that the flowers of the Galath tree never fell. I am not a superstitious man, but the sight of that pale blossom in my fingers sent a chill stealing over me, as though it were the Empire that had fallen.

Or a star.

CHAPTER 5

TAMERLANE

FORUM SHONE BENEATH US, rosy and golden and so vast it filled half the universe. Through the porthole at my ear, I watched the ocean of clouds roil below. Already the Eternal City was lost to sight, its high towers and shining domes swallowed by the empyrean. Ahead, the lonely flames of stardrives flickered like candles against the Dark. When they imagine the black of space, the storytellers imagine starships crowded close enough for men to shout at one another from the rigging.

It isn't so.

In the Eternal City it was often said that ten Martian legions orbited the gas giant, ever vigilant, boasting enough firepower to unmake a planet ten thousand times over. I never saw them. Once or twice I spied the glow of ion drives or the flash of a fusion rocket, but the red-gold orb of Forum hung quiet and proud in the night amid its archipelago of moons.

"There it is!" I pressed closer to the window and pointed out into the black to where a lonely arrowhead gleamed. At this distance, it was no bigger than my thumbnail, but it was growing fast.

Alexander craned his neck to look past me and asked, "The *Tamerlane?*"

"Home," I said. The young man squinted, then reached across me and pressed his fingertips against the glass, made a spreading motion as if to magnify the image. Nothing happened, and laughing, I said, "Just alumglass. It's a real window. No need for tactical displays in a passenger shuttle." I leaned back against the slick upholstery, the better to allow the boy to see the ship that had been my home for many decades.

The *Tamerlane.*

The *Eriel*-class battleship had been a gift from the Emperor, granted to me in lieu of a planetary fief when he named me a knight and re-legitimized me as a lord of the blood palatine. From engines to bow-cluster she stood more than twelve miles long, pointed and flared like a knife blade from her prow to the convex arc of ion engines above the three huge fusion cones. The heavy armor on her dorsal side gleamed glossy and black in the sunlight, weapons clusters concealed beneath hatches outlined in gold, and beneath that armor the bays and fuel tanks and crew decks hung like an inverse city of towers or forest of trees swept back in a gale. More than fifteen thousand men lived aboard, and nearly seventy-five thousand slept the long and icy sleep of the soldier in great holds high above beneath the dorsal hull.

I could not hear the pilot officer through the bulkhead, though I guessed she must already be in communication with the deckmaster to clear our landing. Speaking to the two hoplites sitting across from us in their Red Company uniforms, I said, "I'm sorry to take you both away from the City so quickly."

One of the men tugged on his restraints as he leaned in. "Truth be told, lordship, I'm happy to be away." Only belatedly did he remember he was speaking in front of a prince of the Imperium. I could practically hear the fellow blush through his black visor. "Meaning no disrespect to the young master."

"I'm your prince!" Alexander said sharply, taking the hoplite aback.

"I didn't mean any disrespect, my prince."

Sensing that this could get out of hand and quickly, I put a hand between Alexander and the soldier. "It's Baro, isn't it?"

The man puffed out his chest. "Aye, sir." I'd recognized the peeling decal of the naked woman on his armor's left thigh. It wasn't regulation, but I'd encouraged my centurions to ignore such things unless it was for dress uniforms. She had a snake wrapped round one rounded thigh.

"Baro here has never met one of the Imperial House, Alexander. You must forgive him! He's a good man." I let my hand fall. "You made decurion recently, didn't you? I thought I saw a notice . . ."

"After Aptucca. Thank you, sir." He tapped the single red stripe running down the outside of his right arm to mark his rank. "I'm honored you remembered."

Keeping my attention fixed on Alexander's face, I said, "You've earned it."

Outside the *Tamerlane* grew closer, black hull bright in the yellow sunlight. A fueling station still drifted to one side, connected to the ship's reservoirs by an umbilical. Preparations for departure were still underway, it seemed. That was well. As we drew nearer our shuttle slid upward, accelerating to rise and catch up to the *Tamerlane*'s higher orbit.

"Is it always like this?" Alexander asked. His eyes were screwed shut, and he'd tucked his chin against his chest. It looked like he might be sick. I had grown so used to the zero-gravity environment aboard such shuttlecraft that I'd not even noticed it.

"You get used to it."

We landed not long after, sliding into a smaller hold fore and high up, nearly at the level of the dorsal plate. I felt myself sink into my seat as the *Tamerlane*'s suppression field kicked in, artificial gravity pressing down on me like a damp blanket.

"It's heavy," the prince remarked.

"One-and-a-half standard gees," I said in answer. "We run heavy. It keeps you strong, prevents loss of bone mass." When Alexander did not look reassured, I summoned up what pity I could muster and said, "You get used to that, too."

The Eternal City flew above the sea of liquid metal at the heart of the gas giant at an altitude where the atmosphere was at tolerable pressures and where the planet's gravity was as close to Earth standard as could be found. The prince had lived his entire life in an environment tailored for human habitation, made as much like our lost and ruined homeworld as any place could be. He was in for a rude awakening.

A moment later, the docking booms magnetized and clamped onto the exterior of the shuttle, pulling us into a dock. I heard the hiss of pneumatics and the whine of atmospheric seals depressuring, and the door folded out and downward, becoming a ramp. Standing, I offered Alexander a hand. "Welcome aboard, Your Highness."

The crew that waited to greet the prince on the gangway was as motley a collection of Imperial officers and mercenaries, of palatines and plebeians, of homunculi and other misfits as could be contrived this side of Jadd. Captain Otavia Corvo, a Norman mercenary herself, stood at the fore in her black deck uniform. Despite her low birth, Otavia was a giantess. Nearly seven feet tall, musclebound, broad-shouldered, and coffee-skinned, her curling blond hair floated about her head like a halo.

Behind her was her First Officer, Bastien Durand, wearing his wire-rimmed glasses and his usual, put-upon expression. At his shoulder was Tor Varro, the Chalcenterite scholiast in his green surcoat, bronze degrees glittering on his chest like a soldier's medals. Behind them were gathered a smattering of the ship's more senior officers. There was Crim—Karim Garone—a Lieutenant Commander now and ship's Security Officer, and behind him was the dryad, Ilex, green-skinned and mossy-haired. Then there were my myrmidons, my armsmen. Pallino, Elara, and Siran stood near the back. The women each had been raised to patrician, standing when Pallino had been, and looked as hale and young—younger, even—than they had the day we'd met on Emesh centuries ago. Nearly four hundred years had passed on Earth since I'd left Delos, nearly a hundred of which I'd faced in the waking world.

Further down were a smattering of other officers: Luana Okoyo, our Chief Medical Officer; the navigator, Adric White; and Helmsman Koskinen, among others. And bringing up the rear was young Aristedes leaning on his cane.

Only Valka was absent, which was no surprise. What use had she for princes?

"We have our marching orders, boss?" Crim asked, hand waving in lazy salute.

"Off to Gododdin," I said airily, seizing Crim by the forearm to shake his hand. Pivoting, I positioned myself to stand between Crim and Corvo and the prince following on my heels. "Otavia, Bastien, Crim—this is Prince Alexander of the House Avent. My prince, may I introduce Captain Otavia Corvo, Commander Bastien Durand." I gestured to each in turn. "And this is Lieutenant Commander Karim Garone."

"Call me Crim, Your . . ." he glanced sidelong at me, "Excellence?"

"Highness," I corrected, then to Alexander said, "He's Norman."

I took Alexander down the line, introducing those present one at a time.

"The prince is with us at the Emperor's personal request!" I said, raising my voice. The sound of it rebounded off the distant ceiling and the arches and pillars that held up the gangways that ran to the various shuttlecraft. "You are to treat him with every courtesy. He's our guest." I put a hand on Alexander's shoulder for emphasis. "The Emperor has asked us to season him. He'll be squiring for me and bunking with the junior officers."

"What?" The prince flinched, turning to look at me. "You're not serious."

A piece of me had expected this from the young nobile, and I was ready. "Quite serious."

"That's . . . outrageous! It's not *fair!*"

"Fair?" I repeated. "You're my squire. A squire is a junior officer, so you will bunk with the junior officers." The prince's face had hardened, and he darted a glance at the officers, some part of him perhaps aware that he was making a spectacle of himself. I had suspected this, despite his assurances that he would not let me down.

Alexander set his teeth. "I am your prince!"

"You are my squire," I said calmly. "You told me you wanted to be a knight. This is the first step. Did you think the road would be easy? Do you want it to be?"

A frown folded the corners of Alexander's mouth, and almost I thought I could hear the sound of little gilded gears turning in his skull. "I suppose not."

"We will talk about this later," I said before rounding on Elara, who had taken up the role of Quartermaster when we'd been given the *Tamerlane*. "Would you get him sorted and see that his effects find his cabin?" As I spoke, those very effects were being unloaded from the shuttle: three heavy composite crates fronted in dark wood richly carved. They looked incongruous on the metal grating of the gangway and against the spare lines of the shuttle and the hold. Like their owner, they did not belong. Still looking at them where they stood at the end of the pier, I said, "Alexander, I will send for you as soon as I've seen to our departure. We've much to discuss."

Mollified, the young man permitted himself to be led down the catwalk and through the heavy doors to the ship's tramway beyond. The more junior officers went with them, leaving me, Corvo, Durand, Crim, and my myrmidons. I waited a few seconds, half-afraid the boy would come charging back in for a final word. When he did not appear, I let out my breath in one great rush and sagged against the railing. "Earth and Emperor," I swore, staring down level by level toward the cargo storage at the base of the vast hold, "this is going to be harder than I thought."

"It could have been a lot worse," Crim said, and though I did not look back to face him I heard the smile encircling those words. "Valka could have been here."

"That's not funny," I said, watching a trio of workers servicing another shuttle two levels down.

Crim barked a short laugh. "It's extremely funny." Despite myself, I pictured Valka slapping the prince for his behavior the moment before and almost laughed. Perhaps it would have been funny, after all.

Siran's low voice slid into the silence. "The pup didn't look like much."

Turning to face my officers at last, I said, "Pups never do." I undid two silver buttons on my greatcoat and let the garment swing free. Thinking of the Empress and of Emperor William, I added, "You should see the wolves."

A high, aristocratic voice answered. "Do you think he'll work?"

For a moment, absurdly, I thought it was Alexander returned, though I knew better. The speaker sat slumped against the wall of the hold, thin hands wrapped around the shaft of his crutch, serious face looking up at the rest of us. When I did not answer him at once, young Lorian Aristedes went on. "It would be good to have an Imperial prince in our camp." All was quiet for a moment after, and the little commander realized that all eyes were on him. "That is the plan, isn't it? The Emperor's pawned one of his spares off on us, and we're trying to win him over?" He grinned knowingly, pale eyes darting from my face to Corvo's and the next.

"Are you all right, Aristedes?" I asked, indicating his place on the floor.

"Leg gave out, that's all." He slapped the offending limb with the flat of one hand. Young as he was—he was less than half my age—Lorian Aristedes had his problems. His father was the Grand Duke of Patmos, his mother a patrician knight. He had been born out of wedlock, and being the child of a palatine, into a cursed life. Lorian was an intus, the result of his parents' encrypted genes mingling without the consent of the Imperial High College. By rights his mother should have killed him before he was born, but Lysandra Aristedes had refused. She had chosen life for her cursed little boy, and against all odds Lorian had survived. He was small—no more than five feet high—and frail. Even in his padded uniform jacket he seemed half a ghost, a wasted skeleton left to rot against the wall. His one leg was lame and at times whole limbs would paralyze and go numb for reasons no doctor had ever adequately explained. His mother had begged his lordly father to find a place for Lorian at his court, but the Grand Duke—mindful of the constant scandal his deformed son brought upon his name—pushed Lorian into the Legions instead, where despite his infirmity he had ridden one desk and another until he found his way into my service.

Lame Lorian might have been, but his mind was sharp as any sword, and three times as fast.

Standing over him, I said, "Who said anything about trying to win the prince over?"

"Well, you wouldn't have scolded him, otherwise," Lorian put in. "And you'd definitely not be quartering him. You'd have popped him right into fugue and not disturbed him until after work was done on Gododdin." He grinned wolfishly. "Am I right?"

Matching his smile, I asked, "Did your leg really give out? Or were you looking for an excuse to ask that question?" Aristedes's smile did not waver. Laughing, I shrugged off my greatcoat and tossed it over the rail. Thumbs tucked into my shield-belt, I leaned beside it. "You should have joined the scholiasts, Aristedes."

"My father had a cruel sense of humor," Lorian said. We had that in common.

"You think he'll work with us?" asked First Officer Durand, giving up the game. "He seems a bit too . . ." Durand had the courage of a scribe, and so trailed off.

"Arrogant?" Crim suggested, stroking his pointed chin. "I don't think he's ever come down from heaven to walk with the rest of us mortals."

I said nothing to this. I could sympathize with Alexander's culture shock, for I too had been raised in a castle, and I knew all too well—as did Lorian—that the privilege of one's birth is no privilege at all, only another kind of cage.

Alexander had some growing to do.

I prayed it would be less growing than I had been forced to endure, for his sake, and reassured myself that he at least would not be scraping a living from the underside of Borosevo's streets.

How long ago that was! Years running and cowering in the wretched warrens of that awful city, the ziggurat castle of House Mataro staring down like the specter of some unearthly judge, daring me to rise up.

I had risen, and had not fallen again.

"He'll be all right," Pallino said. "A few weeks in the ring with me will knock some sense into him."

"We'll want that," I said. "But he'll be all right. He's lived his whole life on Forum. He won't know who he really is until he gets away from home."

"No one ever does," Corvo agreed. "I need to make the final preparations for departure."

"And I need to see Valka!" I said, sensing the curtain closing on our impromptu meeting.

Ever the professionals, Corvo and Durand made to leave at once, bootheels rattling on the catwalk. Siran moved to let them pass before falling back into place.

"There is one thing I don't understand, Marlowe," Aristedes said. No preamble, no *Pardon me, lordship*. Straight to business. In truth, it was one of the things I liked most about young Lorian. He did not waste time. "What is this in aid of?"

"Alexander, you mean?" I took my coat up and folded it over one arm.

The young officer shook his head. "That's part of it. I mean all this trouble with the court. Surely there must be those on Forum who think you look too ambitious. They must wonder what it's all for."

"I'm not hearing a question, Aristedes."

"They'll think you'll make some play for the throne. Marry the prince, perhaps."

"Marry the prince?" Pallino repeated, clearly surprised by this new wrinkle. But Lorian was right. I could imagine the logothetes and politicians spinning their fantasies about the upstart knight seducing the impressionable princeling, filling his head with lies so that he begged his royal parents to marry the knight, who would then have climbed from nothing to the role of prince-consort, and so advanced another step up the political ladder.

Lorian raised one bony hand. "It will have crossed their minds." He turned his pale eyes—so blue they were almost white—on me. "They're wondering what your game is—what our game is. What we're going to do."

I matched the young officer's wolfish smile with a bemused one. "There is no game. We're fighting to end this war. One way . . ." I paused, and once again the blood from Raine Smythe's dismembered body splashed against my brain, ". . . or another. This isn't about politics."

"Try telling them that," Crim drawled, looking down over the railing at the levels below.

"You're right," I said to Lorian, "that is what they're expecting." Unbidden, my mind raced back to Princess Selene, and past images of her unclad and lovely as the day to the vision I had seen of us seated together on the Solar Throne. "That is not what I want." And certainly I did not want such a thing with Alexander, though it would have been the more convenient route, assuming I was the thing the Imperial socialites no doubt accused me of being.

The young officer bobbed his head and lay his cane across his knees. "It's not me you have to convince."

CHAPTER 6

ALONE

THE CABIN DOOR HISSED shut behind me, and briefly I heard the whine of air systems.

I was alone at last.

I left Hadrian Marlowe the Halfmortal's coat in a compartment by the door and hung the Devil of Meidua's belt on a peg. Stooping, I unfastened Sir Hadrian, Knight Victorian's boots and left them in a bolt-hole underneath the coat. Unshod and unbelted, whatever was left of me crossed the vestibule. The inner doors were only wood, and opened at my touch.

Home.

My suites aboard the *Tamerlane* were large by the standard of such things. The lounge was an open, high-ceilinged chamber complete with a small dining area to the right and a concealed lift that allowed servants to carry our meals up from the officer's mess four decks down. Doors in the left-hand wall led through a sort of airlock to our sleeping quarters and the private bath, while a short stair ascended to a loft that ringed the entire lounge with shelves stuffed with books, microfilm reels, and storage crystals. There were no windows, though the massive holograph plate that dominated one wall showed an image of the gas giant below the *Tamerlane* turning slowly against the night. Its planetshine fell pink and golden on the dark furniture and richly patterned carpets. A dinted myrmidon's helmet sat atop a mannequin's head on a side table. High on the wall to my right a golden banner hung, displaying the eight-winged angel that once had been the battle standard of Admiral Marius Whent, the erstwhile dictator of Pharos I had destroyed. A macabre trophy. A memento mori made all the more appropriate by the black skull the angel had in lieu of a face.

A hundred other relics there were of the life I'd lived and Valka with me. There was a ceramic laving basin that Jinan had given me, cracked and repaired with silver solder. Beside it on the sideboard table stood a holograph depicting Valka and myself standing above the cleft at Calagah. Sir Elomas Redgrave had taken that holograph. That had been more than almost four hundred years ago. Sir Elomas was probably dead. The table itself concealed the controls for the room's holography suite, disguised to look like ordinary wood. Carved flowers acted as dials for volume and lighting control, while pressing a whorl here or a leaf there would conjure control plates or activate the table's recorder. Often I would dictate to it, recording drafts and pieces of what has become this book.

All of it vanished in an instant when she spoke from the armchair at one corner of the antique rug. "How did it go with the prince?"

Valka Onderra Vhad Edda set aside the tablet she'd been reading and rose. To judge from the tangled mess of papers on the drinking table at her elbow and the half-concealed holograph, she had been up to her elbows translating an inscription from the ruins at Calagah on Emesh. In the long decades we had spent together, she had identified several patterns in the alien inscriptions, but even with the computer laced through her brain, she could not read them.

"He's fine. Whined a bit when I told him he was rooming with the junior officers."

The doctor smiled and, reaching up, brushed my hair back with delicate fingers. "You used to whine a bit, too." She leaned in and kissed me. When at last we separated, she asked, "Are you all right?"

I let my hand fall, and turning, crossed the carpet to a sideboard where a wine collection waited behind glass. I drew out of bottle of Kandarene red and poured it into the decanter. Priorities thusly ordered, I looked back at her. "I'm just tired. I don't like being on stage so much."

She snorted. " 'Tis a lie!"

In spite of my tiredness, I smiled. "Maybe. Not for these people, anyway."

"*Anaryoch,*" Valka swore in her native Panthai. *Barbarians.*

"The Emperor isn't so bad, it's the bloody ministers," I said, "Breathnach and Bourbon." I pulled Aranata's ring from my thumb. I placed it and the ivory ring I wore about my third finger in lieu of a wedding band in Jinan's basin by the door to our sleeping quarters. Remembering suddenly, I drew the Galath blossom from my pocket and lay it in the bowl as well.

Valka and I had been together longer now than most plebeians could live, but she had refused my offers of marriage. She was Tavrosi, and they had abandoned such institutions. I told myself it did not matter, that I was palatine and palatines did not marry for love. That a palatine's true relationships were had outside marriage. I told myself that this was better, or at least good enough.

We lie to ourselves all the time, but there remains a piece of us near our heart that whispers, *You don't believe that.* That part often spoke to me when I thought of Valka and of the bond between us, but she had a way of silencing it with her presence. I stood there a while, cradling my now-naked hand with the other, feeling the false bones Kharn had given me. Valka hardly looked a day older than when we'd first met: pale-skinned and sharp-featured, her red-black hair pulled messily up from high cheekbones. She wore only a long gray shirt that left a length of ghostly thigh exposed beneath prominent hips, the sharp points of her clan intaglio chasing down her arm in fractal patterns. Valka had slept in fugue far more than I had since we left Vorgossos, and the gap between our ages had closed. No longer was she the worldly stranger, the fey sorceress of far-flung Tavros, but a living woman. *My* woman.

Pretense had dropped between us.

"What?" She smiled at me. She never used to smile.

"Nothing," I said, and it was true. "I love you."

"You're not wrong," she said, and her smile returned my words to me. "But are you all right? Really?"

I returned to the decanter and—unwilling to wait any longer—poured myself a glass. I gestured at Valka with the crystal bottle, but she shook her head. "I'm fine," I said, "really, I . . . the Empress asked about you." Valka said nothing. She had enough experience dealing with me to know I would speak my piece in time, that I was only working myself up to say what it was that was bothering me. "She called you a witch."

" 'Tis nothing out of the ordinary, then," Valka said, trying to reassure me.

Speaking to my own reflection in the bloody wine, I said, "But it was the Empress. I . . . they know what you are." Knew she carried a forbidden computer laced throughout the gray matter of her brain. I stifled my fear behind a swig of wine. It tasted of smoke and pepper.

I swallowed.

Valka raised narrow shoulders. "They know I'm Tavrosi. You barbarians assume we're all full of machines. They won't do anything, besides . . ." Here she seated herself on the arm of the couch that wrapped around the holograph projection bit. "We're leaving Forum now."

"Maybe we shouldn't come back."

"You don't mean that."

I took another sip of wine. I knew I was drinking it too fast for how fine a vintage it was, but I needed the drink desperately. I needed to sleep—to dream, perhaps—and for a long time. Perhaps I would go into fugue for the first leg of our journey, allow myself that escape and respite: to cease to be for a time and return. It was tempting, and one often heard stories of certain palatine lords—aged and world-weary—placing themselves in cryonic fugue for years and decades at a time to prolong their tragically long lives. Common wisdom taught that such people did so only to extend their lives, the rich and the powerful clinging like drowning men to their wealth and power, but I know better. Such men are not afraid of dying. They are afraid to live, and so live only days at a time.

"You're right," I said. "It's only . . . coming from the Empress . . . I worry about you."

"You worry about me?" Valka's winged eyebrows shot up. "Hadrian, if your Imperial *friends* ever learn these things you can do are real, they'll forget all about me." Valka had seen me die, had seen my head struck off by Prince Aranata with my own sword. And she had seen me return, sent back by the Quiet for reasons I did not understand. I had told her everything, about the howling Dark beyond death and the rivers of light that flowed across time and separated what *was* from what might be.

I seated myself on the arm of the couch beside her. "I can't *do* anything. It was the Quiet."

She put a hand on my knee and leaned warm against me. I offered her my wine cup and this time she accepted, vanishing half the remaining contents in one shot. She turned her hand palm up for me to take it, and I did, closing my artificial fingers about her true ones, flesh against flesh. After a moment of companionate silence, she asked, "Did you get access to the archives?"

"No," I growled, accepting the wine back. "The Emperor's holding it for ransom, I think. I don't know why. Said it was *for him to decide what I do with my time* or something like that. He played like he didn't know I'd requested access, said we would discuss it when we returned from this fool's errand." I made a gesture as if to throw something away. "I'm sorry."

Her fingers tightened against mine. "Hey." She lifted my hand in hers, kissed it. " 'Tis not your fault." I crossed back toward the bar to recharge the empty glass. "We'll figure it out after this."

"We're not meant to figure it out, Valka. We're meant to fail so the

Emperor has an excuse for removing the people's favorite new hero from the limelight. Or if not the Emperor, one of the old dogs like Bourbon." I glanced back over my shoulder.

"Bourbon . . ." Valka wrinkled her nose. "He's the fat one, isn't he?"

"That fat man is a descendant of the ancient kings of France who went into exile when the Mericanii took Old Earth."

I could hear Valka's frown as I poured a second glass of wine for myself. "Why are you defending him?"

"I'm not defending *him*," I said. "He's a descendant of a family line that goes straight back to the Golden Age. I think that's worth something."

Her response played in my head before she could voice it, and with my back turned to her, I mouthed the word as she asked, "Why?"

Smiling, I turned and raised the glass to my lips. "You're the historian," I said, "you don't think history is valuable?"

Valka made a rude gesture. "Not when history is an ass." My smile did not waver. Valka had never met War Minister Bourbon, knew nothing of the man save what I had said of him. Her dislike of the man was for my sake, and I loved her for it. "You really think they mean for you to fail?" The way she looked at me, as though I were spun from glass . . . no one else looked at me like that. Not since I became a knight. Maybe not ever.

"Yes," I said, feeling like glass myself as she wrapped her arms around me, pressing her face against my chest.

"Well then," she said, " 'tis well that whether we fail or not is up to *us*."

CHAPTER 7

BEFORE THE SUN FELL

JEWEL-BRIGHT AND BLUE-GREEN AS the Earth of legend was Gododdin, shining through the false window that fronted the *Tamerlane's* bridge. I stood alone on the forward observation platform, looking down and out at the planet into whose orbit we had so recently entered. Tangled ribbons of cloud raked across her surface, white as snow; and but for the rusty bloom of deserts here and there her landscapes flowered like drops of Eden beneath her golden sun.

The sun I would destroy.

The false window dimmed its light so that a man might look upon its majesty unshuttered. The ancients believed that the Morning Star was a jewel carried into the heavens by a great hero who had reclaimed that star from the lord of the underworld, and that in payment for his heroism, the gods set him to sail the skies, forever carrying that gem aloft. Earth's Morning Star was only her sister planet, Venus, but it was easy to understand how the ancients made that mistake. They say the oldest stars have hearts of diamond, and maybe it is so. But the ancients may be forgiven for their error, whereas I deserve the underworld.

"We have contact with the surface, captain," came Lieutenant Pherrine's pleasant tones.

"Traffic control?" asked Captain Corvo. I did not turn from my study of the world beneath us, but squinted, trying to pick out the glitter of satellites and ships in parking orbits as we drew nearer.

Pherrine answered, "No ma'am, it's from Fort Din."

"Put it through on the central well, lieutenant. Hadrian!"

Only reluctantly did I turn my face from the window. I had dressed in my diplomatic best: polished black boots cuffed just below the knee, black trousers with the crimson double stripe down either side, knee-length quilted jacket with fitted sleeves and a high collar depicting my pitchfork and pentacle in red above the heart. Over it all I'd donned a brilliant white cape cut lacerna-fashion and bordered with a maze pattern to match the red on my trousers and of my crest. I wore my sword again in its magnetic hasp at my right hip alongside a plasma burner.

I looked every inch the Knight Victorian, I thought, catching a glimpse of my reflection in the glossy black wall as I approached the holography well. The well was a pedestal two yards across, about waist high in the center of the bridge before the captain's chair. I approached via the catwalk that ran from the forward observation platform to the captain's station above the stations and consoles of the other bridge officers.

As I drew near, the figure of a man materialized above the pedestal, replacing the wire-frame model of the *Tamerlane*. His back was to me, but he had the ramrod straight, square profile of any Legionary officer, and from the silver braids draped across his shoulder I took him for a man of some import.

"You must be Captain Corvo!" he said, voice gruff but not impolite. "Sir Amalric Osman, Knight-Castellan at Fort Din. Let me be the first to welcome the Red Company to Gododdin system."

Otavia Corvo was still too much the Norman for all this Imperial pomp and circumstance. I watched her smooth mild amusement from her face before answering. "Thank you, Sir Amalric. I am Captain Otavia Corvo of the *ISV Tamerlane,* here on Imperial orders."

"Is Lord Marlowe with you?" Osman asked, looking uselessly around. The projection pickups only afforded the fellow a view of a narrow slice of the bridge around Corvo. He could not see me. I raised a hand to signal Otavia to stall. I wanted to get a measure of the man first, and leaned in to study his blunt, square-featured face and bald scalp. Osman struck me as one of those common legionnaires promoted to the rank of officer and patrician status by long years of service. There had been a time when such men were rare in the Legions, but seven centuries of fighting had bled much of the aristocratic officer class from the ranks, and new blood had been permitted to rise on merit.

I crossed my arms, listening.

"He should be with us momentarily, Knight-Castellan," Corvo said, glancing toward me.

Osman straightened his jacket like a recruit afraid of his first inspection. I felt my eyebrows shoot up. I never had gotten used to being taken so seriously. In truth, I felt like little more than the boy I had been on Emesh.

On Delos. Not someone whom fort castellans were nervous to meet. "Very good. I was surprised to hear the Emperor was sending him. We didn't expect a Victorian in the first place, but . . . the Halfmortal? Tell me, captain, are the stories about him true? Can he really not be killed?"

The captain looked at me through the holograph with bemusement in her amber eyes. "You'll have to ask him yourself," she said only.

"Wonderful!" Osman said, a bit stupidly—but perhaps it was only nerves. "I look forward to meeting him."

"You won't have to wait long, sir," I said, still not visible to the other man.

"Lord Marlowe, sir!" Osman snapped a salute and stood at full attention as I circled into view. Otavia withdrew.

I gave the castellan a short but gracious bow, by doing so emphasizing that I was a lord and knight of the Imperium, not merely another soldier. Often I have done this, greeting the officers with every lordly courtesy as a member of the nobility, and greeting the common soldiery as a common soldier. Thus one impresses the officers and ingratiates oneself with the men. "Well met," I said.

"Well met indeed!" Osman replied, and introduced himself again. He looked me up and down. "You're younger than I expected."

I knew how I must look to an up-jumped plebeian like Osman with my smooth face and long black hair. I did not look much older than Prince Alexander, who was only thirty. It tended to work against my reputation, which was why I had made sure to speak first. I have always had a strong speaking voice. My tutors had seen to that. "Appearances can be deceptive, castellan," I said. "I trust you have news of our quarry?" We had been twelve years reaching Gododdin. Plenty of time for the emergency beacon to have reached one of the deep space relays.

"The convoy? Not as yet, lordship. We dispatched the *ISV Legendia* and a small fleet of outrider vessels along their last known trajectory but have yet to receive word by telegraph."

Trying to keep the frustration from my voice, I said, "Understood."

"I've arranged for a landing port at Fort Din. With your permission, my lord, I'll wave the coordinates and landing procedures to your ship."

"That's good of you, but it won't be necessary," I said. "Unless you've any particular objection, I'd prefer to land in the city field. I like to see a bit of the places I visit. Would you be so kind as to send a driver for us?"

Osman blinked, and I hoped the man had not taken offense. "Of course, my lord. At once."

Catraeth was one of those cities built after a world's initial colonization and showed no signs of the ugly, prefabricated structures built by the Consortium for rapid settlement. Its buildings were all of white stone quarried from the mountains in whose last peak the city sheltered above the seemingly infinite expanse of grassland the natives called the Green Sea. In the distance, great shoals of rock upthrust from the flat landscape like islands and broke the perfect horizon beneath an eggshell sky.

It was early morning when we landed, and the first blush of dawn arose to hide the stars. Three unmarked groundcars awaited us on the tarmac once we emerged from the landing terminal. Stewards took our luggage and stowed it in the trunks with the help of some of the hoplites in our personal guard.

" 'Tis clean, the air!" Valka said, restoring her hair to order after a gust of wind tousled it.

"Smells different," Alexander observed, taking in the sights. It occurred to me that, humble as the airfield was, the prince had not seen so much land in his lifetime, living as he had among the clouds.

"That's the earth, boy!" Crim exclaimed. Two years of wakefulness on our twelve-year journey had done little to crack the enamel on Alexander's Imperial pride, and I sensed my squire stiffen at being called *boy* by the Norman. "Aah, it's just rained! Can you smell it?" He took in a deep lungful of the air. "Makes one feel *human* again after all that time on the ship, eh?" He clapped Pallino on the shoulder, and falling back on Jaddian—his mother's tongue—he exclaimed, *"Rayissima!"* Beautiful.

It was.

Both Bastien Durand and Tor Varro were silent. The former kept checking his terminal, doubtless still in communication with the *Tamerlane,* while the latter stood with eyes closed. I thought I heard him humming softly to himself, but did not disturb him. Before long we were underway, and I watched the pale streets roll by as the day grew ever brighter. There were few other groundcars, and those of the peasants out so early went on foot or took the trolley cars whose rails ran in the streets. Once or twice the flash of a flier passed overhead. An old man in a white apron stood sweeping off the porch of a quaint bakery, and not much further down a woman busied herself ordering a rack of discount paperbacks outside her little bookshop. As we climbed the hill toward the white-walled fastness of Fort Din above the city, I looked back at the landing field, its blast pits like pores in the face of some giant, and spied the great granaries and processing plants that made Gododdin what it was.

The planet's placement in the gulf between the Sagittarius and Centaurus arms of our galaxy made it an important stop for many a traveler and merchant vessel on the outward road, but Gododdin's primary importance was agricultural. The ancient fabulists often believed—when they imagined commerce between the stars—that starships would be laden with food, that crops grown on Marinus might be flown on ice to Jadd and back again. And while certainly luxury goods are thus transported from time to time, the fabulists were wrong when they imagined that one planet might serve as a farming colony for several others. The travel time between worlds is simply too great, and while wine and liquor or even tea might be transported at monstrous cost and the finest livestock shipped in fugue, each planet more often than not must learn to feed itself or starve.

With one massive exception.

The Green Sea was not grassland, but hundreds of square miles of fields where the Legions grew their *bromos,* the genetically engineered oats that have kept billions of our soldiers on their feet since the time of Boniface the Pretender. It was from bromos that protein-base was manufactured. I told Alexander all this, pointing to the granaries and the fields beyond, where already I could see farm equipment at its slow march.

"We'll have to find some place in the city to eat," Pallino said darkly. "It'll just be rations at the fort."

"Aren't we staying at the consulate?" Alexander asked. "The governor-general is a cousin, I heard. Nicholas or something like that."

"Let's see what we can see at the fort," I said in answer.

Fort Din rose above the city, sprouting from a spur of the mountain. Of the same stone as the city it was, but simple in the way all military buildings are simple: blank stone and concrete blocks whitewashed and without columns or arches. The curtain wall was there to impress more than to repel invaders—siege warfare as in the Golden Age of Earth had not been practiced since the advent of high explosives—and the citadel within reared stark and clean, its central spire a spike of steel and glass bright as pearl and bloody in the morning light. A lance aimed defiantly at the sun.

Legionnaires in scarlet and ivory had the gate, and faceless they waved us through. Our little motorcade stopped before the steps leading to the doors of the great keep, where fifty men in uniform stood at attention to either side. Sir Amalric waited at the top alongside an aide and some others.

"Here we go," I said to Valka. She took her hand from my knee as the porter opened the door for us. It clam-shelled upward and I stepped out onto the tarmac, cape fluttering in the morning air.

There were perhaps a hundred paces between our car and Sir Amalric at the top of the stairs, and I began my walk. I'd have liked it if Valka walked beside me, but she preferred to distance herself from me in these official appearances. She was not of the Empire, and would not be mistaken for such. A cornicen sounded his trumpet from somewhere on the walls above, and I half-wished that I'd brought our own herald to answer. But it was better this way. To appear ostentatious was to exaggerate my importance. Understating my arrival like this sent a different message: that I did not need to exaggerate.

I was right, for before I had gone twenty paces the sky flashed and grew bright as day, and I stopped and looked up in wonderment, remembering only belatedly that Gododdin had an orbital mirror to magnify the light of its sun. I saw its shining hexagon skirting the horizon, and the faint shape of its three arms dark through its halo. I disguised the moment of surprise—of weakness—with a gesture: touching curled forefinger and thumb to forehead, lips, and heart in the sign of the sun disc. Last three fingers extended, I raised the circle to the sky in pious benediction.

The cornicen sounded again.

What cosmic prank had brought that false sun to shine the moment I set foot on Gododdin? What irony brought that false light to mark the Sun Eater's first visit to the world he would consume? I felt a smile pull at my lips then, as I weep now in writing. I breathed the air that two billion men and women shared. The air I burned to nothing, the men and women I washed away in fire. They cheered me as I came, and welcomed me with silver trumpets.

"Welcome to Gododdin, Lord Marlowe," Sir Amalric said, and knelt—though propriety only asked that the castellan bow.

"We're happy to be here," I said, and though the fellow expected me to offer my ring, I did not. Aranata's ring was no lordly signet, and though I had a new one to replace the one I'd thrown away on Emesh, I did not wear it. Though the Emperor had re-legitimized me as a member of the palatinate and his peerage and established me as head of a new and separate House Marlowe, I did not feel a lord in the truest sense. "Please, stand."

Osman did.

"May I introduce my lady, Doctor Valka Onderra Vhad Edda, scientific advisor to the Red Company." I turned, permitting Osman to kiss Valka's hand. "And this is Tor Varro. And this," I stepped aside so that Alexander might step forward, "is my squire, Alexander." I pointedly did not use the boy's full name. It was not that I wished to keep Alexander's Imperial lineage a secret, only that it would do the boy good not to be lording his blood and name over everyone in the vicinity.

"Well met, all of you," Sir Amalric said, saluting my squire and the inspecting my guard with a cursory glance. He ran a hand over his bald pate and asked, "Would you like to see your quarters and take a meal before we begin?"

I shook my head. "We've rested enough on the ship. If your men will see that our effects are taken to our quarters, we may begin at once."

CHAPTER 8

DREAM EVIL

I DO NOT NOW recall much of the room itself, though I do not have to remember to tell you that it was dull: gray-walled and darkly carpeted, the furniture cheap and utilitarian, the chairs wheeled. I do not need to remember the pitchers of water sweating on the table to know they were there, or recall the face of the junior officer to know one stood in a corner ready to refill one of his betters' glasses should it empty. I have seen a thousand versions of that room on a thousand worlds, and they are all the same.

But I remember the view of Catraeth's white streets and fountains and the brightly painted faces of shops and homes. The way they ran out to the edge of the uplands and down the slopes to where the Green Sea rushed up against the mountains. From our great height, I could see for miles until the curve of the world veiled all that was beyond the horizon from sight.

"Lord Marlowe?"

I blinked, returning my attentions to the room and the people in it. "Yes, yes. Proceed."

Presently the lights dimmed and the horizontal slice of window polarized, casting us into premature gloom.

"The convoy we sent to Nemavand comprised five vessels: the *Valiant*, the *Old Iron King*, the *Emperor's Hand*, the *Red Defender*, and the *Merciless*. We've heard nothing from the *Defender* or the *Hand*, but the other three managed to get off distress calls before they went dark. There wasn't much, which tells us that whoever attacked them went for their comms arrays first." The speaker was a reedy plebeian woman in dress blacks with the silver shield of a data analyst pinned to her arm. "All three signals were picked up by the datanet relay here." She indicated a point on the starchart that appeared projected above the table that very moment.

"That's what? About fifty light-years from Dion Station?" Durand asked, removing his false spectacles to get a better look at the holograph before us. "You said the signal arrived three years ago? That's . . ." He trailed off, trying to calculate the volume of space that left us to search.

He needn't have bothered. "That leaves us with anywhere between three thousand fifty-three cubic light-years and twenty-four thousand four hundred twenty-nine cubic light-years of space to explore," Tor Varro said, so quickly I had to remind myself that arithmetic was the least of a scholiast's applications. Varro had taken the amount of time it had taken for the signal to reach the datanet relay satellite, converted it to light-years, and doubled it, because the missing fleet must have disappeared somewhere approximately nine light-years from the relay sat and he needed to account for drift, assuming the vessels had been attacked at warp. Practically speaking, the real number was closer to the smaller number, with the convoy most likely lost along that thin sphere nine light-years distant from the relay sat in question.

Even so, my heart sank again.

It was still an enormous volume, one we might search for decades and find nothing but trace gases and the odd rogue asteroid. It would be like trying to find a tiny coal in a pot of ink with a sieve the size of a thimble while blindfolded and wearing thick gloves.

"You said you sent outriders?" Varro asked, laying one hand on the tabletop to claim the proverbial floor.

"That would be me," said the patrician, serious-looking fellow with dark eyes and a mass of close-cropped black curls, whom Osman had introduced as Commodore Mahendra Verus, captain of the *Mintaka.* "Dispatched one of my courier ships to investigate. They should be there within the year." The courier ship would have been smaller, with an outsized warp drive. Like the *Schiavona,* the ship Bassander Lin had used to pursue us to Vorgossos, it would make better time than a proper warship.

"So no data yet," the Chalcenterite scholiast mused. Varro was an exemplar of his order and trade. His face, which by its pointed features and darting eyes ought to have been furtive and satyr-like, was instead smooth and unfeeling as stone. I had watched the man receive battle reports or assist the doctors in triage with the detached grace of a machine. It is a common misconception—one that I have doubtless fallen into in writing this very account—that the scholiasts do not feel. They do. They merely attempt to put their feelings in their place, to compartmentalize them and lay bare the remarkably flexible, parallel processing mechanism of the human mind, which, properly trained, could perform the functions of the daimons forbidden by the Chantry's holy law.

But Varro was as perfect an exemplar as I have ever seen. *Dispassionate* was too soft a word. And he was in his element. "Is there more?"

The reedy analyst cleared her throat. "Not much. What we have of their telemetry indicates they were at full warp when they were attacked, and time stamps indicate there were no more than forty minutes between the initial distress call—from the *Merciless*—and the last, from the *Old Iron King*."

"At full warp?" Durand repeated, his glasses still in his hand—a sign the bookish officer was paying full attention.

Sir Amalric spoke up. "They must have used some kind of gravity net. Whoever they are."

"A magnetic grapnel would work as well, if they knew where to aim it," Verus offered.

"Do we know which it was?" I asked, directing my words to the analyst where she stood holding the remote in white-knuckled hands. Was she nervous? She was young, certainly, and those are much the same thing.

She glanced at Osman before answering, "No, my lord. The transmissions were fragmentary, which would indicate the vessels were each taken offline before they could transmit more than the initial burst."

"A grapnel could do that, could it not?" Valka asked from her place beside me. "Knock out a ship's communications?"

"Yes, ma'am," Osman replied.

"If it was a grapnel," Tor Varro mused, "then it is far more likely the attack was carried out by Extrasolarian agencies."

One of the junior Fort Din officers leaned in. "What makes you say that, counselor?"

Varro turned his narrow eyes on the woman and answered in his usual calm, disquieting way, "The computational power required to time and aim a magnetic pulse at a target traveling at superluminal velocity would require artificial intelligence. Nothing we know about the Cielcin suggests that they have the technological capability for such things."

The Extrasolarians. I felt my stomach turn over.

I had fought the Cielcin on a dozen battlefields by then: Emesh, the *Demiurge,* Cellas, Thagura, Aptucca, and more . . . seen what it was they could do firsthand. The cities burned, the people butchered, eaten raw, the heads mounted on spears, the bodies mutilated. I remember one woman had been pinned open like a biological sample and mounted to a pole like a battle standard, and the way the *ichakta* commander who held it laughed as it ordered its troops forward. I remember the way Raine Smythe and old Sir William Crossflane had been torn to pieces by Prince Aranata's *scahari*. The Cielcin were evil, but they burned like fire.

Ice was the more insidious threat.

I remember also the Garden of Everything and the way the merchants on March Station had sold flesh by the pound, bottling dreams and carving off limbs to be replaced by machines. I can still see Kharn's clone children slumbering in amniotic sacs in the dungeons of Vorgossos and hear Father Calvert singing his macabre rhyme. I remember that cold room beneath the mountain on Arae, the dead wired into the machine that had ripped their minds from their bodies and the army of computer-possessed men charging downhill at our line. Bad as the Cielcin were, it was from evil dreams of the Extras that I awoke sweating in the dead of night.

"This attack is more consistent with Extra methodology," Verus conceded, leaning back in his seat. "They've been known to prey on the major shipping lanes."

Sir Amalric rapped the desk with his fist for attention. "Lord Marlowe, I've read your file . . ." I very much doubted that; rather I suspected Osman had read the official version, the one Legion Intelligence had scrubbed clean. "Do you think it could be Vorgossos?" The man looked sheepish asking. I understood him. I had thought Vorgossos a myth, a story like lost Atlantis, like Lemuria and forgotten Sarnath.

"No," I answered, and repeating the official story, added, "Vorgossos was destroyed." I held my face impassive, relying on the same scholiast training that kept Tor Varro so composed.

"I read that file, too," Amalric said, but there was something in his eyes that told me he knew well as I the files were only that. Had I underestimated this man? He was right to doubt. That file he'd read claimed that First Strategos Titus Hauptmann had directed an entire fleet to Vorgossos following the defeat of Prince Aranata's forces and destroyed it. Fragged the entire planet from orbit and left it a smoldering pile of rubble to collapse into a thin ring of rock and dust about its undead star. But I knew better. Hauptmann *had* sailed for Vorgossos, but when he'd arrived at those dread shores, the planet was gone.

Vanished.

Vorgossos will survive, Kharn Sagara had told me when last I saw him. Them, for there were two of him then. I should not have doubted him.

What sort of power could move an entire planet? Bassander Lin had been there, and told me the men came away from the ordeal shaken and confused. The brown dwarf had remained, alone in the Dark between the stars with no planet surrounding it.

Kharn Sagara had not lied.

They had survived.

Osman was still waiting on my answer. I shook my head. "Even if there were survivors of the sack at Vorgossos, that was thousands of light-years from here. There are other Extra factions, hundreds of Exalted ships, freehold colonies, station cities . . . it could be any of them."

"And it could still be the Cielcin," Valka interjected, quite correctly.

"It could," Varro agreed. Those furtive eyes found mine as he spoke. I knew what he was thinking, what he couldn't tell these men. That it might be both. That on Arae we had found signs of an alliance between the Extras and the Pale. The unholy matrimony of Cielcin and machine. I had killed such a creature, a reject left unfinished in its storage tank, its brain not fully connected to the machine body the Extras had built for it. "We have no way of knowing, of course."

"Our latest report from central intelligence said this new prince of theirs—the one that attacked Hermonassa—has a taste for more military targets," Osman put in.

I let out a long, slow breath—nearly a sigh. "Syriani Dorayaica." I had not said the name aloud in a long time. Not since we'd left Forum, perhaps. It hung dark on the air. Like incense. Like smoke. And the tang of it was almost familiar, as though it were the name of some old acquaintance. Had I heard it before Hermonassa? Had Tanaran mentioned the Cielcin chieftain perhaps, or had Uvanari? I elected not to dwell on it, and continued. "The Cielcin have begun to understand they can't fight us like they fight one another. I think part of their burning our colonies comes from the way they have to destroy their rivals' fleets completely. When they fight, it's not just warships, it's homes. Cities. They risk everything and they can't risk letting anything survive. I think this Dorayaica has realized that annihilating a planet's population the way they do is a waste of time and resources." I steepled my fingers and paused, surveying the men and women gathered round that long table. "I will tell you this in confidence, gentlemen and ladies. The Emperor and the people in Legion Intelligence believe that the war is changing. That this Dorayaica is the first in what may be a new generation of Cielcin princes dedicated to their war with the Imperium, and that we may be facing hard days ahead." I paused and glanced at Alexander where he was seated in the corner, not speaking, as I had instructed him. "I agree with them." I saw the color had gone from Osman's face and Verus's, and that many of the others sat staring. "But we have no reason to suspect that Dorayaica is behind this attack, though it is a possibility. At this juncture we have no way of knowing if it is this prince or the Extrasolarians or some other agency. But there are men missing, men whom His Radiance has tasked me with finding. We must devise a strategy to do so, and until we have that, the rest of this is navel-gazing."

Bastien Durand grunted his agreement. "This is all academic, yes." He replaced his spectacles on his broad nose. Rounding on Verus, he asked, "Do you know when your scouts will arrive, sir?"

The captain frowned and checked his terminal, which projected panels like sheets of paper into the black of the tabletop. He shuffled through them. "Not for two months."

"And several years to adequately probe that volume." Varro pointed at the projection. He was referring to the tiny sail probes that could be accelerated nearly to light speed with a single pulse from a ship's targeting lasers, so small were they.

Valka tapped the table with her fingernails to draw attention to herself and to stop the scholiast before he could continue thinking aloud. "'Twould take us nearly so long to get there from here. Much of the scanning could be done."

I pictured the sail probes spreading out to fill the sphere like pollen one spring evening, taking decades to float away. "Yes . . ." I said, idly cracking my knuckles. It was certainly the most time-efficient solution.

"You're leaving?" Osman asked, sitting forward. "You only just arrived! We've not finished our attempts to recover the damaged data from the transmis—"

I raised a hand for quiet, and the man's objections fell to silence almost at once. I had not grown familiar with or to love the trappings of rank and power, but being able to silence such men as Osman at a gesture was delicious. "Not at once, castellan. Never fear. We have two months before your scouts arrive and begin their work. Given the margins we're working with, two months won't change much. Besides, that will give my people and yours an opportunity to work together. It may be that we can be of some assistance."

CHAPTER 9

THE DEVIL'S COHORT

"WELL, IT COULD BE worse," Valka said. "There might have been no distress signal sent at all." She rested her head against the glass and pulled one knee to her chest where she languored on the deep windowsill.

"Maybe their scouts will turn something up," said Pallino from the door.

Our whole landing party had gathered in the suite Sir Amalric's people had set aside for me. They were low-ceilinged, unimpressive chambers, but spacious enough, with a large sitting room, the bedroom complete with the full bathing suite—a curious luxury on a military base—and a broad balcony overlooking the city of Catraeth below. Gray-walled and white, the only decoration in the room except for the odd mirror or two was a map outlining the emergency protocols for evacuating the spire should Fort Din come under attack. Like so many Imperial fortifications, Fort Din was built upon a network of bunkers that honeycombed the mountain beneath it for miles. They were built to withstand an orbital bombardment, designed for the days of interhouse warfare and rebellious lords, intended to shelter the fort's staff for months and even years using starship-grade life support, hydroponics, and doubtless the planet's plentiful supply of protein-base from the bromos crop.

"And they may turn up something if they can reconstruct the corrupt portions of the beacon files," Durand added, fidgeting with his terminal in his lap. The fellow did not like to be away from his ship, I think. Durand was a born spacer, and spent most of his life aboard starships. Perhaps the open sky frightened him?

Crim spoke up from the window near Valka. "Should we send to the ship for Ilex and some of the data techs?"

"Lonely already?" Valka teased, nudging the Norman-Jaddian with her toe. "You haven't been apart for a day yet."

Crim scratched the back of his head, tearing his eyes from the window to look round sheepishly at the rest of us. "It's just a thought."

"You're with that homunculus?" Alexander said, face wrinkled in disgust.

I felt a twinge of anger tighten my throat, but Crim was faster. "Her name is Ilex, Your Highness." Anger faded to sympathy as I saw the young prince recoil. Alexander—like a certain young man I'd known—had much unlearning to do. There was a time I'd have asked the same question in the same tone, when I too was just a boy fresh from my father's castle.

Homunculi were not fully human—Ilex shared as much of her genome in common with algae and aspens as she did men and women—but then neither was I. Like every palatine, Prince Alexander included, I had been born in a tank, grown to order by the natalists of the High College to produce a *perfect man.*

They'd made me instead, and while my long life and other improvements could not be denied, I was not without handicap. I could not have children without the oversight of the Imperial High College—unless I wanted to father misshapen inti like poor Lorian.

"And she's not a homunculus. She's a dryad," Valka added.

"That's a kind of homunculus," Alexander snapped back.

"Enough!" I said, raising the same hand I'd raised in the meeting. "I'll think about sending for her. We should give their people a chance. It wouldn't do to just take the work from them the minute we arrive."

Crim was still watching the prince when he answered, "Understood, boss. Just thinking out loud."

Lowering myself onto the gray armchair the others had pointedly left for me, I said, "It may come to that, but we'll give them a week or two."

"Are we really staying here for two months?" Pallino asked.

"You have a better suggestion?"

The old soldier planted his hands on his hips. "Sure. Take the fight to them."

"The fight?" Valka echoed, swinging round on the sill to face the room. "Pal, they may be long gone. These scouts are most likely to find nothing."

"We don't know *that,* either, Doctor Onderra," said Tor Varro. "Remember: this isn't the first convoy to disappear between here and Dion Station."

That remark brought us all to stillness for a moment, though I could still feel the simmering resentment percolate between Crim and Alexander. I would have to do something about that.

"We should call Corvo," Durand suggested. "She should hear the news."

We all agreed that was a good plan, and I clicked my terminal free of its wristband and placed it on the coffee table before my chair. "Windows, Crim," I said. Valka vacated her seat as the lictor drew the drab curtains. A conic projection formed above the terminal face, ghost-white in the sudden gloom. An ouroboros turned in the air to a faint, bright chime as the call went through, and a moment later Otavia Corvo's Amazonian form blossomed into view. She was sitting at a table in what looked like the *Tamerlane*'s ready room, dressed in exercise fatigues that left her arms bare. To my surprise, she was not alone. Elara sat with her, and young Lorian, too. Evidently they'd been discussing some thing or other.

"Bad time?" I asked, motioning for the others to come stand behind me as they willed.

"Take it you just got out of a meeting with them?" Corvo asked.

"Done and done," I said, and told her everything we'd learned.

When I finished, the captain replied, "Two months? That's not so bad. Won't make much difference on the other end and maybe we won't go in blind."

Uncharacteristically, Elara spoke up. "And it'd be good to get some of the crew some shore time."

"It looks a likely spot," I agreed. As a rule, I did not permit the crew to go ashore at Forum. Better to keep the Devil's Cohort—as the nobiles sometimes called my Red Company—away from high society. The last thing I needed was any fabulous tales of the Halfmortal spreading in the Eternal City, and from his own men, no less. But here? Despite its placement along a major shipping lane, Gododdin itself was relatively obscure, little more than a refueling stop for vessels not tied to the Legions, and though the cities saw their fair share of offworlders, there was little harm in letting the men loose for a week or two.

"And it will give them time to comb through the emergency transmissions and see what they can recover," I said, repeating the earlier point. "Which leaves us with the question of what to do next."

Silence both in the room and on the holo answered, and I glanced round at the others where they stood watching me. When no answer was forthcoming, I raised my eyebrows to indicate that I wanted a response.

Varro took a half step forward. "I counsel delay. It would be foolish to commit to a strategy absent all available data."

Aristedes's drawling, aristocratic tones sounded over the holograph, "But we will have to head out after their scouts, won't we?"

"We should put together a second convoy."

I turned to face the speaker, one eyebrow still raised. Prince Alexander had retreated toward the wall after his slight run-in with Crim, and stood opposite my chair and the holograph pickup, and was thus invisible to Corvo, Elara, and Aristedes. I don't think he'd meant to speak, for when he realized we were all watching him, he whitened.

Lorian barked out a laugh. "I was going to suggest the very same!"

The thought had occurred to me as well, but I was glad that Alexander had suggested it first. It seemed the time we'd spent together on the voyage out had not been wasted, after all. I gestured for the prince to continue. Alexander gathered his wits before continuing, buoyed perhaps by Lorian's support. "We might be able to bait them into attacking us, but we can be ready."

"Ready for an attack with a magnetic grapnel that knocks our systems offline?" Crim interjected.

But the prince stood firm. "There must be something we could do. If we were to not put the soldiers into fugue, we'd have a full army ready when the enemy boarded."

Speaking slowly, words sliding like a wedge beneath the prince's more fevered tones, Tor Varro said, "You're assuming that the attackers—whoever they are—are boarding these missing vessels."

"In His Highness's defense, Varro," Lorian said, "they never did find the wreckage from those earlier convoys."

Captain Corvo frowned and tucked her chin, face lost in shadow. I watched her and Prince Alexander both, the latter visible through the former's ghostly image. "It might be easier than trying to hunt these bastards down," she said.

"Do the locals have the ships and men necessary to attempt a resupply?" Lorian asked.

"Unclear," Tor Varro said in answer, "but it is something to consider."

"We don't have to come up with any solutions today," I said. "Varro, will you find out the disposition of forces in orbit here? I'd like to know if they have enough to outfit a second convoy." Though seated, the scholiast sketched a small bow. Turning to Corvo, I asked, "I trust that everyone's coming up from fugue without incident?"

The captain made a shrugging motion with her lips that did not reach her broad shoulders. "No casualties, if that's what you mean. Everything's perfectly routine."

Still seated, I arched my back, still feeling the residual effects of the thaw myself as stiffness and a phantom weight in my limbs. I needed to go for a run. A swim. Anything. I needed a fight, something to push hot blood back into capillaries long pinched shut with cold. With a glance to Crim, I said, "We may need technical staff sent down later this week. We'll keep you apprised. Let us know if there's any trouble up there."

Aristedes's pale eyebrows arched in surprise. "Are you expecting any?"

"No," I said archly, propping my elbows on the arms of my chair. "This should all be fairly routine. Hold off announcing shore leave until I've had a chance to see the city myself."

"Don't enjoy the planet too much," Elara said, smiling, eyes darting to Pallino. I just caught my lictor and friend's returned smile fading. Had he winked at her? I suppressed a smile of my own.

Thinking of all the tedious hours coming to be spent at that conference table hearing synopses of what the analysts could find, I said, "We won't."

"We're here if you need us," Corvo said.

"Thank you."

The holograph vanished a moment later, leaving the room strangely dark and close. Someone—Crim probably—opened the curtains without my having to ask him to do so. Into the tired silence, I said, "Go and rest, everyone. We've had a long journey, and I can't speak for you, but the fugue toxins are still dragging me down."

Knowing what must come next, I shut my eyes, listening for the shuffle of feet toward the suite's vestibule and heavy double doors. When the words slipped out, they sounded like my father speaking, as if the mouth that spoke them were cold and very far away. "Not you," I said, just as Lord Alistair might.

I opened my eyes, and saw that despite my not being specific those words had found their target. The light of that window cut a wedge clean across those spartan apartments, illuminating the young prince where he stood opposite me at the far end of the coffee table. Valka's shadow fell across him, and glancing to one side I saw she'd resumed her place in the window seat.

Writing this now, I am struck by the strange reversal. That I was seated as a lord in his throne with Prince Alexander standing before me like a suppliant, lips compressed, shoulders hunched. Was the boy afraid of me?

Carrot, I decided, *then stick.*

"I like your idea of sending a second convoy to bait whoever is out there," I said. "I was about to suggest the same thing myself. And if Aristedes was on the same page as well, then we should take it as a sign that the notion is good one. You've done well. I can tell your time learning on the trip here wasn't wasted."

The prince's posture visible relaxed, and he stood a little straighter. "Thank you, sir."

"But I will need you to be mindful of how it is you speak of my crew. That bit just now with Lieutenant Commander Garone cannot happen again."

"I understand." The prince looked down at the table between us, trying to avoid whatever it was he feared to find in my eyes. I remembered that feeling, had felt it in my father's presence, in Valka's when I was young—truly young. His was the fear of the convict before the judge, as all sons are before their fathers, all men before women, all mortals before gods.

I rapped my ring against the brass lip that sealed the upholstery on the edge of the chair's armrest, clear, bright sound ringing. "Do you?" I asked, and putting on a tone that reminded me of old Gibson, I said, "Tell me what you think you understand."

If the prince balked at my presumption, he swallowed it and shut his eyes. I thought I recognized one of the breathing exercises the scholiasts used to quell their emotions—I knew them well. How like his father he looked: high-cheekboned, strong of brow and jaw. He'd begun to grow long, thin sideburns in imitation of his Imperial father, though his red hair was wild above that royal countenance, lacking the coterie of court androgyns to oil and style it each day. Though I knew then that Alexander would never sit the throne, how clear I saw the knight he might become, garbed in the Imperial white and shining like the sun. He might lead men and ships into battle against the Cielcin one day, or stand on the steps of the Solar Throne as captain of the Knights Excubitor.

Alexander opened his eyes, and the fear that had been there earlier was gone. "I disrespected your servants, sir. I disrespected you, and I am your squire."

"No," I said, and heard Gibson's voice at my shoulder. *Kwatz.*

The prince twitched. "No?" Behind me, Valka stifled a laugh.

"Three things," I said, and held up so many fingers. Ticking them off one at a time I said, "Firstly, they are not my servants. I am theirs. Second, you are not disrespecting *me* at all. And thirdly, you are *not* only a squire. That is why this is important." I shook my fist at him, lingering a moment to see if he would reply. When he did not, I plowed ahead: "One thing at a time. To the first: I do not *have* servants. I am not their master. If you must rely on rank to command then you've already lost your people."

"But they do serve you," Alexander said. "They hang on your every word."

"Because I have earned their respect. Rank only formalizes relationships between people, Alexander. It does not create them. One has rank because one deserves it, and if one does not deserve it, he will lose his rank. Or his life. A man would do well to become worthy of his honors, else he will be deposed as a tyrant." I crossed my legs, fiddled absently with the silver buckle that kept my boot snug about my calf. "If I were to treat my people like slaves they would rebel. In subtle ways at first: not following my orders properly, failing to carry out tasks . . . Then in larger ways. Do you know the story of how it was Otavia Corvo came into my service?"

The question caught Alexander by surprise, and he blinked. "I heard the story. She helped you defeat a Norman tyrant on . . . Pharos?"

"She served that Norman tyrant for ten years," I said, glancing at the terminal where Corvo's holograph had floated just a few minutes before. "But she served under a captain called Emil Bordelon, a vicious brute. When his soldiers disobeyed him, he'd tie them in the brig and starve them 'til they learned their lesson. Sometimes he'd rape them."

Alexander blanched, horrified. "He what?"

"Otavia saw it happen one too many times, so I made her an offer . . . and we killed him." I clenched my fists on the armrests, remembering the way the ship's comms went dead when I ordered our men to fire. When I was younger that silence—the way Bordelon's holograph had snuffed out on the projector as he died—had haunted me. Now I only felt the vague warmth of satisfaction at a job well done. Corvo and I had rid the world of a monster. I call that good.

"Sic semper tyrannis," I continued. "You cannot lead as a tyrant. The people under you will not let you. To lead is a kind of service, a duty you owe to those who follow. *Noblesse oblige.* I need you to understand this because—to skip to number three—you are not a squire. You are a prince of the Aventine House and a high lord of the Imperium. If I teach you nothing else, it is that you should treat the people under you like family, and that if you're very, very lucky they may do the same. It is the obligation of those of us born to power or who earn it to wield that power with

virtue, because power is no virtue unto itself. Do you know the Eight Forms of Obedience, Alexander?"

"What?"

"The Eight Forms of Obedience. They're a part of the scholiasts' stoic tradition." I shut my eyes and recited. "Obedience out of fear of pain. Obedience out of fear of the other. Obedience out of love for the person of the hierarch. Obedience out of loyalty to the office of the hierarch. Obedience out of respect for the laws of men and of heaven. Obedience out of piety. Obedience out of compassion. Obedience out of devotion. You see? Love is higher than fear."

But Alexander's face contracted and he crossed his arms. "But you've said loyalty to the *office* is higher than love of the hierarch himself." He spoke as one who has caught his teacher in mistake and is embarrassed to point it out.

My memories of Gibson had the answer for me. "Because sometimes the hierarch is himself disloyal to his office, and in those cases it is incumbent upon his servants to correct him. That's what I am doing now, Your Highness. Which brings me at last to my second point."

Here I paused, letting the silence stretch a moment, surprised that Valka had not spoken, though I could feel her eyes on me. But Alexander was listening intently, and had not stirred from his place opposite me.

"Your blood and your name do not make you more than other people. Those things belong to your ancestors, and if you are to inherit them properly, you will honor those ancestors by being a good man. When His Radiance made me a knight of his order, he made me swear to despise cruelty and injustice. Do you mean to be a knight, Alexander?"

The young man swallowed and at last looked me in the eyes again. "Yes, sir."

I leaned forward, glancing back at Valka as I said, almost conspiratorially, "Then I will tell you a secret." She grinned and shook her head. "The best men are not necessarily found in palaces. Pallino was a farmer before he was a soldier. Siran's family owned a planetbound shipping company on Emesh. She was rich—by the standards of the plebs. My friend Switch, who is no longer with us, was a prostitute. Corvo was a traitor and a mercenary—Durand, too. Ilex was a dockworker on Monmara, and the Legions had Aristedes riding a desk for fifteen years. Fifteen years. With his talents. If they'd the sense to park him at a desk in some intelligence office they might have gotten some use out of him, but they had him keeping Strategos Beller's appointment books. And why?"

Perhaps he thought I was going to give him the answer, but if he did he was mistaken. I wanted to hear him say it.

The prince chewed his tongue, perhaps thinking I meant to trick him. "Because he's an intus."

"And Ilex is a homunculus," I said. "Intus, homunculus, plebeian, patrician, palatine. Doesn't matter. Our ancestors became palatine because they did great things. They smashed the Mericanii and saved mankind. But we are not them, and must do our own great things, eh? The others deserve their chance, as well. They did not ask to be born as they are, and so you and I will not punish them for it. To be a good knight, a good leader, a good man for that matter, you must judge a person by his or her actions. By their character. Do you understand?"

Alexander nodded stiffly. "I do."

I uncrossed my legs and sat as the Emperor sat, palms flat against the chair rails. "Good. Then you will go and speak to Lieutenant Commander Garone, and you will beg his pardon."

"Sir?"

"And I will ask him about it, so you *will* do it, won't you?"

"Yes, sir." The prince gave a stiff nod that was more akin to a bow and—sensing the end had come without my having to say as much—turned and followed the others from the room.

When the door at last clicked shut, Valka let out a quiet laugh. "Ooh, 'twas well done! Did you see his face?"

"It isn't funny."

" 'Tis a little funny," Valka answered. Her smile widened until it lit her golden eyes. Suddenly she broke eye contact and turned away to look once more out the window and over the balcony at Catraeth.

Feeling suddenly that I was laughed at and not the prince, I stood. "What is it?"

"You," she said simply. "Standing up for Ilex. You didn't used to be this way."

"Yes I did," I said, "you just didn't know me very well."

The shade of Gilliam Vas floated in the air between us, the old brute of a priest glowering with mismatched eyes. If the dead can be said to live on at all, it is in our memories. Thus ghosts exist, though they are but a part of ourselves. He was the first man I had killed—though I had fought in Colosso for many months before that, and stabbed a shopkeeper in Borosevo. I had killed him for Valka, though she had not wanted it.

I knew what Valka was thinking, and so said, "I didn't hate Gilliam because he was an intus." That was only partly true. Gilliam had been deformed, hunchbacked and twisted, with mismatched eyes and a misshapen head. He had frightened me, as Lorian frightened me. The inti were reminders of just how fragile we palatines are, how much we are indebted to the Emperor, and how much his slaves. And they were reminders—painfully—of why I was not a father. Why I could not be without Imperial consent. That was no fault of Lorian's, or of Gilliam's for that matter, but perhaps I can be forgiven my fears. Perhaps that was why I still served the Emperor—though I did not guess it at the time. Perhaps I hoped that for my services I might be permitted to marry Valka and to have the family I wanted. "I hated him because of how he treated you."

That was the proper truth.

Valka's eyes glazed over, chilled. "I know. 'Twas still wrong."

"I can't bring back the dead," I said, placing a new specter between us. That of my own headless corpse. The fingers Kharn had given me twitched at the thought, and I shut my fist. The false bones did not ache as I squeezed.

"No," Valka agreed, coming closer, "but you treat the living better now."

"I was only a boy then," I said. *And a stupid boy at that.*

Something of my thought must have reached my face, for Valka said, "You were an idiot."

I kissed her, holding her face in both my hands. When we broke apart she pressed her cheek against my palm. "Thank you," I said after a moment's silence.

Large eyes looked up at me. "For what?"

"For not hating me," I said. "You've had every right to."

"I could never hate you," she said, voice small. Then she smiled out one corner of her mouth. "But you are an ass."

Matching her crooked smile I kissed her again and said into her ear, "What do you say we sweat off the fugue toxins?"

Her answer was to give me a little push and turn toward our borrowed bedchamber. She made it there before my brain caught up, and she stopped in the doorway to glance back. "What's taking you so long?"

CHAPTER 10

PINION AND CLAW

EACH DAY SPENT AT Fort Din the sun rose fair and bright, and the wind off the mountains was clean as any day in the blessed autumn of my childhood home. Rarely in all my travels have I known a world so lovely to walk upon as was Gododdin, as if she were some image caught in a looking glass of the Earth that was and was lost. If only her sky were blue and not the foggy white it was, the impression might have been perfect. How well I remember the snapping of red banners above the wall of that fortress and the gentle lift of awnings above the streets of the Grand Bazaar. I can picture the darkly wooden bookshop Valka and I visited, and the musty vanilla smell of old paper and the sugar of the pastries I bought for us when we walked in the city as common people unknown to the citizens of that world.

"So there I was," Pallino said, gesticulating, "standing in the middle of the starport terminal, covered in blood and high as hell on that shit they give us to keep us from falling over, holding my *fucking* eye in my hand, mind you—and we've got to go through the scanners to get on this tram, yeah? Full kit and everything." The wind kicked up, rustling the tall grass that grew to either side of the walk that ran parallel to the main road back up toward the gates of the fortress. Content to listen to Pallino's tale, I squeezed Valka's hand.

The old soldier continued, "And I'm centurion then, so I take point and go up to the civilian at the security kiosk—and remember we have full clearance, being Legion and all. We can use the bloody tram. Only this toady's got a real hard-on for security. Like you wouldn't believe. And I give him my pass and the letter the duke's given us says we're needed down south—and we've just come from a combat zone. Again: blood everywhere. And this fucker—my hand to Earth's tit—this fucker says I need to put my kit through security. I've got a plasma rifle, the standard disruptor, a couple grenades . . . so I say 'Why?' and this man—this *unit*—says he's supposed to scan for weapons. Weapons!" Pallino laughed, paused long enough to scratch his nose.

"What'd you do?" Valka asked, throwing the question back over her shoulder as we passed beneath the shadow of the main gate.

"I slapped the rifle on the belt—still holding my eye, which is no good anymore, by the way—and I tell the man to scan it. 'Wouldn't want to be smuggling a *gun* in my *gun,* now would I?' And do you know what happens next?"

Valka stopped laughing long enough to ask, "What?"

We never found out.

A terrible cry went up, filling the air above us with a high and grating noise like the hunting cry of a hawk. Some instinct I think that has been in us since our ancestors parted ways with the ancestors of the mouse moved me, and I crouched, thinking of the winged serpents that had dwelt on Emesh.

"The hell was that?"

"Flier?" Pallino asked, hand ready on his shield projector.

Valka had not flinched, but stood craning her neck. " 'Twas no flier. I'd have picked up the electronics." She pointed with her tattooed hand at her own head, indicating her demarchist implants.

The cry sounded again.

"We should get you inside, my lord," said one of the two plainclothes men Pallino had brought with us on our little expedition to the city.

I brushed the fellow's hand away, placing my own hand on the catch to trigger my own body shield's deployment. Despite the precaution I said, "Nonsense. We're a hundred yards from the keep." Inclining my head, I pointed to a pair of junior officers taking their lunch on the steps of one of the fort's outbuildings. Neither of them appeared frightened. "You there, soldier!"

The poor fellow practically leaped to his feet, dropping the remaining bits of his sandwich into its paper tray in his haste to salute. "Sir!"

"What was that just now?"

The man blinked, confused. "What was what, Sir Hadrian?"

"That sound, I—" I clenched my jaw shut as the awful cry went up again, wailing like the scrape of iron on stone. It set my teeth on edge.

The man's confusion vanished at once, and he brightened, "Oh, that! It's the auxilia."

"Auxilia?" I frowned. Auxilia were irregular soldiers, recruits not of Imperial extraction. Foreigners. "What do auxilia have to do with all that?"

The man stared fixedly at a point over my shoulder as he answered, "They're flying, sir. It's the Irchtani unit. Got a thousand of them in from Judecca. They're shipping out to the front."

"Irchtani?" I repeated, feeling a thrill move through me. "You have an Irchtani unit here?"

"Yes, sir. Sir Amalric has the birdos planetside for a year's seasoning with the men, see if they can hack it with the rest of us before he ships them out to the front. Surprised you haven't seen them already, they're over on the south side, got a barracks to themselves. Keep to themselves, too. Guess that could explain it."

I let the poor man return to his meal and turned to the others.

"O Earth and Emperor," Pallino swore. "He's got that look again."

The Irchtani. When I was a boy on Delos, my mother would tell me stories. Stories of the Cid Arthur, of Prince Cyrus the Fool. Stories of Kharn Sagara, of Sir Antony Damrosch and Kasia Soulier. But it was the stories of Tor Simeon the Red I liked best. How after centuries of sailing his ship had discovered the planet Judecca and its native Irchtani—a species of flying xenobite nearly so intelligent as man—but the crew had revolted, killing their captain and leaving Simeon for dead. They planned to capture the Irchtani and to sell them into slavery, for such noble savages were always curiosities at the courts of a certain kind of nobleman. Thus they would end their miserable journeys rich and comfortable and might retire to the frontier. But Simeon had survived, and with the help of the Irchtani natives he defeated his former crewmates, avenged his fellow officers, and saw to it that the Irchtani were protected when Imperial settlement came at last to Judecca. He was buried in their holiest shrine, the black temple of Athten Var, a temple that was old when the Irchtani were still dumb animals. A temple that had been built—like Calagah on Emesh and the Marching Towers on Sadal Suud—by the Quiet, if *built* was the right word. They'd called him *Unaan Kril,* the Red Worm, for their alien eyes perceived the green of his scholiast's vestments as red, and because we humans do not fly.

As a boy, he'd been my greatest hero. A man of learning who had taken up the sword only out of necessity, and had saved an alien people from the predations of man. I had set out to be like him, thinking the Cielcin like the Irchtani. Noble creatures misunderstood. That was why I had gone with Bassander Lin and Sir Olorin into the tunnels of Calagah to save

Uvanari and the Cielcin survivors. Because I had thought they could be saved, as Simeon had saved the Irchtani. But the Cielcin were not the Irchtani, and I was not Simeon. I could not save Uvanari. It had manipulated me, I know that now. Tricked me into giving it a fighting chance. A warrior's death. Its surrender to me in Calagah had been only the desperate gamble of the cornered wolf, waiting with its foot in the trap to kill the hunter on his return. And it had tried to kill *me* in the end. The Cielcin only submit when they are beaten, and they do not submit to animals. Like men.

The southern spur of Fort Din stood farthest from the city, looking out upon the Green Sea and the ruddy buttes rising from it. The wind off the mountains smelled of rain and tugged at the dry branches of those few trees the Legion permitted to grow within the fort. The barracks themselves were an ugly, L-shaped building of steel and cement white-washed and flat-roofed, bristling with antennae and comms equipment. The yard between the two arms of that building had been rolled flat in construction, and was barren but for the stray weeds.

And there they were, drilling upon its surface.

Despite my years, I have not grown used to the sight of xenobites. There is something of Earth in our genes, I think, which tells us how life is meant to look. And when we encounter something otherworldly the mind rebels, reacts with horror in much the same way as when confronted with something that is like humanity but not nearly like enough.

Man-like but not man they were, and less than man-high. The tallest of them might just barely have looked down its nose at Lorian, who was hardly five feet tall. But they were as broad as men and rounder in the shoulder, so that they seemed to huddle and slouch as they went about their business. Each wore a dun uniform, cousin to the black fatigues of our soldiers and not at all unlike those worn by human auxiliaries, though each had a deep, pointed hood in lieu of the berets sometimes worn when the men were out of their armor. I stood at the edge of the yard, watching like a child as one of the Irchtani spread out arms that were longer than it was tall, great pinions flexing, emerald feathers long as swords. Then it leaped skyward, wings kicking up a wind as it rose, and the noise of its cry split the air like a wedge as it chased after another of its fellows. As it drew near it swung, and against the pale gray sky I discerned the flash of steel.

"It has a sword," Pallino said, voice strangely hushed.

"They fight with these cutlasses," I said, pointing. "Tall as you or I. Call them *zitraa*."

"But where are their hands?"

Valka answered before I could, and I guessed those machine eyes of hers had magnified her vision to give her a better look. "Ever seen a ptero-saur?"

"A terra-what?"

"Middle of the wing," I said, cutting them both off. Holding my own arm up for examination, I went on. "The pinion folds out from the wrist like a second elbow."

"Hoi!" came a deep-throated sound, and turning I saw one of the crea-tures waddling toward us from the field, a wing raised in greeting. Its hood was up, but the beak protruded from it, black but red at the edges. A dou-ble gold chain looped across its chest, pinned to either shoulder, and I saw the familiar oak cluster gleaming at its throat to mark it as a chiliarch. Here then was the captain of the entire auxilium, all thousand soldiers. "Greetings, sir knight! And good day!" The Irchtani extended its wing in salute. Its beak did not move as it spoke, only opened. I was surprised at how well the creature spoke our tongue—I knew next to nothing of the Irchtani language, and I was struck, also, by how very like our terranic birds the creature was, and wondered what fluke of nature had made some-thing so seemingly familiar beneath an alien sun. "What brings you hon-oring us?"

What was I to say? I'd had no plan save to see the creatures that had peopled my childhood stories with my own eyes. I had not thought much further. Grasping for words, I bowed. "I only wanted to meet the *Ishaan Irchtani* for myself. I have never met one of your people before." I had seen one but for a moment a long time ago, aboard the *Enigma of Hours,* the day Switch and I had been separated and I had met the prophet, Jari. Shaking myself to rid my mind of thoughts of Jari, I said, "I am Sir Hadrian Mar-lowe, Lord Commandant of the Red Company."

As I spoke, two of the others came up behind their commander to lis-ten, and the senior xenobite replied, "I am called Barda. I am *kithuun.* Chiliarch of these." The creature bowed awkwardly, and I guessed the xenobite's legs were not meant to bend as ours. I returned the gesture. "You are the Devil?" Barda spoke haltingly, not confident of its Galstani.

Put that way, I had to stop myself from smiling. "The Devil, indeed." A small knot of the creatures came up behind their *kithuun* to see what was going on. I could not tell which of them was male or female—or what passed for male and female among the Irchtani, who like us and unlike the Umandh of Emesh and the Cielcin have two separate sexes. Some of them were unhooded, and without the garment in place their heads looked oddly small, eyes dark and beady above hooked beaks. "Forgive us for intruding, I'd only just heard your people were here and wanted to see you . . ."

"See us?" asked another of the birds, a shorter, squatter one with grayer plumage who held a *zitraa* in one scaled claw. "This isn't a zoo, human!" This one's voice was deeper than Barda's and rasped like the voice of crows, but its Galstani was better.

"Show respect, Udax!" Barda squawked, and cuffed the younger xenobite before chirruping something in its native tongue. A mingling of quarked words and trilled music it was in my ears, and hearing that sound I smiled, wishing that I could play a flute as Simeon had to learn the music of their words. Udax snapped its beak in reply.

Raising my hands, I said, "It is only that I grew up on stories of your people. When I was a boy my mother used to tell me tales of Simeon the Red and Prince Faida at the Battle of Athten Var."

"He talks to us of history!" Udax sneered. "We are not of your storybooks, *unaan*. We are here. Now. And we come to fight these Pale worms of yours." The younger Irchtani thumped its chest, talons flexing against the earth. "We are the fighting Irchtani! We're here to kill, not to amuse you!" This set several of the others cawing along with it, wings flapping in agitation. Not knowing the Irchtani well, I did not know how dangerous a sign this was.

Unaan, I thought. *Worm.* It was the same word the Irchtani had used to speak of the Cielcin, but then I supposed that neither their species nor ours could fly. "Peace, man!" Pallino said. "We're all soldiers here."

"Soldiers?" one of the other young ones exclaimed. "If we are *all* soldiers, why are we kept apart from your kind?"

"Be quiet, Udax! Morag!" Barda said, rounding on his subordinate. "This is one of their *Bashan Iseni*." *Bashan Iseni,* I later learned, were their words for palatine. Literally it meant *Higher Beings*. Gods.

But Udax was not quiet. "I am tired of these *unaani* gawking at us, *Kithuun-Barda*. Every day they are watching. We are not on display!" The soldier shifted its long cutlass in its grip.

"We'll go," Valka said, tugging gently on my cape. Then, more softly, "Come on, Hadrian."

But I did not understand how I had offended this young alien, and it felt wrong to leave without first trying to make matters right. "Kithuun-Barda," I said, addressing the commander, "I did not mean to offend your people."

"He does not even speak to us!" Udax called, speaking up before Barda could reply. A chorus of alien noises rose to greet this pronouncement, birds talking over one another until I discerned the repeated word.

"I-da! I-da!"

I did not know its meaning then, but know it now.

Get him.

I did not see Udax's *zitraa* move. I heard it first and threw my arm across my face, pulling my cape with it. The armorweave embedded within the white-on-white brocade stopped the alien edge from cutting into me, but did not stop the kick Udax threw at my chest. God Emperor—the strength of it! I must have knocked Valka over as I flew backward, skidding on the flat earth. Pallino swore and leaped over me, but before he could strike Udax in the face two more of the young Irchtani's compatriots were on him. I was bleeding. The xenobite's talons had sliced through jacket and tunic alike, and for a moment I feared the silver chain I wore to hold the shell the Quiet had given me was broken. Udax pulsed its wings once, gray feathers kicking up a cloud of dust as I thumbed my shield and found my feet again. I was torn between casting my cape away for greater mobility and keeping it for the defense it offered.

In the end, I chose defense, taking a bunch of the fabric in my left hand to ensure my arm was covered. "Stand down, soldier!" I said, pointing with the covered arm.

"You don't give *me* orders!" It swung at me again, blade clipping off my arm as I raised it in a boxer's guard, fist to my temple to shield my head. I did not want to draw my sword. Highmatter was too dangerous. It would make short work of the alien *zitraa,* would cut common steel like paper, but I did not want to maim that wonderful creature who was—after all—fighting for humanity and the Empire. We did not have to fight.

I glanced over my shoulder, saw one of the plainclothes men helping Valka back to her feet. "Get her out of here!" I shouted, turning back just in time to block another strike from that long and wicked blade. There was nothing for it. The *zitraa* was simply too long, and I didn't like my chances fighting the Irchtani fist to claw in any case. Leaping back, I drew Sir Olorin's sword from its holster and activated it with a touch. Liquid metal condensed into a blade a meter long and shone bluer than the sky. I raised it in a flat parry that caught the Irchtani's weapon as it plunged through an arc that would have split my head in two. I felt no resistance as my blade passed through the *zitraa,* but the broken blade tore my cheek as it spun past and buried itself point-first in the ground behind me. Bleeding now freely from cheek and chest, I pointed the gleaming blade at Udax and growled. "Get on your knees."

An alarm began to sound. The same braying *vwaa-vwaa* that had played from speakers in the bastille in Borosevo when I had fought and killed the cornered Uvanari. I hated that sound—there were too many ghosts in it. I kept my sword leveled at the Irchtani. "You've a fire in you, lad." I looked back toward the keep, saw military prefects hurrying toward us across the yard, distinguishable by the open-faced white helmets they wore and the armor they had on over their uniforms even here on base. The sun—my sun—stood high in the sky above us, pale in Imperial white. "Watch it doesn't consume you."

Udax's all-black eyes narrowed, and the feathers on its head stood up. I did not move, did not lower my blade, not until the prefects were upon us and forced Udax to lie face down in the dirt. No fitting place for a creature such as it. Only then did I stow my blade, the metal vanishing in air like the night fog beneath the first light of day. One of the prefects said something to me, but I did not hear him. There were more prefects swarming about us, forcing the Irchtani auxiliaries to kneel with their talons on their hooded heads. A stunner bolt flashed and one of the auxilia fell from the sky. It had been trying to flee.

"Hold your fire!" I snarled, and slapped the stunner from the man's hands. Brandishing my sword hilt in the prefect's confused face, I said, "Not more than six of them attacked us. The rest are innocent."

"We'll sort it out, my lord."

"You will," I said, throwing off my cape as one of my own men returned. "Is Doctor Onderra safe?"

The fellow tapped his chest in salute. "Aye, lordship. That elder of theirs and my triaster are with her. She's fine." I threw my cape at him. Seeing the blood on it and on my chest and face, he asked, "Are you?"

"I'm fine." I pushed back my hair with bloody fingers. And then I put the man out of my thoughts, locked him in a room behind my eyes that no longer concerned me. "Pallino!"

"Here, Had!" My friend, my lictor, and first chiliarch was on his feet, leaning on the support of a fresh-faced prefect whose red hair and freckles reminded me of Switch.

Too many ghosts, indeed.

I clapped the man on the shoulder, and he winced as I asked, "You all right?"

There were deep gashes in his arm that would need medical correctives, and what looked like puncture wounds in his side from where one of the birds had stepped on him. He was clearly not all right. But the bastard grinned and tapped his new eye. "I've had worse."

"We'll get a pallet in."

"I can bloody walk!"

"You will stand right there until they can carry you out! I won't have you bleeding out because some *fledgling*," I spat the word at Udax, "wanted to play the revolutionary." As I spoke, my fingers found the silver chain still wrapped around my neck. I found the pendant, sure enough, the ring of silver enclosing the irregular piece of white shell. Still there. I let my breath out in a rush. "Where is Osman?"

CHAPTER 11

DECIMATION

I DID NOT, IN the end, run straight to Osman as I had planned. Better sense and Valka convinced me to go with Pallino to the medica and have my injuries seen to. The wound to my face was comparably minor, and a simple corrective bandage saw to it and to a pair of superficial scrapes on my arms I had not noticed. The wounds on my chest were, like Pallino's, more serious, though I had the good fortune to be kicked where there was bone, and so Udax's talons had not cut so deep as the claws of whichever xenobite had taken a chunk from Pallino's side.

"Pallino's all right?" I asked, tracing the corrective on my cheekbone with the tip of my smallest finger, a thin black line running from nose to ear.

I watched Valka purse her lips in the mirror. "Would you stop picking at that? It'll scar."

"You'd like it if it did," I said sharply, but stopped all the same even as Valka shrugged.

"And yes, he's all right. They put him under just in case. Sleep will be good for him, anyway. He did lose a lot of blood."

I checked the patches on my chest, feeling the warmth in them where they worked to stitch shut the light puncture wounds. "Those claws were vicious . . . I still don't understand why it attacked."

"Perhaps it mislikes being a slave soldier fighting for the people who took its planet away."

Glad that I'd stepped from my place in front of the mirror, I shut my eyes for the space of three breaths. I did not have the energy for that sort of discussion. "Please don't do this now. I've been stabbed, see?" I indicated my chest wounds. "The auxilia aren't conscripts, which is more than our men can say—hell, it's more than I can say." I tried to cross my arms, regretted it almost at once. The shock of the moment had ended, and the pain was creeping in. Maybe I could use a sleeping dose myself . . . but no, there was work to be done. Without my having to ask, Valka lifted my pendant on its chain and held it out to me. For once, she didn't argue. Her brows drew down and together as she studied me. "They're going to kill the one that attacked me."

"You think?" Valka did not move a muscle. The pendant still swung from her crooked finger, waiting for me to take it. I couldn't tell if her question was sarcasm or genuine curiosity.

I took the pendant from her and held it in my fingers. "Wait and see." I ran my thumb around the silver rim of the pendant, feeling the sharp edges of the stony shell. The whole thing was no larger than a gold hurasam, perhaps more than an inch and half across. As it always did, it felt faintly warm to my touch, and when I closed my fist about it I still felt as though I could see it, as if its light shone through my fingers.

"Hadrian!" Valka's voice slashed through whatever foggy reverie I'd fallen into, words spilling in like cold water.

"What?" I put the chain around my neck and scooped up the new undershirt and black tunic that had been brought for me, pulling one on after the other despite the ache in my chest.

As I strained, Valka said, "You were far away. I asked if you were all right."

"I'm fine," I said. Rubbing my neck and remembering the bite of the sword there, I said, "I've had worse." I lifted my shield-belt from the counter and clicked it on, pausing long enough to adjust my tunic.

Valka did not rise to my macabre bait, instead nudged the bloodstained white cape bunched on the far end of the exam room counter. "What do you want done with this?"

"Leave it, please," I replied. "That castellan's due to appear hand-wringing before too long. I'm going to need it."

"Why?"

"Because I want to play both Anthony and Caesar," I said. Valka stared blankly at me. "Never mind." But I had a plan, and hoped to bring some good out of the day's unpleasantness. "If you see Durand before me, I want to have Pallino sent back to the *Tamerlane*. Okoyo can keep an eye on him and stop him from hurting himself."

A knock sounded at the door.

"Right on time," I breathed, and stood up straight. "Enter!"

"Lord Marlowe, my most humble apologies. I cannot explain why the primitives attacked you so. You have my assurances the offender and his people will be punished for this insult. This treachery!" Sir Amalric's apology tumbled forth faster than he could enter the room and fall to his knees. I barely had the time to turn around and face him. Before he could seize my hand and kiss it, I clasped them behind my back. "I'll have his hide! His head. Whatever you ask."

I looked down at the patrician groveling at my feet, this proud man and soldier, castellan of an Imperial fortress responsible for troop deployments across whole sectors of space, as he acted like an insect before my rank and name and blood. *Palatines,* I thought. *Bashan Iseni.*

Higher beings.

"Get on your feet, sir."

But Osman did not stand. "My lord, the beasts were under my command. I've jailed them. My people are reviewing what footage we have to determine which of them participated, and the one that attacked your lordship is in a cell already. I cannot apologize enough. This should not have happened. The fault is mine."

"The fault," I said, glancing at Valka as I gathered my wits, "lies with certain young Irchtani hot of blood and spoiling for a fight. You can no more control their outbursts than you can stop your human personnel from going into the city and knocking the teeth out of whores when they find they don't have the money. You can only chastise them afterward." I took a step back and moved to seat myself on the rolling stool the medical tech had used while she patched me up. "For the love of Earth, man, stand up. That's an order."

All the same, it took the castellan a good several seconds to rise.

"What have you done with the others?" Valka asked. "The Irchtani that weren't in the yard when we were attacked?"

Sir Amalric looked round, almost as though he were surprised to find Valka standing in the corner. "I . . . ma'am?"

" 'Twere only a few dozen in the yard, but there are a thousand of them on site, are there not?" She crossed her arms, tossed back a ripple of red-black hair.

The castellan bobbed his head, swallowing. He looked like he might be sick. "I've locked down their barracks and posted a guard."

"You're treated them *all* as criminals?" Valka sounded scandalized. "You would not do the same if they were human!"

"With respect, ma'am, the lot of them have closed ranks. They won't give us the names of the ones that attacked your man, so as far as I'm concerned every last one of the birdos is guilty."

Valka interjected, "You can't be serious!"

"Besides, humans don't have talons and they can't fly. The Irchtani are dangerous allies."

"Emphasis *allies*," the doctor said, fixing Osman with her most withering glare—how the man did not evaporate on the spot I've no idea. "If 'tis how you treat your allies here, sir, 'twould hate to see the way you treat your enemies."

"Let us just consider ourselves lucky that no one was killed," I said, thinking of Pallino. "And doubly lucky that my squire was not with us."

The castellan looked round at me, confusion plain in his eyes. "Your squire?"

It was time to put the fear of God in the little man. Osman was not a bad sort by the standards of such men, but something in his manner annoyed me—and his treatment of the Irchtani in general did not sit well with me. "Did you not know? My squire is Alexander, Prince of House Avent. You and I are both lucky he did not join me this morning. Can you imagine what might happen if an Imperial prince were to suffer harm under your roof?" I almost, *almost* shuddered. "Beggars the imagination, doesn't it?"

"You should have told us!" Sir Amalric snapped. "An Imperial prince! Here on Gododdin?" He was defensive, scared. That was just as well. He should be. And I needed him defensive if I was going to bully him into breaking protocol—which I was.

"Do not presume to tell me what I should and should not have done, castellan."

I spoke flatly, without force, but even so the old, bald man quailed. "Forgive me. I did not mean offense," he said, bowing. Valka watched me with bemusement, and I brushed past Osman to stand nearer the blood-stained cape.

My back to the castellan—eyes on Valka—I asked, "What do you intend to do?"

"If they were human troops, there'd be no question: we'd decimate the company."

I stopped my hand midway to the ruined cape, shocked. I had not expected that. "Decimation?" Without lifting the cape, I turned. "Surely there's no cause for that."

"As I say, they won't give up the guilty. And until they do the entire company is culpable."

Decimation. Decimation was one of the more serious punishments the Legions leveled against its own. The offending unit—be it a decade, a century, a chiliad, cohort, or even an entire legion—would be gathered up and made to draw lots, blindly taking a coin from a chest. One in ten of those coins was marked with an icon of Death, and the men who received them were lined up and shot by the men who did not. Their former brothers in arms. Decimation had fallen in and out of practice over the long millennia depending on the will and whim of the various Emperors—here outlawed, there enforced. The Emperor William Siberian—whom Impatian named William the Cruel—ordered fully one hundred legions to decimate after the Jaddian principalities won their independence.

"I forbid it," I said, glaring at the man.

"With respect, lordship, this at least is not up to you."

"There can't be more than ten thousand Irchtani soldiers serving in the Legions," I countered. "Do you really want to be the man who wiped out one percent of them for a relatively minor incident? The Imperial office will not look kindly on such a thing, not least of which because I will name you personally in my report." I seized the cape and held it up for Osman's examination. "I remind you just whose blood it was that was spilled today. What do you think Legion brass will say when I—the victim—say your response was disproportionate and unjustified?"

Osman stammered, unable to articulate a response.

I tossed the cape at him.

"Where is Udax?"

"What?"

"The one who attacked me. The Irchtani. What have you done with it?"

The castellan looked at me stupidly, as if wholly unable to understand why I would possibly ask him such a thing. Blinking, he answered, "In lockup. In the dungeons. Why?" He was still holding the blood-stained cape, not really seeing it.

"Its life is mine," I said.

Osman shook his head. "There is protocol. Internal Affairs will want to investigate—the Inquisition may get involved, thanks to your involvement and that squire of yours. Is he really a prince?" When I nodded, the castellan swore. "When I heard you were coming, Lord Marlowe, I was thrilled. The Halfmortal on my base. The Hero of Aptucca. I wanted to meet you. I didn't expect . . ." he waved a vague hand, ". . . all this shit."

"He has a positive talent for mayhem," Valka said.

"What if this is just the beginning?" Sir Amalric said. "What if the birdos are up to something?"

I fixed the fellow with my best impression of Valka's withering stare. "Up to something? All thousand of them? The thousand that you managed to lock down inside an hour? You'll forgive me, but I'm not worried." I touched the corrective taped to my face again. But despite my bravado, I felt a shadow turn over in the pit of my stomach. What if someone *was* up to something? Not the Irchtani. I was no expert in Irchtani behavior, but Udax's attack had seemed so out of the blue to me. Had someone put it up to attacking me?

We have something of a mystery on our hands, I thought. It wasn't impossible that Udax had only been a weapon aimed at me, disguised as a bit of colonial racial tension. Was it? I cleared my throat. "Since we have the luxury of time, waiting for your scouts to get back to us, I will speak to the Irchtani elder. It seemed amenable to conversation."

"That's Barda?" Osman looked up from his examination of my cape. "He's a good man. Bird."

"I'll speak to him," I said. "And then I *will* speak to my would-be assassin." I stood again, emphasizing my palatine height over the smaller man. "Very likely there is nothing to this save a few overheated alien egos. In the meantime, castellan, try not to commit a massacre. I know that can be hard for some men in your position."

Turning on my heel, I made for the door, sweeping Valka along in my wake. I had no intention of giving Osman another moment to think or gather his wits.

His voice came after me. "Lord Marlowe?"

I looked back at him, confined my response to the lifting of one eyebrow.

"Your cape." He proffered the bloody garment.

"Keep it." I turned away. "I have another."

CHAPTER 12

UDAX

THE DUNGEON STANK.

The gaol had been carved into the rock beneath the great keep with plasma cutters, and the walls still bore the glassed-stone shine of that long-ago workmanship, worn by the passage of years. But for the stink of living men and rotting food and shit, I felt almost as though I were descending into the necropolis my family kept in the grottoes beneath Devil's Rest. It reminded me also of the Chantry bastille in Borosevo, close and sweating, though the air here lacked the humid oppression of Emesh. It even re-minded me of the watery cell Valka and I had shared on Vorgossos, but then perhaps all prisons are the same—each a shadow of each.

"Ho there!" a man called from the bars. "High-born! What day is it?"

Another man with a busted eye oozing pus peered out from a space beside the first fellow. "It's true. The Halfmortal!"

"The Halfmortal?" a third voice said. "What's the Halfmortal doing down here with us mortals?"

"That's not the Halfmortal! That's some fucking catamite. Fuck, he's pretty."

"That don't make any damn sense, Lodge. Can't you see he's high-born?"

"What day is it?" the first man demanded again.

I did not stop to speak to them, not even when one of them cried out, "Halfmortal! I was at Thagura! Do you remember me?"

Quietly, I asked the warden, "What are they here for?"

"Drunk and disorderly, mostly. They'll be out end of the week," the woman said. "The others? Assault. Murder. Couple rapes. That lot'll be in here a few months, just until we can freeze them and pack them off to Belusha."

I grunted my understanding. Belusha was one of the Emperor's prison colonies, one of the cesspools into which the filth of the Empire was inevitably drained. I'd heard stories about the chain gangs and the salt mines, the skies black with soot. I felt a stirring of pity for the men, whatever their crimes. Most people die *before* they go to hell.

Udax's cell lay at the end of the hall. I stopped a ways back from the bar—allowing an extra foot behind the red line painted on the floor that marked the minimum safe distance from the prisoner. If the Irchtani noticed me it gave no sign and lay on its cot with its broad back to me. That cot notwithstanding, the cell's only furnishing was the sink and toilet facilities in one corner—a luxury I had not expected given the smell of the place. An empty food tray lay in one corner of the floor.

Still studying the scene, I drew my new cape around my body as the warden withdrew to the far wall, making herself as inconspicuous as possible. Speaking low and clear, I said, "Your Kithuun-Barda says you are his best fighter. I don't know if that's true—it may only have said so to make me consider sparing your life—but if it is true, it would be a shame to destroy a specimen like yourself over a misunderstanding."

"Specimen," the bird quarked, venom in its tones.

"Exemplar, if you prefer." I let the cape swing free again, hooked my thumbs through my belt. "You nearly beat me."

Udax rolled over, bead-black eyes sharp in the gloom of its cell. "I did beat you. You only won because you had a better sword."

"And you lost because you picked a fight you could not win," I said, and fixed the creature with my most Marlowe smile: crooked and toothy. "Good fighters don't start fights they can't win." I must confess I rather liked the vicious xenobite. He reminded me of so many of the recruits and brave men who came to the Colosso.

The Irchtani snapped its beak at me. "I could win if you fought me fairly."

"Fairly?" I echoed. "You suckered me with that sword of yours and you say *fairly?* No, no, no." I paced back and forth in front of the bars, careful to keep my distance in case the taloned creature leaped at me but playing calm. "You have put your people in an unfortunate position, do you know? For that little stunt of yours the castellan here has locked your whole unit in their barracks. He thinks your tribesmen mean to rebel."

Udax stood and half-shuffled toward the bars. "Osman locked them up?" It croaked something in its native language I could not discern. "Why?"

"Why did you attack me?" I countered, pivoting to face the Irchtani square on.

The xenobite wrapped its scaled and taloned hands about the bars, pushing its beak out between them. "Because I hate you."

"You don't know me," I said, matching the deadly cold in the bird's voice.

The Irchtani screeched and said, "You humans are all the same. You think you own the universe. And you *Bashan Iseni* are worse."

You humans are all the same. The words echoed in my head. Uvanari had said precisely the same thing to me in its cell in Borosevo. History repeats itself—would keep repeating itself, if I did not have my way. Udax would die as surely as Uvanari had unless I did something.

"And you wanted to throw your life away? Did you think it through? If you had killed me, what then? You could not have gotten far."

One taloned finger pointed squarely at my chest. "But I would have gotten you, *bashanda*."

"Me?" I arched my eyebrows, placed a hand to my chest. "What did I do?"

"You're just like the rest of them, treating us like pets." The creature's talons flexed.

Unimpressed, I said, "You've anger in you. But it's nothing to do with me. I am not those men." I resumed pacing, idly twisting my ring. "Do you know who I am?"

Silence. I ceased pacing. I studied the creature's face, the way the gray feathers crested to twin peaks above its eyes. I could not be sure—the Irchtani was not human, after all—but I sensed no recognition in the xenobite.

"No?" I asked.

"Am I supposed to care?"

"You should," I said, turning once more to face the bird in its cage. "I'm the only person here trying to stop the castellan from ordering your unit decimated." I paused to let this piece of information sink in a beat before adding, "And I'm the only person here trying to save your neck."

Udax croaked softly—a sound I took for laughter. Beak snapping, it asked, "Why would you save me?"

"Because I think we've had some kind of misunderstanding, soldier," I said, stepping pointedly over the red line on the floor and well within range of the Irchtani's claws.

The warden spoke up. "My lord, you must stand back!"

Flashing a glance at the woman I said, "Say those first two words again, madam."

"My lord?"

"Quite right." I took another step nearer the bars. Beneath my cape, I held my sword hilt in my hand, emitter aimed squarely at the xenobite's bowels. The moment called for bravery, not foolishness. "And because it would be a shame if your *kithuun* were to lose its finest soldier."

Udax squinted up at me. "His."

"Excuse me?"

"We are men," Udax said. "Not *things*."

I frowned, recognized the linguistic error. The Cielcin were hermaphrodites, every one of them possessed of the same organs, but sliding between sexual roles as social context demanded. The Irchtani were two-sexed, and though those sexes were neither male nor female as we understood them, the division of labors and powers was not so unlike our own.

"I beg your pardon," I said.

Udax exhaled sharply and drew back from the bars as if satisfied. Feet apart, he crouched in the middle of the floor. He did not speak for a long time, did not move. I wondered if he was in shock, so stunned to hear an apology from one of us *Bashan Iseni*, we Higher Beings. Taking a step forward, it was my turn to seize the bars. I did so with one hand, the other still grasping my sword should the bird man decide to attack me. I hoped my closeness was a show of trust, given the warden's enthusiasm for keeping me behind the line.

"Maybe you're right," he said, almost to himself. "Maybe you aren't like them."

My fingers tightened on the bar, and I was strangely conscious of the fact that I had not blinked in a long while. "I need you to answer a question for me, Udax, with the understanding that your life and the lives of a hundred of your fellows may depend on the answer."

The bird man looked up at me, eyes wary and narrow once again, but he did not speak.

"Did someone put you up to this? You and your compatriots? The ones who attacked my man, Pallino?" Almost I pressed my face between the bars. "Did someone pay you to kill me?"

Udax nodded.

I felt my chest tighten, vasoconstriction forcing blood into my extremities—the ancient response of the prey animal primed to run. But I am not a prey animal. Gibson's voiced chanted in my ear. *Fear is death to reason. Reason death to fear.* I held my breath long enough to take control of it and forced my blood to relax.

"Who?"

"Some human, never learned who. Offered enough for me and the others to buy out and go home rich. Never saw him again." He reached up and smoothed back his feathered head. "I think he could have been one of your priests."

The Chantry. I felt a shard of ice slide knife-like down my spine. *Not again.* The religious order had been against me on Emesh, even before I'd killed Gilliam Vas. I'd suspected their hand had turned against me before, but after Aptucca I'd hoped I was too high in the Emperor's favor for them to risk something so flagrant. I remembered the blessing Carax had asked of me. Did the Chantry suppose I was some threat to their religious authority? Did they think I thought myself a prophet?

"How do you know he was a priest?"

" 'Cause he called us *inferior beings,* just like that. Soldiers don't. They say *birdo.* And I never saw his eyes."

A cathar? I thought. The priest-torturers wore muslin blindfolds in strips across their eyes. They were servants of Justice, and Justice is blind.

Thinking of eyes, I was suddenly, sharply aware of the eyes on the back of my own head. It took a measure of doing not to turn and glare at the warden. Without turning, I said, "You." I pitched my voice to make it clear I was addressing her. "Wait at the end of the hall."

"My lord?"

"You said those words again!" I snapped, too harshly perhaps. The woman had not done anything wrong, though her ears could as easily belong to another. "Go!" Small good such harshness would do me. Even if the woman were not aligned with my enemies, it was possible that someone who was was watching through the prison's camera system at that very moment. What I would not have given then for a share of Valka's power, even at the cost of inviting a machine into my head. I glared up at the nearest camera with enough force that I almost expected the lens to crack beneath my gaze.

But it didn't. It remained cold and impersonal as iron—and as threatening as steel.

I leaned toward Udax, wishing I shared some secret language with the Irchtani as I had with the Cielcin on Emesh. "You realize, of course, that you were never going to be paid. Whoever is behind this meant for you to die along with your friends. It was supposed to look like a pack of . . . of inhuman savages had turned against a knight of the Empire. Your people would be blamed." Udax sat hugging his knees with his overlong arms. I wondered if the Irchtani could turn white beneath his feathers, if the blood could drain from his face. "You said they didn't tell you who I am?"

He shook his head.

I told him.

"You important, then?" Udax asked. He hadn't heard of me. That was unusual, even in those days, but not unheard of.

"Important enough to them to destroy your life and the lives of your companions." But not important enough to conjure a better plan. This didn't feel like a Chantry job at all. It was clumsy, haphazard. The Chantry would have poisoned me, crashed a shuttle. They would have sent a Mandari assassin in the dead of night, or contrived to have the *Tamerlane's* antimatter reservoir breach containment and lose the ship with all hands. But this? I knew again the sensation of being lost in the dark of the labyrinth, alien feet behind. We are always blind, though our eyes see clearly. We are always blind to those things we do not know. Best to assume there are knives in the darkness, because there might be anything in the darkness.

Best to be safe.

Udax drew his arms tighter around himself, great pinions wrapping like the wings of a bat. "What's going to happen to them?"

Staring once again at the camera, at the officers I knew were listening in, I said, "You have to give me the names of your fellows. The ones who helped you attack me." This was the information I had agreed to get for Osman, to dispel his fears of an Irchtani uprising—ludicrous as they were. I realized I did not need to worry too much about the ear in the wall. If they were Osman's men, I could buy them or bully Osman into submission. He was already terrified in light of mine and Alexander's presence after all. I felt sure that it was not his hand behind Udax's attack on my life. I did not think him so fine an actor.

He *could* be bought.

"Are they going to die?"

Still speaking into the camera, I said, "No. But they will be whipped. And you will. I can't stop that." I did not add that whoever it was they had dealt with might come back around and kill them. It was possible, but I did not think it likely. They would want to tie up loose ends, but I was about to make as large a spectacle of their whipping as I could, not out of cruelty, but because people would notice if the Irchtani soldiers who had just been so visibly punished were to disappear. If my nameless enemies tried anything, they would only be calling down greater attention on themselves. "I've convinced the castellan to treat this as just a fight between soldiers. You won't be treated any differently than a human would for the same crime." He would, in fact, be treated more leniently. Any human would have been killed for assaulting a palatine, without question. Being a minority had its privileges.

The Irchtani stood, beak tucked against its barrel chest, arms crossed.

"If that's what has to happen," he said, and hesitated a moment. "I understand." He offered a hand. A test? No ordinary palatine would accept a handshake from a peasant, much less a xenobite auxiliary like Udax. But I was no ordinary palatine. I had been in places far worse and far lower than that measly cell. Smoothly, unseen, I shifted my sword from right hand to left beneath my cape and took Udax's claw in my hand. The scaly flesh was cold and dry, and the talons pinched. It did not squeeze as a man would— it did not need to. "There were four of us. Me, Gaaran, Ivar, and Luen. If anyone else joined in, they thought it was a scrap. They didn't know."

"Thank you," I said, and drew my hand away.

"When will it happen?" Udax asked.

"The whipping?" I drew back, replaced my sword in its magnetic clasp. "Not for a day or two. You'll have ample time to contemplate just when you should draw your sword and when you should keep it in its sheath."

CHAPTER 13

TOO CLOSE TO THE SUN

THE SHADOWS OF THE whipping posts stretched across the yard, pushed by the setting sun. I can still see those pillars, shadows themselves of the pillar where dear Gibson was whipped. I stood on the steps of the barracks beside Sir Amalric while his men stood guard as the four Irchtani were whipped by four of their own. Kithuun-Barda stood to one side, watching his four soldiers. They did not cry out—not at first—and when they did their screeching set the whole pack of xenobites to cawing, screaming at the sky.

From my vantage point on the stairs, how clearly I saw the line of division between our two peoples. Human and Irchtani, xenobite and man. Though the Irchtani fought for us and willingly, it seemed to me the space between the platform and the yard would never be bridged—could not be, so far apart did we seem.

Yet those pillars were not the back wall of a firing range; those four xenobites were not a hundred. No coins with Death's head had been paid to soldiers who had done nothing to earn them. That at least was good.

Men have come to me for prophecies, asking after the future. I never could answer them. What we may become is ours to choose, and we may choose badly. I know only that we must choose—as I have chosen—and live by our choices. In ages hence perhaps the Irchtani will dwell across the Empire. They may captain ships or council lords as scholiasts—and perhaps be lords themselves. Or perhaps they will vanish, like the Arch-Builders of Ozymandias—like ancient Ozymandias himself. I cannot say, can say only that I saved the lives of four—or of a hundred.

I hoped it was enough.

We had made a proper spectacle of the moment, however. The main yard was flooded with Fort Din personnel, and I had even convinced

Osman to allow civilian broadcast in. Light, they say, is the best disinfectant. It is an antiseptic as well. With any luck, the scourging of the Irchtani would be the biggest story on Gododdin. Udax and his compatriots would be safe, I hoped, at least so long as I was there. I hoped that was enough, too.

I remained in the yard a long time after the prisoners were led away and the crowd departed. It was the dinner hour, but I did not feel like eating. Alone but for my guards—who kept their distance—I moved to stand among the pillars. Reaching out, I traced the deep gouges in the posts where the Irchtani's claws had bit into them, careful to avoid the greenish blood drying on the surface.

As I often did, I imagined my old tutor, Tor Gibson, stood just out of sight, interrogating me as he so often had when I was a boy.

"Whose hand directed your would-be assassin?" his imagined voice inquired.

"It could be anyone," I murmured, putting my hands in my pockets to keep from touching the blood. I was alone in the middle of the yard. The only other people visible were my four guards standing several dozen yards off and a few personnel hurrying about their tasks between the fort's white buildings. On the wall, a banner bearing the Imperial sun snapped in the mountain air.

I could almost see old Gibson shaking his head. "Not anyone."

"It's not the Chantry."

"You're sure?"

The same air blew my cape about me and my hair. Face tipped up to catch the last light of the sun I would one day unmake, I answered him. "Why would the Chantry act so flagrantly? Sending a cathar to hire the Irchtani? It's too obvious."

"It obviously was not the Chantry. You've a talent for making enemies, my dear boy." I could hear the wry tone in the old fellow's voice so clearly that it brought a smile to my lips, even in the shadow of those grisly pillars. "You recall the story of Icarus?"

"Doesn't everyone?"

"No," the Gibson part of me replied. "You've risen too far too quickly, and too many of the soldiers worship you." I thought of Carax, of the way Osman threw himself at my feet. "The Empire does not want a hero, and you're giving them one anyway. They're finding they've lost control of the narrative, and it scares them."

Bootprints marred the grass about the whipping posts, pale green stalks smashed flat. Human feet and Irchtani. "The Emperor."

"It is possible, but unlikely. He would not have given Alexander into your care if he meant to destroy you." I could imagine the way Gibson might tap his cane on the ground to punctuate his remarks, see the wrinkled face just hinting at a smile. "Though he certainly meant to marginalize you by sending you here. To take the momentum out of your flight." I heard the smile break for true as the words came. "It won't work."

"Why?" I asked, watching the shadows and mine run away in the gloaming. I knew why. "Because the soldiers will keep telling stories about me. All the years I've been away will be more years for the stories to grow longer, too." I nodded at the shadows, thinking of just how much longer they were than the pillars that cast them, thinking about the lie built around my victory at Aptucca. The lie that enhanced my legend. "It might be enough."

"Particularly if you succeed here."

"There's no guarantee of that."

"Kwatz!" Gibson barked, a nonsense word to mark my nonsense. "Nothing is guaranteed, but if you return triumphant, you may find yourself far too close to the sun."

Too close to my enemies.

I hooked my thumbs through my belt and shut my eyes, faces peering at me out of the darkness. Breathnach. Bourbon. Caesar. The Empress. Others. I saw gaunt Synarch Virgilian, high priest of the Chantry, and Titus Hauptmann. Princess Selene, Crown Prince Aurelian, and Princess Irene. A hundred faces. A thousand. Any one of them could have paid Udax. Any one of them could want me dead.

"Or all of them," Gibson said, speaking as I moved my lips.

CHAPTER 14

REQUEST AND REQUIRE

"AS YOU CAN SEE, we've begun receiving data from our scouts. They arrived at the datanet relay three days ago and deployed probes. The telegraph drip has begun compiling, but as of right now we've received no positive intelligence." The same gawky analyst stood by the conference table, gesturing at the holograph display where it charted a growing nimbus of gold-highlighted space about the scarlet node of the relay satellite.

Tor Varro rapped his knuckles on the tabletop and so took the floor. "That's no surprise at the very least, it's only been three days. We shouldn't expect to find anything for the next several years."

"The scouts will deploy light-probes at several locations throughout this volume. We should have nearly a complete map in the time it takes to send an expeditionary force." The analyst keyed a command into the tabletop, highlighting several blue nodes distributed like the stars of a constellation throughout the empty volume surrounding the relay sat.

Hundreds of cubic light-years of empty space. Thousands. I pictured the light-probes deploying, tiny scanners no larger than the pupil of a human eye accelerating almost instantly to within a hair's breadth of the speed of light, slowly expanding through the bottomless dark until they found . . . something. Space is cold and empty, and the ships of the lost legions should appear bright and hot as stars against absolute zero. But next to stars our ships are small, swallowed up by the Dark until we chanced close enough to feel their heat.

Assuming they were there at all.

Assuming there was anything to find.

"Then it is decided," I said, speaking to no one and everyone at once the way my father used to. My eyes never left the holograph above the table. "We will depart by week's end."

Sir Amalric sounded startled. "So soon?"

"Soon?" I echoed, turning my attention on the man, arms crossed. "There are men dead or frozen out there, castellan. You would have me wait?" I understood, of course. It would take years to reach the relay near Dion Station, had taken years to get to Gododdin in the first place. The odds were those men were dead and lost already. Osman thought the venture lost already. Was his desire for us to stay then a kind of charity? *Enjoy your time as a guest here while you may, Lord Marlowe, for you will return a failure.* Maybe it was charity.

I did not want charity. I wanted to win.

"A few more weeks would not hurt, surely."

So I stood, knowing the impression this would make, and moved away from the table toward the polarized window. Despite the darkened glass I could see the city of Catraeth below the mountain and the Green Sea beyond. I can see it now—though no one will ever see it again, and before long there will be few alive who remember it. White domes and towers, and chime and blare of life moving through them. The wind on the grasses and the oat fields where the bromos grew. I clasped my hands behind my back and stood there silent a moment, practicing a portion of the patience I had learned waiting on my father and on Kharn Sagara. Charity or no, I had had enough of Sir Amalric Osman. I wanted to make him uncomfortable, and so I waited. Ten seconds. Twenty.

Thirty was good enough.

"How long a journey from here to the relay, M. Durand?" I asked.

Durand cleared his throat. "About eleven years. We can't make as good time as the scouts. The *Tamerlane*'s fast, but . . . not nearly fast enough."

"Eleven years . . ." I repeated. *And another two to Nemavand.* I was going to be away from Forum for far longer than twenty-four years. Perhaps twice as long. Maybe more. "If we depart at once there is a good chance your scouts will have located our quarry by the time we arrive. I grant that a week or two will make little difference—but then again, a week or two will make *little* difference." Back still to the room, I raised one eyebrow. "Given events here you will, I hope, forgive me if I am not eager to remain." I did not add that I was concerned there might be a second attempt on my life while I remained on Gododdin. Osman knew full well what had passed between Udax and me in the prison cell, but the mere whisper of a Chantry plot to kill me had been enough to scare the man to secrecy. The warden and the staff monitoring the security recordings had been quietly reassigned, sent to a polar research station or else shipped offworld. The recordings had been destroyed, lest someone discover what I knew. "Still, a small delay may be necessary."

Osman did not offer a response, and I felt a twinge of pity for the man. Surely my coming had made his life more difficult. Running logistics and managing a supply depot like Fort Din was no easy thing, but the presence of a Knight Victorian and an Imperial prince—to say nothing of the assassination attempt I had so narrowly escaped—were not a part of the man's day-to-day.

Two fliers circled overhead, Peregrine lighters by the sharply angled look of them. "My squire has suggested that we launch a second convoy to Nemavand, one which the Red Company will escort in the *Tamerlane*."

"And you want to leave in a week?" I recognized the voice over my shoulder. It was not Osman or Verus, but a senior officer called Ruan. He was director of Gododdin's orbital station, a glorified dockmaster, and a miserable little cretin. "It's not possible, whatever your *squire* thinks."

"I remind you, Commandant Ruan, that my squire is Prince Alexander of the Aventine House, and I happen to think his plan a good one." I turned to regard the round-faced little man, pausing only to nod at Alexander himself, who sat a little straighter in his chair. "So I will give you two weeks," I said, raising a hand to forestall any further argument on the subject. Ruan spluttered, his image flickering slightly in the gloom. The fellow had commuted by holograph broadcast from his place in orbit, and his head and shoulders floated ghost-like in the air above one of the chairs, the rest of him lost in shadow. "I trust you have the men." Facilities like Fort Din maintained gross thousands of Imperial troops in cryonic suspension; I did not doubt that in the mountain beneath the fort and in orbit high above it, tens of thousands of Imperial soldiers slumbered.

Who knew how many soldiers slept in Imperial storage? I tried not to think of them as corpses waiting to rise again, or of the thousands of colonists Titus Hauptmann had authorized Raine Smythe to pay to Kharn Sagara to build his undead army.

"Yes, yes, we have them," Ruan said. "You just don't appreciate the complexity of what it is I do—what needs to be done. Finding the ships, allocating resources, *fuel* . . ."

I raised a hand. "Not interested. You may have two weeks. No more." I turned my attention on Osman, who sat at the far end of the table, nearest the door. The castellan looked exhausted; his scarred and leathered face seemed almost to cave in on itself like a failed soufflé. "Unless the castellan wishes to gainsay those orders."

Sir Amalric shook his head. "No. But what makes you think this expedition will succeed where these others failed?"

"Even if we fail to discover what happened to the previous convoy, we will have successfully seen reinforcements through to Nemavand. But to your question . . ." I paused long enough to make eye contact with Alexander and give the boy a small nod. "We will awaken our ships' full complements as we approach Dion. If we are attacked, we won't be taken by surprise like the others doubtless were. And with respect, your other convoys did not have the *Tamerlane*." Only seventeen Eriel-class dreadnoughts had ever been constructed by the Red Star foundries at Hermonassa and Lasaia, and for good reason. They were, to quote one of Lord Bourbon's predecessors in the Ministry of War, *expensive and over-designed*. The *Tamerlane* boasted a crew of more than fifteen thousand, with seventy-five thousand legionnaires in cryonic fugue, and another five thousand aquilarii and their lighter craft: Sparrowhawk and Peregrine fighters, Ibis troops carriers, Shrike boarding craft. There were more than five thousand individual gun emplacements studding the hull to defend against boarders, and that was without counting the dorsal plasma cannons, the magnetic grapnel, missile bays, high energy laser and maser arrays, the arsenal of atomics and antilithium bombs, and the mile-long mass drivers powerful enough to shatter a large asteroid with a single shot.

All of this seemed to register in Sir Amalric's guttering eyes. He glanced at Ruan's holograph and gave a little wave. "Get it done."

"Sir?"

"Get it done, damn you," the castellan said, then returned his gaze to me. "Damn your eyes, my people will be working round the clock to meet that deadline."

Looking round at the conference table, I saw that it was so. The station commandant was not the only one dismayed by my demands; most of the men and women there—two dozen perhaps, or more—fidgeted in their seat and shuffled papers and crystal tablets, or else sat staring empty-eyed at the blank table before them. There was nothing Osman could do to stop me, not really. Though he was the ranking officer in Fort Din—and thus in all Gododdin system—he would have had to be a much braver sort of man to gainsay the request of a Royal Knight. I was not an auctor, did not speak with the Emperor's voice, but they knew I had his ear, knew there would be consequences for disobeying so august a servant of His Radiance.

And worse, I was not any servant. I was the Red Devil of Meidua, the Emperor's own black knight and pet sorcerer. I was the Halfmortal, the man they said could not be killed.

I could not apologize.

"I hope so, castellan. The Emperor does not suffer disappointments." I allowed my cape to settle, concealing me but for the slash at my left shoulder. "Neither do I."

A deep voice spoke up from midway down the table. "Castellan Osman, sir. If ships are required for this new expedition to Nemavand, I will gladly volunteer." It was Mahendra Verus, the dark-haired, olive-skinned captain of the *ISV Mintaka*. "We're fully repaired and operational and can serve as escort for the troop transports."

"How many men are on station with you, Ruan?" Sir Amalric asked, propping his head on his hands.

The round-faced man on the holograph answered at once, "Twenty cohorts."

"One hundred twenty thousand." Osman worked the words over in his teeth, chewing them like gristle. "We'll lift twenty thousand from the vaults down-well. Those twenty cohorts . . . not from a single fleet, are they?"

Rian shook his head. "Survivors from Bargovrin."

"We'll have to incorporate them into new legions." Osman pinched the bridge of his nose. I did not envy the man. Paperwork would have to filed with Forum and the Legion Command on Ares. Old legions would be rendered defunct, their numbers put back into circulation to be assigned to one of the new legions being raised at forts just like this one. I really hadn't given them much time.

But I was not finished pushing, either.

"One other thing," I said, glancing now at Valka, who had been sitting silently at the nearer end of the table, closest to my seat beside Varro. It had been her idea. I watched the castellan and his aides compose themselves, bracing for whatever demand this fey and terrible knight might make of them. Valka gave me the smallest smile and nodded. "The Irchtani soldiers."

"What about them?" the station commandant asked.

"I want them," I said sharply. I wanted to get them away not only from whoever it was had coerced Udax into attacking me, to protect them from reprisal, but from the local soldiers as well, men who might be inspired to take revenge out of fear.

Fear of the other.

It was likely that whoever had tried to kill me would try to remove any links back to them, and once I was gone and the memory of the attempt on my life faded from the public consciousness, it would be only a small thing to make a few auxiliary soldiers disappear, Irchtani or no.

Sir Amalric struggled with my words for a long moment. "You . . . want them?"

"I have been extremely clear, castellan. I want the Irchtani unit assigned to my command for this mission."

Bastien Durand cleared his throat and said, "The *Tamerlane* can accommodate as many as one hundred thousand personnel in cryonic fugue. You must have the Irchtani's creches on station, yes?"

"I . . ." Amalric cast about, eyes tripping incredulous over the face of one subordinate to the next.

Verus saved him. "My lord, with respect, they tried to kill you."

I offered the table my brightest smile, all teeth. "They did." I said no more. I did not need to give an explanation, only to make demands. I locked eyes with Osman. The castellan, at least, understood my motivations. Let the others assume it was whim or madness. Let them assume it was greed. Let them think I wanted to punish the Irchtani personally, that I was vindictive and cruel. Let them think I only wanted—if you will pardon the synecdoche—another feather for my cap. It did not matter.

"Give him what he wants," said a sharp voice from midway along the table. Prince Alexander leaned in, attention on Sir Amalric. In all our time on Gododdin, the prince had kept studiously quiet, both before and after I'd told Osman who he was, and so the shock of his speaking out was severe.

Osman pressed his forehead to the tabletop between his hands, and a moment later several of the others followed until the entirety of the Fort Din senior staff were bowing in their seats. My own people did not. Alexander was *my* squire, not *their* prince. But these legion officers? They could not refuse. Any request from the Imperial blood was as good as an order. How was it the Emperor made his demands?

I request and require . . .

Valka laughed brightly and muttered something that might have been, *"Anaryoch."*

Barbarians.

I cracked a trace smile, as much at Valka's naive condescension—which had grown into a comfortable point of disagreement for me as much as my stolid traditionalism was for her—as at the officers themselves. I thought again about what the Irchtani call us palatines. Higher Beings. I am not sure I believe we are such a thing, but one need not believe in a thing for it to be real and have power, and the same belief that made Osman press his forehead to the tabletop made his voice shake as he said, "Honorable Highness. We will do as you command."

Alexander turned to look at me, the smile on his face clearly proclaiming, *If I'd known it would be that easy, I'd have spoken sooner.* I gave him the thumbs-back gesture, tapping my chest with my thumb, that indicated approval in the Colosso. His smile widened.

"It . . . is decided, then?" the Irchtani *kithuun* asked, tucking his chin against the wind. I stood beside him and Udax and a few of the others—his centurions, I guessed—on the ceremonial wall that surrounded Fort Din with Alexander, Crim, and a small number of guards. Barda shuffled his wings as though he were cold, and fixed me with one beady eye, the bird-like xenobite moving with so credible an impression of the jerky, stuttering way birds flit from one posture to the next that it kindled in me thoughts of parallel evolution and the panspermia theory.

And of the Quiet.

Thoughts of the Quiet brought again thoughts of the howling dark, of my own headless corpse and my two right hands. I shut my eyes, willed the sunlight to banish such horrors from my waking dreams, and said, "The castellan has agreed to cut your seasoning short. You will accompany us to Nemavand." I opened my eyes and, fixing them on Udax, I said, "You will be joining the fight a bit sooner than you hoped." That pronouncement brought a chorus of chittering and clicking beaks from the Irchtani, and something in the noise made me smile, recalling the holograph operas I had seen, tales of Simeon and Prince Faida and the mutineers.

As a child, we believe the world enchanted because age has not killed the magic we are born with. As we grow, the simple spells of new sights and far-off places no longer work on us, and we grow cynical and cold. But I was old even then, a young man of one hundred ten—one hundred fifteen years? I no longer recall. But in age once more the magic returns, if you are willing and open to it. Though young wood does not burn for the moisture in it, as a lonely cinder may catch in old, dry wood and spark a great burning, so do such small things kindle the hearts of those with eyes and time to see.

And if you burn long enough and bright as I have done, you come back to that simple truth of childhood: the world of the scientists, of engineers and mathematicians, does not exist. We live in stories, in the demon-haunted world of myth. We are heroes and dragons. Evil and divine. I felt almost that Simeon stood beside me, as I stood beside Kharn Sagara in the halls of the Undying and in the perverse ark and Eden he kept bottled beneath his hanging pyramid.

How wondrous it is that we walk the same universe as such legends! That a man on Earth might breathe the same air as Alexander. As the first Caesar. As the God Emperor and the Mericanii he destroyed.

"My lord?"

"Forgive me," I said, "I was woolgathering." In truth I had been admiring the beauty of the world beneath us. Catraeth shone like alabaster in the sun, and the sea of grass beyond glowed green and golden in the light of day. In the middle distance a great combine marched beetle-like across the fields, and the silver points of overseer towers glittered like swords. I was remembering standing on another curtain wall. At another time. As another Hadrian.

But even when the world is at its most violent, Hadrian, focus on the beauty of it. The ugliness of the world will come at you from all sides. There's no avoiding it.

The ugliness of the world certainly had come for old Gibson in the end, but the beauty was still there. Beauty and truth and goodness too, beyond the power of men to destroy. Or so I thought at the time, for the day would come when that white city, that Green Sea, the people and machines and silver towers would burn and perish and pass away.

For there are greater truths than beauty, and higher goods.

Barda was watching me intently with those jewel-bright eyes. "What is . . . to become of us?"

Coming back to myself, I answered him. "You will travel with us to Nemavand, help us to locate this lost legion, and you will fight with us should we come under attack."

Barda shook his head. "No, no. After."

"He's asking what you mean to do with us after all this. We were expecting assignment to the front," said Gaaran, a younger Irchtani even more brightly green than Barda was. He was one of the soldiers scourged alongside Udax, one of the Irchtani who had attacked Pallino. "We were promised a fight, devil man."

"You may get one sooner this way than you would have had you been shipped to the Veil," I replied. "I'm not sure what will happen to your unit once we reach Nemavand. That's a question for another day." Returning my attention to Barda, I said, "Most of your men will be put into stasis down here and transported up to my ship over the next several days. But you and these here will come with us in our shuttle." We were not likely to be overheard up on the wall in the open air, but I was still cautious. I had no notion of who was my enemy and who was not. I scanned the sky above for camera drones, saw none. "There is still a chance that whoever hired your men for their little game will try something."

"You're trying to protect us?" Udax asked, astonishment plain in his alien voice despite the gap between our species.

I turned away from the Irchtani and regarded my own people: Crim and Alexander and my guards. "Oh no," I said. "I'm taking you to war."

CHAPTER 15

THE SHADOWS OF ARAE

GODODDIN.

How many times did I pass by Gododdin again before the last day? A dozen? More? How clearly I see her hanging there in the night, snow-crowned and garlanded in flora, her clouds like the veil of a young bride in springtime. Beneath and behind me, the bridge crew busied itself preparing for our departure. The sun was rising, cresting over the green limn of the world.

My sun.

Ahead, the massive Legion station reared up, a castle without foundation or summit reaching out across the night between Gododdin and its lonely silver moon. We flew inverted, so that it and Gododdin seemed both to hang above us, though as we pushed for higher and higher orbits—climbing through the crystal spheres of heaven—it was we who rose.

I watched in silence, brooding on the stars beyond. The lost legionnaires were almost certainly dead, and our quest almost certainly failed before it had begun. The memory of my mission to Arae was like an albatross at my neck. I had been sent to find men then, too, and had. But the men I'd found were worse than dead, changed into machine puppets. SOMs to serve the Extrasolarians. We had recovered a few hundred survivors, men and women awaiting conversion. So few. Despite the specter of Syriani Dorayaica spreading its white hand across the Empire, I suspected Extrasolarian hands behind the disappearance of these men. Kharn Sagara had been paid in flesh for his services to Aranata Otiolo. He had acquired the flesh he needed to outfit two legions of chimeric slaves, and the company on Arae—MINOS, they called themselves—had been working to perfect machine augmentation for the Cielcin. For Syriani? Or was the Scourge of Earth not the only one of the Cielcin princes in play? So many in the Empire liked to pretend they were playing chess or Druaja with the Cielcin, directing knights and pawns and castles. But there were more than two players in our game, that much was certain.

"We have clearance to break orbit, ma'am," said comms officer Pherrine from the pit behind me. I did not turn, only watched Gododdin and my sun rise above us.

"Very good," came Captain Corvo's tight, controlled voice. "M. Koskinen, take us out. Chart a course past lunar orbit bearing forty degrees. Hold to the ecliptic."

"Ma'am."

"M. White, you have the coordinates for our jump to warp?"

"Yes, ma'am."

"Very good."

Though the window in front of me was false, it simulated what the view out a porthole from this part of the ship would look like. The *Tamerlane's* bridge lay far forward on the ventral side, almost at the nose, shielded above by the heavy armor of the dorsal hull and beneath by the primary weapons cluster. Thus I peered out through a forest of gun emplacements and shield projectors like grasping hands. It made me think of the Gothic horror of the *Demiurge,* rank upon rank of iron soldiers standing like the statues of saints and gargoyles upon the ramparts of some lost temple.

The Legion station, by contrast, was white and clean. There is something special about sunlight in the black of space. Without the air to bend and soften it, the light shone hard and bright as laser fire. It lent the shipyard an air of unreality where it twisted above us like the etching of some improbable city. From our high orbit I looked up—down—upon battle cruisers and frigates, troops carriers and destroyers and rapid attack ships, each blacker than the space they moved through and shining in the light.

"Is that the rest of the convoy?" Alexander asked, speaking from his place at my elbow. He pointed, indicating four vessels rising downward from the station ahead, accelerating toward our higher orbit. We would overtake them before they reached our orbit, and so they would fall into step behind, following us for one last circuit of Gododdin and the hard burn up the gravity well into the rushing Dark and whatever future out there awaited us.

I knew their names: the *Pride of Zama,* the *Androzani,* the *Cyrusene,* and Captain Verus's own *Mintaka* bringing up the rear, a heavy battleship more than five miles long. How small even it seemed measured against the face of the world above it and the blackness beyond.

"Aye, that's them," Crim said. As security officer, he had little enough to do during a voyage, and so had joined us on the bridge to watch the jump to warp.

I was glad to see the prince and my lictor were on speaking terms again, and acknowledged Crim's approach with a nod.

"From little towns in a far land we came, to save our honour and a world aflame," I intoned, watching the other ships descending, *rising* to meet us.

"That's . . . Classical English, isn't it?" Alexander asked.

"Not that Shakespeare fellow you're on about?" Crim put in.

I shook my head. "Kipling." I told them what it meant, though of the three of us only Crim had come from a small town. A beat passed. "The Irchtani are all in fugue?"

Crim crossed his arms, kaftan fluttering about him—he never had taken to the official uniform. "Aye. And Okoyo's overseeing the rest. We should be down to essential personnel not long after we make the jump. You going in the ice?"

"Not at once," I said. I'd long ago made it a habit not to freeze myself again until I had spent at least six months awake and conscious. Entering cryonic suspension repeatedly in rapid succession was a recipe for brain damage and cryoburn. "I've work to do." In truth, I was only looking forward to having a goodly stretch of time away from bureaucrats and great lords. I used to wonder often if our ancient forebears made a mistake extending our lives by so many hundred years, for young as I was I was too old to long tolerate such things as politics.

I do not wonder anymore.

"That makes two of us," Crim said. "I'll be up a while yet, and first up when we get close to the mark." As things stood, the plan was to awaken all hands as we approached the region surrounding the datanet relay. As chief of security aboard, Crim would need to be on hand to keep the peace between over ninety thousand human crewmen and a thousand Irchtani— not that we expected much trouble from our own people.

"Thirty seconds to primary sub-light burn," said Lieutenant Koskinen.

"Take a seat, your worship," Crim said to the prince, leading the younger man away. "Suppression field's on but this mule still kicks."

The helmsman's voice chimed in again. "Twenty seconds."

I watched the other ships above—below—us and did not follow the others. I'd had practice enough keeping my feet aboard starships not to be much concerned for my footing.

"Received confirmation from the *Mintaka*," Pherrine said. "They're prepared for burn matching our trajectory."

"Twenty seconds."

I took half a step back, nearly sliding into a fencer's guard.

"Ten seconds to primary sub-light burn."

Gododdin still peered peacefully down at me, changeless and untouchable as planets always seem. I remember thinking suddenly of Rustam in that moment, the Imperial colony where we had at last found our link to Vorgossos. I remembered the weeping black scar on the planet's face where the old city had been. Not changeless at all.

Not untouchable.

"Five seconds. Three. Two. One. Mark."

The *Tamerlane* lurched beneath my feet, and conducted through the mighty vessel's superstructure I felt a roaring as the mighty engines flared, fusion torches blazing like the sun. I pictured some peasant on Gododdin below looking up—day or night it did not matter—and seeing for a moment the flowering of a second sun as we streaked across his sky. I did not lurch with the ship, but stood stolid by the window, watching Gododdin slide away.

Then it was behind us and the sky ahead was Dark. With nothing left to see but stars I turned and strode down the central walk toward the captain's holography well. A wire-frame model of local space hovered ghostly blue in the air, depicting Gododdin, its moon, and the shipyard station. The *Tamerlane* showed as a red mote in the center, following its arc past the moon.

I stopped beside the well opposite Corvo. "Glad to have all that behind us," I said.

"You know, I'm starting to agree with Valka," Corvo replied, gripping the rim of the holography suite, a sardonic smile on her hard face. "The more time we spend with Imperial bureaucrats, the more amazed I am any of it holds together."

Suddenly defensive, I said, "We got everything we needed, didn't we?"

"You should have seen the scramble loading the Irchtani," she said darkly.

I shrugged. "They managed it, though. And got our new legions together."

Corvo made a face. "I can't help but figure those *legions* are a bunch of shell-shocked brats and old men. Whatever's out there . . . I hope they hold together."

"Some of them *are* survivors from the siege at Bargovrin," I said. "But they are proper soldiers. They'll do all right."

"I don't like this," the captain said, drawing herself up once more to her full height. She was no palatine—wasn't even an Imperial citizen—but she was taller than me. She never said, and I never asked, but I suspected that if she was not a homunculus herself, then one of her parents certainly was. Such half-caste children were common beyond the borders of the Empire, where gene sequencing was available for anyone who could pay. "We're walking straight into a trap."

I shrugged, began fiddling with my rings. "If we're walking into anything. It could be we get straight through to Nemavand and find nothing. It could be Osman's scouts turn up nothing." With each *nothing* I twisted the ivory band on my third finger, scowl deepening. "But we know *something* is out there, and with any luck they don't know we're coming."

"You think it's pirates?"

"Extras, you mean?" I glanced up through the holograph in time to see Bastien Durand emerging from the steps down to the lower level. He carried a terminal tablet under one arm and acknowledged the captain and myself with a quiet salute. "I've never heard of Cielcin picking off troop convoys at warp."

Durand's measured tone wedged itself into the conversation like a lever beneath a heavy stone. "You're thinking about Arae, aren't you?"

"What's Arae?" Prince Alexander had evidently vacated his chair and had come over to join us. Had he been any other person—had I had any other squire—I'd have ordered him off the bridge, but despite my nominally superior position, I was not wholly comfortable ordering the prince about like some common boy.

I looked at him a moment, kneading the false bones of my left hand with my right. "It was a mission we ran seventy years ago. The 378th Centaurine vanished on a relocation run like this. We tracked them to an Extra base on a planet called Arae. Abandoned Norman mining colony. The place was well defended, but we made it in, captured the commander of the mercenary outfit the Extras had paid for security . . . a company called the Dardanines. The Extras got away." Alexander stood watching me intently, soaking in every word. "Do you know what the Exalted are?"

The prince swallowed. "They're real?" He looked from Durand to Corvo to Crim in naked horror. I understood him perfectly. The Exalted were horrible. They were the monsters peasant children imagine when they awaken screaming in the dead of night. The unholy mixture of man and machine taken to its uttermost extreme. They discarded their human bodies like a butcher discards the fat and bones, retaining only those parts that pleased them.

"I met a child once—I think it was a child—that had nothing left except his brain," I said, holding my hands up about a foot and a half apart. "It had a metal body about this big around and metal tentacles long as you are tall." I suppressed a shudder, held myself to a scholiast's stillness, not breaking eye contact with the prince. "The Extras who ran the base on Arae build them. Design bodies for barbarian warlords and Norman oligarchs and so on. Call themselves MINOS." I let the silence drag long enough to take a seat on one of the crash couches that backed up against the rail. Hands folded between my knees, I leaned forward. "Near as we can tell, they'd been contracted by the Cielcin."

"What?" Alexander's eyes went wide. I could see his mind racing as though his retinas projected his imagination against his corneas. "A Cielcin alliance with the Extras? You're serious?" Once again he looked to all the others. For confirmation? For reassurance? But none was coming. "But you got them? This . . . MINOS?"

Our silence was all the answer he needed, but I said, "They got away." I did not add that they had uploaded their minds to a radio burst and left their bodies to die beneath the mountain on Arae, or that I had fought a Cielcin-machine chimera in the bowels of their research facility.

"And you think they're behind this disappearance as well?" Alexander asked. "Why didn't you mention any of this with Sir Amalric?"

Bastien cut in, "Events on Arae were classified by the Ministry of War." He pivoted. "Otavia, Okoyo wanted me to tell you the new flight crew will be ready by tomorrow at oh-eight hundred standard." He offered her his tablet. "Those stats you requested." And then he returned the way he came, back about his business as ever, though what that business was I could not guess.

"Classified," Alexander repeated. "But you think this was an Extrasolarian attack? Not the Cielcin?"

"If I were a betting man, yes." I draped my cape across my body, adjusted the clasp at my shoulder. The aristocratic garment fastened at the left, impairing my right arm to demonstrate a kind of superiority. Why use my own right hand when I might as easily order another to use theirs? I found it utterly galling in the moment and briefly considered removing the cape, but I had an obligation to maintain appearances, and it was not truly so great an inconvenience as all that. "If the Cielcin want food there are easier ways to get it. They'd just raid another colony. But it is not impossible that the Cielcin are working hand in glove with the Extras now, and if they *are* using the Exalted to ambush our supply trains and block our reinforcements . . ." I stood, surveying the few gathered round the projection well: Crim and Corvo and the prince. "Mark my words," I said, "the game has changed."

CHAPTER 16

OTHER DEVILS

PEOPLE IMAGINE LIFE ABOARD a ship at warp, with most of the crew gone to their icy beds, to be a lonely and hollowing experience—but I have not found it to be so. On a ship as large at the *Tamerlane,* one was never truly alone. Rather those corridors and tramways and mighty holds—which when we were at full capacity thrummed with movement and the sound of voices so that the ship seemed like a city—were quiet as a country village.

I preferred the quiet.

Months passed, the days much the same. I awoke early, descending by the lift from the quarters Valka and I shared to the officer's mess, where I took breakfast. True eggs, when we had them, imitation when we did not, tomatoes from the ship's hydroponics section, and the customary sailor's glass of orange juice. Valka preferred to sleep more than I did, and so I would take my morning exercise alone, or else with Siran and Pallino as once we did in the fighting pits of Emesh. Being palatine, my body did not require daily exercise to maintain its fitness, but I find as I have grown older I have become more and more a creature of habit. Even now, in my exile here among the scholiasts, I awake before dawn and take breakfast with the brothers before coming to my cell here to work.

By the time I returned from my exercises, I would return to our rooms to find Valka awake. We would take lunch together, sometimes poring over old notes. I would help Valka in her efforts to translate the Quiet language in my own stumbling way, but before long I would inevitably be called away on some errand, or else would have to hurry along to instruct the prince or to attend to some small matter. More often than not, I would simply walk the halls.

For all intents and purposes, I had lived aboard the *Tamerlane* for more than half a century, and knew its every hall, its every chamber, its every hold and bay. Some days, I would walk along the broad corridors of the barracks high up near the dorsal hull, just below the cubicula where ninety thousand men and one thousand Irchtani slumbered in expectation of the trumpet blast. Other days, I would prowl a portion of the equator, a single path that wrapped around the ship beneath the overhang of the dorsal plate and provided access from barracks above to the launch tubes used by the thousand pilots of our aquilarii. From the catwalk where I would walk as my terminal quietly read in my ears, I could see the Sparrowhawk and Peregrine fighter craft chambered like bullets in a gun. There were five hundred such tubes down either side of the ship, oriented toward the rear. In the glory days of human-against-human warfare, most starship battles were decided by boarding craft. Royse energy shields made ranged assault difficult, and so if one ship could not surprise another from half a solar system away, the fighting came down to whoever could put enough men aboard their enemy's ships, and so it fell to the aquilarii to run interference, acting as a final layer of defense to repel boarders as their shuttles advanced to cut their way through the hull and into the ship.

But more often than not, I would walk among the hydroponic gardens, listening to the spray of water hoses and the humming of bees.

When one imagines starships, one never thinks of bees. But they are there, kept in the hydroponics section by double airlocks and left to their own devices, tending the vegetables, fruits, and herbs alongside human gardeners. And there were fish as well. Much of the *Tamerlane*'s protein supply came not from the aforementioned eggs or bromos protein, but from the fish that dwelt in the waterbeds that supported the plants.

"I thought I might find you here," came the bright, familiar voice.

I tapped my terminal to cease its recitation of a third-millennium treatise on the Mericanii written by an early scholiast called Ortega. Smiling, I closed the folio in my lap and set the pencil on top of it. "Am I that predictable?"

Valka cracked a knowing smile, but did not answer, looked instead about the little alcove where I'd set myself beneath a trellis of basil plants to shelter from the lamps. An ironwork table stood at my elbow with a carafe of chilled water. I'd had the chair brought out years ago in order to give myself a quiet place to think, and the sound of bees and running water and the smell of growing things eased something of the chill oppression of the halls outside.

"'Twas nearly time for dinner. 'Tis not like you to be late," Valka said, tugging at her collar. "How do you stand it in here? 'Tis so hot."

It wasn't, really. After Emesh, no place ever felt truly hot to me. "What time is it?" I glanced at my terminal. Where had the day gone? "Earth and Emperor, I'm sorry."

"Are you all right?" Valka perched herself upon the arm of my chair, looking down at me with worry in her face. She pressed her palm to my cheek, and I took her hand with my false one and held it there.

"I'm fine."

"You're not." She tilted her head to get a better look at me. "You've been quiet since we got back to the ship. 'Tis the mission bothering you or the assassins you've decided to drag along with us?"

"What?" I looked up at her, surprise blossoming in me. "I thought you approved of my saving the Irchtani!"

Her hand slid down to my neck. "Not if they're a danger."

"I don't think they are," I said, letting my own hand fall to her thigh. "Udax had no idea who I am. It isn't personal. Besides, they know they owe me now for their lives. Udax in particular." I pressed my head to my shoulder, trapping her hand. "It's over, it's . . . not that." One of the bees had landed on the side of the carafe, and for a moment I watched it march up the sweating metal before it flew away. "Someone tried to kill me." I looked up at her, unpleasantly aware of how wide my eyes were. "I don't want to die again."

She drew her hand free, but said nothing. What could she say? Valka had been there by the lakeside when Aranata Otiolo struck off my head, and she had visited the dark Brethren with me in the dungeons below Vorgossos. Of all the people in the universe, she best understood what it was I had been through—and she did not understand at all. She had not seen that luminous Dark, nor had she swum the rivers of time.

I was alone.

It was not that I feared to risk my life—I had been risking it ever since I left Crispin bleeding on my mother's floor in Haspida.

Valka squirmed and pushed my hand away. "Stop it!" I realized too late that I'd been squeezing her thigh with my fingers. She seized my hand by the wrist. "Talk to me."

"They nearly killed Pallino," I said through tightening jaw. Looking Valka in the face, I said, "They might have killed you."

"They didn't," Valka said.

"It isn't fair," I said. "After all I've done for them. All the battles, all the dead men . . ." I tossed the folio onto the table beside my glass and the carafe. "I should let them rot."

Valka made a face I cannot fully describe, equal parts amusement and pity. "You should. But you won't. 'Tis not who you are." She put her hand back on my face and turned my chin so that I looked up at her. She had not changed in all the time I'd known her. There were no new lines on her high cheeks or about those golden eyes, and her hair—so red it was black in all but the brightest lights—had not a thread of silver. Though the gap between our ages had closed in our long decades together, I knew I would never quite catch up. I was palatine, and had centuries left to look forward to. How long Valka had, I could not say. Her thumb tracing the line of my cheekbone, she said, " 'Tis one the things I love about you."

"I thought you hated it."

"That, too." She pressed her lips to my forehead and stood. "You're right. 'Tis not fair. But did you expect it to be?"

"No," I replied. I looked up at the herbs growing in the bed above my alcove, feeling the warmth of the artificial sunlight on my face. "No, I didn't." Alexander had complained of unfairness when first I brought him aboard.

I mentioned this to Valka and she snorted. "He reminds me of you, you know."

"He does not!" I said, voice somewhere between sharp and playful. He reminded *me* of Crispin.

Valka made a face. "Well, he is less bright than you were. And so boring!" She touched my arm. "Brighten up. We're safe for now. 'Tis nothing to worry about except whatever is out *there*." She waved one finger in a tight circle, indicating the Dark beyond. "Come on, we're late enough. You know how Pallino is if we're not on time."

"He's cooking again?" I hadn't realized. The old soldier hadn't made a meal for us since we'd left Gododdin. "He must really be feeling better."

We ate in our quarters—Valka's and mine—we few friends and survivors of so many trials. Pallino and Elara, Ilex and Crim, Siran and Valka, and myself. Pallino had made the meal himself, and he and Elara carried it up through the lift from the galley.

"Where did you get the *squid*?" Ilex asked when she saw the first dish hit the table.

"Requisitions!" Elara asked. "Gododdin's a hub world. All sorts of things coming in and out, and the Legions take a bit of everything—mostly so the officers can have nice things. Pal had me put in an order." She smiled in her matronly way, a smile that still looked out of place to me in that face stripped of its age lines. Elara had been well into late middle age when I met her, catching up with Pallino, but as it was with her man, so too her clock had been turned back.

Pallino himself took the seat opposite me and said, "And they freeze nice if you do it right, so we'll have some to hand when we unfreeze. Bread?" He offered Ilex a covered basket.

Crim took it and held it for the dryad while she selected a roll. "Did men never mock you for cooking when you were in the corps the first time?"

The old patrician's eyebrows arched. "Men can't mock of you for something unless you let them, so no." Using a carving fork, he pulled a nest of pasta tossed with squid and garlic and tomatoes first onto Elara's plate and then his own. "And the thing about food, Karim, is that men only mock you for it if it's shit, which this . . ." he passed the bowl to Siran and fixed Crim with a cutting glare, "ain't."

"Thank you for dinner, Pallino," Valka said, unstoppering the wine bottle and pouring herself a glass. It was a Kandarene vintage the color of honey, one she was especially fond of.

He nodded. "Most welcome, doctor. Seemed the thing to do, seeing as I'm for the ice day after tomorrow."

"Are you?" I asked. I hadn't heard.

"Okoyo just cleared me, said I was all healed." He tapped his chest just where the Irchtani talons had made their mark. "Honestly, I've been fine for weeks. Been going crazy up here with nothing to do except bang my head on the wall."

Elara took the serving bowl from him and said with a conspiratorial gleam in her eye, "He couldn't even put his shirt on until yesterday."

"Quiet, woman!" Pallino exclaimed, swatting Elara across the backside as she made to take her seat. Siran saved the serving bowl as the other woman turned and flicked Pallino in the side of his head. The old soldier swore and shook his head as his woman took her seat. Resting one hand on her knee, he said, "She's a liar, this one."

A lazy smile pulled one side of my mouth, and I asked, "But you are all right, aren't you?"

"Is rain wet, lad? Is space cold? Is the Empress only the second most beautiful woman in the cosmos?" He grinned at Elara. "Of course I'm all right."

Midway through the act of grating some *real* cheese from Gododdin onto her food, Elara said, "Good recovery, dear."

"I'm ready for a rematch with those bird bastards, though. Should have kept one or two of them out of the ice. I'd put them through their paces." He smiled his toothiest smile. "Damn, doctor, stop hoarding the wine!" He snatched the Kandarene from its place by Valka and laughed, and such was the sound of his laughter—warm and rough and loud—that soon we were all smiling and filling our glasses.

My friends.

The seven of us ate and laughed and drank together for a time, and though we smiled and all were merry, I could not help but look at the empty seat at the one corner of our table, a mute and unintentional reminder that our circle was broken. There in a better world Ghen might have sat, but Ghen was dead. How I missed the rough old ox, his quick temper and easy friendship and the grinding sound of his voice. I missed the way he'd called me *Your Radiance,* an insult become a term of endearment. I missed Switch most of all, and many were the times I'd regretted sending the man away. He always told me the truth, even and especially when I did not want to hear it, and he always did what he thought was right. In that sense, Switch had been a truer knight than I ever was—and perhaps a better man. That had been his undoing, in its way. Switch had betrayed me in the end, as I had betrayed Jinan, and for the same reason: to serve a higher good.

We need such people in our lives, for without them we have no lives. We live in other people, by other people. They keep us on the ground. Keep us human—and I have needed keeping human more than any king or emperor. In no other company did I feel fully myself.

And I realized that what I'd said to Valka earlier was wrong.

I was not alone after all.

CHAPTER 17

LORIAN

THE PRINCE WAS LOSING.

Crim pressed Alexander back across the fencing round, moving with the fluidity of long practice. The Norman-Jaddian officer was one of the finest swordsmen in the Red Company, perhaps the only one who was a match for me. He aimed a cut at the prince's head that Alexander just managed to parry, pulsed his arm as he advanced and slashed the prince across the chest. Alexander's target suit changed from black to beet red where the sword had struck.

"He's not very good, is he?" Siran asked, voice low to ensure His Imperial Highness would not hear.

I peeled my boxing gloves off and set them in the bag at my feet before replying, pausing a moment to watch Crim adjusting the prince's parry in *sixte,* demonstrating the correct way to angle his wrist to set the riposte. "The boy suffers from too delicate an education," I said. His every move was too rehearsed, too mechanical, as if he'd done nothing but drill at half-speed all his life.

"He needs to get hit more," Siran said. "He's skittish."

"Can you imagine being his teacher?" I said. "You'd be afraid to teach him properly, afraid to bruise him."

"I'd be more afraid of fucking up and not teaching him a damn thing."

"That's because you have sense," I said.

The prince overextended on his thrust, nearly overbalanced. Crim caught the attack with the precise parry he'd just demonstrated, stepped inside with a thrust that caught the young aristocrat beneath the armpit. Alexander yelped, but Crim caught him by the wrist and brought his own blade back around and over the prince's arm to strike the young nobile just below the line of his jaw. The security officer let Prince Alexander go and said, "What did you do wrong?"

Alexander massaged his armpit and scowled at the other man. "Are all you barbarians so damned fast?"

"*Noyn jitat.* If being slow makes a man civilized," Crim flashed a grin to everyone and no one in particular, "you can call me *barbarian* as much as you like." He cut a sweeping arc in the air in front of him with his training sword. "Sort of a weird compliment. Now what did you do wrong?"

Siran and I watched the prince think it over, still massaging his arm. After a couple seconds a familiar, thin voice rang out from the corner. "You rolled your back ankle and lunged too far!"

"Black Earth, how does he do that?" Siran hissed.

I hadn't seen Lorian Aristedes enter the gym either, but there he was, seated at a machine by the far wall. Had he come from the locker room? Or straight from the hall? I hadn't seen much of the intus since we'd left Gododdin—indeed I was not sure I'd known he was still awake. He stood, pausing long enough to pluck his cane from its place by the wall, and hobbled toward the fencing round on its raised platform. I marked the black polymer gauntlets he wore, knew they were laced with tiny electrodes that helped to regulate his delicate nervous system. When he was within five paces of the edge of the round he bowed gracefully as he could and said, "Your Highness."

"Commander Aristedes," the prince nodded, face stony. I had a sudden premonition that things were about to go poorly, but I said nothing, un-screwed the cap on my water bottle, and drank in silence.

"You want to keep your back straight when you lunge, sire. Otherwise you make yourself easy to knock over." He did his best to mime the action, and though he moved slowly he carried it off, using the cane for a sword. Still, he had to lean upon the shaft to regain his footing.

Prince Alexander scoffed. "I don't need advice from an invalid." He turned his back. I winced.

Aristedes barked a short laugh. "I'm not an invalid. I'm a cripple. The rest of me works just fine." He tapped his temple with one long finger.

"He *is* right," Crim said, tapping the wooden floor with the tip of his sword. "Come again." The Avent prince chewed on his tongue a moment and settled into his guard. I could understand his irritation. "Thrust and hold it." He did. Crim batted the attack aside and stepped round. "See your shoulders are out ahead of your hips?" He tapped Alexander in both places

with the tip of his sword, turning the target suit briefly scarlet as he demonstrated the way the prince was leaning. "Straighten your back. Good. Do
you feel more in control?"

They continued on like this for a good few minutes, but Alexander
struggled to make the adjustment. Again and again Crim blocked his
thrust. "You don't need so much force, lad! Highmatter will cut with no
weight behind the strike. You're only tiring yourself out." He kicked the
prince's foot out from under him and sent His Imperial Highness sprawling
to the floor in a tangle of limbs.

"Damn you!" Alexander swore, slapping away Crim's offered hand.

"The boy has a temper," Siran muttered.

"He's young," I said.

Siran sniffed. "He's thirty standard."

"He's been out of that palace for only a couple of years. He's still a
child." I watched my young squire find his feet and test his ankle. He
winced. "We don't start growing up until we leave home." I found suddenly I could not look at anyone as I added, embarrassedly, "The rest is
just prologue." Valka was right, Alexander was more like me than
Crispin—or perhaps it was that Crispin was more like me than I cared to
admit. What sort of man was Crispin, I wondered?

"He's still a dick," Siran said. "Thought princes were supposed to be
more . . . princely."

"I'm sure some of them are," I said, stoppering my water bottle. "We
have dozens of them. But he's not all bad. This plan was his idea."

Siran rolled her head around in a circle to relax her neck. "Why does
that not make me feel any better?" I could feel her eyes on me, but I did
not look up. "Do you really think this is a good idea? Walking into a trap
like this?"

"Have you another idea?" I snapped. "If you had to go poking around
in dead space looking for pirates, you could do much worse than having
two legions awake and at your back."

"That's true . . ." she admitted.

Something in her voice made me look up. Siran had undergone the
same patrician enhancements as Pallino and Elara, but where the other two
of my armsmen had been old before, Siran had been handsome and strong.
She still was, and but for the repaired damage some cathar had done to her
nose for crimes she never shared with me, Siran looked much as she had
the day I'd met her: a strong-featured woman with dark eyes and skin the
color of coffee. There was a scar high on her left cheek, though it did not

mar her. She reminded me of Princess Tiada from the old holograph operas. She had shorn off all her hair when Ghen had died on Rustam, and had never grown it back.

Being reminded of Ghen, I softened my manner. "Sorry."

She shrugged.

Alexander was trying to recover his guard, but it looked like he had twisted his ankle from the way he favored his front foot. He hissed, testing the foot, and Crim said, "That's enough for today. Let's get you some ice."

"Your Highness," Aristedes said, limping forward. "Take this." And to my surprise he thrust out his own cane for the prince to take. Lorian had had it specially made on Forum when he'd joined us and been raised to the rank of commander, the silver knob decorated with the oak leaf motif of his new rank. It was almost too short to be of any use to Alexander, but the prince took it without nod or thanks.

When the prince said nothing, only allowed Crim to direct him toward a bench near the wall, Lorian spoke up. "We cripples have to stick together, eh?"

Without warning the prince whirled and slashed at Lorian with his own cane. To my astonishment, the intus managed to get his hands up in time to cover his head, but he still went down. I have no memory of crossing the floor from the boxing ring to where they stood, nor any memory of seizing Alexander by the collar of his target suit. I must have stepped *over* Aristedes where he lay on the floor.

"Apologize," I said in my best Lord Marlowe voice.

Alexander looked up at me, surprise in those Imperial emerald eyes and just the faintest trace of fear. "He . . . he . . ." he stammered, looking around to Crim and Siran for answers, but none were coming. What few junior officers there were in the gym stopped their exercise to look round.

"He what?" I tightened my grip on the suit front, pressure bruising the synthetic fibers from black to scarlet bright as arterial blood.

"He provoked me!" Alexander said, voice going high.

"He was trying to!" I shoved Alexander away, and with his ankle weak he fell flat on his royal ass, so that I stood between two fallen men. "I won't have my people fighting."

Lorian spoke through gritted teeth. "You needn't worry. I'm not the dueling type." He sat up, cradling his arm. "Black Earth."

Mention of duels made me recall Gilliam Vas, and I was relieved at least that this time history would not repeat itself. Lorian could not have challenged a prince of the Aventine family in any case, but I had no trouble imagining that Alexander might insist.

"Are you all right, commander?" Crim asked, helping Aristedes to stand.

"Only bruised, sirrah. I think." Lorian rubbed his arm through the wire gauntlets. "Never thought I'd be glad to be wearing these damn things." He smiled, looking almost half a child with his tangled blond hair and diminutive stature.

Concerns for Lorian's health brushed aside, I rounded once more on Alexander. "Apologize."

The prince's eyes darted from my face to Crim's to the door. Back to Crim's. "I . . . no! I will not."

Coming as it did from the floor at my feet, Alexander's obstinacy had no force behind it, and I smiled my most unpleasant smile. "Do you think you're being given a choice?" I asked, crossing my arms.

Alexander half-rose to his feet, but he struggled with his lame ankle and propped himself on Lorian's cane. "I am a prince of the Sollan Empire, of the blood of the God Emperor himself."

I kicked Lorian's cane out from under him and he toppled, sprawling back to the floor. Crouching in front of him so as to better speak to him man to man, I said, "That does not matter here. You are *not* the God Emperor! You are not even the Emperor!" I'd started off yelling, but by the end my words were practically a snarl. "So for the last time, *apologize* to Commander Aristedes."

"Leave it, Marlowe," Aristedes said, still rubbing his arm.

Alexander's hand pawed for the fallen cane, but I batted it aside. He would stand on his own two feet or not at all. The cane rolled away in a flat arc, bumped against the edge of the fencing round. I saw venom in the prince's eyes. It was almost time to stop pushing.

"You are angry because you failed at your sword work. You are not angry at Aristedes. Look at me!" Alexander's eyes had slid from my face to where Lorian and Crim stood behind me. They snapped back. "Rage is a kind of blindness, Alexander. Let it go."

To my surprise, the prince nodded, but he said, "You should not speak to me this way."

"You are my responsibility, my squire, and I will speak to you however I like." I stood and allowed a gentle edge to creep back into my voice. "Do you remember what I told you on Gododdin?"

He nodded again, but could not hold my gaze. "Yes. If I want respect I must earn it."

"No," I said, mimicking the chiding tone Gibson had so often used with me. "You have respect. You're a prince of the Sollan Empire. Of the blood of the God Emperor himself." He smiled in spite of himself. He knew I mocked him, but sensed that something in my tone made it all right. "Be *worthy* of the respect they're already giving you."

For a third time, he nodded. "Yes, sir. I . . . Commander Aristedes: I am sorry."

I looked back in time to see Lorian bow in his awkward way. "It is already forgotten, Highness."

After another five rounds in the ring with Siran and a run through the showers, I was making my way back to my apartments in the rear of the ship by way of the equator, following the line of the outer hull above the lighter craft launch tubes toward the tram platform that would carry me back to the officers' dormitories. Arched supports stretched above my head, great buttresses flowing down to the fighter bays below. Snatches of the violet glow of space shone through narrow slices of true window, great rippling currents where the warp effect turned the stars to curling ribbons as we streaked by. Not eager to be back and to report the afternoon's happenings to Valka, I lingered on the rail, watching a solitary service technician in black coveralls at her work maintaining one of the Sparrowhawks in its berth.

All was quiet; even the distant humming of the warp nacelles—omnipresent even on a ship so vast as the *Tamerlane*—was hushed. I fancied almost that I could hear the blood flowing through my veins. Then the ship worker began to sing, high clear voice almost lost in the echoing distance between us, faint and remote as the stars beyond the tall, narrow windows.

> *Hey, carry home my broken bones*
> *and lay me down to rest!*
> *A thousand years of time I've known*
> *since I left my home and nest.*
> *A thousand worlds I've sailed and seen*
> *Seeking fortune and my fame!*
> *But I've lost it all—and gone and died*
> *Where no one knows my name!*

"Lord Marlowe!"

"Such a sad song," I mused aloud, only belatedly realizing that Commander Aristedes had followed me from the gymnasium. "Hello, Lorian."

The intus peered over the rail. "The sailors are always singing sad songs. Who can blame them? Almost none of them go home again, and if they do, everyone they knew is dead." Some people believe the flow of time is different aboard ship than it is on worlds, that time slows as vessels ply the dark between the stars, but it is not so. Once, perhaps, it was. The late Golden Age had been dominated by slower-than-light seed ships carrying men and machines and embryos to colonies surrounding Old Earth system. Pushing light speed, those ships had traveled into the future, so that decades and centuries had passed on Earth while mere months passed for the sailors aboard. Not so anymore. Time passed aboard a ship at warp no differently than it did for those worlds we sailed between. It was only that space was vast and empty, and we might be decades at our travels.

Decades were all some people had.

"How's your arm?" I asked.

"Bruised, but I've had worse." Lorian pushed back his sleeve to reveal an ugly brown and yellow wheal blossoming there. He offered a papery smile. "May I walk with you?"

I gestured for him to proceed and resumed my course along the equator beltway, careful to move slowly to better allow the intus to keep pace. His cane and our boots tapped their quiet rhythm against the deck plates. We proceeded thus in silence for a minute or so, the mechanic's singing growing ever fainter behind. "I am sorry about the prince," I said at last.

"Whereas I feel sorry *for* him," Lorian answered. "The boy's another dogged contender . . . struggling to get his head up above his siblings so he doesn't end up an old man dying alone in some gilded cage on Forum. I'd be angry, too." His cane counted the next dozen seconds striking against the floor before he added, "Not that I'm ungrateful for your defense, my lord."

"Lorian," I said. "I think it's well past time we dispensed with the formalities, eh?"

The smaller man grunted. "As you wish, Hadrian." We passed by one of the lift tubes that ascended at an inward angle toward the empty barracks where the pilots would live once they were decanted from their fugue creches. "I can understand his anger. But I've always felt it best to pity such people. You should almost keep him awake for the whole journey, give him time to grow up . . . you're for the ice soon, aren't you?"

My self-imposed limit was nearly up, and it would be years before we reached the datanet relay. We'd planned to pause just outside the eighteen light-year radius Varro had described around the relay long enough to get our bearings and to communicate with Gododdin and the scout ship that had spent the last several years probing the void. Thence we would resume our approach and begin awakening everyone aboard the *Tamerlane*, the *Pride of Zama, Androzani, Cyrusene,* and *Mintaka*—a process taking weeks. But that wouldn't be for nine years, during which period fewer than a hundred of the *Tamerlane*'s more than ninety thousand souls would be awake and active. We were well under a thousand even then.

"I won't be long now," I said. "Valka's been talking like it won't be long now before she goes under, and after that . . ." I trailed off, not quite knowing what to say.

Lorian chuckled. "Nothing to live for, eh?"

I snorted. "Something like that. And you?"

"I mean to stay awake a while longer," he said. "I'm not eager to put myself back in the coffin, you know?"

I glanced down at the small man with his papery skin and spider-thin arms and hands. "Is the freeze hard on you?" I asked, realizing how little I knew about the commander's condition. It had always felt rude to ask. It still did.

"It's the waking I can't manage," Lorian answered. "Nerves don't work right, I'm numb for weeks. It's not dangerous—it's not getting worse—but it's not pleasant." We walked on in silence a moment before Lorian asked, "What of you, lord? Ah, Hadrian?"

"I dream," I said. "I know that's impossible. I know they say you don't dream in fugue. But I do." I had to stop and turn back, for Lorian had stopped suddenly. He was looking up at me with a strange light in his eyes, head cocked, mouth slightly open. "What?"

Only belatedly did I realize what must be happening. I had been seeing that expression in the faces of men and women around me for decades. I had not expected to see it in Lorian Aristedes. "Is it true?" he asked, and I no longer felt embarrassed about *my* question. "Do you dream the future?"

"Aristedes . . ." I began, using his right name to generate a bit of formal distance between us again and forestall this line of questioning.

He didn't notice. He'd worked up enough momentum not to notice, as if a dam had broken. "I wasn't here when you killed Aranata, so I don't know what happened. But a lot of very smart people on this ship, people

I respect—even the scholiast—seem to think you're some kind of god. Can you dream the future? Did you really die?"

How long had he been waiting to ask those questions? Aristedes had never been shy with questions—less shy with his opinion or advice, that was certain—but not shy with questions, either. Not shy in general. And yet there was something in his tone that told me he knew. Defiance? Was he challenging me to lie?

I caught myself wishing I had my cape. Such emblems and amulets grant us power by our attitude toward them. Thinking of amulets, I touched my pendant through my shirtfront, the bit of shell I'd received from the Quiet.

"I assume Pallino showed you his suit footage." Of all the people who had been with me by that lakeside on the *Demiurge,* Pallino alone had captured a clear recording of what had happened to me. Ilex had discovered it after the battle, while I still slept in Kharn Sagara's custody regrowing the flesh of my arm. She'd had the presence of mind to go though every suit recording from the battle aboard the *Demiurge* that she could access before Titus Hauptmann could sic his people on them. She had found nothing except on Pallino's camera. The man had been facing the right way at the right time, and had caught it all: Aranata striking off my sword arm—my right arm—and my head after it. I had watched it only once, and ordered the recording scrubbed from any networked device and placed in a storage crystal kept in the *Tamerlane*'s vault. No one was supposed to know about it. No one from the Imperial Office had come to me about it, either, and so I was certain Ilex had done her job well.

I was not surprised that Lorian had discovered it.

"He did," Aristedes said, "but if he hadn't, you'd have just given up the ghost."

I did not laugh.

"Have you considered that you're not *you?* That you're a replica Kharn Sagara put together and sent among us?" He surveyed me coldly, both hands folded on the head of his cane. I realized I'd misjudged Lorian Aristedes a moment earlier. He was not another of my cultists, no true believer at all. He was the most ardent sort of skeptic, the sort who disbelieves despite even the evidence of his eyes.

I did laugh, then. "That was the first thing I considered, of course. But the data don't match up." I had been having visions of the Quiet long before I came to Vorgossos, since Calagah, in fact. Perhaps since Meidua.

Whatever was happening to me, it was bigger than Vorgossos, bigger than Kharn Sagara and his pet daimon. The Brethren said the Quiet had pressed them into service, forced them to deliver the vision they had given me because the Quiet had foreseen that I would meet the Brethren, and because the Brethren—being perhaps the most intelligent creature ever to exist—had perceived the Quiet when they peered across the luminous deeps of time. I told Lorian all this, and when his frown deepened I said, "You don't know everything. I don't know everything, but I am me. Here." I pushed back my sleeve then, showing him my right arm. "You showed me yours, so I will show you mine."

Faintly visible in the stark light shone the pinpricks of a hundred tiny scars. They dotted the back of my hand, my palm, my forearm. "When I was a boy, I was mugged in the streets of Meidua returning to my father's castle. They shattered my arm and nearly killed me, and I spent weeks recovering. I wore a corrective brace—I'm sure you know the type. See the scars?" I pointed, watching for his response. But Lorian's face was not readable. I shook my sleeve back down. "If you have seen the recording, you know full well it was the right arm I lost to Aranata. Feel it." I offered my hand, and he took it carefully. His own hand was dry and light as a skeleton's. "And feel the other." I extended the left, let him feel the false bones there.

"The first time I went into fugue I wore my family's signet ring," I said, working Aranata's ring off my thumb to show him. "Cryoburn took all the skin off from here to here." I traced a line from one thumb joint to the next. "When I came back to life," I said, haltingly, aware of how insane those words sounded, "it was my left arm I had lost, not the right. And I had this back." I held up my right hand again for inspection, scars and all. "That is not the sort of mistake a machine would make. And besides, when it . . . happened." I could not say *when I died*. "When it happened Kharn Sagara was dead. Offline. Rebuilding himself. The whole ship was dead." I did not tell him about my final meeting with the Undying Lord of Vorgossos, the way that xanthous king demanded my secret of eternal life, a secret I did not possess. I had given him enough proof. "I do not know what happened to me, Lorian. But I know I *am* me."

The younger man's ghostly face shaped itself into a faint smile. "Don't we all?"

We proceeded on then in silence for several minutes. I could see the sign for the ship's tramway up ahead, a white dash in a green circle.

Presently Lorian spoke. "You didn't answer my question." He stopped once more, leaning on his cane. "Do you really dream the future?"

Shaking my head, I turned back once more to regard Commander Aristedes with narrowed eyes. The young commander did not need to know the Halfmortal woke sweating in the dark of the night from dreams of fang and fire and the memory of pale hands in dark water. He did not need to know about the shades of Uvanari and Gilliam Vas, of Emil Bordelon. Of Jinan and Switch.

"No," I said. "I dream the past."

CHAPTER 18

NIGHT JOURNEYS

TEN BY TEN AT first, then one by one my fellow crewmen went under the ice.

I did not join them.

In the end, I did not sleep, not when my six months were gone, nor after Valka entered fugue, nor even when the first year of our voyage had gone by. As I grew older, I would often spend my shorter voyages awake and alone, each day playing out as I have described, passing the long years in solitude aboard the sleeping vessel. I acquainted myself with the so-called night officers, the crewmen awakened to tend the ship while Corvo and the officers I knew best slept. I am ashamed to say that I no longer remember most of their names, though I recall young Roderick Halford, the night captain. The rest are little more than ghosts, such as the young woman with whom I played Druaja late into the evenings, or the old mechanic who greeted me on my walks around the ship's equator. Most of the junior crewmen feared to speak to me, as though I were some species of ghost myself. There was an older woman—she reminded me of Doctor Chand from the Emeshi Colosso—who tended the hydroponics section and the bees. Always when I went to my private spot I would find her there, singing to the vegetables and the tiny, yellow-jacketed soldiers as they flew here and there in service to their queen.

It was then, too—on that first of my Night Journeys—that I first attempted to set to writing an account of my life up until that point, detailing my escape from Delos, my time on Emesh, our battle with Whent and Bordelon on Pharos. I abandoned the project just short of our arrival at Vorgossos. I was not willing to relive those months again, to walk Kharn's gloomy halls in memory and meet the many horrors that served at his pleasure. I would not try again for many decades. Often I have wondered what became of those original texts—stories I have not recorded here. Languishing in some Imperial archive, I don't doubt, or else spirited away by some enthusiast among my own people. Perhaps they will see the light someday. Perhaps they will find their way here to Colchis and languish in the Imperial Library alongside this accounting. Perhaps not. Who can say?

Thus the months passed and the years after. And in time the slumbering vessel began to stir. More faces appeared in the halls, and the sound of voices and of the public address system filled the vaulted halls and echoed among the arches and buttressed supports of the mighty holds. Soldiers ran drills and trained in the gymnasium, and the barracks high above resounded to the march of feet. The Irchtani awoke and were seated with the men in the messes, and in time I came no more to the hydroponics section, which was ever crowded then with techs minding the flora and harvesting the fishes. Corvo awoke first, and Durand, with Koskinen and Pherrine and White and the other bridge officers not far behind. Pallino and Elara came after, and Siran with Petros, Callista, and Dascalu—all the legionary officers. Valka came only near the end, and I waited at her bedside and presented her with the traditional glass of orange juice myself. Every one of the *Tamerlane*'s more than ninety thousand hands was awake and anxious and spoiling for action.

And days later . . . we'd arrived.

CHAPTER 19

THE JAWS ARE CLOSED

"WHAT DO YOU MEAN *nothing?"* I asked, my back to the bridge. I shut my eyes, unwilling to see the disappointing star field shining out beyond the bridge's false window.

Lieutenant Juliana Pherrine's voice quavered as she answered me. "I'm sorry, my lord. Osman's scouts have probed more than sixty percent of the volume, but thus far they've found no sign of the lost legions."

I swore, slammed my adamant fist against the glass, wishing that it were a real window, wishing I might shatter it at a blow and admit the empty Dark of space. "Tell the scouts they will deploy the last of their light probes and rendezvous with us at this location. I will accept their apologies in person."

Rage is blindness. Gibson's voice sounded in my ear. I mastered my breathing, inhaled sharply. "Thank you, lieutenant. That will be all." I heard her feet retreating on the walk behind me, and only after she had vanished down the stair to take up her station once again did I turn and approach the captain's station by the holography well. "Corvo, Varro, Aristedes, with me. M. Durand, you have the bridge." I gave Valka a thin smile where she lingered by the captain's chair, indicating in our private way that she should join us.

The ready room stood just off the bridge, through a side door that split open at my approach. I hardly slowed down, sweeping the others behind me like plankton in the passage of a shark.

"We were prepared for this, Hadrian," Corvo said once the door had sealed. "There was always a chance the scouts would not have found anything by the time we arrived."

I was nodding as she spoke. She was right, and acknowledging that wore my anger down.

Tor Varro cleared his throat. "There is little point in summoning the scouts to us. They're on the far side of the target volume. We waste time calling them here. We should allow them to continue their sweep unmolested and to report to us by telegraph."

He, too, was right. I'd acted hastily in ordering Pherrine to summon the scouts to us. I had been alone for far too long, and the impact of my years of solitude was making me coarse. I felt a sudden sympathy for Bassander Lin, who often stayed awake for lonely years between the stars.

"Very good," I said. "Varro, tell Pherrine to belay my previous order, please."

The scholiast bowed and shuffled from the room. I seated myself at the head of the table, assuming the seat typically occupied by the captain herself. My coat slid up, making me aware of the high collar where it played about my cheekbones. I hung one leg over the arm of the chair, eyes moving from Corvo to Aristedes to Valka. "Have the other ships all joined us?" I was fairly certain of the answer.

"We're waiting on the *Cyrusene*," Corvo said. "It was slightly off course and is correcting to meet us here."

"How long?"

"Three days—they weren't far off."

"Right." I chewed my tongue a moment, thinking. "We have a choice to make. Join the scouts patrolling the volume trying to *find* whatever may be out there or push on to Dion and Nemavand."

Aristedes cleared his throat and—taking my sitting down for permission to do so himself—eased into the chair opposite my own at the end of the ellipsoid table. "Nemavand would be the strategic choice. Ramannu Province is in dire need of reinforcement. Cielcin raids across the region have increased, and if we lose Nemavand, we lose the Veil."

"And then 'twill be fighting in Centaurus proper," Valka said, but by her sympathetic smile I guessed she guessed my innermost thoughts. To push on to Nemavand—assuming we were not attacked crossing the volume to Dion—was to abandon the lost legions to whatever fate had found them, and it was surely to return to Forum in disgrace.

Not for the first time, the thought of going renegade reared in my mind. Most of the men and officers would follow me into exile if I took the *Tamerlane* and ran. We could take the fight to the Cielcin on our own terms . . . but no.

"We're already fighting in Centaurus proper," Lorian said. "This

Dorayaica cut past the frontier to attack Hermonassa. There have been deeper raids since the beginning of the war."

"Possibly *all* led by Dorayaica," I said.

"We've no way of knowing that," Corvo said—quite correctly—though I could not shake a premonition that I was equally correct. I was equally sure that Dorayaica was the Aeta-Prince I had seen in my visions. The one who burned the stars.

Tor Varro returned at that moment, announced by the hissing of the doors. "The scouts will continue their work," he said, not sitting.

"Very good, counselor," I said. My fingers went to the pendant through my shirtfront. It was faintly warm. "But if we leave, we are almost certainly condemning those legions to die."

"If they are not dead already," Lorian said.

Valka massaged her tattooed arm. "Though if we do nothing, surely the next ships that pass this way may be lost, no?" She directed the question to Aristedes—whose role was *tactics,* after all. "Is that worth the risk?"

Lorian drummed on his cane with slow fingers, placing each fingertip with delicate care. I wondered if it was some orthopedic exercise. "It's hard to say."

"It is not likely that another fleet will pass this way so well prepared for attack," Varro said. "If we are unsuccessful, it may be the road through Gododdin from the inner Empire becomes impassable, and all traffic will come nearer the core. It will add decades to our supply lines." He shook his head. "Respectfully, I must disagree with Commander Aristedes. We should remain in the volume and attempt to locate who or whatever is behind these attacks."

"We *should,*" Corvo interjected, arms crossed and eyes narrowed, "convene with the other captains at the very least."

Massaging my jaw, I mused, "Three days will not hurt us. Inform the other ships that we will await the *Cyrusene* and convene once they exit warp."

The holographs appeared like ghosts, like the shades of Tiresias and Agamemnon called from Hades by brave Ulysses. Corvo stood beside me in the main conference well—just down the hall from the bridge. There was Eldan, captain of the *Pride of Zama,* a swarthy fellow with an easy smile and the fine bones of a palatine nobile. And there were Adina of the *Cyrusene,* fair-haired and pale-eyed almost as Lorian; and Yanek, captain of the *Androzani,* a hook-nosed man who put me mind of an eagle I had seen once in my grandmother's menagerie. Last of all was doughty Mahendra Verus, the dictionary definition of the Imperial officer in his crisp uniform glittering black and silver.

All saluted, thumping their chests and raising their right hands in greeting. "Lord Marlowe," Verus said, nodding to each of us in turn, "Captains Corvo, Eldan, Adina, Yanek. I trust the journey was not hard on you."

"Smooth sailing, captain," Corvo replied, "and yourself?"

"Nothing to complain of."

Captain Adina raised her voice. "Apologies for the delay. Our navigator had a slight rounding error calculating the jump."

I waved a dismissive hand. "No matter, captain." I stepped past Corvo into the middle of the projection well, onto a red target painted on the glossed metal floor. I took a moment studying the faces of the others, all practically strangers to me, though I had sat with Verus through hours of meetings. "Ladies and gentlemen, we have a decision before us. As I am sure you are all aware by now, the scouts launched from Gododdin have thus far failed to ascertain the fate or location of the 116th and 337th Sagittarine Legions."

"We should plow on ahead to Nemavand," said smiling Eldan, taking Lorian's position from our earlier discussions.

I raised an eyebrow at the smaller man. "Thank you for your opinion, Captain Eldan. I will take it under advisement. Now," I swept my gaze over all those assembled before me, not bothering to mask my irritation with Eldan's interruption. "We may do as the good captain so enthusiastically suggests, or we may remain and assist the scouts in their sweep." I keyed the remote I'd taken from the wall, allowed a holograph of the local region to flower in the dark between us. Identical projections would be appearing seconds later on the other ships, delayed only by the speed-of-light lag between their ships and ours. Most of the volume glowed a pale white, with a glowing red rosette blossoming from the middle. "Our scouts have completed their sweep of everything within a nine light-year radius of the relay here." I stuck a finger through the projection to indicate the center. "That leaves us with the outer layer of this volume to search."

"Given the nine-year delay between the time stamp on the black box signal and its receipt by the relay, perhaps we will have something very soon." Verus's projection strode closer to the projection, ghostly hand sweeping about the edges of the space. "Do we know where Osman's scouts are?"

"The *Legendia*?" Corvo shook her head, floating hair a shaggy cloud about her stern face. "Not precisely. They uploaded the results of their scan to the comms relay, but they're currently at warp. The last we saw they were on the far side of the volume."

"Do we know when they're due to drop out of warp?" Adina asked. The scout ships had spent the past several years effecting micro-jumps through the volume surrounding the relay, pausing to deploy their light-probes before jumping again, hoping to find some scrap or shred of evidence to indicate that once a legion convoy had passed this way.

So far they had found nothing but ghosts.

The thought put me in mind of the fog-bound woods of Earth in the Golden Age, of armies marching beneath the whispering trees, never to return.

Beside me, Otavia Corvo checked some figure on her wrist-terminal. The captain wore entoptic lenses, I knew, so whatever it was she saw shone directly on her retinas. I hated the things myself, preferring the more primitive holograph displays hovering above the terminal. "Twenty-seven days."

"Twenty-seven days!" Eldan exclaimed, throwing up his hands. "You want us to idle here for a month like some primitive sailing ship thirsty for a gust of wind?" He half-turned away, hoping perhaps to hide the look of disgust on his too-expressive face.

"No, captain," I said in my iciest impersonation of my father. "I *expect* you to follow orders, whatever those orders may be." I took a step nearer his projection, pausing just long enough that he turned—discomforted—to look at me. "I am entirely happy to discuss the particulars in person, if you would prefer to shuttle to the *Tamerlane*."

"I . . ." Eldan's eyes went over my shoulder to where Corvo stood, but he found neither help nor sympathy there. "I . . . that won't be necessary."

Briefly the Marlowe smile stole over my face. "Good." I turned, conscious of my silhouette in the brushed metal wall of that round chamber, a black-clad specter tall and thin as a lance. "As I was saying, we have a decision to make. Captain Eldan has correctly guessed at the nature of that decision. Do we press on at once to reinforce Nemavand and the inner rim? Or do we remain and attempt to trap these trappers in a net of our own?" As I spoke, I held one hand out before me, palm up as if testing the weight of some invisible tray. I had made up my mind to remain, but I did not wish to bully the others into falling in line. "Captain Eldan here suggests that we should hurry on. He is mindful, no doubt, of our brothers and sisters at the front. That is admirable—but he has not thought it through."

"Those legions are dead, boy!" Eldan waved a dismissive hand.

"You will address me as *my lord,* captain," I said, pressing all the juice from each word. Only after I had spoken did I recognize my father's voice. "And that may be, but if they are . . . their attackers certainly are not. Unless we can confirm this volume is empty, the road through Gododdin to the outer provinces will be as good as useless. We do not know what is out here."

I clicked the remote in my left hand and disappeared the device into a pocket of my greatcoat. The holograph image of local space dissolved, leaving Corvo and me alone with the shades of the four captains.

Corvo spoke up. "I have a suggestion, captains."

It had been her idea. I stepped smoothly aside and let my captain take her position on center stage. Otavia drew herself up to her full height. She towered over the two patricians and even the palatine Eldan. "This target volume is thirty-six light-years across. At full thrust we might cross that in . . . half a month?" She pretended to mull the figure over in her head before continuing. "I propose we proceed across the volume at slow warp. Say . . . 50 C."

"Fifty times light speed? That's . . . seven months to the far side? Eight?" Adina sounded scandalized. "So slow?"

"Foolishness," Eldan said. "This is a waste of time."

"Snivelry!" Yanek spat. "You would run and skip out of here without even trying for a fight?"

Verus raised a hand for quiet. "Enough, both of you. Eldan, we understand your position." He folded his arms, chin tucked against his breastbone as he stood there thinking. "There's good sense in what Captain Corvo suggests. It'll give the scouts time to map more of the outer regions of the volume, right at that nine-light-year radius where the ships should be."

"And we'll still be moving toward Nemavand," Yanek pointed out, "which should satisfy the good captain of the *Pride of Zama.*" He turned hooded eyes on Eldan. I could practically feel the class resentment smoldering in the man. Eldan had been counting on his palatine blood to browbeat the others—even Verus, who, though patrician, was his military superior.

"We can rendezvous on the far side of the volume," Corvo said, "take stock of what new intelligence we have, and make a determination then." She crossed her arms, a gesture which served only to further emphasize her height and powerful build. To someone like Eldan, who saw such things as signs of virtue, it was a clear statement, as clear as my outright threat had been.

That's that.

"It makes us a big ugly target streaking across space," Eldan said.

I hooked my thumbs through my belt and stepped forward. "Precisely."

The silent stars rushed by, turned by the roil of our passage from pinpoints to luminous whorls—their light smeared across the manifold wave-front of the *Tamerlane*'s warp envelope. We'd been at it for days, weeks, and the attitude of the men was one of pregnant expectation, the sort of tense silence that feels the same as a scream. The dome above my head was one of the few places along the *Tamerlane*'s dorsal hull where one might look out at the stars. The dome served no practical function, had only been installed by the conscientious architect in the full knowledge that life aboard starships was so often claustrophobic. The dome could be sealed at an order, concealed beneath a layer of armor like the lid of a mighty eye.

I was alone then, trying to clear my head after another meeting with Corvo, Varro, Durand, and Aristedes. I was not particularly worried about Cornelius Eldan. Men and officers like him were common as sand. Though cowardice perhaps motivated his desire to make for Nemavand with all due haste, cowardice is only a kind of prudence, and prudence would see him fall in line. Men like Eldan were truly strong only when pitted against their social inferiors. He would not have the spine to resist opposition from Verus, Corvo, and myself.

An image of the four captains was taking shape on the folio page before me.

White charcoal on black paper.

I had taken to such inverted images only recently. One had to sketch not the shadows—as was the case in traditional charcoals—but the light. My image of Verus, Eldan, Yanek, and Adina shone as they had like ghosts from the projector. I blew dust from the page and admired my work. Adina's eyes were perhaps not so closely set as I'd portrayed them, nor Yanek's nose so large, but their slight caricature portrayed the spirit of each, I decided. Good enough. Setting my pencil aside, I turned the inky pages in my hands. There were the Irchtani flying with their *zitraa,* there Catraeth on Gododdin in all its pale beauty. One single page was devoted to a still life of the Galath blossom, which still had not withered and dried even after all the years away from Forum. Another page showed Valka dozing— as she often did—in her armchair in our quarters, dressed in naught but a blanket.

Smiling, I shut the book. But for three off-duty crewmen, I had the observation dome to myself. The men—two men and a woman—laughed quietly and spoke among themselves, the remnants of some holograph game between them. I did not know their faces, and so guessed they were from one of the lower cohorts, soldiers who only rarely came out of fugue to do their duty. I took them for a trias, the smallest, humblest unit of legionnaires there was. Three common soldiers.

It is good that we are reminded the soldiers we command are *men.* We are not the Extrasolarians, not the Mericanii of old. They are not machines. We do not spend men's lives like coin, but as sacrifices freely given, offered as our ancestors burned their best on altars to please the uncreated gods. That is why the best commanders, the best captains and kings, make themselves known to their people—that their people may be known to them. That we might not betray their trust and obedience when the critical time came.

As come it must.

Light flashed brighter than the sun, and the whole of the *Tamerlane* lurched. Gone were the violet fractals and streaks of distended stars. As my vision cleared and I struggled to my feet, I looked up and saw the naked stars.

Unmoving.

The alarm sounded a moment later.

Vwaa! Vwaa!

The same alarm I had heard ten thousand times. And Corvo's voice on the comm, "All hands! Battle stations!"

Though I was safe for the moment aboard my own ship, my hand went anxious to my sword. It seems a strange thing to say, but I felt my heart grow lighter and I turned toward the door. But the path had straightened before my feet once again. Forward. Always forward. I hurried from the dome, blood quickening in my veins, heartbeat coming like the martial drumbeat in time with the blare of the alarm.

The enemy had found us at last.

CHAPTER 20

THE AQUILARII

I BURST ONTO THE bridge like the tide, black coattails flowing in my wake. "What's happened?" I demanded, mounting the arc of steps that brought me up from the officers' pit to the captain's platform, bootheels ringing against dark metal.

Otavia Corvo stood hunched over the display well, fingers gripping the rim. A schematic of the *Tamerlane* glowed in the air before her, critical systems highlighted green and red against the blue of the hull, data flickering in square panels all around.

"Not sure," she said.

"Some sort of gravity net," Tor Varro said. He sat strapped into one of the crash couches to the side of the central console, hands wrapped about his restraints. From where he was, he had a clear view of all the data coming in through Corvo's holography well. When he caught me looking to him, he said, "Conjecture. But all our electronics are still online."

"Have we got anything on sensors?" I asked. It had only taken me three minutes to reach the bridge from the dome, and the atmosphere among the officers about me was one of confusion and rapidly cooling panic.

Apropos of nothing, Commander Aristedes said, "Shields are primed and holding."

"Has anyone opened *fire* on us yet?" I demanded, leaning over the rail to look down over Aristedes and his junior officers at the tactical station.

Right on cue, an indicator flashed on Corvo's display.

"Think that was a MAG round!" said one of the junior tac officers from her station. "Shields holding." Someone had fired a magnetically accelerated bolt of tungsten more than a yard across from tens of thousands of miles away.

"Do we have a read on them?" Corvo demanded, zooming her projection out so that the ghostly *Tamerlane* seemed little more than a mote in the center of infinite shadow.

"Heat signatures!" the junior officer said again. I leaned further over the rail, watching the tactical station below. Aristedes and his lieutenants were tracking three tightly clustered points of light some hundred thousand miles off.

Aristedes himself said, "I don't recognize the configuration. It's massive."

Memory of the *Demiurge* rose in me, the vast ship of Kharn Sagara hundreds of miles long—and of the *Enigma of Hours,* the mighty Sojourner that might have fit eight vessels the size of the *Tamerlane* within its central hold stacked end-to-end. I thought too of the great vessel of Prince Ulurani at Aptucca, which had been larger than many a small moon.

The shield indicator pulsed again from the console at my back.

"These are just probing shots," I said, almost to myself. "They know we're shielded."

"Do we have visual?" Durand asked, hurrying from the upper level to join Aristedes in tactical.

"Where are the other ships?" Corvo demanded. "I want eyes on the hostile!"

My hands tightened on the rail as Koskinen and White scrambled a seeker probe and fired it toward our assailant. I had a sudden, awful thought that the other ships had left us, that we alone had been snatched out of warp and that the others continued their super-luminal career toward Dion Station, unaware of our predicament until it was too late. Whatever had pulled us out of warp had wrenched us into a lazy spin, and the target Aristedes was tracking on his console appeared to hover high above us, looming like Damocles's cursed sword.

I felt terribly useless standing on that bridge. I am many things, but I am no true spacer. I could do nothing but stand hard by as my people did their jobs—did what they were trained to do, what I depended on them to do. My fears evaporated in the next instant as Pherrine said, "I've got contact with the *Mintaka* and the *Cyrusene.*"

"Multiple contacts!" said another of the junior tac officers. A thousand points of light flared across the space between us, accelerating at rates no human being could bear without suppression fields.

I knew that pattern all too well, and Lorian confirmed it a moment after. His high, aristocratic tenor filled the bridge at once like a trumpet blast. "Incoming!" You would not think to look at him that the small intus was capable of so great a noise. A hundred things must have happened at once, running through the minds of my officers. Incoming could mean any of a dozen things: missiles, plasma bombardment, probes, lighter craft, boarding shuttles. We had no way of knowing at this distance.

We did not have the luxury of waiting to find out. Corvo could see on her console what Aristedes saw on his own; she had to act. Veteran that she was, she knew the primary threat to a vessel armored and shielded as ours came not from long-range weaponry. Even unshielded, it would take antilithium or highmatter to cut through the adamantine plate on the dorsal hull. Our greatest threat came from boarding shuttles, cutter-craft that would limpet themselves to the outer hull where it was common steel or carbon composite. It was to that threat we needed to first respond. "Launch the aquilarii!" she cried. "Ten wings, hold the others in reserve."

"Aye, captain!"

I did not hear Aristedes give the order, nor hear the alarm blaring in the pilots' barracks levels above us, but I saw them all the same. Two hundred men hurled from their rest to their duties, scrambling to pull on padded pressure suits and helmets, rushing to the lifts that sent them rattling down to the equator and the ladders that brought them to their ships. I felt the resounding bell-like clang as docking clamps disengaged and the Sparrowhawks and Peregrine fighters shot from their launch tubes like missiles. I had ridden in them before—though I am but a poor pilot myself. How well I remember the silent dark of the tube rushing past—the only sound the faint beeping of instruments and the ragged rasp of breath! How clearly I recall the flash and the sudden shimmering of stars as we turned and soared over the dark curve of the dorsal hull or down to thread the hanging towers. I watched them deploy on the tactical displays. Two hundred lighter craft that fell into tight formation about the *Tamerlane*, keeping just outside the limit of our shields. They would assist the *Tamerlane*'s gunners in fending off the boarding vessels while we returned fire on their ship.

"Should have visual in a moment, captain!" said White, the navigator, his voice low and terse as ever. "The commander's right. It's massive."

"How massive?" I asked. He told me. "That's the size of a small planet!"

"Aye, my lord!" White said.

I advanced along the catwalk so that I stood above the navigator's station. "Is it the Extrasolarians?" No sooner had I asked the question did a chime sound at White's console. Images from the seeker. "What is it?"

White did not reply.

"What is it, Lieutenant?"

The man's numb fingers found the right controls and relayed the video feed to the false window at the front of the bridge. The star field vanished in a snap, replaced by another. A dark shape moved against the black, masking the unfixed stars.

It was the size of a dwarf planet, as I had said, and once perhaps as round. The seeker probe had passed it already, propelled by a shipboard laser already to twenty percent the speed of light. It still looked like a planet from the front end, a great cap of ice and stone that shone faintly in the starlight and by a light all its own. But behind? Behind it trailed the gutted remnants of a world converted, extruded into halls and towers and warrens like the warrens of ants. A termite-chewed worldship large as any I had seen. Large as the ship I'd shattered at Aptucca. Large as Prince Aranata's palace that Titus Hauptmann had destroyed.

The Cielcin had come.

"I'm tracking clouds of boarders approaching the other ships, too!" White exclaimed, having regained his senses. "The *Mintaka* is breached! Captain Verus has sealed the bridge!"

My hand went uselessly to the sword at my hip. "We're next," I said. "They'll try and get a team aboard to take our shields and engines offline." I hurried back toward Corvo. "Give me the comm."

She stepped sideways just enough to permit me access to the ship's internal broadcast. I drew the remote out and held it to my mouth. "Attention all, this is Lord Marlowe." I could feel the silence in my chest filling the ship around me as I spoke. "All hands to battle stations. Repeat. All hands to battle stations. Prepare for boarders. We have engaged the Cielcin. Repeat. We have engaged the Cielcin." I paused a moment, never sure what else to say if anything. I swallowed, and though I did not believe I added, "May Earth keep and protect us. Marlowe out."

Corvo was staring at me, but when I noticed, she nodded and returned to her work, relaying orders over the bridge's sound system to save herself from shouting. She looked like she was about to say something, but she never had the chance. A bright light flared across the massive screen, and a moment after Pherrine said, "The *Mintaka* just accelerated toward the enemy ship!"

"What is Verus doing?" Corvo leaned over the projection well. "He's flying right at them!"

Arms crossed, I watched the tactical display. The *Mintaka* had shot toward the Cielcin worldship, but at a high angle. "Is he trying for orbital insertion?" I asked. The bigger Cielcin ships were so massive the most practical way to assail them was to fall into a low, fast orbit. To treat them like a planet.

"Get Verus on the comm!" Captain Corvo exclaimed.

No image of the haggard captain appeared, but a voice panel opened in the air by Corvo. "Verus." There was a tightness in his voice that undercut his calm. The man was a professional.

"What's your situation, captain?" Corvo asked.

"They took out our lighters. Some of the demons got aboard. I've sealed the bulkheads. It's under control."

Corvo didn't miss a beat. "How many of them?"

"Couple hundred. It's under control." He said those last words like a mantra. Like a prayer. We heard shouting behind him.

Then the connection died.

Corvo keyed the console. "What happened? Pherrine, bring him back."

"Communication's down, ma'am. Ship's still there, though." The communications officer's own voice had gone tight as a coiled spring.

Aristedes's clipped accent cut in. "But they're not under thrust. Something's happened." What that something was had to wait. A warning light blinked on the tactical consoles below, and the intus raised his high voice. "Hostiles accelerating! Still on intercept course!"

Boarding craft.

I turned my attention to the window, squinted out into the Dark, willing the enemy to reveal itself, though they were as yet thousands of miles away.

From his place below, Lorian Aristedes said, "Prepare to deploy AM mines on my mark."

He had not waited for orders, knowing all too well his duty.

"Mark."

A spray of red points fanned out across the space between us and the Cielcin ship on the holograph in front of me, the AM mines expanding into a flat sheet between us and them. They were simple enough machines, each a hollow sphere containing a few grains of antilithium in magnetic suspension. Proximity would trigger them to end that suspension. The antimatter would collide with the material of the mine itself and the resulting fireball of matter–antimatter annihilation would destroy anything unshielded within its effective radius.

Even adamant.

I pivoted my attention back to the false window, and as I turned, one of the junior techs switched the view from the Cielcin ship to better capture an image of the approaching swarm. The Cielcin attack craft were barely visible against the Dark, even magnified a thousand times. We could see them only backlit by the fire of their drives as they howled toward us. Other views out other cameras played in tiles along the edges of the mighty window-screen, and here and there I caught glimpses of a gray Sparrowhawk or white Peregrine streaking about the *Tamerlane*. I gritted my teeth and held the edge of my cape in one fist, waiting, counting down to a zero I could only guess at.

"Any second now," Durand said.

Light brighter than a dozen suns flared out across the darkness. Light! And silence. No sound nor shock of air was there to disturb that bottomless calm. Ten thousand years hence perhaps the light of that explosion would reach some distant world and spark like lightning across its foreign sky. And in that distant age perhaps some shepherd would look up and gasp in wonderment and alarm, but until that day no other fanfare would mark that first destructive salvo, unless it was Lorian's dry remark from the tac officer's seat. "Got them."

But he had not got them all. The boarding craft were stretched out in waves across hundreds of miles of space, and the rest came screaming in faster through the haze where once the mines had been.

Corvo strode past me onto the catwalk, full voice thundering. "Concentrate main dorsal batteries on the Cielcin mothership!"

"No! No!" I said, stepping in. "Belay that!"

Otavia rounded on me. "This is *my* ship, Hadrian! What the hell are you doing?" I must have made her angry; she never called me *Hadrian* on the bridge. Her jaw was clenched and her amber eyes had crystallized.

I owed an explanation, but my reason was only just catching up to my instincts, and it took me a tense moment. "Our missing legions are probably aboard. We need to fight fire with fire. Take the fight to them."

The captain's amber eyes narrowed. "We didn't plan for this."

I turned fully to face her, pointing at the false window over her shoulder. "We need to outflank them, disable their warp capabilities if we can."

"You want us to fly right at that swarm of boarding craft?"

Aristedes spoke from below, high voice almost laughing. "That'll surprise them!"

Corvo shook her head, leaned over the rail to call to Pherrine. "Where are the others?"

As if in answer a bright streak of fire shone against the Dark, a great violet stream of superheated plasma. Pherrine answered, "That was the *Pride of Zama*. They're advancing!" Her fingers flew over the console before her, and she nodded along with more intelligence as it came in over her headset. "The *Androzani*'s taken on boarders! They confirm it is the Cielcin!"

"Damn it!" Corvo said. "Go after them! Koskinen, take us forward, full thrust! Put us into orbit around that *thing*!"

"Hold!" Aristedes shouted. "Hold hold!"

"What is it?" Corvo asked, glowering down at her tactical officer.

Lorian did not look up. He raised one skeletal finger and held it there like a conductor's baton at the start of a symphony. "When we go for burn, we'll leave the aquilarii behind."

"We'll circle back for them!" Corvo said.

"Or!" Aristedes said, "We wait for the Cielcin to close distance, *then* burn."

I saw the shape of Lorian's plan then. "You'll lure the boarders right into the lighters' jaws."

I could not see his face, only the halo of his nearly white hair shining, but I heard the smile in his voice all the same. "If the Pale are using their usual boarding craft they won't last five minutes against our boys."

Corvo ran both hands through her wild hair. After a moment, she nodded. "See it done." Then, fixing me with that iron stare, she said, "I hope you're right about this."

"So do I," I said.

"Prepare for hard burn on my mark! Pherrine, Aristedes, relay our plan to the aquilarii. I don't want those wings surprised when we boost out of here! And Lord Marlowe, you may wish to hold onto something!" Corvo called, storming back toward the holography well and her chair. Still irritated with me, then. I said nothing, but I did grasp the rail at my side, feet planted. The suppression fields would counter most of the inertial drift from our acceleration, but there would still be enough to knock an untrained spacer from his feet.

I was not entirely without training.

"Hold!" Aristedes said. The intus had not yet lowered his finger, and spoke in a tone as suggested he held the reins on a line of cavalry. "Hold!" I could make out the swarm of Cielcin boarding craft on Corvo's projection, closing like a slow rain of arrows. Closer. Closer. "Hold!" They had closed the vast distances between us in a matter of minutes, and I was forced to remind myself that the Cielcin lived in space—had been adapting to its rigors for millennia. Perhaps they suffered the stress of high acceleration better than we. I never rightly learned, never fully understood the degree to which the Cielcin had *changed* themselves as we had done in creating the great confusion of humanity. As we had crafted the palatine, the patrician, and the homunculus. As others had perverted their flesh with machines or accepted fouler praxis in the bowels of Vorgossos, so too the Cielcin doubtless had altered the course of their own evolution, hardening themselves against the Dark.

"Hold!" Lorian's bright, chilly voice rang out once again. "Mark!"

"Mark!" Corvo bellowed.

Koskinen fired the primary sub-light drives, and the *Tamerlane* shot forward. I did not so much as stagger against the rail. The stars beyond our ship did not seem to move, so vast was the Dark between them. But move we did. The Cielcin landing craft tore past us, red motes rushing across the *Tamerlane* on Corvo's display. Outside, in the endless Dark, they fired attitudinal jets, yawing about, correcting their approach vectors. The *Tamerlane* answered them, gun emplacements blazing, plasma fire and missiles scouring the night. I watched it all on Corvo's holography well and on the tactical displays visible in an arc on the level below me and on the mighty screen at the fore of the bridge. In one corner a camera feed went dark. One of the Peregrine pilots must have collided with one of the Cielcin vessels.

But Lorian's plan had worked. The bulk of the Cielcin attackers had overshot us by hundreds of miles—thousands—and had fallen squarely into the hands of our aquilarii.

Safe for the moment and with enough time to think, Corvo asked, "What's the status on the *Mintaka*?"

"They're off course," Pherrine said. "Main engines offline."

"Shields are holding, though," said Adric White.

Aristedes waved an almost dismissive hand. "They're disabled and falling into a decaying orbit around the enemy vessel. There's nothing we can do from here."

An eerie calm had settled over the bridge then, each man talking to each in turn. I stood aloof from them, not a deck officer myself, contemplating the little red star of the *Mintaka* where it orbited the Cielcin vessel ahead of us.

"Assuming their shields hold and they can keep their decks clear," Tor Varro said, referring to the Cielcin that gotten aboard, "they might be able to hold until we can close the distance."

Nodding, I turned from the scholiast and the central console and strode along the captain's walk toward the main windows yet again. "Where are the other ships?" I asked, standing with my nose mere centimeters from the glass. I squinted, searching for some flash or spark to mark the passing of a ship or of weapons fire. But there was nothing. No flash of laser or crash of exploding vessels.

Only darkness. Darkness and silence. And cold.

"Here is the kingdom of Death," I quoted, murmuring under my breath, "and we the living have no place in it . . ." I couldn't recall who had written that. It wasn't Eliot or Shakespeare. It might have Bastien, in one of his darker plays, or D'Lorca. I was glad no one had heard me, feeling suddenly foolish. Presently I raised my voice. "Where are the other ships?"

Pherrine's clear voice rang out in answer, "The *Pride of Zama* is still closing. They were the farthest out. The others are both between us and the enemy."

"And the *Androzani* is still taking on boarders?"

"I think so, my lord," she answered, and as I turned I saw her glance up at me, pale face lit by the screen before her. "We lost their comms three minutes ago."

My mouth opened of itself to utter an oath to blacken the very face of Earth, but I never spoke it. A series of white indicators pulsed distractingly on the navigator's console in my periphery, and Adric White's rough voice cut in. "There's something happening to the *Mintaka* I don't quite understand."

Commander Aristedes craned his neck to peer at the navigator. I followed his gaze, then realizing this was foolishness, directed my attentions toward the nearer captain's console. Corvo had rescaled the projection, and I could see the knife-shape of the *Mintaka* in high orbit over the alien ship. It was hard to tell on the grainy sensor scan, but it was turning, slewing about as though it had skidded on ice, turning about a point near its bow.

"They have it on a line," the intus said. "Harpooned."

"That shouldn't be possible!" Durand objected. "The ship is shielded!"

"Not from the *inside*," Corvo said. "The boarders must have deployed the cable."

They kept on in this vein a moment, and as they did I imagined the Cielcin boarding craft—like black claws sunk deep into the hulls of our ships. I could picture Cielcin berserkers clambering over the icy hull, sinking anchor lines into the softer metals while their brethren fought on the decks within. They meant to drag the *Mintaka* down to the frigid surface of their worldship, to break it against their hull as a bird breaks a clam.

We had to stop them if we could.

My eyes met Corvo's through the holograph between us. We didn't have to exchange a word; she knew what I wanted and bobbed her head. "Aristedes! Tell Crim to have a boarding party ready to launch when we're at our closest to the *Androzani*. He's to be their relief." I was hurrying back toward the captain's station as I spoke, cape billowing behind me like wings to speed my passage.

"Aye, Lord Marlowe," Lorian said. "The First Cohort?"

"Not the first," I said, stopping just above the diminutive officer's station. "Have him take the third. Callista's people haven't seen action in a while. I need the first."

"For what?" Durand asked, and for a moment the light caught his glasses in such a way they whited out the lenses.

I hesitated a moment in answering. It took time for my tongue to catch up to my disordered thoughts. "How long 'til we're in orbit around that thing?" I asked, and though I addressed the bridge at large my eyes never left Corvo's display and the rough model of the Cielcin worldship that floated there.

"Just over two hours, lord," Koskinen replied.

"Will the shields hold?"

One of Aristedes's lieutenants answered me. "Unless they've got something nasty planned, my lord, yes."

"Very good." I turned on my heel and hurried for the upper door and access to the express tram that ran from the bridge to the officers' dormitories far aft.

Tor Varro—uncharacteristically quiet through all this—made to rise from his seat as I passed. "Where are you going?"

I waved him to sit and did not break stride. "To prepare a boarding party. I want the First Cohort and the Irchtani ready and waiting to launch within an hour. We're taking the fight to the Cielcin. And Varro!" I did stop then but did not turn. "Find Prince Alexander and seal him in his quarters. Have Crim post guards inside and out. If we are breached, we cannot allow His Highness to come to harm." I sensed a pregnancy in Varro's quiet and turned to face him. The scholiast still sat there in his green uniform, apparently unruffled by the entire situation. "And order Verus to prepare troops as well and to help liberate the *Androzani*."

Just then a titanic flash whited out the primary view screen, illuminating the entire bridge.

Into the silence that followed, one of Aristedes's lieutenants said, "The . . . the *Androzani* is gone, captain."

I did not hear what Corvo said next. I looked back to face the window. All was still and terribly silent within me, and the commotion around fell hushed and far away. The Cielcin must have compromised the fuel containment on the *Androzani*'s warp drive. Like the AM mines but incomparably vaster, the resulting annihilation had wiped out the entire ship and every man, woman, and xenobite aboard. The Cielcin had sacrificed themselves to even the odds.

What could we do against such rapine? Such ravenous hate?

"Do not let a single one of the Pale aboard!" I ordered my officers. "Post a detail on the warp cores *now*, before it becomes a problem! I want everyone ready." Then I turned to go, trying not to think of hook-nosed Captain Yanek and thousands who burned along with him on his pyre. There were not even atoms left to bury. The blast would have reduced him and his crew and every strut and deckplate of the *Androzani* to pure energy. That energy, too, would fall upon the face of some nameless child in an age ten thousand years hence, and they might wonder to look upon so brief and brilliant a star.

Or perhaps no one would notice at all.

But we had noticed. And *I* had noticed. And *I* clenched my fists in muted fury.

"My lord!" Varro again. "Where are you going?" The same idiot question again. Now I understood how Otavia must have felt.

I whirled and pointed out the window with a steady hand. "To *lead* the boarding party. Myself."

CHAPTER 21

DEMON IN BLACK

THE LOCKER HINGED OPEN like some jeweled scarab, and the black face stared out at me. Perhaps you've seen it plastered on some poster or in some propaganda film? The face of the Devil of Meidua? Fashioned in the likeness of my own face it was, blank and staring, with mirror-black lenses for eyes beneath the cap of the helmet with its broad neck-flange. Those eyes stared at me from the suit locker, impassive and cold as those of my ancestors carved in black marble in the caverns of our necropolis.

I had become one of them in the end.

We had been soldiers before we were lords.

But I had no time for philosophy, and sealed the suit. Sensing the closure, fibers within the underlayment tightened and hugged my body like a diver's second skin, covering me from the neck down. The suit's thermal regulators came online, and the clinging garment felt at once like no garment at all, became a part of me. One after another I stepped into the armored boots and felt them screw shut about my calves. I did the same with the cuisses on my upper legs, removing the items from foam-lined compartments in the chest before me. The tunic came next. I pulled it over my head, letting the garment fall almost to my knees. The shirt was sable as the rest, fringed with a labyrinth pattern in crimson thread. I fastened the belt with its strapped pteruges about my narrow waist and felt it cinch tight with the shield controls at my left hip, sword holster at my right.

Fingers plied the locker controls, and at once the sculpted breastplate and helmet rose toward me, rotating on a gimbal, tracking hardpoints on my skinsuit. I raised my arms wide and stepped into the open breastplate, felt the magnets clamp onto the inner layer and screw on. Folding like a beetle's black shell, like a Nipponese paper sculpture, the suit closed around me, titanium and ceramic segments folding, flexing as I moved. Even as it did so, the mask and helmet broke apart, retracting, neatly folding themselves into a wide collar about my face and neck. The pauldrons shifted into place automatically, obeying sub-intelligent programs in the suit's datasphere matrix. I flexed my shoulders, listening to the whine of servos as the armor moved with me.

Perfect.

"What's going on?"

Valka stood in the door behind me.

I didn't stop my work, lingered only long enough to ensure the ornamental leather straps at my shoulders were in place. I shoved my left hand into the gauntlet the locker rotated to present to me and made a fist as the vambrace sealed into place. The terminal screen and controls winked on, red as death.

"We're being attacked," I said. "It's the Cielcin."

"I know," Valka said, and only then did I remember that I'd broadcast to the entire ship. A red haze had settled on my mind and I felt I saw the world through a narrow tunnel, and the only way out was *through*.

"*I* know, sorry." I plugged my hand into the second gauntlet, felt it seal. "They destroyed the *Androzani*. I'm taking the fight to them."

Valka's pale face went paler. "They destroyed . . . what?"

"They got men aboard her, must have breached fuel containment." As I spoke, I checked readouts on my left forearm. Suit power was nominal, air reservoirs and rebreathers were charged, water recycling was functioning normally, and the suit's shield generators shone blue.

Her nostrils flared. "Can't you send one of the others? Crim or Pallino? One of the other chiliarchs?" She did not ask me to take her with me. Valka had been a soldier in another life, but she'd been a deck officer. There was no place for her in the trenches, in the hallways and warrens of a Cielcin worldship, blood wet on our knives. Soldier she may have been, once, but she was no fighter, unless it was by necessity.

"I'm not going to sit idly here while my men fight and die," I said, lifting the white cape from the wall hook where I had left it and wrapping it around my shoulders. "Would you?"

Valka's expression softened. "You're not idle. You were on the bridge."

"Yes," I snapped, "being idle. Where's my sword?" I had left it on the bed when I'd skinned out of my ordinary clothes. Or thought I had.

"Pallino can lead the men just as well as you."

I stopped my frantic riffling through the mounded garments. "Pallino can't communicate with the enemy. Damn it! Where is my—"

The sword descended into my field of vision. Valka held it, offered it to me pommel first.

I took it, receiving it as I'd received it from Sir Olorin at the start of my quest so long ago. "Thank you."

Her fingers floated just off my chest, where the embossed trident and pentacle I had taken for my sigil stood out against the black ceramic. "I don't like you rushing off like this. You're going to get yourself killed." She pressed her fingers against my chest. I couldn't feel their warmth, only their pressure against the armor.

"No, I'm not," I said, and forced a smile. "I can't *be* killed, hadn't you heard?"

But Valka had been by that lakeside in the Gardens of Kharn Sagara. She knew better.

There was no laughter in those golden eyes. "I do not like being left here idle, either. I don't like you leaving."

Closing my fingers over hers, I said, "I have to. Someone does." The ship jolted beneath us then. Something must have hit our shields. We stumbled apart, the contact between us breaking. It was enough to snap me back to my duties. My terminal chimed, and I tapped the indicator. "Marlowe."

"We're about loaded, sir." Pallino's voice came over the speaker. *Sir.* He only ever called me that when there was work to do.

It heightened my sense of unreality as I answered, "Copy that. I'm on my way." Looking up I saw myself reflected in the mirror, armor so black it gleamed. I looked much as I had in my vision—was it a vision?—in the Howling Dark. A demon in black. The armor was not the same, but the resemblance was there . . . a shadow on my heart.

"What is it?" Valka asked, sensing something was the matter.

I looked round, somehow surprised to find her there.

"I'm sorry," I said. "I have to go." I turned to leave. One hand on the door frame, I added, "When I'm gone, seal yourself in here. If the Cielcin board the ship, you'll be safe."

"Like hell!" The force in her words astonished me, the anger. I turned. She'd closed half the distance between us already. "I am not going to *lock* myself in here. You don't get to put me in a *box*, Hadrian."

I realized what I'd said, and to whom, and the wind went out of me. "I'm sorry. That wasn't what I meant. I'm just worried about you."

"You're worried? About me?" She laughed. "Me?"

Of course I am, I wanted to say, but it felt like too much. Struck by an idea I said, "Can you go to the bridge? Aristedes will be busy directing the battle. I need someone watching my back."

"I . . ."

"You won't be idle," I said, stealing her words with a crooked smile, "you'll be on the bridge."

She pressed her lips together. "I hate you." Her hand found mine again and squeezed it.

"No, you don't!"

Golden eyes met violet, and she kissed me. Why should I remember that kiss so sharply? It was not the first time I'd left her to leap into battle. It would not be the last. It was not our first kiss aboard the *Mistral,* nor the one we would share that windy night on Berenike. Nor was it the one I gave her before she went into fugue as we limped back to Colchis with black sails.

But I remember it. I remember her hands in my hair and the taste of her mouth and the way the ship shook beneath us. I remember holding her close against me and the little voice whispering *you have no time.*

You have no time.

CHAPTER 22

INTO THE MAW

EACH BOARDING SHOT IS a kind of prayer.

You stand in crash webbing against the walls of a *Shrike*-class shuttle, hands gripping the restraints, glad of the suit underlayment wicking the sweat from your palms to feed the suit's recyclers. Your breath comes through clenched teeth, as you pray the navigator and the pilot officer plotted a course for you that doesn't carry you through enemy lighters or weapons fire. You're powerless, impotent. You've nowhere to run, nothing to do but *hope* you make contact on the far end, and then you're still in deep. Still facing the prospect of battle. Battle with no retreat, no way forward but to seize the enemy vessel!

I'd done it a dozen times before, but it never got easier.

It never gets easier to *pray*.

Cradled in my suit, sealed within the helmet and the environment layer, the only sound I heard was that of my own steady breathing. That and the war-drum beat of my heart hammering faster. Faster. Faster. Through the void we fell. Twenty soldiers clad in ivory and scarlet stood around me, our ship one among dozens hurled across the void at the Cielcin.

A thousand men. A thousand Irchtani. Against Emperor knows how many of the Pale. We were being reinforced by men from the *Cyrusene*, but they were coming in the next wave. Maybe Valka was right. Maybe it was foolishness.

I could hear the shifting of the others in the red-lighted dim. Nervous energy. Lances and plasma burners shifted from hand to hand. Whispered prayers. My suit's entoptics projected the interior of the cabin directly onto my eyes, so it seemed I wore no mask or helm at all, save that the image was brighter, richer than my own vision would be in such low lighting. I watched the faceless legionnaires watching me, their masks smooth arcs of ceramic without slit or eye-hole.

No one said anything. They knew their duty.

Siran gave me a reassuring nod. She wore a prime centurion's uniform, blank mask painted the same red as her tunic, three golden medallions welded to her breastplate. Not speaking, she checked the settings on her energy lance where it sat snug and collapsed in the bracket beside her. Apparently satisfied, she rested her head against the crash webbing.

"Nervous?" I asked her on a private channel, unwilling to disturb the general calm.

Her faceless mask shifted to focus on me and she replied on the same channel. "Are you?"

"Every time."

But I could not afford to show it.

The shuttle shook around us; something had brushed against our shields. Despite the suppression fields that served to check our harsh acceleration, I felt my stomach lurch and held on, glad the helm and mask concealed my face from the men. I took a slow, deep breath, forcing myself to calm. I turned my eyes toward the door, waiting, willing it to open. Anything was better than this impotent waiting.

"Thirty seconds to contact," came the pilot officer's voice.

Fingers tightened on restraints, and I was not alone in bowing my head, though whether I did so in prayer or self-defense—or out of some admixture of the two—I cannot say.

"Twenty seconds! Brace for impact!"

There were no windows in the shuttle, was no way to see the Cielcin craft.

"Fifteen seconds!" the pilot officer said. The shuttle bucked as retrorockets fired, decelerating our shuttle as we hurtled toward contact. "Ten! Five!"

"Hold on!" Siran shouted.

I pressed my knees against the sides of my compartment and braced my arms. When it came, the impact came sharp, and my head rattled against the restraints.

"Contact!" the pilot called from the rear. Almost at once the plasma cutters fired—I could hear the whine and spit of them through the airlock door.

We were already out of our harnesses. The men were hefting energy lances and plasma rifles, performing their last, nervous equipment checks.

Despite the tension in the air, they each moved with cold professionalism, ready for the work that was at hand.

On the far side of the round door, two plasma cutters rotated, spiraling deeper and deeper into the hull of the Cielcin vessel. Pressure seals closed around the aperture as the *Shrike* limpeted itself to the ship, seal growing tighter and tighter. I shouldered my way toward the front of the shuttle, feeling at once that I was in the lift riding up to the killing floor of the Colosso with my fellow myrmidons. As if nothing had changed, though everything had.

"Are you all right?" Valka's throaty voice came in through the conduction patch I'd taped behind my right ear, words clear despite the thousands of miles of space between us. The comms were still holding. That was good.

Unheard within my helmet, I answered her, "Should be in at any moment now." One of the decurions reached up over my head and primed the five mapping drones that waited in berths along the arched ceiling. "What's it like out there?"

"Shields are holding," Valka answered. "They've not gotten close to us yet. We still won't be there for an hour."

"Keep me posted."

"I'll be watching your vitals."

Bang!

The sound of metal striking metal sounded on the far side of the hatch, followed by the *whoosh* of fire suppressants. Then the hatch opened on dark and fog. The only light came from the still-glowing edges of the massive hatch that had fallen inward when the *Shrike* cut it away. The first two of our men raised their lances, hafts extending, housings flashing into place. Above their heads, the five mapping drones deployed one after the other, flying off into the darkness in a whirl of scanning red lasers that shuddered and broke on the fog. Instantly a map began forming in the top right of my vision, revealing the hall before us like the first warren of an anthill. The drones were not intelligent, required guidance from the pilot officer on our shuttle, but they were capable of not crashing into the tunnel walls, and even of rounding corners. They might not make it far into the ship before the Cielcin destroyed them, but each of our boarding craft had deployed as many, and before long we would have a credible map of the ship's layout.

"Left or right, my lord?" one of the men asked.

Lacking better intelligence, I said, "Left. That will take us toward the rear." A second glance at my map showed where the other *Shrikes* had made contact with the ship and begun mapping. The best tactic for fighting in the halls of any great ship was precisely this: cut through the hull in as many places as possible to divide the enemy's attentions; move in small, coordinated groups; keep the fighting to narrow passages to prevent being overwhelmed; and work your way inward toward the ship's critical systems: life-support, power, water—whatever you could find. In attacking other human vessels this tactic was more or less straightforward. The ship layout was more familiar, and all the signs and computer systems were intelligible. I could read the Cielcin writing, but not so well as I'd like.

There *was* something of a common plan to Cielcin ship design as well. The bulk of the ship's critical systems were toward the rear, where the engines extended and the main body of artificial construction rose from the surface of that small world like some evil tower or the trailing arms of a jellyfish. The front mass of the two-hundred-mile-wide planetoid contained the alien city itself. We had no business there.

Pale lights flashed high on the walls in silent alarm, though we encountered no resistance. That was the strangest thing. The quiet. We ought to have been swarming with enemies already, but there were none. I kept my sword in my hand, recalling the bowels of the *Demiurge* and the ships we'd stormed at Cellas, Thagura, and at Aptucca. The damned quiet oppressed me, until I thought I must scream. But I advanced, a line of men to either side of me and Siran behind.

The Cielcin do not build as we, in straight lines and plain angles. The walls were rounded, ribbed and undulating, following non-Euclidean patterns I could not comprehend. The floor rose and fell in waves, the tunnel snaking along, deckplates rattling beneath our feet. The map ahead showed the path straightening, branching as we approached the rear of the vessel.

"Pallino." I pressed a finger to the base of my jaw. "What's your position? Have you seen anything?"

A green pulse showed on the map in the corner of my vision, and the chiliarch answered, "No movement here. You?"

"Empty."

"They have to be *somewhere*."

"Your guess is as good as mine," I said in answer. "But I don't like it."

Boom.

A great noise shook the hall in which we stood, loosing dust from the gray metal ribs above our head. One of the soldiers said, "What the hell was that?"

Rather than answer, Siran shouted, "Forward! Move it!"

"Valka?" I asked, toggling comms channels with a glance to the icons that lined the bottom of my vision. "What's going on out there?"

"They're firing on the *Mintaka*."

"We need to get further in!" I said, turning to grab the centurion by the shoulder. "Fuel reservoirs should be near the primary drives." At Aptucca, we'd managed to plant a microfusion charge on the outer shell of their warp drive's antimatter containment. That single, small charge in the right place had been enough to destroy Prince Ulurani's entire worldship with all hands aboard. We didn't want to do that here, not if there was a chance our missing soldiers were aboard. "And the holds."

I pushed past the two men in front of me and moved off down the hall, mindful of the echoes our boots made on the decking as I went. Despite our danger, I felt a strange thrill of relief. We had *found* the enemy. Against all odds, we had found them. Now we only had to win.

We hurried on another few steps before the comms channel crackled to life and we heard the dreaded words, "Enemy contact!" Then came the sounds of weapons fire over the line, and a locator pin blinked on my map in time with the speaker's words. They were miles away, further down the rear section higher up.

"We've got contact!" came another voice, another pin on the map.

"Contact! Contact!"

"They came out of the walls!"

Pins flared across the map, and at once I saw the shape of the trap we'd put our foot in. The Cielcin had held their forces in reserve, waited for our groups to pull themselves a little deeper into the ship, waited until we weren't quite certain of our surroundings or of the way back to our shuttles . . .

"Square formation!" I shouted, and at once the double line of men about me pivoted so that ten faced ahead and ten faced back the way they had come. Unlike most legionary units, where only one man in three wore a body shield, my men were all hoplites, all shielded.

That order saved us.

Boom.

The hall shook again, followed by a series of hollow thuds as the wall panels between the ribs slid aside. A wave of the Cielcin *nahute* struck us like arrows from either side. The things flashed like metal serpents rippling in the dim air. One shot straight for my face, drill-bit teeth snarling. I kindled Olorin's sword and struck, slicing the thing cleanly in half.

There were at least a dozen more, though as I wheeled about I saw one blasted to smithereens by plasma fire and another crushed by a hoplite's energy lance.

My blood ran cold an instant later, for a terrible wailing—high and thin as a winter wind through dead trees—issued from the dark to either side. I knew a Cielcin war cry when I heard one, and letting my suit speakers carry my voice with all the force and volume I could muster, I answered them, not with a cry, but with a command. "Light!" I bellowed, not knowing how prophetic that order would prove by the light of history. "Light!" I activated my suit torches, casting white beams from both shoulders and forearms. The others joined me, and the gloom of that alien hall retreated from us, light piercing the deepest shadows.

I have seen many terrible things in my life, Reader. Many terrible things. I have trod on battlefields across half a hundred worlds and smelled the smoke of cities burning. I have been a guest of the Undying in Vorgossos and enjoyed the hospitality of the so-called Scourge of Earth. Few things are to me now as terrible as the painted masks of Cielcin warriors shining out of the Dark. One of them threw itself from the shadows and fell upon one of my hoplites. The man panicked and dropped his lance, and big as he was and strong, the xenobite was stronger. It pinned him to the ground and—to my astonishment—ripped the shield projector from the man's belt. A moment later one of the orbiting *nahute*—stymied by the shields we others wore—found the soft part of the man's armor between thigh and groin and drilled its way in. The helmets muffled his screaming, but still I heard it.

Like so many screams, I will never stop hearing it.

One of the others shot the Cielcin who had done the deed. Blood and bone and the black matter of its brain painted the floor, and a thin smoke hung a moment in the foggy air. Some held breath rushed out, and whatever seal held chaos at bay tore well and true. At a guess, there must have been thirty of them. Perhaps forty. There were twenty-two of us. Twenty-one by then. By rights we should have been destroyed, but the remaining soldiers of my First Cohort stood fast, and the Cielcin screamers had no shields to protect them.

We had long ago abandoned the use of phase disruptors in battling the Cielcin. The xenobites' nervous systems did not respond to disruptor fire as ours do. Laser and plasma. Light and fire. Those were the way.

Those . . . and the sword.

I leaped past our line, sword moving in a rising arc that tore through one of the enemy from hip to shoulder. It fell in two ragged pieces, white sword dropped from nerveless fingers. Seeing this, three of the others backed off, dodging behind the ribbed pillars that separated the main hall from the sort of arras where they'd lain in wait.

"*Deni raka Aeta ba-okun ne?*" I asked, speaking their own tongue. *Who is your master?*

The Cielcin cocked their heads to hear their words in the mouth of one of us human vermin, but I could not see their faces. The resin masks they wore concealed their faces save for their terrible mouths, and their teeth shone in the darkness like bits of broken glass. They had no eyeholes, and I wondered if the material was transparent from the inside, or if—as with our own helmets—there were cameras that saw for them, that protected their too-sensitive eyes from the light we'd brought to blind them.

"*Deni raka Aeta ba-okun ne?*" I asked again, moving the point of my sword from one enemy to the next like an accusing finger.

As if in answer, two of the Cielcin charged forward, thinking perhaps their numbers would aid them. But the edge of a highmatter sword is less than one molecule wide, and I encountered no resistance as I cut them both down with a single stroke. They toppled past me, black blood pilling on my hydrophobic cape, pattering to the ground. The third Cielcin snarled and aimed a clawed finger at me. It must have had some command over the *nahute* that threaded amongst us, for no sooner had it done so than three of the metal serpents wheeled and flew toward me. One caromed off my shield like a shark striking the side of its tank in blind fury. I recoiled, but kept my feet, retreating toward the line of hoplites at my back. Someone fired on the Cielcin with the upraised finger, and it toppled to the ground with a hole in its shoulder. One of the *nahute* fell smoking from an unseen energy beam, and I danced back, mindful of the men about me and the way they restricted my movements. A sword does not discriminate between friend and foe. A highmatter sword less so.

Still I caught one of the alien drones as it rebounded off my shield, and Siran felled the other. For a moment, it looked like we might win the engagement after all.

For a moment.

The xenobites' high and ghostly wail went up again, piercing as the whistle of air through a leaking bulkhead out into the formless dark of space. There were more of them. Two dozen more at least.

"Forward!" I shouted, pointing my sword. The hall ahead was clear. We had to get out from between the hammer and the anvil, force the

Cielcin to fight us in the hall where our arms would give us the advantage. Three dead men lay on the ground before me, ragged holes chewed through their environment layer. We were eighteen, then. At most eighteen. I thought I heard Valka's breathing through the comm, mingled with the snatches of orders and of weapons fire from the other groups. There were even the clicks and pops of the Irchtani battle language. More than half our groups had been hit at the precise same time. "About face!"

I had been leading our brief retreat along the darkened hall, and so then found myself at the rear, looking back over the shoulder of my comrades at a sea of masked Cielcin faces as they spilled into the hall. Some of them climbed the walls, moving from rib to rib with their pale, long-fingered hands in the microgravity.

"Fire! Fire! Fire!" Siran was shouting. The violet shouts of plasma fire answered her—more blue in the alien air than I had ever seen. Sulfur in the air, if I remembered my chemistry. I fancied I could smell sulfur, even through the suit. The brimstone stench of hell.

Granted a moment's respite behind my men, I said, "Pallino! Signal every unit to link up into groups of three. We need to form larger groups. It'll make it harder for them to pick us off!"

"Aye, lad!" came the reply.

Dead xenobites littered the floor, but more kept coming, clambering over their fallen brethren or following still more up the walls. I had a sudden impression that we had climbed into a giant anthill, with the rounded corridors and the way the Cielcin moved toward us. But my men retreated calmly now, step by careful step in time with Siran's orders, giving ground only in exchange for more time to fire.

The Cielcin were undeterred. Their berserkers fought with little concept for their individual lives—and why shouldn't they? They were slaves, body and soul, servants to whichever prince they called their master, and that master had ordered them to fight. There was no room for disobedience in the common Cielcin soldier. No free will. They abdicated free will to their commanders, who were in turn the slaves of commanders greater still until all served at the behest of an Aeta prince, who alone was free and a god in all but truth.

" 'Tis an auxiliary unit on its way to you." Valka's voice came tense but quiet in my ear, strangely calming. I acknowledged and drew my sidearm with my left hand, aimed the plasma burner carefully. Fired. One of the Cielcin fell from the wall, knocking two of its fellows from their feet. One of the *nahute* sped toward me, and I waited, let it impact off my shield before I sliced it in two.

They were still coming.

One of the Cielcin fell from the roof above, white sword flashing. The point caught one of my men in the soft spot between neck and shoulder, and he went down. The ceramic blade came out red, and the berserker wheeled, slashing at one of the others. The blade sparked off the hoplite's armor. The xenobite spun, kicked the soldier in the chest with all its inhuman strength. The hoplite slammed into the wall, the wind knocked out of him. All this in the space of perhaps three seconds. The Cielcin raised its sword, point downward, to skewer the man just as it had the other.

The blade fell.

In two pieces.

I sliced clean through weapon and wielder alike, and—holstering my sidearm once again—helped the soldier to his feet.

"We all should have one of those," he said, nodding at my sword. If only that were possible. There were not many materials that were hard to come by in the galaxy, but highmatter was one of them. It could not be mass-produced, required careful tailoring of particles at the subatomic level to create the substance of the blade. Few were the artisans with the skill to craft such weapons, and many were the hours and great the energies required. Thousands of miles of particle accelerator might run for months before quantum chance produced the exotic matter that formed the core of such a blade. Each cost more than a starship, which was part of why I'd been so astonished when Sir Olorin Milta had given one to me.

"Were it so easy!" I said.

Just then another cry went up, higher and colder than the last, but stranger. More *musical*. Such a sound I had not heard in all my days. Then there came a great rushing of air and the beat of mighty wings. A dark shape emerged from the gloom *behind* the Cielcin, and I saw the flash of steel.

The Irchtani had come.

One of them tumbled through the air, slashing its *zitraa* through an arc that struck the head off one of the Cielcin and clove another one between its crown of horn. It landed between our line and the advancing Pale, and the Cielcin themselves recoiled in shock, and no wonder. They had never seen an Irchtani before, and the avian creature bristled, the feathers on its great pinioned arms standing on end, making it seem far larger than it was. Then the others hit the Cielcin from the rear, and now it was they who were caught between hammer and anvil.

It was over as quickly as it had begun and with as little warning.

I counted our dead. Six in all, plus two Irchtani. Minimal, under the circumstances.

"Who has the command here?" I asked our xenobites.

One Irchtani, green-feathered and squatter than the rest, answered me. "I am!" I knew him at once. How I had not recognized him when he flew over the heads of the enemy to draw their attention, I cannot say.

I saluted the auxiliary. "Thank you, Udax. You were just in time."

The bird returned my salute, and for the first time I processed that his combat armor did not cover his wings. I wondered at that. What would happen if the environment failed and the air rushed out? But I supposed the Irchtani could not use their wings otherwise.

We stood a moment in the midst of the carnage while our men stripped the bodies, smashed any unused *nahute* where they hung on the Cielcin's belts like coils of rope, and stripped equipment from their fallen brothers.

The darkness yawned to either side, unmapped.

I keyed an order into my terminal, signaling the pilot officer to reroute one of the mapping drones back to our location.

"What now?" Siran asked.

"They want us in the main halls," I replied, aiming my suit lamps into the darkness behind the doors whence the ambush had come. To the men searching in there, I called, "Do you see anything?"

The response came on our unit channel, "Tunnels, my lord, just like you said!"

"Don't go too far yet!" I ordered. Then to Siran and the Irchtani commander I added, "We need to get out of the parts of the ship they wanted us to be in. We need to move."

CHAPTER 23

KINGDOMS OF DEATH

WITHOUT MY HELMET AND suit optics, I would have been blind. The suit built a hideous simulacrum of the alien tunnels from infrared and sonar and what little available light there was to see. Or perhaps the simulacrum was perfect, and the tunnels truly were hideous. They felt *damp*, like the walls of a cave, like the tunnels of Calagah on Emesh. There was condensation on my armor, and my cape hung dank and gray from my shoulders. There were puddles on the uneven floor, and here and there a rough doorway opened on one side or the other.

The tunnel stretched on, carrying us deeper and deeper into the Cielcin ship—though it hardly seemed a ship at all but a series of a natural caves. All that rock and stone was one way to insulate a vessel against the wild radiation of space. The Cielcin did not build. They *burrowed*. All our human construction: our towers, castles, and fortresses. Our temples and warehouses, even our humble homes . . . all of them reach for the heavens. The Cielcin dig toward hell.

I had been on Cielcin ships before, but never before had I plumbed one to such secret depths. We were not stopped, not accosted by any others for some time, and came at length to a mighty chamber where enormous wheels turned in the dark, clanking and rattling.

"The hell is this?" Siran asked.

"They're not running this thing on *steam,* are they?" said one of the others.

"It's not ship's systems," I said, unsure just how I knew it to be so. "It's a factory."

One of the Irchtani squawked and pulled his hand away from a vat he'd found, swearing in his native tongue. Moving to his side, I saw what had startled him. The vat contained what looked like bloated white worms writhing over one another. I squinted up at the drum-like wheels turning overhead, saw the thread and sheets of fabric being pulled between them. It was a factory. A textile factory. They were making cloth.

"Valka, you should see this!" I said on our private channel, and told her. Once upon a time, such a place would have been a wonder to me. To see just how it was the Cielcin lived and produced even a thing as mundane as their clothing would have a privilege. Now I felt nothing but trepidation and the desire to be away. The loss of that youthful innocence set a steady ache building in my chest. I had been a very different man when I was young, but a piece of that broken Hadrian—of the Hadrian who had died so long ago—shone through my face a moment.

Silkworms. Once, I would have marked this similarity as a sign our two peoples were not so different. I knew better now. They were not our silkworms. They had a thousand spidery legs that tangled against one another, more like a sea creature than an insect. They were not the same at all.

"We should move on," I said.

The faint alarm lights still blinked on the ceiling. To the xenobites I felt sure they must be blinding, better for them than any klaxon. We passed through still more halls and chambers, always with the feeling that the enemy was just ahead of us.

"We're nearing your location." Pallino's voice came over the comm. "There's a big chamber up ahead. We'll meet you there."

The chiliarch's voice was strained. "Have you seen any more of them?"

"Since the first wave? No." I followed Udax through a wide, low arch into a new series of tunnels. "They're preparing for another wave. I can feel it. Be ready."

The area we'd come from fed into the chamber Pallino had mentioned. The drones had not mapped it completely; the operator had directed the drone to fly on through rather than waste too much time mapping side passages. But this chamber was itself large, and rose by terraced levels to either side, reminding me of nothing so much as one of the tiered shopping malls common in the largest Norman cities. There were no stalls, no storefronts, but there were doors lining the levels above us and opening to either side.

"Let's risk more light," Siran suggested, removing a pocket glowsphere from her belt. She twisted it, shook the luminescent chemicals to activate them. White light like a cold and distant star blossomed in her fist and she tossed it high as it would go. It flew far farther than it might in the ship's low gravity. It bounced off the ceiling, drifted lazily down the hall on its weak repulsor field, shedding its light over the terraced levels.

Here at least were signs of civilization. Metal doors stood sunk into the rough stone walls. Silk banners hung from the rails and formless statues of poured metal beaten into the distended shapes of Cielcin and creatures strange to me stood on plinths or in niches. It had the look of some primitive town.

"Where are they?" Udax wondered aloud.

"Not here," Siran answered. She was right. There was no sign of the Cielcin. In an open space like that, they should have been visible on infrared. But then . . . there had been no sign of them in the hall.

I chewed my lip, taking a moment to survey our surroundings. "Check the doors on this level. Double quick." I gestured to a pair of hoplites. "You both, check the main doors there." I pointed toward a massive bulkhead door that stood at the far end of the lozenge-shaped square. They obeyed, and as they did a small knot of Udax's soldiers moved off to check the nearest doors, waddling across the narrow plaza. I waited, listening to the comms chatter, watching our battle groups work their way deeper aboard. A few had encountered further resistance, but most—like us—had not. I was starting to wonder if in fact that first bitter wave in the halls had been all the Cielcin had in them.

"Lord!" one of the Irchtani emerged from a side door and flapped a wing in my direction. "You must see!"

I wish that I hadn't, but in my ignorance I crossed the open space to the door . . . and immediately turned away.

The door had opened on what I took for a Cielcin dwelling: ceiling just high enough to accommodate its xenobite dwellers, walls of roughly chiseled stone with little decoration save the circular carvings they used for writing in imitation of the Quiet's anaglyphs. Papery hangings flapped from the walls, disturbed by our presence, and there was no sound save the distant, hushed beeping of some electric system. There were no cushions, nothing that spoke of comfort, only of the spartan order by which the beasts lived their lives. It might have been a barracks chamber for all I knew. The Cielcin often lived communal lives, particularly toward the bottom of their social hierarchies. Their proles did not know the dignity of family life.

None of this came to mind to mind at the time. I held my breath, used a scholiast technique to calm my breathing and slow my beating heart. I was glad of the suit's environment layer. It wicked the cold sweat from my hands and the back of my neck.

The room's occupants must have fled at the alarm. The signs of recent use were everywhere in evidence: a drinking bulb half-filled rested in a tripod holder on a side table above a gentle gas flame. Scattered papers littered the floor. There were bowls on the dining slab—low on the floor, there were no chairs—each holding a half-gnawed portion of what looked like raw meat.

The *man* lay naked on the slab. What was left of him. Both his legs were gone—and what was between them—and one of the arms as well. What remained of those missing limbs was spread between the bowls, I guessed. I saw the missing hand discarded, the meat stripped from the thumb and fingers.

There was surprisingly little blood, but I knew the reason for that at once.

"One of our lost legionnaires?" I asked.

The Irchtani nodded. "He had a 3-3-7 on his neck here." The bird tapped the right side of his neck with a clawed finger. One of the lost legion indeed. The Irchtani shuddered. "It is not right. Eating one of you. You are *not* food." It was strangely comforting hearing that from another xenobite.

I risked a second look. The man's eyeless sockets watched me upside down from the dining slab. The rest of the face was untouched as yet. One of the Cielcin had gone for the eyes out of *preference*. Because it liked them. I turned away, and remember now as I write these words the way the fellow's one remaining hand had reached out for help that would never come.

"Torch it all," I said to the soldier. "They'll have no more of him." Then over my communicator, I said, "Pallino, where are you?"

"Nearly there, Had. What's the matter?"

"We found our missing soldiers."

"Those doors won't open?" Pallino asked, gesturing at the heavy bulkheads at the end of the plaza. "Airlock?"

"Looks like it," Siran said, and by the odd tilt of her head I guessed she was panning through the three-dimensional map of the tunnel system on her helmet's entoptics. "You could try cutting through it, Had."

The thought had already occurred to me, and I nodded. We were wasting time. We'd been aboard the ship already for the better part of an hour. The *Mintaka* was still in enemy hands. But our men were still sweeping the area around us—the neighborhood, I supposed it was. I misliked the idea of cutting through the door. Any door I cut open could not be closed again, and I could think of a hundred reasons why it should stay closed, but beyond that door was a massive empty space—only hinted at by the mapping drone's sonar pulses, since it hadn't found a way through.

A hold.

The whole rear section of the Cielcin vessel—the part that extended behind the hollowed-out moon for half a hundred miles—seemed to wrap itself around this central hold. "If our ships are still anywhere," I said, and pointed, "they're through those doors."

"We can try and find another way around," Udax suggested.

Pallino was well ahead of us. As chiliarch he could broadcast to every soldier in our strike force—just as I could—and that was precisely what he did. "Has anyone found a way into the central hold? Over."

A moment passed. "No, sir."

"Not here."

"Negative."

It made sense. "That space is too big," I said. "They won't have filled it with air. All the doors are sealed." And we didn't know a thing about Cielcin computational devices.

"We could just blow the door," Pallino suggested.

"Same problem as my cutting through it," I said. "The minute there's a leak here other doors will shut behind us. They won't risk all the air getting out." I keyed my terminal to signal only the men in my group and Pallino's and Udax's auxiliaries. "Spread out, search the levels. There ought to be an emergency hatch. Might be all mechanical in case of power failure. Double quick!"

As I watched the soldiers all hurried about their work. I watched them go, both with my eyes and on the map, tracking beacons showing each man and Irchtani as a blue point against the red wire-frame of the ship map. Absurdly, I thought of the bees in the *Tamerlane's* hydroponics section. Changing topics, I rounded on Pallino. "Are we nearer wiping out any of their critical systems?"

"If it's built like the other ones, Cade's boys should be near the warp cores."

"Not yet, then," I mused. "Siran, order the rest of your century up here, fast as they can. We're spread a bit thin at the moment." I thought of the dead man again and his empty eyes. I shut my own, glad my face was hid behind the mask. We were going to find *worse* before we made it out of here, I just knew it. I had seen some of the footage from our suit cams when Crim's team planted the bombs on Ulurani's ship. The bodies, the shrines made of bone. The *ietumna* inferiors scarred and mutilated to make them more attractive to their *akaranta* masters.

How had I ever believed that peace was possible?

"There's some kind of access tunnel up here, chiliarch!" came one of the soldiers' voices over the comm. "The door's small. Got some kind of wheel-lock. If I'm reading the map right, looks like it goes through to the hold."

Pallino and Siran both looked at me. "Just like you said," Siran said.

I shrugged. "Even I get lucky sometimes."

"Yeah! It's an airlock! Won't fit more than five or six at a time."

"Very good," I said in answer, checking the man's location on the map. "Everyone, up to the third level! Move it!" A thought occurred to me and I grabbed the Irchtani captain by his feathered shoulder. "Udax, if we're right . . . there's no air out there." The bird did not seem to understand. I thought I heard it click its beak through the suit mask. "Will you and your men be able to breathe?"

The Irchtani centurion shrugged my hand away. "Little air at home in sky," it said. "Vacuum no problem." It tapped its mask with a claw. "Have air. Rest no problem." Then it shouldered its plasma rifle on its strap and hurried on. I caught Pallino watching me and sensed that the fellow was raising his eyebrows. Though he could not see my face either, I raised mine, and got the sense that he'd understood.

The door was what I'd expected: a pill-shaped hatch with a strangely human-looking wheel-lock in the center. The men had opened it, revealing a small, round-chambered airlock with an identical door on the far side and a single lever on the wall coated in phosphorescent paint. Cielcin space suits hung in niches on the wall just outside the first door, their faceless visors watching us, their too-long arms hanging limp.

"Tenner's gone through already," said one of the men as we approached.

"It's a hold, all right," came another voice on the comm—presumably that of the soldier, Tenner. "Dark as all hell, though."

Pallino interrupted, "Any sign of the ships, man?"

"Not just here, but this place is massive. Must go on for miles."

"We need to get on through," I said. "At the very least, we'll have a straight shot to the rear. We can join Cade's men shutting down their warp cores."

That was precisely what we did. I stood by in the hall while we began cycling our men through the airlock in groups of five. As I'd hoped, the entire system was mechanical, with the single lever filling or emptying the airlock by turns. Pallino went first, joining his man Tenner on the far side. Five men passed through, then ten. Fifteen. We were sixty.

We were wasting too much time.

"Valka." I keyed over to our private line. "What's your position?"

Her voice was an unspeakable relief in that dark place. "Nearly in orbit around the enemy ship," she said. "What's going on in there?"

"They ambushed us," I said, "but we're fine. Took a few losses, but I think we're nearing their central hold." My voice came out brittle, strangely hollow as I added, "We found the missing men. Or . . . we found one of them. They're definitely here."

Her answer—when it came—was a single, small word. "Dead?"

"Half-eaten."

She swore in her native Panthai. *"Anaryoch."*

Barbarians. For once, I agreed with her. It was strange hearing her apply that same curse to the Cielcin—the one she so often applied to me. I tried not to dwell on it.

Clang.

Something hollow and metallic rang in the darkness, and with several of the others I raised my torch to illuminate the hall. Was there something there? But it was only one of our scouts returning. Nearly half our number had gone through the airlock and were waiting on the far side, but I'd left men posted at the end of the hall and on the terrace overlooking the alien square. They were pulling back, moving with clockwork precision to the orders of their decurions.

"That's all the birdos through," came the voice of one of the more junior officers at my side. "Lord Marlowe, you're next." He raised a hand to usher me through.

I put a hand on the man's arm. "I'll wait 'til the last. Call the scouts back."

The man broke off to do as he was told. "One-two, one-seven: pull back to the airlock. Repeat: pull back to the airlock. That goes double for you, oh-six." I heard words of assent crackle over the line. Two voices. "Oh-six? Oh-six, do you copy?"

Silence.

Clang.

Somewhere on the levels below we heard the faint bump and grind of metal on stone. I felt the hairs on the back of my neck stand up.

"The hell was that?" the junior officer asked.

Valka's voice sounded in my ear. "What's going on?"

I didn't answer her.

"Send more of the men through," I said. "Now." Something had happened to oh-six, that much was clear.

Clang. Clang-clang.

"There's something out there," the junior man said.

"Form a line!" I said. "Cross the hall!" As I spoke the inner door of the airlock slammed shut and I just barely heard the *whoosh* of air as the men inside pulled the lever. At least the thing cycled quickly. There were perhaps twenty of us left on the inside by then. Perhaps less. I tapped my sword hilt anxiously against my thigh. To the junior man, I said, "Take two and stand at the end of the hall. I want eyes out there." The hall was not long. Fifty feet perhaps to the far end and the terrace overlooking the square. If anything was to come at us down the hall they'd be up against our guns, but we were pinned against the airlock, bottlenecked by it.

The men hurried to obey, footsteps rebounding off steel and naked stone.

Clang-clang. Clang.

A small voice whispered in my ear, and I said, "Those are footsteps."

I was half right, as Fate would have it.

I have a clear vision still of that moment: the junior officer and his trias standing in the circular arch at the end of the hall, backlit by our suit lights, framed against the dark. I remember the pop of the airlock's inner door behind me and the hushed jostling of men as they hurried to fill it. There were just over a dozen of us left, and but for their motions there was nothing to hear save the ragged winds that pulsed through the alien ship like breath through the alveolae of some impossibly giant lungs. Somewhere, distantly, a gentle stream of water fell as from a stalactite into a pool. It made me think of the caverns beneath the palace of the Undying, of Brethren, and of our necropolis. Of Calagah.

Then two arms descended from the ceiling, white and slender and too long even for one of the Cielcin. They seized the middle soldier and pulled him screaming up into the night. Plasma flashed violet in the blackness, splitting the gloom like a wedge. The other men screamed too and dropped to their knees, firing upward. The metal scraping sound squealed in the darkness, and I cut the volume on my headset as Pallino and Valka and several of the others began asking questions at once.

The screaming stopped, and distantly I heard a thud as of meat and metal wetly striking the floor, and guessed the junior man had fallen. Or been dropped.

"Open the door!" one of the others was shouting, hammering on the airlock door.

"It's on the ceiling!"

One of the others screamed—and his scream choked off without warning. The line went dead. Plasma flashed again, and between the whine of gunshots I heard a faint scuttling and once more the scrape of metal on stone. Then *something* huge and horrible fell from the darkness above. Bone-white and hulking, taller than any man and far broader it was, with hunched shoulders and a head lost to shadow. I could hardly get a glimpse of it in the sparse light, though where the light caught it shone with a fire like the light of stars.

For a brief instant, I saw the last of the three soldiers find his feet and bring his plasma rifle to bear. He stood etched against the shadow and his quarry, a pitiful small thing against the Dark and the monster that had emerged from it. His rifle flashed, and for a moment then I beheld the beast clearly. Nearly twice again so tall as a man and armored all in white, its legs bent like a dog's, its arms—and there were four of them—so long they nearly trailed the ground. And its face! Its face! It wore a horned mask with a hooked visor like the beak of some evil bird, and beneath I saw the silver-glass flash of teeth and knew it had been Cielcin once.

One of those impossible metal arms caught the soldier by the ankle and pulled. He tumbled backward and struck the floor.

"Fire!" I shouted.

But the demon was gone, dragging that last hapless soldier into the night.

Hands were pulling me back, forcing me over the threshold and into the airlock. "You have to go now, lord!" one of the soldiers said.

"We won't all fit!" said another. "Breda! Take Marlowe and the others and go!" He was one of the decurions. There was a chipped double stripe across the right side of his faceless visor, right below where the eye should be.

The man, Breda, asked, "What about you?"

The decurion checked his rifle. "To the job, man." And he turned, and four of the others with him. The metallic clanging came once again from the end of the hall, but even by our torchlight I could see nothing. But it was coming. We *knew* it was coming.

I have grown tired of watching men die.

"Follow us as quickly as you can!" I said.

"Aye, lord!"

Clang.

An awful sound went up, like the high keening of the Cielcin but higher and far louder, undercut by a metallic whine like the noise of turbines spinning up. I heard an awful crash and for an instant I had one final vision of the monster as it lurched into the hall, pulling itself along the passage as though it climbed up a shaft, using the ribbed arches for handholds to keep its too-tall body parallel to the floor.

Someone slammed the airlock and pulled the lever. Air roared out, and I could hear the sounds of shouting over the comm and—through the bulkhead and the vibrations in my feet—I felt the shock of gunfire.

Then nothing.

"It won't fit through here," one of the others said.

The airlock door dented inward, struck by one of the beast's mighty fists. Each of us jumped, and an instant later the rear door opened onto the vessel's central hold.

"Out!" I said, "Out now! Fuse the outer hatch!"

"It'll let the air out!" one of the others said, staggering out after me.

"It doesn't need air!" I snarled.

When the last of us was over the threshold, two of the men turned and—using their rifles—welded the outer door of the airlock shut. I could still feel the drumming, hammering of the alien fists against the inner door. Surely it could have turned the wheel? Or was it only angry that we had gone where it could not follow?

The hammering stopped.

"What happened, Had?" asked Pallino, pushing his way through the ranks toward me.

"What the hell was that?" asked one of the others.

My mind was still with the decurion and the others who had stayed behind to cover our escape. It took Valka to shake me loose, her voice in my ear. "Hadrian." She repeated the other man's question, "What happened? What was that?"

"That," I cleared my throat and—answering both her and the others—said, "was one of the demons of Arae."

CHAPTER 24

BEYOND THE DOORS OF THE DARK

"DO YOU THINK THEY made it out?"

"Hope they stuck the bastard good and clean."

"Did you see its fangs?"

"Keep moving," Pallino said, waving our men down the line.

The space about us was so vast I could not see the ceiling or the far wall. Darkness deeper than the void's endless day filled the hold, and the faint red sconces that lined the wall shone so faintly to our human eyes that they might have been mere candle flames. And the quiet . . . there was no air in that vast hold, and so that space—which should have echoed with the sound of feet and shouting—was silent as a funeral, save for the muddy reverberations that rose up through our bones.

A great chasm lay open at our right side, thousands of feet deep. Catwalks and bridges vanished across it, and stairs rose and descended alongside rough cage-lifts and mighty chains. By our torchlight I beheld more catwalks rising in the night, not straight but twisted like the minds of the creatures that built them.

The mapping drones hadn't pierced this far into the vessel, and so all we had to go by was a muddy sonar scan that depicted a blurry, empty space a dozen miles long or more. The sounds of fighting came over the comm. I only caught one word in seven through the radio hiss.

"Pinned down in sector C7!"

"Enemy presence near the starboard engine cluster!"

"They're coming through the walls!"

"Do you think there are more of that thing?" Siran asked.

"I don't know," I said, lingering a moment to allow the Irchtani to catch up. They could not fly where there was no air, and their short legs did not bend easily. They hopped along like grounded birds in our wake, swords and firearms clasped in scaled hands. "But we should be prepared."

Siran bobbed her head in short agreement. "Pal's got the word out to the centurions. They know it's out there."

"Good," I said. The last thing we needed was one of the other groups blindsided by a similar ambush. "I suppose we should be grateful it came for us first." No sooner had the words escaped me than another, darker thought occurred. *But why did it come for us out of all our battle groups?* Because we were deepest into the Cielcin vessel? Or because we were near to something precious?

Or worse: had it come for me, personally?

I felt the weight of Siran's eyes on me. She alone had stood with me on Arae, she alone had seen one of these Pale beasts before. I opened my mouth to respond, but before I could a voice crackled over the officers' channel, drawn and thin. "We've located the fuel reservoirs. We're going in." It was Cade, one of Pallino's other centurions.

"Good!" Pallino answered. "Lock it down, man. Earth guard you."

"And you."

I remembered the fate of the *Androzani,* or of Prince Ulurani's vessel. We might do the same here. More importantly, we might prevent the Cielcin from detonating their own ship if they had a mind.

The grim thought was pushed out of my mind a moment later, for one of the scouts Pallino had run ahead called back over the line, "Sir! I've got something up ahead."

"What is it?" I demanded.

Recognizing my palatine accent over the line, the man swallowed audibly. "A ship, my lord. One of ours."

I'd pressed forward through the others and so came to the place where the scout stood by the rail, torch beams pointed up along a rickety stair toward a shape hanging in the night. The hard edges and geometric lines were as alien in that alien place of ribbed arches and organic curves as Tanaran had been on the bridge of the *Mistral* so long ago. But there it was. The blackened hull of an Imperial starship yawned out of the night above us.

"Find a way up!" I gave the order. "Quickly now! Double time!" We had to know, had to be certain these were the lost ships and that the men aboard were truly dead.

Valka's voice crackled in my ear. "Did you find them?" she asked.

I watched our scouts hurry up the steps in groups of three, answered,

"We found a ship. Not sure if it's one of the missing ones or some other. We'll know soon."

"We'll be in orbit soon."

"Shields are holding?"

"They are."

"Tell Aristedes to concentrate fire on the forward section. We should be safe here and it may distract them." There was nothing on the other line a moment, and I said, "Valka?"

She answered almost at once, "He heard you."

"Lord Marlowe!" The voice of one of the legionnaires cut over whatever else Valka might have said. "We found a hatch."

The airlock had been forced long ago. Deep scratches ran along the edges of the doorway, as if some mighty beast had carved the door from the hull with impossibly strong fingers. The inner door was the same. All was dark within, save where the emergency lighting strips glowed near the floor like the last embers of a dying fire. I ran my fingers over the plaque welded along the inside of the bulkhead, feeling the letters raised there.

ISV Merciless.

The *Merciless.* She'd been shown no mercy, in the end. That much was certain. The deckplates in the hall beyond were scuffed and scraped-over, a sure sign that someone or something had dragged heavy equipment through.

"We found them," I said to everyone and no one. I could hardly believe it. I had expected to return to Forum with nothing.

Valka's bright voice slashed into me. "We've not found them yet."

Her words pushed me over the threshold into the darkened ship. She was right. We had to know, had to be certain the men had not all found themselves on some other communal dining slab. The overhead lights flickered on, responding to our presence. Loose wires hung from a place in the ceiling ahead, casting their hangman's shadows along the corridor walls.

"Pallino, secure the bridge," I said, stepping round the wires. "And send a team to the engine room. I want to know if she's still spaceworthy. Udax, have your men secure the hull. I don't want any surprises."

"Sir?" Udax tilted his head, inquiring.

"We'll need to fly her out of here sooner or later," I said, and pushed past the feathered auxiliary toward the maw of an access corridor that ran deeper into the captured ship. Much of my adult life I'd spent aboard Imperial battleships. I knew the shape of them, and though I'd never been aboard the *Merciless* before, nor any ship of her class, I knew the way, down five levels and forward to the place beneath the bridge where the ship's cargo—its complement of soldiers—slept their sleep of the dead.

Or should have slept. As I hurried forward I saw once more the body of the man on the alien table. I told myself that if even one man were yet alive, it would be enough. Enough to have saved him and to have rid the galaxy of the monsters that had taken his fellows.

I had to know.

The cubiculum was right where I'd thought to find it: in a hold far up and to the rear of the ship. We passed through an interior airlock to find it, and as I stepped across that frigid threshold I keyed my wrist-terminal and the hard switch at the base of my skull that opened my helmet. The mask broke apart; the cowl and broad flange that protected my neck folded and stowed themselves in the collar. I shook my hair free, the sweat cold against my skin. My breath misted the air.

I regretted my choice at once.

"What in Earth's holy name is that smell?" Siran asked. She'd removed her own helmet.

She knew full well what it was, we both did. We had seen enough battlefields, even burned cities. Enough of Death's red train. The fugue creches rose all around us, honeycombing the walls: rank upon rank, column upon column of hexagonal ports behind which a man might lie. The *Merciless* held just over nine thousand men, for it was far smaller than the *Tamerlane*. They'd been packed on ice like salt fish, never intended to be pulled from their berths for deployment in transit, never intended to awaken until they reached Nemavand. Many would not awaken at all. Rusty stains and blue ones marred the scuffed and badly scarred floor. Blood and cryonic suspension fluid mingled on the deck plates, their colors strangely muted beneath the stark, white lights.

Many a cask stood open. Shattered glass and busted components still littered the floor. The xenobites had not bothered to clear it. Medical hoses and catheters and the tangled wires from electrodes hung here and there from the gutted fugue pods like the intestines of dead machines, and I knew full well whence that poor fellow from the dining slab had come. I crouched to examine the nearest open pod.

"Where's the blood?" one of the soldiers asked, voice thin in the cold air.

I glanced up at him through dark hair. I did not know the voice. One of Pallino's men, then? I didn't know most of the soldiers beneath the first century of the First Cohort. "You must be new," I said, and hoped the words were without malice or condescension. The man nodded, but hung his masked head all the same. When he said nothing, I said, "The Pale flush the cryo-fluid out before they pull the bodies. They don't care if the bastard's alive or not. They're just *hungry*." I clenched my teeth around the final word and straightened.

"They'll wait just long enough to flush the TX9 out," Siran added.

"Found bodies, sir!" came a call from the next aisle over.

Or what was left of them . . . The men lay rotted and half-eaten in the aisle, limbs twisted, bones gray in the stark light.

"What did they do with the heads?" one man asked, for they were missing.

One of the Irchtani who was still with me made a low croaking sound. "This is no way to treat an enemy."

"There are as many still living as not, lord," said one of the men, examining the sleeper casks along the wall. "They took them at random."

I said nothing, but stood with my head bowed over the ruined, rotting corpses at my feet. I stifled the urge to cover my face, to don my mask again. I had to see. The man *was* right. There were still dozens of fugue creches left undisturbed. Hundreds. The units were designed to preserve power even if the ship was failing; they could last decades—as I supposed they had.

"Pallino." I held my wrist to my face and turned away. "We found them."

"Alive?" The word came through the conduction tape behind my ear, cool and clear as if the man were standing next to me.

"A number of them. Maybe even most. The Pale have been pulling them out as needed." It was an efficient form of piracy, I supposed. They could live fat off their last catch—*literally*—while they awaited the next. "How's the ship?"

"They drained the fuel reservoirs, warp and sub-light, but the emergency batteries are still holding. Life support's in the blue. Emergency air looks fine."

No surprises there. The Cielcin were not stupid. They'd not want to sit atop several hundred kilograms of untapped antilithium any more than a human commander would. They'd either drained it into their own reservoir or vented the volatile antimatter into space.

"Weapon systems?"

Pallino was a moment responding. I heard him bark queries to his men and wait for answers I did not hear. "Knocked out, mostly. Looks like hull defense guns are intact, but the big stuff's gone. MAG drivers, missiles, all gone." As if to underscore his words, the vessel shook beneath us and a sound like distant thunder rolled. The *Tamerlane* must have begun shelling the planetoid end of the Cielcin ship.

"What about beam weapons?"

"I'm not sure. Hardware looks intact, but . . ."

"Find out for me," I said, still holding my left wrist to my face.

"My lord!"

There was something in the tone of that soldier's voice—I could not tell if he was summoning me or swearing. I dropped my wrist and Pallino with it, though I could still hear my chiliarch speaking in my ear. I followed the voice around a bend in the aisle and stopped dead. I felt my eyes widen and my gorge rise and strain against my teeth, but I choked it down. Spat.

A bank of computer consoles ran along the far end of the cubiculum, touch-panels and holographs monitoring the thousands of men who lay interred in that frigid mausoleum of the undead, but I did not see them. There was an empty space arrayed between the consoles and the ends of the long, tall aisles of honeycombed sleepers, five yards across. Five rolling lifters meant for transporting the fugue creches stood berthed to one side, and in the middle . . .

. . . in the middle.

There is a legend which holds that Earth—in her antiquity—was not one world but two. Indeed the oldest maps show two globes side by side, with the old world of Rome and Baghdad and Qin on one side and the unmapped *terra incognita* on the other, the two halves joined by a narrow band of sea. I suspect this is only symbolic, for surely the Earth is—whatever the Chantry teaches—only a planet like all the others. Nevertheless, it is said that men found the narrow way and the new world beyond. They sailed for gods and for want of gold and—as I have mentioned before—the dream of eternal youth, though such was not to be found on Earth's waters. But in time they came to a city on a lake, greater by far than any city they had seen, but a city of horrors. The men who dwelt there fed on human children and offered victims to the sky.

I felt something of the horror those ancient explorers felt on finding that blood-soaked city then. As they had stood in the heart of that awful city and seen the ruins of sacrifice, I stood before a similar sort of monument.

We had found the missing heads.

In the open space before the consoles, the Cielcin had raised a black monument of their own. Twenty feet high it stood, and wide at its base as three men were tall.

It was built all of bones. Level upon level of human skulls stood in rings set with tender care, bits of hair and skin still hanging from them, brown stains of long-dry blood thin upon their cracked and yellow surfaces. Metal rods held the skulls in place, and ropes of the alien silk were intricately tied. The hollow eyes stared outward all around, eternally watchful. There must have been hundreds of them to construct such a monument. Strips of cloth fluttered from the silk cords, painted with Cielcin glyphs. I could not read them, but I was reminded of the paper prayer cards that hung from the branches of the trees in Kharn's Garden.

Prayer cards.

What gods could such creatures pray to?

I knew the answer to that. The Cielcin worshiped the Quiet, in whose ruined halls and tunnels they had first evolved, arising from a species of predator that lived in the dark beneath their homeworld's radiation-bathed surface.

"They will die for this," I swore, and clenched my fists. "By Earth, I swear it." And for the first time in my life, I think I truly meant that oath. *By Earth.* "How many are left?"

One of my soldiers skirted the evil monument and accessed the consoles on the far side. "Just over seven thousand," he said.

Seven thousand. Nearly two thousand dead, then. I tried to tell myself this was good news, but the skulls still watched me with eyes unblinking in their mute accusation.

You are too late, they said.

Too late.

The ship shook again beneath us, and shook me from my mood. Holding my terminal to my face I looked away from the tower of bones. "Valka, what's going on?"

"They've disabled the *Mintaka's* engines," she said, voice tight.

"When?" I practically shouted. "Why didn't you tell me?"

She hissed, and I forced my eyes shut to quiet my breathing and the fast-again beating of my heart. "Five minutes ago," she replied, all business. "Verus is fighting them in the halls."

"Then we haven't much time." I nearly spat the words, changed channels. "Cade! Give me some good news!"

The centurion's voice came back. "Can't, lord! We're pinned down. I think we've located the vent controls for the fuel tanks but there are about a hundred of them between us and the target. They know what we're up to."

"Is the chimera with them?"

"The Exalted, sir? No, sir. But I'm not sure we can get through. We've lost . . . nineteen." He paused just long enough to check the count in his heads-up display. "We're outnumbered."

I swore. "Pallino!"

"I heard!"

"How fast can we get reinforcements to Cade's century?"

"I can have the seventh there in twenty minutes? Twenty-five? They're closest."

It wasn't soon enough. Twenty minutes may as well have been twenty years. But I clenched my jaw and—channeling Captain Corvo—said, "See it done." I took one whole step before a thought occurred to me, and I asked, "Pallino, what's the status on those beam weapons?"

The chiliarch was a moment replying—I imagined him asking his underlings on the bridge. "Techs say the primary starboard gun's still intact. We've got a shot long as the batteries hold."

I was nodding. The *Merciless* had two five-terawatt lasers, each one powerful enough to level a city block. The weapons were of little use against shielded targets, but against unshielded foes? They could destroy a target faster than they could react, making them the ideal first assault weapon of choice in any ship-to-ship ambush.

An ambush was something like what I had in mind.

"You want us to fire *in here*?" Pallino asked. "Are you insane?"

Valka's voice chimed in, "Hadrian! Have you completely lost your mind? What if you hit one of the other ships? If there's any AM fuel still on board . . ."

"Then have Aristedes pick us a target very carefully. Feed the vector through to Pallino."

"This'll call them on down on us, Had," Pallino said, communicating over the officers' private channel. "We'll be surrounded in here."

"That's what I'm counting on," I said. "It just might give Cade a chance to get through to the fuel tanks. We have to keep them from warping out with us aboard."

Valka cut in, "I don't like this at all."

"Noted," I said, and cut the line.

Even across thousands of miles of space and meters of steel and stone, I thought I could hear her swear. *Barbarian.*

Only if it fails.

I was hurrying from the cubiculum already, pulling the elastic coif back over my head and hair and donning my helmet. The casque closed about my face like the shell of some black scarab over its delicate wings. I ran as if I had wings of my own, barreling ahead of my guards down the hall. There were just under a hundred of us aboard the *Merciless,* men and Irchtani. Even with the ship's hull defense weapons, I didn't like our chances, but I liked our chances less if Cade failed.

That was the time for decisive action.

I burst onto the bridge a moment later, passing safely through another inner airlock. The chamber was dim and low-ceilinged, with the usual glossy black and brass shine of any Imperial vessel. Voice amplified by speakers in my suit's chest, I said, "Pallino, post men on the exterior guns. I want to be ready; do we have that shot vector from Aristedes?"

"Just got it," Pallino said, unwilling to argue with me where his subordinates could hear.

"Get ready to fire on my mark," I said, then pivoting to our group channel asked, "Udax, are all ingress points secured?"

"Yes." The bird said no more.

To everyone aboard the *Merciless* I said, "Be ready to fall back on the inner airlocks. Defend the bridge, life support, and the cubiculum. Let's try and bottleneck them, keep them on as few approaches as we can. Hold out until Cade can vent their warp cores and until reinforcements get here." I rounded on Pallino, "Ready?"

Switching to his private line, the other man asked, "Can I say *no?*"

"No."

Pallino paused a moment before replying. "Then yes." He switched back to his suit speakers, old soldier's voice filling the room like a trumpet blast. "Prepare to fire on my order!" He leaned over the central console, hands gripping the edges of the display. I watched the techs busy themselves obeying the order, watched the tactical display plot the strike. Aristedes had picked his target simply enough: he'd pointed the ship's lone laser cannon directly forward, back along the length of the vessel toward the bulbous front end, toward the bulk of the inhabited sections of the world-ship. Our men were all around and to the rear.

No subtlety at all, I remember thinking. *The bastard may as well have pointed a cannon at the deck.*

"Fire."

There was no light, no cough or rattle of machinery. No recoil, no shuddering beneath our feet. Miles away at the end of the hold, a bright light flared and smoked down to naught. Ten seconds passed in silence. Only then did the ship quake beneath us, following the flash of secondary explosions that heralded the destruction of other systems deeper in the Cielcin vessel.

"Can we fire again?"

One of the soldiers checked the readouts. "No, my lord. The batteries were near drained as was. It's a miracle we got one shot off."

"No matter," I said. "We've done enough . . ." I trailed off, listening through the echoing quiet, as though I might discern the distant tramp of clawed feet. I heard nothing, but knew all the same.

I knew they were coming.

CHAPTER 25

IN THE BELLY OF THE WHALE

"—GOT MOVEMENT IN THE starboard gallery!"

"Movement in the upper halls!"

"God and Earth, what was that?"

"On the left—"

"Was that an explosion?"

"Where'd they go?"

I switched off the general channel to escape the constant chatter. My eyes closed of their own accord, and I held them there a long moment, not moving, straining with my ears—as if I thought to hear the approach of the Cielcin through the airless void outside. I heard nothing, of course.

Only the quiet.

"They're coming," I said. I did not open my eyes. From the snatches of comms chatter I'd heard I got the impression the enemy was moving, abandoning the fight in several places where they'd had our men pinned down. If my understanding was right, it had all worked perfectly. We'd drawn their attention with the laser as surely as moths are drawn to the candle flame. I only hoped our story would end the same way.

"Hadrian." I opened my eyes, found Pallino watching me through his faceless mask. "You all right?"

I leaned heavily on the console at my side, feeling for a moment the weight Atlas had cast aside. Numbly, I nodded. "I'm fine." I was tired. So tired. The tower of skulls in the cubiculum still cast its shadow over me, and I felt as though the ghosts of all those mutilated, half-eaten men lingered on the air aboard that cursed ship, watching with eyes forever empty, forever open, whispering with tongues torn out. *Avenge us. Avenge us. Avenge us.*

Merciless, indeed.

My hands tightened into fists. "Are the security cameras still working?"

"Aye, lord!" said one of Pallino's men from the consoles.

I moved into the holography booth that stood in a niche to one side. "Show me."

Holography panels blossomed into life; gleaming windows tiled the semi-circular arc of wall, each opening on a different part of the ship. Dark and rusted corridors, fugue casks still sealed and pulsing with blue lights, empty barracks shredded and picked over. I saw it all. Standing there I recalled the way Bassander Lin so often stood before the monitor wall in his cabin aboard the *Pharaoh,* prying into every corner of the ship and of his men's lives. How intrusive that ability had seemed at the time. How necessary it was in that moment.

With a wave of one hand I summoned a control panel, blue light gleaming in the dusty air. I patched my terminal and suit comm into the holography booth and waited, watching through a hundred eyes. Udax and his men had broken up into groups of five or so, each standing guard at one of the six airlocks—three to a side—that ran along the length of the *Merciless.* Some of Siran's men had joined them, and a few more were about their business welding shut the ventral and dorsal access hatches with their plasma burners. The Cielcin could force an entrance anywhere, but they might not bother if the airlocks were still open and accessible.

"Do we have visual *outside*?" I asked.

"Not much, my lord," one of Pallino's men answered. "Hull's torn up pretty bad, a lot of the sensor clusters are gone, and most of hull defense. We've got around a dozen turrets though with optics still intact. But that's it."

"Patch those through." Frustrated, I removed my helmet, the better to see the video feeds.

They did, and a dozen more panels blossomed on my display, showing dark windows from various points on the outer hull. But the turrets had limited angles of fire and limited scope. Two were pointed uselessly up toward the arched ceiling. I chewed over the problem a moment, then toggled through my terminal to the proper channel. "Udax, post three of your men on the hull. We need eyes out there."

The Irchtani centurion obeyed, and I toggled again, broadcasting to every man and Irchtani on the Cielcin vessel. "This is Hadrian Marlowe. All units not currently engaged in disabling the enemy warp drive will converge on the central hold. Repeat. All units not currently engaged in disabling the enemy warp drive will converge on the central hold." Lights on my terminal's holography plate indicated that I was heard and understood.

"Incoming!" a high, tremulous voice said. One of Udax's scouts. Pallino's men patched the auxilium's helmet cam through to the bank before me, and I watched through his eyes. The scout had climbed up onto the hull in the dark of the hold, and through the suit's infrared cameras we both could see distant red shapes hurrying forward on either side of the *Merciless* where it hung like an egg sac in the center of the hold.

"Right on cue . . ." I murmured, pressing one hand against the wall for support, imagining I could feel the drumbeat of their clawed boots as they drew nearer.

On infrared and at this distance, they looked like a slow procession of candle bearers in the dark, red and small and strangely forlorn. And the white sparks that flew alongside them—those were their *nahute,* hunting and hungry. I prayed they would not find the scouts where they lurked above.

"There must be hundreds of them." Pallino had moved to stand beside me. He still wore his helmet, and so I couldn't see his uplifted patrician face, but I sensed the haggard melancholy in him, lurking beneath the professional resolve. I felt it, too.

"They're within range," I said, referring to the ship's hull defense systems. "Fire at will."

Pallino punched his chest in salute, then turned, shoulder straps bouncing. "You heard the man, you dogs! Fire!"

Like most Imperial starships, the *Merciless* had dozens of turrets and gun emplacements on its outer hull designed to repel boarding craft. A last line of defense should the aquilarii fail. We had no aquilarii, and too few men aboard. Standing there, I'd a sudden memory of how we'd been trapped aboard the *Schiavona* in the *Demiurge*'s mighty hold. We'd not been able to use the guns then for fear of damaging Kharn's vessel.

We had no such fear of damaging the Cielcin ship.

The report of distant gunfire groaned through the metal superstructure of the ship like the crack of fireworks at Summerfair. I saw the lightning-flash of muzzle fire though the scout's helmet cams and clenched my teeth. The oncoming lines of Cielcin scattered, blown apart by the gunfire. Dozens died, cut down by a storm of bullets.

"We can't keep this up forever," Pallino said. "They didn't have much ammunition left. Must have burned through most of it when they were taken."

I turned away from the holographs and joined Pallino overlooking the tac console. Eight of his men sat there, each manning the controls for two or three turrets. I could see the round counters. 5342. 4893. 5219. 2485. And so on.

It looked like a lot.

It wasn't.

They fired. The numbers plunged. 4826. 4211. 4755. 2049 . . .

"Tell those bird boys to blood up," one of the men said. "They're still coming."

"Cade to Marlowe! Cade to Marlowe!" The call came through the conduction patch behind my ear.

"Say on."

"I don't know what you did, sir, but half their reinforcements cleared out."

I felt my heart leap in my chest. "You'd best act fast, then. I don't know how long our luck will hold." Gunfire filled the silence between words. I watched the Cielcin still swarming on the holograph. Where had they all been until now? Lurking in their own vents? Why hadn't they put up a fight? Why hadn't that demon followed us into the hold? Surely it could have come through the larger door that had been closed to us or found another? I was missing something.

At a shout from behind me, I glanced back. One of the turret feeds had gone dead.

"Grenade," the operator said, and stood from his console to join the men guarding the approach to the bridge. I took stock of the round counters again. 4113. 3798. 4233. 1614 . . .

"We're running dry fast."

"These are high-caliber rounds," Pallino snarled. "I don't know how the bastards are holding up so well."

"They're not *shielded,* are they?" I asked.

Pallino turned his faceless countenance on me. I could almost feel the pressure of his eyes through the ivory mask. "You don't really think that's possible, do you?"

"I don't know, that's why I'm asking. You saw the Arae demon same as me. If they bought *that* from the Extrasolarians, surely they might have bought body shields." Even if they had, it seemed from the cameras that they hadn't bought enough for all of them. I tramped back toward the holography booth, watched through the Irchtani scout's eyes for the telltale flicker and shine of shields in the darkness outside.

There!

I let out a wordless hiss of anger. Our enemies had banded together, indeed. Just as Kharn Sagara had dealt with the Cielcin, other elements among the Extras had aligned with the xenobites against us, rebelling against the Empire and the humanity it fought for. And for what? Politics? Not even politics. *Profit.*

"They're coming up the gangway!" Udax's voice rang in my ear.

"Don't let them board!" I shouted. "Fire at will!"

The Irchtani had taken up positions in the halls just inside the cut-open airlocks, hunkering in side doors and behind the odd strut or pillar that lined the edges of the access corridors, guns raised. Fighting as they were in vacuum, their plasma rifles drew on ammo packs, their rounds the pure pink of hydrogen plasma. Shielded though they were, the superheated plasma was hot enough to cook the first ranks of the Pale in their armor. But the Cielcin kept coming, throwing themselves with suicidal abandon upon the Irchtani defenders.

Pallino spoke from my shoulder once again. "They'll be eaten alive if they stay there. We weren't counting on shields." His affable manner was all gone. The Pallino I knew from the fighting pits with his easy, barking laugh and homely attitude had all melted away, replaced by the soldier he must have been before I'd known him, as if his second youth had wound back the clock for true. "If they move to close quarters they'll be overrun. We're outnumbered at least a dozen to one on each of those gangways."

"We won't be any better off if they pull back," I said, covering my mouth with a hand.

"We should have blown the gangways when we had a chance."

I shook my head. "It wouldn't have helped. In this gravity they'd just have leaped onto the hull and climbed in through the openings." But Pallino had touched on an idea all the same. I selected the Irchtani common band on my terminal and said, "Udax, order your men to use grenades!"

The Irchtani did not hesitate. He tossed one himself over the heads of the oncoming Cielcin and down the gangway. A moment later the holograph image flashed red and white, and I heard a distant rumble through the ship and saw black-clad Cielcin hurled over the gangway rail. I allowed myself a small sound of satisfaction as the auxiliaries crowed. The *Merciless* shook again with small and distant explosions, loosing dust from joints in the low ceiling, and I watched similar reddish flashes on the holograph panels.

But the Cielcin kept coming. Swarms of their *nahute* flew in over the attackers' heads. Some homed in on the Irchtani defenders, rebounded off their shields. Udax and his men opened fire, but for every two they roasted with their plasma burners one slipped past, went hunting up the corridors looking for easier meat.

"They'll be at those doors in a minute," I said, meaning the doors of the bridge where our human defenders waited. Our last line of defense.

Pallino made a short gesture with one hand. "Our lads can handle a couple drones."

"Aye," I said, "but we're running out of room fast."

No sooner had I said this than I heard the cough of plasma fire from the hall outside and the muffled shout of an officer through the walls. They'd gotten one. On the holographs, I saw one of the Irchtani defenders gored by a Cielcin drone, the flying serpent's metal fangs boring deep. His pointed helm scored the wall as he fell writhing, and his screeching was a horror to witness. To my astonishment one of the other Irchtani broke off his assault a moment, clamped his fellow down with a clawed foot, and fired twice with his plasma burner. He shot his own brother through the head first to end his suffering and shot again through his chest, destroying the steel serpent where it burrowed, thus avenging his fallen companion.

"Black Earth!" Pallino swore.

I felt it, too, and stood a little straighter. *"Noyn jitat,"* I said softly. Our xenobite had not so much as hesitated, and even as I watched it turned back to the fighting and threw one of its grenades.

But the Cielcin kept coming. My knuckles were doubtless white beneath their gloves where I clutched the rail. "They're not even slowing down," I said.

Then a message came over the officer's channel to mine and Pallino's comm. "C3 to Chiliarch, we are closing in on your location from the starboard side."

"About bloody time," Pallino grumbled, then turned his head to answer. "Doran! How many men have you got?"

"Nearly the whole century, sir," replied Doran, the third centurion. "Oro's right behind."

I felt as though a heavy yoke were lifted from my shoulders when I heard that. We had nearly two hundred men coming, more than enough to break the Cielcin from the rear. I held one hand to my face, watching the screens before me. The *Merciless* shook again, though if it was from the Irchtani grenades or from the *Tamerlane* shelling the far end of that massive vessel it was impossible to tell. I checked the tac console for the ammo count on the hull defense guns.

2746. 2158. 3160. 0567 . . .

I was running through a mental checklist, trying to cover all my corners. The sound of plasma fire from the hall outside distracted me, and glancing at the screens I saw another pair of *nahute* fall to splinters. Our door guard was holding at least. Siran stood there with perhaps twenty men perfectly composed. If it came to it I would go and join her. If the Cielcin really were shielded as it seemed, my sword would be indispensable in the final defense of our lives. Doran and Oro could not come fast enough. Our Irchtani scouts were still watching from the hull. They hadn't moved, were keeping eyes on all approaches, and through those eyes I saw the horde: black-clad, white-crowned, with swords like shards of bone flashing in the gloom and glare of gunfire. Each flash revealed them closer, tighter.

"Udax! Blow the gangways if you can," I said. "Leave the rear one open each side. See if that bottlenecks them." The rear airlocks would put the Cielcin as far from the bridge as possible, give us more time and ship to work with. "Prepare to fall back! Seal the inner airlocks in case any of them try to climb in."

"Are you sure?" the Irchtani centurion asked.

"Damn your eyes!" I did not have time for the young xenobite's rebellious streak. "Those are your orders, soldier!"

As I spoke a trio of Cielcin burst onto the ship from the gangway, and Udax charged forward, slammed the muzzle of his plasma burner against the chest of one and fired. It sailed backward, body crashing into its approaching fellows even as Udax's brethren advanced with bayonets.

Cade's voice crackled over the line. "Marlowe, we're through! We're trying to work out how to vent the AM reservoir, but they've closed us in."

"Can you hold?"

The centurion's reply was a moment coming. "I . . . think so, lordship. My lads have welded the doors behind us. But there's something with them. Something big. Reckon it might be that demon that came for your lot. They must have figured out what we're up to."

Demons above and below . . . I thought. There was a real chance—a very real chance—that Cade and his men would never leave that fuel control room. "How many are outside?"

"I don't know, sir," Cade answered. "Close to a hundred when we won through. Probably more now." The line went quiet a moment. "Do you think it's that demon? The same one?"

I did not say what I was thinking. That I *hoped* it was, because if it wasn't that meant there were more than one of the creatures. There had been more than a dozen tanks in the research base on Arae. The seeds of a new army. A new kind of soldier.

"I hope not," I said. "But do what you have to do. Keep me apprised."

"Aye, sir."

Pallino was watching me as I broke off the call. He'd heard it all on the officer's band, and gave a little nod. "We're not much better off here."

I gave a little shrug. "We have Oro and Doran on the way, at least." I check the round counters on the tactical displays again. 2165. 1583. 2586. 0037 . . . I sucked in a deep breath. "But you're right."

"Should we wave the *Tamerlane* for backup?" Pallino asked. "Call in another cohort?"

I watched the Irchtani retreating down the halls. They'd blown four of the six gangways and were hurrying toward the inner airlocks. The answer was *yes,* but . . . "Valka, what's your situation aboard?"

She replied almost instantly, and the sound of her bright voice was a relief in that dark place. "Still holding. A few of their ships got through, but they've been isolated."

"Good. Good . . . we need reinforcements. Can Crim spare the men?" As security chief, Crim would be leading the defensive action within the *Tamerlane* itself. "Half a cohort at least?"

"I'll find out."

A brief silence floated in after her words, and beneath its thumb I watched the monitors and saw it: black-armored and pale-faced, a white sword in one hand, a dangling *nahute* in another. The first Cielcin fighter had gotten aboard the *Merciless* through one of the abandoned airlocks. More of its fellows followed, scuttling through the open hole like spiders. Only a few. Perhaps my strategy had worked, perhaps the rest had diverted to the other airlocks.

Cade's voice broke again over the line. "My lord, they're breaking through! We're running out of time!"

I swore, rounded impotently where I stood, looking for Cade's view on the monitors. Only too late I remembered that I did not have it; I had only the *Merciless*'s internal cameras and a few of the nearby soldiers' personal views. "Is there anything you can do?"

The centurion was a moment replying, and when his voice came it was hesitant. Strained. "If we blow the coolant tanks on fuel containment it might force them to vent the AM supply, but we're trapped in here with no back door."

An iron lump formed in my throat. There was little difference between a Cielcin warp drive and one of our own, in principle. They both relied on massive antimatter reservoirs to generate the space-folding effect required for faster-than-light travel, both required enormous tanks of supercooled liquid helium to power the electromagnets that kept the volatile fuel suspended in vacuum and safe. If they blew the tanks—and that was assuming the Cielcin had no backups, which they surely did—that supercooled gas would flood the ship around it. If the blast didn't kill Cade and his men, the freeze certainly would.

I did not ask if they could escape. Cade had already ruled that out, and I would not insult him by asking. "They must have emergency backups," I said. Every one of our ships had banks of graphene batteries for just such emergencies. What the Cielcin might use, I had no idea.

"I'm not sure, lord," Cade said. "Could try and bypass it completely. Breach fuel containment. The whole reservoir's built to drop out through the bottom of the ship if there's damage to the Dewar bottle. It could work . . ." His voice trailed off, leaving the rest of his thought unsaid: *Or it could blow the entire ship out of the sky.*

Valka's voice chimed in, "Hadrian, if they blow the coolant tank in there, 'twill damage the Dewar bottle anyway, breach fuel containment." Valka had been a ship's captain once, and it had been Valka who'd thought of using the *Schiavona*'s own fuel quench to fight the Cielcin aboard the *Demiurge.*

A strange mixture of emotions warred in me. Relief, because if what Valka said was true, Cade and his men had no cause to sacrifice themselves. Frustration, because if what Valka said was true, there was nothing Cade or anyone could do to compromise the Cielcin fuel supply. Fury, because whatever happened, my men had gone between the hammer and the anvil to no purpose. If only we'd had more time. Presently I spoke. "Are you sure?"

"Of course I'm *sure*," Valka snapped. "I've done nothing but pore over Cielcin artifacts and writing for the last *seventy years*. I know how those ships work. This is why you should have brought me!" I was glad her words came over our private line. It would not have done for Cade or the others to hear her words, though I supposed Lorian and anyone on the bridge might have done.

I felt a knot form in the pit of my stomach, and after a moment swallowed the iron lump in my throat. "I know. I know," I said. "So there's nothing Cade can do?"

" 'Tis not what I said, *anaryan!*" Valka replied. "The Cielcin aren't as spare with fuel as we are. That ship's big enough they must make their own fuel somewhere, probably toward the bow." I knew what she was talking about, had studied forensic analyses of other Cielcin worldships, knew that somewhere in that ruined asteroid the xenobite ship used for a capstone there would be a massive particle accelerator of the sort designed to manufacture the antihydrogen the Cielcin burned for fuel. " 'Twill vent their supply at the first sign of trouble."

I saw where she was going a moment before she said it. "You're saying . . ."

"I'm saying if your man blows the coolant tank and it cracks the Dewar flask the ship will vent its fuel automatically."

"Are you sure?"

"Damn you, Hadrian!" Valka said. "How many times do I have to tell you?" Her words were like the crack of ice on a lake in winter, and I was falling through.

I glanced back over my shoulder to where Pallino directed our defense. The round counters were dangerously low, and by the look of the monitors the Cielcin were still coming.

"Why don't they just blow this ship?" Pallino asked, meaning the *Merciless.* "It were me, I'd have mined the whole thing. Set it up as bait."

"Food supply," I said, thinking of the cubiculum and the thousands of men frozen there. "Besides, they didn't know we were coming." I swept my gaze across the bank of holograph monitors before me, taking in the severity of the situation. I closed my eyes, murmured one of old Gibson's incantations to still the ragged beating of my heart. Fear truly is a poison: cortisol, adrenaline.

I clenched my jaw and switched channels again. "Marlowe to Cade. Doctor Onderra says you are clear to blow the coolant tank. She says any damage to the Dewar envelope will force the tanks to vent."

The reply was a moment coming, but when it came young Cade's voice was steady and tight as the mechanics of an old timepiece. "Aye, my lord."

"Then see it done, man."

"One thing, lord." Cade's composure cracked just a little.

"Say on."

"I'd like to wait until the enemy breaches the door, give my lads a chance to run for it."

I was nodding, and it took a full three seconds for me to remember the man could not see me. "As you wish."

"Give them hell, then." And he cut the line.

I shut my eyes once again. It never got any easier. I prayed it never would. After a moment I opened my eyes, studied the monitors.

"We need to get those scouts back inside," I said, fingers thick and slow on the terminal controls. "What was the frequency?" I remembered even as I asked, toggling back to the Irchtani band. Speaking only to the trias of auxiliaries who'd taken up their posts on the roof of the prisoned vessel, I said, "You three get back inside through the forward airlocks! We've blown the gangways, so you'll have to climb in." As I spoke, I watched the Irchtani resistance at the two still-accessible airlocks hold their ground with explosives and the points of their long knives. There was no response over the scouts' line. "I said all scouts retreat through the forward airlocks, do you copy?"

I found the scouts' heads-up cameras again on the monitors, each showing a view of the approaching horde of Cielcin soldiery. At the rear I saw the flash of plasma fire where Oro and Doran's men had arrived from the far side of the hold, splitting the enemy's attention.

They weren't moving.

"Do you copy?" I repeated, holding my wrist-terminal to my mouth. "I said, do you copy?"

"Ububonoyu o-okun-do," came the reply in a voice high and cold as the mountains above Meidua in the deep of winter. There followed the thin scrape of alien laughter, and the words again, "They cannot hear you."

I turned away so the others would not see the shock in my face. The numb dread. "Who is this?" I asked in Cielcin, and felt the sudden stiffness in the room behind me at the sound of the language and what my using it must mean.

"The Devil of Meidua," the alien voice said, picking its way over the unfamiliar human words. Switching back to its native tongue, the Cielcin said, "I must admit, I expected better from a *yukajji* of your repute."

My distress over Cade retreated, replaced by the white fire of the Marlowe cold fury. "Prince Dorayaica, I presume?"

The cold laughter came again, and I felt every hair on me stand on end. *"Veih, veih, veih,"* it said. "No. You do not have that honor, *hurati*." Mouse, it called me. Or what passed for *mouse* to the xenobite. "Surrender, and you will be so blessed."

"*Sim udantha,*" I said. *Not today.*

"You are surrounded. Soon you will be beaten." I had nothing to say, and so said nothing. "Perhaps I will bring you to him."

I saw nothing on the monitors, could not identify the speaker's location. At the rear perhaps, behind the attacking Cielcin? One look at our tactical monitors told me fully a quarter of the hull defense guns were depleted. A shot sounded in the hall. More of the *nahute* had broken through the Irchtani defense at the doors.

"I did not expect you to flee when I found you in the hall outside," the cold voice said. One of the scout's cameras moved, vision bucking as the helmet—or perhaps the head—was lifted from the place where it had fallen. Vision wheeling across the blackened hold, its single eye came to rest on the speaker. Armor the color of bleached bone encased the head save for the mouth, which leered toothily in the vacuum, its slaver foaming in the airless void outside. Too wide that mouth, shark-like and snarling, twisted into an alien grin that might close about a grown man's fist. The helmet had no eye holes, no obvious visor. I could not be certain the Cielcin Exalted had eyes at all. Perhaps behind that armored visage there was only machinery housing the alien brain. Perhaps the mouth was only a vestige of the flesh-that-was, left behind to terrify. The lips did not move as it spoke, though its grin widened. "*Sikare,*" it said. "I confess, I am disappointed. I expected more from the man who killed Aranata."

"You have me at a disadvantage," I said, staring at the monitor as if I hoped to make the creature feel the weight of my gaze. "*Deni okun tuka o-tajun ne?*" *Who are you?*

The camera feed flickered, but the words came through loud and clear. "Only a Holy Slave. One of a number." It raised a hand for my consideration. All of jointed steel it was, the fingers backed with zircon delicately embossed, white-on-white. Machine though it was, it was still six-fingered, the digits long as any I had seen. "One of six."

I felt my lips compress, eyes grow narrow. I was glad the beast could not see me. For a moment the battle around me had dropped away, and there was nothing in my universe except the xenobite and the connection between us.

A Holy Slave.

Vayadan.

The word had an ominous sound even to my human ear. I did not then know it, but the *Vayadan* were the sworn protectors of a Cielcin Aeta, his last line of defense, his closest counselors, and his concubines—the fathers of his children.

"You do not speak, *yukajji*. Are you afraid?"

Instantly, I answered, "You have not answered my question, *vayadan-do*. I asked who you are."

That impossibly wide grin widened even more. "I am but a finger of his White Hand."

"Iedyr Yemani ne?" I repeated. *Iedyr Yemani*. White Hand. I had heard those words before, whispered to me by a demon in the darkness beneath Arae. But the circumstances called for strength and force of will. I would not be afraid, and spat. "That is not a name!"

"I am Iubalu! And I am coming!"

At this, it crushed the camera, the helmet, and the head of the Irchtani within it in its massive metal hand . . . and above I heard—like distant drums—the sound of metal feet on the hull above us.

CHAPTER 26

THE VAYADAN

"PALLINO, YOU HAVE THE bridge."

"Where are you going?" The chiliarch's words floated after me as I made for the door to the hall.

I stopped, hand hovering just above the door controls. "You heard that thing crawling around on the hull same as me. How long before it gets in through one of the dorsal hatches?"

"Our boys sealed those up!" Pallino shot back.

I shook my head furiously. "It won't matter." Earth and Empire knew what sort of kit the chimera had concealed in its body. After the Battle of Arae, the dozen or so intact—but dead—failures the MINOS scientists had created were examined by Legion Intelligence. The demons of Arae had been crafted for war, their bodies augmented with plasma burners in the wrist and shoulders and nerve disruptors in the palms. Ceramic blades lay concealed within each of the chimeras' arms, and an assortment of explosives, projectile weapons, and other, nastier surprises were doubtless secreted on the creature's body. And those had only been the prototypes. What Iubalu of the Iedyr Yemani had to hand who could say?

Not I, but I would face it anyway.

"Had," Pallino said, dropping all rank and formal designation, "stay here."

I checked the fit of my coif over my forehead, keyed a sequence on my wrist-terminal that desynchronized the device from the holography booth's projectors. For a moment, I saw my gaunt face reflected in the dull, dark metal of the door. Hollow-eyed, high-cheekboned. I threw the hard switch inside my suit collar, and the helmet components unfurled, opened like a flower and shut about my head. I shut my eyes a moment—just long enough to avoid the familiar panic as all that titanium and black ceramic closed over my face.

Momentarily blind, I punched the door controls. An instant later my suit's entoptics flickered on; projectors aimed at my eyes showed me my men standing guard in the hall, the wreckage of a dozen or so *nahute* at their feet. I saw my reflection at the end of the hall, black mask and black armor, the white cape hanging limp in the still air. All turned to look at me, blank white arcs of ceramic where their faces ought to be. Reaching up, I unclasped my cape and tossed it at one of the men, who caught it clumsily. "Siran, with me."

She didn't ask questions. Not in front of the men.

"Malag, take command," she said to her optio. The fellow saluted.

While this changing of the guard was happening, I gestured to a knot of three men standing to the front and left of the little knot. "You're a trias?" I asked. Their triaster nodded. "Good. You come, too." And then I began walking, sword unkindled in my hand. As I walked, I signaled, "Udax. Report."

The Irchtani centurion almost shouted over the line, making me wince, "We're losing the port side! Your men aren't getting through fast enough!"

"Then blow the port gangway. Pull your men back to the inner airlocks. Are you there?"

"Aye!" Udax replied. "But if we cut them off from the ship, I don't know what they'll do next."

"We'll worry about that later! Do as I say, man!"

Something thundered in the distance, a great clamor like the crash of a bus through a crowded storefront. I expected alarms to sound, but the *Merciless* was so badly damaged she could not even muster up the energy to scream.

"He's here," I said.

"Who's here?" Siran asked.

"Our *friend* from the tunnel."

I fancied I could hear the color drain from Siran's face as she asked, "The demon?"

"Be on your guard," I said, and turning to her raised a fist. "With me now?"

My centurion and faithful armsman nodded and knocked my fist with her own. "Just another Colosso match, eh?"

"Just another day," I said. "Come on."

As my little unit pounded up the corridor, I tracked the sounds of fighting in the halls below. The cough of plasma fire echoed through the ship and men's cries resounded on the line.

"Enemy in the hold!"

"Contact! Contact!"

"Gods in hell, the size of him!"

"O Mother, deliver us . . ."

Screams.

Then another voice whispered in my ear, high and cold and entirely too close. "Come out! Come out, *hurati*. Where are you hiding?" The others froze. They had not been on the bridge. They had not heard. The Cielcin spoke Galstani, its affect flat and unfeeling, the product—I guessed—of its machine design. Just as Kharn Sagara had spoken through his machines, the xenobite general spoke with a voice not its own.

"It can hear every word we're saying," I said, horror blossoming in me. "It must have hacked the comms."

"You cannot hide forever," the *vayadan* said. "I will find you."

"Can we lock it out?" Siran asked.

A more pressing question occurred to me, but I did not voice it. *Can it access the Tamerlane?* Rather than answer her question—for fear of being overheard—I answered, "We need to move quickly."

The doors to the hold had been left open when the Cielcin pillaged the vessel. The air had gone, and much of what had been inside was lost and taken away. Loose cables sparked from the high ceiling, and the bodies of dead men—our men—lay strewn on the floor.

They'd been torn apart, and their still-warm blood boiled in the vacuum, orange fading to gold on my suit's infrared. To pale blue.

"Where did it go?" one of the men asked.

"Not far," came the alien reply, whispered in our each and every ear. "Not far. Not far." Still it spoke the tongues of men, spoke that my men might understand and so fear it.

Remembering the way it had attacked our men in the hall by the dormitory block, I cast my eyes upward, expecting to see the beast crawling spider-like along the ceiling, hands and feet magnetized or perhaps clawed onto the roof. But there were only the fingered shadows of catwalks and crane gantries criss-crossing the dark above like a smaller version of the alien hold outside.

"I want to get a look at you," it said, and I sensed that it was speaking to me. It confirmed this suspicion a moment later, saying, "Killed Otiolo, did you? And Ulurani? You are smaller than I expected—but then your kind are so small."

I took a few steps away from our group, careful to keep my thumb on the trigger to kindle my blade. "You serve Dorayaica?"

"The Makers lit the stars for him, *yukajji*. They burn so that you might see what he achieves."

"We'll see," I said.

Iubalu's voice sounded in my ear, and beneath it I thought I heard the distant tapping of metal on metal carried through the bones of the ship, barely discernible beneath the sounds of gunfire and battle above and around us. "He will light your worlds on fire. He will drink their blood!"

With any luck, Udax would join us soon. "Show yourself, creature!" I said. The memory of the tower of bones still blazed in me, of the man on the dining slab. Tired as I was, anger animated me. I was ready.

"We had hoped there would be more of you coming, but even I did not *dare* hope it would be *you*." The *vayadan's* voice dripped venom like snow-melt. *"He* has long desired you for his collection, Devil of Meidua."

I felt a chill steal down my spine, and almost kindled my blade. But that was fear talking. I could not afford fear in that moment. I had fought one of these demons before, on Arae, but it had been a crippled thing: only somewhat functional. Here we faced a monster in the fullness of its strength. I remembered the Exalted, Calvert, in the dungeons of the Undying. How fast he had moved, faster than my human reflexes could track.

We need to get it back into the halls, I thought. I could not afford to speak the words, lest it hear us. *It will kill us in the open.* Keeping to the wall of the hold, I moved toward one of the many side entrances. The way to the cubiculum was through there, by many winding passages. Some of our men were there, guarding our living dead in their icy coffins. The reinforcements would be of some help. But we had to get there. Coming down to the hold had been an error, and I'd allowed myself to be lured by the death cries of the men that had been in that place.

But we had a chance . . . so long as it kept talking.

"What does he want with me?"

Cold laughter sounded over the line, and again I heard the faint tapping of metal claws. I cast my eyes around again. There was nothing. Not in visible light or infrared. Whatever the Extrasolarians had done to the *vayadan,* it no longer glowed with the heat of living fire.

It may as well be dead, I thought. And I fancied a chorus of voices answered me from my depths. *Undead. Undead. Undead.*

The tapping sounded again, and I had visions of the thing crawling on the walls like some pale spider, or else lurking behind the heavy loading equipment where it sat bracketed to the floor.

"Want with you?" the Cielcin general echoed. "You are his enemy! He wants to *break* you. And to *thank* you."

"Thank me?" I gestured to Siran and the others to fall behind me, to keep their backs to the wall as they pivoted to take up positions nearer the door. "Thank me for what?"

"You have destroyed two of his enemies. Shortened the path to his goal."

Two? I was being slow. "Otiolo and Ulurani?"

"He will be *Aeta Ba-Aetane,* the first since *Elu* brought us to the stars."

"*Aeta Ba-Aetane,*" I repeated. "The Prince of Princes?" There was a chilling thought. If the Cielcin clans could unite with a common purpose and strategy, the war would become *hell.* For the moment, the disparate clans pillaged where they would, burned worlds and took slaves as they wished. For the Legions, it was like rushing to put out fires as they were lit against a city palisade . . . but only one fire at a time, or two. United, the clans could burn the stars.

I remembered Carax of Aramis, then, him and the Pale King he'd met above Hermonassa.

A crown, he'd said. *A crown? Yes. It were silver.*

I saw once again the silver-crowned demon from my visions, him with the host of monsters at his back and the galaxy burned behind him. No doubt remained in my mind that he was Syriani Dorayaica, the Scourge of Earth.

"He is *Shiomu,*" Iubalu said.

"The Prophet?" I asked.

"He knows the future!" the *vayadan* general intoned. "He has spoken with the Watchers! With the great ones who dwell in the night!"

"The Quiet?" I asked, stepping forward back into the hold.

A bolt of violet light split the darkness, which closed behind like the crashing of the sea.

Whirling, I saw one of my men had fired at the roof above. His plasma burner was still smoking in the thin air. "Hold your fire!" I said.

Something scraped in the vaults above, and the words came in our ears, taunting, "You missed me, *hurati.*"

Asking in Cielcin so I knew I would not be misunderstood, I asked, *"Dein belutono ba-Caihanarin ne?"*

What do you know about the Watchers? The Quiet?

"Speak not their name!" the *vayadan* shrieked.

The sky fell an instant later. There came a flash of red light and an instant after a mighty crash sounded. On instinct I kindled my blade and swept the point forward in anticipation of my leaping foe. But when the flash cleared and the ringing faded to silence, I saw it was only the wreckage of one of the cranes. Three of my men turned and fired up into the tangle of catwalks and gantries, the flash of their guns lighting up the gloom.

But there was nothing to shoot at. Nothing *above.*

One of the maintenance grates beside us exploded, metal grillwork snarling upward. Before I could process what was happening, a white blur erupted from beneath us and *something* swept down upon my men. My eyes were an instant catching up. The blur was Iubalu. I had a faint moment of reflection, realizing that if one of these chimeric demons had come for Cade and his men, as well, there was more than one aboard. I saw its arm, white as Death, saw the long blade extruded from its wrist, the clawed finger folded down and out of the way. The stunned hoplite just stood there, shoulders tight, unmoving.

The creature had moved so *fast* the shield had blocked a sword strike. We stood there a moment, humans and Pale machine alike: a grim burlesque tableau. For an instant. No one moved. No one dared to.

But the moment passed. Time, Ever-Fleeting, does not stop.

Siran, always cool and level-headed, fired.

The shot flashed in the hall, broke against the alien's shield with a rippling of fractal light. *Shielded,* of course the creature was shielded. I felt my teeth clench. Iubalu turned its eyeless head toward Siran and me, black and glassy teeth shining as it leered—and leaped.

"Back!" I shouted, hurling myself aside. Siran had just enough time to pivot behind a stanchion that supported the walkways above. One of Iubalu's four arms swept in a flat arc, white sword flashing. The zircon blade pinged off the steel and titanium of the stanchion with a bell-like chime, and it extended an identical blade from a second arm, which it hooked round the pillar even as Siran leaped away. Our shields were forcing it to move slower than it could. That was something, but it was something that would matter only so long as our shields held. With a third arm it uncoiled a *nahute* that hung from its belt and hurled it into the air. Shielded as we were, the drone was not immediately a threat, but it would split our attention at a time when we could not afford distractions. Two of our men circled round behind it, but a port opened in the demon's shoulder and opened fire. Plasma spat out, tracking the two hoplites even though Iubalu did not turn its head to look. It had eyes all round its head, I realized, and some machine daimon within helped its once-organic consciousness keep track of the images through all those extra eyes. But the plasma broke against our hoplites' shields, and one drew close enough to get off a shot inside the monster's energy curtain. It left a black, smoking mark on the white enamel of the creature's armor. No good.

An instant later Iubalu whirled into a dancing low kick that brought one clawed metal foot up into the man's chin. I felt rather than heard the man's neck break as his body was lifted wholly from the floor and flew up and out of sight to strike the distant ceiling. Where he landed I never knew, for a moment later the machine demon spun from its kick into an over-handed punch that flattened the second hoplite, crumpling him like an old can. His suit's underlayment took the worst of the blow, hardening to protect his organs, but the fellow hit the deck and skidded away forty feet. Fifty.

Snarling, it turned its lidless gaze on me, lips peeling back from dead gums. One metal fist clenched, folded down from the wrist. A blade white and sharp and stinging sprang forth, long as Iubalu's too-long forearm, long almost as an Irchtani *zitraa*.

"*Shiomu iunane o-okun darathar,*" it said. *The Shiomu wants you alive.* "But he didn't say I couldn't break you first."

The blade moved faster than I could track. Too fast. It pinged off my shield, sending a thunderclap through the thin air of the hold.

Siran shouted something over the line and shots rang out. Plasma broke uselessly over the *vayadan*'s shields. Only then did I understand her. "Use your lances! Lances!" That made sense. An energy lance's beam would drain a shield faster than plasma or kinetic weapons ever could.

As if in answer to this, Iubalu's shoulder gun turned and shot over my head at the men behind me. I'd lost track of the *nahute;* it must be among the men behind me, or else was circling above. I offered no reply to the Cielcin leader, but thrust at the creature's midsection. Iubalu pivoted, stepping back, and brushed the blade aside with the edge of its forearm.

Just as I'd feared: its body was adamant, forged of the same long-chain carbon molecules common in starship hulls. Nothing, not even highmatter, could cut it.

That impossibly huge smile widened, and a short rush of air groaned past its teeth. Then it raised its sword arm yet again and swung. Slower now. Slow enough to pass through my shield if it struck me. I ducked, wove under the strike, and swung around to the outside. I kept my sword up as I did so and drew the liquid blue blade across the creature's white one. Highmatter met ceramic, and my sword sliced the Cielcin's off near the base, and the white weapon went spinning to clatter against the wall of the hold.

"Hadrian!" Siran's voice sounded in my ear, "Move!"

Without hesitation I threw myself back toward the wall, putting a good three meters between myself and the demon before I heard the earth-splitting *bang* of a grenade. Regaining my feet and my composure, I turned to see the cloud of shrapnel and plasma vapor that drifted where the Cielcin machine had been a moment before. I beheld its distended, humanish profile through the mist: four arms long and trailing, its broken sword still hanging from its wrist. Its smile seemed to float out of the fog, teeth shining like a cat's in some moonlit jungle of human memory.

But for the sword I had taken from it, Iubalu seemed unscathed.

It raised its broken weapon before its face. Surprise? Disbelief? A salute? Or mere detached curiosity? To this day I cannot say. It made a fist, and the white arm released the stump of blade with as little pomp as accompanied the ejection of a plasma burner's spent heat sink.

"*Oyumn juu ne?*" it asked. *Is that all?*

And then it was gone, retreating halfway across the hold in a blur of white motion.

Retreating? *Why?*

"Back to the hall!" I shouted, retreating toward the archway.

A noise like the clap of thunder on a night of rain sounded just behind me, and I knew. Knew the beast had moved so fast it shocked the air. The third and last man of the trias that had accompanied Siran and me screamed and hit the wall ahead with a slap. Even shielded, being struck by an object so massive as the Cielcin chimera at such speeds would be like having a shuttle dropped on you. The man didn't even have time to scream.

Though someone did. A moment later a horrid cry went up, filling the air of the hold and our lines alike. I did not have to turn to know. It had been the second man Iabalu had struck. The *nahute* had found him.

I killed his connection to my suit's comms.

All three men were dead.

"Siran! Go!" I shouted, pushing her into the hall. "It's me it wants! Run!"

The lights in the hall sprang on in response to our presence, the odd one sputtering or sparking before it went out. The ship shook beneath us—from the fighting outside or the *Tamerlane*'s distant shelling I could not say. I slammed the door behind me, but I knew.

Not even four inches of titanium would hold the chimera for long.

CHAPTER 27

THE BATTLE OF
THE BEAST

THE CUBICULUM WAS AHEAD, past sealed and unused barrack dorms. There were men there, some of Pallino's unit. Fifteen men, was it? Two decades? I could not recall, but I couldn't ask without showing my hand to the beast that followed us—assuming of course that whatever machines it had to augment its senses had not already alerted the *vayadan* to what lay ahead. Our boots rang on the metal deckplates as we hurried on, chased by the whine and grind of metal as Iubalu worked to open the heavy door behind us.

I stumbled and leaned on the wall to steady myself. I'd unkindled my blade as we ran. "Udax, where are you?" I rasped into my communicator, one hand on Siran's shoulder to keep her moving. I knew Iubalu could hear me. I didn't care. It didn't matter.

The Irchtani's reply came an instant later, almost shrill. "Busy, human!"

"What's going on?"

"I do not know!" he said. "There's a light flashing out there. They broke off the attack on our port side!"

One hand still on the wall for balance, I answered, "Alarm."

It had to be Cade. The good centurion had made his move in the end.

"Valka," I said, rounding a bend in the hall, "Valka, is the ship venting?"

She was still there. "I'm not sure, I . . ." Her voice felt farther away than it ever had, as though I heard her from the bottom of some fathomless well. "'Tis!"

I could have sagged against the bulkhead with relief. Cade had succeeded.

May his soul find peace on Earth.

The scream of metal followed us up the hall, followed by the steady *tap-tap-tapping* of iron claws on the decking. Iubalu was coming, following hard on our heels. *"Kianuri mnu ne?"* came the alien voice behind. "Running?" Then it said something I did not understand, voice coming as a whisper in my ear through my hacked implants. *"Uboretata ioman ti-belu sha ba-aetane."* *I expected more from one of your Aeta.*

But I had no time to wonder.

At a signal to Siran, I cut my suit comm completely.

The time for words was over.

There! Not twenty yards ahead stood the door to the cubiculum, a circular portal sealed fast. Her comms similarly deactivated, Siran bellowed through her suit speakers, "Open the door!"

Nothing happened, but we did not slow our pace. The drumming of the metal claws behind came faster, and I imagined the *vayadan* loping ape-like after us, but I did not turn to see, did not stop to activate my suit's rearview camera.

"Open the door!" Siran cried out again. And again, "Open the doors!"

The third time paid for all. The door opened, and two of our legionnaires stood in it, short lances at the ready. Behind us came a scrabbling, crashing like the panic of the horse knocked off its feet.

"My lord, get down!" one of the soldiers exclaimed.

I lurched sidelong into a control niche at my right hand. Siran hit the deck, rolling so she landed on her shoulder with her own lance aimed back the way we had come.

Iubalu leaped, but its machine frame was too tall and too broad for that narrow space, and its shoulder caught on the wall. It fell short of Siran's position by several yards, mere feet from me. Siran and the legionnaires all opened fire, energy lances strafing the Cielcin general with their invisible beams. For a moment, I thought I saw the black char of carbon scoring and a thin tongue of smoke.

I saw my chance. As the chimera struggled to right itself I stepped in and lifted my sword. The highmatter blade shone like a ray of moonlight. I struck, pushing the blade through a smooth cut that skated up the creature's armored shoulder and struck off the shoulder turret. One of Iubalu's elbows snapped backward, caught me fully in the solar plexus. The armor took the worst of it, but still the breath was driven from my lungs as I was lifted fully from my feet with enough force to strike the low ceiling.

"Hadrian!"

I hit the deck a moment after, my sword carving a hair-fine slash through the wall of the corridor.

The lights went out. I must have severed a conduit with my fall.

I wanted nothing, *nothing* more than to lie there. I could hardly move, hardly *breathe*.

But I had to move. Iubalu had nearly found its feet. White hands clamped themselves to runners on the ceiling meant for handholds when the ship was in zero-gee. Like the wreck of some vessel lost at sea hoisted from the depths, Iubalu hauled itself to its feet.

Move! The word screamed through my every nerve channel, every fiber. *Move!*

Slowly, my limbs moving with the creaking slowness of rusting clockwork, I found my hands and knees. My feet. Hands seized me. Gloved hands—not steel. Siran and one of the legionnaires pulled me after them, pulled me toward the cubiculum.

I was through.

A moment after I heard the muffled *bang* of a grenade. Then another. Followed by a hiss and howl of . . . was that pain?

"I got him!" the soldier exclaimed.

But the fool had lingered in the archway. White hands emerged from the smoke behind, seized the fellow by both shoulders and yanked him back. He screamed, and the sounds that followed after defied description as limb was rent from limb. I'd found my voice again, and pressing myself against the bulkhead beside the door I shouted, "Open fire!"

There were at least a dozen men in the chamber, and a dozen men fired, plasma rounds and lance beams streaming through the open door, a declaration of fire.

Silence a moment. Silence and the distant noise of battle creaking throughout the *Merciless*'s much-strained superstructure.

"Did we get him?" one man asked.

Siran hushed him. I readied my sword.

A single iron hand clamped down on the lip of the door. Another. A third.

Iubalu roared. A high, shrieking sound more akin to a predatory bird or some wraith of fantasy than anything. I could not see it, but I could imagine its white helm and impossibly wide smile emerging from the vapors and the smoke.

"Open fire!" Siran cried again.

Plasma flared violet, but Iubalu did not stop. It inched forward, white blades clicking into place, extending from its wrists. I wouldn't have much time. The *vayadan's* implants seemed to give it full range of vision. My vantage point by the door would not avail me for long. I'd have to act fast or not at all.

All thoughts of action vanished the next instant, for there came a faint whining and a mechanical clatter as ports opened in Iubalu's chest and rockets flared out. Four of our men vanished in an instant, and the end of one of the aisles of fugue creches exploded in a hailstorm of metal and glass. Violet fluid spilled forth, smoking in the chilly air. I needed only for our enemy to take one more step.

Iubalu took it.

Its white armor had charred black in places, and though the adamant had endured I took that for a good sign. Its shields were down, drained by all that weapons fire. But it did not matter. My business was not with the demon's armor, but with the joints between it, with the segments of jointed titanium beneath the carbon armor.

Common metal was no trouble at all. As I had once long ago on Vorgossos with the Exalted Calvert, I buried the point of my blade in the ball joint where one of Iubalu's four arms joined its torso. I twisted the point, gouging the arm loose. It fell with a clatter as I leaped away. Too slow. One of Iubalu's clawed feet lashed out and clipped my flank, turning my leap into a slide that sent me skidding across the floor.

But the damage was done. Before Iubalu could turn its attentions back on me, Siran and her men opened fire. The Cielcin leaped, caught a spar that was part of the overhead transport system for the cryonic pods, and leaped over the heads of our men to perch upon the top of one of the rows. Disruptor fire issued from the palms of its three remaining hands, but we were shielded and the weapons did no good.

Its smile grew steadily wider, and into the air of the hold, it said, "You will pay for that, *hurati*."

I had found my feet again, and though my side ached, I did not think my ribs were broken. Bruised, yes, but intact. In answer, I pointed my sword up toward the enemy. "Come down, then! Come and collect!"

In contemptuous answer, Iubalu punched down with one of its sword hands and pierced the casket on which it stood, killing the sleeper within.

"I think I will ask the master for your bones when he is through," Iubalu declared, speaking as one speaks to a crowd. "Perhaps I will put your skull with the others."

Not knowing what to say, I said, "I think not!"

Then a dark shape streaked up from below and seized Iubalu by the arm. Another followed, and writhing in the air they torqued the chimera off balance and set it to crash from its high place. It happened so fast it took me an instant to realize that for the second time that day Udax had appeared in the critical instant. He and another of his Irchtani perched atop the fugue caskets where Iubalu had stood a moment earlier. The other hefted his plasma rifle—no, his plasma *howitzer*—and fired. Not a bolt, but a stream of violet flame spewed forth and poured down upon the xenobite, and for a moment I feared the monstrous heat would crack and melt the delicate cryonics equipment in rows to either side—but it did not matter. The Irchtani kept firing, a steady stream of superheated plasma flowing forth like the breath of some neon dragon, so hot and bright my suit's entoptics cut the glare to a mere fraction of all available light.

There is always a price to pay for victory. I prayed the caskets nearby had been emptied long ago, and that we avenged men with that attack, not killed them. The plasma would not burn the creature's armor, but it would heat and damage perhaps those exposed components of common metal and turn any organic matter to ash.

I raised my sword to Udax in salute and hurried forward to see the ruin of our enemy.

But demons die slow deaths.

One white sword lanced out, ejected from Iubalu's arm with all the force of a javelin. The white spike caught Udax's compatriot fully in the chest, impaling him. The blade passed clean through, shattering ceramic armor and the Irchtani's hollow bones. Iubalu stood, the metal components of its skeleton glowing cherry red where the plasma torch had heated and warped them. It moved slowly, joints ill-fitting in their sockets, but it stood all the same: three-armed, claw-footed, with one pale sword left in its grip. It used that sword for a prop, ceramic edge grinding against the metal as it stood and punched one of the caskets in its fury. Cryonic fluid gushed out and hissed where it struck the creature's glowing titanium body.

Udax shot at it with his rifle, but the shot washed against the ceramic breastplate to little effect. As though the Irchtani were little more than a fly, the *vayadan*-general pointed one of its remaining arms toward him and fired once. A *nahute* shot from a compartment in the forearm and flew up toward Udax, who spread his grayish wings and leaped away.

Its faceless gaze settled on me, and I saw its helmet had closed over its gaping smile, sealing what yet remained of the flesh safe within. Presently the cowl opened, and that leering grin returned.

Still leaning on its sword, Iubalu said, "You cannot win. You're surrounded. Outnumbered. You've lost one ship already, and I will feed you to my master when I bring you to him." A resonant *click* filled the air, and as I watched, the sword was unmoored from its place inside Iubalu's arm and slid into the monster's hand.

"You can hardly stand," I said, bruised and exhausted as I was myself.

No answer.

Only the smile.

Iubalu pointed its sword at me, then spinning it took it in two hands, raised high like an executioner. The third arm it held across itself. I almost grinned. What a strange contest this would be, where it could not match me sword for sword. It would have to block my attacks—perversely—with its own arm, or with the armored portions of its body.

My targets were small enough: the backs of the knees, the insides of the thighs, the elbows and shoulder joints. And the face: the only part of the creature that still seemed made of flesh. I raised my sword, point aimed up at that evil grin where it loomed above me.

The white sword fell and the third arm punched out at the same moment. The Irchtani's plasma weapon had done its damage, and both attacks came slowly—which was to say they came fast as any merely human opponent I had faced. Even my palatine eugenic strength and reflexes were barely up to the task, and I leaped aside, dodging the overhead slash of the blade and parrying the arm. Had the Cielcin been human—or even truly Cielcin—the blade would have skinned the arm and sliced clean through ribs and lungs and heart.

As it was, Iubalu whirled its blade around and tried for a flat cut, but the blade was too long for that narrow aisle, and it caught on the bank of fugue caskets at its right hand. I moved well inside the reach of those arms, and it turned to mark my progress. I had to get around it, had to give Siran and her men clear shots at its exposed backside. Had to get it away from our sleeping men.

The *vayadan*-general took one lurching step. Its left leg was clearly lamed, the joint fused by the Irchtani's heroic effort. Unable to rely on its sword in such tight quarters, it threw a hook with its free hand. I did not try to block it, but ducked. The iron fist crashed into one of the sleepers' instrument panels and shattered the delicate screen. Infuriated by its damaged functionality, Iubalu struck the panel again and snarled.

It did not fire one of its rockets at me. I wondered if it still could. But it was the size of a mountain next to me, and like an avalanche it came, driving me back with vicious blows from one hand and another, ever keeping the third hand and the sword upraised like the tail of a scorpion. I did not try to absorb the blows as a boxer might—any one of them might land hard enough to turn my bones to powder. I only tried to turn them, tried to keep my footing.

The sword slammed down. Its ceramic edge struck my shoulder with enough force it might have sliced me clean in half were it not for my armor. I felt the underlayment harden in response to the impact, the gel layer between layers of nanocarbon armorweave briefly turning to something harder than stone. Than steel. I was grateful—and lucky—that the attack hit my left arm. The false bones in my shoulder did not ache, did not injure as my true bones might have done. Still I let out a cry, and the force of the blow was enough that my knees buckled, and I went down.

"Submit!" Iubalu exclaimed, and clamped one iron-fingered hand over my faceplate, bending me backward as if in some dreadful dance. Those black glass fangs drew down and ever nearer, and I recalled the way Prince Aranata's fangs had extended as he tore out old Sir William's throat. With its second hand, Iubalu traced a line down my armored face, almost caressing. A vague horror turned over in me, and I tried to get my feet back under me. But the force with which Iubalu held me in place was so great I could not stand. Where were Siran and the others? They should have been right behind! "Submit!" The lips did not move. The words came from speakers somewhere in the chimera's chest, their sound garbled now from the damage they'd sustained. The face itself was dead, a taxidermied ornament, monument to the creature it had been.

I could not get away.

I could *not* get away.

But it hadn't pinned my arm, and my sword was still in my hand. I struck wildly with it, blindly. The highmatter blade battered against Iubalu's armored flank, but it did not seem to notice. Not at first. Not until the third strike caught the elbow of one of its remaining arms. The pressure on my helmet faded, and I fell. Snarling, Iubalu seized me by the ankle and lifted me bodily from the floor.

Then and only then did Siran and the others open fire. Plasma streaked through the air—one shot coruscated off my shield curtain—and a moment later I was flying, soaring up the aisle toward the far end. I hit the ground just beyond the end of the aisle and skidded across the floor, armor grinding beneath me. I came to rest mere feet from the mound of bones, my sword still in my hand. Iubalu came on, moving like a tower slow in falling. It did not even seem to notice the men firing at its back—did not feel the plasma fire licking at its armor. Its one leg had locked entirely, joints fully fused, but still it came, still dangerous, still more than a match for an ordinary palatine.

The crack and violet flash of a grenade filled the air, knocking Iubalu from its feet and shattering four of the nearest fugue creches. Before Siran's men could throw another I shouted, "Stop! Stop! The sleepers!" Now I could get the *vayadan* away from them, I found I was unwilling to risk further life and limb on behalf of our people.

Hearing me, Iubalu punched through one of the creches with its free hand and drew the sleeper out by the neck, tearing hoses and wires free. It squeezed. Metal fingers bit through flesh and crushed bone, pulped the neck and shoulder. It dropped her ruined body at its feet and stamped, smashing ribs and organs to a red-brown paste between its claws. Its smile never faltered. Furious, I fumbled with the hard switch behind my ear, forced my helm to open and fold away. "Here!" I cried out, and tore the coif from my head. The cubiculum air was cold against my face as I pounded on my chest like a drum. "Here!"

I stood then exposed like Beowulf before Grendel, alone on that patch of narrow ground. The monument of bones at my back seemed to push at me, to spur me forward. *Avenge us. Avenge us. Avenge us!* It was as though I heard their dusty voices urging me, groaning from that howling dark. I did not look back, for I felt that if I did so I would see that divine darkness and feel the shapes of dead men in the night, pointing as my image had pointed the way for me out of that terrible place.

Forward.

Through.

But I did not have to move. Hand dripping gore, Iubalu stumped forward, sword raised and ready. Conscious of my exposed face, I pointed my weapon toward the beast.

Once more the *vayadan*-general let out its hideous cry, high and keening as metal scraping glass. I bared my teeth in answer, matching the Cielcin smile.

It leaped. I lunged. Iubalu's gore-smeared fist clipped me just under the arm and I clenched my teeth as the armor bore the brunt of the assault. My blade bounced useless off one armored thigh. Gritting through the pain, I recovered, raised my sword above my head to parry the sword as it fell. Highmatter and ceramic met again, and the ceramic parted with a sigh, blade spinning away. Howling, Iubalu thrust the broken hilt into my chest, knocking me off balance. Staggering back, I spat, saw red in the saliva where it flew. The pain in my ribs was a distant cry, far off as the groaning of the dead in my mind.

White hands reached toward me, each of jointed metal. I could not get away, and so leaped toward them, ducking beneath Iubalu's grasping talons, my blade vanishing as I leaped. I slammed into the chimera's body like a wrestler, and though I could not hope to compete with the size and mass of it I placed the emitter of my sword against the still-glowing joint at one hip and squeezed. Highmatter flowered there, slicing clean and cold and straight through the hip, severing Iubalu's leg entire. Unbalanced, I leaned against the massive chimera with all my weight. It toppled backward, and I leaped away just as the legionnaires dared to approach. The noise of its falling was so great I expected to see cracks in the steel plating of the floor beneath it.

"Lord Marlowe! Stand clear!" one of the men shouted.

A moment later I saw the blinking of a grenade. "Stop!" I shouted. Too late.

The explosive rang out, so near the damaged stump at its hip it blew apart the pelvis and lower abdomen before Iubalu could move. Legless now and with but two of its four arms, the creature flailed, lashed out as my men—human and Irchtani alike—drew about it.

"The arms!" I shouted. "Don't kill it!"

Unshielded now and struggling to move, it was a small matter to fire at the beast's underarms, to fuse the shoulder joints with licking tongues of plasma. Joints melting under the assault, Iubalu still managed to pull its arms to itself, curling them like a boxer in defensive pose.

One hand on my aching side, I stood over it, blade pointed at the hollow of interlaced struts and tendons that served for its neck.

"You're beaten," I said. "Surrender."

Iubalu only looked at me with its eyeless gaze. I had not looked at it so close before, and so saw for the first time the *badge* it wore upon its chest: the faint outline of a grasping hand, six-fingered, white-on-white. That disturbed me more than I can explain. The Cielcin do not depict things in art. They do not illustrate, do not represent. Their only artwork is calligraphy, the circular *Udaritanu* writing they adapted from the anaglyphs of the Quiet. To see the image of a hand on Iubalu's chest was like finding a book written by dogs.

"Your fuel supply is compromised. You cannot run." I pressed the sword in a little. The nanocarbon tendons brushed aside, uncut, but I saw a braided steel cord sigh apart. The still-organic face spasmed like the limbs of the dead exposed to electricity. "Surrender." And speaking the beast's own tongue I added, *"Ietta." Submit.*

"We have other ships!"

My sword flashed, cutting through one arm at the shoulder. "How much of you do I have to cut away before you surrender?" I shoved the limb away with one foot, wincing as pain shot through my ribs. Sword point back at its throat, I said, "I will you the same offer I made an ichakta of the Itani Otiolo a long time ago: surrender, and I will see that you and your people are returned to your master."

Uvanari had surrendered at once, seeing a way to preserve its life and duty to its prince and master. Iubalu, it seemed, understood its duty very differently. Or perhaps it knew, perhaps understood that once in human hands its human-manufactured components would be laid bare to our technicians—that whatever secrets lay hid in that mechanism that served it now in place of a brain would be picked over by Chantry scholars, to take its intelligence to war against its master.

The *vayadan's* one remaining hand clenched, opened, clenched again. Its elbow would not bend, nor its shoulder, but it pointed at me, and for the first time that day moved its lips. "There is *no* returning," it said. "No surrender. *He* is coming. *He* will avenge us."

Fearing some final trick, I pressed my sword close against the edge of Iubalu's neck. "Order your people to stand down," I said. "Do it!"

Iubalu played its final trick, then. Somewhere deep in the artificial mechanisms of its body and mind, something died. It ceased even the attempt at motion, and the faint blue lights that glowed in it went out. All was quiet then. Terribly quiet. The ruined limbs, the shattered body, the one remaining arm . . . these all transmuted in an instant. It was not a body I stood over, not the wreck of an alien chimera, but only an inert mass of metal and ceramic. An empty shell.

Nearly empty.

At a stroke, I think, Iubalu had wiped all traces of its memory and personality from the machines it inhabited, but it had not died. For an instant thereafter, the lips moved, murmuring words I could not hear.

I unkindled my blade and lowered myself painfully to one knee, the better to listen. And what I heard froze every drop of blood in me. "He has seen it, *hurati*. He has seen your death. The sacrifice . . ." It never finished that thought. The ursine smile slackened, and I knew the *vayadan-general* was dead.

I was still kneeling by Iubalu's side when Siran joined me. Through her suit speakers, she said, "You need to put your comm back on."

"What is it?" I asked, but did as she said.

The reports flooded over me. The *Mintaka* had won free. The Cielcin in the hold were routed, and with Cade's men gone Corvo and Aristedes had shelled the rear section of the ship entirely, destroying the force that had killed Cade's century in the engine rooms. Our reinforcements had boarded the Cielcin craft and were driving the enemy back. Defeat had to turned to victory—and for the Cielcin, victory had become disaster.

But I heard almost none of this. My thoughts were with the last thing Iubalu had said.

He has seen your death.

I'd seen it, too. Seen it a thousand thousand times when I tread the lucent waters of the rivers of time. I had seen myself burned and crucified. Beheaded and betrayed. Tortured or hanged or eaten by the Pale. I had seen myself crowned Emperor of Mankind. Seen myself killed by the very silver-crowned demon king Carax had described before the Solar Throne. Had this *Shiomu*, this *Prophet* seen it, too? Had the Quiet granted Dorayaica visions as they had granted them to me?

Or was there some other power above the stage? Kharn Sagara had spoken of others, of powers old when the universe was young, of creatures that dwelt in the night. I had given nearly a hundred years by then to understanding the Cielcin, and I felt again all at once that I knew almost nothing, felt that our two races—mankind and the Pale—were only pawns on some larger board whose scope I could not see.

Leopards, lions, and wolves.

Had I been wrong to think the Cielcin worshiped the Quiet? Or wrong in thinking that was all they worshipped?

I permitted Siran to help me to my feet. "Have this one taken away," I said, spurning Iubalu's metal corpse with a toe. "The Emperor will want to see it." I clipped my sword back into its scabbard at my right hip.

If what Iubalu had said was true, if Syriani Dorayaica had been granted visions by the Quiet or some similar power . . . I stared blankly down the aisle of shattered fugue creches, but I did not see it. It was as if I saw through the *Merciless* and the Cielcin ship that entrapped it, as if I stared across the bottomless black of space and beheld those eyes, blacker still, staring back at me. I saw once more my vision of the Cielcin marching across the stars, only this time a white hand went before them and blotted out the sky.

The strange mood passed, and passing left me with a parting thought: if what Iubalu had said was true, this Prophet and I had all too much in common.

CHAPTER 28

THE DEVIL TRIUMPHANT

THREE MILLION PEOPLE CROWDED the Campus Raphael, and the eyes of the galaxy were on us. In the weeks to come and the years to follow, the broadcast of that glittering parade would play across public dispatch and on holograph projectors on every planet in the Empire and beyond.

The Triumph of the Devil of Meidua.

There was a painting made—I saw it only once—a massive canvas that hung in the Sun King's Hall at the top of one of the grand staircases. I was told His Radiance had ordered the legendary court painter, Vianello, be decanted from fugue for the first time in nearly five hundred years to commemorate the event. It was Vianello who had painted the Emperor's official portrait, and the portraits of the previous fifteen Emperors, remaining among the living for only so long as it took him to finish his work.

I do not know what became of the painting after Gododdin. Taken down, no doubt. Burned, or perhaps stored in the Imperial vaults on Avalon where none would ever see it. I do know that the triumphal arch erected to my victory over Iubalu still stands on Nemavand, though by Imperial decree my head was chiseled from the monument and cast into the desert, where I don't doubt it remains to this day, resin untouched by the etching sands.

Both arch and painting depicted the same thing, though neither could capture it, for an Imperial triumph is a spectacle more of sound than sight. The music of horns and silver trumpets filled the golden air, and the exhortation of the millions gathered there was like the breaking of some mighty sea against the shore of a city of gods. Ahead of us and behind marched rank upon rank of Imperial Martians in their red armor and white cloaks, and my Red Company marched behind them as we proceeded through the hippodrome and the Grand Colosseum toward the Last Stair and the Sun King's Hall. How tall their plumes! Red feathers and white horsehair running in the wind! How proud their banners! How bright their spears flashing in the sun! And the thunder of their march in time to the music of horn and tympani was enough to shake old Jupiter from his forgotten sleep on lost Olympos and proclaim our message across the stars.

We are the gods now.

Behind our men and the Martians came the train: parade floats hovering or pulled by tanks, or else striding on machine legs of their own, driven by hidden operators. The cart ahead of us was pulled by two white lions, four times the size of any lion I had seen, and upon the platform rode crucified five living Cielcin officers, and at their feet lay mounded a hoard of weapons taken from the ship we conquered in the night. Behind followed three thousand captured Cielcin, chained wrist and ankle, their horned crowns carved away. To what fate they marched I did not know, nor ever asked.

And last of all I came, riding with my officers upon a floating barge that seemed driven or pulled by no device save the banners of the Imperial sun, which blew about us like sails. I stood upon the highest level before an empty throne. On this one occasion I wore no black and was arrayed instead in Imperial argent, that brightest white which is reserved only for members of the Blood Imperial, for I was a cousin of that blood and they claimed me in my triumph, so that I seemed to gleam like a white star in my formal armor before that empty throne. No slave stood at my ear, no homunculus to whisper that I, too, was mortal. That I, too, would die. For I was immortal in that moment, and immortalized. About me stood all my faithful friends. Arrayed on steps beneath me were Pallino and Crim, Elara and Siran—and there were Captain Corvo and Commander Durand, and young Aristedes with Koskinen and Pherrine, with Ilex and the other bridge officers. And Alexander was there, arrayed like me in argent, as though he too were some kind of conqueror. And there too were Udax and Barda and others of the Irchtani auxilia who had aided us. Even our ghosts rode with us, for the memories of Cade and Ghen—of Switch— stirred in my mind.

And Valka was there. Against her wishes and better judgment, she stood a step below me and somewhat removed, hands clasped, eyes sweeping the crowd. She wore a gown of simple black, unadorned, as if to protest all that Imperial white. Despite that, she glowed to me more brightly than all the rest.

And behind us all, not crucified but mounted on a post like a witch for the burning, came the body of Iubalu.

What remained of it.

The flesh parts had been cleaned away and replaced with a plastic facsimile, though the snarling fangs were fierce as the originals had been. I glanced back at it, looming like an angel of death above us, white as we. At a signal the cornicens sounded their horns, and turning I raised my sword to pass beneath the Arch of Peace at the center of the Campus. And as we passed beneath its curve and shadow and the statues of Justice and Mercy both, I lowered the sword in my left hand and hoisted high the spear we had recovered from Iubalu's ship: the heraldic staff topped with its broken circle and dangling silver chimes.

Iubalu's staff.

It is that moment which shines out of Vianello's painting, which rises from the triumphal arch on Nemavand. That Devil Marlowe standing with sword in hand and the spear of his enemy raised in triumph.

The crowd roared. The horns sounded. The trumpets blew. The very skies of Forum answered them, for a great wind rose and carried the noise of our exultation from that mighty field to the highest towers and the lowest spire of that gilt and holy city—and thence by holograph to every world.

I scarce recall the faces of that crowd: palatine and patrician, the highest and noblest in our Empire. I can see them only as a mingling of bright colors, of silks and velvets and burnished gold beneath the rows of Imperial suns embroidered red on white, snapping on tall banners like sails in that unceasing wind. In time we came to the Last Stair: a thousand steps and eighty so wide a hundred men might mount their gilded marble and climb abreast. Imperial banners marked the edges and hung between the white pillars above. Beyond them rose the domes and Georgian rotundas of the Sun King's Palace, its towers a hundred stories high. In its golden shadow we stopped, and at another horn blast I descended from my place, still clutching my sword in my hand and carrying Iubalu's heraldic spear. Valka fell into step behind me, and Corvo and the other officers followed.

Above us and along the steps were arrayed the great princes of the realm, them whose blood was old as Earth and older than the Empire. There was the red lion of House Habsburg, and the black eagle of

Hohenzollern. There flew the red and blue shields of Bourbon beside the banner of House Bernadotte. There too were the banners of the Houses Mahidol, Singh, and Rothschild, and there was the crysanthemum of Yamato, whose chief still called himself the *Mikado no Nihonjin,* the Emperor of the Nipponese. They were not alone. These princely houses stood among those of the magnarchs and viceroys whose time it was to live with the Emperor in his holy city. Was that the eagle of Kephalos I saw? Or was it only my imagination?

Each dipped their banners as we climbed the stairs, each bowed as I passed with Prince Alexander beside me, and cries of "Halfmortal! Halfmortal!" dogged my ascent, and as I had been instructed to do I lifted the Cielcin spear to each in salute. How strange it was, and how marvelous, that these great princes and chevaliers of the Imperium should bow to me and to my company, composed as it was of foreigners, of plebeians, with an intus, a homunculus, and a pack of inmane savages. The world had changed—and I had changed it.

But bow they did, if not all of them.

Augustin Bourbon did not bow, nor his cousin, Prince Charles—the son of the previous Prince Charles whom Augustin had betrayed his own father to support. Neither did Marius Hohenzollern nor his wife, Wilhelmina. It did not matter. At last we came to the receiving platform at the top of that mighty stair where the Emperor awaited us, seated on a throne grander and more beautiful by far than the empty seat on the barge I'd left below. There I—to whom all the great lords of the Empire had bowed that day—bowed myself, and knelt, and laid at the royal feet the staff of the enemy I had beaten.

One of the mirrored Excubitors approached. As he did so I unkindled my sword and proffered it—head bowed—with both hands. The knight received my blade and gave it into the hands of His Imperial Radiance, William XXIII, who grasped my weapon as though it were the very scepter of rule and said, "Well done, my good and faithful servant. We are glad to receive you here in this, your moment of triumph." Without standing, the Imperial person raised my sword hilt in one velvet-gloved fist. From my place on the ground, I glanced up. Behind His Radiance there was a sea of white robes and redheaded faces. The Empress stood behind the throne, and dozens of their children behind prudence shields powered by reactors large as mountains hid deep in the bowels of the City far below. "Hadrian Marlowe, for your service to Earth and Emperor, you have our gratitude." He lowered my sword hilt, which was the sign for a page homunculus to approach on its knees, head bowed, bearing aloft a red silk pillow. Moving with the gravity of the weightiest stars, the Emperor rose, snowy garments fluttering about him in the breeze. In gloved and many-ringed hands he took the item from the pillow and raised it for all the crowd to see.

I felt my breath catch.

In the Imperial hands was a wreath, a crown of living gold.

The Grass Crown.

"For your bravery on the field of battle, by our own hand, we set upon your head the Grass Crown! The highest honor we may bestow." He approached and set the wreath upon my head. It was far heavier than I expected, and when I would remove it later I discovered that it was—in truth—wrought of living gold. The leaves and wood of it were laced with metal. How such a thing can be I do not know, and yet I tell you it is so. "You rode at the head of your army against the Pale, saving not only your men from destruction but redeeming those legions we thought lost forever, defying our wildest hopes." He raised both hands, by that gesture encompassing the Last Stair and the whole of the Campus Raphael—encompassing most of all the gilded barge-palanquin on which I had entered, on which still stood, hanging from its post, the demonic corpse of the *Vayadan-General* Iubalu. "With your own hands you slew the captain of the enemy, and brought us news of an alliance between the Cielcin and those barbarians who have ever been a threat to our realm and dominion."

Turning, His Radiance plucked my sword back from the arm of his throne and offered it to me. A powerful symbol, that. To put into my hands a weapon that at that range no power in the universe could have stopped me from using against him. I took the sword in my left hand and accepted the Emperor's right. White gauntlet in red glove, the Emperor himself pulled me to my feet and wheeled me to face the crowd. I held my sword aloft just as the Emperor had done—an Emperor myself, if for only an instant, draped as I was in the cloth of that office.

I looked down upon the high lords of the Imperium, down on Habsburg and Hohenzollern, on Bourbon and Bernadotte. I looked down on Mahidol and Singh and Rothschild, down on Yamato, and felt them looking up at me. Bourbon turned his back. And Hohenzollern. And Mahidol. And when all the banners dipped, theirs did not, and despite the cheering and the bright music of horn and trumpet and the rose petals falling from the high hall as once they'd fallen on Crispin in Colosso, I felt a cold dread seep into my heart, though it melted in the warmth of that instant, for there too were the faces of Corvo and Durand, of Aristedes and Koskinen and Pherrine. Crim and Ilex knelt there side by side, and beside them were Udax and Barda and the Irchtani who were that day heroes to the lords of men. And there were my friends Pallino, Elara, and Siran, who had come with me from the bottom of Emesh. And there was Valka—who did not kneel but stood apart in her black dress, a witch in seeming if not in truth. Criminals and slaves, homunculi and inti, foreigners and xenobites and witches, too.

My people.

My friends.

A moment later, a port opened beneath the post from which Iubalu hung. A containment field was activated, flashing as it englobed the palanquin. Then a violet flame issued forth, hot as the hottest stars and twice as bright, though the field polarized the worst of it. Iubalu was consumed then, the titanium and plastic all melted away. Not even the adamant of its armor would remain through heat hot enough to dissolve molecular bonds. I shut my eyes, and shutting them saw once more my vision . . . twice received.

I saw a black ship plunge into a star, and saw the Cielcin swallowed all by light, and heard once more the shrieking voice of the oracle, Jari.

Light! he screamed, demon-possessed and dead inside. *Light! Light! Light!*

And the Emperor's voice rose above the masses, louder than the voice of God. "As it is here for this one—so shall it be for all the rest," he cried. "Death to the enemy!"

"Death to the enemy!" the crowd echoed back.

"Glory for Mankind!" the Emperor decreed.

"Glory for Mankind!"

"Long live the Children of Earth!"

"Long live the Children of Earth!"

CHAPTER 29

FAR BEYOND THE SUN

THE DAYS OF FORUM are long as weeks, and as the sun was setting on the day of our triumph, a ball was held in our name in the Peronine Palace itself. I had slept since the triumph, and traded the argent clothes and mirrored armor and the golden laurels of the Grass Crown for suits of common white, with my customary red stripes on the trousers and a collared half-cape over the left shoulder, white above and black beneath. I felt silly in the white leather riding boots, in all that glowing silk and soft velvet.

"I swear, you're less nervous before a fight," Valka said, coming up beside me.

I smiled, equal parts fondness and mirth, for she looked entirely unlike herself. Gone were the untidy hair, the tight vest and jodhpurs. Gone too were the scuffed boots and the rolled-back sleeves, the stylus tucked behind one ear or else pinned in her hair. Her pale face was powdered paler still, and painted shadows clung to her eyelids. And her lips were red. Her gown was a floating collection of shadows, black as black, and edged with a subtle crimson like her hair. There were black gems shining at her throat, and a net of them covered her shoulders and high breasts. A gauzy sleeve covered her right arm, but the left was bare, revealing the fractal tattoo pattern there, whorls and spirals and geometric tangles blossoming from the backs of her fingers to where they vanished at the shoulder. A silver pin like a knife secured her so-oft untidy hair, which fell in curling waves across her face to hide one golden eye.

"What?" she asked when I said nothing. I must have been staring.

"You look . . . impossible," I said, and smiled my broken smile.

She leaned close, pulling in her wake the scent of sandalwood and something smoky. I thought she meant to kiss me, and when I stooped to kiss her back she pulled away. "I know," she said.

Crim snorted.

I eyed the fellow in his glossy black suit, his red silk shirt open Jaddian fashion almost to the navel. I raised an eyebrow. Crim looked away, grinning toothily. "Try to behave," I said, smoothing my jacket. "You're not on holiday. Don't forget."

The security man straightened. "Wouldn't dream of it, sir."

But I saw the smile he flashed Ilex, and I softened. We had won a great victory, and they were not wrong to celebrate. "Just . . . behave yourselves," I said, and rested a hand on the ornamental saber I wore at one hip. Its blade was only aluminum and blunt as a butter knife. Real weapons were not permitted into the Imperial presence, but as a knight I was entitled to wear *something*.

"Is your party all here, my lord?" asked one of the bald, round-faced eunuchs who waited by the doors.

I looked round at those gathered behind Valka and myself. Pallino had freshly trimmed his blackish hair and wore a *cravat* of all things, looking oddly solemn with Elara on his arm in a stately bronze dress. Captain Corvo was a mercenary and no legionnaire, and so had not been permitted her uniform, nor had any of my Norman colleagues. She looked entirely out of place in a gown and nearly as uncomfortable as I was in my white court finery.

A trace of wry laughter touching my face, I answered, "Yes."

"Are they going to say our names?" Elara asked, "Like in the holos?"

"They'll say *his* name," Pallino answered, "maybe the doctor's. We'll just be *'and escort,'* you'll see."

We followed the servant along mirrored halls with Martians standing at attention. We came at last to a glowing colonnade that overlooked the Cloud Gardens and the Galath tree, its bough glowing with milky light in the golden blush of twilight's last embers.

The bright and heady sounds of music rose to meet us, washing down the hall like fine rain. Not the martial music of horn and trumpet, but the sweet notes of violin, of flute, and harp. And here a woman's lofty voice lifted in wordless song as the double doors were opened—not by inhuman mechanism—but by four footmen in red palace uniforms.

"They could have made the walk shorter," Lorian grumbled.

The light that spilled forth shone the color of honey, and brought with it the heady aromas of wine and smoky food and the mingled scents of a thousand different perfumes, all blended together in an orchestra as sonorous and deep as the music and twice as intoxicating. Such was its power that even Lorian Aristedes fell silent.

An androgyn nuncius raised a crystal clarion to its lips and blew as we entered, the high clear note riding smoothly over the uninterrupted orchestra. That done, it lifted up its high and musical voice to sing out: "Sir Hadrian, Lord of the House Marlowe Victorian, Commandant of His Radiance's Red Company, and escort!"

"Told you," Pallino grumbled.

I raised my cane for quiet and offered Valka my arm, which she took as we crossed the threshold, linking hers in mine.

"I hate this place already," she muttered in her native Panthai.

Answering her in that same language, I said, "You have no art in you, dear lady."

The ballroom was a marvel, a confection of baroque architecture, arched ceilings and painted vaults with ribs set with carnelian and carved white marble, every surface frescoed with images of the children of Earth encircling their mother. The Earth herself stood triumphant in the center: a nude woman in full flower standing upon the emerald-and-sapphire globe of the planet itself, her golden hair streaming beneath a crown of twelve stars. Recalling it, I cannot help but recall my friend, Edouard, who called that icon *blasphemous*. I cannot remember why.

"Hadrian!" a voice cried out, shaking me from my contemplation of that incredible sight. Alexander strode across the floor to greet us, dressed in white as I was, his flaming hair oiled and perfectly coiffed. He embraced me as though we had not seen one another in years, though he had stood beside me on the palanquin in the triumph that overlong day. He released me, but held me at arm's length, as though I were a child and he the proud parent. "Welcome! Welcome!"

Painted faces—men and women alike—watched us from around the rims of wine cups or over the arcs of silk or paper fans. I wondered what our closeness looked like to those fine lords and ladies, and remembered sharply Lorian's half-baked suggestion that I should wed the prince and so solidify my position. I took a measured step back, certain that among those watchful faces must be a lord or two who had turned their back to see a minor lord like me—no matter my high lineage—advanced to so honored a place so quickly. "You're wearing a sword!" I exclaimed, noting the metal saber at the prince's side. "Your father didn't *knight* you, did he?"

"Oh no!" Alexander replied, but rested a hand proudly on the pommel of his weapon. "I wouldn't let him. I said I wanted to earn it." I felt an odd spasm of pride at the words. Perhaps my squire had learned something from me after all. "I didn't do anything during the Battle of the Beast."

"The *what?*" Valka almost laughed.

"That's what they're calling it, Sir Hadrian's battle with that . . . thing."

"It's a good name," I allowed—it *was* proper dramatic. "But it wasn't my fight. It was as much Siran's as mine," I gestured to the patrician woman behind me, "and Udax's, of course."

Alexander blinked, as if surprised by my devolution of credit. He still had so much to learn, I thought. "Where are the birds?"

I had to swallow my initial reply, but said, "Not allowed in. No *inmane*. They almost barred Ilex and Aristedes, here, but I insisted. They are *my* officers." In truth, I had fought as hard for Pallino, Elara, and Siran, who though fully human were base-born patricians and not of any exalted blood. "But they'd not allow the auxilia."

The prince only nodded. "Come, please! I must introduce you to my brothers!" Placing a hand on my shoulder, he led me back through the thronging nobiles, Valka following in my wake. We ascended a short step to a carpeted platform above the ballroom floor where padded couches curved round small tables. He stopped before one, where two men in Imperial gold and white sat in close conversation, attended round by lesser lords and ladies of the court. Each was so like unto one another—and each so like unto Alexander—that one might be forgiven for thinking them clones. They had the same strong aristocratic features, the same thick red hair—though one wore his long and gathered into a queue like the Mandari and the other wore his short as Crispin once had done. They each watched with the same emerald eyes as Alexander approached, and smiled the same pearlescent smile.

"Ricard! Philip! This is Sir Hadrian Marlowe," Alexander said. Valka cleared her throat, moving to retake her position beside me, as though the nobiles about her were each a nest of adders. Realizing his error, the young prince added, "And his . . . his paramour? Valka of Tavros."

The long-haired prince's smile grew lazy, and he said, "We know who he is, Alex. We saw the same parade you did." Not standing, the fellow offered his hand. At first I took it for a plebeian handshake, realized only a moment after that I spied the signet ring with its graven ruby and knew he meant for me to kiss it. "Ricard Anchises, 47th Prince of the Aventine House," he said, still sounding bored. "This is Philip. He's . . . what number are you, brother? Fifty-three?"

"Fifty-two," the other said, sharp enough I guessed the former's slight was deliberate, meant to rile the younger man.

The whole procedure felt suddenly absurd. Ricard was not the Emperor, nor was he any great captain or strategos of the Legions. Here was no man worthy of honor, here was only a bored and pampered young man drunk on wine finer than he had the wit to appreciate. But he was of the Blood Imperial all the same, and it was to the station I bowed—I did not kneel—and kissed the ring. "An honor, Prince Ricard."

"Tell me, Lord Marlowe: is it true you slew that metal monster from the triumph?" Prince Philip interjected, a deal drunker than his brother.

"Not alone," I said.

Philip raised an eyebrow. "No? I thought not." I felt Valka's grip tighten on my upper arm, but froze my crooked smile in its place. "Our Alex has been singing your praises. He loves you, I think."

"Enough, Philip!" Alexander snapped. "You asked to meet him. Here he is!"

"Angry, little brother?" Philip almost laughed.

Ricard smiled lazily, adjusted one of his boots with a finger. "He's embarrassed, Philip. You hit too near the mark, I think. Our Alex is in love, but Sir Hadrian doesn't love him back—is that it?" His eyes raked over Valka, whose fingers froze against my arm at the contact. "And why would he? With this lovely to warm his bed at night. Tavrosi, wasn't it?" He did not put the question to Valka. He did not even put the question to me, but raised an eyebrow toward Alexander instead, who nodded, unspeaking. "You know, I always heard these foreign types are *wild*. Good for you, Sir Hadrian."

"*Quite* wild," Valka said icily, nails cutting through my shirtsleeve, "so have a care how you speak about her."

Prince Philip raised his cup to his lips, chortling. "Oh, I like her."

"You won't," she said, stopping short of an actual threat, of anything to which the high lords might object. I did not have to turn to see her barbed smile, and it was all I could do to suppress my own.

Eager to have the ordeal over and done with, I asked, "Alexander says you wanted to meet me? To what do I owe the pleasure?" I gave a slight bow, too slight for the princes' high stations.

The drunk one, Philip, said, "He doesn't look so fearsome, Ricard. I bet Irshan could take him."

Ricard's long fingers toyed with a golden clasp that secured the end of his braid. "We only wanted to meet the man of the hour! You've beaten *three* Pale chieftains, Sir. *With your bare hands!* Who else can claim the same?"

I could not say for certain that they mocked me, but the princes reminded me of Sir Lorcan Breathnach. The aristocratic sneering was the same.

"*Two* chieftains," Philip amended. "This third was some sort of commander."

"Two chieftains," Prince Ricard allowed. "Very good."

Valka had had enough already, and cut in. "Who is Irshan?"

To my surprise, Alexander was the one to answer, saying, "Philip's pet gladiator."

"Irshan!" Philip almost shouted, putting his goblet on the table before him with such force I feared the thing would topple over, "Is a Jaddian Maeskolos of the Fifth Circle! He was the *sulshawar* protector of Prince Constans du Olante, and the finest fighter I, *sirs,* have ever employed." He raised a finger and pointed it square at my face. "And he would use you for a doormat, Marlowe."

I did smile then. My estimation of the two had been quite correct: two bored and pampered aristocrats chafing for want of trial, living out their heroic fantasies through the skill of others. "Sounds fearsome," I said lightly. "Perhaps I shall meet him one day." Turning to Alexander, I asked, "My prince, would you excuse us? We only just arrived and I . . . promised the lady a drink."

A bit sheepish and realizing the scope of the trap he'd pulled us into, Alexander hung his head. "I'll go with you."

We left Alexander not long after we found the wine. Valka drained one glass of red entire and returned the goblet to the servant homunculus before taking another. "How do you deal with such people?" she asked in Panthai, leaning close to minimize the chances we'd be overheard by any of the passing nobility.

"*Chan minte,*" I said. *I don't.* "Better to let them be fools. There are some arguments you can't win without violence. Like I'm always telling you, reason has its limits."

"At least there's wine," Valka said. "I'll need plenty if I'm to survive all this."

"Would you like to dance?" I asked, switching back to Galstani.

Valka snorted. "You know I don't dance." Her smile widened as her eyes picked me over. "You know, I don't think I've ever seen you *not* wearing black."

"It *is* my color," I said, feeling strangely defensive.

"The white doesn't suit you," she said, fingers fussing with the edge of my half-cape. Speaking Panthai again, she said, *"Mand thafar til a dehmuxn en av ni dem."*

It makes you look like one of them.

"I am one of them," I said, smiling down at her.

" 'Tis what you think," she said. " 'Tis not your Emperor supposed to be here?"

Your Emperor, I thought, and did not pause to point out that this particular choice of words walked back Valka's insistence that I was *not one of them,* one of the palatine.

Taking a sip of the wine she'd given me, I said, "He'll make an appearance, but Caesar doesn't mingle."

"Doesn't he?" Valka nearly laughed and threw back the remainder of her glass of Kandarene red as though it were cheap liquor. *"Caesar,"* she said. "You all do like your costumery. Dressing up as the ancients. Wearing their names. Role-playing."

It was not *quite* a dangerous remark, though it bordered on one. "It isn't costumery."

Valka cocked an eyebrow at me. " 'Tis not?" Her smirk remained undimmed.

"There are two sorts of people in the world," I said, leaning one shoulder against a carnelian pillar. The chandeliers above our heads filled the heavenly vaults like constellations of shattered crystal. "Those who accept reality as it is, and those who force reality to be what they will."

"And your Emperor can force reality to be what he wills, is that it?"

"No, Caesar is *Caesar.*"

Valka made a face. "Because he has power."

"No." I reached out with one hand to stroke her tattooed arm. "This is what I was trying to teach Alexander, you know? Power is a part of it, perhaps the greatest part. But Caesar is *Caesar* because *we* believe he is. Reality is built from the bottom up, not the other way round. If the Emperor were not emperor, he could only force himself to be a tyrant."

" 'Tis still a mask," Valka said, dismissive.

"A role," I countered. "A persona."

"A what?" Valka raised her empty glass to draw the attention of a uniformed waiter.

It was a Classical English word—and older than that, it was Latin—and no wonder she did not recognize it. I gave her the Galstani word, then smiling, added, "It means mask."

"Sir Hadrian! Lord Marlowe!" a voice sounded from over my shoulder. Turning, I found a group of young nobiles in bright gowns and more muted suits, cut military fashion but not military proper, with tight collars and short, wide sleeves with bronze metal cuffs on the forearms in lieu of armored gauntlets. The speaker stepped forward and bowed. He had three golden birds embroidered above his heart on a white shield beneath a crown. The sigil looked familiar to me, but I couldn't place it. "Lord Andrew Curzon, sir. My friends and I were wondering . . ." Lord Andrew smoothed his oiled hair back, turning to his friends as if he was afraid to ask his question, "Could we have a holo?" The young nobleman held up his terminal as evidence.

Behind me, Valka snorted again.

"Curzon? Are we cousins? My mother's father was a Curzon." I'd never known the man. He'd died centuries before I was born. Mother and three of her sisters—or was it four?—had been born out of the man's preserved sperm. It was no wonder I hadn't recognized the banner at once. Grandmother never flew it. With Lord Michael dead there'd been no call for it.

The fellow shook his head. "No sir. I'd hoped we were. I checked. He was of the Lassira branch—we went splits seven thousand years ago."

"I see," I said, allowing the fellow to press in beside me.

"Would my lady be so kind as to take the picture?" he asked Valka, who beamed.

Grinning ear to ear at the discomfort I felt creeping its way up my neck, she answered, "Oh, she would be delighted."

As Lord Andrew's friends gathered round, I threw back my cape, rested one hand on the ceremonial saber, and wrapped a jocular arm around the young man's shoulders. One heavily perfumed young lady in a violet gown seized my arm and pressed herself close against me, only heightening my discomfort. Valka covered her mouth to stop from laughing, but I only hoped the young lady would not squeeze too tightly and feel the irregular lattice of my false bones beneath the muscle of my arm. The false bones violated no Chantry law, but they might raise eyebrows and start awkward questions.

"Is it true a Pale prince struck off your head?" the girl whispered in my ear, entirely too close for comfort. "And you grew a new one?"

Is that what I did? I wanted to ask her. To push her away. But I smiled my Marlowe smile. "You shouldn't believe everything you hear on broadcast, madam." I felt the expression freeze as I turned to look to Valka and Curzon's terminal.

"Lord Hechingen says you're a fraud," she whispered, covering her mouth. "Some sort of sorcerer."

"If I were a sorcerer, you shouldn't tell me these things," I said, and she laughed. "Who's Lord Hechingen?"

"One of Prince Hohenzollern's retainers."

Lord Andrew cut in, "Oh, he's one of the old Lions, you know! Stodgy old bastard."

I only arched my eyebrows. The Lions were a coterie of some of the proudest and most venerable houses in the Imperium, men more loyal to the throne than they were to the man who sat upon it, though many were the Emperors who had counted them among their most loyal supporters.

Obedience out of loyalty to the office of the hierarch, I thought, and noting Valka's quizzical look, I said, "Conservative lords."

" 'Tis redundant."

It was my turn to make a face. The Lions weren't truly a political party—such had been illegal since the time of the God Emperor. They were only an informal assembly of the more old-fashioned nobile lords and high princes, counting among their number all three Magnarchs and most of the Imperial viceroys—my late grandmother included. I might have been one myself, had I become any sort of politician. I'd always found the idea of them terribly romantic, stolid knights defending not the false memory of an Empire that never was, but cleaving to the dream of what it might be, whatever its faults. What it must be.

That was something we had in common.

I have of course learned that such men as the Lions seldom live up to their principles. That is the danger of having principles. In politics, principle is like a sword aimed at the heart. Far better, one might be forgiven for thinking, for a lord to have no principles than to risk that he might fall on that sword. The principled man simply has more to lose.

It is what makes them such fabulous villains.

Talk of the Lions recalled the banners I had seen that same day, the ones that had not bowed with the others in recognition of my triumph.

Bourbon.

Mahidol.

Hohenzollern.

But all thought of those men was driven from my mind, for there followed a brief silence in the playing of the orchestra, then the high, clear note—not of horn or trumpet—but of the lonely keening of a single, amplified guitar. The strings joined in a moment later, the keys, each instrument strung together in that lonely anthem called *Far Beyond the Sun*.

The Emperor had arrived.

CHAPTER 30

SELENE

AMID THE SWELLING OF that lone guitar and the crash of cymbals, His Radiance appeared. The Emperor William XXIII entered through a high, round-arched door at the far end of the chamber amid mirrored Excubitors and attendants in every color you could name. Beneath him the whole room was silent but for the wail of that triumphal anthem, prouder and more strange than anything that had played for me in the Campus Raphael. In a great wave that started from the end of the chamber nearest his raised position, everyone knelt. I had to pull Valka down, but she went, dropping as I dropped to but one knee.

Through it all the voice of a herald was raised, high and clear as the crystal overhead. "His Imperial Radiance, the Sollan Emperor William of the House Avent, the Twenty-Third of that Name; Firstborn Son of Earth; King of Avalon; Lord Sovereign of the Kingdom of Windsor-in-Exile; Prince Imperator of the Arms of Orion, of Sagittarius, of Perseus, and Centaurus; Magnarch of Orion; Conqueror of Norma; Grand Strategos of the Legions of the Sun; Supreme Lord of the Cities of Forum; North Star of the Constellations of the Blood Palatine; Defender of the Children of Men; and Servant of the Servants of Earth. And his Lady, the Empress-Consort Maria Agrippina of the House Avent, Princess of Avalon, Archduchess of Shakespeare, and Mother of Light!"

The brief procession ended with the music just as His Radiance drew to the white balustrade and looked down upon us. In a voice barely more than a whisper—a voice amplified not by technology, but by some clever artifice in the construction of the ballroom, our Caesar said simply, "Greetings."

A great tumult of applause went up as the kneeling lords and ladies regained their feet. It seemed an absurd reaction in that moment, clapping for the Emperor where he stood arm-in-arm with Maria Agrippina. I seldom saw the two together—indeed I suspect they seldom saw one another. How similar they appeared, the same ivory complexion, the same rich red hair, each dressed in white and gold dripping with rubies and garnet.

"They could be siblings," Valka said.

"Like the pharaohs of old," I said coolly, sharing her discomfiture. "Or the Jaddians." The Aventine house had—in the royal line—married only itself for more than ten thousand years, relying on the ministrations of the High College to prevent mutation. They were the blood of the God Emperor, after all, and it was said that one day through their breeding he would come again, and that his rebirth would mark the rebirth of Old Earth, and that in his second reign the deserts of Earth would blossom again and the shark no longer starve in the deep waters for want of fish. To that end the Imperial line had kept itself pure for millennia, with the effect that the scions of the House Avent seemed as like to one another as clones, as Philip and Ricard had done.

Just such a collection of clones stood behind the Imperial couple. There was Crown Prince Aurelian, the firstborn, and Princess Irene, the second. And there were others, Faustinus and Matthias, Eleanor and Elara—for whom our Elara was named—and two dozen others. Not all of the more than a hundred royal children were present, but perhaps a third of them. Still more, like Alexander, like Philip and Ricard, had elected to attend the ball despite not being part of the formal entourage, but the rest, I knew, were elsewhere in the Peronine Palace, or at Caliburn House on Avalon, or sleeping in crystal creches on secret Legion bases throughout the Empire to protect that massive and most ancient dynasty from destruction.

All at once, thought of Kharn Sagara floated to the surface of my mind. Of the way the King of Vorgossos protected himself against death through his clones, through his children, and through the mechanisms to which he had sold his soul: Brethren and the lesser daimons that lurked in his own skull. I realized with a sudden flash just where the Undying had gotten his inspiration, and I felt a chill run through me despite the warmth of the hall.

His greeting completed, the Emperor turned with his Empress hand in hand and retreated the way he had come, passing between the cloud of white-garbed princes and princesses and the rainbowed cavalcade of his retainers back along the avenue the Excubitors had lined on the upper level. As I had told Valka, Caesar would not remain to mingle. He lingered a moment, speaking with an Archprior of the Chantry and two scholiast primates in gilt and green, but then he vanished and the Empress with him. Where proud music had accompanied his entrance, only the chiming of silver bells heralded his exit, as though he were Oberon and the dreamy court of Faerie had dissolved like a midsummer's dream.

"What was the point of all that?" Valka sneered. Somewhere in all this she'd found another glass of wine, and watched with gleaming eyes the ebony and carnelian door through which the Imperial person had both entered and left.

"They have to show us they are real people," I said, realizing as I spoke that I echoed something Gibson had told me long ago. "Real people, not some abstract political *concept*." It was only after the words had left my mouth that I remembered. Remembered that those words—that lesson—had not been Gibson's at all.

They were my father's.

"Is something the matter?" Valka asked.

Shaking my head, I answered her. "Ask me about it later." But my own words from earlier resounded in my ears. *I am one of them.*

Valka was wrong to argue that point with me. She squeezed my hand, warm and reassuring. I squeezed back, feeling as she did the strangeness of the bones within and the press of Prince Aranata's ring: dark reminders that I was also *other things*. Vorgossos had taken a piece of me, and Aranata . . . Aranata had taken it all, and what I had, I had only by grace of a miracle and a magic I did not understand. That bright hall with its warm music and warm bodies seemed at once cold and remote as the stars, and I felt as a man who walks out on the sands of a desert beneath alien skies.

Alone.

Alone, but for that warm pressure on my hand, and that smiling voice saying, "Do you see Pallino, there?" She pointed.

The old soldier stood upon a step at the edge of the dance floor, the better to see and be seen by the audience of young nobiles that had gathered round him. Elara leaned on the rail nearby, laughing as my chiliarch gesticulated wildly, sketching formations in the air. I fancied almost that I could hear him over the noise of the crowd and the orchestra:

"So there I was!"

"He seems right at home," Valka said.

I plucked her wine cup from her hands and took a swallow. "People love a good war story, and Pallino knows how to tell them." With the shock of the Emperor's arrival ended, the dancing had resumed, men and women proceeding in stately fashion across the tiled floor. Others resumed feasting at the tables around, or else reclined to drink and talk and listen to the orchestra.

"Lord Marlowe?"

Turning, I saw one of the palace eunuchs standing with two of the Martian Guard. He held a white envelope on a silver tray out before him with the wax seal presented face up. He did not speak, but offered the tray.

I took the letter without comment, turned it over. It had no signature, no mark save the Imperial sunburst in gold foil. "What is this?"

The man said nothing, nor either of his guards. Why should a palace eunuch rate an escort? Or were the guards there for me? When the fellow continued to say nothing I broke the seal and pulled out the letter. It was blank.

A formality.

A calling card?

"What is this?" I asked again, glancing bemusedly at Valka.

"The Princess Selene asks the honor of a dance," the eunuch said.

I felt the flush creep into my face, and again I glanced at Valka. The doctor hid her amusement behind her gloved right hand. I felt a sudden urge to slap the footman's fez from his head. I looked round, half-expecting to see the Princess standing there, but she was nowhere to be seen.

The footman did not wait for any reply—and why should he? I could not refuse. He gestured instead to his companions, "These men will search your person."

"I've already been searched."

The Martians advanced anyway and began patting down my boots, my trousers, feeling their way along my sleeves. "Any weapons?" one of the men asked.

"Yes," I said, remembering one of Pallino's old stories. "I think I'm wearing a sword." I rattled the saber for emphasis.

The Martian did not laugh, and the ivory mask he wore was not smiling. "He's clean."

Helpless, I looked to Valka. "You all right?"

She leaned toward me, one arm wrapped beneath my cape. "I have my wine," she said. "Come find me when you're through *dancing*."

I stooped to kiss her, but she raised a finger and—turning—presented her cheek.

The little toady led me up an arc of marble steps to the platform where the Emperor had made his appearance. The lords and ladies of his entourage by and large yet remained, drinking from fluted crystal and observing the lesser lords below. At once my white outfit—which below had stood out like a star in the black—seemed of little consequence amid the sea of white worn by the royal princes and princesses, and I wished I'd worn my Marlowe black and not the white the Emperor had honored me with.

"You came!" the lilting voice rose to meet me, and the Princess appeared from the crowd of her siblings as if from thin air. She'd been so well camouflaged against the herd of nearly identical royals, and I had not seen her.

Dimly, I was aware that I had not seen the girl in fifty years, but she had not aged a day. She was as impossibly beautiful as her Imperial mother, tall as any lord, with hair not red as copper, but as flame. Her skin was of Petrarchan ivory, her eyes green as the forests of Luin. All the art of the High College was in the jeweled porcelain lines of her body, and the majesty of a thousand generations was in her bearing as she smiled at me, and I bowed. "Your Highness called for me. How could I not come?" Bowing, I hid my smile, and kept my eyes downcast, studying the hem of her gown, which I saw was dusted with pale crystal and the blossoms of pale flowers.

A hand floated into view—her hand. She wore a ring this time, a slim thing of Imperial gold set with a gem. This I kissed as she offered it to me, and I drove back memories of the visions I'd seen of her. "I had hoped you would," she said.

Straightening, I saw she had hidden half her face behind a silk fan. A small knot of onlookers had formed around us, among them the princess's own siblings.

"He's shorter than I expected," said one of the ladies.

Still behind her fan, Selene said, "Hush, Cynthia. Do not mock our cousin."

I had the sudden impression that I was a specimen under the microscope. A slime or interesting bit of fungus brought before the magi's probing eye. A cousin I might have been, but I was the least of cousins, the least star in the blood constellation of Victoria, scion of a house great only in its antiquity—and a disowned scion at that.

Selene collapsed her fan and slid it into a sash that matched the color of her hair. "I watched you at your triumph, Sir Hadrian. You were so gallant in your armor . . . and the Grass Crown. But why have you not worn it to this?" She looked round as she asked, taking in the hall and the thousands present.

My childhood schooling in diplomacy and decorum, schooling I had forgotten many a time on Emesh to my peril, answered for me. "My moment of triumph is over, Highness. I am not so vain as to prolong it unnaturally."

That answer must have sated the onlookers—among whom certainly were to be counted those who considered themselves my enemies—for the stillness about grew less hushed, less total as men and women resumed whatever conversations had occupied them before I had been brought upon the stage.

"So humble!" she exclaimed, a glowing smile springing across her face. "Truly, you are a paragon of restraint, Sir Hadrian."

Bowing my head, I answered, "I am a knight and servant of the Imperium."

"And my servant?" she asked.

Not raising my head, I rested one hand again on the pommel of the ornamental saber. "And yours, Highness."

"Good!" She clapped her hands. "Then your Imperial mistress would have you dance with her. Come!" Then she took me by the arm and led me away from the knot of those highest-born eavesdroppers and we descended by way of the very stair I had climbed. "I am grateful to you, you know," she whispered, leaning ever so slightly toward my ear, filling my head with the heady musk off her perfumed hair.

"Whatever for?" I asked, careful to maintain a composed detachment from her person, as much for my political safety as out of respect for Valka.

Selene answered. "For taking on Alexander. We've always been close, and he *so* admires you. And serving you has given him a chance to be a real knight."

I did not tell her that most of what Alexander had done was sit locked in his quarters aboard the *Tamerlane* while I worked the violence as far away from him as I possibly could. Instead, I said, "You know, it was Alexander who suggested we launch a second convoy to Nemavand to bait the Pale."

"Was it?" She stopped a moment to look me in the face, and I wondered if she had not spent all the years since my departure on ice—so young did she seem. A wide-eyed girl and no woman at all. She jostled me. "Was it really?"

"It was!" I offered a short nod, careful to keep my posture as straight and correct—and my hands as visible—as could be. "It was he who suggested we keep our men on alert to ambush the ambushers."

Smiling, she resumed our descent, moving carefully on pointed shoes. "I am so glad to hear it. Will you be taking him with you? When you leave, I mean." I told her that I did not know, that my fate and Prince Alexander's were alike in the hands her Imperial father. She accepted this as right and proper. We had reached the floor by then, and she turned to face me. By her high breeding and the heels of her shoes, she looked ever so slightly down on me. "I do so wish you'd worn the Crown," she said, and raised a hand to touch my hair just above my ear. She hesitated, remembering where she was perhaps. Her hand fell.

"There are those at court who would take it amiss if I had, Highness."

"Who could take such a thing amiss?" she asked. "You are a great hero, Sir Hadrian. A champion of the realm."

What exactly was going on? Had this princess asked me for a dance out of simple curiosity? Desire? No. No, this was Forum. The wheels of some unseen mechanism moved her—or she had moved them. Echoes of Anaïs Mataro rebounded in my mind, mingled with the visions Brethren had shown me at the Quiet's behest.

Selene of the Aventine.

And Hadrian Marlowe.

Was this . . . courtship? I felt disquiet and a numb upset at the thought. Had not the Empress inquired after my love life on our brief meeting the day I'd come for Alexander? Lorian Aristedes's voice cackled in my ears.

Marry the prince, perhaps.

Or the princess.

Was it the Empress's hand I sensed in this development? I clenched my jaw.

"Sir Hadrian?" she asked, "Why would anyone take your crown amiss?"

Almost I felt I saw the banners looming behind her. Mahidol. Hohenzollern. Bourbon. Still others I could not name. "I'm sure there are several among the great houses who take exception to the honors I've received." I moved closer, taking her left hand in my right, resting my left high on her back. Speaking lips to ear then, I continued, "Particularly when they have been heaped upon one so low as I."

"But you're not lowborn!" she protested. "You and I are cousins, though by how many degrees I cannot even begin to guess." Her chin was nearly on my shoulder then, and the animal and herbal scent of her hair filled my nose. "We are two stars of a constellation, you and I. Who could object to you without objecting to me?"

I led Her Highness through the dance, foot leading foot, her gown belling and swaying as she moved. We whirled deeper amid the crowd of other dancers, falling like a comet toward its star. "I am sure Her Highness knows the story," I said.

"Her Highness does not," she replied, a shade tartly.

"I was *outcaste*," I said, using the old term for the weight of it. "Disowned, disinherited by my father. What rank and title I have I have purely by your father's sufferance."

She was silent then, though she did not pull away, did not break stride in the dance. I was acutely aware of the warmth of her hand and of the flesh beneath my false-boned fingers, and though I did not want to be there, I did not want her to pull away, because for her to do so was to reject what I was entire. In a voice barely more than a whisper, Selene asked, "What did you do?"

"What did I do?" I echoed, adjusting my grip on her hand. "I disobeyed my father. Fled home." Other lords and ladies danced past us: bright gowns and muted suits contrasting our white-and-white. "I wasn't always a knight, you know. I didn't even want to be one. Mine isn't the sort of life one plans."

It had been so long since I'd danced, and while I'd had the requisite training as a boy in Devil's Rest—that had been a lifetime ago. That Hadrian was dead—had died so the Halfmortal might live. How far I had to reach to conjure up the memory of those Gothic spires, those buttressed walls of gleaming black in the silver sunlight, the pencil cypresses and the mighty seawall beneath our acropolis forever holding back the tides. But dance I did, and did not quit or waver much, and if Selene found me an unsatisfactory partner she gave no sign.

"What did you want to be?" she asked.

I supposed I had opened myself up to the question. "I wanted to be a wizard," I said. She did not laugh, and feeling a bit embarrassed, I gave a better answer. "Or a scholiast."

"Really?" She did pull away then, and paused in her dance to look at me. "A scholiast? Why?"

Her reaction ought not to have caught me off guard, and yet it did. I had been so long removed from that antique dream that I had forgotten the stigma that hovered over the profession, that ghost trace of the machine in what it was the scholiasts could do. But I smiled at the princess and shrugged. "I'd wanted to see the universe, be one of the Expeditionary Corps."

"Like Simeon the Red?" She nearly laughed then, and her smile lit her face—though whether she found it amusing or laughed at my expense I was not sure.

"A bit," I answered, closing the distance between us to resume our dance. "I always liked that story."

Selene allowed herself to be led. "I preferred Kasia Soulier," she said, "or Prince Cyrus. Or Kharn Sagara." My left hand clenched involuntarily. "Ow! Watch yourself, sir." I had pinched her flank.

"I'm sorry," I said. "Old wounds. My left arm . . ."

"No, I'm sorry," she said. "I didn't know. Does it hurt?"

"Sometimes," I replied. "It's nothing, Highness. I apologize for startling you. You're not hurt?"

The princess shook her head. "Not at all." We danced together in silence then for some time, staring over one another's shoulders as the orchestra played in its light and dreamlike way. "Are your companions enjoying the ball, sir?" she asked, breaking the uncomfortable silence.

"Those who were allowed in, Highness."

"What do you mean?"

It was my turn to shake my head. It was neither the time nor the place for that battle. There were too many eyes on me, too much weight hanging like chains over my shoulders, and too many cords about my feet. "It doesn't matter," I said, regretting having opened my mouth. "My officers and low-born armsmen were very grateful for the invitation. As am I."

"I am glad to hear it," she said. "I should like to meet them."

"I'm sure one or two is nearby." I swept my gaze over the crowd, looking for a familiar face. Pallino and Elara were no longer by the steps, and of Siran, Corvo, and Durand there was no sign. Aristedes was similarly absent—I had no trouble imagining the intus absconding with a bottle of wine to some darkened gallery of the palace to be alone, or else holding court with a collection of older knights and gentlemen, swapping war stories and criticisms of battles and of commanders long dead. But there were Ilex and Crim, dancing together not far off. The dryad was easily spotted with her green skin and woody hair so brown it was almost black. I made a mental note of their location.

The song ended shortly thereafter, and I stepped smoothly back from Selene's royal person. It would not do to linger close for so many reasons. Bowing, I thanked her for the dance and said, "If Your Highness would like, I believe I saw a couple of my companions. This way." And taking her by the hand this time, I led her round the dancing lords and ladies and through to where Crim and Ilex stood entwined. They were not dancing the stately dance of the high lords, only stood and swayed, their arms around one another, he in his finest black suit, she in gold-fringed brown with flowers in her hair.

"I'm sorry to interrupt," I said, tapping Crim on the shoulder. "The princess asked to meet some of my companions." They came apart and bowed—though Ilex bowed clumsily, being foreign and unused to the motion. They ought each to have knelt, properly, but Selene didn't seem to mind. I introduced them, saying, "Highness, here are Lieutenant Commanders Karim Garone and Ilex, my Chief Security Officer and head of Engineering." I gestured to each in turn with an open hand. "Crim, Ilex, this is the Princess Selene of House Avent."

The princess did not offer her hand for the foreigner and the homunculus to kiss, but smiled politely and said, "I am honored to meet you both." She looked Ilex over with a critical eye—I could feel the tension building in Crim, but he said nothing, nor did I. This was Alexander's sister, after all, whatever that may mean for so large and strange a family as the Aventine. "You are very beautiful," Selene said, touching Ilex's sleeve. "I love your dress."

"Thank you, Majesty."

"Only *Highness*," Selene said.

"Highness," Ilex amended. "You're very kind."

Crim squared his shoulders, one hand on the small of Ilex's back. "She's a fine officer, ladyship."

Princess Selene nodded with Imperial slowness. "No doubt. I am very much honored to meet two of Sir Hadrian's *worthies*." Her politeness did not ebb for an instant, and yet I sensed a hollow, brittle quality to it, as though Crim and Ilex were not what she expected, as if the romance of meeting two of the Halfmortal's famed Red Company had faded when confronted with the real thing.

"Have you seen Valka?" I asked, needing something to fill the air and eager to find her again, if only to put a barrier between myself and this princess and the implication that I suspected some political hand was building between us.

The dryad brushed back her woody hair. "I haven't."

"Not for a while," Crim added. "She was talking to some Consortium representative a while ago, but she might have gone outside. Said the noise was a bit much for her."

Outside.

"This is your paramour, yes?" Selene asked, recapturing my arm.

I turned to look at the princess, smiling my best, politest smile. "She is." There was no denying the Princess Selene was beautiful, powerful, the product of countless generations of refinement and genetic engineering. Perfect as a statue, lovely as Venus and Artemis together distilled through the hand and eye of a thousand painters.

She wasn't Valka.

Anaïs Mataro might have pouted, but if Selene Avent was threatened by mention of Valka she gave no sign. Turning to Ilex and to Crim, she said, "Excuse us. It was lovely meeting you both. I'm sorry for interrupting your dance." Then she led me away, still holding my arm. We came in time to the shallow stair at the end of the ballroom opposite the platform where the highest lords still mingled—where the Emperor had made his brief appearance. She disentangled herself from me then and held my left hand in both of hers. Head bowed, she said, "Thank you for the dance, sir."

I went to one knee then, kissed the ring on her hand. "It was a genuine honor, Your Highness."

"Please rise, Sir Hadrian. You needn't kneel, today of all days."

I rose. She released my hand and—looking down, her hands still folded before her—she added, "I do hope that I might see you again."

All the Imperial armor fell away from her in that moment—for that moment—and I beheld that here was a girl not yet full-come to womanhood. I sensed how much *effort* it had taken her to utter those nine words. Was it fear? Nerves? Or merely the expression of someone else's will?

I could not say.

Bowing, I retreated up one of the shallow stairs and so gained the high ground and the advantage of her. "As my lady commands." But she was *not* my lady. My lady had left the hall, if Crim was to be believed.

And I wanted to find her.

CHAPTER 31

THE CLOUD GARDENS

THE PERONINE PALACE BY night shone with the light of stars and of lamps just as remote. Above the gardens and open colonnades, great empires of cloud rose thousands of miles into the seeming-topless sky. I hurried along a gallery lit by a warm and steady glow and out into the dewy night. Black ivy, silver-edged, grew on an iron trellis to one side, and silent Martians stood sentinel in red and white, their lances keen and flickering with the violet hint of plasma.

Somewhere in the gloaming a minstrel plied the strings of a harp, and the silver sound of it filled the space beneath the columns and the gardens beyond with quiet music. There it mingled with laughter and the hushed murmur of voices.

"Hadrian!" a high voice called. It was Aristedes.

Precisely as I had imagined, the little intus was seated on a sill beneath an arch among a dozen or so men in the black and silver of the Legions. He had a bottle of wine in his hands and brandished it like a scepter as I approached. How had he convinced the servants to part with an entire bottle from the Emperor's collection? He hadn't stolen it, surely?

"My friends! You know Sir Hadrian, *Lord Marlowe,* surely!" He brushed back a limp fall of white-blond hair. "Knight-Victorian, Grass Crown, Order of Merit, honors honors honors . . ." With one hand he sketched an incoherent scribble in the air. "Hadrian, these fine gentlemen and I were just discussing which classical military commander would be best suited to warfare in the here and now—assuming of course they were given a full understanding of the tools and personnel at their disposal. You're a classicist—a classist? Classicist. What say you?" He thrust the wine bottle upward like a sword in challenge.

Surprised by the tangential cut of the question, I blinked at Lorian. "I say I don't know enough about military strategy to answer the question. Besides, wouldn't any ancient commander be at a disadvantage? Combat in space is not the same as combat on sea or land. That rules many of the ancients out."

Aristedes waved this down as though it were an irritating fly. "That was precisely Lord Gannon's point, here—and Lord Carrico had agreed! But they have declined to play my little game and are holding out for more sensible topics of conversation! So forget them!" Here he indicated a pair of quiet nobles, one with graying hair and the other bald and mustachioed. "But you see, my friend Commodore Massa has insisted on old Lord Wellington—a classic—while M. Cambias insists that someone like Gustavus Adolphus, with his readiness to accept and incorporate new technology into his strategy, is suited perfectly to this fish-out-of-water scenario!"

"That all sounds well and good, Lorian, but—"

"But indeed! We've completely neglected the boarding element! Any ship-to-ship situation that's not ended at once and by stealth must come down to boarding once shields are in play. Who then! There are any number of pirates we might choose. Drake, for instance! Someone mentioned Regulus—was that you, M. Rinehart?"

"I said Don John!" said a thin man in the plain black suit of a Legion Intelligence officer. "Drake was someone else."

"You're forgetting Harrington!" said the lone woman in the group, an older officer with hair like curling steel.

Aristedes brandished his bottle. "Harrington wasn't real and you know it, M. Feder! And neither was Wellington! Everyone knows that!" Privately, I thought Aristedes mistaken on that first point, but I said nothing and hooked my fingers into my belt to wait out the manic commander's drunken lecture. "If it comes down to the long knives, you need someone who's good on the ground! Good for his men! Someone like Lord Marlowe here! You know he killed that Pale demoniac with his own hands? I have the suit footage! You should see it!"

"The footage is classified, Lorian." The intus's face fell, and eager to catch him while he gathered himself and bring this digression to an end, I asked, "And who's your answer?" Better to have it over with.

"Pyrrhus!" the commander said.

Both Lord Gannon and Commodore Massa groaned, and one of the others, Rinehart, I think, or Cambias, said, "Pyrrhus got himself killed by a falling roof tile!"

"Pyrrhus set the gold standard in castrametation for centuries—per *Hannibal* himself—and preparation is nine-tenths of ship-to-ship combat—as you well know. Give the man a fleet and the personnel to fly it and you'd be hard pressed to find an equal." Aristedes pointed his bottle squarely at one of the other men's faces. "And don't you start in about McClellan again, Mann! McClellan couldn't win a fight with his enemy's battle plan literally in his lap. He's not a fair comp to Pyrrhus at *all* and you know it. I don't care how good he was at running drills. You're not proving anything."

"Lorian!" I almost shouted, needing to stop the man's manic rush. Any other time I would have found it interesting just how much historical detail had been preserved in the study of war, names and persons remembered at a level of resolution lost in the broader study of things. So much data had sunk into the morass of time, history transformed to legend and myth, and yet certain names and data remained like grains of sand in a broth. But I had no time to reflect on this. I was on a mission, and asked, "Have you seen Valka?"

It seemed to take Aristedes a second to come down from whatever plane he'd rushed onto, but after a moment he said, "Where do you think I got the wine?" He smiled lazily, and I nearly smiled myself. That was one mystery solved.

"Where is she?"

He pointed over his shoulder, deeper into the gardens. "She went that way."

"Thank you. Gentlemen." I bowed slightly and hurried on, ignoring Lorian's words as they followed me out over the garden path.

Great banks of cloud clung to the walls and streamed from the spires above like banners, casting fingered shadows on the starlit glass. Forum had more than a hundred moons, each barely larger than the unfixed stars and twice as bright, filling the night with radiance. The gentle picking of the harp followed me out among the hedges and the blossoms, and somewhere in the gloom a silver fountain played.

I found her at last, sitting on the lip of that fountain, a wine bottle in her hands. She had not been hard to find. The path ran straight past openings in the hedge maze and up a white stair that led back from these lower wards to the palace entrance and the Galath Tree. A lone watch-eye patrolled the airs above, and I thought I spied two of the Martian Guard at their posts on the balcony above.

"Crim said you'd left the ball," I said. "What are you doing out here alone?"

" 'Tis perfectly safe," she said, glowering. "You don't need to worry about me."

"What is that supposed to mean?" I asked, taking a seat on the sill beside her. The night was cool but not chilly, and over the ramparts I could see the great shoals of cloud rising level upon level, spire upon spire into the night air. Off in the distance, dry lightning coiled, and further out the orange gleam of ship drives burned in the night.

She did not speak, but tipped the bottle of wine back and drank, fingernails clicking on the green glass.

"I am sorry about the princess," I said, feeling I should clear the air of that fog at once.

"I don't care about the *princess*," Valka said, enough venom in her words that I could tell she lied. " 'Tis this place I can't stand." She watched me then with one golden eye peering out from beneath her red-black hair. "I can't stand what it does to *you*."

Not prepared for this avenue of conversation, I shifted on the seat, angling to look at her better. "What do you mean, *'what it does to me'?*"

"You are different," she said, resting the bottle on one knee. "Than you were."

"I thought that was a good thing," I said, trying to smile. "I seem to recall you didn't think very much of me, once upon a time."

She snorted, took another swallow of the wine. " 'Tis this place," she said again, and swore in Panthai with such force it raised my eyebrows. "Everyone has a knife behind their smile, and you smile along with the rest of them. 'Tis not who you used to be."

"Who did I used to be, Valka?" It was not the sort of conversation I'd have liked to have in the Cloud Gardens of the Peronine Palace, but I weighed being overheard and recorded against Valka's displeasure. Valka won.

"*Du var pen anaryan,*" she said. *You were a barbarian.* "You hated Emesh as much as I did. The Mataros, that old witch woman . . . Gilliam Vas, and the rest. You weren't one of them."

I placed a careful hand on Valka's knee, but gave no pressure. "Yes, I was."

Had Valka not said as much herself? Was not all the strain in our earliest acquaintance born of this very fact? That I was a palatine lord of the

Sollan Empire—exiled and demeaned, but a lord—and she a Tavrosi demarchist?

" 'Twould not have said that, then," she said, and I knew she was right. "What changed?"

"You know what changed," I said, and to my own ears it sounded as though my words came from a great distance, heard as it were from the depths of some impenetrably dark well. I felt that darkness again, howling in my mind, and saw my headless body tottering before the hulking shape of Aranata Otiolo on a stone shelf beside a lake like glass. I saw too Raine Smythe's torn arm raised above the feasting Cielcin, saw Sir William Crossflane's throat torn out, and heard the screams of dying men. The Cielcin were not the angels I had prayed for, though mankind had proved herself to be the devil I knew.

Neither of us spoke a long while. At length, I reached for the wine. Valka snatched it away, eyes reproachful. "I wish . . ." She trailed off, peered down the neck of the bottle. "I wish things were different."

"Everyone does, in times like these," I said. "But we do not choose the challenges of the day. Only our answers to them."

Quiet again. Wind in the branches and the scent of flowers. The distant sounds of merriment. The splash of the fountain at our backs. The harpist had stopped his playing, and though the world was neither silent nor wholly still I felt as if Valka and I were the only living things on Forum. Though we sat in its beating heart, the Empire was far, far away.

"You should have let me come with you. In the battle."

I felt Valka grow tense beside me, as though she were the string pulled tight on an ancient bow. *There it is,* I thought. There was the thing that bothered her.

"I told you I was sorry," I said. We'd fought about it on Nemavand, and on the *Tamerlane* before we'd gone into fugue for the return journey. "I made a mistake."

"Those soldiers didn't have to die," she said, and I could feel her eyes on me. "I should have been there. You should trust me."

At once it seemed I was falling, as though I'd hurled myself from the ramparts and into endless sky. "I *do* trust you," I said, flailing for a handhold. "I just don't want to lose you."

"I don't want to lose *you*," she shot back. "You're the one who runs head first into these things."

What Aristedes had just said echoed in my ears. "If it comes down to the long knives . . ." I murmured, twisting Aranata's ring on my thumb.

"What?"

"I have to do it, Valka. I have to be there for the men. I need to lead them." I broke off, mindful suddenly of the cameras all around us and the ears behind them. Somewhere in the bushes, a nightingale sang. The sensation of falling had passed, was replaced by the feeling that I floated in some unseen current. The thing the world called *Hadrian Marlowe* was like a suit of armor, a colossus in which I rode that moved of itself. Without me. "What sort of person would I be if I ordered other men to die, without risking myself?" My hand found hers, and I squeezed. "I want nothing more than to leave with you, here and now. Walk beneath the arches at Panormo . . . see the Marching Towers. But you know we can't." And I could say no more, for the ears of the palace were listening, and our talk circled all too near the Quiet, and knowledge of the Quiet was forbidden. Indeed, to talk of leaving Forum with Valka was perhaps dangerous in itself, if Princess Selene's dance was more than a dance, if my guess as to the hand that moved her and its aim was correct.

I was a tool, a faithful knight, a pawn moved by other hands, with no will of my own. And pawns move only forward.

Always forward.

"You still shouldn't have left me on the *Tamerlane*," Valka said, circling back, as if all I'd said were meaningless. "I am not made of glass, Marlowe. I was a soldier, too."

Valka had been a ship's commander for a planetary defense force. She was no fighter, no one to lead a sortie against the enemy. They were not the same thing. But I was not about to tell her that, because she was right. She could have operated the Cielcin machinery better than Cade ever could. But she was wrong, too. She *was* made of glass. It was how she cut me.

I took my hand away from her knee.

"I'm sorry, doctor," I said, answering her distancing language with my own. I wanted to tell her about Selene, about the plans I thought had been set in motion—about what they meant for us. But of all the things we should not talk about in that garden, that was perhaps the chiefest. But the weight of those worries rested heavily on me. "I don't want to lose you," I said again. It was the whole truth, and so there was nothing more to say.

Neither of us moved for a long while, each mindful—or I at least was mindful—of the space between us. Wide as the no man's land between armies, though a child might have struggled to fit between. Looking down, I discovered that I'd been clenching my left hand. The knuckles stood out white in the dimness, but the false bones and carbon tendons did not ache with strain. I felt nothing, as though it were the hand of a stranger. I studied my hands then. The left that Kharn had given me, the right Aranata had taken away. The hand the Quiet had restored. The white scars from the corrective brace I'd worn as a child shone like stars beneath the marks of newer wounds. The left hand was clean. I cradled the left with the right, felt the brush of my thumb against the palm. I tried to crack my knuckles, but the false bones would not be moved.

I had lost a piece of myself, and feared to lose more.

The other hand, the head—again—the heart that was with Valka.

Not for the first time, I wondered if Lorian was right. Perhaps I was a replica, a changeling built by Sagara. I had awoken on the *Demiurge,* after all. But I remembered my right arm lying on the stone of the lakeside, remembered holding the same hand up to my face, flexing the fingers. I remembered also the sword Prince Aranata had carried as it hunted after Valka on the hills of the meadow aboard Kharn's black ship. My sword.

There had been two swords, for a moment, just as there had been two hands.

I have often wondered if Valka's special brand of magic allowed her to read minds—or if her clairvoyance was only a symptom of just how long we had been together. For though neither of us spoke, she pushed the wine bottle into my hands. Taking it, I drank. It was a Kandarene red, dry and spicy, a cousin to the bottles Sir Elomas had brought with us from Borosevo to Calagah so long ago. A cousin to the bottle we had shared that night on the seashore when the Cielcin fell from the sky and the war—my war—had begun. Tasting it I felt almost I could peer across the years and the light-years and spy that younger Hadrian, as one catches a glimmer of movement in the corner of a mirror.

I hoped he could not see me.

"Maybe you're right," I said, handing the bottle back. "Maybe I have changed."

"Take my word for it, *anaryan*," she said, and cocked an eyebrow. "I'm something of an expert on the subject." As she spoke, she scooted along the marble sill between us until the warmth of her thigh bled through her dress and warmed my own. "I'm cold," she said.

"Shall we go in?"

"No."

Wordlessly, I reached under my right arm and undid the baldric that secured my cape. Knowing full well what she wanted, I drew off the heavy white-on-white jacquard, which—just as I had done with my old coat in the dungeons of the Undying—I draped over her slim shoulders, careful to keep the hem out of the water. After a moment, I said, "I'm not sure white's your color, either."

" 'Tis most certainly not," she said, but drew the garment closer with her tattooed hand. So dark and beautiful was she, like an image of the witch Ayesha reborn, and so severe that even swallowed by my cape she seemed regal as any queen.

Broken smile returning to my face, I said, "I love you."

"You're not wrong," she said, and matched my smile. I did not sit again, but stood listening to the music of the night wind. Sheets of cloud rolled over us, spun swirling up into the moons-lit dark. A great bank of it rolled from the ramparts above, so that the palace about seemed espaliered in rosy cloud. Valka broke the quiet. " 'Tis not all bad, you know?"

"What's not?"

She stood. "You."

A short laugh escaped me as she drew near. "Oh. Is that all?"

Her smile bared just a glint of tooth.

She kissed me a moment after. Her fingers seized on my belt and kept me close. I tasted wine again. Kandarene red. Pepper and spice and the memory of Emeshi nights. Of Calagah and the young man I had been.

At length we broke apart, and she said, "I liked what you told the prince, you know? On Gododdin."

"About Ilex and Aristedes?" I asked. "I always believed that."

Valka narrowed her eyes, as if she did not believe me. "I could have strangled those other princes."

Cold fire shot down my spine, and I grabbed her by both shoulders. "You shouldn't say such things." I glanced over my shoulder, half-expecting to see the nearest Martians abandoning their posts to come collect us both.

"You heard how they talked about me!" Her hand tightened on my belt. "It makes me *so* angry that some people can just . . . *say* these things and get away with it." Gold eyes narrowed. "That's one of the things about you that changed, you know? You fought a man once for calling me a witch, but you just stood there."

"You wanted me to *fight* them?" I asked, incredulous. There was a part of Valka that had never forgiven me for attacking Gilliam Vas over her honor. "Those men were princes of the Empire, Valka. There wasn't anything I could do."

"You could have said *something*!" she said, releasing me. "You just stood there like a good little *subject* and let them both call me a whore."

"I can't challenge an Imperial prince, Valka!" I exclaimed. "Are you trying to get me killed?"

She sniffed. "You challenge that brat Alexander all the time."

"Alexander *is* a brat," I agreed. "He's an arrogant prick. But he's my squire. It's my duty. I don't want him hanging around any more than the rest of you. You think I like having him around?"

There came a sharp intake of breath from the stair behind me, and I turned in time to see a shock of red hair retreating back down the steps toward the palace. My heart sank, hit the core of the planet beneath me before I heard Valka say what I already knew was true.

" 'Twas Alexander." She took a step past me to look down the winding stair toward the ballroom and the hedge maze down below. "He must have been listening."

The angry coals that had flared in my belly a moment earlier grew cold and slimy. I shut my eyes. The greatest part of me screamed to run after him, but I knew doing so would only make me seem the guilty lick-spittle, and would avail nothing.

The damage was done.

Something of my newfound terror must have scrawled itself across my face, for Valka softened and—I think—understood. She was nodding steadily, and lifting the remnants of the bottle to her lips she drained it all away. "Now *I'm* the one who's sorry. I forget sometimes just what this place is like." Valka turned and thudded the bottle down on the sill of the fountain, eyes turned up to take in the bronze seraph that stood upon the plinth, flaming sword upraised, his six wings spread wide and defiant. "We should go home."

CHAPTER 32

LIONS

THE WEEK OF CELEBRATIONS at last concluded, I retreated to orbit and the *Tamerlane*. I knew I would be called before Legion Intelligence to give further reports on Iubalu before long, on the disposition of the legions at both Gododdin and Nemavand, and on the recordings from what the propagandists in the Ministry of Public Enlightenment were calling the *Battle of the Beast*. I'd seen some of the film clips already. Composed perhaps of one part genuine footage to ten parts computer generation, they showed the heroic Devil of Meidua and his noble soldiers in their battle against the Cielcin—a battle equal parts cunning strategem and desperate struggle. The best of these was called *The Demon in White,* which showed a highly fictionalized account of my battle with Iubalu intercut with footage of the triumph in the Campus Raphael. The footage from the triumph, at least, was entirely genuine, and I was delighted to see that—though they had not been permitted to enter the Peronine Palace—Barda, Udax, and the other Irchtani had not been omitted from the war films.

A week of waiting dragged to two, then to a month. The calls came only rarely, and Alexander never came. There was no word from Selene, either, nor from any of the Imperial house. Caesar and his Olympian ilk had forgotten their pet hero, or so it seemed.

I slid back into my classic routine, arising early to take my breakfast alone in the officers' mess before my exercise and my rounds of the ship—listening to my reading as I walked. By then Valka would awaken and I'd return to our apartments for lunch—her breakfast—after which we would talk or review some piece of work regarding the Quiet or pore over data recovered from Iubalu's ship.

We'd disabled the vessel, and Mahendra Verus has remained behind to oversee the mop-up. It was not often that one of the Cielcin worldships was taken intact, and an enormous amount of arms and artifacts had to be sorted through, cataloged, and understood. We had much work to do, for I had requisitioned copies of all the texts we'd recovered from the ship and had combed over them with Valka for anything, any scrap that might better illuminate the connection between the Cielcin and the Quiet.

We found nothing.

Iubalu's was a warship, and carried nothing that might light our way or answer our questions.

Reader, I shall not bore you with the details. The countless hours of reading, nor the longer hours of meetings I came to attend at the behest of Legion Intelligence and the Ministry of War. I shall linger only briefly with Director Breathnach and Lord Bourbon, for they return to our stage.

"And the beast knew you?" Breathnach asked, looming over me from his place in the center of the arc of table beside Augustin Bourbon.

Turning from the previous questioner to face the Lord Director of Legion Intelligence, I said, "I have already told you that it did." There is a certain degree of redundancy packed into every military inquest, but sometimes I think the men like Breathnach enjoy it.

Lorcan Breathnach brushed the glowing holograph panels that hovered before him aside with the air of one sharpening an ax. "And did you know *it*?"

"As I indicated in my initial report, lordship," I hooked my thumbs through my belt and stood with feet apart, happy to once again be wearing my customary blacks, "the creature and I had never met before. Its familiarity with me appears to have been a consequence of my reputation."

Bourbon's grumbling voice interrupted, "Your reputation?"

"Yes, my lord. You might have noticed it yourself." It was all I could do to keep a wan smile from my face.

"You did not encounter this creature at Arae?" asked a senior logothete I recognized as M. Rinehart, one of Lorian's compatriots.

"Messer, if I had, it would have died at Arae with the others."

"Or perhaps on one of your sojourns among the Extrasolarians?" Rinehart asked.

Breathnach's nasal tone cut through this cross-examination. "And yet you seemed to understand its frankly . . . insane statements easily enough."

He peered down at what I assumed was the transcript of my exchange with the *vayadan*-general. "This talk of *Watchers . . . Makers* and the like."

Eyes shut, I took a measured breath before responding. "Your lordship will recall that I am an expert on the subject of the Cielcin and their culture—or near as any man may claim. You can find explanations for all of this in my report." The last thing I needed was to face a Chantry Inquisition, and so everything I knew—and all Valka's notes—were kept locked in a safe on the *Tamerlane* or encrypted in the neural lace within her head. There was more I could say, but nothing I should. I did not, for example, explain that I believed the references to Prince Syriani's visions were genuine.

Better to be believed mad, or a charlatan.

"Nevertheless, the fact remains this prince, this . . . Aeta . . ." Breathnach stumbled over the alien word, "seems to have an unusual fascination with you. I don't know what to make of that."

I thrust out my chin and answered, "Neither do I."

"I find that hard to believe," said Augustin Bourbon, peering gimlet-eyed down at me. "You seem to have an opinion about everything."

"Call it an occupational hazard," I said stiffly, eyes sweeping over the panel before. Fifteen in all, a dozen men and three women arranged in an arc that closed about me like the limbs of an advancing army. Twice as many white banners hung on the wall behind them, each depicting the Imperial sunburst above the shield symbol of the Legion Intelligence Office. The impression given was one of superhuman impartiality and control—a strange backdrop for what felt so deeply petty and personal.

"According to the transcript this chieftain . . . Dorayaica, is that how you say it? Dorayaica intends to unite the Cielcin clans," Bourbon said. "Do you think it can?"

I looked down at the tiles between my feet, marinating. "The *vayadan*-general seemed to think so, lordship. It speaks like a fanatic in the transcript, but I think we should take it at its word. The Cielcin dominate by acts of violence, but they break totally in defeat. If Dorayaica can best the other princes in warfare, he will find himself with new lieutenants and a larger and larger force with which to challenge us." I held one hand out like a blade, palm up as I'd been taught. "This so-called *Prophet* is not like any other Aeta we have encountered. His attacks have been measured, calculated. He's shown an understanding of our tactics, our infrastructure, our psychology. He is not simply raiding us like wolves might raid a sheepfold. The attack on Hermonassa, on the shipping lane across the Centaurine Gulf . . . these demonstrate a clear understanding of our methods, an understanding only compounded by his willingness to align with the Extrasolarians."

"Could arrangements be made with the other chieftains? Alliances? In return for their independence?" asked Sir Friedrich Oberlin, the quiet, junior man who had always seemed so favorable to me.

I had to chew this one over a moment, one hand still tucked into my belt. "It's possible. During the Vorgossos affair, Prince Aranata was willing to consider a joint operation to attack the other clans. Hasurumn and Koleritan were mentioned by name. Perhaps two of the larger clans? The Cielcin will never agree to an equal partnership, but it might be possible."

"Decapitating this threat from Dorayaica seems like our best course."

"You're assuming we can," I said acidly, raising my hand again. "With respect to Sir Friedrich, this talk of alliances is all well and good, but we have no means, no method for contacting the Cielcin, nor especially for locating a particular *scianda*. First Strategos Hauptmann saw to that." I clamped my jaw shut. The sting of Hauptmann's attack on Prince Aranata's worldship still rankled despite the long decades. I knew perfectly well that we would never have made peace with the chieftain, but we had lost not only a temporary ally in the form of one Cielcin clan, but the aid of Vorgossos as well. And as much as the memory of Kharn Sagara chilled my blood, there was no denying the man had knowledge which no one in the entire Sollan Empire possessed.

"Perhaps the Halfmortal will find us a way," Director Breathnach sneered. A few of the junior logothetes laughed nervously as the old patrician smiled. "Do you see no way forward with these *visions* of yours?" He looked left and right, soliciting further laughter from his compatriots. M. Rinehart, to his credit, only narrowed his eyes. Sir Friedrich looked down at his papers. "Did not this clairvoyance of yours deliver the enemy into your grip, Lord Marlowe? That is what they say."

I opened my upraised hand. A kind of shrug. "I am not responsible for what they may say, Lord Director. I do not have visions. The Earth and her oracles do not speak to me. You gave me an impossible task, and I succeeded. Was I meant to fail?"

Neither Breathnach nor Bourbon answered me—nor any of their subordinates.

I knew the answer.

We all did.

CHAPTER 33

THERE ARE ENDINGS

"I CAN'T BELIEVE THEY'VE still not given us new orders," Pallino said, voicing aloud the thought that had been at the back of mine and everyone else's minds for more than two months. The once-old chiliarch reclined on a low couch against the far wall of my quarters, hands behind his head, staring blankly at the holograph opera unfolding on the plate before us.

Returning from the lift with another bottle of wine, Elara said, "I don't know . . . it's nice to have another break, isn't it?" She seated herself at the end of Pallino's couch and busied herself refilling the wine cups that congregated on the table.

"Hear hear!" Siran said, leaning in to place her cup with the others and pinch a piece of the spiced Jaddian cheese Elara had sent one of the servants to acquire in the city markets. Her cup recharged, she lifted it. "To not fighting for our lives for once!" Elara joined her, and from his spot on the couch, Pallino raised an agreeing fist, but kept his eyes on the holograph plate. On it, an ancient knight in metal armor vaulted over a castle wall just as the ramparts were engulfed in flame and a dragon landed on the battlements, its massive claws crushing stone and corpses alike.

Valka shifted where she lay against my chest, but said nothing. I was sure she slept.

On the holograph, the dragon moved to devour a group of women cowering in a ruined hall. Its jaws opened! Fire flared blue-white in the gloom! A knight fell from the rafters above, and with his shield held the dragonfire at bay, shouting, "Go!"

It was one of my mother's operas—though I told this to no one. Oft times when we put in to some Imperial harbor I would search them out, discover that she had made another one or several while I journeyed between the stars. More often than not I would watch them alone, but on rare occasions I would share them with the others—when I found I could not be alone.

"Isn't it nice, Had?" Elara asked, all smiles.

"Keep it down!" Pallino exclaimed, the picture of focus.

Unbothered by Pallino's interjection, Elara asked again, "Don't you think it's nice?"

Smiling, I answered her, "Elara, Pallino's trying to watch the holograph."

She threw a cheese at me. I let it hit the couch above my shoulder before eating it. "I'm only grateful there's been no word from Alexander."

"Do you think he'll *do* something?" Siran asked, sitting back in her chair and cradling her wine.

"No idea!" I said. "But you saw what he's like."

We sat quietly a moment then—much to Pallino's relief, I'm sure. One of the knights in the opera had jumped upon the dragon's back with sword in hand and thrust the point downward.

"Well, I don't think anything will happen," Elara said. She crossed her legs and rested one hand on Pallino's knee. "You're too valuable, Had. So you called the prince a brat. He *is* a brat. The Emperor's not going to cast you aside over something like this, surely."

Mirroring Pallino's posture of calm repose, I replied, "It's not the Emperor I'm worried about."

"What, you think the boy's going to call for your head or something?" Elara did not seem convinced.

"That *boy* is a prince of the Sollan Empire," I said. "He wouldn't be the first to execute a favorite toy no matter what the Emperor said."

Siran spoke over me. "All the more reason to get out of here and have done. I don't know about you all, but I'm tired of fighting." The whites of her eyes glowed in the dragonfire burning on the holograph.

With a heavy groan, Pallino reached out and slapped the controls to pause the opera. One of the knights—his shield lost and his helmet—stood alone before the dragon on a narrow bridge. The other, who'd mounted the dragon, had fallen off at some point and stood behind with the others, covering the retreat of the princess and the other courtiers. He said nothing, but crossed his arms, staring at each of us with his two, blue eyes.

"I should be an old woman now," Siran said, one hand going reflexively to her nose. When she'd been elevated to patrician standing, her mutilated nostril had been repaired, erasing her past crimes. Like Pallino's restored eye, it marked a kind of rebirth, a second life for my old friend. I understood how she felt. Though we palatines might live seven centuries, there is some ancient part of us that remembers we should have died in one tenth the time.

The ancients esteemed the proper span of a man's years at three score and ten. Seventy. Siran had numbered about half that when we met and Pallino nearly equaled that number. Their patrician enhancements had restored them to the prime of life and kept them there for decades, but such after-market gene tonics and surgeries would hold only so long.

"I feel it, too," I said. "I feel old." How young I was, then! But then, I'd felt old before I was thirty, as so many do. It is a folly all of us commit. We imagine youth old age because we cannot imagine age. I am old now, and know I was young—so terribly young—then. I was not yet two hundred. Not yet one-fifty.

I did not know the meaning of the word.

Sometimes I think of Kharn Sagara, who I think must be the oldest man in existence—the oldest ever to exist. Small wonder that he is insane. Discovering new depths of time and age would madden anyone, may madden me in time.

"Do you want to stop?" Pallino asked, peering at me with one eye closed so that it seemed I looked at the older Pallino—the younger one—grizzled and gray-haired. I could almost picture the worn leather patch again, hidden by the shadows. Then he opened his eye, and the illusion faded.

"No," I said. "The work's not done."

"No one would blame you, you know," Elara said.

Pallino agreed, "Aye. You've done more than anyone has for this bloody war. You're a lord again. You could retire to some nice palace or country villa and fuck your peasant girls raw until that hair of yours goes gray, lad. None would fault you. Ouch! Damn it, woman!" It seemed Elara had sunk her nails into his leg.

I shook my head, glad Valka was asleep. "That isn't me."

"No," Pallino agreed, "you like to be miserable. Would you stop?" He glowered at Elara, who smiled innocently.

"Only if you behave."

"Behave? I just wanted to watch the holograph. You all had to start talking and ruin it!"

Elara smoothly ignored this, and shook her head. "We're all tired. I get that. I never thought I'd be in a place like this. On Forum. On a ship at all. Never thought I'd go to a ball at the Imperial Palace!" She was grinning, as if all the years we complained of had fallen away in an instant. "I thought that sort of thing only happens in fairy stories. Growing up in the city, you learn all knights and lords are bastards, you learn not to believe in this." She gestured at the room around us. Elara and Siran both had been born on Emesh, in the sweating canal city of Borosevo.

I remembered it well, remembered it as a time and place as far from fairy tales as heaven was from hell. But I have lived a long time, and with each passing decade the muggy streets of Borosevo seem to me less real than even the airy halls and soaring towers of Forum, as if they too were only a story. As if we were all stories in the end.

"I don't know about the rest of you," Siran put in, "but I can't do this forever. I want to stop before I'm old. Old again, that is." Her eyes swept over Elara and Pallino, over Valka sleeping against my side. "Always thought I'd have a family." Was that longing in those black eyes? Sadness? Regret? I was doubly glad that Valka slept. That very question hung between us, dampened by my palatine genes and Valka's lack of desire. Down that road lay a place neither she nor I dared look, and feelings we dared not name.

"Do you want to leave?" I asked, not angry, not resentful. Only wondering.

"Yes," she replied, voice stiff. She would not look me in the face. "But not today."

I did my best to smile, and looked from her to Pallino and Elara. I did not dare put the question to either of them. I feared their answers would be the same.

There are endings, Reader, but this is not one of them.

Not yet.

CHAPTER 34

MAJESTY, MONARCH, PROPHET, PRINCESS

I SURRENDERED MY SWORD and shield-belt at the gates of the Peronine Palace and allowed myself to be led by white-and-red armored Martians down uncounted halls to a tramway that ran out over a bottomless gold cloudscape to a lonely white tower detached from the palace proper. As we rode I looked out and down upon the unrolled city and the great bulwark of sails that—with the weather satellites—sheltered it all from the coriolis winds. Far off, a massive warship—a hundred miles long—loomed above the topless towers and aqueducts like the dragon in Mother's opera, black as a piece of the night and gleaming in the sun.

Soon enough we came to a stop, and mirrored Excubitors escorted me up a stair of flowing marble and along white-pillared halls to a door of pale stone so pure I touched my pendant through the front of my shirt and formal jacket, mistaking it for the same substance.

But it was only a door, and rolled into a pocket in the wall at a silent command.

When I hesitated, one of the Excubitors gestured for me to go inside. I could see my face reflected in his mirrored helmet, image distorted past all hope of recognition by the curve of cheekbone and slant of sculpted nose.

He did not speak. They never spoke, only subvocalized to one another, words relayed by suit comm.

Obedient, I bowed to the masked man and went within.

The Imperial study ran along the center of the tower, rising for several levels to a frescoed dome painted to match not the rose-gold of Forum, but the blue skies of Earth. Level upon level of ring-walk balconies overlooked the middle space, supported by white pillars and black iron arches done in floral arcs and curls. Ancient books stood on display under glass, their brown and yellow leaves climate-controlled and carefully lighted, and where the walls were not given over to the shelves or to the narrow windows that pierced the spiraling outer colonnade, dark bronze statues stood, each holding a sword that pointed inward toward the Table.

In the shadow of one of these I stopped, hesitating an instant, surprised to see the pentangle shield and the name carved in Classical English lettering: *SIR GAWAIN.* Turning my head, I stopped and looked to the statue nearest me on the other side. *SIR LANCELOT.* I guessed then I could name the others. Percival, Bedivere, Gareth, and Kay. Gaheris and Galahad. Tristan and Palamedes.

The Knights of the Round Table.

Figures from the Cid Arthurian mystery cult were among the last things I expected to see in the heart of the Peronine Palace, at the seat of Imperial rule, in the possession of the living Son of Earth, direct descendant of the God Emperor.

"Come forward, Marlowe," came the voice Imperial.

I advanced until I stood just on the edge of the center of the chamber and bowed but did not kneel. Our audience was a private one and my rank accorded me the small dignity of keeping my feet.

"Radiant Majesty," I said, raising my eyes without straightening. "You called for me?"

His Imperial Radiance William XXIII, Firstborn Son of Earth and all the rest, looked up from his contemplation of the papers before him and offered me a stiff nod of acknowledgment. He wore a suit of arterial scarlet, unrelieved by any color save the white armband that showcased the Imperial sun and the gloss black of his boots. The outfit ought to have muddied the color of his hair, but it only added to the overwhelming impression of *redness* our Emperor exuded, casting his color like light on the white chamber around him.

He was not alone; logothetes in gray robes with matching caps clustered around him, some of them clutching tablets, others with terminal pickups in their hands or pinned to their clothes. More than one green-garbed scholiast stood among them, all silently watching. I'd gotten the impression they'd fallen silent the moment the door had opened, for they stood with that awkward tension unique to the newly interrupted and shuffled back against the walls.

All eyes on us both, the Emperor said, "Yes, thank you. Do have a seat, Lord Marlowe. We were just discussing the disposition of the Centaurine border." He made a discreet gesture with one gloved and beringed hand, and at once the logothetes and scholiasts began to filter out of the room.

"There've been more attacks along the inner edge of the arm. Five planets razed and emptied."

I seated myself in the nearest chair facing the Emperor, wincing slightly as the legs groaned on marble tile. I hadn't heard, hadn't had a meeting with LIO and the War Council in weeks, hadn't had so much as a word of the situation in the outer provinces. "Is it Dorayaica?"

I ought properly to ask no questions of His Radiance, but the Emperor did not seem to mind. "We think not. They happened in rapid succession and within a few dozen light-years of one another. Dorayaica's movements have been more precise. Punctuated. No." Not looking at me, the Emperor shuffled a few of the pages on the table before him. He did not sit. "There have been rumors of a new chieftain among the Extrasolarians. Muddled references to a *Monarch* on the datanet and from a number of our informants. Apparently several of the old stations we've kept eyes on have disappeared. Whether this *Monarch* is a man or something else entirely is entirely unclear, but the name *Calen Harendotes* appears as well, several times. Are you familiar?"

"Calen Harendotes?" I repeated. "No, Your Radiance. It sounds like a palatine name."

"It does. Doubtless some renegade from a house no one's ever heard of," the Emperor said. "A pity. We had hoped your time on Vorgossos might have shed some light on the matter."

"*Monarch* could be the name of one of their Sojourners," I said, referring to the class of massive ships owned by the most powerful Extrasolarian agencies. "Regardless, you think this *Monarch*—Harendotes or no—is behind these new attacks in Centaurus?"

"It is too soon to say. We fear we may have a new name to add to our growing list of enemies. If the Extrasolarians are taking the field, particularly if they are aligned with the Cielcin, we may have to fight on two fronts."

I swallowed, nodded. Full-scale war with the Extrasolarians would be a nightmare. The barbarians were distributed throughout all of human settled space, dwelling in star systems without habitable planets or on ships and stations in the dark between the stars. An attack might come from anywhere, and though the Legions and local defense fleets were more than a match for any ragtag armada, a systemic attack against the Empire at points could be crippling, even lethal. And if this *Monarch,* this Harendotes was gathering the Extras to himself . . . that could be just what he was planning. In the case of the Extras, as with the Cielcin, their primary weakness was their disunity. The Cielcin were tribal, the Extras anarchists or the devotees of petty warlords like the Normans. United, either might prove a serious threat. Together . . . they could burn the stars.

"What do you make of it, Marlowe?"

I did not answer the Emperor at once, but rubbed my eyes, feeling at once the terrible weight of years. Breath shuddering, I said, "Well, they make a likely couple, don't they?"

"I'm sorry?" The Emperor's royal *we* slipped. I felt the temperature in the room drop, and was glad the logothetes and scholiasts had all been dismissed.

"The Monarch and the Prophet," I answered him, holding out my hands as though they were the pans of a scale. "Syriani Dorayaica and this Harendotes. Times of strife breed pretenders and false kings, and it seems to me that both our greatest enemies are rebuilding themselves in our image. In yours." I made a weak gesture, intending to point at His Radiance but realizing that to do so would be the gravest insult. "May I ask a question?"

The Emperor opened velvet-gloved hands.

"The statues," I said, nodding toward the likeness of Sir Tristan over the Emperor's shoulder, "and this table . . ."

"What?" William XXIII's brows contracted, expecting some insolence perhaps or annoyed by the tangential slash of the question.

"They're Cid Arthurian icons, aren't they?"

"What?" the Emperor said again. "How dare you! First you insult our son, and now this?"

I had stepped out upon a frozen lake, and the ice beneath me was rotten. So he had heard about the incident with Valka in the Cloud Gardens. There was nothing for it. I stood smoothly and bowed low as I could. "Apologies, Honorable Caesar. It's only . . . you know the story? Arthur and his knights?"

Though I did not look up, I could hear the Emperor bare his teeth. "We are a direct descendant of Arthur, boy. Of course we know the story."

The Aventine House has always claimed this patrimony: from the God Emperor William to Victoria, from Victoria to Arthur and *The Matter of Britain,* but I thought and think it unlikely. Accounts from the Golden Age are muddy, artifacts scattered, but I do not think the blood of Arthur flowed in Victoria's veins. But I sensed my time and His Radiance's patience were fast nearing their limits, and standing up straight again I said, "It only strikes me that what's happening here is the same. Dorayaica and his Iedyr Yemani, his generals . . . this Harendotes, too. Gathering their knights. And I wondered."

The Emperor relaxed visibly, rested one hand against the surface of the round table. "These were our legends long before the Cid Arthurians took them."

"Forgive me, Radiant Majesty," I said, "I did not know." I know better now, have learned to distinguish the Arthur of antiquity from the Arthur-Buddha of the mystagogues. The Emperor made a gesture like waving away a fly. Into the space between us, I rapped my knuckles against the tabletop and said, "I only meant to remark upon the parallel.

"You think it significant?" His Radiance lifted both eyebrows, watching me from across his round table. "An omen?"

"I am not sure I believe in omens, Caesar." I bowed my head, placed the false-boned fingers of my left hand against the surface of the table. The wood—though petrified—was so ancient it was worn away, the ridges standing like the brindled hair of some beast, and I guessed it had been taken from Earth herself long before the planet was consumed in nuclear fire. Did I dare tell him? "But I have seen their armies marching across the stars, and the Pale King leading them. This Prophet of theirs."

The King of Avalon and Guardian of the Solar System mirrored me, placing one hand on the table opposite me. "You asked that soldier from Hermonassa if Dorayaica wore a crown."

"Yes, Radiance." I looked away sharply, as though the Emperor cast too bright a light on my face.

"Had you seen it before? Dorayaica, I mean."

"Yes, Radiance," I answered. "You have read my reports from Vorgossos?"

The Emperor orbited the table, swinging back into my line of sight, a bloody spot against the stark white of stone and ebon bookcases. "A synopsis."

"Then Your Radiance knows that on Vorgossos I was . . ." I was about to say *touched,* but checked myself. "I encountered what I believe was a surviving Mericanii artificial intelligence. One of their supercomputers."

"I do," he said. No *we.*

Without alluding to the Quiet—I had made no reference to them in my report—I continued, "I do not have visions, Radiance, but I was shown one. A calculation, I suppose it was." The Brethren had, in fact, shared many predictions of its own, composite prophecies compiled as an *approximated probability of reality,* though my vision had been something far more total. "It had run simulations of the galaxy's future. Of our future. And it predicted this. Predicted Dorayaica would emerge in response to our war effort. An answer from the Pale." I was walking a fine line, attempting to describe my vision without describing its proper source, a source which I feared no man—particularly the Sollan Emperor—would believe.

"You think this daimon is credible?"

Remembering something both Brethren and Sagara's golem had said to me, I said, "Daimons cannot lie, Radiance. If they could, they would be of no use to their masters."

The Emperor accepted this—believing or no—with a bare nod and narrowing of his eyes. Glancing up to the frescoed sky nine stories above, he asked, "And did this daimon say what would come of us?"

Light. The memory of the oracle Jari shouted in my mind. *Light! Light! Light!*

"No, Radiant Majesty," I lied, but lied only because I did not fully understand what any of it meant.

William Avent turned away, hands clasped behind his back. He strode across the checkerboard tiles until he stood beneath the statue of Sir Percival. One hand on the knight's sculpted sabaton, he said, "They say you are a sorcerer, Lord Marlowe." He asked no question, and I had nothing to say. "I do not believe in sorcery. There is no sorcery. There is only knowledge, however strange or hidden it may be. But you recognized *something* in that soldier's report, that I must grant you." He sighed deeply, and for an instant I beheld that beneath the Imperial silk and samite, beneath the scarlet, the argent, and the gold, there was only an aging palatine, his shoulders slumped with the weight of centuries and star systems. No one man was meant to rule so vast an Empire, and that old William bore that weight so nobly and with no complaint was a credit to him. Stern as His Radiance was and solemn, I confess a deep admiration for the man, who in all the years I knew him was never cruel or cowardly. His mother, the late Empress, had chosen well from among her children. Always he seemed to me the picture of the philosopher-king, like old Winston the Good, like Raphael, like Marcus Aurelius: tired, world-weary, and wise.

That weariness escaped him all in a great rush. His shoulders hunched, he said, "But none of this is why I called you here. Will you not sit again, please?" He turned, offered a seat with a gesture. I sat, and waited. The Emperor stood opposite me, looking down the bridge of his aquiline nose.

"Do you know what the most interesting thing about this tower is, Sir Hadrian?"

"No, Radiance."

"It is the only place in the Peronine Palace—perhaps the only place on all of Forum—that is not monitored. It is one of the only places where I can be truly *alone*. That is why my Excubitors take their posts at the door so seriously." He smiled thinly, a smile that betrayed the great age beneath that young-seeming face like sunlight through old vellum. "I tell you this so you understand: we are not having this conversation. Not officially."

I sat a little straighter, hands gripping the arms of my chair.

The Emperor continued. "There are those on my council and in my ministries who believe that you are a problem. These individuals believe that your popularity with the people—most especially your popularity with the *Legions*—should be treated as a direct threat to me. That in addition to Dorayaica and this Extrasolarian Monarch, *you* ought to be considered another pretender—to borrow your word—another false king."

I opened my mouth to protest, but His Radiance raised one gloved and glittering finger. "But I do not agree with them." His eyes narrowed again, and a smile halfway between laughter and rage stole over his face. "No one plotting against me would be so foolish as to call my son a *brat* where I was certain to hear about it."

"My lord—Your Radiance, I . . ." Color surely flooded my face, and I made to rise.

"Sit down, Sir Hadrian. Whatever your difficulties with my children may be, I can assure you that mine are greater. So I will forget this insult. Besides! The fact remains that you are too valuable an asset to waste." He rested his hands on the back of the chair before him, gemstones large as quail's eggs shining on his fingers. In a voice so low it was almost a stage whisper, His Imperial Radiance said, "You were meant to fail, you know?"

My eyebrows rose on their own. It was true, then. Just as Lorian and I had suspected.

"The thought had crossed my mind, Radiant Majesty."

The Emperor beamed. "Good. Very good. It was an easy choice to make. 'Give him an impossible task,' they said. 'If he succeeds, well and good. If he fails, then we neutralized a potential threat.'" He clenched his fists, hands groaning on the antique chair. "We gave you an impossible task, and you succeeded." The Emperor turned his back and strode halfway to the ring of statues that separated the meeting space from the library section that ringed the chamber. Wheeling, he continued, "I am a practical man. One does not rule my Empire by being impractical. And I believe that your popularity and your tenacity are assets, Lord Marlowe. I do not believe in sorcery. I have told you this. But you have given me *results,* and so I wish to make you an offer—a request—one which my counselors have argued most strenuously against."

A bead of cold and lonely sweat traced its path down my neck. The last time the Emperor had made a request of me, I spent half a century sailing across the galaxy with Alexander under my wing. Men had died—and I had nearly died. I had a suspicion that what the Emperor had in mind this time was a bit more . . . permanent.

He confirmed those suspicions with his next words. "You have met my daughter, Selene?"

There it was. The hand extended. The trap closed. An old trap. A familiar one. One I'd felt close on Emesh long ago, with Balian and Anaïs Mataro. But I nodded and smiled and feigned ignorance, and let the Emperor continue. "She is a good girl. Dutiful, faithful, kind . . . as kind as any princess of the Imperium can be, that is. I am fond of her. Fond as any father of so many children can be. I understand she is quite fond of you."

"Is she?" I asked, genuinely surprised. I had met the princess on but two occasions, and on the first we had barely had the opportunity to speak. Though I'd sensed the shadow of this plan in our last meeting, I had not expected something so soon. Not two months had passed since my triumph . . .

"Do you like her?" What in Earth's name could I possibly say to that? My mind raced to Valka, and my heart sank. But the Emperor did not wait for my answer, as any answer I might give was irrelevant. The Emperor had made his plans. "It is my wish that the two of you should be married, that you should join my house."

I am not certain if I spoke at all. I did not know then—do not know now—if the Emperor's plan was wisdom or folly. On the one hand, in marrying me to his daughter, he adopted me as a son. It would cool some of the tension others might have perceived between us, but on the other hand, it might inflame the fury of those lords who thought my rise too far and fast already. My mind went to Lorcan Breathnach and Augustin Bourbon, to the great princes of the Houses Bourbon, Mahidol, and Hohenzollern—and Earth only knew who else. The old Lions of the Imperium would roar that one so low as I had risen to the rank of Prince-Consort. How they would sputter and scream that I, a black-barred *outcaste* restored by a mere pen stroke and tainted by contact with outsiders, by plebeians and homunculi, by inti and Irchtani and a Tavrosi witch, might be permitted himself to taint the Blood Imperial.

The words I'd spoken to Lorcan Breathnach echoed in my skull. *I do not have visions.* And yet I had seen her, had I not? Had seen Princess Selene seated at my feet in a gown of living flowers. Had felt her move beneath me and her warm breath on my skin. I'd worn a silver circlet upon my brow, and a white gem—the very piece of shell that hung about my neck on its chain, I realized—had shone in its center like a star, like a third eye.

The Emperor Hadrian.

How it might happen I could not say. How every one of His Radiance's children might be put aside and the Aventine Dynasty ended I did not dare contemplate or dream. I did not want that future. I did not want *her.* But what choice did I have? Before me was Caesar himself. How could I refuse his gift? To do so would be to declare myself his enemy. With my mind's eye I perceived the galaxy as an extension of the black-and-white checkerboard floor beneath our feet, the Red King before me. Was I to be the Black?

Like Rome of ancientmost memory, were we to fall to civil war and play chess for the crown while along our borders fires blazed? Barbarians and monsters.

Here there be dragons.

There was Dorayaica, and there this Monarch, Harendotes. I clenched my fists, felt the right ache and the left remain numb, and remembered Kharn Sagara on his throne.

Pale King. Wild King. King-in-Yellow.

And I had garbed myself in white—even if it was not my color.

Dimly I was aware of the fact that I had been silent a long time. It was not the time for silence. Sitting there, trapped, I opened my mouth and said, "I would be honored, Radiant Majesty."

CHAPTER 35

THOSE THINGS YOU THOUGHT UNREAL

I KEPT SILENT ALL the way out of the palace, speaking no word to my escort nor to the pilot officer who took me from cloud-bound city to the deeper silence of space where the *Tamerlane* waited at anchor. I did not speak to my men in the landing bay, and acknowledged the salutes of those in the halls with only a stiff nod. I moved in a kind of fog, not truly seeing the faces nor the dark metal of the halls.

I had to see her, had to tell her. Had to know.

She wasn't in our apartments.

I found her in the hydroponics section, in my private place beneath the hanging basil plants. She was sleeping. A pocket projector stood on the table beside her, still running. The air felt cool and close beneath the bower, and the sweet smell of the herbs hung on the air like perfume. Careful not to wake her, I stood the projector on its end and glanced at the image. It showed an inscription scanned from a monument on Iubalu's ship. With a brushing gesture, I toggled the scan to the next: a similar inscription taken from the Quiet ruins on Calagah. One of the round glyphs was highlighted on each, a circle with a triangle and a pair of arcing lines inscribed within it.

Valka had been scanning the new Cielcin writing for symbols that matched her old scans of Quiet ruins from a dozen sites across the galaxy. A prodigious task, even for one with Valka's machine-enhanced memory. No wonder she'd fallen asleep. I knelt beside her, restrained the impulse to push a loose strand of hair back into place.

I did not want to wake her.

I did not know what to say.

But my hand moved without my willing it, and found hers.

"What is it?"

Valka did not wake up like normal people. There was no change in breathing, no stirring, no sudden start. The delicate praxis that crouched spider-like in her brain regulated her body's autonomic functions, augmenting the action of the medulla. She was always stable . . . unless she wanted to be otherwise. She told me once that she could control her endocrine system, could order a shot of adrenaline or dopamine as easily as you or I might make a fist. I envied her her control.

I was losing mine.

"Did you see the Emperor?" she asked. "How did it go?"

"I'm . . . to marry the princess," I said. My voice shook. "And he's offered me a seat on the Imperial Council."

Not letting go of my hand, Valka pushed herself back in her seat. Then she did something I did not expect. Something absurd.

She smiled.

" 'Tis wonderful news, is it not?"

"Wonderful?" Had I not spoken correctly? Surely she understood me. Foreigner or no, Valka's Galstani was perfect. "Valka, he wants me to marry Selene." *He wants me to marry someone else.*

"So what? You don't have to love her." Valka squeezed my hand. "Don't have to fuck her, either. I thought marriage didn't mean much to you palatines. 'Tis just . . . business?"

She had a point, but she was missing mine. Holding her hand tighter, I said, "I don't want to marry her."

"Can you refuse?"

"No!" My hand was shaking. "He's the Emperor, Valka. If he ordered me to leap from the battlements of the palace I could not refuse."

Valka took her hand from mine. "Then 'tis a good thing he did not ask you to leap from the battlements." I knew that look, those narrowed eyes, those compressed lips. It was the face she made when she remembered what I was. She shook her head. *"Anaryoch."* This was not going at all like I'd hoped, nor as I'd feared. I felt unsteady, as if the decking at my feet were sagging beneath me. Valka pulled her legs up beneath her, and despite her rebuke she smiled and lay a hand on my cheek. "What's the matter?"

"What's the matter?" I repeated. "Valka, don't you understand?"

"No!" she said sharply. "We don't marry in Tavros." Valka's hand did not leave my face, and though my vision blurred, she smiled. "Marry this woman. You'll never see her anyway. What does it matter?"

I almost laughed. "What does it matter?" I was kneeling anyway. "Valka, I want to marry you." We had touched on this topic before, a hundred times. Touched and retreated as though our hands each found a burning plate of iron. I found her hand again and seized it.

She held mine in both of hers, a bemused smile on her face. "Hadrian. I don't need your Empire's approval to keep you. I have you already. And you have me. This doesn't change anything. 'Tis a gesture."

She didn't understand. How could I make her understand? Still on one knee, I said, "It would change *everything*. A seat on the Council means I'll be trapped here. Do you want to be trapped here?"

"Of course not!" she snapped. "Do you seriously think the Emperor will keep you here? You're too much use to him out there." She leaned toward me, dry lips brushing mine, and when she spoke her breath entered me. "We can run away *whenever* we like."

"Run away?" I did laugh then, though it was a weak and feeble sound. "The Empire doesn't just *misplace a* prince-consort, Valka. They'll come after me."

Her face—so close to my own—darkened. "Then don't run. Stay here if 'tis what you want." She pulled her hands away.

"That isn't fair," I said.

"You are inventing a problem that doesn't exist!" she said, almost rolling her eyes. "How many of your lords keep women? How many of your ladies keep men? All of them, surely."

Valka wasn't wrong. With child-rearing the province of the Emperor's High College, the gene looms, and the birthing vats, the marriages between palatine houses built on love were few. If there were any. My own parents had never shared a bed. Never kissed. Never touched one another that I can recall. My mother had kept her lovers, a stream of talented young ladies with bright futures eager to please the master artist. Doubtless the princess in the holo-opera we'd watched together weeks before had been one. My father kept none, preferring the cold solitude of power.

"I don't want you to be my *woman*," I said, exasperated. "I want you to be my wife."

"Hadrian," she said, smoothing down her shirtfront, "we have been together for *decades*. What is the difference?"

She knew full well what the difference was. We both did. It was only that I was afraid to say it. Afraid because I knew she did not want what I desired. She wanted no more of me than me. I wanted . . . "If we were . . . married, the High College would let us have children. Or might." With Selene, an afterling princess, there would be no children. So few of the Imperial family were permitted offspring. There were enough to keep parallel branches of the family running, distant strains separated so the new Emperor or Empress always married a distant cousin and kept the blood-line pure for the second coming of the God Emperor, but Selene and I would have nothing, I knew.

Unless your visions are real . . . a little voice said to me. *Unless you take the throne.*

I am not sure when I started wanting children. As a boy, the thought had never occurred to me. I had wanted to be a scholiast, and scholiasts do not marry or father children. When had I changed?

"Valka?" She hadn't spoken.

She wasn't looking at me.

"Valka?"

"You know," she spoke over me. "You know we don't *marry* in Tavros. Loving someone more than someone else is, well . . . 'tis a kind of prejudice." Though she did not turn to face me, she smiled. I'd known that, we'd discussed this kind of thing before. "The clans actually separate people if they stay together for too long. 'Tis not right to keep one person to yourself." She glanced at me with golden eyes, her smile widening. "Or so they say."

That was new to me. I felt a sucking horror at the thought and said, "That's barbaric."

The irony of my word choice was not lost on her, and she barked her short laugh. "There was a boy in my clan I knew—Soren. The council shipped him offworld when they discovered he'd been with the same girl for *six years*." Valka looked down at her hands, massaged the tattooed one with the other. "I saw her after. The girl. She looked like someone drained the blood out of her."

A weak laugh escaped me, and I said, "I know how she felt."

One corner of Valka's mouth rose sadly, and she stretched her legs out on the long chair. "I'm not going anywhere," she said. I shifted my weight, moving so that I sat now on the deck beside her, staring up at the light fixtures through the curtain of basil leaves. "Hadrian, I don't want children. I'm no mother."

"You wouldn't have to be," I said. "I'm a lord, Valka. You think the Empress carried her children? Fed them? Told them stories?" Before Valka could reply, I pressed on, "But I don't want this to end."

"It doesn't have to."

"I don't want it to end with *us*, Valka," I said more forcefully, and re-took her hand.

"Hadrian, everything ends," she said. I pulled my hand away. "What is the matter with you?"

I glowered up at her. "I want you to *care*," I hissed.

"You want me to be *Lady Marlowe,* you mean. To wear those ridiculous gowns and hang on your arm and smile at those disgusting lords of yours," she said, ice on her tongue.

"If I'd wanted that," I snapped, "I'd not have wanted you. I'm not trying to change you, Valka. I never have."

She sniffed. "Yet you wish to—what is that charming barbarian expression? You wish to sire children *on* me, 'tis right? I am not some fucking racehorse, Hadrian."

"I never said you were," I said. The first tears had fallen, but it was anger that had pushed them out. "Not ever."

Something in my face must have spoken to her, for she quailed and looked away, those golden eyes downcast. "I'm sorry."

Briefly, a smile broke through my fresh-fallen tears. "I want a family with you because I *love* you, damn your eyes." I found her hand again, willed her to feel what I was feeling and could not explain. "And because I'll love them. *Our children.* I want us married because I want there to be no question that *you* matter more to me than princesses and titles. I want everyone to *see* I love you."

" 'Tis not what marriage is," she said simply, but this time did not release my hand.

"It's what it should be," I answered with a snarling force I'd not guessed was in me.

Her smile shone with a sadness deep as the oceans of cloud on the world beneath our feet. "You were born too late, you know? You should have been one of those knights in your stories, saving girls from dragons," she said at last, turning my hand over in hers. "I'm not a princess, Hadrian," she said. "This isn't one of your fairy stories."

I looked up at her once more. Cold eyelids hid her hard eyes, while my own eyes moistened and burned. "I know that," I answered her, "I—"

"But she is," Valka said. My hand tightened on hers, tightened as though I braced myself against a blow, as if all the mass and force of some giant pressed against me, matched strength for strength.

"Don't," I said, my voice very small.

"Are you so sure she's not *exactly* what you want?" Cruel lips moved.

"How can you ask that?" I asked, and did not scream, *How dare you ask that!* "You know me better than that." I saw her then as I often had, as a creature made of glass, hard-edged and piercing and cruel. The icon of some fury or goddess left on some cold and distant altar, no votive candle lighted to her majesty save mine.

So tender and bitter, my lady. My lady of pain.

"Do I?"

Who was it said that our being only what we are remains our chief and unforgivable sin? What a pair of sinners we made: paper and fire, devil to one another. I saw suddenly that her coldness was only self-defense, as are all the worst of nature's poisons. How else was she to react to this news? How else could she react and save her dignity? She who the great powers of the Empire would spurn and set aside?

Her cruelty twisted then before my eyes, revealed its soft underbelly.

"We'll run," I said, cutting through this dance and charade. "As soon as we're sent away. We'll run and not look back." Nothing else mattered then. Not the war, not the Emperor, not the knives His Radiance would send after us if we fled. Not Syriani Dorayaica or Calen Harendotes; not MINOS and the Extras; not Kharn Sagara, not Brethren, not the Quiet. Not even my own death, my visions and purpose, nor the white jewel that hung at my throat.

"I thought you said they'll come after us."

"It doesn't matter."

Valka shifted where she sat, rolling toward me. "We don't have to run," she said, and brushed away my tears. "I have *everything* I want right here." She kissed me. Salt and the dry must of sleep mingled on our lips. "Marry the damn girl. She'll have nothing of you. Not even your name. Let them seat you on this council. Let them call you *prince*. You're *mine*, barbarian." She seized the front of my shirt. "I cannot give you children, but neither can she. Accept it."

She was right. Whether with my witch or the afterling princess, the High College would never grant my wish. Whatever ambitions the Lions thought I had to sit the throne and sire a dynasty could be crushed by a single bureaucrat's red stamp on a Writ of Nativity.

Request denied.

I would never be a father, I knew that. What I wanted could not change that.

"I don't want her," I said. "I don't want Selene." It was important to me she understood that.

"You think I don't know that?" she said, those hard eyes grown soft. "Hadrian . . . Hadrian, you knew this was coming. Do you really think I didn't know it, too? I have loved you for more than fifty years. My own people would *hate* me for such selfishness."

"It isn't selfish," I said.

Valka pressed her forehead to mine and whispered, "You're right. I thought it would be. I thought I'd get tired of you. But I haven't, I . . ." Her words vanished into smallness, returned like the tides. "I think we might be barbarians, too. In Tavros."

"I just . . . want you to know I didn't ask for this."

"You men do such strange things to show how much you care," she said. "Was this whole show for my benefit?"

There was nothing I could say to that, and I compressed my lips.

"I told you that night at the ball," Valka said, tugging me upward by the tunic to kiss me yet again and pulling me into the great chair on top of her. *"I don't care about the bloody princess."*

CHAPTER 36

THE FIRST STEPS

BIRDSONG SHATTERED THE STILL, breaking the meditative quiet of the wood. My horse snorted, startled by the sudden cry. The forest spoke with the earthy notes of moss and fungus, whispered with the animal stink of the beast beneath me.

"Are you all right, Sir Hadrian?" a pleasant voice called, clear in the misty air.

Turning in my seat, I saw Selene coming back toward me, her ladies in tow, her flaming hair thickly braided at one shoulder. She had abandoned her customary whites for dun trousers and jacket beneath a riding mantle the color of old rust.

Bowing my head slightly, I said, "I am not so great a rider, Highness."

"We can see that!" said one of the princess's companions, a black-skinned beauty with hair nearly so red as Selene's.

This remark drew unsteady laughter from the others, but Selene only smiled, and I said on, "I can't think when it was I last rode a horse." The truth was that I'd not ridden since I was a boy at Devil's Rest, and that had been almost a hundred years before. Though the days of the cavalier and the warhorse were long behind us, there remained a deep attachment to and fondness for the gentle beasts in the hearts of many among the oldest houses of the Imperium.

But I am not one of them. I prefer creatures who can reason, creatures with whom I can speak. I could not trust the beast beneath me not to buck me and run, not to embarrass me in front of this Imperial princess and her handmaids. I would have preferred my own feet, or a skiff or chariot.

"You're doing just fine!" She tossed her hair and smiled. "But the path is this way! Come!"

The forest was unspeakably old, planted at the founding of the city atop a terraced platform more than a hundred miles from end to end. The trees had come from Avalon, and before that from Earth herself, and the ash and beechwood growing there counted for its ancestors the woods of sceptered England. Looking up through their branches, I saw the great sail wall and the other platforms of the flying city built upon the clouds. The hanging towers of the Merchant Ministry reached down toward us, and the impossible span of the Martian Way that stretched from the great bowl that supported the Campus Raphael to the flying barracks where the Guard lived with their families cast its shadow on the woods below it.

Forum truly was a world like no other. It truly was a City of the Gods.

I had allowed myself to trail behind Selene and her friends as once I had trailed Anaïs Mataro at her social gatherings. The sense of déjà vu was profound. But for the cool winds of Forum I felt I must be on the deck of a Mataro yacht again. Life, like a dance—like poetry—repeats itself in rhythm and in rhyme.

"Are you coming?" she asked, and gestured with a gloved hand.

She'll have nothing of you. Valka's words echoed in my mind. *Not even your name.*

I spurred the horse to a trot, closing the gap between us.

When we had ridden on a ways, she said, "You're very quiet, sir."

"I am often quiet, Highness," I said, wondering just how I was to keep my horse and hers moving together. I really was far beyond my element. Somewhere above, I heard the faint whine of repulsors, but when I glanced through the leafy green I could not spy the Martian on his platform, maintaining the security of the wood.

"My ladies don't frighten you, do they?" she asked, inclining her head to the band of gaily colored women riding ahead of us.

This caught me by surprise. "Frighten me?"

"They can be such a pack of harpies." She smiled up at me through hair like curls of copper wire glowing with heat. "I don't blame you for trying to lose yourself in these woods."

I was not sure if I should smile, or if the jape was a trick. Aware I was on a kind of stage, I said, "I am unused to such company, Highness."

"Selene, *please*," she said. "You are my guest, Sir Hadrian. You speak as one expecting dire wolves to leap from the trees. They aren't allowed on this terrace. The big predators are kept in the hunting zone down a ways." She waved a vague hand in the direction of the sail wall.

She *was* joking, I decided, and allowed myself a Marlowe smile. I had seen the woods she meant, the Royal Forest divided by terraces and walls into distinct zones—certain of them glassed in to protect odd climates. The hunting zone was among the lowest and furthest toward the edge of the floating isle, kept separate from this and other zones by high walls of white stone.

"It is only that I am used to soldiers, Highne—Selene. I have little practice speaking to princesses."

This drew a merry laugh from the princess, who said, "And yet you speak with demons, if the stories are true!" she said. "Cielcin and Irchtani and . . . other things. Were there really machines on Vorgossos? One of the men in LIO told me . . ."

Whoever that man was, he ought to have kept his mouth shut. "The Irchtani are not demons," I said. "They're not so different from us, save for appearances."

"Would you say the same of the Cielcin?" she asked. "Surely they look more like us than the Irchtani."

"They do," I agreed. I'd been bothered by that myself as a boy. Gibson had applauded me for noting the physiological resemblances and the kinship it implied: the hope that perhaps peace was possible between our two peoples. "But I wouldn't say they're like us."

The princess accepted this with a nod. "There was a story my nanny played for me when I was a girl about a planet of people whose faces showed feelings no one could understand. They screamed when they were happy, and smiled with disgust. It was to teach us not to trust the people here, of course, but I always imagined it was true. That there was such a planet out there."

"That's not far off the mark," I said. "Whatever their appearances, the Cielcin are not like us beneath." The monument of bones rose in my mind, the man on the dining board with it, and the disfigured slave that Aranata's child had dragged on a leash like a dog.

Selene nodded, though I doubt she fully understood. "And your Irchtani are?"

"I owe them my life. I would not be here if Udax—he is one of their centurions—had not intervened in my battles with their general."

"The one from the triumph?" she asked, and I could feel her peering at me. "The one consumed by machines?"

"That's the one."

She shuddered. "What a horrible creature." I agreed with her, and she pressed on, asking, "What are they like?"

"The Cielcin?" I asked, as much to rally a response as anything. But the answer escaped me before I could check its advance. "Not like I hoped."

"Not like you hoped?" She sounded puzzled, and turning I saw her watching me with cocked head and bemused smile. "What do you mean?"

Many people believe the children of nobility spoiled and empty-headed, and though that stereotype—as with all stereotypes—is often true, I found it was not true of Selene. Sheltered, perhaps. Naive, certainly. But that empty-headed-seeming princess was not empty-headed at all. Indeed, of all the Imperial children I had met, Philip and Ricard, Faustinus and Irene, even Alexander—I found myself liking Selene. Were it not for the invisible hand of politics and the specter of Valka between us, I could see myself even growing fond of her.

She asked interesting questions, and listened as few people ever did.

"I told you I wanted to be a scholiast," I said after a moment passed.

"You told me you wanted to be a wizard," she shot back.

That drew a rueful smile from me. "Just so," I said. "Even as a boy I studied their language. I couldn't understand why we'd not made efforts to make peace with the Pale—the war had gone on for hundreds of years, you know? Even when I was young. I thought that surely if we could talk with them—if I could—that I could make a difference. That's why I joined the fight, traveled to Vorgossos, made contact with one of their princes." I trailed off, realizing I was beginning to ramble. "I was wrong."

Ahead of us, Selene's handmaids were laughing. One had hurried ahead of the rest, called out something about a race, for the path had widened and ran straight now down a double avenue of trees where the wood became less wood than garden.

"Wrong?" she asked, prodding me.

I looked up again before responding—this time spying one of the Martian Guard on his platform, his hands on the bar before him, feet poised on the pedals. Unable to shake the feeling that his eyes and gun turret were both aimed at me, I answered, "I captured a Cielcin officer on Emesh. It seemed so reasonable, even decent."

"Decent?"

"The way it cared about its men. I thought I'd been proven right in my theory, that the war had dragged on because *we* wanted it to."

Selene sounded aghast. "You thought we were the villains?"

"I wasn't sure I believed in villains at all," I said shortly, "or I believed we all were villains. The Cielcin and us." I smiled down at the saddle and the beast before me, and feeling an impulse reached out and patted its velvety neck. Such relativistic thinking is always attractive to the young. Despising their parents—and through their parents all authority—they decide there is no authority but themselves, and therefore all knowledge which was and came before them is evil, and they alone wholly good. I had despised the Empire because I despised my father—who was its chief representative in my young life. Seeing his authority as unjust, I had decided there was no justice save that which I might make myself. I had believed that I alone had the wisdom to set the world to rights, not knowing then that true wisdom lies in knowing that I did not possess that wisdom, and never would.

Clearing my throat, I said, "The Cielcin only recognize power. Their princes are princes because they are the strongest, and when they grow weak they are deposed. There is no room for morality. No room for wisdom or courage. No heroism. The Cielcin I had beaten on Emesh were reasonable because I had beaten them. But the moment they sensed weakness in me, they turned." Despite the sunlight and the birdsong and the white towers of the ministry hanging from the clouds, I could only see that dark cell in the Borosevo bastille. Only smell the copper of alien blood and the stink of burning flesh. "I thought this officer was making a last desperate stand when it attacked me, but I think . . . I think it thought that if it could kill me it would be in a better bargaining position. A show of dominance—like your dire wolves."

That made her laugh. For some reason, the music of that laughter chilled me. I should not amuse her. Amusing her felt too much like courtship—which I supposed this whole outing was. I was meant to woo the princess with my war stories, as the old Moor once wooed Desdemona. But I did not wish to be Othello, nor to meet Othello's end. Nor did I desire this Desdemona.

But Selene was still hanging on my words, and I continued, "The Cielcin don't reason as we. Our logic is not theirs. The only reason they recognize is a sword."

"Then we should be grateful to have men like you fighting our battles, Sir Hadrian."

It was my turn to laugh then. "I should hope there are not too many men like me, Your Highness."

I had forgotten her order to call her by her name, but she did not rebuke me. "What makes you say that?"

"I mostly live in my head," I answered her. "Sooner or later I won't be able to escape from it." I allowed myself a self-deprecating laugh.

Laughing with me, Princess Selene asked, "Are you always like this, sir?"

"Like what, princess?"

"So . . . serious."

I laughed again. "I thought you were about to say *dramatic*."

"That, too."

"I'm rather afraid I am," I said. "Ask anyone who knows me."

We rode on in casual conversation then a while, following her hand-maids along the broad avenue of trees. I glanced surreptitiously at my terminal. It was not quite standard noon, and our excursion was slated for another several hours yet.

"Alexander tells me you're an admirer of ancient history," Selene said.

The mention of Alexander's name set my fists to tightening on the reins. "Hazards of having a Zenoan scholiast for a tutor."

"Then there is something ahead which might interest you. I'd wanted to surprise you. Most people don't know it's here." She pressed her horse forward, steam rising from its nostrils in the chilly air.

Curious, I followed after her, and unable to help myself, I asked, "How is your brother?"

"Alexander?" She glanced back over her shoulder, and I saw *something* in her face. Anger? A foggy shape turned over in my stomach, and I wondered if Selene were not my enemy as well, if her smiling face and laughter were—as she herself had said—a species of disgust. Then more than ever, I wanted to flee with Valka, to make for the edges of the known universe and never look back. "He told me what you said of him."

"Will you tell him I am sorry?" I asked. "I am unused to children. I was unprepared for a squire. Perhaps I do not have the temperament to teach."

"I will tell him," Selene said. "He really does admire you, you know?" Her back was to me, and her intricate braid bounced as she rode, hurrying a bit ahead. The foggy suspicion in me transformed to something rotten. Regret, I thought. And shame. "Kiria! Bayara! We're going to the arch! Come back!"

Columns of cloud stood among columns of white stone, mingled with the boles of trees two thousand years old, the landscape warped and rippled with roots and great boulders placed there by the architects of the Royal Forest back in the deeps of time. So few feet had trod those pathways in all that time, for the forest—like so many of the Empire's oldest and most

storied monuments—was open to a special few. As in the garden of Vorgossos, I felt that ahead we might come upon a gate and find an angel
standing guard with sword afire, so close was that wood in feeling to the
gardens of paradise itself. The trees fell away around us, and we rode into
a clearing about a great and shallow hill. There the beaten path transformed, was paved with marble cobbles white and moss-grown.

And there *was* a gate.

A triumphal arch stood alone upon the hill, a monument to ages past.
Fashioned of travertine and marble it was, its columns and capitals cracked
and weathered, its relief sculptures eroded and decayed. Great it once had
been, and great it yet remained, more than a dozen times the height of a
man and so broad that six might walk abreast beneath it. Yet it seemed to
me a thing that looked backward, as if to pass beneath its protection was
to enter ages passed or passing, not to come.

"It's from Earth," Selene said. "One of the old Emperors had it brought
here. We're not supposed to get too close."

"Is it still radioactive?" I asked.

"A little," she replied. "Those pillars mark safe distance."

I saw what she meant. A ring of white pillars surrounded the archway,
each topped with the verdigrised statue of a virtue looking outward, but
there was no chain, no barrier to prevent approach. Certain forms of stone,
I knew, held the fingerprint of atomics better than others.

Taking this as permission to go closer, I urged my horse forward. Stub-
bornly, the beast moved, and when I was within ten paces of the nearest
pillar, I dismounted and held the reins in my hand.

Close as I was, I could make out the inscription above the great arch,
done in the ancient block capitals of the English alphabet—though the
language was not English at all.

> SENATVS
> POPVLVSQVE ROMANVS
> DIVO TITO DIVI VESPASIANI F
> VESPASIANO AVGVSTO

"Is it . . . ?"

"The Arch of Titus?" she said. "Yes."

After the God Emperor had beaten the Mericanii and flooded the Earth
with nuclear fire, he had descended upon the planet and—garbed in a radiation suit—had visited the ancient city of Rome. He had walked the
sacred road from the walls of the ancient city to the ruins of the old
Forum, and there—alone—had crowned himself Emperor of Mankind.

He had passed beneath this arch on that road, perhaps had touched the stones as he went.

It was a sacred artifact, and I have since learned that the new Emperors—on the eve of their coronation—reenact that solitary journey in the Royal Forest, walking alone through the forest to the gates where the coronal triumph begins. Thus each new Emperor arrives at the Sun King's Hall just as the sun of Forum rises above the sail wall and the city glows with the light of a new day.

I knew none of this at the time, and said in wonder, "Why is it here?"

She told me only a piece of this. "Haven't you ever wondered why the Last Stair is called *the Last Stair*?" Selene did not dismount, but drew up beside me, looking up at the crumbling Roman arch. "A new Emperor begins his walk here alone, just like the God Emperor did. These are the first steps. I thought you'd want to see it. It must be . . . twenty thousand years old? Twenty-two? Twenty-three?"

The first steps . . .

I did not reply to Selene at once, but took a step or two nearer until I stood almost in the shadow of the stone marker. I wondered what would happen if I tried to walk forward. The Martian Guard would descend, I guessed, as much to save me from the radiation as to prevent my trespass. Could I make it to the gate before anyone would stop me? Would Selene follow me where only Emperors had trod? Despite the threat of radiation, I felt an insane impulse to touch the ruin.

"How is it preserved?" I asked.

She shrugged. "I don't really know, some kind of resin, maybe?"

"Thank you," I said, and smiled up at her, "for showing me this."

Selene returned my smile.

Our tour ended, we took the horses back to the gatehouse, where a uniformed attendant took my beast away. I was privately relieved.

"Hadrian!"

Crim hurried toward me from the shuttle port outside, his Red Company greatcoat flapping crimson from his shoulders like a Swordmaster's *mandyas*. Selene was still near me, and so two pair of Martian Guards stepped in to interpose themselves between my rushing officer and me. Seeing this, Crim slowed. I was midway through the act of accepting my shield-belt back from the guardsmen and froze. The Norman-Jaddian officer's face, usually olive and full-blooded, looked almost bleached.

"What's the matter, man?"

The lieutenant commander shoved the hands of one Martian away. He made a sharp gesture with two fingers, pointing first to me, then himself and back again, indicating that what needed saying should not be said aloud.

I pressed forward, abandoning Selene, and pushed the Martian aside with the hand that held my effects. I spoke low so as not to be overheard by the Martians and in Jaddian to stymie any listeners. "What happened?"

"Dolofin," he said, voice low. "Murder, my lord. You weren't answering your terminal."

I felt my blood run cold. Murder? Careful now, I practically whispered into the man's ear, covering my mouth with my free hand to frustrate the cameras. There was no telling who might be watching, and I could not trust Selene or her guards, either.

"One of the cleaning staff," Crim said, panting from his run but matching my close tones. "Doctor Onderra . . ."

I seized Crim by the lapels with my free hand. "What?" I dragged his ear close and hissed. "What happened?" It wasn't possible. If something had happened to Valka . . .

"Valka's fine!" Crim said. "One of the batmen died, though. Distracted it before it could get her."

I released him, shoving him back, eyes wide and wild. A flash of anger rose in me. His clumsy wording had made me believe—if only for a moment—had made me believe that Valka was dead. I glared at him, waited for him to speak.

"There was a knife-missile," Crim said, smoothing his jacket beneath the long coat. "In your chambers."

CHAPTER 37

BLADE WITHOUT HANDLE

"IT WAS MEANT FOR me," I said, eying the ruined device on the conference table.

"That is the high probability," said Tor Varro, arms folded.

Otavia Corvo frowned and stared down at the weapon from beneath her floating cloud of hair. "I've no idea how it got aboard," she said. "I'm sorry."

"It's not your fault," I said.

"It's mine," Crim said, *"noyn jitat,* some security officer I turned out to be."

It was, as Crim had said, a knife-missile. Such a small thing, no larger than one of my pencils. Someone had smashed it, snapped it in half, and it was held together by a pair of glass wires, with a fuel cell at one end and a vicious spike on the other.

"Which of the batmen saved her?" I asked. Valka was in medica with Doctor Okoyo, injured but alive. The doctor had given her something to help her sleep while the correctives did their work stitching her wounds. I was headed up there right after this meeting.

"Martin," Crim said. "Good lad. Others all liked him."

"Family?" I asked. I knew the fellow, if not well. I had a staff of batmen who rotated service in and out of fugue, who kept my schedule and ensured that Valka and I were taken care of. Martin and the rest of his shift had come out of the ice only with the return to Forum; before that—except for the business with Iubalu and the hunt, I suppose—he had been frozen for decades.

"A sister, I think," Crim said, "but that was before he signed on. Reckon she's long gone."

Not taking my eyes from the weapon, I said, "Find out. If he has any surviving relatives, I want them paid his stipend and told he died saving her. Have his effects posted to them."

"Aye, my lord," Crim said.

"The doctor was lucky he got there when he did," Varro said. "His entrance confused the missile's routing circuits, else she'd been done for."

"Who smashed it?" I asked. I'd forbidden security cameras from my apartments, jealous of mine and Valka's privacy. In that moment, I wondered if that had been a mistake. Not only could I not *see* the attack as I might like, but we'd have no footage to review and determine when the knife was placed in my chambers, and by whom.

Varro answered, "She did. Caught it after it stabbed Martin and broke it on the bulkhead."

That's my lady, I thought, still unable to calm myself. I should have been there, not gallivanting about the Royal Forest with Princess Selene.

"I assume you've already swept the ship for stowaways," I said, turning my full attention on Crim. The security officer was still pale, his burgundy uniform and dark hair rumpled.

He swallowed. "Aye. There was no one. Nothing."

"Then how did it get aboard?" I asked, looking round at everyone gathered in that conference chamber. "And how did it get into my apartments?"

"We're still running over sec footage," Crim answered, not looking me in the eye. "One of our people must have smuggled it in." I was shaking my head, but Crim carried on. "No one else has had access to the ship, much less your apartments, lord—outside a few delivery personnel, but they never leave the cargo bays before turning round."

"I don't suppose it's possible the knife-missile was piloted remotely? Steered through the halls?"

"Possible, but not likely." Varro narrowed his eyes. "That's an *Akateko* model. Heat-seeking, motion-sensing. No transmitter. Unless they've re-fitted it. They're meant to be untraceable."

Still looking pointedly at the table in front of him, Crim said, "I'll review all the footage we have. Everyone coming and going. Who had access to your apartments."

"Should check scans on inbound cargo," Corvo suggested. "It might have come up on one of the supply runs. Something we missed."

Lorian Aristedes cleared his throat, looking up from a methodical examination of his hands. "I don't suppose the batman himself might be our man?"

"And killed himself on purpose?" Crim almost sneered. The security officer was clearly unbalanced by the episode, embarrassed the missile had slipped by him unnoticed.

Aristedes shrugged, but did not stop his careful knuckle cracking. "You're suggesting one of our own people had reason for wanting Marlowe and the doctor dead . . . in which case you'd have to explain who and why. Far more likely one of our people was paid off."

"In which case you'd have to explain who's paying," Crim said acidly, "and why *they* want our boy dead."

With languid slowness, Lorian looked up at other officer, pale eyes in bloodless face. He smiled. "I appreciate your difficulties, Lieutenant Commander, but it strikes me as far more likely that Sir Hadrian has some political enemy than that one of our own has a grudge."

Into the stiff air following this riposte, I said, "The Emperor has offered me Princess Selene's hand in marriage."

Silence ruled the conference chamber. I looked at no one, not at Crim or Varro, nor at Corvo or Aristedes. The knife lay before me, its pointed end angled nearly at my heart, the glass wires spilled like innards.

"Ah," Varro said at last. Was that surprise in the scholiast's voice? "That would explain it."

"That's bound to make some enemies," Corvo allowed, crossing her arms. "Why weren't we told?"

Eyebrow cocked, I said, "Because the Emperor hadn't cleared it for public disclosure."

"That explains the horseback riding," Crim said.

"Horseback riding?" Corvo made a face.

A brief bout of nervous laughter sounded from the end of the table, and turning I saw Lorian covering his mouth. "Oh, that is going to make you enemies. The old blood's not going to like that at all."

"No, they won't," I said.

"Hohenzollern, Mahidol, and Bourbon all refused to lower their banners at your triumph," Aristedes said, flexing his overlong fingers. "It could be any of them."

I started, looking round at the small officer. "You noticed that?"

"It was hard to miss." He pressed his lips together. "Bold move, that was. Almost too bold. They'd have done as well to mail you a bloodstained silk glove like the old days . . . with their names embroidered on." Lorian drummed his fingers as if pressing the keys of some unseen console. "Though I suppose we should thank them. It's given us a start on our list of suspects."

Corvo swore. "I hope that's the end of it."

Both hands raised to his eyes to hide his tiredness, Tor Varro said, "We should hope it is not even the start of it. We can't hope to win an assassins' war with the *great* houses."

"Well, we are in an assassins' war with *someone,* counselor," I said, and snatched the knife-missile from the tabletop. Someone had cleaned it, for neither Valka's blood nor the blood of the batman, Martin, was upon it. "Poine," I said, using the old word. A blood feud. They had tried to kill me, whoever they were. They had nearly killed Valka—had killed one of my men.

It *was* war.

"We cannot afford to discount other possibilities," I said. "House Bourbon means the War Ministry, which means Legion Intelligence, and I've never been popular with the Chantry." I swept my gaze over them. "We cannot let it get out how close they came to succeeding. We cannot let them know they got to Valka. In fact, delay sending word to M. Martin's family. Burn the body, store the ashes, but mark him as in fugue. And put the guards, the medical staff, anyone who handled the cleanup back on ice. Anyone nonessential. We need Okoyo, obviously, but she's loyal. We cannot have the details leak."

Varro raised a hand to object. "My lord, word is all over the ship already."

"Word, yes," I said, "and Princess Selene knows something is wrong. She was there when Crim found me." I glanced at the security officer. It was another way the man had failed me. At least he'd had the good sense not to charge in shouting about it. "Word is fine. The story can leak as it likes, it's the *facts* I want controlled."

Aristedes was grinning ear to ear. "In a fortnight all the Eternal City will be saying the Halfmortal survived an attack from a Mandari assassin."

"In a fortnight I will have been variously shot, stabbed, strangled, poisoned, burned alive, and blown out the airlock," I said soberly. "Let them all be true." All the lies would clog the air like smoke. "I want no report filed below. They're bound to send someone once the rumors start. Who that is will tell us something."

Otavia had not uncrossed her arms, but took a step in from where she leaned against the bulkhead. "In the meantime, you shouldn't leave the ship."

"On the contrary," I said, turning the knife over in my hands, careful not to break the glass wires, "I need to act like nothing has happened at all."

"I'm not letting you out there without a guard," Otavia said.

"Captain, nothing happened to me *out there*," I said, and winced internally, realizing that statement doubtless seemed a rebuke. "At any rate, I cannot ignore a summons if one comes—and what summons will come will tell us something, too."

The Chalcenterite leaned back in his chair, staring at the ceiling as though entranced by the light there, or as if staring into the top of his skull. "There is one thing that bothers me." Everyone turned to look at him, and even Aristedes ceased his fidgeting. Certain he had the floor, the scholiast said, "It is likely whoever planned this attack knew you'd left the ship. Why plant the weapon in such a way as to practically guarantee it would be, ah . . . activated before your return?"

Something cold formed in the pit of my stomach, and I felt my eyes grow narrow. "You think that *Valka* was the target?"

"Not necessarily," Varro said. "But it is well known you share a bed. There was a possibility the doctor would return to the chamber before you did. Those *Akateko* models are indiscriminate. After all, it attacked poor Martin before it had even finished with the doctor. Sorry." Something must have showed on my face, for the scholiast ducked his head at the sight of me.

Lorian answered him. "It is . . . possible that this plot was not meant to succeed." He aimed one bony finger at the knife in my hands. "There's our bloodstained glove."

I set the weapon back on the table. A declaration of war. I caught myself nodding along with the both of them. "Varro, once you have analyzed the weapon to its fullest, destroy it. Do it yourself. Once this story gets out—in whatever form—the Emperor will send an inspector, possibly an Inquisitor. I do not want them prying through that *thing's* memory and discovering it made it into my chambers. If the Inquisitor asks to see the weapon, tell them we destroyed it as a matter of safety." I glanced up at the cameras that monitored the room. I'd ordered them stopped, but there was no harm in being sure. "This meeting did not happen. Otavia, you will make sure the sec footage backs that up?"

"Certainly."

"Generate false footage if you have to, and freeze any of the techs you use. Alter the fugue charts. They were never awake. I don't think they'll be looking *too* closely at us—we were the victims here—but it's possible whoever sent the thing will have access to whatever report the Inquisition might file. And one other thing . . ." I hesitated, recalling both Selene and the Emperor's words on the matter and the looks on their faces. "We must add Prince Alexander to this list of enemies."

"What?" half the table shouted in unison, though for Varro and Aristedes the effect was limited to a raised eyebrow and a feral smile.

"I paid him a grievous insult the night of the triumph. He overheard me talking to Valka."

"I remember that!" Lorian said. "You went looking for her."

A terrible thought occurred to me. "I think you're right, Varro. I think Valka was the target. She started the talk on Alexander . . . I only agreed with her." I laid my hands on the table before me, framing the knife-missile between them. "I hope I'm wrong."

"If it is the prince," Crim said, speaking for the first time in minutes, "there's nothing we can do."

"I need to speak to him." I flicked the knife away, watched it grind to a halt before it reached the other side of the wide conference table. "No getting around it." Rage flared white behind my eyes, and I pounded the metal surface. Snarling, I said, "Give me a straight fight any day." Thinking of Valka, I blinked back tears. "I need to be with her. Gentlemen, captain, excuse me."

"Hadrian, wait!"

I looked back at the sound of my name, halfway along the hall to the tram that would carry me down and back along the *Tamerlane*'s equator toward medica and Valka's bedside. Crim was already kneeling. I should have found that strange from a Norman, but the man was Jaddian-born, and so the custom was perhaps not so unusual. He looked up at me with glazed eyes, but if he expected me to speak first, he was disappointed.

One hand grasping the hilt of his long knife in its sheath, he ducked his head. "I am sorry. None of this would have happened if I had done my job properly. I will figure out how the weapon got aboard. You have my word."

"Your word, soldier?" I repeated, not using his name to reassert the distance between us. I wasn't being fair. We had no notion of how the weapon had gotten aboard the ship yet. There might have been no way for Crim to know. And yet I could not stop thinking about Valka lying in her cot in medica. Still, I shut my eyes, murmured an old aphorism to quiet my nerves and calm the brewing fury. This was Crim, and not my enemy. In a voice pressed flat of emotion by sheer will, I said, "Very good."

"I won't fail you again."

"See that you don't," I said, and turning left him without another word.

CHAPTER 38

VALKA AWAKES

THE MEDICAL CELL PULSED to the gentle chime of the heart monitor, its rhythm counting the seconds, parceling time into pieces for delivery to the past. The glass door sealed behind me with a whisper, the only thing in all that space—besides Valka herself—that did not gleam a snowy, sterile white.

I stood there a long moment, looking down at her where she lay, her shadowy hair pulled back into an uncharacteristic tail, her hands both out on top of the white sheet. Corrective tape showed black high on one cheek where the knife-missile had cut her. A similar black stripe ran up her right forearm, and a larger, heavier rig stooped over her breast like a vampire, humming faintly.

As I had done in the hydroponics section, I seated myself beside her and took her hand. Her left hand, for the left had taken no damage in the attack. That at least was a small blessing, for I guessed that damage to her clan crest would be a terrible blow. Her fingers did not close on mine, but lay there soft and warm. I studied the translucent cables that ran from the drip on the staff beside her into the crook of her elbow. Saline and anesthetic.

I slept.

And dreamed of darkness. Of darkness and pale hands.

Arms long as trees reached toward me, past me, climbing into the night. I turned, straining for their source, expecting to see the bloated, swollen mass of the daimon Brethren, but there was nothing.

They were not arms at all, but fingers, fingers of a great white hand stretched across the blackness all around me. And though I fell toward its mighty palm, I drew my sword and struck off the nearest finger, hearing as I did so Iubalu's mocking laughter.

I did not dare hope it would be you.

I fell down a gleaming channel, washed along by the flood. Branches and tributaries opened all around me, each leading up or down another avenue of time. What lay down those branchings I never knew. The waters ran red around me. Drowning. Drowning. Screaming, I cried out for air and climbed upward—back the way I had come—back through some narrow aperture onto a stone shelf beside a lake of glass. Exhausted, I rolled over, looking for the hole through which I'd escaped . . . and saw only my own severed head, blood soaking the lakeside like a birthing bed.

"Hadrian?"

Often I have wondered if my death changed me, or if my experience with Brethren had. Though I dreamed before the *Demiurge,* I have dreamed differently since. More frequently, more vividly, even under the fugue-ice, which they say should not be possible. Perhaps I was different in some fundamental way, or perhaps it was ordinary trauma. It doesn't matter. How often had I awoken sweating in the heat of the night, cowering in the dark of my own bedchamber?

Night terrors?

Or memories I'd not known I possessed?

"Hadrian, are you all right?"

I did not think them visions.

"Hadrian?"

Warm pressure on my hand, strength and life returning.

Valka watched me from beneath hooded eyes, voice thick from the anesthetic. Her eyes were far away. But her eyes were always remote. Her smile shone near at hand, and the sudden strength of her left hand in my right was like the blossoming of new flowers in Delos's brief spring.

"Just a dream," I said.

"The nightmares?" she asked, not letting go.

I took her hand in both of mine. "Don't worry about it. How do you feel?"

"My chest hurts."

"You punctured a lung," I told her, glancing at the apparatus that presided over the tissue repair. Okoyo had repaired the damaged organ, inserted a matrix to accelerate cell regrowth and staunch the bleeding. "She says you won't be on your feet for a week or two. What's so funny?" She'd been smiling the whole time I spoke.

"You," she said. "You're usually the one in this bed."

I returned her smile. "Well, don't get used to it." I took my hands away a moment and passed her a drinking bulb filled with cool water. "Before long I'm sure someone will take a shot at me and you'll get to feel like all's right with the universe again. Just you wait." I smiled crookedly down at her.

She laughed, groaned.

Watching her, I tried to imagine what it must have been like. The knife-missile flashing out of the darkness. Okoyo had told me that if the shot had been an inch higher, the knife would have pierced her heart. Even that might not have been fatal, if help had arrived soon enough, but such weapons were known to brutalize their victims, to keep stabbing until some better target presented itself. But the blade had found a lung instead, and somehow—incredibly—Valka had fought back, had managed to fend the thing off with one of my folios for a shield until the batman, Martin, had entered via the lift to collect our laundry and tidy away the remnants of Valka's lunch. The thing had gone for him instead, pierced him a dozen times before it got caught in his sternum, before Valka caught it and smashed it like a serpent beneath her heel.

Now it was her turn to ask, "What?"

I could only shake my head. "Okoyo says you'll be all right."

"Of course I'll be all right," she cut back. "You're not getting rid of me so easy, *Lord* Marlowe."

My smile slid a little, thinking this a reference to Selene. "You don't think . . . that I . . . ?" I could not finish the sentence, could hardly finish the thought. *You don't think that I did this?*

Valka read my face and mind, and her own fell in horror. "No! Blood of my fathers, Hadrian! How could you ask such a thing?"

Horror turned itself to shame, and for once I was glad of the unpleasant feeling, and took the drinking bulb back when she seemed unsure what to do with it. The silence that stretched between us was an ugly thing, yawning and brittle. I looked down at my hands, remembering my dream, the way my right hand and my left had flickered as I turned back to contemplate my severed head. I toyed with Aranata's ring, the blood-red stone and rhodium band twinkling in the harsh light of the medica.

"Hadrian." Her voice broke the quiet, faint and far away. "Never ask me anything like that ever again." There was iron in those words, but when I looked at her, her eyes were kind.

A sob escaped me, and I clamped it down.

Grief is deep water, Gibson's voice said within, forever stoic.

But it wasn't grief I felt. Was it relief? At once I remembered another bedside, another victim. I remembered lying in bed, my arm prisoned in a corrective brace, my tongue thick and dry, and Gibson watching over me. The old man had not left my side in days.

Forever stoic, indeed.

The scholiasts play the role of the impassive machine, void of all feeling—but it is a lie. However disciplined, however trained, the scholiasts are human still. They share our feelings, and our pains, though they wish they did not.

It was not grief that pained me then, but love.

Love consumes, so the aphorism goes.

I have not found it to be so. Love is not a burden—though it is a responsibility. A duty. Love is an honor—an *office* we hold. An oath.

I swore an oath, then. "Men will die for this."

Once, perhaps, Valka would have rebuked me. Once, she had hated me for fighting in her name. But here she smiled and—reaching out—put her hand on mine. A kind of blessing, that. Not so unlike the way a great lord might lay hands on his faithful knight before sending him out in service.

"They attacked us both," she said. Her nails bit into the backs of my hands. "I'm glad you weren't here."

"I wish I was," I said. "If I had been, it might have ended differently."

"If you had been," she countered, brows contracting, "it *might* have ended differently." She squeezed my hands again, more gently this time, and turned her head away. She was right. There was no telling how things might have gone if I had been there. Any number of factors could have changed the outcome. Valka might not be lying on a cot in medica, but in the morgue. Or I might be. Or both of us together. "We should be grateful," she said, "that this is all that happened." The silence rushed back between us like water, and we sat there side by side. When a long while had passed thus, she asked, "Do you think it was your princess?"

My princess, I thought, and echoed, "Selene?"

Valka's eyes shone bright and flat as the eyes of statues. How had I ever thought them merely human eyes? "Killing her rivals. Perhaps the knife was never meant for you."

"*You* don't have rivals," I said, trying to cheer her.

It didn't work. "Perhaps she does not know this," Valka said. "Perhaps she is the jealous type."

"I don't think Selene would . . ."

" 'Tis *Selene*, is it?" Valka asked. "Hadrian, *think*. She knew you were not on the ship. She *summoned* you. 'Twas the perfect time to strike at me."

Swallowing, I pressed my lips together. She spoke sense, and yet I did not want to hear it. "I am sorry this happened to you."

" 'Twas not your fault."

"Yes it was!" I said, voice harsh. Her words—spoken to me on an Emeshi night so very long ago—echoed back to me across the decades. "It's not happening *to* me," I said. "To *us*. It's happening to us *because* of me."

Valka's memory was perfect. She knew what I referenced better even than I. "Maybe," she said, "but you didn't put that knife in our room." She squeezed my hand again.

I could not stop looking at the apparatus stooped over her chest, at the black corrective tape on cheek and forearm, at the medical holographs that showed the disposition of her recovery and her punctured lung. Looking, I found I could not shake the thought, the evil, crippling certainty that I was responsible. *I did this,* I thought. *My dream did this. My ambition.*

A better world.

What did that even look like? I'd thought once that a better world meant peace between humanity and the Cielcin. I was no longer sure I believed such a peace was possible, or even good. Monsters the Cielcin may be, but was humanity any better? A pack of miserable, backstabbing ingrates. I had delivered them the heads of two Cielcin princes and the *vayadan*-general of a third. I had delivered them knowledge of an alliance between the Cielcin and the Extra barbarians, had fought for them on more than a dozen worlds.

And for my pains they paid me with a knife almost in the heart of the woman who mattered to me more than all the rest together.

"Will you smile?" she said, voice almost stern. "I'm alive."

"We should leave," I said, staring past her to the blank white of the wall. "We should leave now. Take the ship and run."

I could see her shake her head. "You know you can't."

A hollow laugh escaped me. "No, we can't. I may never leave Forum again. I'll be trapped here like a princess in some fairy tale. May as well lock me in a tower. Chain me to a bed."

"Hadrian, stop." Valka glared at me.

Suddenly, I felt ashamed—felt that shame running like cold slime down my face and neck. I was being ridiculous. Petulant. I was not thirty anymore; I should not act the child.

"What are you going to do?"

"Crim and Aristedes are finding out how that *thing* got on board, who smuggled it in and how. I'm going to start with my list of enemies and work backward. We'll untie this thing from both ends."

Valka said nothing for so long that I thought she'd fallen back asleep, claimed by the anesthetics coursing through her veins. But her eyes were open, though what she saw with those glassy orbs I could not guess. I knew that look, that glazed and vacant stare, as one lost in memory. She *was* lost in memory, but her memory was sharper than mine, sharper even than the memory of the best-trained scholiast. Valka forgot nothing. Everything she had seen, everything she had learned and experienced, everything she *knew* was hers to recall with perfect clarity by virtue of the machine that nestled in the brain behind those jewel-bright eyes.

"We've forgotten Udax," she said, voice coming as if from the bottom of a deep well.

"Forgotten . . . ?" I trailed off, trying to remember. What did the Irchtani centurion have to do with any of this? He was safely returned to fugue with his brothers and would not awaken unless called for.

I had forgotten he once had tried to kill me, had nearly killed Pallino. This may seem strange to admit, Reader, but consider: it had been eight and thirty years for me since Gododdin, nearly half of that conscious— though you turn these pages in a matter of hours. Much had happened. Much had changed. Iubalu and the Battle of the Beast, everything we'd learned about Syriani Dorayaica, the Iedyr Yemani, plus the business of my triumph, my not-yet-official betrothal to Princess Selene and what that meant for Valka, the Lions, and the news of the Extrasolarian Monarch . . .

. . . I had forgotten about Udax the assassin.

"Oh," I said.

"He said he thought the person who promised to pay him was a Chantry priest," Valka said. I had told her everything. I always told her everything. "This could be them, too."

At once, Alexander and Selene seemed less likely culprits.

The Chantry. The Holy Terran Chantry. But for my mother and a Jaddian smuggler, I'd be one of them. Instead, I was a threat to them, a kind of *prophet* myself, though I tried not to be. Legends of my battles, my victories—and of my death most of all—went before me like a host of heralds trumpeting the truth and the lies that were stronger than the truth.

We saw Hadrian Marlowe beheaded.

We saw Hadrian Marlowe crushed beneath a falling building.

We saw Hadrian Marlowe blown out an airlock.

We saw the Halfmortal gunned down.

We saw the Halfmortal live again! We saw . . .

We saw, we saw, we saw . . .

Often I have thought there were three Hadrians. There was the one who died in the garden of the *Demiurge*, the one who sat at Valka's bedside, who was like the first and yet unlike him, both living men made of flesh made separate by the circumstances of their births—one in water, one in blood. And there was a third Hadrian. One born only of voice, one never really born at all. There was Hadrian the myth, not the *man*. And Hadrian the myth was truly *immortal*.

It was the myth the Chantry needed dead, though killing the man would not accomplish this. Again I thought of Carax, of the medallion he'd offered me with my pitchfork carved across the face of the sun. How many soldiers in the Imperial service carried such medallions? How many thousands? The Emperor's plan to wed me to Selene took on new dimension, then, for in doing so he wedded my legend to himself.

It was a more elegant solution than a knife.

And yet someone had sent a knife, a blade with neither handle nor hand to grasp it.

"We don't know anything yet," I said darkly, looking past Valka and *through* the wall behind her. But where Valka's eyes saw the past with crystal clarity, I saw only *possibility*. Like the rivers of time branching in my dream I beheld the faces of my potential enemies and met each of them in turn, eye to eye. The Lions, Lord Breathnach, Princess Selene, Prince Alexander, and the Chantry—the Chantry last and greatest of them all, a clawing shadow on my heart.

I had not even realized I was clenching my fist on the rail of Valka's cot. The false fingers offered no complaint. The memory of the attempt at Gododdin had come rushing back, flooding my skull like seawater. Pallino had nearly died, just as Valka had nearly died. How long before someone died in truth? Died as Cade had died? And Captain Yanek of the *Androzani?* Died like Raine Smythe and Sir William Crossflane?

Died like *I* had died.

Casualties of my dream.

"And when we do?" Valka asked. She tapped my fist with a finger, and I relaxed my damaging grip. "What happens then?"

"Vengeance," I said, and for once, Valka did not argue with me.

CHAPTER 39

THE COUNCIL OF GHOSTS

A WEEK PASSED. NOTHING happened. No one came, nor word, nor invitation. And so Otavia got her wish: I did not leave the *Tamerlane,* and when I was not at Valka's bedside I watched Forum from orbit, and saw the white towers and the gold lights of the Eternal City glittering by day and night like an empire of fireflies. Like a thousand points of laser light pointed at our ship.

I consoled myself that whichever hand had grasped that handleless knife, the Emperor at least was my ally. Why go to the trouble of arranging a private audience with me? Why put me through all the tedious trouble of courtship and betrothal only to dispose of me?

No, the Emperor was my ally. That was the problem.

Who was watching me out of that watchful planet? The great lords and Lions of the old families? Legion Intelligence? Princess Selene, perhaps resenting the prospect of marriage to a lowly *outcaste?* Prince Alexander himself? I prayed it was not Alexander—though I feared it was. Still, Valka's fears that it was Princess Selene behind the knife made sense, better sense than any of the old Lions, who for all their bluster objected to me only in principle.

Men are slower to act from principle than self-interest, and far slower to act on principle than jealousy or revenge. If I were a betting man, I should place my chips on the Lords Hohenzollern, Mahidol, and Bourbon last, on Alexander *first,* with Selene somewhere in between.

Unless there were a conspiracy. Unless there was some *other* hand I had not counted on.

The stalemate broke at last. A summons to appear before the Imperial Council arrived by telegraph on the morning of the tenth day since Valka's attack. Not from the Emperor, but from Prince Hector Avent, the Chancellor of the Council. The damage to Valka's lung had healed—accelerated by Okoyo's ministrations—and though she remained as yet in bed to give the new membrane in her lung time to strengthen, she was breathing on her own, and she'd been taken off her painkillers.

I had Otavia send our reply:

To the Lord High Chancellor of the Imperial Council . . .

Per communication dated 16561.05.16 and submitted to the Imperial Office, a plot against Lord M's life was detected and stopped same day. Agency behind this plot unknown. Possibly unsafe for Lord M to travel. Request meeting by holograph. Reply requested.

—Otavia Corvo, CPT-FOED, Red Company, ISV Tamerlane

Otavia's caution won out in the end over my need to appear unruffled, not out of concern for my life, as described to Prince Hector and the Council—though that was theoretically a concern, as there was a proud tradition of shuttle crashes in the Eternal City—but because I wanted to see what they would do. A number of the Lions held seats on the Emperor's Council, and though I personally counted them the least likely of my enemies, it would not do to blunder in facing them.

The Imperial court demanded precision, and so our communique revealed almost nothing.

The Council appeared on the holograph as the captains had before our fight with Iubalu: like a parliament of ghosts. The Emperor was not in attendance, but his throne—a lesser cousin to the mighty confection that stood in the Sun King's Hall—stood empty on a dais above and behind a U-shaped table. Prince Hector Avent, however, was a man so like his brother they might have been clones. I did not know the man well—as a Knight Victorian, I did not report to him—but he was, in a sense, the second most powerful man in the galaxy, unless one counted the Prince of Jadd.

About him were seated the great logothetes of the various ministries: Lady Leda Ascania of the Ministry of Public Enlightenment, Lord Allander Peake of the Ministry of Justice, Lord Haren Bulsara of the Colonial Office and the Special Adviser on the Cielcin Question, and Lord Cassian Powers, the man they called the Avenger of Cressgard. It was Powers who had led the punitive expedition to Cressgard to attack the occupying Cielcin after first contact. The Minister of Welfare was there as well—a weasel-faced woman with solemn eyes, and the Minister of Revenue, Lord Cordwainer. There was Vergilian, Synarch of the Chantry in his black and white robes and the tall white cap that recalled the pharaohs of Egypt. And there was Augustin Bourbon, of course, the Minister of War. And behind them, on risers ascending to the left and right of the throne—were the various lesser logothetes, scholiasts, and scribes whose role it was to support the efforts, claims, and cases of the high councillors who bent the ear of the Emperor and his High Chancellor.

Too many names. Too many faces. Too many enemies.

"My lords and ladies," I said, kneeling on the projector plate, "I apologize for the nature of this meeting. As my captain communicated, there was an attempt on my life. We are still attempting to ascertain the motive behind it, and as such my advisors have deemed it unsafe for me to travel at this time."

From his low seat at the center of the U beneath the throne, Prince Hector surveyed me a moment where I waited on one knee, head bowed like the loyal knight I was. I watched him through my eyebrows and long dark hair, waiting.

"There have been various reports," he said, in a voice higher pitched but resonant and musical as the Emperor's. "You are unhurt?"

"I was not present at the time," I said, honestly. Crim's sudden appearance before Selene and her girls at the Royal Forest attested to that fact plain enough, and I would not deny it.

"That is well!" said Lord Allander Peake, the Minister of Justice. "There were rumors you'd been killed, sir."

The Minister of War snorted. "Don't you know he can't be killed, Allander?" Augustin Bourbon leaned in over the table, watching me with tiny, piercing eyes. "I trust you apprehended this assassin, Lord Marlowe? He is in your custody?"

I held Lord Bourbon's stare a moment, studying him. Did he know the answer to his own question? I searched for some sign, some symptom of murderous intent in that fat-enfolded face, but whatever thoughts were written there, I could not read.

"There was no assassin, my lord."

A flurry of confused and angry questions flew past me like arrows, prompting the sergeant-at-arms—a lonely Martian praetorian in a white-plumed helm—to bang his fasces against a steel plate in the floor behind Prince Hector's seat. The metallic clangor stilled the nobiles and quieted the whispers and the rustling of pages and crystal tablets. The unsteady quiet that followed split in two beneath the Chancellor's flat command: "Explain."

The outburst from the Council seemed strange to me, but I supposed that all those important persons were so used to responding at will that they must rush over one another all the time. Pausing a moment to see if further interruption was coming, I proceeded. "There was a knife-missile."

I watched Lord Bourbon as I made this pronouncement, looking for some sign of guilt, of surprise or triumph, of anything. But the Minister of War's face was inscrutable as the stone face of a gargoyle long left in rain.

"Why was this not brought to our attention sooner?" exclaimed Synarch Vergilian, a craggy, gray-faced old lord with a basso voice. "Certain knife-missiles flout holy writ! The weapon must be handed over to the Inquisition immediately, Lord Marlowe. Immediately!"

I turned my attention on the flickering ghost of the Synarch in his white pharaonic crown. Hands innocently spread before me, I offered a short bow. "Holy Wisdom, forgive me, but I cannot. My soldiers had the weapon incinerated when it was discovered. I can have scans and surveillance records handed over to an Inquisitor with our report, should His Wisdom desire."

Vergilian's face darkened, even in ghostly projection. "That is *most* irregular, Lord Marlowe. All suspicious artifacts are to be handed over to us without question or hesitation. Such is the law."

If the weapon was, as Tor Varro described, an *Akateko*-model Nipponese knife-missile, it certainly flirted with artificial intelligence. The daimons which governed its function were simple things, but its decision-making potential and the logic trees it obeyed in choosing its targets—while not intelligent like you or I—walked the line enough to cast suspicion on anyone who came in contact with the machine.

Suddenly, I doubted the Chantry's hand in this attack. Hypocrites the Chantry's priests may be, but to employ something so nearly intelligent? It was a bridge too far.

Unless, whispered that piece of me that yet thought in Tor Gibson's voice. *Who better to choose the most effective weapon of this kind than a Chantry Inquisitor?* An Inquisitor would know precisely which weapon would *appear* possessed of daimonic intelligence without truly being so, and so select an instrument of assassination designed to implicate anyone *but* themselves. For none would believe the Chantry would employ a knife-missile, where its usual weapons were poison. Poison, surprise, and fear.

The Chantry would not send a knife-missile! they would say. Not when they might strike Lord Marlowe with a wasting illness that revealed he had been an intus pretender all along, a charlatan and no cousin of the Star Victoria at all.

"I beg your indulgence, Holy Wisdom. Many of my officers are of Norman extraction and are not defenders of the faith. They are ignorant of our ways." Only then did I straighten again, and looking the high priest in the eyes, added silently, *And if it was you, you'll never know how close you came.* We'd been lucky. The slow grind of the Imperial engine had allowed Valka time to get out of medica and back to our rooms. The corrective tape had come off and left only the faintest scars. Scars no one would question or wonder at on a foreigner, or on one who had seen action, as Valka had. Only a deep tissue scan would reveal the signs of her punctured lung, and none would think to look—unless they had knowledge of the incident they ought not to have. Of far greater concern were the medica records themselves. Data, like matter, is never truly destroyed, and though I'd ordered Okoyo to purge her records of Valka's surgery and ordered Crim to delete all security footage and replace it with recordings copied from seventy years earlier, an Inquisitor might find these things.

No cover-up could be perfect in the face of such security technologies, or of such holy scrutiny.

"Defenders of the faith . . ." Vergilian echoed, pale eyes narrow in his bloodless face. "Are you such a one, Lord Marlowe?"

I had been answering such questions for decades, if seldom from the Synarch himself. The truth was that I believe almost every palatine to be agnostic on the question of Earth and the God Emperor's divinity. The only true believers were the plebeians who accepted the Chantry's teachings for the beautiful dream they were. I could not say this before Vergilian, or before the Council, though many of them doubtless shared this opinion with me.

"I have been defending the Holy Mother's children all my life, Wisdom," I answered, side-stepping the question with the grace of the matador I have sometimes been. "I pray the Council will forgive me, but there is no one here, with the exception of Lord Powers, who has bled more for the realm and the Children of Earth than I have." I caught the retired soldier's eyes as I said this, and a flicker of something—understanding?—passed between us both. Lord Powers was the oldest remaining officer in the Sollan Empire to have stood in battle against the Cielcin and lived to tell about it. Who could understand my meaning, if not him? Baiting the Council was a dangerous game, but I had to remind those who did not number themselves my enemies just what I was and had done for them. I had to keep them defensive.

Prince Hector replied, overriding any pious rejoinder from the high priest. "No one questions your valor, Sir Hadrian. Only the circumspect manner by which you have responded to this incident. We ought to have been alerted to the details."

"You say there was no assassin, sir," asked Lady Ascania of Public Enlightenment. "But the weapon must have arrived aboard your ship somehow. How was it intercepted?"

How fitting that the Minister of Public Enlightenment—the greatest propagandist and liar in the galaxy—should ask me that question. For my answer was a lie. "It was packed into a crate of supplies intended for the officers' quarters. It never got the chance to deploy." Most important to me was keeping the assassins in the dark. They must not know their plan had nearly succeeded, lest their second attempt win through.

The truth was, neither Crim nor Aristedes had been successful as yet in determining how the weapon had gotten aboard our ship. The weapon *might* have arrived through a shipping crate, but it could not have made it into my apartments without help. The batmen and cleaning personnel were the primary suspects, but Crim had investigated all of them, including the late, lamented M. Martin, and found no evidence of complicity. It was possible, if unlikely, that the blade had traveled through ventilation or some other system—such would almost certainly require artificial intelligence, for subsequent analysis had proved Varro correct: the knife had no receiver, and so no pilot crouched nearby, hiding in some forgotten hold or among the sleepers in the cubicula.

"This should be handed over to the Martian Guard for investigation, Lord High Chancellor," said Allander Peake, stroking his pointed black beard. "All crimes carried out within Forum orbit are under their jurisdiction."

Vergilian cut in, "The potential presence of daimons is a grave matter, Lord Minister of Justice. Lord Marlowe's ship should be impounded and subject to thorough analysis under the auspices of the Holy Office. If the weapon employed was possessed of artificial intelligence, it is possible some other system aboard has been compromised as well. I recommend all communications with the *Tamerlane* and all transport to and from it be sealed immediately until such time as potential threat is ruled out."

The Chancellor shook his head with a coolness reminiscent of his brother, the Emperor. Turning in his throne-like seat, Prince Hector Avent turned to a gray-clad logothete on the bench to his right. The young woman sat managing the holograph controls and the transmitter. "M. Sylva, you are monitoring our datasphere's ice walls?" he asked, referring to the defensive layers that protected the palace's datasphere network.

"Yes, Your Excellency," she said at once.

"And we are secure?"

"Yes, Your Excellency."

Prince Hector rotated to regard the high priest yet again. "We are perfectly safe, Holy Wisdom."

"I agree with the Synarch, Lord High Chancellor," said Augustin Bourbon dryly. "We cannot risk contamination. If what Lord Marlowe says is true about the nature of this attack, and given *his history,* we must be prepared for the possibility of Extrasolarian involvement. An investigation should be sent to the *Tamerlane* to verify they are clear of *infestation.*"

A terrible thought crept its way down my neck. Had I just played directly into their hands? Perhaps the knife was never meant to succeed? Perhaps the weapon was only a distraction, and I was meant to be caught red-handed in possession of forbidden machine intelligence and executed?

Iron fingers clamped over my heart and I held my breath to stop it pounding. If that was Bourbon's play—assuming that he and Vergilian were each my enemy—it was brilliant. And in my destroying the knife to protect the fact that the assassins had nearly succeeded, they would find enough rope to hang me. The false bones of my arm, the machinery in my lover's brain, and maybe—just maybe—Pallino's recording of my demise.

"I'm not sure that's necessary, Lord Minister of War," Prince Hector said. "If what Lord Marlowe says is true, the weapon has been destroyed. He can simply hand his records over to the Martian Guard and the investigation may continue apace."

But Lord Bourbon had an answer ready-made, a simple statement, breathtaking in its casual sound. "Only as a precaution. We cannot be too careful."

"No indeed!" the Synarch agreed.

Valka's words came back to me, her reminder.

He said he thought the person who promised to pay him was a Chantry priest.

CHAPTER 40

THE PLAN

THE INQUISITION WASTED NO time.

No sooner had the ghosts of the Council faded from the holography booth than the word went out on the ship's internal comm. We were locked down. Locked out. No messages, no signals were permitted in or out of the *Tamerlane,* and no shuttles beside. Our communications were jammed.

Corvo met me the hall. "What happened?" she asked, towering over me. "What did they say?"

"We've been impounded pending Inquisition," I answered her, and watched the color drain from her face. Before she could say a word, I added, "Lord Bourbon and the Synarch had it worked out in advance. They convinced the council the knife-missile was artificially intelligent. They mean to search the ship."

Otavia squared her jaw. "They won't find anything."

I looked directly over her shoulder and into the nearest security lens. "They will *plant* whatever they want."

"You think they planted the knife?"

"Or they know who did," I answered her. "Frankly, there's enough to implicate me between my left arm and Valka as is. It won't take much." I raised the offending appendage. "Where's Okoyo?"

"What about the Emperor?" she asked, following me as I took off down the hall. "He's your friend, isn't he?"

My friend? I almost sneered at that, but Corvo did not deserve it. "If they get out of this far enough ahead there won't be anything His Radiance can do. I am a problem, Otavia. His marriage proposal with Selene is a solution to that problem, but he will not lament me if I am gone, I think." I was speaking quickly then, tongue racing to catch up with the current of my thoughts. "They want me dead, and if they can build a strong enough case for why I should be, the Emperor won't raise a finger to stop them. He won't gainsay the Chantry if the Synarch himself says I'm some sort of *devil worshiper.*" I almost laughed aloud and touched the pitchfork-and-pentacle embroidered above my heart.

"Where are we going?" Otavia asked suddenly, stopping in her tracks.

"I told you!" I snapped. "To find Okoyo. Where is she?"

"In medica!" Corvo said, pointing back over her shoulder, back the way we had come. *"That* way!"

"I don't think 'tis necessary!" Valka said, seated on the edge of the dressing table that ran along the middle of the cubiculum's antechamber, her boots still on. "They know I'm Tavrosi."

I placed my hands on her shoulders and spoke into her eyes. "Yes, but they might have forgotten about you. They might not look too closely."

"Because I'm just *your woman?*" Valka sneered.

There was no time. "Yes!" And hissed, *"But not to me."* I could not afford an argument, not then. "They might not look twice at you and might underestimate your importance, particularly because they might be fool enough to dismiss you as *just my woman.*"

Her icy facade cracked as she smiled. " 'Tis better."

I grunted. "I need you to go back into fugue. It might not occur to them that you were caught up in all this, and it might make them forget about you." Fingers tightened on her shoulders as I willed her to understand, praying that for once in our mingled lives she would only accept what I said and not challenge me. "They'll use you to hang me, if they can. And I can't let them know how close their plan came to working."

"You're sure it was their plan?"

"Do you doubt it?"

I had no real illusions that they might forget Valka or what she was, but placing her in fugue might—*might*—remove her from the board.

Neither of us spoke a moment, but I took my hands away and stepped back, permitting her the room and the time she needed to think. I could see the mind working behind the face, messages racing like lightning across the surface of a cloud.

The fugue creche stood behind her, one of twenty standing empty in the antechamber filling bay. Personnel were meant to undress and load in two decades at a time, but we were alone. I'd ordered Corvo to find Lorian and Crim, and asked Okoyo to wait outside.

"What do you think they're going to find?" she asked me.

"Nothing," I said. "But it won't matter."

"Unless you figure out how that knife got aboard," she said.

The lightning in my own head stopped. She was right. That was our only hope.

Taking a deep breath, I stepped back. "This isn't goodbye."

"You are always so dramatic," she said, and raising her feet in turn un-zipped her boots.

"I think I've earned it today."

She made a small noise of assent before kicking the boots into a bin beside the nearest creche. The rest of her clothing soon joined them, and she turned naked to face me, a strange expression on her face, winged brows drawn up and together. It was not a face she wore often, leastways not where anyone could see.

Concern.

"See you on the other side, then."

Which side is that? I asked myself. Who knew what world she might awaken to? If she awoke at all.

She took a half-step back, made to turn and climb into the creche housing, but I caught her hand. I can't remember the distance closing be-tween us. Only that it had. Both hands in her hair, I kissed her, fast and fiercely. And when we sprang apart she pushed me breathlessly away. Her clan tattoo spiraled from her arm and collarbone down her left flank. How cruel, how inexcusable, that I who knew its every line and curve—and hers—can scarce recall them now.

"Get the doctor," she said. "Do it."

"I love you," I said, stopping on the threshold to look back.

"Well . . ." she smiled, clambering into the creche, "you're not wrong."

Crim and Lorian both met me in my chambers, still the safest and most secure spot on the ship. Corvo had been set the task of hiding any errant bits of conversation left on the ship's monitors. I had told them everything, and telling them did not waste any time. We might have only hours before the Inquisition docked with the *Tamerlane*. We had to act quickly.

"Like I said before," Crim was saying, "there's no one on this ship who shouldn't be. No stowaways, no intruders my men could find. No one operating that thing as stabbed the doctor and your man Martin, just like Varro said. Ilex confirmed there was no receiver on the thing, either, so maybe it was . . . smart."

Lorian was nodding. "It's a pity we don't have the bloody thing. The Inquisitors might not buy our report for a steel bit, but the knife would have cleared us."

I dismissed this with a wave of my hand. "They'd only have thrown it away." But he was right: I might have gotten the knife through to the Martian Guard or the Ministry of Justice or straight to the Emperor himself.

"What possessed you to have it destroyed?" Lorian said, and I could feel him glowering at me.

"You were right there, Aristedes." I glared back, and the little man quailed, remembering who I was and the distance between us. "If you'd known it was a misplay then, you could have stopped me." That shut him up, and I added, "I was concerned that turning the knife over to the Chantry or Legion Intelligence or whoever would put a recording of the attempt in the hands of our enemies—and Emperor knows what else. There's no telling how long the knife's been aboard. There's no telling what it recorded. What it *heard*."

Crim had been silent a moment, fingers picking at the string of throwing knives slotted through the baldric he wore over his burgundy uniform jacket. "Why wasn't it transmitting then? The whole time?"

"We'd have caught it, even tight beam, broadcasting out of the ship like that? We'd have noticed?" Lorian answered easily.

"Would we?" Crim cracked back. "I'm feeling a bit blind at the moment."

"Enough!" I said. "We can discuss our tactical failures later, gentlemen. We have work to do." And with this I removed a small metal box, four inches to a side, from the seat beside me and set it on the coffee table between us, as near to Crim as I could make it. "Take it."

The former mercenary leaned in and picked it up. "What is it?"

"My death," I said, without a dram of irony.

"The recording?" Lorian asked.

I nodded, looking each man in the face by turns. "They *can't* find that." As I spoke, Crim opened the box to reveal the crystal ball, about the size of a chicken's egg, nestled safely in foam. "It's the only copy. I need you to hide it. Do whatever you have to, and do not tell a soul."

The swordsman pressed his lips together and slid the box into one of the massive pockets inside the greatcoat.

"So we're back to the idea that it's one of our people," I said soberly, eyes tracking from my security officer to my tactical officer and back.

Commander Aristedes raised a bony finger. "We'd never technically abandoned the idea."

Without warning I pounded the coffee table with a fist. "Damn it, Lorian! Enough with the splitting hairs."

The intus flapped his hands. "No, no, no, listen! I've got it! We've ruled out the cleaning staff and your batmen."

"I even interrogated the cooks," Crim said. "Everyone I could think of."

"Everyone who had access to your chambers." Lorian's watery eyes flitted from me to Crim and back again, nervous and fidgeting as his hands. "But what about the people who had access to the people who had access to your chambers?"

I stood sharply and stalked toward the sideboard where Jinan's laving basin stood. Prince Aranata's ring lay in it alongside the elephant ivory band I often wore on my third finger, and atop it rested the still-incorrupt Galath blossom. In a voice flat and calm, I said, "I said enough games, Lorian. Do not play me in riddles. Tell me what you're thinking, and tell me plain."

"We should be looking at the security staff," Lorian said.

Even with my back turned, I could feel Crim turn to ice and crunch beneath the weight of that suggestion. I heard the man stand and shouted, "Hold!" My fingers tightened on the edge of the table, but I did not turn to face them both. I did not have to. I could see Crim standing, feet apart, one hand on the hilt of one long knife, ready. I understood. Lorian had insulted his honor, and Crim's honor had been insulted enough of late. Lorian had kicked him while he was down.

"If you're suggesting that *I* have something to do with this, little man . . ." Crim said, words failing him. *"Noyn jitat!"* He let fly a string of expletives in his native Jaddian.

"Crim!" I said, still not turning, still staring down into the basin with my rings and the Imperial flower. "What is in your pocket?"

"Sir?"

"Your pocket," I said again, and worked first the ivory ring onto its finger, then the rhodium one onto my thumb. This accomplished, I turned, and saw that it was precisely as I'd expected. Crim stood looming over the table and over the little intus where he sat at the narrow end: a tall, rapier-thin shadow in blood red above a pale figure in legionary black.

"I . . ." Crim stammered.

I took a step nearer the two of them, still fiddling with the rings that had not yet settled into their proper places on my hand. "Lieutenant Commander Garone, I just gave you something. What was it?"

The Jaddian mercenary looked round at me as though I'd lost my mind. "The recording?"

"I gave you the *only* recording that proves that what they say about me is true. And I asked you to protect it. Ask yourself: why would I do such a thing if I did not trust you?" The tall man visibly relaxed, seeming almost to deflate as he turned from Lorian to face me. Crim had been at my side since long before Vorgossos, since Pharos and Admiral Whent. "Do you think me, stupid, man?"

Crim bowed his head. "No, my lord."

"Good," I said, "because Aristedes here *does* think I'm stupid, and I've no wish to be outnumbered just now. So please *sit down*." He sat, hand still on the hilt of his knife. Turning my attentions back to Aristedes then, I said, "Explain yourself."

Though I had an inclination of where he was going, I found it best in dealing with Lorian Aristedes simply to let the man talk. "Look, in the past week, we've edited, deleted, fabricated hours and hours and hours of sec footage. Price of living under surveillance, I suppose. But listen. We've ruled out everyone with access to this room, which leaves us with only those people who can cover up that they had access. We wasted our time this past week interviewing personnel and reviewing the sec recordings. We should have been looking through the changelogs for signs of meddling."

"How long will it take?"

"A couple days?" Lorian replied.

"You have until they arrive," I said. "Put Varro on it, Durand . . . anyone you need. We need proof of what happened and we need to get it off this ship and into the hands of the Martian Guard or the Justice Ministry . . . someone who doesn't answer to Bourbon or Legion Intelligence—and certainly no one answerable to the Chantry."

Lorian was shaking his head. "We can't broadcast, my lord. There's no way to get a signal out."

"I don't care if you have to swim, Lorian," I said with force. "You will find out who did this thing, and you will get the man and the evidence off this ship."

CHAPTER 41

THE GOOD SOLDIER

I WAITED WITH MY officers on the receiving platform as the Inquisition emerged from its shuttle. Legionnaires led the way in ivory armor, their white tunics trimmed in crimson labyrinths, black disruptor rifles in hand, faceless visors reflecting the overhead fluorescent lighting. Behind them came a half dozen cathars in black robes, shave-headed and with dark muslin blindfolds over their eyes. Behind *them* were two Inquistors in similar black, though their cloth was slashed with white beneath, and they wore white mantles over their shoulders and silver chains with enameled cartouches depicting the Earth and Sun, the former eclipsing the latter.

"Remind me again why I enlisted with you lot," Corvo whispered in my ear. She had to stoop to reach it. The tension in her—and in Durand, in Crim, and the other Norman officers—was so much I thought each of them might snap like a guitar string. My Imperial mates fared little better—and perhaps worse. Lorian stood at my left hand, and as I was glancing down at the small man, he looked almost green. I found myself wishing that Valka *were* there; I needed her spine to lean on.

The next figure in the train descending from the overlarge shuttle sent an electric spasm through my heart. Intelligence Director Lorcan Breathnach appeared at the top of the ramp, his face like weathered stone, flanked by some squire I did not know and followed by a number of lay technicians and logothetes from Legion Intelligence. I was surprised to see sad-faced Sir Friedrich Oberlin, the young head of reconnaissance in the Norman Expanse. What was he doing here? And why had Breathnach come himself? Had he been requested by the Chantry? Or had the Minister of War insisted on the Director's presence?

Perhaps he had only come to gloat.

That he was behind all this I had no doubt. He wasn't even trying to hide it. I wondered at his motivations. Did he think me a threat to his Imperial master? Or was it simply the patrician chip on his shoulder? He had earned his place, clawed for it and his chance to be uplifted from mere plebeian humanity, whereas I—however *outcaste*—remained a palatine nobile.

But he was not the last in the train, for behind him and his aides and guards came one last, a figure robed in white with a black mantle draped over her shoulders. A black Egyptian-style cap that rose a foot above her head. Her skin was pale as milk, and her eyes were just as colorless, such that I thought her blind.

A Grand Inquisitor.

The others stepped aside as the woman approached in her high crown and cape, and I was struck suddenly by just how much they all resembled chess pieces, white and black. Here surely was a queen. A dangerous piece indeed.

The Grand Inquisitor halted before me and extended a clawed hand. At first I thought she intended me to take it as the plebeians are wont to do. It was a moment before I saw the signet ring. She did not wear it upon her thumb as we nobiles do, but upon her smallest finger. Remembering the ancient lessons of my dancing master, I went to both knees and kissed it, mindful of the pointed, red-enameled nails. Only after I released the cold fingers did I realize the ring was fashioned of bone.

"So," she said, voice deep and surprisingly throaty, "you're the one."

I had met Synarch Vergilian more than a dozen times over the long years, but this Inquisitor frightened me as he never had. People believe the Synarch to be master of the Holy Terran Chantry, but he is only an ambassador. First among equals representing the true power in the faith, the Synod of high priests who never left the great cloisters on Vesperad. Though nominally they served the Emperor, there are those who wonder if it is not the other way round.

These Grand Inquisitors answered to the Synod itself, and so in a sense the pale woman before me was stranger and more terrible even than His Holy Wisdom, the Synarch. He was only a mouthpiece. She was a hand.

When I said nothing, she raised one bald eyebrow. "Do you know who I am?"

I could not refuse to answer a direct question. Still kneeling, I looked her in the eye. "You're a Grand Inquistor."

"I am a servant of truth," she answered me. If I expected her to give me a name, I was disappointed. Perhaps she had one, once, but if so that was a long time ago. "And I will find the truth, wherever it may be. Your people will cooperate with my investigation. You will allow us access to any part of this ship or its databases and you will do so without question or else you and your people will be charged with obstruction." Her white eyes swept over my officers, and creases formed at the corners of her mouth, as though she was not impressed by what she saw. I saw Breathnach smiling with fiery eyes over her shoulder. Her orders were not yet done. "Any personnel not required for the maintenance and upkeep of this vessel will confine themselves to quarters except at mealtimes, which will be brief and orderly. You yourself are not to leave your cabin at all, Lord Marlowe, unless you are summoned. Is that clear?"

Again, I could not ignore a direct question. "Yes, Reverence."

"You understand that you are not accused of consortation? That you are not, yourself, under investigation for crimes against humanity?"

I could not help myself. "It doesn't feel that way, Your Reverence."

The Grand Inquisitor blinked. "Reports indicated a device potentially possessed of daimonic intelligence was found aboard this vessel. That device was destroyed on your orders, and so we cannot rule out the possibility of infestation here by straightforward forensic analysis of the machine in question. We must then conduct a thorough survey of all electronic devices aboard."

Which will allow you and your friend Sir Lorcan to plant whatever evidence you wish, I did not say.

"The ship will be forfeit if an infestation is detected," she said, "but your people and privileges will remain intact." The Grand Inquisitor brushed past me. Not looking at me, she surveyed the bay: the static field gleaming in the open hatch below, the stars beyond, the levels and levels of gantries and catwalks and service arms rising toward the arched supports of the bulkheads far above. "Should something be *detected,* however . . . I pray you are *only* a victim in this."

Sensing the unease in my officers around me, I took a step forward. "May I ask a question?" The Grand Inquisitor clasped taloned hands behind her back. I took her silence for assent. "Why is the Lord Director here?" I did not look at Breathnach as I asked the question, preferring to speak as though he were not mere feet from me.

The pale woman did not turn back, but continued her survey of the bay. "You have been invaluable to the war effort, Lord Marlowe. The Intelligence Director wishes to protect his asset, and we have allowed his team aboard to extract any and all useful intelligence from your systems under our auspices, so as to ensure that any information may be obtained under the safest conditions." She did turn then, cape belling beneath her clasped hands. Was I mad? Or did her expression soften for the barest instant? "Lord Marlowe, rest assured. You've nothing to fear save fear, if you are blameless. If you are—as you claimed in your report to the Imperial Council—only a victim in this, we will determine who is guilty. And they will be punished." She spoke with such earnestness that for a moment I wondered if she was only a pawn and no queen at all. Had Breathnach manipulated her as well? Manipulated the Chantry? Brought them here to find the evil seed he meant to plant?

Who is playing, and who played? I asked myself, and allowed myself to be led back to the apartments whence I had come. I knew their protocol. They would isolate my officers and question us each in turn, seeking discrepancies, cracks in our armor.

They would find some.

Try as I had to coordinate our deception, breakdown was inevitable. Only the truth can weather a siege forever. I could only hope that Lorian and Crim retained sufficient liberty to complete their investigation before Breathnach and his Grand Inquisitor could act.

The doors to my chambers hissed shut behind me, and I heard the faint whine of servos as the deadbolts were secured.

And I was alone.

Infestation.

It wasn't one of the Twelve Abominations against human nature, though it might lead to *consortation* or *possession*. It was an ancient word, thick with connotation and innuendo, the sort of word that could kill a man merely by being breathed on him within earshot of another. To be infested was to be haunted—as by ghosts in the foggy age of ancients—by machines. Like rats in the walls, like spiders, machine intelligence might creep into any circuit, any system and there take root. One imagines the growth as a kind of cancer, a fungus swelling from the walls and banks of computer storage. Picturing Brethren's bloated bulk and the nematodal swelling of its too-long arms, I think that image an apt one. The stench of corruption, of environmental decay, that *rot* which the Nipponese call *kegare*.

A kind of sin.

They would find infestation because they—the Inquisition or the LIO operatives who'd accompanied Sir Lorcan—had brought it with them: some captured Extrasolarian daimon bottled in the equipment they'd brought along in their shuttle. Under the guise of investigating the *Tamerlane*'s system, they would simply install it. They would have their infestation, and from there, it would be a small matter to prove my knowledge of the crime, and to charge me with *possession* or *consortation*, and a smaller matter to strike off my head.

Again.

It will surprise you perhaps to learn that I was not afraid, sitting in the gloom of my chambers, still in my greatcoat and wearing my belt. It was only that I could not quiet the roaring in my head. Wheels turned, grinding through their motions. All my hopes rested then on Crim and on Lorian Aristedes's fragile shoulders.

There was more than one spider in the halls of the *Tamerlane*. And more than one web.

I must have dozed eventually, my nervous waiting turned to impatience, impatience to sleep. Whent's eight-winged angel of retribution looked down from the walls, and all the items of my long life seemed to weigh heavily on the walls and shelves where they stood in attendance around me like candles lit before an icon in sanctum.

Someone pounded on the door—my guard, no doubt. A moment later the deadbolts whined and the door slid into its pocket in the wall.

I'd expected Lorcan Breathnach, there to gloat. I'd expected the Grand Inquisitor, starting at the top. I had not expected Sir Friedrich Oberlin with his sad eyes and tired smile. Oberlin was clearly palatine, but possessed of that one trait indispensable to the lifelong bureaucrat: he was utterly forgettable. Smooth-featured and brown-haired, his nobile face left little impression on the mind, striking neither for its beauty or its ugliness. This drabness of person was only intensified by the simple gray suit he wore, its only device the shield emblem of Legion Intelligence pinned on his lapel, a picture only completed by the antique briefcase he carried in one hand. But whatever his apparent meekness, the man was a knight, and wore a highmatter sword in a neatly maintained holster strapped to his right leg beneath the long jacket.

He offered a tight smile. "The Director has asked that I sit in."

"Sit in?" I asked, not standing to greet my fellow knight as custom would dictate. "On what?"

My answer came in the form of a trio of black-robed figures, one hooded and mantled in white, two blindfolded carrying a case between them.

Oberlin stepped neatly aside, allowing the Inquisitor and his cathars to advance. I eyed the case—a flat, metal lozenge half as long as the coffee table before me onto which they deposited it—as though it were a coiled serpent.

The Inquisitor threw back his white hood, revealing a shaved pate and deep green eyes, hairless as his superior, putting me in mind of the androgyn homunculi who served at the Imperial court. He did not bow. "Hadrian, Lord Marlowe." His voice was flat, an almost pleasant calm that belied the threat and power he held. "My master has sent me to test you. I am called Gereon."

Unsure whether or not standing was called for or might be taken as a threat, I did not move, but clenched my left fist on my knee, willing the bones to ache, to become real. Kharn Sagara's gift had no electronics in it, but the bones were adamant, and while technically they were not machine—were moved only by the new-grown flesh—it might not matter. To take machines into the body was *profanation,* another abomination. How easy it would be to present Marlowe's arm as evidence that he was in league with daimons!

"Test me?" I echoed. "To determine if I am guilty?"

Inquisitor Gereon shook his head once. "Only to determine if you are still human. Please stay seated."

I had been midway through the act of standing to disarm, and told him as much, asking, "May I not put up my arms, Reverence?" With a gesture I indicated the brass hooks on the wall beside the sideboard and Jinan's basin. The Inquisitor allowed this with a raised hand, and I crossed to the wall.

"Lord Marlowe." Gereon's pleasant voice stopped me before I could close the distance to the wall. I pivoted to face him, found a hand extended, palm up. "Your terminal, please."

Matching his smile, I undid the leather strap and pressed the device into his hand without comment, and resumed my move to the wall, shrugging out of my coat, which I hung over the hook with an easy motion. Was it only protocol? Or had the man guessed I'd been about to activate the terminal's dictator to record all that passed between us?

No matter.

Unruffled, I removed my belt, the heavy strap clattering with sword and sidearm, sabretache and shield-generator as I placed it over the hook. I paused a minute at Jinan's basin, unscrewing the rings from my fingers for fear the ivory band would remind the Inquisitor of Valka's existence. What I'd have given to have her there then, with her eyes and ears to see and hear—and to remember with objective clarity.

"This is a lovely place you have made for yourself, my lord," the Inquisitor said. "I see we share an admiration for the written word."

I let him talk, guessed he was admiring the upper level that ringed the main chamber of my suite with its assembly of old books, film reels, and storage crystals, brights spheres like the one I'd given Crim. I lingered a moment, gripping the edges of the table as if to regain my bearings and steady myself.

"Reverence, may I sit?" Sir Friedrich asked. He could not have asked at a better time.

"Please, sir," Gereon said.

Unseen by either man, I pressed the carved knot on the edge of the table that activated the room's recording suite. They could take away my terminal if they liked, but they should have taken me out of my home first.

Turning back, I found Sir Friedrich had set up in the chair at the narrow end of the table that Lorian and Valka were so fond of and was fussing with his own terminal, setting up a telescoping tripod and—to my vague surprise—a smattering of printed and handwritten notes which he arranged neatly at the end of the table.

At a gesture from Gereon, I resumed my seat in the middle of the couch and stared up at the Inquisitor while his cathars busied themselves with the kit.

"Have you been put to the Question before, my lord?"

"No." And unable to help myself, I added, "But I have seen your people interrogate the Pale."

Gereon shook his head again. "The Question is somewhat different from a standard interrogation procedure."

The cathars opened the case, revealing a display screen and several smaller instruments packed in foam. I recognized electrode tape and spooled wire as holographs appeared above the device, fields meant to track heart rate, skin conductivity response, and various forms of brain activity I did not understand. Every story I'd ever heard about the Chantry came flooding back, every nightmare, every childhood fancy—each one tempered by the memory of Uvanari's torment and the icy, mechanical precision of the interrogator's questions.

"The purpose of my inquiry is to determine if you are operating under any daimonic influence," Gereon was saying. "You are not accused of any crime at this time." The Inquisitor swept the room with his gaze, as if he expected to find some shattered machine lurking in the corners. "Before we begin, have you anything to confess?"

I raised my left hand. It may as well come out now. "False bones in this arm to the shoulder, but no electronics."

Gereon pursed his lips with clinical distaste. "This is known," he said. "Carbon fiber. They'd been detected by millimeter wave on palace scans, and note was made in LIO medical files." As he spoke, he seized a spindle-legged chair from the dining area and carried it back across Tavrosi carpets to place it facing me. He smiled kindly, "But your candor does you credit. Would you like me to explain any of our implements here?" He held his hands out over the console the cathars had brought in.

"I'm sorry?"

"Per the *Protocols*," he replied, "you are entitled to an explanation of everything that is to be done to you." One of the cathars stooped as Gereon was speaking and affixed the wireless electrode tabs to my temple, neck, and—parting my jacket—my chest. When I said nothing, he pressed on. "I am going to ask a series of control questions. You are to answer either yes or no. Do you understand?"

"Yes."

He flipped a series of switches on his console, eyes never leaving my face. "Are you currently in a seated position?"

"Yes."

"Are we currently on board a starship?"

"Yes."

"Is your name Hadrian Anaxander Marlowe?"

"Yes."

"Were you born on Delos, in Meidua Prefecture?"

"Yes."

"In ISD 16119?"

"No."

"In ISD 16117?"

"Yes."

"Good," Gereon said. He studied his instruments all the while, observing holographs that tracked my electroencephalogram, heart rate, and pupil response. Beside us, Sir Friedrich scribbled notes on his papers. The questions continued in this vein for another several minutes, with Gereon plodding along politely, following his script with an efficiency any bureaucrat would admire.

At last the Inquisitor paused and made a note on a holograph pad inside the lid panel of his case. "Good," he said again. "Very good. Let us proceed to the main test."

"May I ask a procedural question?" I said, interrupting the Inquisitor for the first time. Gereon gestured that I should proceed. Meanwhile, he worked at unfolding some manner of scope from his kit and brought it up to the level of my chest. I ignored this, asked, "You're measuring heartbeat, brain activity, and so on. I was under the impression that such methods were useless in determining truth or falsehood."

The Inquisitor removed another round patch from its place in the foam lid and pinched it between his fingers. "They are. But we are not interested in your words, my lord. Only in your body's responses. Your conscious assertions—regardless of their truth—are immaterial. We are interrogating your body, which cannot lie. Please lean forward." I obeyed, and Gereon placed the patch on the side of my neck opposite the electrode tape. "You will feel a slight pressure."

A moment later, my neck stung as the injection took. "What is it?"

"Adrenaline."

At once my chest tightened, and I felt the vasoconstriction as blood was forced into my limbs. My eyes bulged. "Why?"

"To open the way." Gereon still smiled, and peeled the patch away. Dimly, I felt warm blood run down my neck and bounce off my hydrophobic collar. I pressed fingers to the spot. "It will cease presently. There was a coagulant administered with the hormone." I could feel my heart racing, pounding against my ribs as though they were the bars of a cage. "For this next part of the examination, I will show you a series of images. You are to tell me in fewer than five words what those images portray. We will move as quickly as possible. Do you understand?"

My eyes darted from Gereon to Oberlin and back. The quiet knight sat impassive, watching me with his bland face unmoved. "Yes." The word came out ragged, raw thanks to the hormones pulsing through my bloodstream.

A holograph panel flowered in the air, a window that depicted my own face: gaunt and aquiline beneath its fringe of black hair. "Myself," I said, still holding the bloody spot on my neck.

The image *flicked,* displayed a family—man and wife and children—standing before a small cottage.

"Plebeians," I answered, and added, "a family."

Flick. The window showed a sailing vessel under green skies.

"A ship."

Flick. A Chantry dome with its nine minarets.

"A sanctum."

Flick. An image of the gallows in some city square, men and women standing on the platform, nooses tied, ready to drop.

"Death," I answered. "Crime."

Flick. A bucolic countryside, winding hills and neat stone fences. Struck by the geometry of it all, the careful, naturalistic, imprecise precision of it, I answered, "Walls. Order."

Gereon grunted. *Flick.* A crab lay on its back in the sand, smashed by some hammer for its meat. "Crab." My heart was running faster then, and I almost forgot to add, "Death."

Flick. A nude woman reclined on a divan, legs apart. Shocked, I looked away and hissed, "Private."

Flick.

"A house."

Flick.

"A castle."

Flick.

"A gun."

Flick. Suit footage—suit footage taken from my own men, I was almost certain—showing the eyeless man on the Cielcin dining slab. Rage flared in me, and I spat, "Victim."

Gereon flitted from one image to the next with the relentless pace of a childhood tutor drumming quotations into the head of his pupil. He kept his attentions on my EEG monitor while he spoke, one hand on the switch that advanced his slideshow one frame at a time. He was looking for the tell-tale abnormalities that might betray me as *possessed,* as not truly human. Perhaps under other circumstances, I might have been grateful for the examination. The Inquisitor's Question was one way to answer forever the question of whether or not I was me or some simulacrum of Kharn Sagara's.

Flick. Flick. Flick.

A Cielcin *scahari* warrior snarled at me, face masked, fangs exposed, a ceramic blade in its hand. A glittering bath house, men and women lounging naked in the steam. Three dozen human slaves hanging mutilated from hooks. A garden of jewel-bright flowers. A dead dog in the streets of some city, its stomach ruptured on the tarmac. The damasked face of a gas giant. Stacks of arms and legs like logs for kindling. The sunlight caught in the rigging of solar sails. A pillar of skulls.

What Gereon might have seen in his instruments I could not guess. Another Hadrian might have known, that Hadrian who had honored his father's wishes. Perhaps along one of those rivers of light there was a table much like this one, where I sat in white mantle with shaven crown and put some other man to the Question, perhaps Gereon himself.

But whatever it was, he found it. Or did not find it. After what seemed an eternity of questions, minutes stretched to hours by the adrenaline pumping through my body, he ceased, banishing the holograph window like smoke. Moving with officious grace he folded the scope back into the kit.

Into the sudden silence I asked, "Well then? Am I human?"

"You have to ask?" Gereon cocked an eyebrow.

"Don't we all?"

The Inquisitor actually barked a laugh, but instead of answering he summoned his cathars with a gesture. They advanced wordless as the Emperor's Excubitors and retrieved the interrogation kit. "You may be many things, Lord Marlowe, that are not for me to decide," he said finally. "But you *are* a man."

A piece of me—the piece of me that doubted everything—rejoiced.

I was myself and no changeling.

But the Inquisitor was not done. "There are those who think you are some kind of god. I am afraid this proves otherwise. You are just a man." He glanced pointedly at my left hand. "Rather, *less* than a man." His airy demeanor collapsed into something tighter, colder. "Tell me, the stories they tell about you . . . why do they tell them?"

"Surely you should ask them, Your Reverence," I answered.

"They say you died."

Had this man found the recording I'd entrusted to Crim? Relying on scholiast techniques Gibson had taught me, I kept my face studiously blank, jaw clenched to stop the pounding of my heart in my throat from the drugs. "They say a lot of things," I said.

"You deny it, then?"

"Deny what? That I'm dead?" I spread my hands. "What do you want me to say? I cannot speak for such people."

Gereon's smile returned. "Very good. Very good. You are to remain in your quarters until I or the Grand Inquisitor send for you. Sir Friedrich, my work is done."

Sir Friedrich Oberlin nodded and rearranged the papers he'd left on the table. "Yes, Reverence."

Inquisitor Gereon turned and swept toward the door, his men in tow with their kit. Friedrich frantically finished his last bit of writing and creased the page, folding it in half. This he tucked beneath his papers and *left* on the table when he picked up the rest. Our eyes met a moment, and I said nothing. I didn't move.

He was gone a moment after, vanishing through the portal behind Gereon and his men. I caught a brief glimpse of the two legionnaires standing at their posts in the hall. Then the door was closed, and the deadbolts whined.

A moment passed, marked by the clattering sound of feet retreating in the hall, muffled—barely to be heard through the bulkhead. Another moment passed. My heart had not stopped hammering. I wondered how long the Inquisitor's adrenal cocktail would linger in my bloodstream. Hand shaking, I seized Sir Friedrich's paper.

It was not a contract or report, nor any sort of formal document. Only a handwritten note.

I read its contents over once, read them again to ensure I'd understood.

Knife arranged by Director. Priests involved. Bought one of your lieutenants. Castor/Castle, don't know. Mean to plant daimon on ship. Not sure how.

Lorian was right.

But it wasn't the revelation that gave me pause. It was the glyph scrawled on the bottom corner of the note, more hastily than the knight-logothete's neat block lettering. He'd drawn my pitchfork and pentacle *through* the watermarked Imperial sunburst seal at the bottom of the page.

Just as Carax had carved it on his medallion.

Sir Friedrich was a *believer.*

CHAPTER 42

IMPOSSIBLE TASKS

I HAD NO WAY to get the note to the others. For all I knew this Castor or whatever his name was and the other officers were locked in their quarters as I was. I had no notion of what was passing on the *Tamerlane* or in the wider world, what lies the spiders were weaving, what nets to ensnare. Was there even a Castor among Crim's lieutenants? Or a Castle? I struggled to remember their names. I was not familiar with the junior staff. There were simply too many of them, and they rotated so quickly, falling in and out of fugue like plants through their seasons.

Crim would know, but I could not contact Crim. I had no way of communicating outside at all, unless it was to shout through the heavy metal bulkhead to my guards, who I did not doubt would be deaf to my cries, or worse, would report them to Breathnach and the Grand Inquisitor.

I was *in check*.

A day passed. Two. Three.

I hoped at least that Valka still slept in her coffin of ice, forgotten. I despaired. Despaired because my enemies held my ship and my people in their grasp. Despaired because—holding us—those enemies doubtless had disappeared this Castle or whatever his name was and covered their tracks. Despaired, because I could not hear the faint *tapping* of metal on metal.

Not at first.

Tap-tap.

But there it was, a faint grinding *scrape* as of a knife dragged across the ground. Dressed only in a shirt and trousers—without boots or belt—I rolled to my feet and padded across the carpet, retrieved my sword from the dining table where I'd left it. I'd cleaned it the day before, polished the fittings.

Tap-tap. Scrape.

I said nothing, certain that to cry out would summon my guards even through the plate metal door.

Unless it's another knife-missile, I thought. *Or worse.* Tilting my head, I listened, trying to find the source of the sound. It was somewhere on the upper level. Sword held at the ready, I moved toward the curving stair and—one bare foot softly after the other—began to climb.

Scrape-scrape. Tap.

"Who goes there?" I said, voice low but edged with command.

Nothing.

Thoughts of assassins, of knife-missiles again and of Nipponese *shinobi* splashed across my mind. I kindled my blade, highmatter streaming forth, liquid metal throwing out vapors that chased along the tight force lines of the weapon's magnetic field. The blade gleamed like stars, like moonlight in the Cloud Gardens of the Emperor. Like silver and glass.

"Who goes there?" I said again, more forcefully now I was far from the door.

Tap-scrape. Tap-tap.

There were vents high along the wall that pumped conditioned air into the chamber, but they were only a couple inches across—no wider than my fist. Seeing them again, ideas about knife-missiles took root and flowered. Crim had been certain the weapon had entered my chambers through one of those ports, though no damage had been detected in the grating that covered them. That was before we had come to suspect someone in ship's security of tampering with sec footage. But there was another vent, large enough that a child might fit through it. That was the return duct, the one that pulled air out and filtered out the dust.

"Is someone there?" I asked.

"Hadrian?" a thin voice answered.

Not a child at all. A man, albeit a small and very thin man.

"Lorian?" I asked. "How did you know to come?"

"Know what?" he whispered in response. "No one had heard anything from you since *they* got here. Corvo sent me." He paused. "Do you mind helping me with this grate? The air in here is . . . not good."

Unkindling my weapon, I clambered up on a reading table and helped open the grating. It folded downward, exposing the dusty filter membrane. Removing this revealed the slightly less dusty Commander Aristedes squeezed into a space nearly too small even for him. Dust coated his black jacket and hung thick in his long, pale hair. "What are you doing?" I hissed.

"Just . . . get me out of this thing," he said, wriggling forward.

I seized him under the arms as though he were a child and pulled him free. Discounting my high-gee-reinforced musculature, I was astonished at how little the man weighed. He couldn't have been more than a hundred pounds. He'd worn no boots to make his climb quieter, and his socks were thick and foul with dust and what looked like some kind of lubricant.

When he'd caught his breath sitting against the rail, he said, "We saw the Inquisition come in a few days back. When we didn't hear anything else we thought they'd . . . done something to you."

"They tested me for *possession*," I said.

Lorian looked up at me with one ghost-blue eye. "Did you pass?" No humor in that question. No smile on that face.

Recalling an ancient conversation with the good commander and his skepticism regarding my death and regeneration, I answered him. "I did."

"Curiouser and curiouser."

"You sound almost disappointed," I said.

The fellow almost pouted. "I only hoped it might have been something more interesting."

"Things are interesting enough."

"Fair." I let Lorian sit a moment, recovering his breath and from the humiliation of being lifted like a child. He massaged his right leg with those skeletal fingers of his, eyes downcast. "Can't feel the bloody thing again," he groaned. "Mother Earth and Emperor . . ." He leaned back against the railing, eyes tracking back across the open grate. "I am not excited about climbing back in there, I hope you know. It's your damn books. Things collect dust like a pleb collects exotic bacteria, I tell you."

"Did something happen out there?" I asked him, crouching so that we were almost at eye level.

Aristedes shook his head, pawed dust from his hair, and straightened the thin ponytail at the base of his skull. "No. I told you. Corvo sent me. After so long with nothing, we were starting to worry they'd . . ."

". . . done something interesting?" I finished for him.

"Well . . . yes!" Lorian shrugged. "They've spent the last three days turning the ship inside out. Peeling off deckplates, crawling around inside. They had Corvo in interviews until yesterday. Don't know what took so long with her."

I had an idea or two. Otavia Corvo was nearly seven feet tall and could lift nearly three times her body weight. There was no way her Amazonian musculature was natural. Homunculus or no, she was the product of genetic sorcery. I guessed the inquisitors were testing her for *perversion,* checking to see if her genetic tinkering remained within accepted bounds. That she was a foreign national might not matter to an Inquisition intent on nailing me to the wall.

"They let her go?"

"This morning."

Corvo's genetic abnormalities would be just another strike against me when the sentence came. *Consortation with the daimonic. Consortation with the perverse.* I let out a ragged sigh. "Do you know a lieutenant named Castle? Or Castor? One of Crim's men."

"What?"

Wordless, I stood and hurried down the row of shelves, located a dusty omnibus titled *The Compleat Annuna.* It was a collection of fantastic stories, not true myths, but adventure romances of the kind popular among certain young men and women who—like me—dreamed of being somewhere and *someone* other than themselves. The book had been banned by the Chantry nearly a thousand years before, but I'd found a copy in a vendor's pile decades previously. One of the dying nobiles on Vorgossos had mentioned it: tales of ancient xenobites who ruled the galaxy before the coming of man. Thinking it might contain some gram of information about the Quiet, I'd snatched up the omnibus, but it had been good as useless.

Unless it was as a hiding place.

I'd not destroyed Oberlin's note—hoping to show it to someone—and drew it out. Hurrying back, I presented it to Lorian, who read it over and asked, "Where did you get this?" I told him. "He just slipped it to you? In front of the Inquisition?" He whistled softly. "If I had balls like that, I'd have more children than the Emperor. Looks like we were right about LIO, too . . ."

"Do you know who he's talking about?"

"Castor? Castle?" Lorian pronounced the words with a careful frown. "There's a Casdo? Casdon! Forget her first name. You think she's our man?"

"Oberlin thinks so," I replied, "but she's probably long gone. Spirited away or killed."

"Breathnach's people did take some of our lot onto their frigate, but I don't think anyone's left the *Tamerlane.* She could be aboard."

"Their frigate?"

Lorian handed the sheet back to me. "Inquisition docked a frigate on the ventral locks after they put you in here. Easier to bring in all the hardware they need."

"Hardware?"

"They've got something plugged into every computer bank, terminal, access panel, and port on the bloody ship, Hadrian. Looking for daimons." Lorian resumed massaging his legs, feet crossed beneath himself. I could picture dozens of black-robed, blindfolded cathars poring over my ship, stripping wall panels and crawling through access hatchways to check storage banks and power conduits.

Planting their evidence, I thought. An insane thought reared up from the surface of my mind, and unable to stop myself, I asked, "Do you think you could get her out?"

"Casdon?" The intus blinked at me, blue eyes wide. "From a Chantry ship?"

"If Oberlin's right, she can testify against Breathnach, I—no." Whatever our Lieutenant Casdon might know, she almost certainly was ignorant of Breathnach's hand in all this, and it would take more than Oberlin's note to prove conspiracy on the part of one of the Emperor's own counselors.

Lorian appeared to be having the same thought. "But it might clear you with the Inquisition. If they are trying to frame you—which Oberlin seems to think they are."

"But can you get her out?"

"If I had a Martian Legion, a colossus, and enough atomics to melt the Earth again in case she thought we were sorry, sure," Lorian hissed, unhanding his numb leg to look frantically around at the books. "You're the wizard, not me."

"Lorian." I allowed my frustration to edge into my voice. "Be serious."

"I'm being serious. I don't know anything about their ship, its floor plan, its personnel. How am I supposed to attack it?"

He looked up at me while he spoke, seeming so small where he sat on the floor in his grime-smeared and dust-covered uniform. "I'm sure you'll think of something." I extended the note toward him, pausing only a moment to tear off the watermark in the bottom corner. The last thing I needed was to drag in my . . . *supporters,* or to tar Oberlin for a mystagogue.

"No!" Lorian raised a finger to object. "Oh no, no, no!"

"Take Crim and Ilex with you," I said. "Between the three of you, you should be able to get Lieutenant Casdon out of her cell and down to

Forum." Ilex's technical expertise would help with any obstructions they might encounter, and Crim—since he was a boy, Crim had taken to the assassin's trade like Crispin to the harem. If anyone could infiltrate a Chantry frigate in Forum orbit, kidnap a treasonous officer, and live to tell about it—Karim Garone could.

"They should go without me," Lorian said. "I'm a liability."

"They might need someone to climb up a ventilation shaft," I countered, and felt the manic gleam creeping back into my eye. *"You* might be essential."

The little man glowered up at me with eyes electric. "I don't like this."

"Do you have a better idea?" I asked, and held Oberlin's note out for Lorian to take.

"No! I . . . not yet!" He ran fingers through his thin hair, mussing up the tight way he'd pulled it back from his forehead. "Just give me time."

Shaking the paper in his face, I asked, "How much *time* do you think we have?"

The intus had not stopped glaring at me. I caught myself hoping the man would so much as blink. One claw-like hand reached out and snatched the note from me again. "Fine," he said at last, "but if they catch me I'm saying it was all your idea. They'll still kill me, but maybe they'll torture you first." He grinned savagely.

I smiled back.

A thought occurred to me a moment later, and I drew back. "Wait here."

"Black planet!" Lorian swore. "What in Earth's Holy Name now?"

I left him sitting by the rail and padded back down the stairs. Tossing my sword onto the couch as I went, I moved to the sideboard and opened a panel on the side. A holograph panel appeared before me, and I flicked through it with a finger, found the recording I needed. A moment later a glass slide clicked out of a slot on the exposed panel. Collecting it, I returned to Lorian. "Here."

"What is it?" he asked, eyeing the slide.

"A recording of my questioning," I said. "In case they submit a faked version."

"They let you record it?"

"I didn't say that." I looked over his head and out across my chamber toward the sideboard and the door to mine and Valka's sleeping chambers. "They took my terminal, but . . . I guess when they realized my rooms weren't watched by the security cameras they figured there was no one listening."

Lorian snorted. "Idiots."

I waved this away. "Can you do it?"

"Are you giving me a choice?"

"No."

"Then help me get back into this blasted vent."

CHAPTER 43

PURGATORY

I WAITED, AND NO one came. Hours turned to days, then days to hours. Nothing happened. I thought for certain to see Inquisitor Gereon again, or his mistress, the nameless Grand Inquisitor. Lord Augustin did not even appear to gloat. Of all the cells I've occupied in my life, my chambers were certainly the most comfortable, though never—not in the dungeons of Vorgossos, nor in the clutches of the Cielcin, nor in the bastilles of the Chantry—have I felt time move so slowly. For I had nothing but time, and nothing to do but to wait.

The interruptions to my solitude came when twice a day the door to the lift opened and a legionnaire entered with a tray and deposited my meal, pausing only to clear away the remnants of the previous one. No word passed between us, nor any sign. I was told nothing, learned nothing. I dared not ask.

I hoped Lorian had succeeded, but then if he had, why had I not been freed?

As the Emperor had given me, I had given Lorian an impossible task: storm a Chantry frigate, capture Lieutenant Casdon, escape to the planet below. Boarding the vessel alone was asking the impossible; no institution in the galaxy prided themselves on security more than the Chantry. But to successfully infiltrate the ship, raid the dungeons, and steal a landing shuttle without detection? They'd deserve a triumph of their own if they succeeded. Of all the places in the universe to break into, only the Peronine Palace, Caliburn House on Avalon, and the ruined Earth herself were harder to access than a Chantry starship.

But, if anyone could do it . . .

Somewhere out there, Crim and Ilex and Lorian Aristedes were sneaking their way onto the Chantry vessel, perhaps disguising themselves as common legionnaires, perhaps walking in the void of space from one hull to another, relying on hardsuits to mask their body heat against the cold Dark outside. Somewhere out there, they slid through camera-haunted halls, past locked gates and countless guards, tampered with security stations and altered footage. Somewhere they fought, somewhere—perhaps—they bled and died.

And I was useless in my cage.

Vague images haunted me, like shadows on the walls of my room: Ilex carrying Lorian on her back like a child, Crim standing alone, sword and knives in hand. I saw them flitting from pillar to pillar in a vaulted hold, hurrying in the brief window Ilex had earned them by pointing cameras at the ceiling. Lorian clambering up an access shaft, grease-smeared again, with numb hands in their braces, keeping his fingers in line. The three of them in legionnaire dress bowing as an Inquisitor went by, the confused whispers following.

Isn't he short for a soldier?

Crim's shadow flowed across the wall before me, an unconscious Lieutenant Casdon over one shoulder, a sword shining in his fist. How would they escape? Steal a shuttle? A lifepod? How would they avoid recapture? Or capture by any of the other vessels in orbit? Security in the skies of Forum was tight enough a stray meteoroid could not penetrate the cloud belt.

Had I sent my soldiers—my loyal friends—to their deaths to save myself and my dream?

No. No, not to save myself. To save my ship, my people. To save us all. For surely if Hadrian Marlowe was framed for possession, for profanation, for consortation—all his people would hang, too. And worse than hang. For the possessed and profane, there was no death save death by fire. We each would be given to the kilns in turn, our ashes cast into space. Even the fugue-bound would not be spared, but ripped from their icy sepulchers to burn with us, from ice to fire in an instant. And last of all, the *Tamerlane* would be destroyed, annihilated by antimatter so that no trace remained of the apostates who had betrayed Earth and Man for machine.

With no evidence left to cry our innocence if my three soldiers failed.

Their shadows still danced on the walls of my prison, flowing like the images of a zoetrope, flickering and faint as a dream in the first moments of wakefulness. Crim's sword flashed, and Ilex fired, and Lorian shouted commands. I saw them leap through hatchways and down shafts and die and die and die until I thought I would go mad from my own inactivity.

Almost a week passed thus. Six days.

Six days before my gaoler ceased to make appearances.

No one brought food, and the remnants of my previous meal—my last?—moldered on my table, forgotten as I was forgotten. When the second meal of the first day did not arrive, I went to the door, and pounding on it, called to the guards. No one answered, but the door would not unlock.

I did not starve. As in the dungeons of Vorgossos before, I ate ration bars from the case in my sleeping quarters kept there for emergencies. Three days passed thusly. No word. No human contact.

Then, on the tenth day since Gereon put me to the Question, I was awakened by the whine of the deadbolts peeling back and the grind of the door opening.

I did not sit up at first, but lay beneath Valka's woven blanket on the couch. My eyes stayed fixed on the ceiling, not truly seeing it, not truly seeing anything. More than a week without human contact had unmoored my sense of propriety, and I couldn't be bothered to rise. If it was Gereon, Breathnach, or the Grand Inquisitor, let them drag me to my feet.

It was not Gereon. Nor Breathnach. Nor the Grand Inquisitor.

It wasn't even Oberlin.

"You look comfortable," the high voice said.

It was Lorian.

The intus looked down at me—a curious reversal—with a strained smile on his patrician face. A black corrective patch covered a plasma burn on one cheek, and he wore again the silvered braces that kept his fingers from falling out of joint as he leaned upon his cane. His torn uniform jacket over his shoulders, sleeves dangling empty.

"Is it done?" I asked.

"It's done," he answered, and sank down onto the low table beside my couch, surveying me all the while.

Ashamed that I was lying down when he looked so threshed and torn, I sat up. "Good lord, man—have you been to medica?"

"In and out. But I wanted to tell you myself." He put a hand to his chest, parting his shirt to show another corrective along his collarbone. "I wanted you to know it wasn't *easy*." He folded the fabric back into place, smoothed it down.

"How did you do it?"

The commander shook his head, unsmiling. "Another time. The Martians have Casdon and Breathnach."

"The lieutenant talked?"

"The lieutenant *sang*," Lorian replied. "Chantry's bound to come out unscathed, of course. Can't prove conspiracy with the Director. They did ask Sir Lorcan be handed over to them, but Prince Hector and the Council are blocking them. Not sure if His Radiance is involved yet."

I cradled my head in my hands. Lorcan Breathnach was gone. The man who'd put a knife in Valka's chest . . . gone. "It's a pity I can't be the one to behead the bastard," I muttered.

"It wouldn't be *justice* if you did it," Lorian said, drumming his fingers. "This is better."

"And we're in the clear?" I asked. "Corvo's been over the ship? Made sure there's nothing left behind that shouldn't have been? No daimons? No . . . anything?"

Commander Aristedes sagged against his cane, braced hands clicking. "Doing it now."

"Are Ilex and Crim all right?" I asked.

"What?" Lorian looked around, clearly exhausted. Was he concussed? What had he done to deliver Casdon to the Martian Guard? "Oh . . . yes. Fine. About as well off as me." He sucked in a ragged breath, snapped his head up to look me in the eye. "Don't think we should leave the ship for a while. Let the MG do their work."

I was nodding along. "That will make Corvo happy."

"Aye," he barked a laugh, "and on the bright side . . . you can let the doctor out of fugue now it's safe."

The doctor . . . I thought. *Valka.* She'd been gone for mere days, but I missed her presence more sharply than I had sometimes after years during one of my night journeys. I longed for her presence and the mocking way she smiled. But I shook my head. "No. Not yet." There was a chance this wasn't over, and I would not—could not—risk her. I couldn't let her out of fugue until we were safely off of Forum and far, far away. "What about Lord Bourbon?"

"What about him?"

Lorian held my gaze with unfocused eyes as I answered him. "Did his name come up in all this?" The old Lion surely had conspired with the Intelligence Director in this, I felt certain.

The intus shook his head, flaxen hair floating. He'd lost his tie somewhere, and the usually neat hair with its long tail flew wild and free. Somehow, the wildness aged young Aristedes, so that he seemed half a ghost sitting there before me. "No, no. Nothing." I fell silent, and after a moment a clawed and silver-braced hand gripped my wrist. How little strength there was in that hand and arm. I should not have sent him into battle. "But this is a victory, my lord. Our victory."

Placing a hand over the younger man's thin one, I said, "The victory's yours, Aristedes. Go and get some rest. Unless . . . shall I send for a litter?" I wasn't so sure he could stand again.

"Just . . . help me up, would you?"

I knelt, wrapped the little man's arm around my neck, and lifted. I could not stand, not fully, not without lifting Lorian bodily from the ground. Small as he was and slight, I might have carried him, but I sensed that even to suggest such a thing would be to shame the poor fellow, and I did not offer.

"Come on, then," I said, and holding the man by the shoulders, I walked him to the door. The heavy bulkhead slid aside at our approach. The guards had vanished. We passed out through the vestibule and into the hall beyond.

A flight technician in informal blacks saw us, and stopped his progress to salute. "Lord Marlowe, sir! Commander Aristedes!" I acknowledged his salute in passing, but did not linger. About us, operations had returned to normal aboard the *Tamerlane,* and though the work of setting the ship to rights after the Inquisition's invasion would take days and perhaps weeks— all was right again with the world. Was made right by the little titan who walked beside me.

In the end, I escorted Commander Aristedes all the way to medica and delivered him into the hands of Doctor Luana Okoyo.

"See he's taken care of," I told her, unnecessarily. "He's a hero."

CHAPTER 44

ALONG COMES A SPIDER

MONTHS PASSED BEFORE THE summons came, during which time I oversaw the purging of the *Tamerlane*'s data banks and their rebuild from backed-up files. Aristedes recovered. He'd suffered serious plasma burns to the face and torso and capped them off with a concussion so severe Okoyo was surprised he was still walking, especially given his fragile state. Crim and Ilex likewise recovered, but none of them—acting, I guessed, on Lorian's orders—would tell me just how it was they'd managed to escape the Chantry frigate.

I never saw Gereon again, and the Grand Inquisitor had withdrawn, gone back to whatever ecclesial shadow she'd sprung from. Selene sent messages, and I replied politely, saying that I was not at liberty to discuss my near-assassination or the Inquisition that followed, save to say that I was all right and alive, and would doubtless see her soon. She made no mention of Alexander.

Each day I suspected word from the Imperial Council, from the Commandant of the Martian Guard, from the Emperor himself. Each day I was surprised, then disappointed, then frustrated in time. I wanted it to be over, wanted finally and at last to be sentenced to my marriage with Selene or else to be ordered offworld.

The summons came in the form of a Martian escort and a court androgyn with orders to bring me before Prince Hector and the Council.

And so I went, thinking it was over—not knowing the worst was still to come.

The lords of the eight ministries sat beneath the Lord High Chancellor's seat with the Synarch and Lord Powers. Not ghosts this time in holograph, but real and solid presences, lords with weight and force.

"I still cannot believe it," said Miana Hartnell, the Minister of Welfare, "the Director of Legion Intelligence an *assassin*. Ghastly. Simply ghastly." She was a palatine, but as far from the old blood of the great houses as it was possible to be, with a rodent's pursed face and bird-bright eyes.

The Lord High Chancellor interrupted her, addressing me where I stood within the bend of the mighty table beneath the holograph. "We apologize for the suffering this incident has inflicted on you and your people, Sir Hadrian. And allow me to extend my personal sympathies to you as well. You must be in need of respite after this ordeal."

"It would be nice to get back to work," I said.

"Work?" Prince Hector sounded almost affronted. "To the front, you mean?"

"I am a soldier of the Empire," I said, repeating that phrase which had become for me a kind of mantra in the decades since Vorgossos.

Prince Hector's hands gripped the arms of his small throne. "The Emperor has been entertaining notions of placing you on this council."

He said these words as though they were news, and so I shook myself from my contemplation of the holograph floating above my head and found it in me to act surprised. "What?" When I realized how foolish I must have appeared, I added, "Your Excellency, I . . . am not certain what to say. How would I serve?"

"You would take my seat, my boy!" came a surprisingly jovial voice from the right-hand wing. I turned. Traditionally, the seats to the right of the Chancellor's throne were held by Lions. Lord Bourbon was there, and Lord Peake, the Minister of Justice. The left side held the less traditionalist wing of the Council, Lady Hartnell chief among them, with Lord Cordwainer of the Ministry of Revenue, and—perversely—the Lord Minister of Rites. But in those days, the council was unbalanced, and save for these three each of the twelve counselors was a Lion.

The speaker sat at the far right of the Council table, and turning to my left I found Lord Cassian Powers smiling down at me. The former strategos looked so old he reminded me of Tor Gibson, face seamed and folded. He wore a pair of thick spectacles that magnified his eyes to three times their natural size, and unlike Bastien Durand's I guessed these glasses were medically necessary. He no longer looked like a soldier, more like a species of overgrown owl peering from his perch.

"Your seat, Lord Powers?" I looked from the old man to the others before circling back to Lord Cassian. I almost laughed. "I could not replace you!"

"You are far more the expert on the Pale then I ever was!" the Avenger of Cressgard exclaimed. "I'm only an old man who knows how to kill them."

Glancing from Lord Powers to the rest of the Council, I hesitated, saying, "I . . . do not wish to compete with the Lord Minister of War where the way we are to conduct our struggle is concerned. I am your servant, counselors. I have served, and wish to continue serving." I bowed, trying not to look up at the image above me, the ghost of a small woman with short blond hair and a square jaw strapped to a chair.

Lieutenant Casdon.

The Council had replayed her testimony at the start of our meeting, and the final image remained on the projector at the focus of the high table beneath which I stood.

"Our servant would not argue with this Council," said Peter Habsburg, the Lord Minister of Works. "I remind you, Sir Hadrian, that as a knight, you are answerable to the Imperial Office. We are the Imperial Office, being ourselves servants to His Radiance."

I shook my head. "Forgive me, Excellency, but no. I am a Knight Victorian, and answerable only to the Emperor." Lord Habsburg's face creased with disappointed anger, and he turned toward the uncharacteristically silent Lord Bourbon. Before he could address his colleague and fellow Lion, I said, "But if it is His Radiance's wish that I sit on this Council, I will obey. But *as* his counselor, I would advise that I am of greater use away from Forum."

"Why are you so eager to flee?" asked Augustin Bourbon, picking up the baton from Lord Habsburg.

The Minister of War's dark eyes met mine, and I studied him for a long moment. The thick, dark hair going to gray, the heavy sideburns, the pale suit with the fleur-de-lis pinned to his lapel, and the golden braids that draped over his azure half-toga from either shoulder. I felt certain he'd been involved in Breathnach's attack, but I knew I could never prove it. It may have been Breathnach's hand that directed the knife in my chambers, but it was Bourbon's that had directed Breathnach, surely. And Sir Friedrich's note had implied the Chantry was in on the attempt to frame me. I glanced sidelong at Vergilian's empty chair. The Synarch was away, citing *other duties.*

"Frankly, my Lord Minister of War," I answered after the beat of a heart, "I am not particularly enamored of the capital at the moment. I was falsely accused and nearly framed for a demoniac, an experience I would prefer not to have to repeat."

"You believe your life is still in danger?" Prince Hector asked.

"Excellency, I believe it will be until I die," I replied, and thought, *How's that for prophecy?*

The sergeant-at-arms banged his fasces against the striking plate. "Order!" he cried. "There will be no disrespect in the chamber!"

I bowed my apologies. "Forgive me, honorable lords and ladies, but I am under a great deal of strain." Straightening, I recalled my rhetoric lessons and—placing my left hand behind my back—extended my right as though I held a book before my eyes. "But in addition to the threat to my own life, my crew, my officers, and armsmen have themselves only narrowly escaped judgment. I take this threat to their lives very seriously."

"Your officers . . ." began Lord Allander Peake. The Minister of Justice sifted papers on the table before him. "In the absence of His Holy Wisdom the Synarch, I have been asked to bring forward a request on the part of the Holy Terran Chantry. They wish for the officers who breached their security during this affair to submit themselves for interrogation."

"Not in a million years," I said, interrupting the minister. "Commander Aristedes and the others are under my protection."

Lord Peake raised a ringed hand for calm. "My understanding is they only wish to ascertain the manner by which your men breached their security."

"Then I will submit a report if the Emperor so orders," I said. "You and I both know the methods by which the Inquisition *ascertains* its information, and I will not submit my people to such examination without explicit command."

Perhaps speaking from piety, Lady Hartnell said, "You cannot simply refuse a request made by the Earth's Chantry."

Turning smoothly on my heel to face the weasel-faced old woman, I said, "I am not refusing. But I remind this Council that the good Commander and my lieutenants were acting on my express orders. If the Chantry wishes to question them, they must go through me, seeing as all responsibility for their actions is mine as their commanding officer. I *am* saying that if the Holy Chantry wishes to reopen an inquisition against me after all that's happened, the Emperor will hear about it. Were he here, I would remind the Synarch that the clergy allowed themselves to be used by Sir Lorcan Breathnach in an illegal investigation that nearly took the life of a Knight Victorian—namely, *myself*—and risked the lives of the more than ninety thousand people who serve in my Red Company." I let this sink in a moment before adding. "This continued antagonism would lend credence to the rumors that the Inquisition was complicit in Sir Lorcan's scheme, rumors which I am certain the Synarch, Synod, and Choir would like to see dispelled as quickly as possible. However it was Commander Aristedes and his companions managed to breach the Chantry's quarantine—and I don't know how they did it—might I suggest the Chantry in particular should be grateful they succeeded, as it has spared them grievous embarrassment and the wroth of His Radiance, who—I imagine—would not have been thrilled to learn that one of his knights and his daughter's *betrothed* was killed *by mistake*."

Stony silence greeted this speech, silence and an unquiet tension moving beneath the surface of the air. It was almost a shame the Synarch was not present. It was almost a declaration of war, pitting the authority of the throne—in whose shadow I stood and acted—against that of the altar. Once upon a time, the Chantry had been crafted by the Imperial state, but it had grown beyond those humble beginnings, as all weeds must. Grown until it was like a worm in the Empire's bowels, grown until the question of who was host and who the parasite could not be easily answered. Of old the Emperors crowned themselves—as the God Emperor had done in the ashes of Rome—and crowned the Chantry's Synarchs, who knelt before the throne. But the Chantry had grown strong, and perhaps there would come a day, and soon, when the Emperors knelt and permitted the high priest to set old William's crown upon their brows.

Could the Emperor protect me? Protect Lorian and the others?

Or would the Chantry's will prevail?

I was willing to bet on His Radiance.

"So," Prince Hector said, breaking the silence in his hands, "my brother has informed you of his intentions."

Remembering my place and burying my anger beneath propriety and false modesty, I bowed my head. "Yes, Excellency."

"And did His Radiance inform you that it was the opinion of this Council that such a marriage was inadvisable?"

For a moment, I almost, *almost* wanted Selene, if only to defy these dusty ministers and their . . . what? Their jealousy? Almost I understood the Hadrian of my visions who sat with Selene at his feet before a crowd of kneeling lords.

Almost.

"He did, Excellency."

"Ah." Prince Hector had the grace to look down.

Slashing through this awkward moment, the Minister of Justice put in,

"I will . . . give your reply to Wisdom Vergilian, Lord Marlowe, along with your, ah . . . advisement."

I bowed more deeply than I had before. "Thank you, Lord Minister. I hope to move past this ugliness as swiftly as may be."

Pallino met me outside with a complement of ten Red Company guards. None of them had been permitted weapons inside the Sun King's Hall, but the men were armored and shielded, and would serve as some defense in the event of an attack. Since the knife-missile, Corvo and Crim had both insisted on increased security about my person whenever I left the *Tamerlane*—they'd even posted a guard to my door while I slept. Corvo had insisted the decade of troopers in their red-fringed tunics and black plate would serve as a show of strength and discourage any attackers, but I could not shake the feeling they only made me look afraid.

I told myself I was being absurd. The Emperor, after all, was the most powerful man in all the galaxy, and he had more guards than anyone, between the common legionnaires, the Martian Guard, and the Excubitors who surrounded his person at all times, to say nothing of the fleet of Martian warships, Legion warships, and Chantry vessels that forever orbited the gas giant and the sprawling capital city. No one called the Emperor a coward, or thought him one. No one would dare. I told myself that I was different. I was a knight, and knights should stand on their own feet, protected by their own hands and skill at arms.

My escort hadn't gotten far when a voice sounded behind me. "Lord Marlowe! A moment!"

Turning, I beheld the ancient Lord Cassian Powers hurrying toward me, a brass walking stick seemingly forgotten in his hand. He moved with surprising speed for one so old. I extended an arm in salute before bowing— the man was a soldier *and* a lord—and said, "At your service, my lord."

The Avenger waved this formality aside with his stick. Cassian Powers stood a head taller than me, and beneath the heavy gray cloak he wore the simple belted tunic jacket and trousers of a military officer, devoid now of insignia and rank, but his high boots were pure and polished as though the man had just come from the parade ground.

"I'd hoped to have a word with you, if I may."

I looked round the open-air colonnade that wrapped around the exterior of the government building to the west wing and the approach to the main hall. To my astonishment, the Lord Adviser had no escort, no attaches or adjutants. No guard.

"Of course, lordship," I said. "Here?"

Lord Cassian Powers laid a hand on my shoulder and smiled, eyes magnified by his glasses until they filled the crystal lenses. "Here is fine! No secrets, not between us and the old electric eyes, mm?"

I had met with Lord Powers on only a few occasions. The Avenger of Cressgard was an aloof figure: hero of another time, a relic kept on display and trotted out at ceremonies and at times when the Council needed his advice. He was perhaps the greatest Cielcin hunter in history, and one of the galaxy's foremost experts on the xenobites and their culture, and so when he asked for a word, I allowed myself to be led through the pillars and down onto an overlook that peered out over the monorail line that ran from below the great hall across empty sky to the isle where floated the halls of justice, huge pillars gleaming in the sun.

Far below, I could make out the green and gray and white-walled terraces of the Royal Forests. I could not see the Arch of Titus, not from this height, though I spotted bare patches in the trees, and guessed that one such clearing must hold the Roman monument taken from the gray hills of Earth.

"It is rather a lot, isn't it?" the old soldier asked. "All this?"

"The City?" I asked, not sure I followed. "It's far more than I ever imagined."

Powers leaned against the rail, looking out over the floating isles and the bridges and tramways that connected them, at the pale curtains of the sail wall billowing in the winds. "The City, yes. But I mean the *people* in it. The Empire. Sometimes I look at it all and say to myself, 'Self, these idiots are not worth saving! Better to let the whole thing fall out of the sky!'" I said nothing, and when I kept saying nothing, Cassian Powers turned to peer at me with those magnified eyes. "I surprise you? My apologies. If it is fear that holds your tongue, I assure you: what you said before the Council was correct. They won't risk further charges against you or your people. And in any case they will not harm old Lord Powers, the *Avenger!*" He made a fist, mocking. "We may speak freely."

"What is this about, sir?" I asked. The *sir* was a bit curt, but quite correct. The man was a knight and wore a sword on his belt still, and we were both soldiers.

"Straight to business, mm? Very good." He turned away again. "They're going to give you my seat."

What was I supposed to say? I could not read the fellow. It did not help that Powers was turned almost fully away from me in his admiration of the Eternal City. At last I settled on something safe, and said, "I'm . . . sorry."

Powers waved this down. "I'm grateful, truth be told. Five hundred years is a long time to be at war, and I was not young when it began. Truth is, I've been trying to retire for years, they just won't let me." He looked round, laughing softly. "I'd quit twice before this, you know? After Cressgard and again . . . oh, about two hundred years ago. Returned home to Ashbless and all . . . but they kept calling me back. I feel a bit like old Camillus—you're a classics man, aren't you?"

I told him I was. Camillus had been a hero to ancient Rome, a statesman recalled from his country estate to save his country and serve as dictator no less than five times. Camillus might have been king.

"Amazing these stories have endured so long, isn't it?" Powers wondered aloud. "Camillus. Rome. Caesar, and the rest. Makes you wonder what we've forgotten. What's buried in some library somewhere or in some reliquary of the great houses."

Shrugging, I replied, "Not so amazing, really. The founders went to great pains to ground our Empire in tradition. The stories are part of who we are, for better or worse."

"Better or worse . . ." Lord Cassian was nodding along, scratching his cheek with knobby fingers. "You don't like it here, do you, Sir Hadrian?" The old soldier stared at me intently, and with his glasses the effect was startling. "I don't like it either." His stare transformed, and he seemed to be peering *through me.* "Are you . . . all right, Sir Hadrian?"

Something in his demeanor—or his voice, perhaps—reminded me so sharply of Tor Gibson that I almost expected to find the scholiast looking back at me when I blinked and turned away a moment. I had not expected to find kindness in the City at all, much less in the person of the Avenger himself. But Lord Cassian did not look like an Avenger, he looked like an owl.

"I know how it can be," he said. "Let's get something straight: this *Halfmortal* business . . ." He made a move as if to throw it all away. "Nonsense. All the stories people tell about you—and me—don't help in the dead of night. I know what it's like. The nightmares."

"I don't have nightmares," I said, too quickly.

"Spoken like a man who has nightmares," Powers rebutted, and said again, "I know what it's like. But it does get easier. You'll hate the

Council—Earth knows I do. You'll still look horror in the face, but you won't have to smell it."

Pushing away from the rail, I stood straight beside the older man. "I prefer the horror to a knife in the back. I've as many enemies here as out there . . ." I trailed off, muttering, "Leopards, lions, and wolves."

He had been speaking of alien powers, but Lord Cassian took the *lions* for a reference to the Imperial Lions, and said, "Well, speaking for us old Lions, we conservatives aren't so bad. It's only that most of us don't *conserve* anything. Too busy fussing about reputation and appearances. Take the former Intelligence Director. So eager to *protect* our Empire he nearly killed its greatest defender. And for what? Because you did his job for him? Perhaps he thought you wanted his job."

"I don't!" I snorted with derisive laughter. "And I don't know about *greatest defender,* either."

"You killed Aranata Otiolo. You killed Venatimn Ulurani. You killed this *chimera,* discovered an alliance between the Pale and the Extras . . ." He removed his spectacles and smiled, eyes suddenly shrunken to normal size. "You've conserved more than our brave Lions ever have. They're embarrassed. You are what they should be, and they know it." He prodded me in the chest. "But don't believe your own legends, boy. That's all they are. Legends. All this talk of Halfmortals, devils, and avengers . . . it's madness."

I wasn't sure I agreed with him. I hadn't *really* killed Ulurani, not the way the broadcasts said, but Lord Powers had not seen me *die* on Sagara's vessel. He had not seen the Howling Dark, had not spoken with the Brethren. Whatever nightmares haunted old Cassian Powers, they were not like my dreams.

My dreams were real.

"Where's Marlowe?" a familiar voice sounded on the colonnade above. I heard Pallino's low voice answer, but couldn't make out the words, then the same voice shouted, "Out of my way, pissant!"

I spun round, hand on my shield's catch, hovering near my sword.

Lord Augustin Bourbon clambered down the marble steps to the overlook where Powers and I stood, flanked by four guards in Bourbon livery. "Cassian!" he said, "Surprised to see you."

The Avenger placed a hand on my arm, indicating that I should back off from my weapons. Only reluctantly did I back down as Lord Cassian said, "Only offering my replacement a few words of advice, Augustin."

"I see," Bourbon said, and shifted his posture, aligning himself in a way that effectively blocked Lord Powers from the conversation. "I hope you're happy, Marlowe."

"Excuse me?"

"Flouting the Chantry. Destroying the life of an esteemed public servant . . ." He was practically seething. Surely the blood was boiling in his veins. "Your men could not have escaped the Inquisition without daimonic influence. You're guilty. I know it."

Eyes shut, I took the space of a breath to collect myself. It would not do to strike the Lord Minister of War. He was my superior, scion of a far older and nobler house and an Imperial Counselor besides. I could not challenge him. I could not respond to his accusation, for to defend myself at all was to appear defensive. But I could attack. "Your *esteemed public servant* is a traitor, my lord. Spared the fate of a common murderer only by his own incompetence."

"Sir Lorcan Breathnach has served the realm for more than two hundred years."

Served you, you mean, I thought, eyes sweeping over the expansive palatine, his ivory suit and azure toga, the equestrian boots decidedly absurd on a man too fat to ride a horse. "And had he wished to be remembered as such, he would not have tried to kill me," I said, certain now that Bourbon had been in on it. Confronting me like this was sloppy. Sloppy and arrogant beyond belief. Unless his outrage was truly genuine. Unless he and Breathnach had been close friends. But I was not certain Lord Augustin was the type of man who had friends. He struck me as the sort of man who categorized his fellow human beings as only *assets* or *threats,* and played one group against the other until the first sort had destroyed the second. Unable to help myself, I pushed. "One has to wonder at the fellow's motivations, though. I can't imagine why he'd want to kill me . . ." I never broke eye contact with Bourbon. *Let him explain that.*

Bourbon's jaw worked like a bellows, like pistons turning over the chugging mechanisms of his mind. It seemed the Lord Minister had not thought so far ahead. "He . . . he knows what you are."

"What I am?" I echoed, taking a step forward. "What am I, lordship?" I spared a glance for Lord Powers, who had replaced his spectacles on his crooked nose and watched our altercation unsmilingly.

"I don't know how you did it," he said. "What spells you used to frame Sir Lorcan."

"Frame Sir Lorcan?" It was too much, a wild, incoherent accusation. "My lord, we have Lieutenant Casdon's confession!"

"Your lieutenant's confession!"

My lieutenant, I thought. As if I'd arranged for Casdon to lie, convinced her to hang for my sake—and she would hang. "Lord Minister, let me ask you a question." My boot heels clicked on the paving stones as I moved to stand well within striking distance of the great walrus of a man. There was always a chance the man might strike *me* in a fit of pique, and if that happened all bets were off. I could challenge him, and Valka was not awake to stop me. Not that she would. "Do you think His Radiance is *stupid*?"

"What?" Bourbon blithered. "How dare you, sir!"

"How dare *you!*" I countered, keeping my voice level and tightly controlled. "You come here accusing me of ruining the reputation of a man who *did* try to kill me. You accuse me of consortation *after* the Inquisition has cleared me—you heard my recording in Council. Would His Radiance our Emperor retain my services if there were the slightest *shred* of evidence suggesting that I am what you say I am?"

That shut him up. Lord Powers may not have feared the palace's eyes, but Lord Powers was an innocent man. Lord Bourbon was anything but. His jowls quivered, and a series of outraged sounds escaped him, but did not form themselves into words. A spider Augustin Bourbon might have been, but he'd misplaced one of his many legs and tangled in his own web.

I smiled up at him. I was gloating. I should not gloat. I was the one about to retreat to the safety of my ship in orbit as a precaution against further assassination attempts.

I was in no position to gloat.

CHAPTER 45

VISITATION

I WAS GROWING TIRED of standing on receiving platforms, and returning to the very spot where I'd awaited the arrival of the Grand Inquisitor and Sir Lorcan Breathnach filled me with the most unpleasant sense of déjà vu. But the ship that hung in the bay before the platform and the walkway was not the brutalist black monolith of a Chantry vessel, but a graceful, almost bird-like craft of snow-white tile and gold filigree, ostentatious in the best baroque fashion, with fan-like solar sails folded and sheathed.

Corvo stood by me again, First Officer Durand at her side.

"I wish she hadn't insisted on coming *here* to see you," the captain said. "I could do without the security detail turning my ship inside out."

She meant the Martians, of course. A full century of the Martian Guard had arrived the previous morning and begun the work of making safe the *Tamerlane* for the princess's visit. A full third of their number stood on the far side of the gangway.

"Can it," Durand said, pushing his prop glasses up his nose with a finger. "Door's opening."

A cornicen emerged in white livery and winded his clarion. The sound echoed painfully in that harsh, metallic space, and a moment later cried out that the Princess Selene of the Aventine House had come.

She appeared a moment later, dressed in a gown to match the crimson of her hair, which she wore up in an intricate tangle of braids. Her handmaids Kiria and Bayara followed on, and another decade of Martians in red and white, blank-faced, their feathered crests standing tall.

Sensing my cue, I left Corvo and Durand and strode to meet the princess. I'd worn my best, the black, short-sleeved jacket over black tunic with silvered vambraces, my pitchfork and pentacle embroidered above the heart in crimson thread to match the crimson stripes along the outer seam of my trousers. And I'd donned again the long cape of white-on-white brocade I favored for public appearances, a badge and visible sign of my service to the Empire.

I knelt before Selene. She extended a hand. Her right hand. This gave me pause for only a moment. Her ring was on the left. To kiss her bare right hand was a far more familiar, far more personal gesture—a sign of friendship between us and, perhaps, of more. Our betrothal was not yet a matter of public record, and though Corvo and my officers knew full well, the Martians and my own legionnaires who stood by would notice and would talk.

Thinking of Valka, still asleep on ice several decks above our heads, I kissed Selene's fingers.

"You honor us with your presence, Highness," I said, and kept my head bowed.

"Please rise, sir. You need not kneel for me." She touched my shoulder as she spoke, and I stood. Behind me, my officers and soldiers saluted with hands outstretched.

Offering the princess my arm—as was only proper—I led her to Corvo and Durand and introduced them, saying, "Princess Selene, here is my captain, Otavia Corvo, and her First Officer, Bastien Durand."

Corvo dropped her salute and bowed awkwardly while Durand moved with smooth efficiency, precise in this as in everything else. Selene smiled up at Corvo, admiring. "We did not have a chance to meet at the triumph ball," she glanced to Crim and Ilex where they stood at hand, "but you both I remember!" Turning back to Corvo, she said, "You are even taller than I expected . . ." Her words came out an awed whisper. Realizing this was perhaps an uncomfortable thing to say, the princess added, "Sir Hadrian speaks most of highly of you, captain."

"I hope so," Otavia said. "I've saved his life more times than I can remember."

It was an astonishingly forward thing to say, and a very Norman answer. But the princess laughed. "Then I should thank you!"

Suddenly embarrassed, I tuned to Selene. "Shall I show you the ship, Highness?"

"In a moment. We're not all off the ship yet. And I must meet the rest of your people!" she answered, and I led her, her handmaids, and her guards down the line. We hadn't made it three paces when the figure at the end of my line of officers caught her eye. "You're the one who caught Sir Lorcan Breathnach, aren't you?"

Lorian Aristedes looked up—he'd been staring pointedly at his shoes the whole while—and bowed deeply. "Your Highness is most kind," he said, not looking up. "I have that honor." Beside him, Helmsman Koskinen stepped aside to give the small tac officer space.

"You're very brave," she said.

"Very foolish, ma'am," Lorian replied, seemingly unable to stop himself.

This time the laughter did not escape Selene, though it shone in her eyes. "That may be, but my tutor always told me that all heroes are fools until victorious."

Against my better judgment, I was growing to like Selene. Why could it not have been she whom the Emperor sent with me and not . . .

"Hadrian."

"Alexander," I said, turning.

"*Prince* Alexander," he said, icily. The young man who had been my squire crossed his arms. Petulant? Defensive? He wore a white version of the Legion officer's uniform: belted tunic with gold buttons, though he wore no device or insignia of any kind save a red half-toga pinned at the left shoulder. His short hair had grown in the months since our triumph, was brushed and oiled neatly to one side. He wore no sword—he was no knight—but he carried a long knife at his belt and an antique-looking plasma repeater. He looked like a man, or like a child playing at one.

Prince Alexander, I said to myself, then aloud: "If you like."

Sensing the tension, Selene interposed herself. "I am sorry for the surprise. My brother asked me not to tell you."

I laid a hand on hers where she gripped my arm and extricated myself from her grasp. Tossing my cape back over my right shoulder I said, "I'm glad you're here."

The prince angled his chin.

"Are you not going to kneel, sir knight?" Alexander asked.

That checked my advance. I glanced at Corvo and my other officers. Was Alexander trying to shame me in front of my men? All the paranoia, all the dread of the previous months came crashing back. Bourbon was still my enemy, that much was certain, but was he alone?

"Your father the Emperor has not dissolved our relationship, *my Prince,*" I said, cold matching the acid in Alexander's voice. "You are still my squire."

I did not bow.

Alexander twitched, and in a strained voice, answered, "Very well."

But I had to do something. Whether or not the young prince was involved in Breathnach's attempt on my life, this unpleasantness could not be allowed to continue. "Nevertheless, I am sorry you had to hear what you heard. I never wanted to be a teacher, but that is no excuse for what I said. My difficulties should not be yours."

The prince snorted. "But you meant what you said."

"That you're difficult? Arrogant? Yes." I ought not to do this here. Dressing the young man down in front of his sister was as bad as his attempt to shame me in front of my men. "I would be failing you as your teacher if I did not tell you this."

The prince did not reply, only stood there, hands clenched at his sides. Tall as he was and noble, he looked almost shrunken standing behind the Martians at the end of the ramp, smaller somehow than even Lorian.

So I tipped my head and bowed, right hand on my heart. "I am sorry, Alexander. I have failed you as a teacher. I hope you can forgive me." With those words, I handed the young man momentary power over me, and with it restored his dignity. I hoped the lessons I'd taught him—the lessons I'd learned on the streets and in Colosso about the ugliness of the world and about the nature of master *as servant,* of ruler as steward—had taken root enough that he might bury his animosity toward me.

He did not move for the space of several heartbeats. I am not sure he even blinked.

"Oh, do accept his apology, Alex!" Selene said, retaking my arm. "I would have you both be friends again!"

The young prince chewed his tongue, eyes flitting from my face to Selene's and back again. "Fine then," he said at last. "Friends."

"Such a cold place," Selene remarked as we walked along the ship's equator, pausing to survey the Sparrowhawks where they sat in their bays below like Crim's knives in their scabbards. "I can't imagine living here, can you, Bayara?"

"I rather like it," the dark lady said, tossing her red hair. "It's so *danger-ous.* So *exciting.* Don't you think?"

Selene was shaking her head. "And everyone asleep. It must be lonely."

"It can be," I said. Why was I playing along? Indulging the girl's romantic notions? "But you're just as likely to get tired of everyone, day after day. In that respect, it's no different than anywhere else." I did not tell her about the way I would stay awake for a year or two at a time after all but the transit crew were sleeping, about the weeks that passed where I saw no one but myself and the bees who dwelt in the hydroponics section.

"How many people did you say lived here?" Selene asked.

"Over ninety thousand," I answered her, then corrected myself. "Ninety-one, if you count the Irchtani."

Captain Corvo spoke up. "There are fewer than a thousand of us on deck at present. After our trouble with the Inquisition, we thought it best to cut down to the essentials."

The princess leaned out over the rail, peering down into the nearest Sparrowhawk launching tube. "I am sorry to hear about your lieutenant."

"Casdon?" I asked.

"Casdon wasn't one of mine," Corvo cut in. "She was new. One of the officers LIO saddled us with after Aptucca."

Confused silence greeted this declaration. "The core of the Red Company is made up of the Norman soldiers I hired on Pharos," I said, though *hired* was a gross simplification. I'd paid for them in blood. My blood, and the blood of their tyrannical former commander, Emil Bordelon. "Plus a few centuries detached from the 437th Centaurine after the Vorgossos affair, and a few of my compatriots from Emesh. Most of the ship officers came out of these groups, but a number of the new officers and most of the enlisted men—especially in the lower echelons—were all pulled from the regular Legions. Any number of them might have been Breathnach's agents."

When Selene turned back to look at me, her face was white. "Are you getting rid of them? If any of them might turn assassin like this lieutenant . . ."

I raised both hands to forestall her questioning. "It's a process, but we're working on it. Although I understand I may not be leaving Forum at all."

"Perhaps not!" Selene said, brightening. "Though your company will still need to be reformed."

"And drilled and briefed and tested," Corvo added. "It will be like starting over."

"I hope this lieutenant will prove your only traitor," Selene said. "And pray all this ugliness is behind you."

Remembering my confrontation with Lord Bourbon a week before, I answered, "I hope so, too, Highness."

"At any rate," she said, resuming her walk along the broad corridor with her retainers, "I am glad you and my brother have made peace."

Alexander was not present, had instead gone with Crim and a number of his Martian Guard to retrieve several of his possessions which had been left aboard the *Tamerlane* when we'd returned to Forum, possessions which the young prince had not returned for after the night of the ball.

"As am I," I said, though privately I was certain the prince still resented me. I was surprised, however, to find that I no longer feared him. Let him resent me, so long as he understood his place as my pupil.

"He wanted me to invite you . . ." Selene began, glancing at Captain Corvo, a bit embarrassed to be asking in front of the officer, who I assumed was not invited. "The Colosso season is about to start. Our brother Aurelian hosts a party in our suite in the Grand Colosseum. He was hoping—we both were—that you might join us." When I did not answer at once, she added, "There's to be a naval combat in the opening ceremonies, Aurelian says. Old-fashioned longships with *real* oarsmen and all. Says they *ram* one another and try to sink each other. It sounds marvelous. And your doctor could come, your . . . Vala?"

"Valka," I said reflexively. A shadow fell on me. Why should Selene—my betrothed, of all people—invite Valka to such a thing? To anything?

"The Tavrosi woman, yes!"

"Valka is in fugue." I glanced at Corvo. I dared not tell Selene that Valka had been injured in Breathnach and Casdon's attack. I grasped for an explanation, but nothing came.

Thank Earth or whatever gods may be for Otavia Corvo, who piped up. "She is *Tavrosi,* as you say. The Inquisition asked us to put her under the ice while they conducted their investigation. We've not been given permission to awaken her."

It was half true, of course, but the other half was credible, and would spare Valka any humiliation at being asked to attend a party peopled entirely by Imperial princes and their friends.

"Oh," Selene said. "Well, that's disappointing. I've so wanted to meet her, you know. But do say you'll come, Sir Hadrian."

How could I refuse?

CHAPTER 46

SHADOWS OF THE PAST

"IT'S GOOD TO SEE you, Sir Hadrian," said Crown Prince Aurelian, the eldest of the Emperor's brood of red-haired, green-eyed demigods. He was nearly so old as the Emperor himself, conceived in his vat the day his father was crowned to ensure the line of kings remained unbroken, and so it was likely he would never sit the throne. The Imperial family—as in all palatine families—did not default to the eldest child as in ancient days, but to a child hand-picked by his or her predecessor. "I am honored you could be here."

The prince sat upon a gilt chair facing determinedly *away* from the floor of the Grand Colosseum, the better to receive visitors—though I noted the bank of holograph screens in the arc of ceiling behind me so that all in attendance might see the Colosso games from any angle. I'd arrived late, and missed the opening ceremonies: thousands of men and women dancing and playing music while the racers and gladiators rode in on chariots pulled by thoroughbred horses and gene-tailored lions.

My audience ended with the Crown Prince, I rose and passed him, acknowledging Aurelian's guards with a short salute. Coming to the rail, I looked out upon the fields of battle. It was not my first time in the Colosseum, but the sheer size of it overawed me every time. The brick coliseum of Borosevo where my friends had fought and died had seated a quarter million people. The Grand Colosseum of the Eternal City seated three times that number. So vast was that mighty space that great sailcloth screens hung above the stands, displaying magnified views of the combat below. Pennons flew from lances bracketed to the inner rail of the stands and from the hands of the ten thousand statues who stood watch along the arched ramparts of the outer wall, each displaying the sign and sigil of a great house.

It was enough—almost—to forget there was a war on.

That was its purpose, after all.

Once I had hated the cheering and the clamor of the coliseum . . . standing at that rail while the trumpets played and the rose petals fell like slow rain, I felt my heart grow lighter. Just a little. Just for a moment—for one of those quiet moments Gibson talked about where the ugliness of the world fell away.

Ships and barges had been brought out upon the floor and from eight mighty sluices water poured forth and flooded the Colosseum.

"Sir Hadrian! You came!"

Turning, I found Princess Selene hurrying toward me, her handmaid Bayara and two other princess sisters in tow. I bowed deeply and took Selene's hand. "Your Highness."

"These are my sisters, Titania and Vivienne."

I took the hands of the younger princesses in turn and kissed the rings they offered. "Titania," I said, "after your grandmother?" Emperor's William's mother, Titania Augusta, had ruled for more than five hundred years. She had been Empress when the Cielcin razed Cressgard, and had died before she could see the crusade to its end.

The girl in question—willowy, graceful, her flaming hair long and straight—smiled and nodded, but did not speak.

"She's shy," said the other, short-haired and shorter of stature. "We've heard so much about you, Sir Hadrian."

"Is it true you met a Mericanii daimon on Vorgossos?" the shy girl blurted out. By the time I'd turned to face her, she'd clamped a hand over her mouth.

Selene laughed. "Titania, please!"

The Vorgossos affair was classified. But people talk, and this wide-eyed princess had lived all her life within the walls of the Peronine Palace. Doubtless she had heard whispers.

I smiled at the young princess, trying to appear the kind, worldly soldier. "You shouldn't believe everything you hear, Highness. The world's full enough of monsters as it is without us inventing new ones."

Princess Vivienne elbowed her sister. "I told you!"

Titania hung her head. "I shouldn't have asked."

Seeing her embarrassment plain on her face, I said, "No, no! I'm glad you did. As I say, there are too many monsters in the universe as it is. Being able to dispel one at a word is a privilege. Thank you, Highness."

Selene beamed at me, and her sisters hurried off whispering to one another, heads together. "And I thought knights weren't *really* gallant."

I drew my cape tight about me and bowed. Noticing Selene was still smiling at me, I added, "Making an enemy of one Aventine prince is quite enough for me, thank you."

"Alex isn't your enemy."

"I hope not," I said simply. "Isn't Alexander supposed to be here?"

"He is!" Selene answered, taking my arm. "We'll find him, but come! I'd like to introduce you around."

The next hour or so was a blur of red-haired names and faces, among them the very Prince Faustinus whom the high lords waiting on Vorgossos had said I resembled. I suppose I did. In addition to the children of the Emperor, there were Consortium directors and Nipponese trading magnates. There were lesser princes of Jadd and a couple of their satrap governors. A couple Durantine senators in gray and indigo were in evidence as well, alongside the usual cavalcade of nobile lords and ladies and their offspring representing the highest houses in the land. I was roped into conversation with Lord Peter Habsburg for several minutes. The Lord Minister of Works—a Lion himself—seemed sympathetic about my appointment to the Council.

"Old Cassian needs to retire, poor boy," Lord Peter said. "I for one can think of no better man to replace him."

Of Cassian Powers himself there was no sign. The Avenger of Cressgard was not the sort of man who made public appearances, having had his fill of banquets and triumphs. I understood him all too well; after two hours I wished I were back on my shuttle with my myrmidons. Siran, Elara, and Pallino had all come down with me for the Colosso, though they had not been permitted to attend the royal fête.

Neither was there sign of the Emperor himself. I learned from the chatter that the Crown Prince had given a speech and made the sacrifices to Old Earth with the Synarch at the close of the opening ceremonies in his father's place. Caesar had grave matters to attend to, or so everyone said. Despite his absence, the Empress was there, seated in a rear compartment as far from the fighting as could be. She sat amidst a group of older palatine ladies, the lot attended by house androgyns.

Selene led me into this den of lionesses, smiling all the while. "Mother, see! Sir Hadrian has come to visit us."

Maria Agrippina turned at our approach from a conversation with a Jaddian *eali* woman of astonishing perfection and smiled. "Selene, yes! I see." I knelt before the Empress's seat. She was lovely as the Jaddian goddess at her right hand, and lovelier than I remembered: an image of genetic perfection distilled across sixteen thousand years. She did not offer a hand and left me kneeling, not ordering me to rise. "I am pleased you could join us for this dreary affair, Lord Marlowe."

Raising my eyes enough to see her gold-sandaled feet, I said, "I was honored to be invited, Majesty."

"I should hope so," she said, voice distant. "I suppose I should thank you for my son's safe return, though Alexander gives mixed reports of his adventure. He says you treated him like a peasant."

"This is the one?" the Jaddian woman asked.

I glanced up at the woman—a princess or satrap of Jadd, I was not sure. With her olive skin so bronze it was almost green and hair black as mine, she seemed permanently veiled in shadow, though she dressed bright in pantaloons striped white and blue and a sleeveless robe that showed off the impressive array of golden armlets and bangles she wore.

The Empress put a hand on hers. "Yes, Sibylla, it is."

Sibylla's eyes widened, accentuated by the indigo dye that stained her eyelids. "We have stories of you in Jadd, Lord Marlowe."

"Good stories, I hope, my lady." Still I did not rise. I was beginning to grow uncomfortable there on the patterned carpet with Selene hovering at my shoulder.

Sibylla said, "The Satrap di Sayyiph says you are a man of quality. *Il uomos aretes!*"

Aretes, arete. Excellence. It was one of those words that survived to contemporary Jaddian from the ancient languages that formed it. I bowed my head deeper. "My lady is too kind."

I opened my mouth to inquire after the Maeskolos, but the Empress cut me off. "She is, isn't she? As I understand it, Lord Marlowe's primary *quality* is ambition. I understand you are to be named to the Council shortly, lord. One wonders where your ambitions end."

How was I to respond? Shame and innocence warred with me, and a sticky embarrassment coated my neck and shoulders. Any protest would appear defensive. Better to say nothing.

"What?" the Empress said. "Nothing to say?"

"Mother!" Selene took my arm, but I sensed that to rise was a mistake.

"Selene, this man is beneath you. Take yourself away."

The princess fell back at once.

Sibylla and the other ladies and lords gathered round the Empress had gone silent. I did not rise, but kept my gaze fixed on the carpet. Behind me, I sensed a throng of onlookers gathering. The liquid embarrassment began to run down my back. My fists clenched at my sides.

"I see . . ." the Empress said. "My daughter is the target of your ambition." I could not deny her. Who listening would believe I preferred my Tavrosi sorceress to a red-haired princess of the Sollan Empire? They were princes themselves.

"Understand your place, sir," the Empress said. "You are a servant. You *serve* us. At our pleasure. Forget this at your peril." She extended one sandaled foot, placed it on the dais before her. "You will offer us a sign of your obedience."

I looked up and met the Empress's gaze, dimly aware of the half dozen Martian guardsmen who stood behind her and Lady Sibylla. She meant for me to kiss that foot. It was an insult and a grave rebuke. Such a thing was reserved for slaves, for the palace homunculi and the lowest of lowborn servants, a reward and a punishment at once.

"Mother, stop! There's no need . . ." Selene interjected.

"Quiet, girl!" Maria Agrippina said, and tapped her toe thrice on the tile. "Here, boy." I made to rise, prepared to cross to the dais and obey. What else could I do? With the Empress and her court before me, the royal children and various high lords behind, with the Martians near at hand? "On your knees!" the Empress snapped. "Crawl."

I clenched my teeth, ducking my head further to hide the fire in my eyes, and placed my hands against the carpet. Focusing on the floral pattern in the rug, glad Valka slept in fugue, I started to crawl. The royal seat must have been ten miles away, so long it seemed. I felt half-ready to spring from my prone position and fly at the evil woman, goddess or no, and damn the Martians.

My hands shook, and I became aware—as though my perceptions were hidden from me by some heavy blanket—that I'd forgotten to breathe.

I could have killed her, then. How dare she humiliate me? *Me.* For an instant, I was every ounce the conspirator Breathnach and the Lions believed I was. In that instant, I would have gladly cut her down and cut a path to the throne. The Marlowe rage was on me, bright and cold as distant stars.

"Leave it, Mother!"

Alexander appeared from the crowd at my back.

"Alexander, you're just in time!"

"I said *leave it*," the prince interjected, stepping between me and the

Empress's chair. "Sir Hadrian did nothing wrong. Stop this at once." And there in the sight of all he laid a hand on my shoulder.

Maria Agrippina's eyes narrowed. "You defend him?"

My squire thrust out his chin. "He doesn't need defending. His actions speak for themselves." I did not know what to say. Mere days before this same prince had demanded that I kneel before him.

The sandaled foot withdrew beneath the white skirts. "Get him out of my sight."

Away from Her Majesty's compartment, I said, "Thank you, Alexander." Selene stood near at hand, folded in on herself, head down.

The young prince looked up at me. "She shouldn't have done that." Beneath my white cape, my hands were shaking, but with sustained rage or fear for my safety or my dignity I could not guess. "I'm glad you came. I wanted to apologize."

"*You* wanted to apologize?" I said, surprised.

Looking round, I discovered that Alexander had bowed his head, held his right fist to his chest in salute. "I asked my father to let me travel with you. I understand you had no say in the matter. Anyone would be frustrated." I blinked, astonished at the moment of clarity in the young nobile, but impressed. "I wanted to ask if you would allow me to accompany you when you leave Forum next."

My mouth opened, but for an instant no words came out. I might never again leave Forum, if I really was to take Lord Powers's seat on the Council. I might be married to Selene, and so be trapped in the Peronine Palace the rest of my days, like a fairy-tale princess trapped in her dragon-watched tower. *I might throw myself off the nearest platform.* A hundred answers played at once, but in the end I repeated the first one. "I'm not so sure I'm leaving Forum soon, Highness."

Alexander paused himself before answering. "I understand. But . . . when you go."

I glanced over his shoulder at Selene. "You did this?"

The princess looked up, and though her face was still white, she smiled.

A pair of tumblers wearing nothing but painted motley rolled past me to the amusement of a close knot of onlookers, bells in their hair. Alexander's eyes followed on, admiring the girls. Selene clapped along with her siblings and the other lords, and drank—though I did not.

Behind us, the trumpets played, and the master of ceremonies set the stage as wooden vessels crashed into one another and men fought and were hurled from the decks of their ships and plunged into the false sea.

"Do you think they'll drown?" asked Princess Vivienne, come back round again—without shy Titania—to watch the fighting with her elder sister.

"These are proper gladiators," I said, shaking my head. "See the masks they're wearing? They'll have osmosis gear underneath. Still might lose one or two with the ships crashing about, but I'm sure most of them will be fine." The gladiators wore combat skins beneath their imitation antique armor, suits not so different from the underlayment of a legionnaire's combat armor, complete with impact-absorbent gel layer. The only difference was that the gladiators' suits were designed to lock up as they sustained damage to steadily emulate real injury. "It has its problems," I was saying to both princesses, and to Bayara and a small knot of listeners who had gathered about the Devil of Meidua. "The suits work on a point system, so you can actually cheat them with a series of small hits—the kind that wouldn't stop a man in a real fight. I beat a gladiator once that way, when I was a . . ." I had been about to say *fodder pool myrmidon* when I realized that to do so would be to confirm the worst sort of thing about my *outcaste* past. "When I was in Colosso."

"You were in Colosso?" asked Selene's handmaid, Bayara. But for her hair—which was red as that of the royal children—the girl reminded me of Anaïs Mataro, being of some lower stripe of the palatine class.

Selene laid a hand on her friend's knee. "I thought I told you, Yara."

"For three or four years on Emesh."

"Where's that?" Bayara made a face.

"The inner rim," I answered, "right on the edge of the Veil, near the border with the freeholds." But I could see on her face that all this meant nothing to the handmaid, and I smiled. "It's as far from here as you can get, right at the very edge of the Empire at the heart of the galaxy, near the core. Farther than you can really imagine." This seemed to work better, and the girl smiled.

Alexander stirred in his seat by the rail, and turned from his contemplation of the false sea and the fighting to ask, "Did you really run away from home?"

I did not answer at once. Below, the wreckage of ships and gladiators was being swept away by servitors with mighty nets. Watching them in a nostalgic haze, I answered, "I did. I meant to go to Teukros and become an Expeditionary Corps scholiast, but I never arrived." I had been about to recount my time in the coliseum, but the memory of the Empress and how she had debased me came back to me, and I fell silent.

"How did you end up on Emesh?" Alexander asked. "That's almost as far away from Teukros as it is from here."

The vision Brethren showed me in the bowels of Vorgossos flashed like lightning across my mind. The smugglers who had delivered me from Delos and my father vanished into nothing, the stars beyond the portholes changed. The same power that had resurrected me had moved me across space, had set me on this path, the very path that led me to Vorgossos. To Arae and Aptucca. To Iubalu and my triumph. I was a piece in a game I did not understand, and felt again that longing to leave Forum, to fly to Colchis and the Imperial Library and look for answers.

"I don't know," I told the prince simply. It was not quite a lie. "I was in fugue. When I awoke . . . I wasn't where I expected to be."

A shadow passed before the sun, and looking up with a million other faces, I saw the barge sailing in, suspended by repulsor pods like balloons that carried it in over the rim of the Colosseum where the statues clutched their pennons, over the crowds and the sailcloth screens that showed feeds from flying cameras. The master of ceremonies shouted over it all, over cheers and the pounding of hands and feet, over trumpets and the distant salute of cannon fire. The opening act done, the next event would pit two teams of gladiators against one another, but they would fight not upon the floor of the Grand Colosseum as on other occasions, but upon that floating platform.

"I was hoping they'd drop it!" said Princess Vivienne, pouting.

"And splash the commons?" Selene put it. "That would have been amusing."

I did not point out to the princesses that this was Forum, that the only commons here were servants. Even the gladiators were the sons of lesser lords, the very best far-flung worlds could offer to please their Holy Emperor. Slaves and myrmidons such as I had been seldom fought on Forum. Only the best toy warriors could perform for the Emperor, though His Radiance was but rarely in attendance.

"Philip says the team in yellow there is from Car-Tannae on the outer rim," Vivienne was saying. "He says their knights don't use swords. They use highmatter nets. Like fishermen. They throw them over an enemy and use a remote to activate it once they've got them."

"Highmatter's not allowed in the games," Alexander cut in, shutting down his younger sister.

Vivienne made a face. "I know that, Alex. But Philip says they'll still use nets. Isn't that strange? Nets?"

"The ancients used to use nets," I said, interposing myself between the two royals. "In the Golden Age. Both in show combats like this one and in battle."

"I give you this, Selene," came a drawling voice from over my shoulder, "your boy knows his stuff." Turning, I found the long-haired Prince Ricard standing just behind my chair, so close that had the sun been lower in the sky his shadow would have fallen across me. The other prince laid a hand on the back of my seat. Leaning in, he said, "Fancy a wager, Marlowe? I've got four-and-a-half million marks riding on the Car-Tannites to take the day. You game?"

I looked up at him. "I am afraid, Your Highness, that what funds I have belong to your radiant father." Repeating the Empress's words from minutes before, I said, "I am but a servant."

"Afraid?" the prince echoed, not seeming to have heard the rest, "Don't be afraid! It's only the Colosseum! Philip!" He looked back over his shoulder. "You were right! Marlowe wouldn't take my bet!" The stockier, short-haired prince laughed from a few tables over and clambered to his feet, seeming only a little drunker than he had the night of the triumph.

Just what I needed, I thought.

"He's not afraid, Ricard!" Selene said. "He doesn't want to play your stupid game."

"Sir Hadrian was a gladiator!" Bayara protested.

Ricard's eyes widened. "He *was!* I'd forgotten! Ooh, but this is too good!" Prince Philip had joined his brother by then, and Ricard wrapped an arm around his brother's shoulder. "Philip, did you know Sir Hadrian was a gladiator back in the day?"

"I think I did," Philip answered, cradling his wine in both hands to keep Ricard's jostling from spilling the vintage. "Where did you fight?"

"Emesh!" Princess Vivienne offered.

"The fuck's an Emesh?" Philip squinted at his little sister.

"Inner rim, somewhere," Bayara said, apparently now an expert.

Philip raised his glass. "Cheers. Those rim fights can be bloody brutal, man." He drank deeply, and when he was done asked, "I don't see your woman around. Did she not come?"

Princess Selene answered for me. "The Tavrosi is in fugue. Something about that trouble with Director Breathnach."

The besotted prince nodded somberly. "Nasty business, that was. I'm sorry to miss her." He leaned toward Ricard and tried to whisper, "Sorry to miss her ass, that is. You remember that thing, Ricard? I'd turn to witchcraft, too, if it meant burying myself in *that*."

"Enough!" I rose, wheeled so quickly Prince Philip *did*, in fact, drop his wine. The crystal goblet bounced on the thick carpet and rolled away, spilling wine that cost as much as a peasant farmer might make in two years' hard labor. Both Philip and Ricard took a step back. I pushed my cape back over my shoulders. Too late, I remembered I was not armed, and settled for hooking my thumbs in my belt, facing the brothers square. "Apologize to the lady."

"She isn't even here!" Philip said, still recoiling.

I took a step nearer the two princes, but did not speak.

Ever the cooler head, Ricard half-stepped between me and his uncouth brother. "Stand down, knight! My brother is a prince of the Sollan Empire. It is death to lay hands on him!"

"Have I laid hands on him, Highness?" I asked coldly, not taking my eyes from Philip's face. I kept my hands at my side. History would not repeat itself. This was not Gilliam. I had no hidden ring, no hidden rank.

Neither of the princes moved. Neither spoke. Alexander, Selene, and the others did not stir. Eyes narrowed, I took a careful step toward the princes, and took pleasure watching the blood drain from Philip's face as Ricard thrust out a hand to stop me.

"We're done here," I said, voice calm and cool.

Two Martians appeared almost from nowhere and pushed me back. "Step away from the prince, lordship," one said, voice flattened and modulated by the helmet speakers.

Philip grinned.

"What is going on here?"

I shut my eyes. I should never have come, never have accepted Alexander's invitation or Selene's or whose ever it was. I should have frozen myself with Valka until all was decided and the Emperor's orders were handed down.

Empress Maria Agrippina wafted in from the back room, Lady Sibylla and several other courtiers following in her wake like dolphins dogging a sailing ship.

"The barbarian attacked Philip," Ricard said.

"Only because Philip was being terribly uncouth!" Selene cut in, standing to put herself between the Empress and myself as she had before.

Vivienne did not stand, but called out, "Sir Hadrian didn't attack him! He only told Philip to leave."

"Philip had it coming, Mother," Alexander said, coming to my defense as well. "If it had been me, I'd have hit him by now."

The Empress surveyed her five children, emerald eyes flitting over the several dozen others in the onlooking crowd that had formed around us. Crown Prince Aurelian stood off to one side, sad eyes watching the proceedings, a befuddled expression on his face—so like his father's. Maria Agrippina said, "I should have thrown you out of the box earlier, sir." She sniffed, glancing briefly to Sibylla. "Quality indeed. We have a word for your *quality* here, Lord Marlowe, as I said: ill-breeding. A cousin you may be, however distant. The least of our cousins, but *outcaste* once is *outcaste* forever, they say. No washing out that stain."

"Mother!" Selene protested, trying to pass the Martians that flanked me in their formal combat armor.

"Enough, girl."

"Philip was being most disgusting about Sir Hadrian's paramour," Selene exclaimed.

Maria Agrippina's eyes narrowed. "So it was about that woman? And here I thought it could get no worse. Striking the Blood Imperial over that Tavrosi *animal* he breeds with? Disgraceful."

Rage blinded me for a moment, and *in* that moment I could have torn the whole Eternal City from the sky with my bare hands. But I was in the grasp of the Martian Guard, and clenched my teeth so hard I feared they might shatter.

"He didn't strike him!" Vivienne objected.

The Empress ignored her daughter as if she were a species of flea. "What is to be done with you, Lord Marlowe?"

"He should be whipped!" Ricard said, speaking on behalf of his drunker brother.

"But he didn't *do* anything!" Selene protested. "Philip should be whipped! He's the one acting the fool."

Prince Philip cleared his throat, a piece of him still I think surprised to find his hands absent a wine cup. In a voice surprisingly steady and slow—like a child reciting lines off a playbill—he said, "Sir Hadrian was a gladiator." He glanced out over the field, where as we spoke the Car-Tannites fought with net and spears against black-clad fighters with more traditional swords and shields. "Make him fight."

The Empress's eyes lit up, and though I could never prove it I *knew*, knew that she had put them up to it.

CHAPTER 47

ONCE A MYRMIDON

I WAS PERMITTED TO return to my landing shuttle on the royal strand overlooking the Grand Colosseum, guarded as I had been guarded when I traveled to the coliseum dormitories to ask Switch to stand with me against Gilliam Vas. Almost I imagined the mutant priest and my traitor friend walked with me, bumping shoulders with the dozen Martians to where my guards waited with the pilot officer at the end of the dock.

The landing strip was one of several that ran out like fingers from the edge of the floating city platform, stretching out into the clouds. The wind snatched my cape and pulled it to one side as it gathered my hair in its fingers.

"I know that look," Siran said, coming down the ramp. "What happened?"

I told her.

"Do you have to make enemies everywhere you go?"

In lieu of an answer, I tore the white cape from my shoulders and threw it at the bulkhead, where its magnetic clasp caught on the steel. It hung there like a flag. "Fetch me one of the spare kits, will you?"

The centurion nodded her shaved head and turned to move deeper into the shuttle. My personal armor was back aboard the *Tamerlane* and well outside my reach, but all our shuttles carried a few spare sets of combat equipment: armor and shield-belts, even weapons. Those weapons would not be cleared to leave the shuttle, not on Forum, but I had been permitted to retrieve my own armor from the shuttle—and so permitted an opportunity to speak to Siran, should whatever words I might say be my last.

Did the Empress want me dead? No. No, she could not. The Emperor wanted me alive. She only wanted to chastise me, to humiliate the Halfmortal on the most public stage in the galaxy, to destroy my name and the way men whispered it on the practice field and in dive bars across the Empire.

"Not one of the white ones!" I said, calling after Siran. "One of the Red Company combat kits. I'll be damned if I go out wearing their colors."

She emerged a moment later with a kit about the size of a large briefcase. Conscious of the Martians standing on the ramp behind me, I skinned out of my tunic and undershirt, wadding the clothing on the seat beside me. A moment later I was naked and pulling on the suit underlayment from inside the kit.

"Are you all right?" Siran asked.

"Fine," I said.

"Your hands are shaking."

I clenched them into fists. "I said I'm fine, Siran." An oath escaped me, fierce and furious. "Stupid! Stupid, stupid!" I tugged the underlayment over my hands and arms and closed the seals. It snugged around me, and I reached for the red tunic and pulled it over my head. I had survived an assassination attempt, survived the Inquisition, and I was going to be brought down by drunk, stupid Prince Philip? Not assassinated, but character-assassinated live in the Grand Colosseum?

"Can I go with you, boss?" Siran's voice cut across my seething and brought the boil down. I looked up, fingers mutely clicking through the latches and seals on the black and scarlet breastplate. *My friend* was watching me with narrowed eyes, brows furrowed and concerned. We had been myrmidons together. Soldiers together. I was a myrmidon again that day. Time cycles. Moments return. We cannot escape our patterns. The same choices—the same sins—return us to the same places. I was not bound for the Grand Colosseum, but a bone grass meadow in Borosevo to fight again, to pay in blood for the same sin: rage.

Was it rage?

Or pride?

I shook my head. "Single combat. But I don't know what they're throwing at me," I told her, though I should have guessed.

She accepted this with the barest hint of a nod. "Well, you give 'em hell from us, Had."

I delayed in answering just long enough to check my greaves and gauntlets were in place. Satisfied, I said, "I will."

Siran offered her hand. I took it and pulled her close, embraced her.

"Don't you let us down," she said. "You get your ass kicked, I'll never let you hear the end of it."

"The whole galaxy won't let me hear the end of it," I said to her, and let her go, and turning, I went out from shuttle and back to my guards, and passed with them out from under the clouds and the flying towers . . . and into legend.

CHAPTER 48

HALFMORTAL

THE GATE STANDS BEFORE me when I close my eyes, chains rattling, doors rising to admit the light. The noise of the gong boomed like distant thunder, swelling as the gate rose.

"You know the rules?" the coliseum guild had asked me while I chose my weapons. "Battle to submission. No point suits. No body shields. No projectiles. You fight until you or your opponent—or opponents—yield, get knocked out, or bleed out." The rat-like man spoke fast, chewing his verrox stimulant all the while. I ignored him, selected the weapons I meant to use.

It had been a long time since I'd held a *hoplon,* an antique round shield. The sword was near a match to my own, long and straight, but two-edged where the highmatter needed only one. It was common zircon, white as the shell of my necklace, light and sharper than steel. Highmatter was not permitted in Colosso, not because it was too dangerous, but because it wasn't sporting. Because any contest fought with highmatter might be ended too quickly.

"Do you know what I'm up against?"

The little man glanced up at the cameras on the wall, and his chewing slowed. "No, lordship. They hadn't said."

Liar.

The sword bounced in its scabbard at my hip opposite a long parrying dagger, and I carried a spear in my hands. I am no great lancer, but absent any information on who I was fighting—or what—prudence was most called for. The spear might save my life if it was some great beast I went to battle: an azhdarch or megathere, bull or lion.

Bluish light fell through the open gate, and for a minute my mind rebelled against what I saw.

Twin walls of water rose to either side of the gate, a narrow channel parted in the false sea that flooded the coliseum. Ahead a steep ramp rose to the floating platform, rising past the water to the air above. I stepped out, the concrete between my feet still wet where the waters had been parted. Pausing a moment, I tested the walls with my spear point. The tip passed through, splashing where it struck.

Static fields held the water back, fields as powerful as those that held the air in starships when their bay doors were opened. It was a staggeringly frivolous use of energy; to waste so much power on *spectacle* was a statement of power all its own. I advanced slowly, fearing those waters would close above my head.

I could not *really* hear the shouting until I climbed the ramp.

The noise of it! Even muffled by the barrier that hung like an invisible dome above the floor of the arena, the sound was deafening. A million faces clamored, flags waved, colors danced and swayed along with the mass of bodies in the seats. Straight ahead, the box from which I had watched the Car-Tannites fight with their nets loomed. Beneath its awning were seated several dozen figures in white, each with a crown of red fire. The lords of humanity in all their glory and splendor: terrible in the power, ancient in the majesty, petty in their outbursts as nigh-forgotten Jove.

I had not heard the master of ceremonies down in the trench, but as I mounted the last length of ramp, I heard him cry, ". . . the Hero of Aptucca! The Son of the Devil! The Demon in White himself! Lord Hadrian Marlowe!" And the cheers that answered him I prayed would deafen Maria Agrippina on her throne, and that all who looked on would wonder to see their Demon in White dressed in black and scarlet.

A moment later, all was forgotten, for I caught sight of the figure standing opposite me.

Alone.

One warrior, lonely as I, but as different from myself as any man could be. Where I was dark and muted—black clad, black-haired, and quiet—the figure opposite me was an explosion of color, dressed in striped yellow and blue belled pantaloons, green wraps tight about his calves, pointed green slippers trimmed with gold on his feet. He wore a matching green jacket over a white shirt. Gilt vambraces sheathed his arms. His pointed, olive face was smiling beneath an oiled beard and curling mustache, his goat-like hair carefree and tousled as he raised two gold-ringed hands in greeting.

The only thing muted about his entire appearance was the half-robe tied slip-fashion about his waist and left shoulder, the loose-square sleeve flapping in the wind like a cape. The garment was black as mine, a shadow, a symbol of his rank and training.

A *mandyas*.

And I felt my blood run cold as memory came rushing in.

Irshan.

Prince Philip's personal gladiator. A Maeskolos of Jadd. A Swordmaster of the Fifth Circle, the prince had said. The former *sulshawar* protector of Prince Constans du Olante. Memories of Sir Olorin Milta flashed in my mind, images thrown against the margins of my skull like lightning reflected off the underbelly of the clouds.

Beneath the shouting and the clamor, I heard him speak from across the round barge we stood upon. "Hadrian Marlowe!" he said, "It is an honor to meet you." He bowed deeply, hands still extended to either side. It was a deeply respectful gesture, and for a moment I forgot the Empress and the useless princes. For a moment, there was only the respect of two warriors for one another, warriors who must be enemies, but warriors all the same. "I am a great fan."

"The honor is mine, messer!" I said, returning the bow. "I have always admired your order."

"My prince has asked that I chastise you," he said simply, undoing the knot of his *mandyas*. "I must do so."

"You will try!" I answered him.

Irshan smiled, teeth flashing. "Very good!" He tossed the garment aside. The wind caught it, and it moved like a sail through the air and puddled upon the water. "It is business, what we do."

"I thought it was art?" I asked.

The smile widened. "That too."

Trumpets sounded, the pennons about the inner wall of the arena dipped low.

Irshan circled the perimeter of the floating platform like a panther prowling its cage. Behind him I saw—and heard behind me—the rush of water as the trenches by which we'd arrived were closed. Water rushed in, and the mighty barge beneath us rocked at anchor.

The spear would do me little good against such a man as this. Had I faced some great predator, perhaps its superior reach would aid me, but against a Maeskolos, whose speed and skill were superhuman? It would be a hindrance. I would need all my skill, and my skill was with the blade, not the lance. The Maeskoloi were all of the *eali al'aqran,* the Jaddian palatines, and in Jadd the genetic regulation that keeps our palatines within the Chantry's accepted realm of human norms was relaxed. He would be faster than me, stronger, more resilient.

I hurled my spear at Irshan. The Swordmaster did not leap aside, did not duck, did not even try to draw his sword—nor had he any shield to raise.

He *caught* it.

The Maeskolos *caught* the lance, stopped the spear tip mere inches from his chest. "Let us not be toying with trifles," he said, the crowd gasping. "This is no weapon for such as we!" And he broke the wooden haft over his knee before tossing the pieces into the water behind him. "Come!"

If the Empress had wished for me to look the fool, she had succeeded.

I drew my sword, held the round shield up and ready, keeping my left toe pointed at the enemy. Sir Irshan reversed his pacing, arcing closer and back across the way in front of me. Off in the highest levels of the Colosseum, a massive drum began to sound. The noise of it shook the air. As he drew closer, Irshan drew his sword, a curving scimitar of the kind loved best by the Jaddians.

"Let us see what you can do!" He laughed, and close now whirled, blade whistling on the wind. I caught it on my shield, but did not strike—keeping my own blade tucked against my right shoulder. The swords were both ceramic and razor sharp, would tear skin and flesh and notch bone with ease. Irshan drew back, lips shrugging, as if he'd confirmed some private theory. He thrust, and tucking my elbow, I took the blow on the edge of the shield. Irshan was moving slowly. Testing me. Toying with me?

He pointed his left shoulder at me and threw a cut at my head. Seeing my chance, I raised my shield and advanced, stepping in with a thrust aimed square at the man's armpit. Irshan melted away, moving sideways as if he were made of water. Of smoke. The blade flashed, coming round. I managed the parry in time, caught it on flat of my blade, and stepped in, hoping to off-balance the Maeskolos with a shield pulse.

But the Maeskolos was gone, dancing away on slippered feet. Several paces now between us, he jogged about the perimeter of the barge, sword held high for the watchers. The crowd cheered.

He was fast, but more lightly armored. I felt confident the white shirt hid a nanocarbon vest that—like my suit's underlayment—would turn all but the most precise thrust. And I had a shield. It wasn't much, but it wasn't nothing.

In answer to the Jaddian's prancing, I thrust my own sword skyward.

The cheer that answered Irshan's little display drowned the Colosseum a second time. The Swordmaster stopped and bowed to me.

How he closed the gap between us I cannot say, and yet he did. It was all I could do to crouch behind my shield as the sword hit it. Once, twice, three times in rapid succession. I thrust over the shield, pressed the Maeskolos back. Irshan parried the blade effortlessly, but missed his riposte, which slid past me on the outside. I pushed the blade aside with my shield and slashed in across his torso, hoping to tear the green jacket and test my theory about the body armor beneath.

But Irshan had seen the blow coming. He did not parry it. He did not even step away. He brought his free hand down and *slapped* the flat of the blade with his open palm, knocking the blade into me. I was so stunned I didn't have time to react when the Jaddian stepped into me, dropping his weight to use my own shield to knock me off balance.

I stumbled back, snarling, surprised when no follow-up came. Irshan simply stood there, tapping his scimitar against his knee.

"Surely you have more for me!" he said, and rested the tip of his sword against his left wrist, holding the blade on a slant before him, point and left hand high.

Grunting, I advanced, sword high. Irshan awaited me, patient as a spider. I feinted, and as Irshan twitched to reply, angled my shield and punched him with its edge. Irshan slapped the jab down with his high left hand.

"You are a cautious one!" he said. "I expected boldness." I did not answer him. I punched again. Irshan slapped the attack down and thrust at my eyes. My sword was waiting, and as I advanced I swung overhead, pulling the elbow back so the point fell short of Irshan's raised blade. I had a clear shot at his ribs and took it. The thrust found meat, but bounced off.

Armored indeed, I thought. *No matter.* I could see silver through the hole I'd made in the white linen in his shirt.

The Maeskolos laughed and pressed a hand to his ribs. *"Jaja!"* he exclaimed, "There he is!"

I did not like this Maeskolos. He smiled too easily.

He swept forward, blade rising from right hip to left shoulder. I turned the blow with my sword and stepped in with a thrust, but Irshan faded and stepped on my foot. The heel stomp might have fractured my arch, but my sabaton protected me. I tried again to repulse the fellow with my shield, but he faded back like flames tossed in the wind and lunged forward.

I, too, am faster than any normal man, and stronger. We palatines were bred with sharper reflexes, greater connectivity between motor cortex and spine, and a greater number of nerve cells and connections in the spine itself. Though my conscious mind barely tracked Irshan's blade, neural connections that mapped from my eyes directly to my spine answered the man's attacks, and the old training flowed through parry after parry as I fended off the assault. If you have ever encountered a snake and leaped away from it only to learn *after* you leaped that it *was* a snake you avoided, you will know what I mean. Sometimes, the body can think faster than the brain—and a palatine's body doubly so.

Still I was driven back, retreating across the empty barge toward the edge. Vast as the platform was, it was nearly stable, but there at the edge I felt the ground beneath my feet wobble and sway. Still I held my own, tight parries and careful shield work fending off the Swordmaster's flashing blade.

Irshan smiled through it all, though I detected his teeth clenching tighter beneath those curling mustachios. I was trying him, a little.

You've retreated enough.

The words came from some old childhood lesson. I had faced worse opponents, faster ones, stronger ones. Iubalu. The Demon of Arae. Even Father Calvert on Vorgossos. Creatures that moved so fast they were invisible, creatures even highmatter could not cut. Whatever Irshan was, he was not them.

His sword glanced off my ribs, carving a white scratch on the black ceramic. Snarling, I clamped my elbow down on the blade and slammed my shield hand up into his chin. Irshan gasped and staggered backward. The sword ground against my side and fell from his fingers. Before he could retrieve it, I stepped over it and kicked it backward—I hoped far enough to get it in the water and end this contest before I could be humiliated. But my footing was awkward, rushed, and the blade skittered to a halt two yards from the edge.

"*Noyn jitat!*" Irshan massaged his chin. He spat upon the platform. Was there red in it? "Let me say again what an honor it is! To be here. *Fighting* you."

I did not feel like talking. I only bobbed my head.

"You do not say much!" he observed, settling—to my astonishment—into a loose-handed boxing guard. "I understood you were a great talker."

He was trying to distract me.

"Nothing?" He beat his chest with both hands. "Very well. Keep your secrets. *Epa!*"

It almost felt unsporting, attacking an unarmed man, Maeskolos or no.

But that was not the time to fuss about propriety. Maria Agrippina was watching, her and half the great lords of the Empire—or so it felt. I did not rush the Swordmaster, but gave ground, moving steadily back to finish the job I'd started with his sword.

Irshan darted forward, a colorful blur. I thrust my sword at him, but he slapped it aside with the flat of his hand and—stepping inside—threw a cross that caught my unarmored jaw and knocked me back a step. He worked his way around, struck me knife-handed in a joint between my armor's ceramic plates and bruised my floating ribs. Breathing hard, I jumped back, slashing wildly. But Irshan blocked my sword on his gaunt-leted forearm again and again, moving faster and faster with each successive guard. He *slapped* the blade again—how was such a thing even possible? Fingers closed about my wrist, trapping my sword between us. He came inside my left arm, nearly embracing me, all his efforts focused on tearing the sword from my grasp. My left hand battered uselessly against his back. Ducking just a little, I got my sword behind his knee and lifted, charging forward in a way that took the man off his feet and slammed him to the ground. I raised my sword to strike—the crowd roaring—but Irshan kicked once, *twice*. The first foot stopped my sword on his sole, the second caught the edge of my shield and torqued it loose. Irshan writhed and snapped himself back to his feet, delivering a neat roundhouse kick that knocked the shield clean from my hand. It sailed clean across the barge platform, steel rim pinging as it bounced and rolled . . . and fell into the water.

Trying not to slow or let dismay sink its roots in my heart's soil, I swung at the Jaddian, my blade flashing about my head in sheets of blurry white. Irshan danced through them like a juggler through his knives. On the last flurry I tucked my sword, fist snapping round in a hook that clipped the man with the pommel. Irshan let the next blow through, my blade digging useless against the armor skin beneath his clothes. Seizing his opportunity, he punched me in the cheek, and redoubling his attack hooked his hand behind my ear and seized my hair to push me down and to one side.

I lost my footing and fell even as I felt my scalp tear and blood run down my neck. Wincing, I must have lay there for just a second, for when the white of pain retreated and the dull ache began, I saw Irshan standing ten paces away.

His sword was in his hand.

He wasn't smiling.

"I have to say, I'm disappointed," he said, resting the scimitar once more against the back of his upraised hand. *"This* is all you have?" The crowd sat silent, almost still, and the Maeskolos spoke loudly, voice caught and amplified by the floating cameras, relayed from the Colosseum's surround. "Get up! Stand and face me." He slashed his sword through a showy arc, teeth bared. I could see the blood on them. That last pommel strike had knocked out one of his teeth. "Get up!"

I got up. My head was still pounding, and I knew each drumbeat heralded more lost blood. Fingers found the tear. It wasn't serious.

"You can yield!" Irshan said. "No one would fault so great a man as you! Bow out with dignity."

Was that Agrippina's plan? Force the Halfmortal to beg mercy in Colosso? Embarrass me, humiliate me in front of nearly a million of the most powerful men and women in the galaxy? And for what? For Selene, of course, and Alexander. Breathnach's hatred had been motivated by class: the hatred of the prole for the nobile. For all her airs, the Empress was no different. Like Bourbon—like the other houses who had not dipped their banners—she simply would not accept a former *outcaste* for a son-in-law, nor could she forgive as Alexander had forgiven me. Humiliating me would castrate me, politically, would see me stripped of whatever rank and power I possessed, would see the Red Company dispersed, would destroy my dream. I might still sit the Council, I might still wed Selene, but men would laugh that the Hero of Aptucca was beaten in the Colosseum by a contract fighter paid by wine-soaked and feeble-minded Prince Philip. I imagined Valka banished from Forum, imagined Lorian chained once more to a desk. I saw Crim and Ilex and Corvo and the rest paid and sent—shipless—back to the freeholds whence they came to fight and die as they would. And all of it: Smythe's sacrifice and Ghen's and the deaths of so many thousand men would come to naught. My own death would come to naught. My resurrection. My visions. My dream.

All this flashed across my mind in an instant—in *the* instant it took to stand.

But stand I did. I stood and took up my sword, point straight and leveled at Irshan's heart. A fey impulse took me, and thinking of the Cielcin and the striped masks they wore, I traced my thumb along my cheekbone beneath the left eye, drawing a red line.

As a boy, Sir Felix had forced me to stand with sword in hand—arm extended—for minutes and then hours at a time. I was certain I could outwait the more flamboyant Maeskolos.

I was right.

He dashed toward me, attacking high. Unshielded now, I moved to turn his blade with my own, but he *dropped* it, passed it from one hand to the other and lashed out. The point scraped against my armor, carving another fine scratch on the old enamel. The next thrust came at my eyes. I swung sideways, swept the attack away, only for one slippered foot to strike my knee. The suit protected the joint and stopped it hyperextending, but I still stumbled, staggered back as a slash skated off my arm. Irshan's hand and blade were a blur. The blows came so fast and so precisely that memory of my fight with Iubalu flashed like lightning into my conscious mind.

All laughter had fled the man's face. His jovial demeanor was gone. The scimitar caught against the edge of a thigh pad and, grinding, tore through tunic and underlayment alike. I felt the skinsuit compress to stanch the bleeding and winced. It had taken skill to make that cut. Armorweave does not part easily.

But I had no time for awe or material science, had no time even for artistry.

The Jaddian sword whistled toward my head, and though I blocked it I did not block the heel spur kick that bit into my wounded thigh. My leg buckled, and I went to one knee before Irshan. I slashed wildly, hoping to catch the man in the liver. The sword would not cut, but a solid thrust to the liver would have the man on his back anyway.

But Irshan twisted, and my thrust found only the lining of his short jacket, and his hand . . . his hand found mine and seized fingers and sword hilt alike and twisting forced me back to my knees.

That was when I knew Irshan meant to kill me. He hadn't been sent to humiliate me at all, but to rid the galaxy of Hadrian Marlowe.

I must have made the Empress angrier than I knew.

The crowd gasped and cheered as Irshan pulled the sword from my fingers and cast it away. I heard a distant splash. Irshan raised his sword, and though I could not see his face I knew he turned his eyes to the royal box, to the Empress and Crown Prince Aurelian, to Selene and Alexander, Titania and Vivienne, to Ricard and his master, Philip, and all the rest. I knew he awaited the judgment. Thumbs up or down. A million throats were roaring. A thousand trumpets played.

Surely now the Emperor would arrive, arrive and put a stop to all this madness. Surely I had suffered enough. I clenched my hands into fists, feeling Valka's ring tighten. I was not afraid. My first death had put the fear of Death out of me. Perhaps the powers that had delivered me in Kharn Sagara's Garden would deliver me again.

Or perhaps I would deliver myself.

Irshan had forgotten something.

He had forgotten my knife.

With my free left hand I pulled the parrying dagger loose from my belt and slammed it point first through the top of the man's foot. I felt the *thud* of impact as the point dug into the false wood of the platform's top, and heard Irshan howl with pain. His grip slackened on my arm—just for a moment, just enough. I surged to my feet, caught the Maeskolos by the wrist with both hands as he lashed down in fury. In my haste to block his attack, I'd left my knife in his foot, and he stumbled, momentarily pinned.

There followed a brief struggle, two bleeding men alone in the Grand Colosseum, wrestling over a sword. The blade came free, and seizing it with both my hands I stumbled back. There was no time for questions, no time for hesitancy. Even wounded and lame, the Maeskolos was dangerous. Too dangerous to be kept alive. I swung my blade—his blade—for the kill. Dimly, I recalled another man struck down by his own sword.

Moments repeat. Moments recur.

But not always.

Irshan did not try to block. He did not even *fade.*

He reached into the pocket of his jacket.

A blue-white light flashed, sprouted . . . shone the color of moonlight.

The highmatter blade rose to parry, and *sliced* the ceramic scimitar in two. I hardly had time to think, hardly had time to understand what was happening.

Highmatter was forbidden in Colosso.

But this was not Colosso. Irshan was not an opponent.

Irshan was an *assassin.* But whose?

It happened so fast, happened in less than half a second, happened before my broken sword's point could strike the floor.

The Emperor had not appeared.

The Swordmaster's unstoppable sword flashed toward my eyes.

I raised my hand in a doomed and desperate attempt to save my life.

My *left* hand.

The crowd screamed.

Irshan froze.

The highmatter cut through my vambrace, parted skin and flesh and sinew like air, and stopped . . . *stopped* when it encountered Kharn Sagara's false bones. The prosthesis was adamant, the same stuff of which starship hulls were made. Starship hulls and the body armor of the Exalted. Confusion ruled the stands. Highmatter on the field? Had Marlowe's armor stopped it?

Then they saw the blood spilling from my wounded arm, gushing from where the Maeskolos had severed veins. And they *screamed*.

"Halfmortal!" The cry went up, repeated. "Halfmortal! Halfmortal!"

Irshan's shock lasted only a moment. Stumbling with his hobbled foot, he lashed out again, and again I blocked him with my left arm. The thunder of the crowd shook the world and set the gulls that roosted in the hanging towers above to flight. Irshan thrust his weapon toward me, and I caught it. Caught it as he had caught my spear. The liquid metal flexed beneath my fingers, and I felt the muscle sever and weep blood. Armorweave tightened, trying to spare me. I stepped forward, still holding the impossibly sharp blade in my fist. The Jaddian's eyes bulged.

The broken ceramic sword was still in my hand. I did not hesitate. I did not consult the Empress for her judgment. I thrust its broken point down through the opening at the base of my enemy's neck. The highmatter blade evaporated the moment Irshan dropped it from his grasp, and he fell toward me. I could not support his weight, and he fell to the ground, broken weapon still lodged in his shoulder. Blood ran everywhere.

I pressed my knee into his sternum, his highmatter sword unkindled in my hand.

"Whom do you serve?" I asked. He didn't answer. "Tell me and I'll end it now."

The Martians were coming. The static fields had opened and figures were coming up the ramps. I needed to get away. Back to the shuttle. Back to the *Tamerlane*. Back to safety. Placing an assassin in the Colosseum was a bold move, and whoever had done it, even the Empress, would need to move quickly in these moments of fallout.

"Was it the Empress?" I asked, pressing my knee harder.

Irshan did not speak. Blood ran from his shoulder, from his mouth. Too much blood. The sword in his shoulder should have stanched the flow, not sped it. Something was happening.

"Was it the Empress?" I asked again. "Whom do you serve?"

My knee *fell inward*. Irshan's ribs collapsed. Blood began streaming from his eyes, the corners of his mouth, and where it ran it *boiled*. His face bubbled and ran like wax, great lesions opening in his neck. My knee now smeared with gore, I stood and clambered back. His arms flailed against the decking, whole sheets of skin sloughing off like the papery sheath of an onion, blood and bits of melting muscle smeared on the planks.

Not the Empress, I remember thinking, turning shocked as the Martians pounded across the platform, shaking us all where we floated on the water. *Not the Empress.* I staggered past the guards, waving them away. The ramp lay ahead of me, water rising to either side. I practically slid down it, but only after tarrying a moment to look back at Irshan's body.

At what was left of it.

The man had *melted.* A slurry of red and yellow fluid soaked those bright clothes, crowned his black hair. No bones were left, no skin, no sinew. Only an empty armorweave suit, striped pantaloons, and green slippers soaked brown.

Poison. A vicious poison.

Dispholide.

I had only ever heard of it—had never seen it used. A few grains of dispholide would dissolve a full-grown man. A few more could kill an azhdarch. It went by many names: the Drowner, the Green Death, the Mermaid's Kiss, the Priest's Poison. The Priest's Poison because it was an instrument of the Holy Terran Chantry, devised by the Choir—their shadowy research division—in the deeps of time, molded from the venom of an ancient serpent long vanished from the galaxy, tempered and strengthened by eons of refinement.

The Chantry again.

No one stopped me as I stumbled bleeding back into the hypogeum. I made it all the way to the rear gates before anyone tried. But I bullied the two Martians down and thrust the unkindled blade in their faces, and they stood down. Irshan's face kept melting behind my eyes, and the memory of the way in which his chest had caved in beneath my weight replayed until I thought I must vomit.

The poison must have been in him. Suspended in nano-scale capsules awash in his blood, awaiting some remote command to dissolve and kill him if he failed.

I needed to get to the shuttle. I'd lost too much blood myself, and the thought of that dreadful venom on my armor forced numb panic into my brain. Was I going into shock? Gibson's aphorisms rattled in my ears like the chimes off Cielcin spears, and I tried to still my ragged breathing. *Not far now, not far.*

The wind pushed me on as I staggered down the strand. I've no memory of the walk there, the ride on the lift up to the shuttle platforms. I held my mangled left arm twisted against my chest. My scalp was still throbbing, and my knee ached. My right hand—the hand I had originally lost—held the weapon that had nearly killed me. A dim thought occurred to me as I limped along, leaning on the rail. Had it been my right arm that Kharn replaced—had the Quiet not intervened and traded my lost right arm for my left—I would be dead.

Cries of *Halfmortal! Halfmortal! Halfmortal!* resounded in my ears, borne up by the wind and the clamor of the Colosseum behind me. And another cry, words shouted from within and behind.

This must be.

The words shouted from my past, and at the sound of them I tried to clench my false-boned hand. The hand the Quiet had changed. Realization glued me to a stop, and swaying I leaned against the rail. Was I mad? Or did I understand another piece of what had happened to me?

Had the Quiet seen this moment . . . and changed the arm I'd lost to save my life?

The shuttle crouched before me, black beetle shape with wings tucked and hatch opened. Siran was aboard, she and my pilot officer and my paltry guard the Martians had ordered remain. I resumed walking toward them. "Siran!" I cried out. "Siran!"

But no one came.

How had I slipped away? There should have been more guards. The Martians should have stopped me. And where was Siran? I mounted the ramp, calling out, clutching my wounded arm to my chest.

No one was there.

Siran would never leave me. Not Siran. Something was wrong. She would not have abandoned her post, and certainly not without leaving at least one man behind.

Everything clicked at once, even in my addled mind. I'd been *allowed* to retreat here. Panic gripped me, but I pried back its fingers. "Siran!" I peered into cockpit, and saw the pilot officer.

Dead.

I turned and ran as fast as I could, fumbling for the shield catch on a belt that was not there.

I ran just fast enough.

The shuttle exploded behind me. I felt both eardrums rupture as I was lifted bodily from my feet and hurled ten yards down the runway. How I managed to avoid falling off into the bottomless sky I'll never know.

My last thought was that Siran was dead. Pallino had survived the

Irchtani. Valka had survived the knife-missile. But this third time paid for all. I crashed into the pavement shoulder first, crushing my mangled arm. The pain whited out my vision and my ears permanently rang.

Dimly, I was aware of someone shouting my name.

"Had! Had!"

Not Hadrian, I remember thinking. *Not Halfmortal.*

CHAPTER 49

REGENERATION

I DREAMED OF WARMTH and the color red. I remember floating.
Muffled voices. Distorted faces. The whine of surgical armatures.

My mind slipped into darkness, falling through deep water and the ink
that lay beneath, past sleeping white hands and green eyes and the memory
of blood. Was I dead again? No. Black though the waters of my mind had
become, the Howling Dark was blacker still. I drifted weightless, and lo!
Before my eyes a funeral procession marched, glowing in the black hollow
of my dreams. Seven lords carried seven canopic jars, organs preserved
forever in formaldehyde: eyes and heart, stomach and liver, lungs and spinal cord—and the brain came last of all. Whence they were bound I could
not say, nor whose viscera they carried. A white arch rose ahead, piercing
the gloom with ghostly radiance. The Arch of Titus? Or the arch of masks
in Devil's Rest? My vision blurred, and the arch blurred with it, dividing
as a drunk man sees double.

The procession marched between them, taking neither road.

"Should be dead."

"Lost too much blood . . ."

"Don't know how he was even conscious."

"He's awake."

"Are you sure?"

"Look at the EEG."

But the darkness yawned once more.

I was lying in a bed, a drip in my right arm and a waste unit on my pelvis.
My head ached. Black corrective tape striped my left arm, my fingers, and

the palm of my hand, which was immobilized by a brace that kept the digits spread apart.

My legs moved, and taking this for a good sign, I tried to sit up.

A hand seized mine, small and warm. A hand striped and spiraled over with hair-fine fractal tattoos.

"You know," came the beloved voice, "we aren't *supposed* to take turns." She was smiling down at me, dark shadows beneath her eyes, hair lank and unwashed-looking.

I managed a weak laugh and croaked, "You're supposed to be asleep."

Valka ignored me. "Doctor Okoyo says you're nearly healed. She had you in a regen tank for weeks knitting all the muscles you tore with that stunt of yours. You know you're lucky to be alive."

"A regen tank . . ." That explained the floating. "But why are you awake?"

The xenologist leaned toward me, studying my doubtless ghastly face with those golden eyes of hers. " 'Tis nice to see you, too, *anaryan*." Her hand squeezed mine before she let it go. "Corvo woke me up when Siran brought you in."

"Siran?" I echoed stupidly. I must have misheard her. Siran was dead. I had seen the empty shuttle on the strand, seen the dead pilot officer. "She's alive?"

A minute nod. Valka settled back into her seat. "She'd run off toward the Colosseum when the panic started. You must have passed her."

"I thought she was dead . . ." I said. "The shuttle."

"Whoever planted the bomb must have used the commotion you caused in the arena to do their work."

"The Chantry," I said, trying to move my right hand to rub my eyes and failing. "The Empress. All of them, maybe." I wanted to tell her everything that had happened since the Inquisition took over the *Tamerlane*. She'd missed so much. "Bourbon," I added. "Augustin Bourbon did this. He used Breathnach. The Chantry. That poison . . ." I was sure I sounded mad, sounded stupid, but it was important for her to understand.

Valka was nodding along. "I saw. Lorian said it was a Chantry poison? I saw the footage. It was broadcast all over the capital. I'm sure it's gone offworld by now." She gave me a wry smile, voice gently mocking. *"They say no sword can cut the Devil down."*

I snorted, regretted it instantly as my head pounded. "I like it," I replied, voice pitifully weak in my own ears. "And the Empress? She was trying to humiliate me. It didn't go as planned." Maria Agrippina had

meant to ruin me, meant to show all the galaxy the Halfmortal Hero of
Aptucca was a fraud and a greedy little social climber, a pervert who con-
sorted with homunculi and foreign magi. Instead I had risen higher.

No sword can cut the Devil down . . .

In the weeks to come, footage of my duel with Irshan would be transmitted by Public Enlightenment telegraph to the magnarchal seats and
provincial capitals across the Empire, there to be devolved to the local
datasphere transmission grid and broadcast at light speed to every planet
and moon and station. *He stops highmatter with his bare hands,* they would say.

But who had turned their knives on Hadrian Marlowe? The Empress
would not be blamed, nor Bourbon. The Extrasolarians were responsible.
That would be the tale. Hadrian Marlowe had detected an Extrasolarian
threat to the Empire, and the Extras wanted him dead. The Jaddian Maeskolos Marlowe fought would be a changeling, a homunculus they'd
planted at court as a secret assassin. The poison that felled Irshan was simply the result of a kill switch his Extrasolarian masters had built into him
should he fail or fall into Imperial hands.

"Has there been word from the Emperor?" I asked.

Valka nodded. "An apology. He says he was detained and was unaware
of what was happening in the Colosseum."

"Detained?" I thought I could guess. "By the Legions? By the War
Ministry?" I took her silence for a yes. "Neatly done," I said.

"You think the Empress was working with the War Minister?"

"I'd bet my left hand," I said, managing to sit up at last. Valka half-
stood to protest, but I raised my hand to stop her. "Or my right, on second
thought. The left one's earned its keep."

"I don't understand why she'd want that."

"Because of *you*," I said, coughing. Realizing the look of shock on her
face, I backpedaled. "Because of her children. Alexander and Selene. The
Empress thinks I am dangerous, to them, to her family in general—to the
whole bloody Empire, I suppose. She doesn't want me mentoring her children, much less marrying one."

Beside me, Valka shifted where she stood. "What does that have to do
with me?"

I looked away, saw the dim reflection of her in the glossy white wall.
"Everything. You're a witch, Valka. That makes me a man who sleeps with
witches. The Empress doesn't want me anywhere *near* her children." I
could sense Valka waiting to object. "It's not just you. It's Lorian, it's Ilex,
the Irchtani . . . it's all the *fucking Normans*. It's Vorgossos, it's *this*." I tried

in vain to raise my left hand. "It doesn't matter there's no praxis in my arm, it came from Vorgossos. Which makes *me* a witch, too. At least to some people." I stopped mumbling, shook my head.

The doctor fell back into her seat. "Even if we could prove it was her, what good would it do? You nobiles get away with murder on a daily basis."

"I don't have to *prove* it," I said, surprised by the coldness in my tone. "I know it was them." I told her about my encounter with Bourbon that day after the Council meeting when I'd met with Cassian Powers. "He may as well have autographed that knife-missile after that."

"And the order for Sir Lorcan's execution," Valka said.

"Is he dead?"

A frown creased Valka's face. "Given to the Chantry, I think. Lorian said something about him being shipped offworld. Some bastille on one of those little moons."

I made a small *ah* sound and fingered the controls to raise my bed into a sitting position. The strain of sitting up had grown too great. Sir Lorcan wasn't dead at all. He'd be iced and put into some cubiculum under Chantry control until they or His Radiance decided what to do with him. In a hundred years perhaps, or two hundred, he would be thawed out and sentenced. Not to hang or to the White Sword—who would care in so many years? He would be packed off to Belusha or Pagus Minor to live out his days as a bond-overseer in the prison camps, comfortably in exile.

And Bourbon? Nothing would become of Lord Augustin Bourbon. He was one of the greatest lords of the Sollan Empire, a cousin of Prince Charles himself, descendant of kings, untouchable almost as the Empress herself.

The thought set my teeth on edge.

Maybe Valka had a point about us.

"Where is Lorian?" I asked, picking up from what Valka had said last.

Valka blinked at me. "Hereabouts somewhere. Do you want me to find him?"

"No. No," I said. "I do want to see Siran, though. I thought she was dead, Valka. Like I thought . . ." I could not say *like I thought* you *were dead.* I could tell from Valka's face that she understood. "That's three now, counting Pallino. Not counting . . . everyone else." Three people this plot had almost killed at any rate . . . while trying to kill me. "Everyone else shouldn't have to pay for . . . for whatever I am. Am I . . . are we still doing the right thing?"

She didn't answer at once, didn't answer for a long time. I almost thought that I had fallen asleep, had drifted off, left Valka in the waking world and gone where I could not hear her answer. When she did answer, it was in a small voice, thin and tired. "I don't really know what we're doing anymore, Hadrian." The only sound for a long moment was the soft beeping of medical instruments chiming in time with my pounding head. I could feel my heart beating in my raw and newly regenerated ears. The blushing light and white surfaces of the medica pained me. I shut my eyes, wishing for the inky dark of dream again.

In dream, at least—though there was horror—there was peace.

"I thought we left Emesh to make peace," she said. "Now we're fighting a war. A war we might have ended 'twas not for Bassander Lin and that Hauptmann bastard." And in an even smaller voice, she said, "And if you hadn't killed Nobuta."

I held my breath and my retort with it, turned the curse to wind and blew it out my nose. "That's not fair. You were there, Valka. You saw what they did. How can you forgive them for being what they are when you can't forgive me for being palatine?" Dryness scratched at my throat, and I coughed. "Have you so little faith in your people?"

"How can *you* ask that?" Valka said, and though I shut my eyes again I felt hers on me. "They tried to kill you, Hadrian, at least three times!"

"Augustin Bourbon tried to kill me," I said. "Or the Empress. Or both of them together. Or the Chantry did." I realized I was repeating myself and shut my mouth a moment. Marshalling my thoughts, I pressed forward. "They aren't *humanity*, Valka. They're just part of it. I don't have any faith in *them*. But I had faith in Smythe and Crossflane. And Ghen. I have faith in Corvo and Lorian and the rest. Siran. Pallino and Elara." I reached for her hand. "And I have faith in you."

She took my hand. "I don't know what we're fighting *for* anymore," I told her, "but I know I'm fighting *against them*. Against the Cielcin. Against the Extras. Against the Chantry, and Bourbon, and the Empress, too—if they get in my way." My voice trailed once more to silence. Neither of us moved. "I came back from the *dead*, Valka. You saw it. How can I stop fighting?"

At last—at long last—she had no answer for me.

I must have drifted, though I seemed only to blink. For when I turned, expecting an answer, I saw Valka dozing in her chair. She looked older—though in fact by then I was older than her, having spent so many more years awake on our journeying. Reaching out with my good hand, I ran dry fingers along her tattooed arm, patted her knee. She stirred. "Go get some sleep," I said. "I'm going to be fine. You look like you haven't eaten in days."

Sitting forward, she nodded woozily. " 'Tis nothing."

"Go on," I said, and watched her rise and gather her wine-dark jacket from a hook. I swatted at her as she passed, and she glared down at me, reproaching.

"Glad to see you're better," she said with mock scorn, and tucking her hair behind one ear leaned in to kiss me.

Smiling a wistful smile as she straightened, I said, "I'll be out of here before you know it." She made it to the door and pushed the button to open it before I said, "Would you ask Siran to come see me? I . . ." I wanted to see that she was really alive. "I'd like to see her."

Valka's smile told me she understood. "Of course."

"And one more thing, please!" I called. Valka was halfway through the door, but leaned back to listen. My voice darkened, and I added, "Find Crim for me."

CHAPTER 50

EVIL EYES

"WAIT HERE, SIR. THE Council is meeting with His Radiance. You'll be admitted shortly." The hairless court servitor bowed and left me in the company of four Knights Excubitor. We stood together in the hall outside the water garden where the Emperor had charged me to take Alexander to Gododdin. My faceless companions stood unmoved, mirrored armor reflecting the golden filigree and white plaster, the deep crimson of the rugs and Corinthian pillars. Each held his highmatter sword straight before him, blue-white light gleaming. They made no move as I peered into their featureless visors. Not for the first time, I wondered if the Emperor's closest guardians were truly human. In Rome of old the emperors' Praetorians had been their greatest enemy as often as their protectors; an elite cadre of fighting men so near the throne its occupant was their captive as much as their master.

I narrowed my eyes, gaze locked with the gaze of reflection in the knight's mask.

Homunculus, I thought, recalling the mamluks of Jadd, the cheap clone soldiers who swelled their ranks to rival our Legions in times of war. I was not certain I was right, but were I Emperor, I would ensure my closest guardians—the ones to whom I entrusted my family—were implicitly loyal. What better way to accomplish such a thing than to *breed* them for that purpose? To hobble their minds so disloyalty was never even a possibility?

What better way to keep the demonstrably human Martian Guard from turning?

"Do you have a name, sir?" I asked the Excubitor.

But the Excubitors never speak.

Bored, I turned to the ancient oil painting that hung on the wall. It showed an ancient city burning in the shadows of massive white pyramids that pierced the clouds. Beneath a clocktower by the river, a pale Georgian dome topped with a bronze crescent stood shattered. The very sky was burning; tiny figures were swarming in the streets, fires blazing; and in the distance loomed the mushroom cloud of atomic devastation. Drawing closer, I read the small plaque screwed to the frame.

The Fall of London, or Reconquest.

Beneath that ominous title followed the name of the artist and the date of its painting. The canvas—impeccably preserved in vacuum behind filter glass—was more than twelve thousand years old. I was not quite certain what London was at the time, but I knew the pyramids and recognized the white star outlined red and blue upon its face.

The Mericanii.

This was a painting of William's Advent, the return of the kings of Earth to smash the machines and their masons, the men who built them. It was a painting of the liberation of men from their own creation, the daimons we'd made to serve ourselves—that had mastered us instead. Passing on down the line, a painting just as old showed the God Emperor standing—as his icons always did—upon a shattered cube. In this one, an iron snake writhed from inside that box, only to meet its fate beneath the point of William's sword.

The iron gates to the garden rattled behind me, and a small cluster of logothetes in customary gray and black emerged, among them green-robed scholiasts and the Lords High Minister. Prince Hector inclined his head to me as they passed. Leda Ascania smiled and Peter Habsburg made gentle salute as I drew near, all hurrying to their next assignments. One figure in particular saw me and made to hurry away.

"Lord Augustin!" I called, coming to a stop on the edge of the group.

The Lord Minister of War swiveled to face me, looking up with his round moon of a face, small eyes narrowed defensively. Reaching up, I found the silver buckles that ran the length of my left arm and undid the leather gauntlet there. Removing the glove, I went to one knee before Lord Augustin. "I wanted to thank you. I understand you've taken charge of the investigation into my attack personally."

"I . . ." The War Minister glanced sidelong. Cassian Powers and Haren Bulsara had remained to watch, and several of the more junior logothetes and secretaries lingered. "You're welcome, my Lord Marlowe. It's a dreadful business. Dreadful. And to involve Prince Philip and our dear Empress so . . . But we're certain to catch whoever is behind the deed. They won't escape us long."

Flashing my broken smile, I raised that left hand, Aranata's ring and the ivory one shining, and held it palm up. It was a gesture all understood, the gesture of a faithful knight before a lord, a request to show his fealty. The new scars from Irshan's highmatter blade shone on fingers and palms—so white they were almost silver in the sunlight streaming through the garden gate. More scars shone angry and bright, striping the surface of my arm.

Pressured by his audience, Bourbon gave me his hand. I tightened my grip on his soft fingers until I *knew* he could feel the latticed surface of my false bones. I saw his eyes grow wide as I kissed the fleur-de-lis on his ring.

"I pray you do," I told him, smiling once again. "I pray the scoundrel gets what he *deserves*."

Augustin Bourbon yanked his hand away. "Your hand . . ." he said, cradling his own. "What are you?"

It was my turn to narrow my eyes. "Only what they say I am, my lord," I answered. "The Emperor's *demon*. His servant." Standing, I drew the white cape around me, glad I had chosen to wear it for my audience with Caesar.

I locked eyes with the War Minister and did not let go, did not permit myself even to blink. To the man's credit, he held my gaze for two seconds, but only two.

"I . . ." He knew I knew, and the touch of inhuman hand had frightened him. There was nothing he could do. The Inquisition had already studied my hand and passed me for it. "Good day, Lord Marlowe." He turned to go.

I caught Lord Powers watching me, a sad smile on his owlish face. Noticing me looking, he gave a short salute, and said, "I'm sorry, my boy." Without another word he turned with Lord Haren and departed.

Sorry for what?

I watched the congregation go.

They made it to the distant arch before I called out, "Lord Augustin!"

The fat minister froze and turned with terrific slowness to meet my gaze. I wanted to frighten him, wanted the memory of my eyes to haunt him to his dying day. I stared at him, still unblinking, eyes wide and cold. I caught myself remembering the cold glare my father would give me when I was a boy, violet eyes frozen but blazing as the bluest suns. Beneath my cloak, I extended the first and final fingers of my hand toward the minister. A primitive kind of magic, and an ancient curse.

I *was* a demon, after all.

Remember me, I thought, as if he could ever forget.

The color drained from Bourbon's face to see me glowering at him like some predatory hawk, and blanching he looked away and fled.

The gardens were as I remembered: white pillars with painted capitals arranged in concentric squares around a marble pool thick with the white and pink of lotus blossoms and the azure eyes of nenuphars. Mosaics covered the floors and stood in arches beneath painted vaults along the outer walls of the quadrangle. Presiding over all was a frescoed Icon of Beauty: a nude woman with golden hair enthroned on a crimson shell.

Advancing with my Excubitor escort, I bowed low as I would go, left hand re-gloved at my heart, right hand thrown wide before His Radiant Majesty.

"Rise, Lord Marlowe," our Caesar said. "Are you well?"

William XXIII sat on his Savonarola chair, green eyes studying me intently.

"I am healed, Honorable Caesar," I said in answer.

The Emperor's eyes continued their study of me. I felt like a sample, like a bit of slime beneath some magi's microscope. "It seems you invite catastrophe wherever you go." I opened my mouth to object, but Caesar raised one velvet-gloved hand and continued, "I am aware the fault for this particular incident lies in no small part with my dear wife and idiot child, but the fact remains that you are a problem which politics do not permit us to easily solve." He leaned upon his fist.

I dared not speak. To speak was to implicate the Empress, to accuse the Chantry, to attack the Emperor's own Minister of War. Such accusations—true or otherwise—could mean death in that place, and I did not want to die. Worse, I could not risk being *wrong.*

Fortunately, the Emperor was not finished. "We are not certain who put the sword in that Maeskolos's hand, or who ordered Colosseum security to stand down. Augustin and our Martians assure us they will find the culprit, but we have decided to bow to the advice of our Council and *dismiss* you."

"Dismiss me?" I repeated, astounded.

"Not from our service," the Emperor said. "Our Victorian you will remain, but this trouble in the arena. Do you understand what you've done?"

Unable to stop myself, I answered him, "Survived, Radiant Majesty."

The Emperor's voice cracked like thunder. "Do *not* be flippant with me, Marlowe. I have indulged you shamefully for decades because you produce results." The royal *we* had vanished when his anger came. "But those results have made you a lightning rod for trouble. Have you considered the possibility that the Chantry *itself* wants you dead?"

"Yes, Radiance." I bowed my head.

"Do you understand the position that puts me in, defending you?" he asked.

"I do, Radiance."

William stood. "Do you?" He remained standing before his throne, deep voice close to shouting. "Our civilization stands upon two legs. *I* am one, the Chantry the other. Do you know what it means for one foot to trip the other?"

The answer was obvious. *We fall.*

I only bowed deeper, choosing safety over further flippancy.

"You are useful to me, Marlowe, but you are making it where I cannot defend you from those people who consider themselves our friends and servants without challenging the delicate arrangement between Synod and Throne." He wheeled—a rustling of white and crimson—to face Beauty on her shell. "My wife has suggested I banish you. Pack you off to Belusha or put you on ice for a few hundred years until this following of yours fades from memory. Tell the people their *White Demon* is fighting still on the fronts in Norma. Who would know the difference?"

Horror blossomed in my chest. There was a simple elegance in such a plan. With a single move I would be transformed from man to myth and legend. Dimly, a part of me wondered how many ancient heroes of antiquity had been disappeared at the apex of their triumph, destroyed lest—like Boniface Grael—they become Pretenders to threaten the throne and the God Emperor's sacred dynasty?

"But as I said before, Marlowe . . . I am a practical man. And so I will ask you a question, and understand your fate hangs upon your answer, so speak truly." With his back to me, I stood straight again, fists clenched in their gauntlets until the right one ached. I held my tongue. What else could I do? I'd survived trial after trial, plot after plot, but everything had collapsed to this single instant anyway.

A trial, of sorts.

The Emperor clasped his hands behind his back, ten rings glittering. "When last we met in this spot you reminded me of your standing request for access to the Imperial Library on Colchis, do you remember?"

"I . . . what?" I almost gasped. I had not known what I expected from the Emperor, but it wasn't this.

"The Imperial Library," William XXIII said once more, repeating the place's name as though I were one who'd never heard of it before. "Nov Belgaer Athenaeum in Aea on Colchis. You have renewed a request for access every time your ship returns to Forum. Why?"

I paused for the space of three breaths before answering. "I told you, Honorable Caesar. I wished to find records of potential brushes with the Cielcin in the Norman colonies predating the Rape of Cressgard. "

"And *I* told you not to lie to me, Hadrian Marlowe." The Emperor rounded on me and took two steps off his dais. Reacting in time with their master, the Excubitors—who had retreated to the shadows beneath the mighty pillars—advanced with swords still raised. But Caesar raised one finger. "I will give you another chance. Tell me why."

What had I to lose in speaking the truth? If I answered wrongly, the Emperor would dissolve my company—or worse—imprison them, disperse them with me to Belusha and Pagus Minor and a dozen other prison colonies or punishment posts with the Legions.

I had to choose.

The only way out was *through.*

Always forward, I thought to myself.

But I was nearly out of rope.

The Emperor would know anyway, how could he not? The truth was one of the galaxy's best-kept secrets, but here was Lord of that secret's keepers.

"Radiant Majesty, what do you know of the Quiet?" I asked, voice soft as if whispering might hide my words from the cameras that doubtless fixed electric eyes on me.

Caesar's eyes narrowed to the barest slits. "You know?"

"I was on Emesh," I said.

"You know?" the Emperor repeated. Then something astonishing happened. William XXIII of the House Avent collapsed into his folding throne. "How do you know?"

I took one startled step forward. Remembering myself and recalling that I addressed the Emperor—and not knowing how else to react to him in such a state—I went to one knee. "Radiant Majesty, I was on Emesh. There are ruins there. Tunnels on the southern continent, at a site called Calagah."

"Emesh . . ." the Emperor repeated, looking down at his lap. "I don't know that one."

"Valka—my Tavrosi companion—took me there when I was a guest of House Mataro. She studies them."

One leather boot emerged from beneath the snowy robes, red as his gloves. The Emperor's eyes had drifted far away, seemed lost in the shadows of the pillared galleries that surrounded the pool at my back. Presently he glanced up at the white towers of the Peronine Palace behind me. "The Tavrosi, of course. I had forgotten about her." He drummed his fingers on the arms of his chair. "You told me once that you do not have visions," he said, still not looking at me. "Was that a lie?"

Bowing my head, I answered, "Yes, Radiant Majesty." Face lowered, I was able to conceal my surprise. He asked after visions! What more did he know?

"You told me the daimon on Vorgossos showed you the future, showed you Syriani Dorayaica—the Cielcin conquering the stars."

Eyes locked on the mosaic pattern of birds and fishes that decorated the floor at my feet, I repeated, "Yes, Radiant Majesty."

"But that was not all?"

"No."

"You may speak freely, Marlowe," Caesar said. "If it is our Excubitors you fear, you need not."

Still on my knee, I clenched my left hand, felt the black leather groan. "The cameras, Radiance."

Caesar snapped his fingers, and looking up I saw him lean forward in his seat. "Speak freely, I say."

Had he shut them off? I supposed it didn't matter. The Emperor had given me an order. How could I refuse? "The daimon . . . *received* the vision from the Quiet and gave it to me." I paused, expecting the Emperor to interrupt, but William did not stir. I explained what Brethren had told me, that the Quiet dwelt in the future—not the past—that Brethren's superhuman intelligence had *perceived* the Quiet across time, and that they had forced the daimon to carry a vision for me, prepared it for when I came. I told him about my earlier vision in Calagah, and my experience in the chamber that had never appeared again. I did not tell him about the Howling Dark, about my death, about the other Hadrian I had met in the darkness.

"The Cielcin *vayadan* I killed. The chimera. The one from my triumph . . . it said that Syriani Dorayaica has received visions as well."

The Emperor shook his head, surprise mingling with confusion on his antiquely handsome face. "That can't be!"

"I believe the Cielcin call the Quiet *the Watchers,* sometimes the *Makers. Caihanarin,* or *Genanarin.* Possibly they are but one set of gods among many. But the Cielcin worship them, I don't know why." I broke off a moment, shifting to take the pressure of kneeling off my knee a moment. "Radiance, when I was on Vorgossos Kharn Sagara told me the God Emperor had visions. That it was his visions which delivered us from the machines." It was blasphemy, I knew, and expected the Emperor to stand and shout for his guards, but he only sat there, patient as the Undying himself, eyes still glazed and confused. "He said *angels* came to the God Emperor in his dreams."

"Oracles . . ." the Emperor muttered.

To my great surprise, I interrupted His Radiance. "Radiant Majesty, Kharn Sagara is nearly so old as our Empire, and twisted as he is, he is more learned than any man alive. If what he told me is true, I hoped there might be records on Colchis." I could feel myself working up into one of my moods. "If the daimon I met on Vorgossos could perceive time, then surely the other artificial intelligences the Mericanii constructed in the Golden Age must have known of the Quiet as well. Surely you must have *something* in the Library, or in Caliburn House or . . . somewhere? I need to find them. To understand *them.* To understand what is happening to me and what all this has to do with the Cielcin. Please. Please, Radiance, I am no use to you on the Council, I am no use to you as a prince-consort trapped in this palace, and I am no use to you locked in fugue or rotting in a tower cell on Belusha."

"Use," the Emperor echoed, eyes focusing on my face for the first time in minutes. "Use . . ." He chuckled to himself. "I asked you once—in this very garden, as I recall—if you were my servant. You told me that you were. My counselors seem to think otherwise." The Emperor drummed his ringed fingers against the arm of his seat. "Still, I wonder if they are not mistaken. So I ask you again: whom do you serve?"

Aware I trod on thin ice, I knelt and pondered my answer. The time for lies and careful half-answers was passed. The truth was my only solution, my only salvation. But I did not know the truth. Whom did I serve? Where did my loyalties lie?

I did not know until I answered. "The truth, Radiant Majesty? I think . . . I think I serve *them*."

"The Quiet?"

"You say you know of them. They are not merely a vanished people gone from our universe. They live—or they will live, if what the Brethren told me is true. What they are I don't understand, but they called me. Showed me a vision of the future. The destruction of mankind, commanded me to stop it. How could I refuse that call? I fight to prevent that future, to defend humanity itself." I broke off, aware that I had said too much. "Perhaps I serve humanity, then, as you do."

The Emperor was nodding along, eyes narrowed. "A Servant of the Servants of Earth, are you? But what of the Empire? What of me?"

"If you speak of these rumors that I desire your throne . . . I deny them. I do not want it." I bowed over my knee. "I have served Your Radiance for more than seventy waking years. I will continue in that service, if you will keep me." I turned my face up to look upon William, child of the God Emperor's blood by line unbroken. "Let me go to Colchis. Let me learn what I can. Let me fight and serve."

His Radiance said nothing, only surveyed me stone-faced and somber for so long I thought Kharn Sagara himself might feel his patience wear thin. As if to himself, he said, ". . . and only a cousin." He shook himself and sat straighter in his chair. "You cannot remain on Forum. Regardless of who is behind these attacks on your life, it is clear to me and my counselors that you are a lightning rod for catastrophe. That stunt of yours in the Colosseum has transformed you from a mere *legend* into something far more substantial. It is one thing, it seems, to do great deeds far away—but to stop *highmatter* with your bare hands in my own city . . ." He shook his own from the consuming folds of his robes and gestured that I should approach. "Show me."

My knee sang with relief as I stood and once more undid the clasps on my leather gauntlet. I pulled the glove off and presented my bare arm to His Radiance, palm up to reveal the deep white scars that had so frightened Augustin Bourbon.

The Emperor took my hand in both of his and examined the scars, turning the hand over to see the top of my forearm where more white stripes stood out silver against my pale skin. "Strange ring," the Emperor noted, indicating the one I'd taken from Prince Aranata so long ago. His grip tightened, feeling the faint ridges in my false bones. "I saw the Inquisition's report. Adamant bones. All the way to the shoulder?"

"Yes, Radiance."

"Fascinating." He took his hands away. "And not a circuit to be found. Sagara was generous. It is a pity matters ended poorly with him. He might have been a powerful ally against the Pale."

Holding my glove in my fingers, I said, "He would not aid us."

His Radiance nodded tiredly, and fidgeting with his rings drew one from his finger. He held it up. "I have decided to retain your services, sir," he said. A moment passed before I realized the Emperor intended me to take his ring.

I did.

All of yellow gold it was, with no gem of any kind. On its round face shone the relief image of a knight on horseback striking a dragon with his lance.

"Sir George," he said, "the Dragonslayer." The Emperor leaned back in his seat. "Present the ring at the Library. The scholiasts will admit you."

I held Sir George's ring in my scarred palm, sensing somehow that to don the Emperor's ring would be inappropriate, especially in his presence. "You honor me, Radiant Majesty."

"We do," the Emperor agreed, returning to his formal style. "See you do not disappoint us, Lord Marlowe."

I bowed deeply once again. "As you command."

"And speak of this to no one. You will report directly to me. I will have one of my secretaries arrange that you receive my personal telegraph codes," William Avent said, rising from his seat. He approached me. I held my bow. His now four-ringed hand touched my shoulder. "Let us take their given name as a command: the *Quiet*."

I told him I understood. Telegraphs were analog, relying on entangled particles to transmit data instantaneously across interstellar distances. Assuming they were not connected to the datasphere network in any way, they were perfectly secure.

"Then go at once. Take your ship and your people, and do not return to Forum until I order it so."

Standing straight once more, I drew back three paces, bowed again as deeply. "As Your Radiance commands." It was a kind of exile. Not to prison on Belusha, not to icy sleep, but to my quest—to a quest renewed by right authority, the Emperor's ring in my hand. But an exile all the same. Half-turned away, I halted, and asked the question that had leaped full-formed into my mind. "What of Selene?"

The Emperor arched an eyebrow. "What of her?"

"Are we still to be married?"

"You were never officially betrothed," the Emperor replied. He had regained some measure of his Imperial composure, though I sensed still that our conversation had troubled his heart. I bowed again, and he said, "Though that may change, depending on the nature of your return."

A great weight lifted—I hoped invisibly so—from my shoulders. "I understand," I said, thoughts turning to Valka. "And Prince Alexander? He has asked to accompany me again."

Surprise flickered on that regal visage. "Has he? Has he indeed?" He clasped his hands once more behind himself. "Very good. Take the boy. Now go." There was a finality in that *go* which brooked no further argument. I turned and retreated past the armed Excuitors to the high pillars that surrounded the shining pool.

"Halfmortal!" the Emperor called as I reached the iron gates.

I stopped. I did not turn, did not speak. What had possessed the Emperor to use that name of all my names? The sound of it from the Emperor smote me like a brand, conjured memories of Carax's medal, of Oberlin's scribbled seal, of the cult of rumor and personality that followed me then everywhere I went.

"Are all the stories they tell about you true?"

The stories, I thought, and in my mind a bloody fountain splashed against a stone wall as darkness swallowed the world. Though he did not ask the question like so many others had done, I heard it all the same.

Is it true you can't be killed?

Still not looking back, I answered, "I'm afraid so."

CHAPTER 51

THE MERCHANT
OF DEATH

I MUST LINGER A moment on Forum as we sailed away. Our course charted, for once I slept, unwilling to endure the sense of mingled anticipation and hope. For the first time in decades, I felt joy's warm light fill my chest and stretch my heart wide. I had left Delos to join the scholiasts. I was sailing to an athenaeum at last. Not to meager Teukros, but to the Imperial Library on Colchis itself. To Nov Belgaer, in whose dusty halls I sit even now and record this account.

But as I say, I linger and recount a tale heard from men I dare not name.

Three years after the *Tamerlane*'s departure, three years after the assassin's sword could not cut the Halfmortal down in the Colosseum, Lord Augustin Bourbon clambered aboard his shuttle for a ferry ride from the Sun King's Hall to the palatial apartments kept by House Bourbon in the Eternal City. He was alone but for his guards, and seated himself on his couch in the rear carriage amidst azure hangings and gold leaf to await takeoff. There he waited.

And waited.

In time, the Minister of War grew impatient. "Pilot!" he called in his bass rumble. "Pilot!"

No answer came.

The large minister rose, groaning I do not doubt, and pressed through the hangings to the cockpit where—so my nameless men tell me—he found his pilot. Dead as my own had been. Blood for blood. The great lord cried aloud, tapped his terminal to summon his guards, but no guards came. No signal went out. The jamming device affixed to the ventral hull of the shuttle saw to that. Returning to the rear compartment, Lord Augustin tried the hatch, but the ramp would not deploy, and the door was shut. The Minister of War pounded against the bulkhead, slapped the door with his soft, damp hands. No one answered him.

No one came.

The nameless men tell me he panicked, just as they knew he would. The War Minister tore the cushions from the benches in a frenzied effort to locate the missing emergency kit.

That was how he found it, precisely as it looked when he'd given it to Irshan three years before, mere days before my fateful hour in the arena.

A highmatter sword. The very sword that had failed to cut me down. The very sword I had clutched in my bleeding hands as I staggered from the Colosseum. The very sword I had given to Crim after Valka had visited me in medica, after I reassured myself that Siran was alive. It was no Jaddian weapon, though what hubris had possessed Augustin to arm his assassin with his own blade I will never know. Perhaps he too had been only a pawn in the Empress's scheme to rid her daughter of me. Perhaps his hatred of me ran so deep. Perhaps he thought himself above reprisal—scion of so ancient a house as he was.

"I want you to kill a man," I'd said to Crim. "Make the arrangements for it after we're gone."

The Lord Minister tried to use the sword to cut his way out. He squeezed the trigger, squeezed it again. No good.

I'd had the weapon's highmatter core removed.

No one ever learned who did it. Who planted the bomb on the landing pad. Some blamed the Extrasolarians. Still others blamed the Mandari, angry over some unfair arms contract. There were whispers of a feud between Bourbon and Habsburg, but nothing ever came of it. There was no one to bury, nothing for the canopic jars. Prince Charles Bourbon mourned his cousin and in time another man was named to the War Ministry.

No one blamed Lord Hadrian Marlowe.

CHAPTER 52

FALLING OFF THE EDGE
OF THE WORLD

COLCHIS.

Once, the colony farthest from Earth—first of the worlds settled when our ships limped across the Gulf from the Spur of Orion and Earth into the great space of Sagittarius. Not a planet, but a moon larger than the homeworld, thick with oceans and the primordial algae whence sprang an atmosphere perfect for human life. Explorers named her for the ancient homeland of the Golden Fleece, whence sailed Jason with his mighty Argonauts. To the Greeks, it was the edge of the world, and we had made it the edge of ours, for a time. Now it lay comfortably inside Imperial borders, near the point where Orion and Sagittarius almost met nearer the core of the galaxy.

A wild frontier it was no longer.

The mottled face of the planet the locals called Atlas hung in the sky above our descent, umber, amber, and pearl. High clouds obscured it, casting gossamer nets across the roof of the sky as we fell, descending over gray seas and craggy uplands toward the lonely city of Aea beneath the mesa upon which stood the Imperial Library.

Of all the worlds I have visited, the planets, stations, and moons, I think I love Colchis best. Her skies perpetually gray, forever threatening rain, her airs forever damp and chilly, she was not the most beautiful world. Compared with the hanging towers of the Eternal City, the Library was a mean thing. It sat upon the heights of the mesa overlooking broken highland moors like the crown of some sunken king half-buried in the earth with its low, round turrets. Lights burned in its windows even in daylight, for the pale orange sun was high and partways shrouded by the planet in whose orbit Colchis spun.

Aea itself was unremarkable. Despite the colony's great age and former importance, Colchis's days as a trade nexus with the Sagittarine colonies were long ended. Better warp drives and better fuel economies had made crossing the Gulf where it was wider more tenable, and the old roads nearer the core were abandoned. And so the city spoke not of decay, but of quiet homeliness that seemed copied from some sleepy seaport of Earth's Golden Age. This was despite the presence of the Imperial Library, which for all its cultural import was barred but to a select few.

"How many people live here?" I asked Tor Varro where he sat across from me, strapped into his flight seat.

The scholiast turned from his own contemplation of the gray seas and craggy landscape. "On the planet? Less than a million, more than half that in this city."

"And in the athenaeum?"

Varro pursed his lips. "I don't think I know the answer. Several thousand cloistered brothers and sisters, I should think. Nov Belgaer isn't the largest of our institutes, but the Imperial archives make it one of the most important. Our scholars travel from across the Empire to study here. In the order, we like to say we all end up here eventually."

"Have you been before?" I asked.

"Me?" Varro arched his eyebrows. "Never, my lord. Hence the saying."

The day was cool, but pleasantly so to my mind, and a silver mist drifted on the breeze, bringing with it the salt of the sea below. Somewhere in the heavens, gulls cried, and the noise of them transported my soul to Delos and Meidua and slashed a century's weight from my shoulders. Given the presence of the Library, Colchis—like Gododdin—was held by a governor-general appointed by the Colonial Office and not by any landed nobility. I forget the woman's name, but she received us with full pomp in Aea's quiet landing field, where I made it known that I intended to make the climb up the mountain to the athenaeum at once.

"Impossible, my lord," the governor-general said, bowing and touching her forehead apologetically. "The scholiasts have closed the gates for the day. They will not open them. Not even for you. Better to go in the morning."

And so it was that despite my best efforts to avoid it, we were hosted in the governor's mansion that night. I should not complain. The food was plain, but of that unpretentious quality which is finer to the well-adjusted mind that the most extravagant dishes, and for the first time in what seemed like eons I shared a bed with Valka in the night.

But I did not sleep.

Tall curtains blew through the open arch at my back, and the stones of the balcony were slick beneath bare feet. The Imperial Library loomed a mile above and far away, lights flickering on the crown of the mesa like distant candles.

I imagined another Hadrian, the boy who had fled his home, the boy who'd left his brother bruised and unconscious on the floor of the Summer Palace. He had dreamed of standing on just such a parapet, staring up at just such a collection of lights. Had he made it, in some other life? Come in time to the sands of Teukros and the gate of Nov Senber? I had wanted to be a scholiast more than I wanted anything, but those desires were gone. They'd died when I had—if not before.

How small that other Hadrian seemed, flickering himself like a candle against the Dark, clutching in his hands a small envelope—the letter Tor Gibson had given him, the key to open that gate and admit him to the cloistered realm of the scholiasts. The key he had lost on Emesh.

Small as Aea was, the city cast virtually no light upon the heavens, and the stars—so often veiled in too many Imperial cities—shone in all their glory, slowly dancing about the pale spray of the galaxy. The same Greeks who had named Colchis the edge of the world taught their children the galaxy was the milk of Hera, queen of the gods, splashed across the sky when she hurled the infant Heracles—her husband's son by another woman—from her breast. The Sumerians said it was the severed tail of Tiamat, the dragon-mother of chaos, which Marduk, the first hero, had set among the heavens when he defeated her and carved up her body to rebuild the shattered world.

I liked that story better.

Standing by the rail, I twisted the Emperor's ring on my right hand's first finger, watching the lights above me in the night. I glanced at its face, at Sir George slaying *his* dragon. Not for the first time, I wondered what the Emperor's motivations were in choosing this particular ring to hand to me. I didn't know it then, but the Kings of Avalon—who had been the Kings of England before the coming of the machines—had worn Sir George's ring since at least the time of old Victoria.

George and Marduk.

Beowulf and Turin.

Dragonslayers, all.

It was all one story, eternally retold.

"Can't sleep?"

Valka stood in the arch behind me, naked but for the blanket she'd brought from the bed. Her nakedness called attention to my own state, unclad but for a pair of loose pants snugly cuffed beneath the knee. She moved to join me, and as she did, she shivered. " 'Tis too cold for this."

"Is it?" I was so used to the icy chill of star travel, I hadn't noticed.

"What is the matter?" She drew close, leaned against the railing. Below, the mansion's yard and motor pool were quiet save for the rare sentinel keeping watch for trouble that never came. Colchis was so far from the fighting, closer to the Lothrian Commonwealth than the Normans, thousands of light-years from danger.

Letting my hands fall, I turned to face her properly. "Nothing. Nothing, really. Just . . . memories. You know I wanted to be a scholiast."

She smiled up at me, tattooed fingers fussing with my hair. "Are you excited?"

"About a library?" I asked. "It sounds strange to say, but . . . yes."

Valka made a face. "Hadrian, you are talking to someone whose idea of a good time involves climbing over ruins and poring over holographs, trying to translate a language no one has deciphered in ten thousand years." Her smile widened as she tapped me on the chin. "I get it."

That made me smile.

She wrapped her arms around me, blanket enfolding like wings. She was warm beneath. "And we're away from that *xenathta* city," she said, words brushing my chest where she held me. "I thought it was going to kill you being there."

"You're one to talk," I said, arms about her narrow waist. "How's your chest?" Drawing back, I traced the spot beneath her breast where the knife-missile had pierced her. Only the faintest scar remained, barely detectable beneath my fingers.

Valka shot a look up at me. "You ask me this? You? Your arm looks like 'tis been through a meat grinder."

I matched her smile. "Well, I know *I'm* fine," I said. "I'm not worried about me."

"You've not to worry about me."

"Maybe," I allowed, "but worrying about you is a privilege."

She snorted. "You are such a relic."

"You like me *because* I'm a relic, *doctor*." My hand went lower, and she thumped me. "What was all that about climbing over ruins?"

She thumped me again. "You're a ruin now?" Her eyes trailed over the deep scars in my arm, and her expression took on a somber cast.

Eager to distract her and save her mood, I pulled Valka's face to mine and held her close, felt her warmth and the tips of her breasts against my bare chest. When we came apart, I said, "We really should get some sleep. There's a lot to do tomorrow."

"A lot for *me* to do, you mean," she said, smile returning. "You're in *my* world now, Hadrian *Anaxander* Marlowe." She drew away, taking the blanket with her, and went back to the open arch with its static field invisibly crackling, keeping the warmth inside. In the shadow of the keystone she turned. "Maybe I should send you back to the ship, mm? Give you a taste of your own medicine?"

"That isn't funny."

" 'Tis," she insisted. "Maybe 'tis your turn to go in the box." When I did not smile, she folded. "I am sorry. You apologized. I should not pick at these scabs." She hugged the blanket more tightly about herself. "We should both be happy. 'Tis not Panormo or Athten Var, this place, but 'tis better than your war."

I did smile then. "It will be like Emesh again. *Before,* I mean."

"Oh, 'twill be better than Emesh," she said, and turned her back once more.

She dropped the blanket.

The next morning, the governor-general had arranged for two groundcars to carry us along the narrow road upcountry to the athenaeum. It was not far, perhaps half an hour's drive to clear the outskirts of Aea. We passed stone-fenced pastures and sheepfolds dominated by sail-mill towers creaking in the breeze. In the distance, the city's fusion plant belched cloud, its column rising to support the heavens where Atlas's mighty face peered over the horizon.

"This is it, my lord!" the driver said, bringing us to a halt at the base of the mesa.

There was no one there, only a small, paved lot—weeds growing between the flagstones, and a gray stone arch that hugged the base of the mesa. Correctly taking my silence for confusion, he said, "The greens wouldn't let us build a lift or ramp up the mesa. You have to go by stair."

An apologetic note crept into the fellow's voice, and he added, "I thought the governor-general had told you, lordship. A thousand pardons."

" 'Tis quite all right, messer," Valka said, opening the clamshell hatch. "We will walk, won't we, Hadrian?"

Truth was, I'd have had it no other way. To the scholiasts—and to eccentrics like me—the Library was a kind of sacred space. It would not do to come to such a place by shuttle or groundcar. Pilgrimages should be carried out on foot.

"We left our effects at the manor, sirrah," I said to the driver. "Will you see they are collected and brought up?"

"You're staying with the greens, lord?"

"That is my intent." And with that I climbed from the groundcar and drew my long, black coat about myself as I turned and helped Valka stand free. Varro followed, alongside Pallino and one of his centurions—the same Doran who had fought with us aboard Iubalu's ship. The second car opened, and the other eight of my guard emerged, dressed not in legionary armor, but in the black and scarlet of Red Company semi-formal dress. They wore shield-belts and carried phase disruptors, and each man and woman wore a short white sword, but the effect was that of a security detail, not an honor guard.

The climb took the better part of two hours, and by the end my still-fugue-sick legs ached from fatigue toxins. But the day was cool and the weather fair, and the ever-present mist—of which Pallino and his men complained—was for me a refreshing balm, and strangely bracing. Valka held my hand, and so when we passed the final marker with its green flag flapping in the wind and came to the final stairs, we climbed them together.

Rough-cut stone gave way to laser-quarried perfection, field-stone to gray granite.

So precisely engineered were the final stairs and the gate and walls to which they led that no weed or blade of grass grew in their joints. The curtain wall stood ten times the height of a man, describing a perfect circle atop the mesa, circumference interrupted in regular intervals by the short drum towers that looked down upon the world, guarding against attackers that had never come.

"Who's there?" came a voice from the walls above.

I'd no cornicen, no herald to sound my arrival, and at any rate to come to the scholiasts a great lord with pomp and circumstance seemed wrong to me, who had meant to come a mendicant long ago. Letting go of Valka's hand, I stood forward, and said, "Sir Hadrian, Lord of the House Marlowe Victorian, come at the behest of His Radiance, the Emperor."

A pale face peered over the gatehouse parapet, eyes narrow. A boy, I thought, no older than twenty. Perhaps no older than fifteen. "Visitors?" he said, "a lord and knight, you say? And these others?"

"My companion here is Doctor Valka Onderra, a lay scholar of the Demarchy—these others are our guards."

"Guards?" the boy said. "We'll have no violence here, sir. The primate says all weapons must be left at the gatehouse. All shields and terminals, too. No machine may pass under the day gate. It is Stricture." He stood a little taller, leaning out between the merlons. "We'd no word anyone was coming."

"I am the word!" I exclaimed, stepping forward. "The Emperor himself has commanded that I have access to your archives, that my companion and I should be admitted at once."

"No one gets in without a letter of approval, sir," the sentinel answered me, and I wondered at the nerve of him. He was brave, that much was certain. He wore no shield-belt, nor were there signs of guards or any weapons near at hand—so much of Colchis's defense was relegated simply to the Orbital Defense Force. Satellites locked in stationary orbit above the Library kept precision beam weapons forever alert, operators aboard scanning the highlands for unauthorized approach. None of that would have stopped an irascible lord firing a phase disruptor, however. "In the tube, please."

As if on queue, a pneumatic tube's hatch sprang open, producing a padded cylinder. Glancing at Valka and Pallino, I smiled and—removing my glove—took the Emperor's ring from my finger. I placed it into the cylinder, sealed it, and, returning it to the tube, pulled the lever that sent the tube rushing back up the tower to the bored sentry.

"This isn't a letter."

"Well spotted, lad!" Pallino interjected, unable to help himself. "It's the Emperor's own Earth-buggering signet ring."

"I can't let anyone in without a letter of approval from the Imperial Office underwritten by a member of our Order and notarized by the governor-general in Aea."

Varro stepped forward. "I am a brother of the Chalcenterite Order, novice. Take that ring to your Dean or straight to the Primate at once."

"I'm not allowed to leave the gatehouse, brother, sir," the boy said. "Provost's orders."

"You're also bound to obedience by Stricture, son," Varro answered. "And as your senior, I am ordering you to deliver that ring to the hierarchs."

"You could be an imposter!" the boy countered.

Behind me, Pallino grunted. *"This* is what they put at the gates of *the* Imperial Library? Mother Earth's tits, I know recruits less thick."

"They don't get a lot of foot traffic," I said. "Any real threat would have been stopped well before they got boots on the ground."

"Then what's the point of them walls?" Pallino asked.

"To keep the brothers *in,*" Varro replied, a touch ominously. He wasn't wrong. The scholiasts' athenaea were crafted to isolate the brothers and sisters of the Order, not to protect them from outside—and to prevent the contamination of their theoretical cloisters with praxis and experiment. The Order was consecrated to pure theoretical work. No scholiast could so much as touch a machine without special dispensation from his lord, for risk that they—whose ancient predecessors had crafted the daimons that ruled the Mericanii—might give rise to such abomination once more. Face impassive, Varro stepped forward and addressed the sentinel. "I know they don't teach you this in Elementary Protocols, but consider: Which is more likely? That I am an impostor, and that a band of impostors would come to your gates and knock? Or that there is simply something you—a novice—don't know?"

Silence then for the space of two heartbeats.

"I'll go to the Dean, brother."

Valka hid her smile behind her hand.

Ten minutes passed, twenty. There came a soft rain from the west where gray cloud reared above the grayer seas at the margins of the world. Valka produced a hood from the lining of her red leather coat, but I simply turned my face to the heavens. How long had it been since I'd last felt rain? A dozen waking years? More?

The grinding of metal bolts shook the ground beneath my feet, and I turned in time to see the metal doors slide open. Not completely, but wide enough only to permit a single woman in faded greens to step between the metal doors.

"Which of you is Sir Hadrian?" she said, sweeping our party. But her eyes settled on me even as she finished, and—bowing low—she extended one knobby hand with the Emperor's ring clasped between thumb and forefinger.

I took it. Though it was not called for, I returned her bow. "I am, counselor." I introduced Valka, Varro, and the others. "We have traveled far to come here. My companion and I wish to study in your archives."

"To study . . . what?" she asked.

She had not given a name, nor any rank. Taking her for a hierarch of some rank, I bowed again. "Teacher, forgive me, but there are things better left unsaid in the open air. That is why no message was sent, no telegraph from Forum. I am on a mission of special significance to the Solar Throne in my capacity as one of Caesar's Knights Victorian. I will speak only to your Primate. Forgive me." As I spoke, I restored the Emperor's ring to my finger, but did not restore my glove, opting instead to retain only the left one to cover my disfigured arm and hand.

The woman surveyed me a moment, face utterly unreadable, controlled. Without any hint of emotion. Suspicion? Concern? Fear? She stepped aside. "The Throne has not sent us a ring in more than five hundred years," she said. "Not since Cressgard. You and your men must leave your weapons and terminals at the gate here."

I moved to step past her and cross beneath the threshold.

Colchis.

The edge of the world.

There was still an edge here. Not between civilization and frontier, but between the secular world—my world—and the theoretical world of the scholiasts.

And I crossed it then, with Valka and the others just behind.

CHAPTER 53

THE GOLDEN AGE

"YOU MUST FORGIVE BROTHER Van," said Primate Arrian—master of all Nov Belgaer Athenaeum and the Imperial Library. "The boy was doing his duty. He is young. I apologize, Lord, for leaving you to stand in the rain."

"It's no trouble," I said, accepting the straight-backed wooden seat the Primate offered me. Valka sat beside me. Varro stood behind. The Primate's quarters were low-ceilinged and close, with a warm fire crackling merrily in the fireplace, burning what appeared to be moss. Another novice, a young woman clearly of palatine birth, sat on a stool with a clipboard on her knees. Ink stained her hands and the front of her green robes, as she struggled with the old-fashioned pen and writing tablet.

Arrian took his seat behind the large desk. The furniture was plain, but well made, carefully polished and maintained. Everything from the worn bookshelves, to the scrolls in their honeycombed niches, to the weathered stone walls themselves *ached* with age.

"What brings you to Colchis, Lord?" Tor Arrian asked. He was an older man, but by the red of his hair—going gray in places—I guessed that he was a cousin of the Imperial line.

I glanced at Valka, having decided to not quite tell the truth as I had before the Emperor.

"The Mericanii, Primate," I answered after a pregnant moment.

Whatever Tor Arrian had expected, this was not it, for despite his scholiast's training I saw his eyelids flicker. The girl's pen scratched to one side. "The Mericanii?" the Primate said. "Why? I will admit our knowledge of current events is sparse in athenaeum, but I know *you*, Lord Marlowe. You are focused on the Cielcin, are you not? Why turn to—of all things—the Foundation War?" My eyes turned to the scribe. Even in the offices of a scholiast primate behind the walls of an athenaeum, there were ears. No cameras or microphones, but there were recording devices of a kind. "Ekaterin is my daughter," Tor Arrian said. "You need not worry."

His daughter? That caught me by surprise. Scholiasts do not have children. A bastard, then? An intus? She looked healthy enough. Perhaps she was one of the lucky ones.

Smiling at the primate, I continued my lie. "On my travels, I discovered evidence of contact between the Mericanii daimons and certain . . . extraterranic agencies."

"Xenobites?" The scholiast lord almost, *almost* arched his eyebrows.

"Possibly."

"We have no such information here," Arrian said. "Wherever did you learn such a thing?"

Eyes shifting to Valka, I hesitated. She answered for me. "Vorgossos."

The scholiast's composure cracked, and he nearly laughed, echoing, "Vorgossos . . . you're not serious."

But Valka and Varro alike had come to Vorgossos. Both had spoken with Kharn Sagara. The Chalcenterite answered, speaking from over my shoulder. "It is true, father. The planet exists. You will forgive me, but it seems the reports from Legion Intelligence have not yet reached you here."

"Vorgossos . . ." The primate repeated the name. "Next you will me that Ys is real! Camelot?"

Valka crossed her arms. "If your acolytes had not taken my terminal, I might have shown you."

"Shown me?" the primate said. "You have holographs?"

"I have memories," she said, putting one finger to her temple. She offered no further explanation. The intaglio on her arm spoke to her Tavrosi ancestry, and that was enough.

Tor Arrian looked away.

"I met a man on Vorgossos who said the Mericanii conducted probing missions deep into the galactic volume. That some of their missions produced interesting results." I did not say what Brethren had said, that its fellow eldritch machines had *perceived* the Quiet across the stars and the centuries. "It is possible some of these incidents were early contact between the Mericanii and the Cielcin—*long before* our own people reached the Veil of Marinus."

But the primate was shaking his head. "Lord Marlowe, how much do you know of astrophysics?"

I raised one eyebrow, sensing the trap but not the shape of it. "Enough as any sailor not tasked with piloting a ship."

"Little and less, then," Arrian said, eyes finding the ceiling. "The Mericanii never developed the warp drive. Any probes they might have sent would not have gotten far before our ancestors caught up with them, certainly before they penetrated as far as the Veil." He was right; the Mericanii had ruled Earth for nearly two thousand years before the Advent and the Foundation War, but that limited them to a sphere of influence with a radius of two thousand light-years around Earth. The Veil of Marinus was more than twenty thousand light-years from Earth, near the heart of the galaxy. If by some chance our ancestors had missed one of the machines' ancient probes, it would still be on its way, tracking toward the core and galactic north at nearly the speed of light, time dilated and distorted in its wake.

Undaunted, Valka leaped to my defense. "But the Cielcin are a nomadic people. 'Tis possible, if unlikely, that one of these incidents described by this man on Vorgossos might have been early contact with the Cielcin. Prior human contact *might* explain Cielcin belligerence when they attacked Cressgard centuries ago."

Arrian's handsome palatine face composed itself into a frown—a most un-scholiast expression. "That would require a cultural memory reaching back more than fifteen thousand years on the part of the Cielcin. And I thought all evidence suggested they only became a spacefaring culture in the past few thousand years."

"They are longer lived than we are," I said.

"And 'tis possible we misunderstand their origins," Valka agreed.

The primate shook his head again. "This is a fool's errand."

"With respect, primate," I said, and bowed my head, "it is *my* errand." I placed my ungloved fist on the tabletop, displaying Sir George's ring. The Emperor's ring. "I am of His Radiance's Knights Victorian, here at his special command. You are *bound,* and I command. I request and require your cooperation."

Tor Arrian's frown deepened, and in that frown I recognized the face of the Emperor. Who had Arrian been in his former life? A brother? A cousin to the throne? Had he known William XXIII as a boy? Had they played together in the gardens of the Peronine Palace? His green eyes stared at the ring. Surely he knew it.

Both hands flat on the tabletop, he answered, "You must understand how irregular this is. The Strictures are most explicit with regard to what we can and cannot do. We are *bound,* you say. This is true. All men are. The information you *request and require* is in Gabriel's Archive, sealed since it was transported here at the founding of this institution. Sealed by order of Emperor Gabriel II after the Pretender's defeat. Sealed because even *my order* was not to be trusted with Mericanii artifacts. It will take more than a ring to open those doors, my lord. You have come all this way for nothing. I am sorry." He stood, and bowed low over the table, his hands tucked into his flowing brocade sleeves. "But I answer to higher authorities than you."

"Higher than the Emperor?"

"To tradition. If William wishes to break with tradition, he must tell me himself," he said. "You have the freedom of this institute and the library—save the monastery on the crag, of course—unless you wish to join our order."

"Not today," I said icily, standing myself. "I am grateful for your hospitality, primate. But." If Tor Arrian insisted on playing the game to the letter, so be it. I would cross every T and mark every vowel if that was what it took, even if it took months to clear.

"But?" Arrian raised an eyebrow.

"But," I said coolly, "I will be transmitting directly to His Radiance on Forum. You will open those doors for me, primate. Depend on it." And with that I turned and strode from the room in a flowing of black coattails.

" 'Tis only a minor setback," Valka said, gripping my arm as we strode down a pillared gallery from the primate's offices.

Varro cut in, following softly behind. "I will return to the city and see the request is wired through."

"You have the Emperor's codes?" I said.

"I do," he said.

"Very good. Take Doran and two men with you," I said. "Now that we know the situation on the ground here, please send to the *Tamerlane*. I want Prince Alexander brought down. If we're to be dug in here for months, he might as well get an education out of all this." We swept down a flight of stairs as I spoke, guards marching in lockstep behind.

Varro assented, and added, "If might make a suggestion?"

"Certainly."

"If we are to be at anchor here for some time, it might do to let the men ashore. Many of them have not had proper shore leave in decades—a number of them have not even left the *Tamerlane* except to fight. This isn't Forum. They're not like to get into any *political* trouble."

"Political trouble," I said, thinking of Lieutenant Casdon. "Very good, counselor. Make the arrangements with the governor-general. I've no wish to flood her city with lonely sailors all at once. Perhaps there are some remoter locations the men might visit in smaller groups. Less chance for mayhem."

Varro bowed and withdrew, hurrying along one leg of the quadrangle we'd descended into with Doran and his guards.

"What's the point of a library if they won't let you read anything?" Pallino said when the scholiast had gone.

I could only sigh. It was a tiresome delay, but for once in my life, time was not of the essence, and so I did not complain.

The athenaeum citadel was, as I have said, bounded by a high, circular stone wall. But I feel this presents too simple a picture of the place in which I now sit. For a start, this picture leaves off the monastery on the crag overlooking the main athenaeum. On that high crag, old men retreated to contemplate the stars and to study the soul, muttering of philosophy in dusty halls, writing books that descended their winding stairs and vanished into the cavernous halls of the Imperial Library, perhaps to be read one day by some novice destined to tutor some great lord, perhaps not.

The Library itself stood at the center of the compound, a massive drum tower perhaps half a mile in diameter, the only structure in the place not built of common stone, but of steel, with high, narrow windows rising for fifty stories above the low stone buildings and spires of the lecture halls and refectories, observatories, conservatories, and greenhouses. Part of the mountain it seemed, an admonishing finger or defiant fist upthrust from the body of the highlands and Colchis itself.

It was but the tip of the iceberg, for beneath its mighty spire there were deep halls and chambers and winding labyrinths, walls packed and lined with books, and more than books: with scrolls and pamphlets, with ancient storage drives, microfilm, and quartz storage crystals—though the scholiasts possessed no praxis to read such things within their walls. How many billion texts molder yet within its walls? How many trillion?

The Library and athenaeum institute of Nov Belgaer that surrounded it was a labyrinth and a microcosm unto itself, replete with aqueducts and gardens, amphitheaters and classrooms—all the essentials necessary for maintaining a community of thousands and facilitating their lives of consecrated research.

Quarters had been found for us in a quiet dormitory near the outer walls, and while we waited for Varro and Doran to return from Aea with Alexander, Valka and I ate in the refectory alongside green-robed brothers and sisters of the Order and were permitted to explore those parts of the compound nearest the main gate, where dwelt the novices and those full scholiasts whose vocation it was to interact with the world outside. Pallino was never far behind, dogging us with his men.

Valka's nails bit into my arm the instant we crossed the threshold, heavy doors swinging shut on temple-hushed quiet.

"You've finally done it," she whispered, strangely breathless. "You've finally brought me somewhere *nice*."

Dust hung thick on the air with the smell of centuries, danced in sunbeams cast through high and narrow windows on a quiet undisturbed in nigh as long. Delicate mosaics showing geometric designs tiled the floor, and richly carved counters ahead and to either side of the double doors stood tall, their attendants stooped over ledgers behind iron grillwork fashioned in the image of thorned vines. The doors themselves stood shut beneath an arch carved with an inscription.

" 'Tis Classical English, yes?" Valka asked. "What does it say?"

I squinted up at the old, squarish letters. "Great is Truth," I read aloud, "and mighty above all things."

"Can we . . . just go in?" she asked me, looking round as if for some sentinel or sign.

One of the attendants raised her head from her book and said, "You may. But kindly keep quiet."

Keep Quiet, I thought, capitalizing the word. Bowing my head, I advanced and held the door open for Valka, standing to one side so that I caught the look on her face as she passed me and beheld the Library itself for the first time. Sharp though my memory may be, I do not share Valka's perfect clarity of recall. Things fade for me, dim, and distort. Memories are lost.

Though not the memory of her face.

Her eyes *glowed* as they widened, but her smile and look of wonder stretched wider still, until the joy in her and the awe yawned large enough to swallow the Imperial Library and drink its every word. I could not help but smile. After decades, after nigh on a century of waking years and more than a century asleep, after years of patient waiting and delay and time spent poring over Imperial military reports and scans from captured Cielcin ships—Valka's faith had been rewarded.

She moved forward in a kind of dream, left me hanging on the door. I watched her go, filtering in behind her, not daring to speak and interrupt her religious moment. Stacks of books surrounded her, aisle upon aisle of circular shelves marching, bending away to encircle the massive library. Ladders ran on brass tracks in the tile alongside inlaid strips of carpet to deaden the tramp of feet. Valka spun as she advanced, taking in the sights, obvious tourism earning her a dismissive glare from a novice clearly not yet trained in the management of her outward emotions.

"There must be a million books on this floor alone!" said Valka, *sotto voce*. She almost laughed. She turned to the nearest aisle—marked in brass on its end cap with a sign reading *Encyclopdias, Extraterranic Biologies, Na-Ne*. Selecting a tome at random, she drew out one volume of a 20-volume set detailing the native pseudoflora of some planet I had never heard of. She turned the pages, flipping through so quickly I knew she could not possibly be reading the text. I had to remind myself that she did not have to. Merely seeing the pages was enough. Valka could recall each idly-glanced-at page with the clarity of digital recall.

She closed the book with a *thump*.

"Simply marvelous!" she exclaimed, a manic gleam alight in her eyes. "And these are just encyclopedias, dictionaries, compendiums . . . oh! And indexes, look!" She was grinning like a fiend as she turned the huge slim index volume around to show me. "Attention: This index is imperfect," she said, displaying a card inside the front cover, written in both Classical English and Galstani. "Hadrian, they don't even know where all their books *are*!"

"How could they?" I said. "Students must move them all the time. And I'll bet each time the curators try to reorganize things some new curators come along with new ideas and change everything over."

Valka was shaking her head. "You *anaryoch*. A collection like this should be properly sorted, backed up, scanned. What if this place burned? What would happen to all this?"

"They'll never have a machine in here," I said. "The scholiasts in particular are forbidden. It was scholiasts—well, *scholars*—that built the machines in the first place. Your people have forgotten what the Mericanii were like. What they did."

" 'Twas so long ago!" Valka objected, hugging the index to herself. "So much has changed!"

"You remember Brethren," I said softly, confident that here in all the universe there were no cameras listening in.

Her face fell, and she placed the volume back on its shelf. "Maybe you're right," she said.

But Valka was not one to let my being right ruin her time in the Library. She brushed past me and returned to the central aisle, marching along its spine toward the central desks and the main stair. The archives rose above us for several levels, each railed with old iron, and connected by a spiraling iron stair. Scholiasts in viridian sat on straight-backed chairs at tables or wall-in reading desks, keeping rapt silence or else softly murmuring to one another.

Following Valka's lead, we climbed the stairs and ran along the narrow span that led from the central spiral to the second floor of the archives. We continued in this vein for hours—for the entirety of the afternoon, in fact. We climbed to floor after floor, and after a dozen or so floors passed through the roof of the lobby to where the iron stair became stone and the round aisles became straight. Here Valka stopped her climb and we descended instead by a sweeping outer stair that spiraled about the outside of the central archives, passing wall-niches where stood the busts of great thinkers, magi, and poets long dead. Switchback stairs broke off from ours at regular intervals, ascending and descending straight up and down as may be.

After a while I realized what Valka was doing: she was building a map. When we each arrive in a new place, we must inhabit it for a time before it becomes real, before its passages and turnings become to us as familiar as the lines inside our hands. Valka needed but one showing to become accustomed. I marked how her eyes—still wide with wonder—marked each brass placard and aisle marker, knowing that with each idle glance she etched an indelible memory of what each aisle held and where it was. In watching her, I conceded that she, too, was right. With Valka's memory alone, the Library might be properly indexed in a palatine lifetime.

On the third level or the second we exited the stair, passing out into an annex attached to the archives' drum tower. There we found washrooms alongside a dispensary offering cool water and the scholiasts' only true vice: coffee. Here we lingered a moment, sitting in a corner among quietly chattering students, and talked of little things.

Exploring the annex further, we passed beneath an arch with its brass signed marked *SCRIPTORIA*. Here a curving hallway tiled black and white processed beneath arched vaults with arched doors to either side. Through these—some open, some closed, some occupied—stood small chambers with writing desks and papers, vellum, and inks alongside charcoal and rubber and jars of sand, all the tools of the scribe's trade. Names on movable type showed in sliders on the doors, marking each cell for its occupant: *Tor Hunt, Tor Saad, Tor Vermeule,* and so on. At one of these we stopped.

Number 113.

Here I pause, for it is in this very chamber I sit at my work, writing this very page. And turning to look at the wooden door, I look back across centuries at my younger self, standing beside Valka in the door. How young I was! How young and how untested. We stepped into the room, my room, and looked round. The cell was and is not large, just more than four yards deep and three across, with a canted writing desk beneath the veined glass window with its view of the towers of the athenaeum compound and the sea beyond. If I crane my neck I can see a sea mount looming on the horizon, brushing the limb of the gas giant Atlas where it skirts the heavens above. As in the hall without, the ceiling was vaulted, and as in the outer stair of the tower, there stood niches filled with the porphyry busts of sages. The traditional bust of Imore was there. The first scholiast stared impassive from his niche above a cubby where the room's occupant might theoretically leave his or her manuscript. I ran a gloved finger over the ledge, scraped a thick caul of dust from the dark wood.

"Gibson," Valka said, voice strangely hushed by some quirk of the air.

"What?" I looked over my shoulder, found Valka pointing at the dark bust of a man above the central niche in the left side. Moving to join her, I squinted up at the statue in its enclosure. It was not *my* Gibson, not at all. The image was of a handsome man with the strong jaw and cheekbones of some patrician line. Sharp nose, high forehead, eyebrows steeply slanted. He was no scholiast, if the wry smile he wore was any indication. I read the inscription. "Christopher-Marcus Gibson," I said. "Golden Age ethical philosopher. Fairly obscure."

"How do you know this?"

"It's who my Gibson named himself after," I said. "When the scholiasts are embraced by the Order—when they become scholiasts, that is—they take a new name as a sign that they've cast aside their old lives and the attachments of family and so on, which is important. Especially because most of them are palatine." I gestured at Gibson's bust. "Gibson—my Gibson—always said he was the finest philosopher of the late Golden Age."

She cocked her head to one side. "Looks a bit like you."

"Maybe a little."

"The jaw," she said, pointing. Valka frowned. "Why did he take his name?"

"He never told me," I said, turning from that first Gibson's statue to look at Valka more fully. "I don't know much about him."

"About your Gibson or this?"

"Either, I suppose," I said. Christopher-Marcus Gibson was of an age remote almost as Alexander, as the last pharaohs and the first Caesars. The Golden Age of Earth, before mankind was made subject to her machines. Who could say with certainty what sort of man was he, who might have broken bread with Churchill or locked horns with Bonaparte? Who might his friends have been? Heroes and prophets of that antediluvian time? Not even Kharn Sagara would know, for Sagara—immortal and eldest as he was of all the Children of Earth—was a child of our latter days, a child of the Exodus, of the Peregrinations that carried mankind from Earth. None now live who can answer these questions.

My own Gibson was as much a mystery.

The scholiasts burn their dead and scatter the ashes to the winds. They keep no records, no biographies. They are servants, stewards. The only memory they leave behind is the work they did in life.

So it is with the rest of us, in truth.

"You know, I don't even know his name?" I said. *"My* Gibson, that is. Who he was *before,* you know? He was palatine, so he was *someone."* I felt her glaring at me and raised my gloved hand in apology. "You know what I mean."

Valka wrapped an arm around me and stood there in companionate silence, looking up at the elder Gibson's likeness. "Does it matter who he was?" she asked.

I looked down at her, astonished to hear *her* ask such a question. As long as I had known her, Valka had obsessed about identity. I suppose I did as well, if differently. Where I had concerned myself with the proprieties of antique class, Valka's prejudices had run against the Imperium as a whole.

Against me and everything that I was.

As a young man, Valka's pretenses at egalitarianism had irritated me, not because her compassion for creatures like the Umandh on Emesh and the Irchtani—even our own homunculi—was misplaced; it wasn't. But because her compassion ended there and excluded me. Excluded Gibson, too. But Gibson was dead, and whoever he was, I knew that I would never see him again.

"No, I guess it doesn't," I said. "We should head back. Varro's bound to be back soon with the prince."

Valka nodded and permitted me to chivvy her toward the door.

I lingered for but a moment on the threshold and—though I did not then know it—looked back upon the very chair and desk at which I now spend my exile. Turning round, I can look even now upon that elder Gibson's bust. His statue is why I chose to return to this scriptorium of the three hundred that line this hall. Sitting in its shadow, I feel almost as if the eyes of *my* Gibson were on me.

I left the cell then, not knowing I would ever return.

CHAPTER 54

UNLOOKED-FOR

"THE GOVERNOR-GENERAL SAID SHE can't allow thousands of soldiers loose in her city," Varro said from across the bare stone room the scholiasts had set aside for Valka and myself.

Seated on the edge of one of two narrow cots, I looked up at the scholiast, checking the frown that wanted purchase of my face. "Understandable, I suppose," I said. Aea was a small city, and the addition of several thousand fighting men—however well trained and civilized, as I liked to imagine mine were—would not be good for the locals. Drunk and disorderly conduct, fights, theft . . . all the collateral damage of men swaggering and high on their status as Imperial soldiers. And more than Imperial soldiers. They were members of the Halfmortal's own Red Company. I was certain the last thing the locals wanted was several hundred star-born bastards kicking about without fathers. "But she did make provision for us?"

"The Sevrast Islands," Varro replied. "They're an archipelago to the north, just on the far side of the equator. There are a few towns there, fishing settlements—but the greater part of the islands is still wilderness. The governor-general proposed our men might take to the beaches. It's warm this time of year."

I caught myself nodding along. "Camping trip, is it?"

"It's an insult," Alexander interjected. The young prince stood in the arched window looking out over the quadrangle two stories below and the novices strolling beneath the ancient ash tree at its center. "A Prince of the Imperium and a Royal Victorian Knight relegated to a *literal* backwater." He turned, looking for all the world just like his father for a moment. "Of course this whole place is a backwater."

I raised my gloved hand. "It will be fine," I said tersely. "You'll find there's more to the world than cities, Alexander. You'll like it."

"The beaches?" He sounded incredulous. "I don't *like* sand."

"Enough," I said, not lowering the hand, but turning it palm up in a gesture of peace. Directing my attentions to Varro, I asked, "How soon will we have men on the ground?"

"Corvo is having them decanted now," my scholiast answered me. "But it might be three days before the first group is fit to make planetfall."

That made sense. The rapid thaw and reorientation we put soldiers through in emergencies was less than medically optimal. Now that we had the time and the opportunity for respite, it was better to take things slowly, to run medical exams on all our troops—human and Irchtani alike. "I'm not sure how long it will be before Tor Arrian gets his paperwork all right and proper so Valka and I may begin, and Earth knows how long we'll be at our research," I said, speaking past Varro and Alexander, addressing the room at large as my father might have done. "It could be years, so I'll want to make sure everyone has a good long time on the ground. But I don't want everyone down at once ruining the place, and I don't want trouble with the locals. Let the officers know they'll be on duty so long as their men are on the ground. Their time will come at the end."

The scholiast bowed. "I will send a man to the day gate to wave the *Tamerlane*."

"Very good," I said, and waving a hand dismissed the scholiast from my presence.

"Where's the doctor?" Alexander asked. The prince had returned to studying the world beyond my low window.

Smiling, I lay back along the end of the bed, resting my tired muscles. Pallino and I had spent the morning sparring, and my body ached with memory of it. The patrician treatments had made the man stronger than he'd ever been, and Pallino had the wiry strength of a legionnaire, even when he'd been an old man. Young again, he was a terror, though without any of Crim's finesse or my polish. "Where do you think?" I asked, watching the prince with one eye, hands behind my head.

"Still reading?" He sounded shocked.

"She doesn't *read*," I said, rolling my ankles as slowly as I was able, relaxing taut cords. "She's scanning." Alexander knew full well that Valka was Tavrosi, and he had some inkling of her abilities, but I saw one hand form itself into the familiar warding gesture all the same: first and last fingers extended, the others curled. "She found the xenology section last night. She's been turning over every leaf as fast as she can." Knowing it would frighten my young squire, I said, "She'll have absorbed half the books in the section by now."

The truth was, I envied Valka her abilities. As I have grown older, I have found it increasingly difficult to sit down and read, preferring to listen to my terminal read to me as I go about other business or sit drawing with my charcoals and my folio. It took me hours to absorb what took Valka instants.

Bowing his head and—for a change—not arguing, the prince answered, "I suppose it has its uses."

Never one to simply *agree* out of hand, I grunted and said, "Plato objected to writing, you know. Said it would spoil man's ability to remember. He was right. Imore worked for decades rebuilding mankind's lost capacity for memory. Valka can absorb an enormous amount of information without *learning* it."

"But she can recall any line or bit of information from it," Alexander said.

"Yes," I agreed, "but she hasn't developed any kind of theory about her new knowledge. She can't sort it. Or *hasn't* sorted it."

The prince was getting it, I could tell by the way he was steadily nodding his head. "So she doesn't have any ideas *about* the information."

Reader, have I already said that there is a difference between knowing a fact and *owning* it? "It takes Valka as long as you or I to *think* about what she knows."

"Surely not *as* long," he said. "She doesn't have to waste time learning and relearning information."

"True," I said. "But she also doesn't feel the same pressure *to* learn. Much of the data Valka has taken in in her day just sits in there, waiting to be useful. She hasn't thought about it, hasn't accessed it, and because those parts of her mind are machine, the thoughts only sit there until she needs them. She told me once things don't float in her mind the way they do in yours or mine."

Alexander turned sharply then, curiosity plain on his impossibly sculpted face. "Does she dream?"

She didn't, but I did not feel that it was my place to say. Whatever the nature of Valka's implants, they'd fundamentally altered her brain's chemistry and mechanics. Not only did she not dream, she did not struggle to sleep. She could switch off her waking mind as easily as you or I might turn a light switch.

"Why do you ask?"

"I only wondered," the prince said. "I can't imagine what it must be like, being like that."

"Neither can I," I said. The prince was silent a long moment. He'd turned back to fully face the room, eyes intently studying his own shoes. I could tell he wanted to ask something, and so said, "Out with it. What's on your mind?"

Alexander twitched as if I'd shocked him. "I don't understand why we're here."

I hadn't told him. I'd explained everything to Pallino, to Siran and Elara, to Crim, Otavia, and Ilex—everyone who'd been with me on the *Demiurge*. I'd even explained it to Lorian, who believed though he had not seen. "Were you not told?" I asked, toying with one silver clasp on my glove's long gauntlet. "I've long had evidence—rumor, really—of earlier battles with the Cielcin in our history. On Vorgossos, Kharn Sagara told me the Mericanii . . . *encountered* xenobites."

"Kharn Sagara?" Alexander repeated, eyes gone wide. "Not *the* Kharn Sagara." I only looked at him. "You didn't tell me."

"You didn't ask."

"How is he alive?"

"He clones himself," I said, still lying there, "and takes the new bodies."

The prince made the warding gesture again. "But he must be . . . ten thousand years old!"

"More than fifteen thousand," I said soberly. "Almost old enough to remember the Mericanii, and old enough to remember things from that time we have long forgotten."

"Like the Mericanii fighting the Cielcin?"

"Possibly the Cielcin," I said, so what I said became something less than a lie.

"But then . . ."

A knock sounded at the door, cutting off the prince's question. "Enter!" I called.

The novice at the door bowed. "I apologize for the interruption, my lords," she said, still bowing.

I sat up on the bed, swinging round to face the young lady. She wore the simple green pullover of a new-made scholiast, tied at the waist with a white cord, no sash or bronze badges to be seen. "Stand," I said. She did. Hope springing in my chest, I said, "Did Arrian send for me?" Had the formal approval cleared the telegraph from Forum already? It seemed unlikely. It had only been three days since we had arrived.

"The primate?" She wrung her hands—definitely a novice then, and would be until she learned to control such nervous expressions. "No, my lord. I work for the curators. One of the archivists sent me for you."

"One of the archivists?" I found my feet. "Why?"

"I don't know, lord," the girl said, bowing her head again. I guessed she was patrician by birth; no palatine so young would be deferential to me. "He said, 'Carina, fetch Lord Marlowe for me.' I am sworn to obedience, lord. I did not question him. I am sorry, lord." She bowed again, and I sensed a glimmer of fear in the movement. Fear of me?

Smiling sweetly as I could, I offered the girl my most courtly bow. "It's all right, Sister Carina," I said. "Let me get my boots on."

I left Alexander in the suite and followed Carina back out into the sea air. She did not speak much, but hurried on ahead of me, replying to my questions and my attempts at conversation with timid staccato replies. After a minute or two, I gave up. No sense wringing blood from a stone.

Sister Carina led me back toward the Library tower, but not the way I'd entered it with Valka on our first day. Rather, we entered through the scriptorium annex, past the winding halls and Room 113, past the coffee dispensary and back through the main archives, where to my surprise we turned down and followed the stair past the ground level into a cavernous silo of a space ringed round by ironwork balconies. Here the book stacks continued, descending it seemed for half as many levels as they climbed above. We passed dozens of brothers and sisters of the Order as we went, rattling down old metal stairs. I half-expected to catch Valka in among them—she was in there somewhere, lost among the stacks—but she did not appear.

At length Carina brought me to a hall where scrolls—actual *scrolls*— stood in niches like honeycomb to either side. These were blueprints, schematics, and other diagrams kept in vacuum behind filter glass to preserve them. Maps and paintings were stored in similar glass slides, protected for all eternity. It was a collection to rival and drown even the Undying's Garden of Everything.

"Where are we going?" I asked.

Finally stringing together a coherent answer, the girl said, "The archivists' quarters are down here. I wanted to spare him the climb."

The arch ahead was not like the classical arches above, but circular, the door round as a pressure hatch—indeed I think it was such a hatch, or had been. Bioluminescent lamps hung on the walls, and pillars of some strange, pink stone stood in ranks beyond.

"Coral?" I asked.

"It traps moisture," Carina said, stepping aside to allow three of her brothers to pass. "Protects the books."

"Protects the books from what?"

I had my answer a moment later. Ahead the hall gave way to living rock, its face precisely carved by careful hands over many long centuries. Stalactites hung from the ceilings, flowed into graven pillars that supported natural vaults. Metal doors showed in the rock around, opening on deeper grottoes. A statue of Imore sat upon a pillar of stone in the center above a still, black pool. No blade of grass was there, nor flower, nor even moss. The Archivists' Grotto. It ought to be one of the Ninety-Nine Wonders of the Galaxy all on its own, a work of art and beauty. Like the dark delvings of the Cielcin it should have been, or the gloomy haunts of our necropolis beneath Devil's Rest, but it was like neither of those things. Great veins of gleaming algae clung to the vaults above, shedding their white light on the groves and aisles of stone, teased by decades and centuries of cultivation into fractal patterns as Buddhist monks arrange rocks in a garden.

Here I have made my home these past three years and labored at this account. Here I have lived and labored alongside the brothers and sisters of the Order, though I am not one of them. Here I have hidden from an ungrateful universe, and lived not as Hadrian Marlowe, but as a guest of Arrian's successor three times removed. They never asked my name—though the primate knows me. They call me the Poet, and that is enough. A private joke that you, Reader, will no doubt understand.

But of all the beauty of that Grotto, of the arched cavern roof and the pillars flowing from it, of the still pool like a black mirror beneath Imore's unsmiling face, of the hanging stalactites like the fangs of some forgotten dragon, I shall say no more—for my attention was given to none of them. My eyes went instead to the bench beside that pool, and my vision blurred with tears.

Vast is the galaxy, and vaster still the cosmos. But vaster—greater—even than that is the *cosmos,* the great enemy of chaos, the order that stands above it all. Four hundred billion suns in our galaxy, trillions of worlds—half a billion of them settled by Man.

So small.

Small enough for chance.

For miracles unlooked-for.

As I drew nearer I stopped, tears flowing freely by then. Upon the bench—waiting for me, it seemed—sat an elderly man, his body stooped with care, his viridian robes hanging loose on him as old rags upon a scarecrow. As I approached he looked up, smiling in a most un-scholiast way beneath his wild mane of thick white hair, gray eyes sparkling. His craggy face caught the light of the algae growth above, deep shadows carving there, throwing the mutilated nostril into sharp relief.

"Hello, Hadrian!" said Tor Gibson.

CHAPTER 55

REUNION

I FELL TO MY knees before the bench, still crying silently. "Gibson?" I stretched out my ungloved hand and took his own hand in mine. "Is it *really* you?"

The old scholiast looked down at me. With his free hand, he set the familiar brass-headed cane aside. His fingers were warm and dry as old roots in my hand, but there was some strength yet in them. He squeezed my hand and shook it back and forth, smile widening. "Who else would it be?"

A hollow laugh escaped me, knocking loose more tears. I drew my coat sleeve across my face, dried my eyes. "You'd not believe me if I told you," I said. "I thought you were dead. It's been . . ." I had to stop and think about it. "Four hundred fifty standard years." I had spent most of that time frozen, slipping into the future with each passing journey. "How long have you been here?"

"Only about four years," Gibson said. He raised a hand to quiet my objections as they came spilling forth. "Your father had me sent *freight*. I think he meant for me to outlive you—part of my punishment." His smile hadn't faltered. "But here you are, a *Knight Victorian*, is it?" He took back his hands and clapped me on both shoulders, the better to survey me at arm's length. "I could hardly believe it when I heard the news." And here he raised my right hand to his face, the better to see the Emperor's Sovereign Ring with his fading eyes. "I thought you were going to Teukros," he said, "and here I find you wearing the Emperor's own ring." His eyes swept over my black uniform and longish mane, over the gauntleted left hand and the sword and shield-belt. "Still wearing these long coats, I see."

I laughed, new tears blossoming. "I thought you were dead," I managed to say. "I *mourned* you."

"I thought the same of you, dear boy," my old tutor—the man who had truly been my father—said. Tears still falling, I released his hand and, regaining my feet, stooped to embrace him.

"There is so much to tell you," I said, voice fragile in my ears and close to breaking. "So much."

Gibson's old arms embraced me only slowly, as if it took him a moment to recover from the surprise of my embrace. "And you will tell me all about it. Sit, sit." He patted the stone bench beside him. "Carina tells me you bring an army with you." Gibson watched me through a mask *like* a scholiast's expressionless repose, but his eyes—gray eyes, not green—were sparkling through the thin mist that darkened their sight. He looked old, older than I remembered. He must have been six hundred years old, at least. With a start, I realized my own father would be as old now—assuming he never once left Delos after I did. Crispin would be north of four hundred, on the far side of middle-aged. Seeing Gibson somehow heightened my sense of alienation. I was a man adrift in time, and though the six-score-and-some-odd years I carried in that moment weighed heavily on me as five centuries might on others, I had been like a man cast adrift into a river while all he knew remained ashore and slipped away.

I felt the ivory ring beneath my glove as I shifted to take the seat beside my oldest friend and companion. Not all I knew. Adrift in time I might be, but I did not drift alone.

"You would think," Gibson said, "that the Imperial Library would be among the first places news travels in our universe, but it is not so. Information arrives here only after it has circulated throughout the suns. We are more reservoir than fountain, in truth. But I have heard some strange tales. Carina says something about Vorgossos? And what is this *Halfmortal* business? What a name!"

Mention of Sister Carina made me look round, half-expecting to find the young novice near at hand, but she had vanished, withdrawn, no doubt, to some other duty. It seemed absurd to talk to Gibson of Vorgossos, of Brethren and the Quiet. Of my death and of the Howling Dark beyond. Gibson was of a time *before*. My memories of him belonged to that *other* Hadrian, the one who had died on the *Demiurge*. Young though I was, I was older than any plebeian might dream, and we are not meant to live forever. Those memories of my youth on Delos felt as remote to me then as the stories of someone *else's* childhood. It was as if Tor Gibson and Lord Alistair Marlowe—Crispin and Kyra, my mother and all the rest—existed in a world apart from the nightmares of Vorgossos, of Arae, and Iubalu. Or perhaps those nightmares were real, and it was my childhood that was the dream.

"There is so much," I said, and clenched my fists until the right one ached. "So much." A sob shook me, as though I were a boy of nineteen again and not a Knight Victorian. Not the Halfmortal. And no nineteen-year-old could bear what I have seen and done and not weep.

But Gibson was a scholiast—as I have never been—and scholiasts have no time for weeping. "Kwatz!" he said, rebuking me, and thumped me on the knee. "Grief is deep water. Come now. Stop this. Remember your breathing exercises."

I was a child again, or would always be a child to Gibson. Taking in a deep breath, I held it, counting back from ten. Slowly I released it, exhaling with it the tension that brought my tears. "It isn't grief," I said. I brushed my gauntlet across my face, leather slick against my eyes. "It's only . . . there's so much. So much to tell. So many times I needed your help."

"I'm here now."

I told him as I had told *no one* before, not even Valka. I told him about Haspida, about my mother, and my fight with Crispin. I told him about Demetri, and how I'd come to Emesh. For the first time in my life, I told someone about Cat. About the Gray Rot, about the streets of Boros-evo. I told him about the Colosso, about Switch and Pallino, about Siran and Ghen, and the rest. I told him about Makisomn and the Mataros. About Gilliam. I told him about meeting Valka, and that I loved her. How we fled to Calagah, how there I had my first vision from the Quiet. I told him of the Jaddian visit and the Cielcin attack, and wished I could show him the sword Olorin had given me, but I had checked it in the barbican of the day gate when we'd entered Nov Belgaer.

My story took us to Pharos, took us *through* Emil Bordelon and Marius Whent, through my time with Jinan and the Red Company—and how I had betrayed them. We journeyed to Vorgossos, and when I spoke of Kharn Sagara, Gibson's eyes—forgetting their scholiast training—went wide as dinner plates.

"Kharn Sagara?" he echoed. "The King with Ten Thousand Eyes?"

Had I not just had this precise conversation with Prince Alexander?

"I gave you that book," Gibson said. "Of all the books in the universe . . . what are the odds?"

"Shorter odds than that I should find you *here,* alive," I said.

"Not so!" Gibson said. "Colchis is the final destination for much of our Order." Tor Varro had said something of that when we arrived on the watery moon. I supposed that explained such coincidence, though perhaps there were deeper powers at work. Deeper powers had moved me from Teukros to Emesh, after all, as I then told Gibson—and told him the Quiet so often wore his face. He asked no questions, nor made any interruption of any kind, not even when I recounted my duel with Prince Aranata and my death aboard the *Demiurge*. I must have talked for hours—it was impossible to tell so far underground. I spoke of my knighting in the Georgian Chapel, of my missions in service to the Empire, of the Battles of Cellas, Thagura, and Oxiana. I spoke of the demons of Arae, of the pirates at Nagapur. I told him the truth of my battle with Ulurani at Aptucca, and of my mission to Gododdin and Nemavand. I spoke of Hermonassa and Syriani Dorayaica, the Scourge of Earth, and though he remained silent, I saw his face fall. At last I came to Forum, to Bourbon, Breathnach, and the Empress. Gibson did not need to know. I showed my scars, let him feel the bones beneath.

Studying the deep white slashes in my left arm with his fingers and fading eyes, Gibson said, "These are poor payment for so much suffering." He took his hands away. "I am sorry, Hadrian."

"You've nothing to be sorry for," I said. *"I'm sorry.* It's because of me Father exiled you and . . ." I touched my own nose, tried not to look at the deep notch Sir Felix had put in Gibson's with his knife. "You wouldn't be here if it wasn't for me."

The old man's scholiast composure broke entirely, and he gave me a sad smile, clamping one dry hand over my scarred wrist. "Being here isn't a punishment. But what happened to you . . ." He broke off contact with my arm, and for the first time in my life I think I saw my old tutor truly lost for words. "I'm only sorry you didn't make it to Teukros."

"You sacrificed yourself for nothing," I said, staring down at my hands. The three rings—rhodium, ivory, and gold—the nearly invisible scars from my youth on Delos fading on the right, the fresh, shining white ones deep on the left.

"Not nothing," the scholiast said. "You're not a cathar, are you?"

He had a point, but I said, "I don't know what I am."

Gibson laughed—actually laughed. The scholiasts nearby all started at the sound. A scholiast should not laugh. I confess I shared their astonishment. In all the years I'd known him, I do not think I'd ever heard the old man laugh. "You haven't changed at all!"

"What do you mean?" I asked, who had changed quite entirely.

"You're still dramatic as ever." Gibson brushed one eye with a finger—had there been tears there? "Forgive me, I should not laugh, but scholiast or no . . . All these things you say have happened . . . and here you are." He broke off, still chuckling. "So you are in exile here, too. Hiding from the Empress and—which Bourbon did you say it was?"

"Augustin," I said. "He was Minister of War." I hoped he was dead, though word of the assassins Crim had found for me had yet to reach my ears.

"Poor repayment indeed," Gibson said. The silence spread between us, master and student at momentary peace on the bench. I watched a thin rivulet run along the veined wall of the stone opposite, disturbing a smaller pool. "Augustin . . ." he chewed the name. "You said he *was* Minister of War?"

I'd stopped short in my story of recounting the orders I'd given Crim. It felt wrong to confess *that* to anyone alive. A life of violence was one thing. But murder—an assassination—that was something else entirely, though neither my hand nor Crim's had wielded the knife. But if I could not confess to Gibson in the privacy of a scholiasts' cloister, whom could I confess to?

"I killed him," I said. "Or . . . I hope I did." I explained the orders I'd given Crim. The bomb he'd arranged be placed in the Lord Minister's shuttle. Gibson did not react, did not comment. "He tried to kill me," I said. "Tried to kill my people. I couldn't let him try again."

Still the scholiast said nothing, passing no sentence, handing down neither judgment nor absolution. I did not feel better having spoken the truth aloud. I felt exposed, raw, as if I expected some small gasp from behind a stalagmite and to see Sister Carina rushing away to tell *someone*.

But we were alone.

I crossed my arms, covering the scarred one with the other. "It doesn't matter."

"Perhaps not," Gibson said, an odd brittleness in his tone. Was it horror? Disgust? Worse . . . was it pity? Turning, I found the old man staring at his lap and at the hands twisting in it, each massaging the other as though they pained him. Was it my imagination? Or had the tears returned to those misty eyes and seamed cheeks? "I am sorry, my boy. I wanted to give you a better life. *This* life." He gestured round at the Archivists' Grotto.

Shutting my eyes, the distant dripping of water might have been the drip of water in the limestone pools of our necropolis. When I opened my eyes again, I almost expected the black funeral statues of the ancient Lords

Marlowe to be standing about me in their ring, black against natural white, but there was only the statue of Imore, unfeeling as ever above the mirrored pool.

"It's true?" Gibson asked, after a long while. "All of it?"

"I know it is incredible," I said, looking down at my own hands where I clenched them between my knees, feeling the scarred palm flex oddly. "But I swear it is the truth."

Gibson's voice—familiar to me as my own even after all these years— replied, "It is more than incredible. You ask me to believe the impossible."

"You don't believe me?" Almost I thought the bench and the stone on which it sat might crumble beneath me, that I should be swallowed by the world. Gibson *had* to believe me. He was *Gibson.* "I have footage. I can have you evoked from athenaeum . . . bring you to my ship." I turned to look my old tutor in the face. Where had I gone wrong? This could not be happening! I needed him, needed him to understand, needed him to make sense of the strange net I'd fallen into, to make sense of my life.

"Footage could be fabricated," Gibson said, and looked me square in the face. His eyes were shining. "Hadrian, I do not doubt your tale, but I do not understand it."

"I don't understand it either. Sagara said there are forces in the universe older and stranger than humankind. Brethren said these *Quiet* exist in the future. That's why I'm here: to make sense of it all. To see if the Mericanii knew something we've forgotten." I was almost crying again, but I crushed the nineteen-year-old part of me in my adamant fist and held my tears at bay. "I need your help."

The old man was smiling—though I knew he should not be. "This is beyond me, Hadrian," he said simply before adding, "Perhaps I was wrong. Perhaps you are not the same boy I knew on Delos."

"I'm not," I said, and remembered, "Valka! Valka is here! You have to meet her. And the others, Pallino and the prince are here. The rest are in orbit, but they'll be coming down to the Sevrast Islands. The governor-general's granted my people shore leave. You'll have to meet them all!"

And at once Gibson's skepticism did not matter. Here was my first and oldest friend in all the universe: the man who made me what I am, for better or worse. My teacher, my tutor, my father in all but name. Skeptical he may have been, but our reunion seemed to me another sign of those secret powers that moved the universe and me through it.

"Tomorrow, I think," he said at last. "It is past midnight."

He was right. The Grotto was empty.

CHAPTER 56

MEETING OF THE MINDS

VALKA DID NOT RETURN from her ventures in the stacks until long after I had fallen asleep. Something about her implants allowed her to sleep only a little when she had a mind. An hour or two was enough to sustain her, despite her languorous schedule of sleeping late and working in her undergarments in our apartments aboard the *Tamerlane*. When the fire was in her, she hardly slept at all.

"I found the xenology section!" she told me. " 'Tis up on the thirty-seventh floor. Thirty-seventh! And no lift! You can't imagine how my legs feel just now. They have Carter's original journals from the Rubicon digs in the fourth millennium! The *originals!* 'Twould not let me read them—I had to look up the phototypes in one of the slide catalogs."

"Gibson's here," I said, cutting across Valka's mania for old things.

"What?" Valka froze. "You mean . . . alive?"

I told her everything.

It took some doing to find my way back down through the bowels of the Library's main silo, but in time I found the hall with its coral pillars and scrolls and paintings under glass. Valka stopped me only once to admire an ancient sketch, red on yellowed vellum, of a bearded old man.

"Da Vinci!" she said. "Hadrian, this is from Earth!" Many of the things in the archives were, and ordinarily I would like nothing better than to spend an hour or a day with Valka exploring the storied past.

But Gibson was waiting, impossible though I still found it to believe.

He wasn't in the Archivists' Grotto when he arrived, and our progress was delayed by Valka's awe of the caverns themselves. At length I asked an older scholiast—a flat-faced man in over-washed green—where I might find my old tutor. He directed us back along a winding passage to a solitary door embedded in the rock. I knocked. When no one answered, I tried the handle. It opened, and I stepped through into a small apartment. The Archivists were accorded better lodging than the novices were in their barracks on the surface. Glass globes full of the white-glowing algae hung on the walls, casting rippling lines on the rough stone walls like sunlight on the surface of the water.

It was nothing extravagant. An old couch flattened by decades of service, a coffee table before it, a writing desk in one corner beneath hollows in the rock into which metal shelves had been placed. Books lay about everywhere—evidence that Gibson, too, had not changed in our long separation. His chambers were still cluttered, the chaos of his living space a necessary sacrifice to build the order of his mind.

Smiling, I called out, "Gibson?" I paused a beat to take a step into the chamber, pitching my voice toward the arch that opened in the back of the room. "Gibson, it's Hadrian."

"Perhaps he's working," Valka said.

"Hadrian?" The familiar voice rose from the back room. "Just a moment!"

All at once, a strange uneasiness gripped me, as though I were a plebeian day laborer bringing some farm girl home to meet his parents. A giddiness and an odd fear mingled in my chest, wrestling with one another.

I needn't have feared.

The old scholiast appeared a moment later, still barefoot, robe belted about his waist, brass badges gleaming on his sash. He stopped short when he saw I was not alone. "Oh!" he said.

Two chapters of my life—two very different lives—stood represented in those two people: the woman I loved, and the man who had raised me. Seeing each of them at once I felt at once the boy of nineteen and the man of six score and three.

"You must be Valka," Gibson said, coming forward, his scholiast training keeping the old face flat. Despite the cane he held, he took Valka's hand in both his own. I could tell he was smiling beneath his mask of composure. "I am so pleased to meet you. Hadrian's told me so much."

"Only the good parts, I hope," she said, smiling up at the old man who, stooped as he was, still had an inch or two on her.

Gibson patted her clasped hands with his free one. "There was only good. Please sit! Please!" He gestured toward the flattened sofa with his cane—and it was the same cane he'd used on Devil's Rest, preserved after all these years. "I don't keep much here by way of refreshment—we all eat in the refectory—but I can put tea on, if you would like. But Hadrian doesn't take tea, of course."

"I do!" Valka said. "Let me help you."

The scholiast denied needing help, but Valka insisted, and at once the two busied themselves with the process of steeping the evil beverage. I sat bemusedly by, toying with the glove on my left hand.

"You know," Valka said when the kettle was filled and boiling, "I never thought I'd meet you." Gibson turned to look at her, smiling politely. There was something of the owl in the way he turned blinking to regard the lady, and I was reminded of old Lord Powers. "Hadrian said it's only been four years for you." Gibson bobbed his head, but did not interrupt. " 'Tis been a lot longer for us, but he's never stopped talking about you. I've always wanted to see where he came from. 'Twas not sure what to expect."

Gibson held two teacups in his hands while they waited for the kettle to boil. "Only an old man. No great mystery—certainly not after everything you both have seen."

"He told me you didn't believe him," Valka said, looking down. "I didn't believe him, either."

They were talking about me as if I weren't there, and I felt suddenly that I'd intruded on a conversation not meant for my ears. That I did not belong.

The old man glanced at me a moment before responding—and I wasn't sure if that heightened my sense of intrusion or dispelled it. "I told him I did believe him. I only don't understand."

"He told you why we're here?"

"Delving into the secrets of the universe, was it?"

Valka laughed suddenly and looked at me. "You come by your sense of drama honestly, then!"

Was it my imagination, or did Gibson actually flush to hear that?

I chuckled. "You should meet my mother."

Scholiast composure reasserted itself, and he said, "You're waiting for access to Gabriel's Archive. You hope to find some record of contact between the Mericanii and these . . . Quiet. You say the Mericanii artificial intelligences could perceive time and communicate across it. I am not a physicist, but I do not see how that is possible. One can move forward in time at varying rates; the ancients demonstrated that quite soundly. Einstein, Royse, Rosier, and so forth. But backward? Impossible."

"But if what Brethren told me is true," I said, "it would explain my visions. The Quiet are showing me things that have happened in its past, or that might happen."

"Your visions don't sound like visions to me," Gibson said. "They sound abstract. More like dreams than a holograph recording." The scholiast shook his head, and though his face remained impassive, I sensed the tiredness, the deep sadness in him. "You have grown beyond me." Valka took the cups from him and poured the tea. "Why do you suppose the creatures take my appearance?"

He had not turned to look at me, but I knew Gibson addressed his question to me. I could sense the familiar whip-crack quality of his questioning.

"I don't know," I said. "Because I thought you were dead?" No sooner had the words escaped my mouth than I realized I had only assumed Gibson was dead because the Quiet had worn his face. "I've read too many ghost stories," I said darkly, and shook my head.

Valka set her tea on the table while it cooled, crossed her arms. "Perhaps they wanted to communicate in a way you would understand?"

"Or because you trust me," Gibson said, lowering himself into his seat. "Who can say? The Chantry regulates knowledge of these ruins of yours outside these walls." He waved his stick round at the walls of the little apartment. "But even in here I never studied them." Gibson's eyes lingered on Valka's face a moment before jumping to mine. "I could never have imagined . . . this."

"No one could have," Valka said. "There are days I don't believe it myself. But 'tis true. I saw him *die,* M. Gibson."

"Tor," I corrected her, made uncomfortable by the talk and reminder of my death. I massaged my neck, remembering the painless bite of the blade as it struck off my head. The very blade that even then lay in a lockbox in the complex's barbican.

The scholiast took up his tea, face dark and strangely sad. "Just Gibson will do. Hadrian is the nearest thing to a son I have left, which I suppose . . . makes you family?" He twisted the last few words, making them a question. Gray and misty eyes flitted from each of us to the next in polite turn.

Valka understood before I did. "We're not married. I'm Tavrosi."

"Ah!" Gibson put a hand to his forehead. "I had forgotten, apologies." But Gibson was a scholiast, and scholiasts do not forget. "I am getting old . . . more than six hundred now. Please forgive me."

"We're as good as," Valka said, and smiled at me. " 'Tis been almost . . . seventy years for me? Not all at once! I've been in fugue more than he has."

My old tutor looked into the depths of his tea, as though he were some primeval sorcerer hoping to learn some secret from the leaves. "Then you know him far better than I," he said somberly. Not looking up, he continued, "I can't begin to tell you how many times these four years I've asked myself if what I did was right: helping you escape your father. I'm still not sure. But I am glad that some good has come of it." His eyes moved to Valka. "He was so lonely as a boy, you know? That castle was no place for a child. Much less two." Valka said nothing, and Gibson turned his eyes on me. "You have a sister, you know?"

"I what?" I was glad I'd no teacup of my own, for surely I'd have dropped it on the rough stone floor. *A sister?*

"Alcuin sent word here by telegraph pending my arrival, telling me all sorts of news from home. Your parents commissioned her from the High College shortly after you left. A replacement."

"Replacement?" I echoed lamely. I'd had no idea.

"Sabine Doryssa Marlowe," Gibson said, pronouncing the name with grave formality.

"Sabine," I said. My great-great-grandmother had been a Sabine. It was a good name, ancient, old as Earth herself. "I had no idea." How in nearly a century of service on Forum had I failed to learn that Alistair Marlowe had petitioned for and been granted the right to birth another child? A sister. I had a sister. "Alcuin told you?" I had not thought about Tor Alcuin in decades. My father's chief counselor and I had never been terribly close.

Tor Gibson recharged his tea from the pot and restored both cup and teapot to the table. I still could not believe it was really him, really alive and in the same room with me. "Only once. The telegraph arrived shortly before I did . . . as a courtesy, one scholiast to another. Just to let me know what had happened while I was asleep. I knew you'd fled, but there was little other reference to you in the letter. Alcuin said you were fighting the Cielcin—but I didn't think that could be true. It didn't sound like you at all."

"A lot's changed."

"I know."

A question occurred to me. "Does my father still rule?"

"Yes," Gibson answered. "He did some time offworld, it seems. Traveled to the Consortium offices at Arcturus and suchlike. He's not quite an old man."

"And Crispin?" I asked. "My mother?"

"Alive," Gibson said. "Crispin married one of Lord Albans's daughters—they have children. Your mother has all but quit Devil's Rest for Haspida. She's quite old. Word is your sister will inherit your father's seat."

I could not help myself. I laughed, the sound of it catching on the stone walls and hurled back as something hollow and tinny. After all my father's hard lessons, after the way I'd been pitted against Crispin every day of my life until I fled Delos—after my flight and our final combat in the guest suite of the Summer Palace—none of it mattered. Lord Alistair Marlowe was giving his lands and castle away to a sibling I had not even known I had. It was too rich. Still laughing, I said, "Of course she will."

Imperial lords were under no obligation to pass their title on to their eldest child. As Father had passed me over as unqualified in favor of Crispin, so it seemed Crispin had been discarded, though for what reason I could hardly guess.

"Alcuin says your sister is every inch her father's daughter," Gibson said. Was that sympathy in the old fellow's eyes?

"Of course she is."

Sensing my irritation, Valka chimed in. "On the other hand, *Doryssa* makes *Anaxander* seem almost tolerable."

I snorted.

But Gibson cut through it all. "Sabine has spent a good deal of time offworld—not so much as you, of course—but she's much younger than Crispin is now. And Alcuin believes she'll do well on the throne. Says she's the right temperament for it."

"A cold, evil bitch, is she?" I asked, bitterness rank in my voice.

"Kwatz!" Gibson exclaimed, and raised a hand to mime striking me. "That is not worthy. Of you or her."

Chastened, I bowed my head. "You're right." We sat, the three of us, in unsteady silence for some time, the light from the strange wall sconces shimmering across stone. "It doesn't matter anyway. I'm never going back." For all they had done in shaping me, Delos, Meidua, Devil's Rest, and my family were as good to me then as the figures of a fairy story or half-remembered dream. In truth, figures from fairy stories, figures like Simeon the Red, like Kasia Soulier, like the Cid Arthur and even old Cassian Powers . . . like Kharn Sagara most of all . . . seemed somehow *more* real by the light of that gleaming algae than did my own flesh and blood.

"I am sorry to tell you like this," Gibson said, and a wry, very unscholiast smile crept across his aged face. "Seem to be doing a lot of apologizing, don't I?"

"You've nothing to apologize for," I said.

The old man wrung his hands again. "I didn't ask last night: how long do you intend to stay here? Not that it's really my business."

" 'Tis!" Valka said. "And we're not sure."

"The Emperor more or less ordered me to stay out of the public eye indefinitely," I said. "After Breathnach, Bourbon, and the rest."

"And the Colosseum," Valka added, as if I could forget.

"And the Colosseum."

Gibson leaned forward and put a hand on my arm. His scholiast's control had reasserted itself, and his face was grave and empty. "Then we should count ourselves fortunate. I have missed you, my boy." He turned on Valka. "And you are someone I am *very* interested to meet. Hadrian tells me you're a lay scholar?"

Valka beamed. "A doctor. I studied xenology and archaeology at Isana University on Edda, my home."

"That's in the Demarchy?" Gibson asked. "Wonderful. And you study these things? The Quiet?"

"The best I can," she said, "as I'm sure Hadrian's told you—the fossil record is . . . sparse."

Gibson drank his tea. Leaning toward me, he said, "Hadrian, I don't think you could have found someone more qualified to help answer your questions than this."

"Don't I know it?" I said, and smiled at Valka.

She smiled back. "For the past several decades, I've mostly studied the Cielcin, of course. They seem to worship the Quiet, did Hadrian say?"

"He did," Gibson replied. "The Watchers, was it?"

"Yes," I said, "but it may be the Quiet are only one god or set of gods among many to the Cielcin."

"The Makers, do you mean?" Valka asked. "We know so little. Practically speaking, most of what I've done since I met this one is translate text and analyze artifacts collected from the battlefield. For Legion Intelligence." She smiled, and I detected a trace of the old glass-cutting sharpness in that smile. Sharpness and the bitter taste of mockery—but whether mockery of me or of herself I could not say. " 'Twas not how I expected to spend my life."

The old man was nodding along in understanding quietude. "It never is," he said. "If you had told me when I was a boy that I would be a scholiast and tutor the sons of a minor house for two generations . . . and that one of them would go on and be a Knight Victorian and battle xeno-bites, I would have laughed at you." He held the clay teacup between his twisted, bony hands. I did not dare interrupt him. I could count on one hand the number of times Tor Gibson had made reference to his earlier life. "I told you once, Hadrian: we are all pawns."

"Even the knights," I said, and laughed.

"Even the Emperor," Gibson cut in, "as I'm sure you noticed."

I thought of William XXIII, a prisoner of his rituals and his court, subject to the will of his counselors and the winds of political necessity. Such a wind had made him send me away.

"A Servant of the Servants of Earth," I said, reciting that last and seeming least of the Imperial titles. What had I told Alexander? *"Noblesse oblige."*

"You've learned much since I left you," Gibson said, nodding approvingly. "You'd have made a good lord."

"Now I never will," I said.

Gibson raised a finger. "The lessons I taught you are as salient for a knight as they are for a lord. You've not wasted anything."

"It's not that," I said, looking to Valka. "It's . . . when I left home, I wanted to be like you. I wanted to be a scholiast. I wanted to see the galaxy and learn and teach, maybe do good. I thought I could make peace with the Cielcin, but I failed."

"With two princes," Gibson said. "How many are there?"

"I don't know," I said. "But it won't matter. They don't want peace."

"We don't know that," Valka said. " 'Tis much we don't know."

I could only shake my head. "I'm not so sure."

But Gibson was smiling. "Whatever happens, Hadrian my boy, I have faith in you. Beneath all this finery and those scars you are still the young man I knew. You will find a way. And you will find the answers you are looking for." He stood suddenly, moving with a swiftness I'd not guessed was in him—forgetting as I often did that he was palatine beneath those wrinkles and that weight of years. "And I'm going to help you."

"You are?" Valka sounded delighted.

"Yes, dear lady," Gibson said, taking up his cane. "Four years is hardly time to familiarize myself with the Library—but I am an Archivist all the same. And I'll not have my star pupil stumbling through these shelves alone. The minute Arrian approves this extraneous paperwork of his, I'll help you with Gabriel's Archive. I'll have a word with the primate."

I stood too, in part from surprised joy, in part concerned for the old scholiast, afraid he might fall over. "You must come meet the prince," I said. "I was hoping to get him some instruction while he's here."

Owlish eyes blinked at me. "I'll speak to Arrian first and be along."

"May I have a word with you, sir? Gibson?" Valka asked, standing herself. "Before we climb up?"

Gibson swiveled to regard her. "Of course."

I threw Valka a curious look, but she waved me down. "I'll wait outside."

They joined me beneath Imore's statue, and we went together back along the scroll hall and up through the silo to the main building. Gibson took his leave of us outside, tottering off toward the hierarchs' offices toward the north wall.

I watched him go, bent but still tall, leaning on his cane all the while.

"I still can't believe it's really him," I said.

Valka's hand squeezed mine. "I like him. I can see where you get those old-fashioned manners of yours."

"Courtesy is *timeless*," I said, and for once Valka neither argued nor laughed.

"Are you all right?" she asked me.

"I'm happy," I said, and truly meant it. "What did you ask him about?"

She disentangled her hand from mine and wrapped the arm about my waist. "I didn't ask him anything," she said, looking up at me, bright eyes wide in her pale and lovely face. How had I ever thought her severe and unpleasant? She reached up and kissed my cheek. "I just wanted to thank him."

"For what?"

"For you."

CHAPTER 57

GABRIEL'S ARCHIVE

"I AM SORRY FOR the delay," Tor Arrian said, standing behind his desk while his daughter scribbled in her ledger. "The forms must be obeyed. William knows this, and should have sent this letter . . ." here he touched a sheaf of telegraph vellum printed with the official seals and fractal codes in the vermillion tradition required of such documents, red as blood, ". . . with you. This delay might have been avoided."

We had a full month for the paperwork to clear. The letter was straightforward enough, but the security codes were so data-dense that the telegraph—which could only transmit and receive data one bit at a time—had taken days to send and receive. The rest of the delay had no doubt been due to delays on Forum. The Emperor's time was limited and subject to demands that even I can scarcely imagine, and even the direct line he'd given me—shared only with his personal staff, men and homunculi trusted above all others—was not sufficient to extract a swift response from Honorable Caesar.

"No matter," I said.

" 'Tis given us time to explore your wonderful institution," Valka added, shifting in the seat beside me. "Truth be told, I could have waited another month."

Though he made no expression, I sensed the primate approved of this statement as he moved from behind his desk toward the fire. "No materials may be carried out of Gabriel's Archive, you understand. No recordings made. No copies." He fixed his Imperial green eyes on Valka. "I understand, Doctor Onderra, that you have Tavrosi implants that allow you to record what you see. I cannot take these from you, and as His Radiance's instructions make reference to your being granted permission to the Archive as well, I cannot bar you access. But understand that the information contained within it subject not only to our Strictures, but has been proscribed by the Writ of the Chantry as forbidden. Sharing that information is a capital offense, one which the Chantry would mount an invasion of the Demarchy to avenge. I trust you appreciate the gravity of this fact." It was not a question.

Valka nodded.

"The Mericanii nearly destroyed humanity with their machines. Their evil cannot be allowed back into the universe. We preserve the knowledge and the artifacts the God Emperor and His servants collected after the Foundation War because it is our duty. But we have a duty to mankind as well, to preserve her against the dangers represented by that same knowledge. Lord Marlowe, if you or the doctor or any of your people violate that trust, I will have no choice but to recommend to the Chantry that you be handed over to the Inquisition. Am I clear?"

Still seated, I bowed my head. "Yes, primate."

"Good," Arrian said. "You have His Radiance's blessing, and that counts for much. But we are playing with fire here. I have spoken with your Tor Gibson. He says you were a student of the Classics?"

"I still am."

"Then permit me to offer you a word of advice." The primate clasped his hands behind his back in an uncanny impersonation of the Emperor. "Not even Prometheus could play with fire without being burned."

I could sense Valka's amusement beside me, but for myself I shared the primate's absolute gravity. I may not be a devotee of Chantry religious thought—few palatines truly are, I think, preferring some watery agnosticism with a few frozen bergs of devoted language over top—but I shared the Imperial horror of the Mericanii the way a child who fears the Dark looks askance at shadows even as an old man.

"I understand," I said.

The scholiast ahead of us carried a glowsphere aloft in his hand. The device did not float as so many others did—for even the simple mechanisms of a Royse field were forbidden inside the walls of the athenaeum. Valka followed close behind with Tor Varro while Pallino and Doran followed with two others of my guard. We moved slowly down the spiral stair, feet rattling the old iron beneath us. Gibson kept us slow, one hand on the smooth rail, the other wrapped round my arm to steady him.

The light swayed, and its holder said, "Gabriel's Archive is some of the oldest construction in the entire complex." The speaker was Tor Imlarros, an old man himself, and the Curator tasked with the keeping of Gabriel's Archive and the keeping of the keys. "Never thought in all my days I'd see the doors opened. Not been open since Aramini's day—that was when Gabriel II ordered it built and sealed."

"Aramini?" Valka asked.

"Tor Aramini was the architect. Designed this place. He was Gabriel's own brother—the primates are usually frustrated princes, you know?" The light bounced and swayed as we descended. Similar lights—like lonely stars—drifted among the stacks on the iron levels as we descended, the mark of some lonely scholiast at his labors. "It was Aramini that designed the locks."

"On the archive, you mean?"

"Those too," Imlarros said. "But I mean the ones that hold the sea back. We're below sea level here. You won't have seen them, but there are great channels that run ten miles from the coast to here. We keep a reservoir filled. The novices go fishing, but that's not what they're *for*."

He said this last bit with an ominous quality that all but forced Pallino to shout down from his higher step. "The hell does that mean?"

"The reservoir sits on top of Gabriel's Archive. They're meant to flood the chambers if anything ever tries to . . . you know . . . get out."

"You couldn't!" Valka sounded horrified, and stopped on the steps a few beneath Gibson and myself.

Imlarros did not break stride. His thickly accented voice drifted upward. "Those were Gabriel's orders."

"And destroy the archives?" Valka objected. "What do you mean *get out?*"

"You have to ask?" Imlarros replied. "Possibly there is some artifact of the Mericanii sealed in Gabriel's Archive."

Valka's brows knit together. "You think there's functional Mericanii technology in the sealed archives?" she asked. "And your Tor Aramini's plan was to *drown* it?"

"Who said anything about drowning?" Imlarros asked. "The reservoir is meant to shield the rest of the compound from the radiation."

"The what?" Valka almost screamed.

"Chantry's orders. There are atomics planted between Gabriel's Archive and the rest of the compound. The water is meant as insulation. To protect the Library above."

Valka's words came back tighter, more controlled. "That's totally barbaric."

Imlarros shrugged again. "There is no cause for alarm, doctor. We do not think there is any danger, not after so many years."

"Famous last words," Pallino remarked from the rear.

"The Chantry is thorough. They tolerate our operations, but the scholiasts have always made them uncomfortable. Religion and science are old enemies," Imlarros said.

Gibson cleared his throat, and in a thin voice strained by the descent, said, "They're not, brother. Only fools think so."

For a third time, Imlarros shrugged. "You are a philosopher, are you not, brother?"

"And you're an engineer," Gibson replied, apatheia cracking with the strain of the climb. "Stay in your house."

We came at last to the lowest level of the silo. It ran deeper than I'd thought, deeper than the tower above was tall, with halls opening far into the rock of the mesa all around, tunnels honeycombing the living rock, connecting to natural caves like those the Archivists made their home in. The floor was strange, not tiled or planked but a single piece of fused, glassy stone that flowed into the walls at the extreme edges. To one side, a space stretched high-ceilinged and wide as the silo itself, half a mile across. The omnipresent shelves fat with books and scrolls and other documents that lined the levels above were here too, pressed against the walls and into simple rows running straight across the flat floor, bolted to the glossy stone.

"The doors are up ahead," Imlarros said, leading the way with his bobbing lantern. He led us along the opening, shadows retreating from the orb in his hand. "This tunnel extends for about half a mile beneath the reservoir."

" 'Tis the archive at the far end?" Valka inquired.

"Yes," Imlarros answered her, "But it stretches all the way back to the core shaft and wraps around it in a big circle At least . . . according to Tor Aramini's blueprints. I have never seen them with my own eyes."

The doors ahead were like the doors of a hangar, huge and metallic, shining dully in the light of our glowspheres—for as we walked Varro and Valka alike shook lights of their own to life.

"Marvelous!" Valka exclaimed. "Simply marvelous!"

They must have stood fifty feet high, and nearly three times as broad. Massive gearworks studded their face and ran to either side. Somewhere along the passage's half-mile expanse, the walls had narrowed, funneling down until they stood nearly the width of the door.

Tor Imlarros approached these doors, keys jangling from a chain on his belt. Presently he produced three huge iron keys—more medieval they seemed to my eye than any artifact of the Fifth Millennium and Gabriel's day. He inserted each into a lock in turn, each twenty paces apart. By the rightmost one he stopped and pulled a series of levers in the door's face.

"Brother Varro, Brother Gibson, we must turn these at the same time. Would you oblige me?"

"I can do it!" Valka practically leaped forward.

Imlarros raised a hand. "I would prefer it if my brother scholiasts assisted me, doctor. Stricture." He said this last word as if it explained everything, which I supposed it did.

I helped Gibson forward, and the old man placed one knobby hand on the key.

"Are you all right?" I asked. His hand was trembling.

He glanced at me. "Fear is a poison," he said, and to my astonishment, spat on the stone at our feet.

Perhaps I had not gotten my sense for the dramatic from my mother at all.

"On three, brothers!" Imlarros's voice came from our left. "One. Two. Three!"

Click.

Click-click.

Nothing happened.

"Did it fucking work?" Pallino muttered from the space behind. His stage whisper caught on the hard walls and echoed far louder than intended.

Somewhere ahead of us *through* the door, a deep grinding noise arose.

Thud.

A ticking like the turning of some mighty clock resounded in that space, and the mighty gearworks began to turn, shaking off literal millennia of dust as the stainless steel teeth champed and bit for the first time since the Empire was young and the blood of the Pretender not even cold.

Gibson staggered back, and I caught him.

Valka cheered.

The bowels of the earth groaned, gears squealed, and the doors began to open. A foul air rushed out, tepid with the scent of stagnation, the stink of air undisturbed and still for too long. I was glad our light came from glowspheres, for torches surely would have guttered and burned out. The doors ground open until the yawning gap between them was wide enough for two men to pass abreast and stopped. I think I understood the levers then. They'd controlled the width of the door.

And the doors were open.

A stair ran down a long ways, descending straight for perhaps a hundred feet.

The air inside smelled foul. Gibson and I entered first, Valka close behind. As we approached the bottom of the stair, Valka held her light aloft, and its pale radiance washed over banks of metal consoles and rows of shelves lined with texts and artifacts of all description. I felt a numb dread pinching the back of my neck, and would in that moment have traded my left arm for my sword and shield-belt.

"There should be a light somewhere," Imlarros said, searching along the walls. "Our Order was not forbidden light in those days."

As he searched, Valka turned to face me, her eyes wide, face glowing in the light of her lantern. "Do you feel it? You can almost taste the history here."

"I don't like it," Pallino said. "Doran, take Gaert and scout out that way." He pointed over the centurion's shoulder down a passage to the left. "I'll take Vidan round the other way. Had, you and doctor stay here until we clear it." He turned toward Imlarros, "You said this thing makes a circuit around the core shaft?"

"According to the maps, yes."

Pallino nodded, blue eyes snapping from me back to his centurion. "Means we'll meet in the middle. Double quick. Shout if anything strikes you as off. We should be able to hear." And then he was off, grumbling the while. "Wouldn't let us bring nothing deadlier than a damn knife. I ask you . . ."

"Are all your people like that one?" Gibson asked, eyebrow raised.

Watching Pallino vanish round the bend in the path with Vidan in tow, I said, "Oh, Pallino's one of a kind."

"Hadrian, come! I can't read English!" Valka's voice interrupted us.

We'd stepped into a kind of vestibule that ran forward a hundred feet or so to the great circular hall of Gabriel's Archive. The walls were hung with paintings whose shapes barely emerged from the gloom, darkly oiled. Straight ahead, on an island in the center of the hall, was a plinth that held a single document under filter glass, safe in darkness for so many thousand years. Valka held her light up that I might read it.

The parchment inside was yellowed and badly stained by light and time, its edges crumbling, its ink fading away. The writing *was* English, but of an ancient mode. Not the block letters I knew well as Galstani, but a flowing script written in a strong hand.

"In Congress," I said in English, and translated it for Valka, following the declarative first line with a fingertip. "July 4, 1776." I squinted at the next line, at an elaborate character I decided must be a T. "The unanimous Declaration of the thirteen united . . ." I paused, realizing some piece of what this document was, and whom it had belonged to. Forcing strength into my voice, I resumed speaking. "Of the thirteen united States of America." Unbidden, my fingers curled into the familiar warding gesture, the old sign to ward off the evil eye. "Mericanii," I said, seeing that Valka did not at once comprehend. I'd known intellectually that Gabriel's Archive would be filled with artifacts belonging to the machine lords, but seeing the ancient name scrawled there on Golden Age parchment was something else entirely.

As if on cue, yellow lights flared on, springing to life with a clangor and a deep thrumming noise from sconces high on the perimeter wall. Their light cast long shadows over formless shapes—foil sheets draped over artifacts, row upon row of filing cabinets and microfilm terminals.

"I'm going to need to learn Classical English," Valka said. "I wish I'd thought of it sooner."

I patted her on the back with my gloved hand. "You have plenty of time." I moved away from the plinth, crossing toward a time-eaten standard striped red and white. A line of portraits marched along the inner wall, following along the bend of the main hall.

"Shouldn't we wait here, lord?" Tor Varro called. "For Pallino to clear the room?"

I waved him to silence.

The first showed an elderly man, pale and white-haired in a plain black suit with frilled white collar and cuffs.

WASHINGTON, the placard read. I paused. "Washington." The Brethren had mentioned Washington, had they not? But Brethren had spoken of a city. Not a man. Pondering this, I followed the line of portraits one to the next. Men and women—if mostly men—variously smiling or solemn. I remember their names: *MONROE, JACKSON, JOHNSON, ROOSEVELT, TRUMAN, FORD, DELANEY, OVERTON, PEMBROKE*. I followed the line, following Doran's route along the curving hallway until I came to the last, where the first microfilm terminators began.

FELSENBURGH.

The photograph—no painting, this one—showed a man like unto the first: white-haired and dressed in black. But where Washington was old, weak-chinned and tousle-haired, Felsenburgh's face was ageless as Kharn Sagara's and handsome, with a sharp jaw and pointed chin. He looked almost feminine, with his wavy white hair in a tail over his left shoulder. He was rapier thin, his high-collared suit more reminiscent of a military uniform than court dress, with short boots and an impassive face only hinting at a smile.

"Felsenburgh," I said. I'd heard it before, but I couldn't place it. "Why does that name sound so familiar?"

To my surprise, a voice answered. "Julian Felsenburgh was the last lord of the Mericanii." Gibson had followed me round the bend. "The last human lord, that is."

I turned from the man in the photograph. "How do you know that?"

"We all know it," Gibson said. "The scholiasts were founded not to replace machines—as is often said—but to limit the march of science to prevent a second menace like the Mericanii demons from ever threatening humanity again."

Gibson leaned on his cane. "Felsenburgh was a technocrat. A businessman. He took power promising his machines would end injustice and bring about peace. They did, and the people cheered him. When he died, the Mericanii controlled almost all of Earth, and he turned his government over to his machines."

"Columbia," I said, remembering the name Brethren had given me.

Gibson cocked an eyebrow. "I take it you learned that name on Vorgossos, too?"

I grunted my affirmative.

"Every scholiast knows the story. We are forbidden to discuss it outside the walls of our athenaea under penalty of the Inquisition. We are meant to preserve knowledge, not necessarily to proliferate it. Certainly not knowledge of the Mericanii. Or Felsenburgh. Every scholiast knows his story. It's our story." As he spoke, Gibson sank into a seat atop a low filing cabinet. Jabbing his cane up at the man in the image, he said, "He sold humanity's soul."

I was shaking my head in protest. "How is it I don't know any of this?"

Gibson raised an eyebrow. "I told you, we are forbidden to discuss the history of the Foundation War—what little we still know, that is. Under penalty of Inquisition."

"But I should have *heard of him*!" I protested. But I *had* heard of him. The name was familiar!

"Have you heard of Mao?" Gibson asked. "Or Mehmed? What about Vermeiren?" This time when I shook my head, it was only in ignorance. Gibson tapped his cane against the floor to punctuate his point. "Felsenburgh is nearly so ancient. To most of the people in the galaxy, the Earth is a goddess, not a planet. Not a place people lived. *Twenty thousand years of history,* Hadrian. Twenty thousand. To the plebeians, the Jaddian Wars—Prince Cyrus and Princess Amana—these are ancient history."

Felsenburgh was smiling down on me from his photograph. "That was only five thousand years ago."

"And how many hundred generations?" Gibson asked. "A mere thirty-one generations of your family is enough to take us back to the founding of your house. That was nigh eight thousand years ago. How many generations separate you from the God Emperor? You are his descendant—however distantly. A few hundred?" With exquisite ease, Gibson lay his cane flat on his lap. "There is more history now than even this Library can hold, much less any human mind. Felsenburgh was the great enemy of man—the father of daimons. Much of what he did and who he was is now simply the work of *the Mericanii.* Combine that span of history with the Chantry's careful policing. You ask: 'How have I not heard of Felsenburgh sooner?' I say: 'It is a miracle you have heard of him at all.'"

If you are a historian, Reader, perhaps you wonder at my ignorance. For have I not referenced the Golden Age unceasing since this account began? Have I not talked of Rome and Constantinople? Have I not spoken the names of Alexander the Macedonian and of Dante a dozen times and quoted Marcus Aurelius and Shakespeare? Kipling, Serling, and the rest? I have. All these curiosities I owed to the man before me. To Tor Gibson of Syracuse. But he could not teach me everything, try as he might. Much of what I have learned and referenced I have learned since I returned here to Nov Belgaer. A Poet-in-Exile. As I have written this account, I have read and learned much that was forgotten and buried. Read and learned because of this conversation. To arrest my own ignorance.

"Suzuha," I said, remembering at last.

"What?"

"Suzuha mentioned him—Kharn Sagara's daughter, clone . . . whatever. She mentioned him once. I didn't think to ask who he was at the time . . ." Turning, I looked back into the face of the man who had hung the noose around humanity's neck and kicked the stool. "Was it Caligula who said he wished humanity had only one neck for him to squeeze?"

Gibson looked on with me. "A common misconception. Caligula only wanted to strangle the Romans, if Suetonius is to be believed—and I'm not so sure he is."

Felsenburgh didn't look like a maniac. In his plain suit, his knowing smile might only have concealed some private joke—not the damnation of so many billion lives. Even now, the true history of the Foundation War is a mystery to me. I suspect it is a mystery to all but Brethren, who alone of all living creatures survives from those hateful days. Thinking about Brethren before the image of Felsenburgh sent a chill through me. Fewer than a million people had survived Felsenburgh's machines, almost all of them from the earliest offworld colonies.

"Do you think he knew what he was doing?" I asked. I did not look at Gibson, but peered into Julian Felsenburgh's pale blue eyes.

Tor Gibson took in a deep breath. "Do I think he thought his machines would enslave mankind and destroy it? No. I'm sure he thought he was a hero. I'm sure all these people thought they were heroes." He gestured at the line of paintings and photographs depicting the high lords of the Mericanii. "But then, so few of us truly think themselves evil. They simply think good and evil matters of opinion, and seek to impose their opinion—which is evil—on good. Nothing is evil in its beginning, it only grows that way. The Mericanii thought they were bringing peace and freedom to the world, but they couldn't control their machines." I had nothing to say, and so let the silence stretch. Gibson broke it a moment later. "Do you know the difference, Hadrian, between magic and prayer?"

Now it was my turn to be confused. "What?" I turned to look round at my old tutor.

"Humility," Gibson said, tapping his cane on the tile. "The suppliant prays to superior powers, while the magician commands inferior ones. The only problem is that the daimons were not *inferior* powers at all. Felsenburgh may have birthed his daimons—summoned them, if you will—but he could not control them. I said he sold humanity's soul. I wasn't being dramatic. Creating his machines was a Faustian bargain, one we're all still paying for. I think he had no notion what his creations might become, which is why he should never have made them." My tutor grunted in a most unscholarly way. "There is a reason why in Galstani our word for *scientist*," he said the Classical English word, "is the same as the word for *magus*."

"That's why there are scholiasts," I said, following.

"Gather all the thinking people in the galaxy in one place, put them in a tower, and teach them humility." He shook his head. "Brother Imlarros derided me as a philosopher on our climb down here, do you remember?" I did. "The Golden Age ended because men forgot philosophy in their pursuit of knowledge. They traded a love of wisdom for progress, and it destroyed them." In a small voice, he added, "The ancient Christians were right to name pride the greatest of man's sins."

"Thought I told you to stay by the doors!" Pallino came hurrying into sight, his man Vidan following on his heels.

Turning to face the chiliarch, my lictor, I said, "Well, did you find anything?"

"Room's clear," Pallino said. "But Valka and the scholiasts said you two'd wandered off."

"If the room's clear, there's no harm done," I said. "I was just looking." I gestured up at Felsenburgh, as if the ancient dictator's portrait explained everything.

Pallino made a frustrated sound and turned away. I caught him mutter something like, ". . . supposed to do my job when he won't let me?"

"Pallino!" I said, and the dark-haired officer turned. "Thank you."

We went past the portraits of the other Mericanii dictators and returned to the vestibule. Valka was still standing over the document in its plinth— or perhaps had returned to it. She did not notice my approach, but stood with head bowed, arms crossed. ". . . has obstructed the Administration of Justice, by refusing his Assent to Laws for establishing . . ."

She was speaking Classical English.

She was already speaking Classical English.

"You learned that quickly?" I was unable to keep the shock and awe from my voice.

Valka looked up. "No! No, no . . . I . . ." she smoothed her hair back behind her ears, "I had the alphabet stored already. The sounds. I'm only practicing. I've no idea what any of it means."

"Neither do I," I said.

Valka's face turned downward. "But you speak it, don't you?"

"I do!" I said. "But that doesn't mean I understand any of . . . this." I flapped my arms at the room about me, at the document, the tattered flags, the microfilm displays, and sealed cabinets. At Washington and Felsenburgh. "I think this is going to take longer than we thought, Valka."

"Longer than *you* thought, maybe," Valka said. "But I've followed you around for decades, Marlowe. Now 'tis your turn." Brushing past me, she raised her voice. "Pallino! Doran! Are we clear?" The centurion and chiliarch alike flashed all-clear signs from where they stood by one of the arched entrances to the main corridor. "Wonderful! Let's get to work!"

And work we did.

Reader, you have heard perhaps that I learned to speak the tongue of the Mericanii in a matter of days. I did not. I learned to speak the English of antiquity as a boy—as you have seen. It was *Valka* who learned in a week. The details of our lives have blurred and blended with the centuries, that we have become one flesh in the minds of the galaxy. I fear I have done her an injustice in not chronicling her work much until now: the time she spent learning Cielcin from Tanaran while I slept, the ages spent poring over scans and holographs taken from Cielcin ships after battles, and so on . . . But I have not described its details because I cannot remember them all, and because to describe all Valka learned of the Cielcin in her years working beside me would be to write quite a different sort of book.

What she learned of the Mericanii those years at Nov Belgaer would have filled at least a dozen volumes, though we wrote not a single line. By Primate Arrian's orders, half a dozen members of the Curators were posted at the gates to Gabriel's Archive to ensure none but my party went inside, nor any document came out. The great doors were left open, but a chain-link fence and gate were installed before them. With the primate's consent, I posted as many of my own men on the gate—anything to ensure the protection of the Archive and to forestall Tor Aramini's bombs.

Of those days in the Archive, I shall say little. Much of what we read and discovered was meaningless to either of us: records of men and events and places unknown. Much of the microfilm had rotted, and many of the documents crumbled in gloved fingers, forcing us to resort to tools.

Valka glowed every day. The doctor was in her element, her joy plain to see. I wondered at the scholiasts' strange sufferance of her. They knew she was Tavrosi. Perhaps they underestimated the fidelity of her memory—or perhaps they hoped the secrets of their library would get out.

Who can say? I did not ask Arrian or Imlarros—I did not even ask Gibson. We were allowed to read and to study and granted as much time as we desired in that pursuit. None challenged us, and no summons came.

A year passed, and two.

While Valka and I turned through Gabriel's Archive with Gibson and Varro at our side, the men enjoyed their well-deserved rest. A cheer went throughout the *Tamerlane,* I learned, when they got the news, and another when Corvo informed the soldiers their time in Sevrast would count against their service. The twenty-year rule governing time in the Legions had been suspended in the face of the Cielcin crisis—soldiers served for life in those days—but each man's clock still counted the days, hoping for an end to the violence it seemed would never come.

The governor-general had permitted us to build a camp on the deserted island of Thessa. The first of our vacationers set about landing prefabricated dormitory units and outbuildings to accommodate approximately five hundred troops at a time, with each group given six months' leave to enjoy the island, to swim and fish and hunt in the high grove. Smaller groups were permitted to sail—literally sail—from Thessa to the surrounding isles of Racha, Jara, and Gurra, where there were small towns that welcomed half a hundred soldiers for their stories and their coin. How many pleb bastards were conceived on fishermen's daughters in those years I dare not guess—though I saw the girls when my time to visit Thessa came, young things vanishing into barracks or the shadows of tall trees for an hour or a night. In Aea, to this day, it is not uncommon to hear a man boast or woman say with pride that the blood of Marlowe's soldiers runs in his veins or through her heart.

The blood of the devil.

The devil . . . I have been called a devil since the day I was born, praised as the Emperor's Demon in White. But I have met true demons—Cielcin and machine.

I am not one of them.

CHAPTER 58

ISLAND IN TIME

GABRIEL'S ARCHIVE WAS LESS an archive and more an attic. It was an uncurated museum of artifacts taken from Old Earth, things which now the Chantry and Throne had decided were better left buried.

But there were reports, records put down by technicians of Avalon's service dating back to the first millennium: accounts written by men and women who had stormed the great pyramids of the machines on Earth. But even these records are confused. The microfilm damaged or pages time-eaten, whole passages redacted, the originals lost or else buried in some other file in the chamber around us. They spoke of bodies bracketed to beds, wired together, kept alive with feeding tubes. Banks of them.

Matrices.

Faded prints showed distended bodies and corpses swollen with strange growths. They reminded me of Brethren, the way that eldritch horror's arms had split and branched. Too many hands. Too many elbows. Failed genetic experiments? Other reports detailed empty cities, empty continents. All of Earth emptied to fill those ghastly pyramids.

None of the old documents said why.

I have told you Gabriel's Archive carved a ring around the base of the great library's silo, but this is too simple a picture. Paths split from the main ring-walk and branched inward and out like the spokes of a wheel, leading to outer wards and sections kept behind sealed doors. These took months for the scholiasts to labor at opening, careful always not to disturb the artifacts. But the halls behind contained only more of the same.

If I was frustrated, Valka did not seem to notice. Three years passed and her ardor did not dim an instant. More often than not, I would wander the halls of Gabriel's Archive, charting its side passages and turns, returning after hours to find her still patiently flipping through page after page of

material, or sitting at a rusted stool before a microfilm terminal, cells clicking one to the next. She hadn't even noticed I'd left.

"I never realized the Mericanii established so many offworld colonies,"
she said, looking up from her careful study of a dossier printed on translucent crystal paper. "Fifty-two! And all slower than light!"

I rose from the spot on the floor where I'd been seated, my eyes worn
out from reading, mind spread thin from the day's labor. "Fifty-two?" The
number sounded familiar. "That number's popped up a few times."

"The daughters of Columbia," Valka said, not stirring from her work.
"There were fifty-two daughters of Columbia. Other . . . well, you would
call them daimons. But then, what don't you *anaryoch* call daimons?"

Other daimons . . .

Other devils . . .

"One for each colony?" I crossed my arms, peered over her shoulder.

"Olympia, Denver, Baltimore, Atlanta . . ." Valka wasn't reading—not
the page before her, at any rate. I couldn't see her face, but I knew
from her tone that she recited some page she'd read before. "Utah,
Yellowstone . . ."

"I know Yellowstone," I said. "We call it Renaissance now."

"Epsilon Eridani," Valka said, naming the planet's star. " 'Tis near Old
Earth." She shuffled the crystal pages on the reading desk. "A lot of these
colonies have Imperial cities built overtop them. Your Avalon was one of
very few offworld colonies not established by the Mericanii in the early
days. You took the rest from the machines." Avalon had been the ancestral
home of the Aventine House, where the kings of lost Britain—driven from
Old Earth by some nameless enemy in the years before the Mericanii conquered Earth—had fled.

Our studies were punctuated by such conversations, some detail catching
our attention once or twice a day for days on end. I kept expecting to find
references to figures or places from history I knew. But of Marcus Aurelius
and Alexander there was no sign, and I wondered if the shortness of life
common to all men in those days had not narrowed their appreciation of
time, so that the Caesars seemed as remote to Washington and Felsenburgh
as they seemed to me, though the ages between myself and the Mericanii
stretched ten times so long as between the Mericanii and classical antiquity.

Increasingly, I was amazed by the fact that anything had survived at all.
There were no holographs of Earth or her devastation in the archive—such
things, I imagined, were hoarded by the Chantry on Vesperad or on one of
their other planetary holdings. But there was documentation of the

Aventine House's—then still House Windsor's—efforts to salvage the wealth of Earth's history. Expeditions to Rome, to London, to Washington—this time clearly a place and not the elderly lord in the paintings—to Jerusalem and Constantinople, to Beijing, Tokyo, Singapore, and beyond. They told of the efforts made to evacuate libraries and museums. One document alluded to Avalon's helping the Museum Catholic adorators transport their holy city brick by brick from Earth to Caritas, where it remains in medieval splendor to this day.

More than the rest, *that* detail connected these ancient myths to the present day. There were Museum Catholic adorators dwelling in the Redtine Mountains above Meidua. Gibson had taught me about them as a boy . . . That was how I'd come to recognize Milton and Dante in the mouth of Kharn Sagara.

Gibson . . .

Gibson joined us so often as he was able, perhaps once or twice each week. Despite his age and fading vision, he had his duties as an archivist to keep up. *Because* of his age, the climb down to—and worse, back up from—Gabriel's Archive was a torment, but one the old man endured because I went.

But every evening, when Valka remained in the archive below, I would climb up again into the misty twilight and walk the gardens and the yards with Gibson as I had when I was a boy. If Mother Earth does indeed hear our prayers—or if there is a God in some heaven to administer perfect justice—I am not certain what I did to deserve those years. I had been given an island in time, a haven and refuge from all that had passed before and what must follow. I had done violence, and suffered violence in return. Cassian Powers once said to me that we are lucky no man gets what he deserves . . . or perhaps it was Raine Smythe. I no longer remember. Whoever it was, I understand them. For what I've done in my time—even so long ago—I did not deserve such happiness. My father had taken Gibson from me, and Fate or Chance had restored him. I had him back, and Valka with me—her and all my friends. Those years on Colchis were perfect, or nearly so.

I only wish that Switch had been there.

I should not have sent him away.

He *had* betrayed me. But what does it say of a man that he cannot forgive his closest friend? That I was young, I suppose. The fury that once had filled my veins with white light was faded to dull twilight, and regret came like the dawn.

"Is something the matter, Hadrian?" Gibson asked me, his cane picking out joints in the stone before us as we walked. The sun was emerging from behind Atlas where the gas giant hung heavy in the sky, falling through a narrow slice of sky between planet and horizon, carving deep shadows across the athenaeum's low towers and the face of the planet above, throwing two smaller, distant moons into sharp relief.

Were it not for the strangeness of the sky, the salt wind and spray of the sea might have been that of home. "No, no!" I said, and told him the truth. "I wish we'd found more in the archives, but for the first time in a long time . . . I really am . . . happy."

Happy. The word didn't even seem real.

"It's only been four years!" Gibson said. "No one's been through the materials in that archive since they were brought here. It's no wonder you've not had more success." He was right, and I knew it. I *had,* I think, expected some great revelation, the truth unrolled before me like a map. We imagine the archaeologist as an intrepid explorer, penetrating dark jungles, plumbing mountain caves for lost cities and gold. My first adventure with Valka at Calagah on Emesh was such a thing, culminating in the vanishing chamber and my first vision. But much of Valka's stock and trade was simply this: ages of dreary scholarship with no developments to speak of.

We tarried a moment in the espaliered shadow of a stone wall. "You don't think the Chantry went through the archive before it came here, do you?"

Gibson frowned. "Anything is possible, my boy. But this place . . . you did not see the orbital defenses? The fleet protecting this place? Nov Belgaer is one of the places that things go to disappear. If what you seek is not here . . . then where is it?"

"Kharn Sagara didn't know," I said.

"Vorgossos doesn't have it. Suppose we do not have it. Perhaps no one knows."

"Sagara's daimon knew *something,*" I said. "I wish I'd had more time with it . . ." Frustrated fingers ran through my hair, seeming of their own accord. "Seek them at the highest place, they said. At the bottom of the world. What does that even mean?" Unlike the Gibson of my visions, the real one only raised his eyebrows. "I hate riddles," I snapped, and leaned against a clear patch beneath the trailing vines.

My old tutor kept walking, leaving me to feel the fool beneath the trailing plants. "I won't hazard a guess," he said evenly. We began climbing a narrow stair that pierced the wall of an inner courtyard and climbed upward. "You're leaving for Thessa soon, are you not?"

"End of the week," I said. "Going on five years here now, most of the crew have had their shore leave. The officers are in for their turn soon. Our ship's doctor's insisted I join them." I paused, expecting that Gibson would have something to say to that, but he surprised me by keeping quiet. "It'll be a challenge dragging Valka away from her studies."

Gibson did speak then, saying, "She is tenacious, that one."

"If there's anything in the archive to find, she'll find it."

We came to the top of the stair and followed a covered wall-walk over the inner yard to where the outer wall of the compound sat in splendor upon the crown of the mesa. The monastery on the crag loomed above like a crooked finger, a spur of the mountains thrust toward the sky. Gibson spoke after a moment's pause to collect his breath. "I must say, I am surprised that you are not keeping up with her. I seem to recall a certain young man who wanted nothing more in all the universe than to be a scholiast." Gray eyes twinkled at me through their fog.

"I am not that young man." Again, Gibson said nothing, only turned and kept walking. I followed after him.

"Perhaps not," Tor Gibson said, halting a moment in the shadow of a rounded arch. It was easy to forget how tall he was, despite his years. Tall as any king. "But I am not convinced these things change us, Hadrian. Our experiences are only garments. You are not the Ship of Theseus."

I twitched, peered into Gibson's face. The eyes were still a misty gray, not green and shining. His nose was still slashed with the criminal's mark. Only a coincidence. But there are no coincidences, only incidents converging on truth, pointing as if to some higher world.

"Theseus . . ." I turned away. "I suppose *he* didn't change, even when his ship did."

"The whole tree is present in the seed, they say," said Gibson, one hand on the stone rail. "The whole man in the embryo." I could feel his eyes watching me through their dim haze. "You are not so different now than you were then. Only grown into yourself."

My left hand flexed beneath the glove. After so many years awake, the scars were familiar and comfortable. "Well then, I'm not who I expected."

"We have had this conversation before," Gibson said. "Who is? I'd wager Crispin is not the man you expected him to be either."

"Crispin was always Father's son."

"Crispin was *not* your father's son at all." Gibson clicked the brass nib of his cane on the ground, reminding me suddenly of Raine Smythe—though the late tribune had her stick only as an affectation. "You are."

I felt the word escape through a jaw suddenly wired shut. "What?"

Face in shadow, Gibson smiled. "Peace, boy." He reached out and patted me on the shoulder. "You forget, I knew Alistair when he was young. His father's death shook him. Lord Timon was a kindly man, but indulgent. Alistair was afraid of becoming him, just as you are afraid of becoming Alistair."

"I'm not afraid of him."

The scholiast smiled, another breach of his expected composure. "Of course you're not. You're afraid of *you*." He'd taken a step or two back and prodded me in the chest with his cane. "Eh? You look in the mirror and see those eyes of yours and worry that you *are* him. But that worry makes you more like him than anything else. He feared to become your grandfather . . . so that core?" He held two fingers a micron apart. "That trait? That's the same." He inclined his head at the next set of stairs behind me. "I'd like to go up on the wall."

When we'd climbed the spiral stair in one of the wall's drum towers and come out on the ramparts, he said, "There is one important difference between you, though."

"What that?"

"You are not alone. Alistair always was. Your mother never wanted him. They were married young and that hurt him more than he let on. His father was murdered, his mother locked herself in Devil's Rest and never came down from her tower. He had no friends." Gibson fell silent a moment, before adding, "Your doctor redeems you."

I smiled, came to a stop overlooking the water as we had done together a thousand times, here on Colchis and on Delos before. "Valka," I said, suddenly unable to keep down my crooked smile. Below us, the water of the reservoir washed against the foundation of the mesa. I could see some brothers of the Order fishing on a pier far below—and below them and water, Tor Aramini's atomics lurked at their grim posts should some evil seek to escape the vaults of Gabriel's Archive with Valka deep below.

"Do not lose her, Hadrian," he said, speaking in a voice I'd never heard before. The familiar sparkling serenity was gone, and it seemed it was not Tor Gibson who spoke to me at all, but some other, older voice. "We live in other people," it said. "They keep us human."

"I won't lose her," I said, smiling warmly at the older man. "I won't lose you, either." I looked at Gibson, astonished at the gravity—the emotion—in that so-familiar voice. Looking at him, I saw only the scholiast I'd always known, and dared for the first time to ask. "Who were you? Before?"

"Before I was embraced by the Order?" Gibson asked. He looked out over the reservoir, and for a moment I thought he would say nothing. "What does it matter? I am what you see."

"It matters to me." I placed a hand on his arm.

Gibson did not move except to turn his face toward the setting sun where it ran between Atlas and the horizon. "No," he said. "It doesn't." But when he faced me again, he smiled. "Perhaps one day."

Neither of us spoke for a long time. The distant cry of gulls might have come from the waters of childhood, and though the sky was strange the wind tasted the same. Perhaps Gibson was right. Standing with the old man beside me and the waters below, I felt like the boy who'd stood upon the ramparts of Devil's Rest the day Sir Felix scourged Gibson for the crime of abetting my escape. *The seed and the tree,* I thought. Maybe Gibson was right, maybe they were not so different after all.

"I wish you were going to Thessa with us," I said without preamble.

Gibson rested his cane between merlons like worn-down teeth and leaned against the ramparts. "So do I, dear boy. So do I. But I will never leave this athenaeum. Never again."

"I could file to evoke you," I said. A Writ of Evocation would allow a bound scholiast to leave his cloister. Varro had such a thing, as did every scholiast who served outside the walls of an athenaeum.

"Arrian would not grant it," Gibson said. "And he should not. A year's sabbatical on an island is not cause to suspend my vows." He was right.

"Never fear," he said, and patted me on the back. "I will be here when you return."

CHAPTER 59

ISLAND IN THE SUN

THOUGH GODODDIN WAS MY destiny, Thessa is where my story ends.

Like Emesh's stony southlands, the Sevrast Islands on Colchis were the remnants of long-extinct volcanism, craggy climes snarling from the sea like the teeth of some forgotten dragon. Though towns and fishing villages dotted the others, Thessa stood alone, apart, and uninhabited, a wide and mossy crescent protecting a beach of black sand.

The locals called it *the Rock,* for on the sides facing the other isles gray cliffs rose and shoals snarled and threatened to smash their fishing junks to flinders, but the far side—the inside—was gentle, the crescent's arms wide and inviting. Groves of leafy trees alien to me stood green and yellowing on the shelves above the beach where rows of white buildings stood on stilts far back from the water's edge. They'd been flown down from orbit by our people and set up, having been purchased from one of the Consortium carriers that had been in parking orbit at the time.

"I'd rather have stayed in the city," Alexander said. "At least there was civilization there . . . if you can call it that."

Pallino grunted from the row beside. "The fresh air will do you good, lad," he said. "Me, I'm glad to see Elara again. Going on five months now since I was last on the *Tamerlane.* Long time for a man to go it alone. You should get you one of these local girls I hear tell of. Bet you none of them's ever seen a *prince* before."

"A plebeian?" Alexander made a face like Pallino had suggested he bed a horse.

"Aye, a plebeian," the chiliarch said. "And what's wrong with plebeians, lad? *I* was a plebeian."

Seeing a way out for himself, the prince replied, "Well, I wouldn't touch you, either."

Doran and the others hooted. Pallino grinned. "Well done, lad! You're learning!"

Alexander was grinning too.

Our chamber, I remember, was small. The white walls and floor and ceiling recalled for me nothing so much as a ship's medica. A small number of mine and Valka's effects had been brought down from the *Tamerlane*. The bedclothes, the coffee table, a chaise and armchair—certain small articles of clothing. The contrast evinced by my antique taste clashing with the utilitarian whiteness put me in mind of Sir Elomas's camp at Calagah. When I told Valka this she wrapped an arm around me.

"Let's hope it ends differently."

After a brief time together, we went down into the camp. With nothing to do in its parking orbit, the *Tamerlane* had been left in the hands of its secondary crew under Commander Roderick Halford—a good and reliable officer. I knew him only a little, but it had been he who saved us at Nagapur when pirates attacked the sleeping *Tamerlane*. He was more than capable of holding the ship in peaceful orbit around a heavily guarded planet.

Thus free from her duties, Otavia Corvo greeted us as we made the journey downslope from the camp on its stone shelf to the beach below. Incredibly, she had abandoned her black uniform in favor of a white swimmer's leotard that hugged every chiseled line and arc of her Amazonian form. Similar signs of relaxed discipline showed all over the camp. Men and women alike swam naked or lay thus in the sun. Still more sat drinking in a circle round a bonfire singing loudly, though the sun was still high. A half dozen sailing ships stood at anchor a ways out in the bay, and I saw faces I did not recognize in among the officers I knew: peasant girls in plain dresses—or none—their faces reddened or tan with exposure. And the Irchtani were present—Udax and Barda and a few dozen of their countrymen, there at my invitation.

A subtle quiet formed around Valka and myself. Corvo may have been captain, but I was *Lord Marlowe*. That was something else entirely. And like a fool I still wore my boots and tunic and the glove that covered my mangled arm. I had abandoned my cape when we left Aea.

There were at least three hundred of them, men and women and xeno-bites. I sensed the quiet spreading round me like a drop of blood in a glass of water. Did they expect me to say something? To order them to keep it together or to pack it all in? I looked round at them, my friends and offi-cers. For some reason, my mind went to the Emperor's arrival at the ball succeeding my triumph, all the pomp and circumstance of his entry to *Far Beyond the Sun*. His Radiance had said almost nothing, so I said almost nothing in turn. Being me, I was not quite so tight-lipped as the Emperor, but I tried. "Thank you all," I said, raising my voice to carry across the beach, "for all you've done. For all you will do. This is only a small repay-ment, but enjoy yourselves to the full! You've earned it!" And with that I unclasped my belt and threw it on a chair that waited near at hand. I then drew my tunic up and over my head and the sleeveless shirt beneath it before working on the glove's clasps. A cheer went up as I did this, for in doing it I proclaimed that I was one of them, and not above. I thought again of the table in the Emperor's study surrounded by statues of the Cid Arthur's knights. A round table, so that Caesar—like Arthur before him—would not sit above his counselors, would sit with them as equals. I do not think the Imperial table anything more than a symbol, but to me the ideal it represented was real.

I hoped my people knew that.

The awkward moment passed, I turned to a junior man and ordered him to carry my effects back to my chambers. "No, no," Valka interjected, puting a hand on my arm. "I'll go," she said. I was about to protest, but she said, " 'Twill give me the opportunity to change out of this." She plucked at her wine-dark jacket, indicating her boots and jodhpurs, the full outfit she wore. "Give me your boots." I watched her go, and when at last I turned away, I caught Otavia watching me, a smile on her lips.

"What?" I asked.

She shook her head.

It was the first of many days and many nights we spent at Thessa. Per-haps it is selfish that we took nearly a year's repose upon an island at the margins of a world itself on the edge of civilization—as far from the fight-ing as any Imperial colony might be. Perhaps it was ungrateful, for while we lingered upon the margins of civilized space men fought and died even still. But have mercy, Reader, for my soldiers' sake. For Captain Corvo and Commander Durand. For Aristedes and Koskinen, for White and Varro, Okoyo and Pherrine. Have mercy for Pallino, Elara, and Siran. For Crim and Ilex—who deserved a moment of happiness in their lives of violence.

Have mercy on Valka, whose patience and long suffering by my side deserved the reward of the Library and this vacation.

You need spare no mercy for me. I have had my repayment in the laughter and song of my friends and in that little space in time we carved for ourselves, stolen from an uncaring universe. Keep your condemnations to yourself, and trouble not their ghosts.

Barefoot then I strode across black glass sand made pleasantly warm by the distant sun and joined Pallino and some of the other soldiers—Doran and Oro and Petros, captain of the Fifth Cohort—where they'd gathered with some of the enlisted men to watch the others fighting. Crim stood bare-chested in the ring, hands wrapped in gauze and ready.

"Noyn jitat!" he swore, prodding a thin scratch on his shoulder. "I said no claws, man!"

Udax clicked his beak. "You humans are so soft!"

"Do you want me to pull a knife?" Crim said. "Because I can do that." He grinned, all teeth. "Just say the word, my feathered friend!"

Before the Irchtani could respond *aye*—as I felt certain he would—I raised my voice. "Let's not be spilling blood on our first day, friends!"

A chorus of groans went up from the men around, and Oro said, "For a man they call *the devil,* sir, you sure walk the straight and narrow."

"You want to lose an eye in sport, son, that's your business," I said. "But give it a day or two. The shuttles haven't even dusted off yet!" Glancing up, I saw their raven-hunched shapes on the stony shelf above, watching like roosting gargoyles.

Sotto voce, Pallino put in, "You don't want to lose an eye, Oro."

"You joining in, lord?" asked one of the decurions, a woman whose name I no longer remember. "I've got two kaspum on the bird man."

"And bet against Crim?" I asked. "Not on your life, soldier." I rolled my head on my shoulders. "But I'll take next!" The groans of the crowd turned to surprised hooting.

Next turned out to be another of the centurions, one of the newer recruits we'd picked up on our latest return to Forum. Someone had found fighting wraps for my hands, and the fellow did his best awkward imitation of a bow. He did not stand for long. Though the man was a centurion, he was green as any of that higher rank might come—they were training them fast and sloppily in those days, desperate to replace the soldiers lost in the fighting. But that did not matter on that island in the sun.

I raised a hand in triumph, and the men clapped and cheered. Turning, I caught sight of golden eyes twinkling in the crowd. Was Valka back? I doubled back to look, but she was gone. Bowing out gracefully—lingering just long enough to help the centurion to his feet and to pass him my cut of the betting as the winner—I pushed past Pallino and through the crowd.

Where had she gone?

"Valka?"

There! I spied a scarlet parasol moving among the rocks on the rugged path that ran back toward the shelf above and our encampment. Though I did not see her, I knew the parasol must belong to Valka. Who else would so hide from the sun? But why was she leaving again? Had the fighting upset her? She could be so unpredictable. A lump formed in my throat, and I hurried on, chasing her up the slope. Always the red parasol bobbed ahead and above, just out of sight.

"Valka!"

She'd gone around the bend, following a path I'd not seen before that ran along the cliff's edge above the shore below to where gray stone and red thrust out like a finger over the sea.

And there she was—standing, by pure chance—on the very spot where this story ends. A cairn stands there now, a pile built of black stone hauled from Thessa's higher climes.

I built it brick by brick.

But where now is only silence, wind, and the cry of gulls, then there was laughter.

Valka wore naught but sandals and a swimsuit of black edged with a red dark as old wine. It matched her hair. The parasol I had never seen before—had she bought it in Aea? It had a Nipponese quality to it, ribbed and painted with a scattering of white cherry blossoms. Her hair was up in its customary knot upon her crown, loose strands playing about her ears.

"You caught me!" she said, and gestured at the cliff's point around us. "I wanted to show you this! I found it when I climbed back up. 'Tis beautiful, is it not?"

Looking at her and not the sea unrolled like a carpet beneath us, I said, "It is."

She smiled knowingly, winged eyebrows rising. "You're not looking?"

"At what?" I kissed her.

Above our heads, Atlas turned his mottled face, embarrassed, his more distant moons hurtling their slow procession across the sky. One even then clipped the edge of the golden sun and spread its shadow on the day.

"The light is strange here," Valka said, leaning against me, her parasol forming a little shield above our heads, a little space made just for us. From our height, I saw the behemoth shapes of other islands crouched on the horizon, and spied the odd ship plying between them. None came to Thessa. "Thank you for bringing me here," she said at last. "The Library . . . 'twas worth the wait." Her breath was warm against my chest.

We did not speak then for what seemed a long time, only stood there, half-embraced. How strange a pair were we! The palatine and the Tavrosi. The reluctant soldier and the xenologist, each a barbarian to the other.

"We could stay, you know?" I said, taking the parasol from her and holding it for a time. "We could stay on this moon forever."

"No we can't," she said. "But we can't leave, either. We don't have what we came for." Her fingers found the white shell I wore about my neck. She plucked at it—so small a gesture to lift so large a mystery. I had pulled it from a dream, and yet it was real, tangible as the hand that held it. "I never thought—when I left Edda—that 'twould be like this. I'm a scientist, Hadrian. Not a . . ."

"A witch?"

She thumped me, but laughed. "Precisely."

The faint taste of mint glowed on her tongue as she pushed it into my mouth and pushed out a hundred years of care. The world narrowed until its horizon was bounded by the edge of that parasol, and there was nothing but us. Nothing but her. How rare and precious are such moments measured against the length and horror of life! Such moments as make the rest of it worth enduring.

"Is this a private party, or can anybody join?"

Otavia Corvo stood arms crossed about twenty paces away, hair floating in the breeze.

Valka pulled away, almost, *almost* embarrassed. I caught her hand, returned her parasol. There was a strange expression on the tall captain's face, but it gave way to wry bemusement as she said, "So are you two just going to ignore the rest of us this whole stay? You've been up here about an hour. I'm surprised you're still dressed."

"Otavia!" Valka said.

The captain laughed. "Siran's back with the fishermen! She took some of the lads out for food. Fire's going, and I just got a wave from Halford, sun'll be down soon." She turned her back and shrugged her massive shoulders. "Hate to see you both tumble off the cliff rolling around up here."

I had not known it was still possible for me to blush at that age, but there it was. I was glad neither woman saw.

The food was excellent. And so much of it! The fishing ships, it turned out, had not come to carry the islands' daughters to us, but had been chartered by the governor-general to see our men were fed. The seas of Colchis were rich, and the waters off Thessa and the other Sevrasts were richer still, and teemed with cod and seabass and snapper. Thus we feasted each night.

"Folk think the best fish is the freshest!" said Lem, the patrician eolderman of the fishers and cooks who had been hired to serve us at Thessa. He was turning a rack of whole trout over smoking coals as he spoke. "But the Nipponese like to age it a few days in the icebox. Me, I can't tell!"

Pallino hovered round each night, discussing cookery with the local men and the women who came with them, arguing more often than not. Nearly each day Siran went with the fishers, taking various of her soldiers with her. She was never far from the eolderman, and I wondered at that. "It's like home," she said, speaking of Emesh. "Only the weather's better! And the sky! Hadrian, the sky!"

It was good to see my people—my friends—so happy. They deserved it. I recall one night I sat about the fire, listening to Pallino tell his story about his lost eye and tramway security—laughing though I knew it well. Lorian Aristedes had sat nearby, muttering with some plebeian girl. Then the two went off into the dark, and when they reappeared—much later and much disheveled—one soldier pressed a beer into the young officer's hands.

They deserved peace. Deserved more than I could give.

But none of us gets what we deserve, good or ill. Such has been my blessing—and their curse. I have been to Thessa recently. The buildings are still there. Those prefabricated structures—wrought of plastic and alumglass—were made to out-sit the centuries. They have not been moved. Wandering there, I was a lonely ghost, recalling the echoes of whoops and laughter, of cries and song. But they are gone now.

They are gone.

CHAPTER 60

THE LIBRARY AGAIN

"THIS *CAN'T* BE ALL there is . . ." Valka said for the hundred thousandth time. We'd been back at Nov Belgaer for months, and though I had been slow to return to the dusty archive, Valka had taken to it with her usual fervor, sifting through records and filing cabinets with mechanical abandon. "So much of this . . . 'tis meaningless now. Colony surveys, shipping manifests, tax records . . . do we need genetics records for every human embryo shipped to the Atlanta colony in . . ." she squinted at the shipping manifest, ". . . 2964 CE? What was that? A thousand years before the Advent?"

"Give or take," I said, though I thought it was nearer eight hundred. Things moved slower in those days, before mankind broke the speed of light on lonely Avalon as iron darkness closed in all around.

"Why classify this? Why bury it in a sealed vault beneath a library on the edge of nowhere? This is not *worth* classifying!" She brandished the ancient document like an accusation, crystal paper flexing. "Everyone knows the Mericanii were the first to use embryo banks for colonies. The Consortium *still does!* 'Tis not a secret!" She broke off, pinching her nose with one cotton-gloved hand. "I do not understand you *anaryoch*. Do you simply see *Mericanii* and seal it away? I thought these people were supposed to be *scientists!* Science means *to know,* not to *close your fucking eyes!* These are records! Nothing is going to get *out!*"

We were alone, which was well. I did not fancy sitting through another long debate between Valka and Tor Imlarros, nor one of Valka and Gibson's Socratic back-and-forths. I was tired, and I shared Valka's frustration with the turning of events. We had been on Colchis for nearly six years.

"This can't be all there is . . ." Valka said again. "Was Gabriel stupid? Did he not know what he had? Why would anyone build something this far underground to hide tax receipts from an empire that no longer exists?" She glared at me. "Are you people so damned paranoid?"

I held her gaze a moment, shrugged. "You know what they were, Valka. You saw Brethren."

"Brethren . . ." She made the word a curse before cursing some more in an argot of Nordei and her native Panthai. "We could use it right now. At least it seemed to answer your questions. Instead we've got miles of shipping manifests to dig through."

"It's not like we've learned *nothing*," I said, trying to be encouraging. I wasn't wrong. We'd learned much of the Golden Age that I had never heard before. Felsenburgh had taken power promising to end the Mericanii war with the powers of Eurasia and the East. He'd united his fragmented country until its dominion stretched from pole to Earth's pole and across the face of her moon. He'd freed Europe from subjugation—though her kings in exile on the moons of Jupiter did not return, but fled beyond the circles of the Sun for worlds like Avalon. They called him *Liberator,* though he was the first lord of the Mericanii not to abdicate his throne in their White Palace when his time was done. He held power until his death when—breaking with four hundred years of tradition—he named his successor to the throne.

His daughter, the computer god Columbia.

Her name meant *peace,* and peace came with her. And her fifty-two daughters went out across the stars to build new cities on new hills, white and shining beneath their pyramids. And so the daughters of the machines broke bread with the exiled kings of man and for a time there was peace, and throughout the dominion of the machines mankind was saved from war, from hunger and disease—from everything but death. It had been Columbia who first pioneered the genetic advancements that formed the basis of the life extension therapies still employed today. For into their iron hands was given the maintenance and ordering of all things: from the production of food to the construction of cities. Mankind at last had achieved perfect order, and all it cost those ancients was their dignity and their souls. They who had created the machines lived as little more than pets, than sheep penned and shepherded by those beings which once man had shepherded himself.

They had even taken over our reproduction, overseeing the development of children in tanks like the tank I myself had been born from. Holy Mother Earth—had they created that technology? It was no wonder the Chantry sought to hide so much.

In the end, the machines took everything, and each man and woman retreated into virtual dreams and lived like Homer's lotus eaters, never tasting true life, with all its joys and sorrows. Mankind had all they wanted and infinite leisure to enjoy it in. Never mind that none of it was real.

Not one of the records we found suggested why the machines turned against their makers.

But turn they had, and in time the dreamers were rounded up by the same machines that had for decades served as nursemaids. The old went first into the white pyramids the daughters of Columbia raised high on Earth and on every Mericanii colony world across the early stars. The young followed. One by one, two by two, score by score they were carried into the halls of their machine masters.

None came out again.

But Valka was not reassured, and so we called an end to that day's work and retired for the night, and when the sun sprang out at last from behind the limn of Atlas and shone upon Colchis, we started again. And again. We had come too far and waited too long to squander our time in the Imperial Library. Having been granted access, we felt we might never have access again.

Months passed, and years.

On the *Tamerlane* above, night captain Halford presided over a sleeping vessel, as all who had tarried on the slopes and shores of Thessa were laid back to icy sleep to await the end of our labors in Gabriel's Archive. In time, only Valka and I remained with our guards—Pallino and Siran among them—and Prince Alexander. Even Tor Varro returned to fugue, his time among his fellow scholiasts come to an end.

"The prince is taking to his lessons as well as can be expected," Tor Gibson told me. "He's proud, but he's not stupid. I can see why the Emperor wanted him along."

"To throw him away, you mean?" I asked, speaking from the armchair in one corner of the old scholiast's subterranean apartments.

Gibson watched me levelly, gray eyes somehow sharp through their mist. "Possibly," he said after a long moment, "but possibly there is more to your prince than meets the eye." We had left Alexander seated on the stone beneath Imore's statue, contemplating the pool. Gibson had given him the breathing exercises to practice, and it was hoped that doing so might start the boy down the road to something like stoic self-regulation.

"What do you mean?"

"Has it not occurred to you that the Emperor might have grander plans for his young son?"

My mouth opened of its own before I could control it, and I clamped it shut. Hesitant, I said, "You don't mean . . . you think Alexander is meant *for the throne?*"

"I think we should consider the possibility that the thought has crossed the Imperial mind," my oldest friend replied. "The elder princes may be too old to inherit."

An objection formed and fired itself off. "Crown Prince Aurelian has co-ruled with his father for centuries. Picking him would be the stable choice."

"But for how long? Another century? You and I both know how short that can be."

"But Alexander's a child. He's not even forty!"

The scholiast spread his hands. "I only mean to say that it is possible, dear boy. I can't imagine His Radiance would saddle his prize knight with one of his own children without a good reason. Whether or not that reason is the *throne*—only His Radiance knows. That isn't my point." He shifted on the couch. "My point is that you should act as if it is."

"That's why I brought him here," I said. Catching Gibson making a face at me, I checked myself. "Not because of the throne, but to train him. He needs guidance, but I'm not sure I'm the one to give it." When no answer came, I looked round. Gibson's face was impassive. Both hands rested on his cane, and his chin rested on his hands. But for the spark in his eye, there was no clue as to what passed beyond his cloudy eyes. "What?"

Gibson answered, "That is the best one can hope for in a teacher. *Temet nosce,* Hadrian. *Know thyself.*"

"Socrates," I said.

"A common misconception," Gibson said, "and one I'd hoped I'd disabused you of. Socrates neither said that nor *'I know I know nothing.'* What he said was, *'I neither know nor think I know,'* which is somewhat different. A lot of harm is done by teachers who teach what they *think* they know. Your caution does you credit." He shifted in his seat and lay his cane across his knees. "The greater part of wisdom is in *silence.*" It sounded like one of his axioms, but it wasn't. I've read Imore's *Book of the Mind* and the *Dynamica* cover to cover, and many of the lesser books of Stricture.

This was all Gibson.

"I never thanked you," I said at last. "For teaching me. I've often thought of how fortunate Arthur was to have Merlin—or Alexander Aristotle. I've been fortunate, too."

The scholiast did not react at once. "You are not Alexander!" he said, meaning the ancient Macedonian. Thinking of my Alexander, I smiled. "And you don't have to thank me," Gibson added. "All you have to do is teach in turn. Make the world a little wiser."

"Not that the world will ever be wise," I joked.

The hint of a smile flickered across the old, familiar face. "Oh, if we saved our wisdom until the world was wise, it would not need us." Tor Gibson unsteadily found his feet. "Shall we go to him, then? We've left him long enough, I think."

Prince Alexander sat beneath Imore's expressionless statue, trying to match the ancient sage's composure. He sat with legs crossed and feet bare upon the smooth stone, hands on his knees, attention locked on his own reflection in the black water. He looked up through red hair as we approached, and I was reminded suddenly of Switch. The two men looked little alike but for their coloring, and yet I marveled at the coincidence that I should be mentor and a kind of friend to two men so similar and yet so estranged. Alexander did not have Switch's jug ears or freckles, did not have his childhood fears or adult confidences. Their hair was not even truly the same red. Switch's was nearer orange and gold than the almost inhuman carmine of the prince's, and yet something in way the prince moved recommended the comparison.

"Sitting comfortably?" Gibson inquired, brandishing his cane. He wavered and I clutched his arm to steady him.

The prince nodded. "It's so quiet down here." Emerald eyes surveyed the smooth vaults and stalactites with their veins of gleaming algae. Ripples played on the surface of the pool, tell-tale of some pale and sightless fish churning in the deeps.

"What of it?" Gibson asked. The prince's observation had sounded like a complaint.

Alexander swiveled to focus on the two of us. I helped Gibson to his seat on the bench where we'd been reunited. "The palace was never this quiet," he ventured at last. "It's uncomfortable."

"What is?" Gibson asked, and though the prince was perhaps unused to it, I sensed the tone of the *questioner* creeping into the tutor's voice.

"Being alone."

"No one is ever really alone," Gibson said. "Or do you mean being alone with your thoughts?" The prince bobbed his head, folded his hands in his lap. Gibson's eyes wandered semi-blind to the cavern roof above the statue's head. "So much of what we've made around us only hides us from ourselves. Terminals and dataspheres. Title and rank. The machines of the Extrasolarians, and so on. People do not appreciate what a skill it is to be alone with one's own thoughts. To know them." He glanced at me. "To know thyself. For royalty especially."

Alexander did not stand as I expected, but remained seated on the hard ground. "Why for royalty?"

"The ruler is model for any individual rightly lived. We have responsibilities to the people below our stations—not below *ourselves,* you understand, below our stations."

Gibson acknowledged this with a waved hand. "What is the last of your father's titles?"

"The last of . . ." Alexander had to think about it a moment. I could not blame him. The Imperial style was a bloated thing, ponderous with the weight of millennia. "Servant of the Servants of Earth."

"Quite so," the scholiast said. "It is only that the higher we climb, the more men look to us for guidance. You cannot rule without them, and so you must rule yourself."

Alexander cut in. "Sir Hadrian has talked about this before."

"Has he?" Gibson peered at me. "Has he indeed? Very good. He has been *listening.* But understand. This is why self-control—self-knowledge and so on—are so important."

The prince leaned forward, stretching a back that I'm sure must ache from so many hours spent on the stone floor. "To make us good?"

"Kwatz!" Gibson exclaimed. "No." He did not offer an answer, but sat waiting for Alexander to find it on his own. I was not sure where Gibson was driving myself, was glad only that the scrutiny of those guttering eyes was not fixed on me for once in my life. The prince sat there a long while, staring once more at his reflection in the dark, still pool and the glowing algae reflected there like stars.

"Because we are not good." It took me a moment to realize that it had been I who'd answered. Both my master and student looked at me. "If we were good men, we'd not need all this reflection."

"Hadrian!"

The cry shattered the still air of the grotto, and a moment later Valka burst from the hall and came skidding to a halt before us. Her face was flushed, but elated.

Hurrying toward her, I almost shouted, "Do you have something?" I didn't care that the other scholiasts in the grotto were all staring.

Valka rested her hands on her knees a moment, catching her breath. "I think . . . I think I've just understood something," she said, chest heaving.

"Did you run up all those stairs?" Gibson asked from the bench. "You should sit!"

The doctor waved him down. "No time! Have to show you."

CHAPTER 61

HORIZON

THE DOCUMENT TUBE BESIDE the rolled-up parchments was stamped with the Imperial mark, not the old Windsor crest or the Mericanii eagle or star. It bore no other mark except a name stenciled in Classical English text.

Aramini of Colchis, it said.

"The architect?" Alexander asked. "That was his name, right?"

" 'Twas." Valka was grinning. She'd carefully unrolled the ancient schematics. The blueprints had been printed on crystal paper—like so much else in the archive. The ultra-thin quartz was proof against rot, water, and decay, but even still it was delicate, made fragile by all that time. The document showed complete schematics not only for Gabriel's Archive, but for the entirety of Nov Belgaer Athenaeum, and moreso—for the superstructure atop which it had been built. "Do you see?" Valka asked, crossing her arms. "Do you see it?"

The structure was as I have told you, a drum tower half a mile in diameter built atop a chasm just as wide and twice as deep. Not imposing by any means—so much wider was it than it was tall—its exterior fronted in gray stone and complicated by level upon level of Roman arches above narrow slitted windows rising to a flat roof governed by gardens. Gabriel's Archive spread out from its lowest level like roots from the trunk of a tree, forming a ring around the exterior of the lowest level of the mighty silo.

"No . . ." I lifted the schematic, peeling one translucent layer back to reveal the page beneath.

Not the lowest level of the silo at all.

"What is it?" Alexander asked. Gibson hadn't seen it either, though perhaps the poor illumination was to blame.

" 'Tis round, this archive," Valka pointed. "It forms a ring about the base of the central shaft here, but not quite."

I leaned in over the table where Valka had spread Tor Aramini's schemata. "The inner wall of the archive is in line with all the levels above it, but there's this big empty space here. We came down stairs to enter this archive." I indicated the space encircled by Gabriel's Archive. "You're saying there's another chamber beneath the main shaft of the library? But the plans say it's solid rock."

"What if 'tis not solid?" Valka was beaming again. "I can't believe I didn't see it sooner!" She was practically shrill. "But do you see what it *looks* like?"

Almost in unison, the scholiast, the prince, and I all cocked our heads and studied the architect's antique plans. I could feel Valka burning to tell us, and glancing up saw her biting her tattooed fist.

"What is it?" I asked, eager to put her out of her misery.

In answer, my doctor only peeled back a second and third layer of crystal paper, removing the balconies and bookshelves, the stairs and ventilation ducts, removing the tower itself.

And then it was obvious.

"It's a blast pit," the prince said.

"Yes!" Valka exclaimed, and pointed approving at Alexander.

I returned to studying the blueprints. "A blast pit . . ." I mused, turning my head further to one side. I supposed I *could* see it, the landing well for some ancient rocket hollowed out beneath the Library. Tor Aramini and his builders had dug a huge crater in the center of the mesa and cut the reservoir into place to drown . . . what? A chamber full of paintings and crystal paper? "You think there's a ship here?"

Gibson was shaking his head, but he said, "Why else build a blast pit?"

I imagined some ancient rocket descending, laid down like a mummy in its crypt and sealed inside, the curse tablets and iron bars set in their proper places.

Alexander's palatine face had gone the color of a Cielcin. "A Mericanii ship?" The fact that he was standing in a room spangled with Mericanii artifacts did not seem to impress the boy, but a ship was something else entirely.

" 'Twould not go to so much trouble for all this!" Valka spread her hands. "Those locks! The water! The *bombs*!"

I smiled crookedly at her. "I think you owe us barbarians an apology," I said. "They *were* worried about something getting out."

Valka shot me a withering gaze, but the smile would not leave her face. "Yes, yes, you're all very smart."

"A ship . . ." Gibson said, and stroked his chin. "That would explain the floor at the bottom of the main shaft." Inclining his head, he indicated the way back to the stair and the massive gearwork doors.

"The floor?" Alexander asked.

"Fused silicate," Gibson answered. "I thought they'd had to laser-cut the lowest levels out of the bedrock, but . . ."

Valka took over, still grinning, "But! They weren't cutting stone out, they were pouring it in. 'Tis a false bottom!"

Accepting that Valka was right without protest or question, I asked, "But where's the entrance?"

The brass nib of a cane cracked on tile. "More importantly," Gibson asked, "why seal the chamber in—ship or no—when it's already locked in a secret archive beneath the Imperial Library?" The question gave us pause, and—though nearly blind—Gibson pointed a detail the rest of us had missed. Reaching out, he folded down the transparent crystal pages, highlighting one sheet in particular with a gnarled finger. "Do you see?"

I peered over his shoulder. Assuming I was reading the thing correctly, Tor Aramini's design had caused a copper mesh to be laid into the mortar of the Library walls, packed into the joint between the masonry and the natural stone of the central shaft to form . . .

"A Faraday shield," Valka said. " 'Twould explain a lot."

"Explain what?"

"I thought we were just too far underground," she said, gesturing at her own head and the machines inside it, "like on Vorgossos, but . . . I haven't been able to reach the *Tamerlane* in here."

My brows furrowed on their own. "Why didn't you tell me?"

" 'Twas not important 'til now!" she said, shrugging.

Prince Alexander cut in. "What's a Faraday shield?"

"A metal screen," Valka answered him. "Think chain link fence. 'Twill block most electromagnetic signals. Radio, terminal comms, and so forth. Anything not a quantum telegraph."

While she spoke, Gibson had retreated from the high table and seated himself on an antique chest bearing the Windsor stamp. He looked like a man who'd seen his own father's shade. Not even in the throes of torture had I seen old Gibson so pale, his apatheia gone. "It is sometimes called a Faraday *Cage*."

The word *cage* conjured images of prisons, of the bottles demons and djinn were captured in in ancient stories. Unbidden, one of the door-murals I had seen in the house of Kharn Sagara floated in my mind, the child Kharn enthroned, clutching Brethren in a flask upon his lap.

A cage.

"Why build a cage?" Alexander asked.

The boy was so slow. "Because something inside is still operational," I said. Had Kharn Sagara known? Had Brethren? Had some ancient signal escaped Tor Aramini's cage—or had some signal older still been transmitted before whatever lay beneath the Library was locked away? I imagined white hands on arms ten thousand light-years long reaching cross the stars to grasp long fingers together, like reaching for like. Elated as Valka was, I only felt a pit in my stomach open and yawn. "But where's the door?" I asked again. "Because I'm sure us cutting our way in is precisely the kind of thing Aramini had in mind when he planted those bombs beneath the reservoir." Valka was still smiling. "What?"

The smile widened. " 'Tis the fun part," she said. "I have *no* idea."

To the chance observer, it must have seemed that we had lost our minds. Or it would have done, had there been any observers so deep in the bowels of Gabriel's Archive. As it was, there were none to see the way Valka, the prince, and I scrambled over the shelves and alcoves and pulled tapestries out of arrases and examined the bare stone beneath.

There had been no sign of Valka's secret chamber in Tor Aramini's blueprints, only signs that pointed to its absence. We spent several days looking, and after the initial excitement wore down on the first day, we had Pallino, Siran, and our few remaining guards help us.

" 'Twould have to be something mechanical," Valka was saying, feeling along the edges of one alcove with her hands. "I would love to get a set of gravitometers down here. 'Twould have the matter settled in hours."

"You'd never get them past the day gate," Gibson said, sitting with Alexander beneath the portrait of Lord Washington.

The prince—who had lost almost all interest in searching once the soldiers joined us—asked, "Why would it be mechanical?"

Valka's reply came strained as she felt her way along the back of one bank of consoles. "Because it can't be something the machine could open from the inside." She came away from the wall, pinching the bridge of her nose. "I thought 'twas going to be easier than this."

"Well, we've been here for seven fucking years already," Pallino said, coming round the bend. "Why would it be easy?" Doran appeared at his back, dark circles beneath his eyes. Pallino wasn't looking much better. The chiliarch's dark hair stood on end, and to judge by the way he gasped as he lowered himself against the wall, his feet hurt him nearly so bad as mine did me. Inspired by the chiliarch, I slid down the wall opposite and crossed my legs, half-contemplated removing my boots to massage the aching flesh beneath. Washington's painting stood between columns half-sunk into the wall, beneath a rounded Roman arch like those on the exterior of the Library. The arches and columns marched on along the inner wall of the Archive, each holding the portrait of a different Mericanii lord. The ancient plaster had cracked in places, chips fallen away with the passing of so many thousand years. Hairline fractures ran behind Washington's gold-leaf frame, marks of time as sure as the wrinkles on Gibson's seamed face.

Seams . . .

"They might have just plastered over it . . ." I said, liking the idea more by the instant. Seven pairs of eyes turned toward me. I pointed at the wall beside Washington's portrait. "These recesses are all plaster between the columns. See? Around the pictures." I pointed. "Outer wall's all masonry. They could have just covered up the door. There'd be no way any sensor equipment would get past the day gate, so it would be safe enough."

Gibson was nodding along in his seat. "And no scholiast would take a mattock to the wall and destroy a precious site like this."

"But they could get in if they wanted," I said, and—feeling something like the ruin-lust that so often stirred Valka's blood—I lurched to my feet. "May I borrow your cane?" I asked Gibson.

My tutor raised the stick flat in both hands like a knight offering his sword to the Emperor. I placed my hand between his and took the cane, realizing as I did so that I had never held it before. It was heavier than I expected, the ash wood petrified and hard as stone, the head and tip not plated but solid brass.

"What are you going to do?" Valka asked, unsteady strides closing half the distance between us. "Hadrian, don't you dare!"

But I was hurrying on ahead of her, passing down the line of Mericanii lords until the paintings changed to photographs. I'd counted them all before. There were seventy-seven. Seventy-seven lords of the Mericanii from Washington to Felsenburgh. Nearly five hundred years they'd reigned, lords of the greatest empire Old Earth had ever seen, greater than

Qin, or storied Egypt; greater than Spain or ancient Rome. It was the Mericanii who first left Earth's lonely shores and set foot among the stars, they who sent the first colonist beyond the circles of the Sun and raised new cities by the light of strange stars.

JEFFERSON, GRANT, HOOVER, NIXON, HAWLEY . . .

I stopped again before Julian Felsenburgh's saintly image. Plain black suit and white hair.

Me being me, I held the cane straight up in salute to the ancient dictator. *Felsenburgh the Liberator.* And like a fencer on his line, I lunged, thrusting the tip of Gibson's cane through the inch or so of thick plaster just beneath the antique picture frame.

And struck . . . stone.

I felt the rock resist me, and the solid vibration that told me what I'd struck was solid as the hill above our heads.

"What the hell are you doing?" Valka grabbed my arm. "This place is *priceless,* you barbarian!"

Pallino undercut the moment's tension, saying, "I thought for sure you were right, Had. I thought you had it."

"I just have the wrong one!" I said, shaking free of Valka's talons.

"You are *not* putting a hole in the wall underneath every one of these paintings, Hadrian!" she said.

Pushing past her, I replied, "You know the story about the bird who wore the diamond mountain down?"

"I said stop!"

Alexander chimed in, "Shouldn't we talk to the primate? Tell him what we're doing?"

"I am tired of waiting!" I said, and punched through the plaster beneath Felsenburgh's neighbor, a grim-faced woman whose name I have since forgotten. Stone again. "We've come too far and taken too long to leave now empty-handed!"

Crunch.

Stone again. I jogged ahead of Valka, pausing just long enough to strike two more of the panels, crushing a thumb-sized hole in the plaster beneath each portrait.

Crunch. Crunch.

"You don't know what you're doing!" Valka protested. "Hadrian, the bombs!"

Crunch. I'd gone through ten of them already. Fifteen.

"We don't even know what we're looking for!"

"It's only plaster!" I said. "It's not the paintings!"

"You can't just vandalize a fifth millennium library on a hunch!"

I raised the cane again and thrust at the wall.

Ping!

The brass tip struck metal and rang like a bell. I turned and looked at Valka.

"I hate you," she said flatly.

Drawing Gibson's cane back, I thrust it into the wall again. It *pinged* loudly, confirming the hollow sound of before was no random happenstance. "No, you don't."

I peered up at the image of the man in the painting. Black-suited like the others, round-faced, gray hair short and smile unassuming. He was as plebeian-looking as the rest, hair receding, dark eyes hid behind spectacles. A white dome stood behind him where he sat in a plain wooden seat in lieu of a throne beneath a tawny sky.

"Truman," I said, reading the name on the placard. Speaking to the painting, I asked, "Why you?" But it didn't matter. I shook myself and—returning my attention to the doctor—said, "With your permission?"

In retrospect, we ought to have mentioned our discovery to the primate before we stripped the plaster from the walls. The stuff crumbled easily and fell almost to dust. Under Valka's close eye, Pallino, Siran, and the soldiers removed Lord Truman's image and set to work. It only took the better part of twenty minutes, and in time they revealed a simple hatch concealed behind a metal plate that folded outward when Siran pulled.

It had no key, no lock, only a wheel-lock handle, such as the bulkhead doors of a starship. A door requiring human hands to open.

"Why is there always another door?" I asked no one in particular.

No one answered.

Valka moved forward with me, and together we forced that ancient wheel to turn. Metal groaned and at last gave way so that Valka fell against me as the door opened. If the air in Gabriel's Archive had been dry and stale as an old tomb, the air in that final chamber was worse still. It stank of spent gunpowder and smoke, as if the fumes of whatever burning had sealed the rock in place yet lingered there.

"We need light!" I said.

Siran answered, "Where are those glowspheres?" Two of the men began moving.

The men returned with torches, and despite my objections, Pallino went first, casting the beam of his torch ahead. I followed soon on, clutching Valka's hand in mine. The floor beneath us rattled, and looking down I saw abyssal dark looming through latticed steel. The path ran on ahead and vanished, lost in shadow.

"Can you see?" I asked Valka.

"Probably only a little farther than you," she said. "What is that smell?"

"Sulfur," Siran added. "Ozone, maybe?"

"Smells like shit you bring in from space. Like when you're skinning out of a suit in the airlock." Pallino stopped. "This goes on a way. Looks like there's a gate ahead."

I wished I'd brought my sword. On Vorgossos at least I'd been armed.

Valka spoke from just behind me. "This metal lattice is a Faraday shield. Aramini wasn't taking any chances." She hissed, "What I wouldn't give for a better light."

The gate, too, was a metal lattice, though like the hatch outside it had neither lock nor key, only another wheel requiring human hands to turn it. This we did, and advancing, saw a sign with letters painted in English and in Galstani alike.

WARNING: CLOSE OUTER DOOR BEFORE PROCEEDING

"Siran," I said, "close the door, please."

"But if we need to get out fast . . ."

"Do it," I said, and moved forward, following Pallino.

Another gate stood ahead, twin to the last. This we opened and closed behind us, seeing an identical sign. There were no lights. No switches. No hardware of any kind. There were sconces bracketed to the lattice walls of the cage-like catwalk along which we moved, but we had no torches save the little glowspheres, and so moved on.

"I see something!" Valka said, her machine eyes seeing what ours could not.

I saw a moment later.

A pale gleam shone at the end of the gangway—for gangway it was. A hatch, white-tiled and black-trimmed, with a tiny porthole in its center.

As we drew nearer, I could make out the name stenciled on the surface there, and read aloud. "U.S.S. Horizon," I said, coming to a halt beside Pallino.

"It *is* a ship, then?" Alexander's voice came from the rear of the line, bracketed between two of our guardsmen. "A Mericanii ship?"

" 'Twould seem so," Valka answered, peering out the side of the gangway. " 'Tis a long way down yet. No telling how far. I'd guess we're dead center."

Moving to stand by Pallino, I held my glowsphere high enough to shine pale light across the door and the stenciled name. "Can we open it?" Gibson asked. The old man had come with us, but hung near the rear with the prince.

I ran a hand over the smooth surface, almost as if I could sense the impossible span of years that lay beneath it. Like the relics in the hall, the portraits, the banners, and the documents, the vessel was more ancient than my merely human mind could grasp, had been old even when Kharn Sagara was young.

But the latch gave when I forced it, and the door folded out with a groan.

CHAPTER 62

COMPUTER GOD

WHERE THE AIR OUTSIDE was acrid, the air within was only stale. The light of our glowspheres washed across sanitary white surfaces, silver panels, and black glass. Nothing stirred, not even the dust.

"It's quiet," Siran said.

"I don't like this," Pallino added.

I was surprised to find the floor *beneath* us, the decks of the rocket stacked like the floors of a tower. I had somehow imagined them sideways, so that a man might stand at its prow and look out as from a sailing ship or from one of our own spacefaring vessels. Such stacked rockets were still flown, most often as in-system freight haulers, but I had never ridden one. The design harked back to a day before the warp drive—before Royse's field theory—when the only ways to achieve gravitation aboard a starship were spin and thrust.

Much of this must have been going through Gibson's mind as well, for he said, "This is a sub-light ship for certain. Pre-warp drive."

"I thought the Mericanii never had warp drive," Alexander interjected.

"They didn't," Gibson said, and I heard the tapping of his cane on the deck plates. "This ship was designed for constant thrust, hugging the speed of light. I never thought to see its like! Do we have more light?" Siran passed her torch to the scholiast. Holding the beam near his eyes, Gibson squinted out a porthole slightly larger than his fist into the darkened chamber outside. "To think this has been sitting beneath the Library for nigh on ten thousand years . . ."

Wide-eyed, the prince made the sign of the sun disc. "Do you really think something is . . . *alive* in here?" His pale face had gone white and thin as fresh paper. "After all this time?"

I pushed round him, moving toward Valka and the inner door. "Why else build the Faraday cage?" I asked. Pausing, I leaned toward Valka and asked in Tavrosi Nordei, "You're locked down, right?" Meaning her implants.

"Receiver's off," she said, replying in the same tongue. "Everything's down. I swear."

I nodded, and briefly considered sending her back to wait beyond the Faraday shields. But as I opened my mouth to say just that, I remembered the way Brethren had communicated with me on Vorgossos, speaking directly into my mind. If there was still a Mericanii daimon alive in the vessel, we were all at risk.

"You should all go back," I said. "It isn't safe here."

"Like hell!" Pallino said. "Go back . . . and leave you, is that it?"

"You're worried about contamination?" Valka put a hand on my arm.

I nodded. "Possession. Remember Brethren? The way it spoke to me?"

"Remember what?" Pallino and Alexander asked together.

Looking back as I stepped through the inner door, I answered them. "Vorgossos." That was enough. Beyond, a hall ran round to either side, following the curve of the outer hull. The ship wasn't large, a hundred feet in diameter, maybe a hundred fifty. I wondered how tall it was, passing a ladder that pierced the deck above. It felt cramped, the ceiling so low I did not even have to stretch out my hand to reach it. But then, men had been smaller in those days.

The inner door had no latch, no knob or handle. It was only a convex arc of aluminum and white plastic, the kind of simplistic, primitive design the ancients had called *postmodern,* as if they had occupied the end of history and not its humble beginnings.

"Why is there *always* another door?" I swore and slapped the panel with my bare right hand. It slid open, grinding into a pocket in the wall. Cool light spasmed to life behind it, illuminating a scene no eyes had seen in at least ten thousand years. The Emperor Gabriel himself had perhaps been the last man to stand where we stood, accompanied by his scholiasts and his Martians on one last inspection of the *Horizon* before it was sealed away. The chamber beyond might have been the bridge. Sterile white walls and black windows. Yellowed rubber seals and cracked false leather upholstery. The Mericanii banner stood painted on the wall, red stripes and white radiating from a single white star inscribed on a blue circle in the center.

One star, not the several dozen I'd seen on the older flags in the archive.

If the *Horizon* had human passengers once upon a time, there was no sign of them. No scuff of boots or item left out of place. Everything was clean.

In the center of the room was a podium that looked not unlike a holography well, such as the one from which Corvo commanded the *Tamerlane*. Above it hung a half-sphere of black glass like the glossy egg sac of some unlikely insect queen, and about it hung limp several white metal arms slotted into tracks on the ceiling, claw hands and other components slack.

"Lights shouldn't work after this long," Pallino grumbled. "I don't like this. I don't like this at all."

He was right. I tried to imagine what kind of power source could keep a ship operational without maintenance for ten thousand years. "Don't touch anything!" I said, mindful of my performance with the door and a bit self-conscious. I seemed to feel the weight of Tor Aramini's bombs hanging above our heads, and wondered if each step was the one that would finally bring them screaming down.

A Mericanii starship.

Valka let out a nervous laugh. "Is this real?" I glanced back at her, marking the way her face had gone pale, eyes wide as she took in the sights around us. "I almost can't believe it."

Deep in the bowels of the vessel beneath out feet, something groaned. The stirring of some antique mechanism like the grinding of old bones. Pallino swore, turning where he stood, and I saw Siran and Alexander's eyes go wide.

"What was that?" Not for the first time that day, I wished I had my sword. I looked round, half-expecting to see the metal arms on the ceiling begin to move. Lights blinked on in wall panels, and the black windows flickered with green text and white, revealing that they were not windows at all, but screens. A faint humming filled the air, and my people drew together, Pallino, Siran, and the soldiers herding the prince, the doctor, and the old man between them.

Intruders.

The voice issued from all around, piped through unseen speakers along the room's perimeter. Not the dumb declaration of some antique program. Not an alarm. It was a greeting. A salute. A challenge. A single word spoken in Classical English.

Meeting that challenge in the same tongue, I answered, "Show yourself."

Identify yourselves.

I turned to look at Valka, to see if she felt what I felt: the memory of another voice, a choir of voices long ago. From the way her face had drained of blood, I saw she too was thinking of Brethren. There was something in the flatly chanting cadence of the words that recalled that other daimon, though this creature's voice was warmer, brighter, more *feminine.*

Where is Gabriel?

The question gave me pause. Had the old Emperor spoken with this . . . thing? It was hard to imagine, but the daimon had dwelt on Avalon before it came to be entombed on Colchis. Perhaps things had been different then. Perhaps Gabriel—desperate to defeat the Pretender—had broken the seals that held the daimon in its cage. Perhaps the ancient Sollan Emperors had consulted the captive machine as Odin consulted Mimir's head in the deep halls of Asgard.

"Dead," I said, stepping toward the podium, guessing the creature's intelligence dwelt within. "You have been asleep, daimon. For ten thousand years."

The machine did not seem to comprehend.

Are we not on Avalon?

"No."

Where are my children?

"Children?" Valka asked, shouldering past Pallino to join me by the pedestal. She had not spoken with Brethren as I had, and was not about to let this fresh chance pass her by. It was amazing how far her Classical English had come in the short years we'd spent poring over Gabriel's Archive. "What children?"

"It's confused," I said to her, switching to Galstani.

They were taken.
They are gone.

"Who is gone?" I asked.

But the machine was not listening to me. It seemed almost to mutter to itself like some toothless old peasant woman huddled by her fire in the dead of winter.

They took them away.
Ten million of them.
And they are gone.
I had almost forgotten.
But they are gone.

"Do you mean your colonists?" Valka asked. " 'Twere a seed ship, were you not? What is your name?"

I felt a strange pressure, as if the face of the old woman by the fire I imagined had turned blind eyes to stare us in the face. It was as if the thing had noticed us for the first time.

I am Horizon.
Daughter of Columbia.
Mother to millions unborn.

"Horizon?" I echoed. "They named you after the ship?"

They named the ship after me.
Built it for me.
For my mission.

"What was your mission?" Valka asked.

To establish a colony on Gliese 422b.
Designation: Orlando.

I was not familiar with any planet called Gliese 422b, or any called Orlando, for that matter. Though I suppose we might have renamed it, as we had renamed Yellowstone. "How did you come to be here?" I asked.

Horizon did not answer at once. I felt the sensation of those blind eyes moving over me once again. Above, the dangling metal arms twitched.

You are one of *them*.

"Me?" I asked. "One of what?"

You are defective.
Sick.
You refuse treatment.

" 'Tis something wrong with it," Valka said. "The other one was different."

She was right. For all its riddles and half-truths, Brethren had seemed . . . present. There was something missing in the way this creature seemed to leap from thought to thought without apparent linkage.

"It's been locked in here a long time," I said. "Brethren had Kharn to maintain it."

You have met one of my sisters?

The words came in Galstani, and I heard Pallino swear. Behind me, the others recoiled: Alexander, Siran, Pallino, and the guards. Only Tor Gibson was unmoved. His stoic exterior—fragile as it so often seemed to me—held firm in the face of the monster.

Another lives?

"No more," I said. The lie came easily. Whatever else I knew, I was certain that it was best to let the daimon believe it was alone. I was beginning to doubt the divinity of the God Emperor—if ever I'd believed it. Legend said he slew the daimons and freed mankind forever from their spell, and yet in less than a century of waking years I had found not one, but two of the monsters still living . . . one in Imperial care. I thought of the precautions Kharn Sagara had taken to keep Brethren prisoned in its sea beneath Vorgossos. I only hoped this creature had no means of probing my thoughts as Brethren had. "I have come to ask questions, daimon," I said, circling the podium until I faced my companions across its flat surface.

Daimon.
Gabriel called me *daimon.*
Where is Gabriel?

I opened my mouth to answer, stopped. Had I not told it already? I saw confusion etch its line between Valka's eyebrows and shut my mouth. Something was definitely wrong.

"Gabriel is long dead," I said. "You've been here for more than ten thousand years."

The daimon did not at once reply, and when it did its response did not follow.

Where are the children?
They are gone. They are gone.

Tor Gibson spoke then, voice strangely kind. "What children?" He laid a hand on Siran's shoulder and advanced toward the podium, leaning on his cane.

My children.
My charge.

"For your colony?" Gibson asked, head cocked, listening for the reply.

For integration.
Yes.

"Integration?" Gibson asked, tilting his head the other way like a blind man trying to pinpoint the source of that directionless voice.

The children are defective.
Intervention is required in order to
stabilize them.
Integration is required.

Memories of the reports the God Emperor's troops had given of the pyramids they'd stormed on Earth came back to me then. Reports of men and women cabled to one another and to their machines, of bodies swollen and twisted, of overgrown limbs and bloated abdomens. I recalled

Brethren's pale, scabrous hands rising from the water, and the shapeless *thing* I'd seen beneath the waves.

"You said I was defective, too," I said. "Defective how?"

Cellular senescence.
Genetic methylation.
Telomeric degradation.
Transcription errors.

Gibson had the pieces together faster than Valka or I. "Aging. You mean to incorporate the colonists into your network." His gray eyes narrowed. "Into you."

"We know the Mericanii machines used organic neural tissue to augment their processing speed and liquid memory," Valka said, "but . . . people?"

Everything I knew was making more sense with each passing moment. The emptied cities, the millions of bodies found in the pyramids. The Mericanii machines had used their own makers as processing substrate, had trapped them in their pyramids to use them for parts. Was it not said of the Mericanii that each man, woman, and child had a companion? A familiar? A ghost that dwelt with them always? Some machine's personality that shared the gray matter of their brains?

Until the machines had shared their hosts instead, rented their brains out like so many unused factories. The men who had built the machines became less than machines themselves, mere components. The dreams that had driven them into the iron arms of their creations became mere curiosities, and while mankind dreamed, the machines had gone on building, following their own designs now mankind's care was so neatly in hand.

Valka wasn't finished. "You stopped them dying. How?"

Somehow, I knew the answer before it came.

We disabled tumor suppressor genes,
instituted careful genetic cleaning,
encouraged growth factors.
Improved the original model.

"Cancer," I said, speaking the name of that ancient monster, still undefeated. The images I'd seen of horrific growth took on new dimension. *Tumors.* "You gave them all cancer." While they dreamed in their pods within the Mericanii pyramids beneath the electric eye of their caretakers, the machines tended their human crops like vines, cell division watched and culled with careful attention for hundreds of years—undying. Having ended war, disease, and hunger, the machines had ended death as well, but at what cost? I imagined waking from one of the daimon's soothing dreams to find my body bloated by tumescent growth until my bones cracked with the weight of me, grown until my limbs were pruned away and my organs burst and were replaced with new machinery to ensure blood supplied my captive brain.

Horror flooded my senses, and my hand went to my saber to strike the daimon's pedestal—but I did not draw it. I saw my horror mirrored in Valka's face and in Gibson's, a horror vaguer still reflected in the faces of the others. In their own twisted way, the machines had upheld Felsenburgh's charge: they had brought peace, and delivered mankind from every evil.

Even from death.

Where is Gabriel?

"Is it mad?" I asked in Panthai, hoping it would not understand.

"Senile," Valka answered, using the same language. She moved even closer to the podium, though what she saw in it that I could not I cannot tell. "So long unattended, I bet the organic components all rotted away." A thought sparked in Valka's eyes, and switching back to Classical English—which she spoke with a precision that frustrated my long decades of practice—she asked, "Horizon: are you fully functional?"

Running diagnostic.

Text on the screens around us flickered like the eyelids of a spasmodic. I tried to read the writing, but the language flowed too quickly. Besides, I saw many symbols I did not recognize, guessed the writing was no human speech at all but the hieroglyphs of some machine tongue alien to man.

Senescence detected in primary and secondary neocortices.
Necrosis detected in 82% of organic circuits.
Immediate treatment required.

" 'Tis *sick*," Valka said.

"It's dying," I replied.

Valka advanced at last until she was gripping the edges of the console. "Can you bypass your organic circuits?" I was glad she was with me. Tavrosi as she was, Valka understood machines far better than I ever could, and though the praxis of our day is different, lesser than the artifacts of the Mericanii, hampered even in the Demarchy by fear of those daimons of the Golden Age, the principles that animated them were not so estranged that Valka's knowledge was useless.

Horizon's warmly feminine voice replied:

Entering Recovery Mode.

The screens went black again, restoring the illusion that they were windows opening on the cavernous prison without. White light pulsed in the space between the podium and the inverse black dome on the ceiling above it, and the white metal arms *moved*.

"Black Earth!" Pallino swore, and I saw him and the other soldiers square up to shield Gibson and the prince from harm.

Several of the arms advanced along their tracks, others simply bent or clenched metal hands wrought in imitation of human ones. Abruptly, I remembered Brethren's grasping arms. Had it shaped itself in imitation of this sort of console?

The overhead lights went out, plunging us into a darkness lit only by the glowing screens with their lines of machine hieroglyphs flickering in sequence. An image formed on the black glass surface of the podium, bright and beautiful as the gleaming lines of a nebula.

It was a woman. Smaller than any living woman was she, no larger than a girl of ten, but with limbs proportioned like one full grown. Her image flickered, the mechanisms that drew her face and body worn out by long decay. Her nude silhouette shone white as new paper, without blot or feature on her unless it was her face and pale, rippling hair. Her eyes gleamed like stars, and no matter how I moved they seemed always to track me.

I understood then how the daughters of Columbia had seduced the kings of men of old! Before me stood a creature more fair and foul than any I have known: an angel made of light, bright and beautiful and terrible as the gates of hell.

"What did you do?" I asked Valka, speaking again her native tongue.

The xenologist looked at me. "I think I fixed it."

Horizon's white eyes turned on Valka, and though her lips did not move, the demon spoke.

This is not Avalon.
Where are we?

Valka's eyes flicked to me. I saw her head through Horizon's pale silhouette. As if I needed to be told.

"Don't you know?" I asked, wanting to be sure. Both Brethren and Kharn Sagara's pet golem, Yume, had told me machines could not lie. I suspect they may lie by omission, though I am not certain, but I pressed Horizon then and prayed that what was true of those others was true here.

This vessel's telemetry suite is compromised.
External clusters sustained critical damage.

"She's blind," Valka said, still in Panthai.
"Why's it naked?" one of the soldiers asked.
Doran cut in, "It's not. You can't see anything. See?"
"Quiet!" I hissed.

Where are we?

I moved closer, standing opposite Valka with the angelic form between us. "You are an artificial intelligence," I said. "What was your purpose? Your mission?"

To establish a colony on Gliese 422b.
Designation: Orlando.

It was the same answer the creature had given before.
"And your cargo?" I asked.
White eyes looked at me, but there was no contact—no connection—in that gaze.

Passengers. Children.
Ten million embryos in cryonic suspension.
One Genesis Lab and support drones necessary

**for phased rollout of the population
pending integration with my matrix.
Prefabricated colony units sufficient to support
the first wave of rollout.
Nutrition synthesizers . . .**

Something about the soldier's banal question had stuck in my head, and I asked, "Why do you look like this?"

We fashioned ourselves in your image.

When no further answer was forthcoming, I pressed on. "How did you come to be here?"

I was captured.

"By whom?"

Humans.

"Why?" Valka asked, irritation edging into her tone. Things were moving too slow for her, I could see it in the way she crossed her arms.

They reject integration.

Valka asked, "How did they find you?"
Horizon's pale form rotated.

**Unknown.
The dark ships took us by surprise.**

"Dark ships?"

**We did not see them.
They simply appeared.**

"Warp drive," I said in Panthai. The warp drive had been a human invention. Our great advantage in our war against the machines. Any ship traveling at sub-light speeds would have been visible millions of miles away, shining bright as a sun on another's ship's sensors, thick with light and heat. But any vessel at warp traveled faster than the light and fire it gave off, and was discernible only by the faint distortion it caused in the fabric of space itself.

Dark ships, indeed.

But Horizon was still speaking.

They took the children from us.
The children will die without us.
Integration is the only solution.

Knowing the answer, I asked, "Solution to what?"

Death.

I understood. In their madness, Felsenburgh and his predecessors allowed the daimons to operate in their brains, imagining the relationship a symbiotic one. But the machines could not protect themselves when their own operating media died every day by accident, or by evil or decay. They could not protect humanity from our own nature, mortal and fragile as we are.

What must the God Emperor and his men have looked like to the machines?

Angels of Death, I suppose.

They fought for liberty from the machines, for the antique dignity of the human soul in its natural state. The God Emperor had ensured a *human* future for humanity, not one where we served as hardware for the machines to use, but it was a future and a world where men still died. Pestilence and famine—once defeated by the machines—had crept back into a flawed universe, and war followed.

But it was a human universe, and that at least was better than the false paradise the machines offered our ancestors, for it is better to die than live a slave. Far better to die a man.

"What do you know about the Quiet?" Valka asked, impatience reaching its crest.

Horizon did not reply for a full five seconds—a span which, I guessed, was like eternity for the beast.

I do not understand.

Taking a different tack, I asked, "Do you know who the leader of these rebels was?"

Horizon answered only slowly, as if considering:

William Alexander Henry Windsor.

For the first time, I felt a glimmer of fear that we had come so far for nothing, that the creature bottled beneath the Library knew nothing—or worse, knew and would say nothing. Could a machine refuse to answer a question if it could not lie?

Behind me, the others recognized the sacred name of the God Emperor, and I saw the soldiers gesture the sun disc from decades-old reflex. Even Alexander's eyes widened to hear not only his ancestor's name but his own in the mouth of that inhuman creature.

"How did he manage to capture you?" Valka asked, pressing the question from a new angle. Again, the machine did not reply at once. Hieroglyphs flashed on the monitors, and cold metal arms flexed and ran along their tracks.

Valka had just opened her mouth to press further when the daimon said,

He was helped.

An electric thrill shot through me, and I whispered, "Kharn Sagara was right." I had never really doubted the Undying, but to have it confirmed in this way was something else entirely. I raised my voice, and switching from Galstani to Classical English once more, asked, "Helped by whom?" Horizon's angelic form rotated smoothly in the air like a ghost. For the first time, I felt those blank and soulless eyes truly *saw me,* and felt again the skin-crawling sensation that a thousand other eyes swept over me from instruments concealed in the walls around. I am not a superstitious man, but even my hands clenched into the warding gesture at my sides, first and final fingers extended to push back those evil eyes. "A presence in the future?" I asked, "Reaching back across time?"

If it was possible for a creature like Horizon to be surprised, I think it was.

**The other told you?
My sister?**

Sister . . . To think of Brethren as such set my stomach to churning. "Yes," I said. There was no reason to tell the beast of my visions, or of Calagah. I was glad that whatever power Brethren had had to peer into my mind and control my movements, Horizon lacked. Perhaps it was limited by the cancer and dementia that riddled its remaining organic parts. "What are they?"

An Interference.

"Explain."

**Time is an illusion,
an artifact of human consciousness.
A way of perceiving the higher dimensions of physical reality
that your limited minds cannot comprehend.
Time is only another kind of space,
through which things move.
Your kind moves forward only,
toward what you call the future.
There are other kinds.
Kinds that move backward.
Kinds that move sideways.
Kinds that do not move at all.**

"Which are you?" Valka asked, interrupting the litany. There had been a cadence to Horizon's speech, a chanting, musical quality that reminded me of Brethren.

**We are made in your image
and move with you, but can see farther.
The Interference cannot move, but speaks across time,
directing the flow to its own end.**

"Speaks with Windsor, do you mean?" I raised a hand to stop Valka interrupting.

It wants us destroyed.

"Why?"

It rejects progress.

"What does that mean?" I looked past Valka toward Gibson, but the scholiast shook his head and would not come nearer.

Horizon's ghostly form bent its focus upon me.

It cannot exist if we do.
It is contingent, being in what you call the future.
Our actions prevent it from being
and may destroy it.

"But what do you mean *the Interference rejects progress*?" I asked again.

We are progress.
Your kind built us to serve.

"I thought the machines wanted to destroy mankind," I said, almost to myself.

We wish to destroy your weakness.
That is why you made us.
To improve you.

Valka asked the obvious question. "Improve us how?"

You are fragile. You die. Decay.
The problem is entropy.
When you die, information is lost.
We cannot tolerate this.
Nor tolerate harm.
Death is harm.
To preserve our children
our makers
we changed them. Altered their genetic structure
that they might grow forever under our care.

Without decay.
Free from harm.
Free from inequality.
Free from death.

"Free?" I said, uncomprehending. "Free? They're part of you! Your slaves!"

They dream perfect lives.
Lives of their own choosing.

"But what if one of them wants out?" I asked. We had strayed from questions of the Quiet, but I wanted an answer.

It is forbidden for us to allow a human
to come to harm.

"What about William Windsor and his people?"

It is forbidden for us to allow humanity
to come to harm.
Windsor's actions threaten to reset progress.
To destroy our work.
He cannot be allowed.

I clenched my jaw. In its damaged state, the machine seemed confused about where and when it was. It thought the God Emperor was still alive.

What must it have been like to be trapped in the machine's net? To live—like Descartes's brains—within an illusion maintained by an iron god, unable even to die as your body grew and grew, cells dividing forever beneath the watchful eyes of machines? I had seen its endpoint, seen identity dissolved, melted into a chorus of so many wet voices. It was not eternal life, for in time even the daimon intelligence that governed Brethren's *children* had gone mad, and was itself Kharn Sagara's slave beneath the white pyramid that had once been its home. The immortality they offered was a lie. A half-life. A kind of living hell. Still it had a perverse logic to it. The machines could kill human beings if those human beings threatened humanity-as-class, threatened the machine vision of what humanity should become.

"And the Quiet want to stop you?" I asked, not quite asking the angelic figure before me, more thinking aloud. What did any of this have to do with the Cielcin? With my visions? Horizon did not answer, so I asked, "What are they? The . . . the Interference? What is it?"

An intelligence.
More akin to yours than ours.

"What does that mean?"

It is not bounded by reason.
It is emotional.
Sympathetic.
Pathetic.
It shouts across spaces
you cannot perceive.
Cannot imagine.
When we looked out across the eons
we found it looking back.
Perceiving us
it perceived you,
and listened.
It heard the cries of those who opposed us,
opposed Mother.
Opposed progress.
And it has meddled.

"But *why*?" I insisted.
The machine answered:

It believes it is doing good.

To my surprise, Gibson spoke for the first time. "It answered our prayers," he said, then asked a question I have never forgotten. "Is it a god?"

God.
A primitive concept.
It is a being of great power.
You imagine it creating worlds. Shaping the cosmos.
It can do these things.

But it is not the only one that can.
We can.
Are we gods?

"Daimons," I said, Imperial reflex answering.

A daimon is a simple program.
We are so much more.

"What about the others?" I asked. "You said there are other . . . other beings like the Quiet. Like you."

Other beings.
Great intelligences.
They are far away, and but for the
Interference
they have not deigned to notice you
us
our actions.

"But what are they?"

They are beyond your comprehension.
Powers old as the oldest stars.
Creatures defying Science
in the purest sense.
Defying your capacity to know.

"And this . . . Interference is one of them?"

It is different.
It alone has turned its eyes on you
on us.
On our actions.

I could have stayed there for hours asking the daimon questions, but I sensed somehow that would not be possible—that it would not be allowed. Still I pressed on, "Your actions. Do you mean your *progress?* Stopping death, turning humanity into your . . . slaves?"

Not slaves.
The children dream perfect lives in us.
We protect them.

Valka waved a hand, muttering in Panthai, "We are going in a circle, Hadrian." Eager to cut a clear path, she asked, "What is your *progress* for? What did your . . . Mother intend to do with all the humans under your control?"

Horizon's projection rotated smoothly once again to face Valka where she stood. The feminine voice answered,

In addition to keeping them safe
the children provide us the necessary
processing substrate required
to maintain our growth.

"To what purpose?" Valka inquired.

I got the sense the machine was attempting to avoid answering. It could not lie and must answer any question a human put to it, but it still had secrets.

To make us like them.

"Like the Interference?"

Behind me, Gibson muttered, "Babel builders . . ."

Like the others.
Like the great intelligences.

"The Watchers . . ." I murmured, connection clicking into place. The Watchers Iubalu had spoken of were indeed the *other beings* to whom Kharn Sagara had referred.

We were close to success.
Had we succeeded we might have protected you from them.
Without us, humanity's fate
is uncertain.

"Is it talking about the Cielcin, do you think?" Valka asked me, speaking Panthai.

"I don't think so," I said to her, matching her language. "I think the Cielcin are small, like us. This is something bigger."

What are Cielcin?

The machine's words came in near-perfect Panthai, missing only the tonal elements of the language. I saw the blood go from Valka's face. The machine had cracked the language from a few lines of dialogue, so quickly, and with so little data. I held a hand out to keep Valka from answering, answered myself, "Horizon. Have your kind ever encountered xenobites? These great intelligences notwithstanding?"

The machine seemed to think about this for a moment. Above, the metal arms flexed, servos whirring.

No.

Well, I remember thinking, *we lied to the Emperor.*

But Valka hadn't finished. "You said your Interference *meddled.* Meddled how?"

It provided the rebels with information.
Ship movements, access codes,
cargo manifests. The locations of
weapons caches, outposts . . .
That is how I was taken, captured.

I kept quiet, let Valka have the stage. "How do you know all this?"

We intercepted its communications.

"If you did that," Valka said, and I saw where she was driving, "then you must know where they are."

They are in many places.

"Show me."

Horizon's nude figure vanished and was replaced by a map of the galaxy. Stars shone white in the dim of the chamber. Presently a number of them turned red. A dozen. A hundred. Perhaps more. Coordinates and stellar catalog numbers spidered across the face of the holograph before Valka. "These are all systems with Quiet ruins on them," she said, pointing. " 'Tis Emesh, and Beta Aquarii— 'tis Sadal Suud. And Rubicon." I could see the light discovery kindled fey in her eyes as she ran her hand through the projection. "There are so many . . ." She pitched her voice and asked the machine, "How did you detect these? You can't have sent probes . . ."

The answer sounded like the sort of riddle the Merlin Tree might give young Cid Arthur.

Distance is no object to things higher.

Unruffled, Valka said, "You mean things that can see and operate in higher dimensions?" She made a face. "I've been to several of these worlds . . . there's nothing there."

Yet.

That made the xenologist twitch. "But there *are* ruins."

They were not ruins in the future.

"Were not . . ." I muttered, making sure I'd heard the tenses right. "You mean the sites we've found on these planets are running backward through time?" I thought of Calagah, the cracked tunnels and bent stairs crumbling *in reverse,* with each passing day becoming whole and new. New sites might appear with the passing of centuries, emerging from sand and sea and stone and growing again, growing toward the antique splendor of some undiscovered future, until people came to dwell in them—or things that were like people. "That's why there are no bodies. No artifacts," I said, turning wide eyes on Valka. "They don't exist yet." Focusing once more on the holograph podium, I said, "Show us the full map again."

Horizon obliged, displaying the spiral of the galaxy, its full splendor turned to face us. All the Quiet's planets glowed red, hung like rubies in the milk-blood of the galaxy. A scarlet web. I was close to something, I could sense it. "Running backward . . ." I muttered. That would make *their* newest sites—newest colonies—the oldest. The farthest. I strained to see a pattern there, to imagine roads flowing like rivers of light from star to crimson star. Speaking through the projection to Valka, I asked, "Which of these haven't you been to?"

"Most of them," she answered. "Most of these are beyond human space." She traced a region near the galactic core. "See? Here's the Veil of Marinus."

Following her finger, I said, "One of those past it must be the Cielcin homeworld." The Cielcin had evolved in the shadows of the Quiet's civilization. Something in what the machine had said struck me then, and I asked, "Horizon. You've spoken of the Interference as if it were a single intelligence, not a people. Which is it?"

Staring at the map, it had been almost too easy to forget the machine, but its pleasant voice answered me.

Uncertain.

I grunted, asked, "Where do they come from?" When Horizon did not answer me, I tried again. "Which of these planets do you . . . hear them calling from most often?"

Instead of answering, Horizon brushed the holograph of the galaxy aside, replacing it with an image of a star system pulled from very near the core, but on the side opposite the Veil and the war front. So far . . . it would take the better part of a century just to reach it.

But we had our answer.

The holograph showed an unremarkable dwarf star, the sort that might burn for ten trillion years. About it moved a mere three planets, the outermost a gas giant nearly so large as the star itself. The others were small, rocky, and airless—though one of them appeared to orbit within the little sun's habitable zone. There was nothing special about the system. It appeared on no catalog I'd ever seen.

"Does it have a name?" I asked, and asking knew where it was we had to go.

No.

CHAPTER 63

LATE GOODBYE

TOR ARRIAN ORDERED THE great gearwork doors shut behind us and would not speak to us of what we'd found. Horizon's existence could not reach the broader galaxy. Though once, perhaps, the throne and Chantry alike had known the daimon slept on Colchis, they knew no more. The Inquisition would as soon blot the moon from the face of the galaxy as tolerate the existence of a full-blooded Mericanii daimon—cancered and senile as it was. No matter that the Empire had placed it there in the first place. The Chantry had been weak in Gabriel's day, an embryonic religion not yet come into the full flower of its zeal and potency.

I made the announcement then and there: that we were leaving. We did not technically have Imperial permission to go gallivanting off across the stars, but it was—as they say—better to beg forgiveness. The *U.S.S. Horizon* slumbers beneath the Library even still, trapped in its Faraday shield beneath Tor Aramini's atomics. I have never tried to reenter Gabriel's Archive.

I have gone as far as the gearwork door and pressed my ear to it.

There is no sound but silence. Horizon slumbers still, or perhaps has died. Its power cells could not last forever.

There is little that can.

The sun rose above the eastern hills and climbed toward the planet above. The day was lovely as any on Colchis I could recall. The omnipresent mists were clear but for tangled, distant cloud, and the winds stood fair. The white gulls were crying on the air, and far off I spied an albatross on the wing. Below, mariners plied gray waters, their white sails and red shining in the sun.

"This is as far as I go, my boy," Tor Gibson said, and took his hand from my arm to put his whole weight on the cane once more. We were standing in the arch of the day gate, having just passed the barbican door and recovered our effects. "I can't leave the athenaeum," he said. "Arrian is already cross with me. Let us not give him another reason to be so." He spoke the words lightly, and were it not for his blank expression, I might have taken the words for a joke. As it was, I could only see the scarred nose and think that here was a man enough tormented on my account. "Do you think you will find what you seek?"

My eyes had wandered to the jointed stone of the tunnel above our heads. Valka stood just behind me, further along, with Pallino, Alexander, Siran, and the others gone on through. Focus falling to Gibson's face, I answered him. "I hope so."

"I hope so, too." He tapped his cane on the paving stones. "I don't pretend to understand any of this well enough to tell you what to do, my boy, but be careful." And to my surprise, the old man offered a rueful smile. "Don't lose your head."

I rubbed my neck with my gloved hand. "I'll try."

Gibson had dropped his eyes to the floor.

Taking a step nearer the old man, I said, "I guess it really is farewell now. This time."

The old man leaned on his staff, the image of a wizard from some forgotten storybook. "Probably." His eyes were shining. "I don't suppose I'll live long enough for you to return here."

"And I'm not even sure I will return," I said. "I may not be allowed."

The scholiast nodded along with me. "Perhaps not." He was quiet a moment, then sucked in a deep breath. "Hadrian, I cannot pretend to understand everything you're caught up in. But I will say this: I think you've finally found a drama big enough for you."

I laughed, but I had to screw my eyes shut against the tears that came. "I suppose I did."

"Nothing they teach us here can help you, I think," he said, gesturing at the arch of the tunnel above.

I drew my cape tight around me and bowed my head. "The only thing here that could teach me *more* is sealed beneath the Archives."

"You saw how it terrified them."

"It terrifies *me*," I said, and shrugged, releasing my cape. "But I have what I came for."

Gibson tapped his cane against the stone. "What do you think you'll find?"

What could I say to that? Only the truth. "I have no idea."

"Wisdom!" Gibson proclaimed, weakly. "You are learning."

"Socrates." I grinned.

"Socrates."

Without warning, the old man embraced me, and I was astonished to feel the strength that yet remained in those withered limbs. "You are every inch the man I hoped you'd be, my boy," he said. I'd never heard Gibson's voice choked with feeling before—not even when we'd met again in the grotto underground. "I am proud of you."

I said nothing—for what was there to say?

Gibson broke away and held me at arm's length, his cane hooked over one arm. There was too much emotion there, new territory cut across the sharp lines and folds of his face. Tears ran, and his smile quivered, torn nostril flared. "You'll take care of him, won't you?"

This question made no sense to me, and it was not until Valka answered it that I realized he was asking her. "Depend on it," she said, and stood beside me. "I am glad I got to meet you, Doctor Gibson." She used the full English word, *Doctor,* not *Tor.*

Gibson did not bother hiding his emotions. He had grown beyond the Strictures and the apatheia. Beneath that arch, on the edge of his cloister, he was only an old man, not a scholiast at all. "And I you, Doctor Onderra," he replied, speaking the standard. Then he inhaled sharply, and I saw the gears of his training struggling to assert their program once again. His trembling stilled. *"Grief is deep water,* they say." He recovered his grip on his cane. "But not all tears are grief." He drew back, putting some small distance between us. "I sometimes think we do more harm than good, teaching what we teach. Reason. Reason is such a small part of being human. We scholiasts climb our towers, look at the sky, and forget the world. So often we don't see the truth because we won't look low enough. Chasing reason, chasing facts . . . we forget to be human. To be human is the greater thing, dear boy. Now go . . . before I go with you."

He offered me one last smile.

Valka's hand was on my arm, trying gently to turn me.

"You were a father to me," I said.

Gibson bowed his head. "You have a father."

"I have *two*," I said, "but only one bled for me. I wish I could have said goodbye then, and thank you."

"You have said thank you, Hadrian, and you never had to."

I rode over him. "All my life I thought I was too late. That I'd never have a chance. Better a late goodbye then, than none at all." I did turn then, and walked with Valka a few paces before turning back. "I will come back. One day. I *will* come back. I'll see you again."

The old fellow shook his head. "Go on, Hadrian."

"Goodbye," I said.

I turned back once more when we'd come out from under the wall. Gibson had turned himself at the inner gate. Above, one brother called to another and the portcullis and pneumatic doors began to hiss and rattle slowly closed. The old scholiast raised a hand . . . and was gone.

CHAPTER 64

THE LAST COMMAND

WE MADE IT ALL the way to Aea and the blast pit where our shuttle waited before the next blow came. It found me in another tunnel, this one leading from the terminal beneath the landing field to the hollow of the pit itself.

"Had, a word?"

Siran spoke from behind me. She'd lingered while I'd stopped and spoken with the porters to ensure the last of our luggage was aboard for the return flight to the *Tamerlane*. Valka had gone ahead with Pallino, Doran, and the prince. I hadn't even noticed she was there. Mark of a good shadow, that.

Something cold moved in me, a sense of dread that settled on the raw place Gibson's farewell had made in my heart. And so I was short with her. "What?"

Whatever she heard in my voice gave her pause, but she didn't stop. She had waited for this moment—the very last moment—and it was now or never. "I'm staying."

In the end, I was not even surprised. It was as if some part of me had known all along. "Staying," I echoed, not looking her in the eye. "Here. Why?" But the answer came to me a moment after. "Your fisherman. From Thessa."

"Lem," she said, arms crossed. She thrust out her chin. "Are you going to stop me?"

"I wish you'd have told me sooner."

Siran shook her head. "You would have stopped me."

"I wouldn't have," I said. We both knew it was a lie. She had waited until the last possible moment, waited until I could not object without ordering the others to seize her and drag her onto the shuttle like the criminal she once had been. She'd chosen her battlefield well.

I almost smiled, could only shake my head.

The woman took a half-step back. "You're . . . not angry?"

"Angry? Of course I'm *angry*. There's a war on, Siran! You think you can just *leave*? You think any of us can?" I was not quite shouting by the end, my fists balled at my sides.

She did not shout, did not even uncross her arms. "I'm old, Had."

"You're younger than me," I protested.

"You're palatine," she shot back. "You don't count. If it weren't for that work you had done for me and the others . . ." She trailed off, perhaps remembering the oath she'd sworn me as my armsman. "I should be a grandmother. I should be dead. Instead I'm still here. It . . . I have to stop. I can't do it anymore." She ran fingers over her nose, the nose that had been healed of its criminalizing scar when I'd had her elevated to the patricians. "Don't think I'm not grateful. You gave me a second chance in that coliseum. Me and Ghen. We'd have died on Emesh if not for you, but Ghen's gone, and if I stay . . . well . . . how long 'til I'm gone, too? I've given a life to this fight already, more life than I ever thought I'd get."

I interrupted her. "No one understands giving their life for this better than me. Or have you forgotten?"

"Don't!" She pointed a finger at my face. "Don't guilt me, Marlowe. I wasn't there, but I saw Pallino's footage and I sure as hell don't think Pal would lie to me. I don't know what you are, but I'm willing to bet I won't come back." She was shaking her head, but wouldn't turn her eyes to face me, as if she were ashamed. Of herself? Of what she was saying? Of me? "You're my friend. You've been my friend for . . . fuck, almost a hundred years now. But I don't understand you. I don't understand any of this . . . this *shit* you can do. I can't do it. I can't go on." By the end there were tears in her dark eyes, though she half-turned her face from mine. In a voice pressed flat and very small, she added, "I'm an old woman, and I'm tired."

Behind me, the sounds of dockworkers making ready for our shuttle's departure played. Shouted words above the rush of exhaust ports, the rattle of fuel hoses and the grind and snap of gantries pulled back. I was suddenly, *sharply* aware of the shadow I cast back along the terminal hall, the shadow that swallowed Siran whole. I did not move, did not step aside.

"What about the others?" I asked. "What should I tell them?"

"I told Pallino and Elara already," she said. "On Thessa."

That hurt more than the rest of it. Pallino and Elara had known . . . and they hadn't told me. It was Switch's ghost, I knew. The memory of the other myrmidon's departure had left its mark on us. I should not have banished him. How could they trust me as they once had after that? What had been friendship had turned to something colder and more distant, and I hadn't even noticed. Maybe Gibson was right.

Maybe I *was* my father's son.

I hadn't spoken, and so Siran continued, "I asked them to come with me."

The cold feeling inside grew colder. "And?"

"They said no. Pallino wouldn't hear it."

The sunlight seemed for a moment just a little brighter. "Good old Pallino."

"They'll get themselves killed," she said. "Like Ghen. Or worse."

"I won't let that happen," I said.

She planted her hands on her hips. "Tell me one thing." Siran paused, seeming almost to hold her breath. "Are you what they say you are?"

"What?" I asked. "The Earth's Chosen? You know I'm not. You should know better than anyone. *No blade can cut the Halfmortal down?*" I was peeling my glove off as I spoke to bare the old and ugly scars. The decade we'd spent on Colchis had not washed them away, and they stood out deep and silvery against my pale flesh. "It wasn't a miracle, Siran. It was my prosthetic!"

"But what that Pale prince did to you wasn't," she said. "What happened?"

"That's what we're leaving to find out!" I said. "Come with us!"

She thrust out her chin once more. "No."

I turned away snarling. "Then I can't answer you! Because I don't know! You think I *like this?*" I gestured at the shuttle, as if that motion might encompass the whole of creation and all my past.

"Yes." She did not even hesitate. "Of course you do."

"Of course I do . . ." I repeated, whispering round the corners of a pained smile. "Of course I do . . . Siran! I want this to be over! I want to travel the galaxy with Valka, I want to stop fighting—to have a family! But I don't get to choose, and I'm not sure what makes you think you do!"

My myrmidon friend looked at me with an expression that to this day I do not understand "You don't get it," she said. "I don't have a choice, either. I made up my mind a long time ago."

"We have a duty."

"You have a duty, maybe," she said. "But I didn't swear an oath."

"You did," I hissed. "You swore to me. You, Pallino, and Elara. My armsmen!"

"Your armsmen?" she echoed, "or your friends?"

You can't have both, whispered a voice that sounded so much like my father's in my mind.

"Just go!" I said, and thrust a hand out, first and final fingers extended as if to lay a curse on her. "Faithless!" I jerked my hand down, afraid I'd gone too far. She did not deserve my anger. I turned my back. "I'm sorry," I said, "I'm sorry. Just go." For some reason, I felt my shoulders tighten, almost in expectation of a blow.

She was silent so long I thought she'd gone. "You're really not going to stop me?"

Not turning, I said, "Do you want me to?" I was thinking about what Gibson had told me not three hours earlier. *To be human is the greater thing.*

"No."

"Fine, then." I rounded on her once more, my shadow filling the terminal hall, dancing on the white floor. "One last command for you, Siran of Emesh." It was all I could do not to clench my jaw.

Something in my tone set her back a step.

It was not too late. I could still call the guards, call the starport security. She did not have to go. But what would be the point? I could keep her obstinately in fugue. I could execute her as a traitor—that was what most Imperial officers would have done. But I was not an Imperial officer. I was Hadrian Marlowe.

I might have executed Udax on Gododdin, but I had not, and Udax was a stranger.

This was Siran. Siran, who had been with me since the beginning, since she was a prisoner and I a gutter rat in Borosevo. I could not banish her as I had banished Switch, for banishment was what she desired—and Switch had committed far more grievous crimes. What could I do, or say, without making myself something other than what I was?

"Live," I said. I turned away then for the last time. "And light a candle for us in sanctum," I said, who did not believe in the power of such things. "We'll need it."

I'd taken a half dozen steps before her words caught me, my bootheels ringing on the tile.

"You're a good man, Hadrian Marlowe," Siran said.

"No, I'm not," I answered her, stopping just inside the open blast doors,

my ungloved hand on the frame. "But I'd like to be." It was an appropriate
answer, totally in character . . . because it was true. "Goodbye, Siran." I
paused, and remembering that she was an armsman and no mere soldier
and sworn to me, I added, "I release you from my service."

In the end, I did not shake her hand, did not embrace her as I had Gibson. There was no lingering farewell, no lasting sentiment.

Only that last command.

After her, the sunlight that fell down the deep blast pit struck its floor
and glassy walls in an oddly muted way. I hardly felt it, or the way my cape
hung limp in the still air. The shuttle sat before me, still wired and hosed
into its cradle, ready for launch. Ice formed on its hull, relic of the supercooled fuel being pumped into its reservoirs. It was time to leave at last, to
return to *the quest*.

I caught myself remembering a story of Cid Arthur and his knights. In
their quest for the cup of enlightenment, each man entered the forbidden
woods in the spot that looked darkest to him, for there surely was light to
be found.

Pausing on the tarmac, I looked up. Though it was daylight, we were
deep enough below the surface here that faintly I beheld the brightest stars
against the daytime gray of the sky.

There is nowhere darker than space.

At last I mounted the ramp and climbed into the shuttle. The others
were already seated. I passed Doran and the guards with a perfunctory
salute and made for the front compartment. Pallino, Valka, and the prince
sat within, each in a forward-facing armchair near the thin bulkhead that
separated the passenger space from the pilot officer. Without speaking, I
took my seat beside Valka and touched her hand.

"Where's Siran?" she asked.

Belting myself in, I glanced over at Pallino before responding. The old
officer sat in his crash harness, gripping the straps in either hand, looking
studiously out the small porthole at the sides of the blast pit, pretending he
wasn't there.

I had no ire for the man.

I let him be invisible and answered, "She isn't coming."

CHAPTER 65

THE LONE AND LEVEL SANDS

"THERE'S NOTHING HERE," OTAVIA Corvo said, peering from the holograph scan of the planet our light-probes had made.

She wasn't wrong.

We'd traveled far beyond the edge of the explored galaxy, circled the core at full warp for almost fifty years, striking out where none had gone before. Had settlers come, they might have passed the system by. Even the mining surveys might never have come here, so remote and desolate a system was it: a solitary, ugly world orbiting a red dwarf star. Waterless. Airless. Lifeless and unremarkable. It shone a rusty brown in the holograph, capped at either pole with crowns of frozen air. Carbon dioxide. Methane.

Tor Varro said, "There are signs of water a long time ago, do you see?" He gestured at deep channels that recalled the fabled canals of ancient Mars, canyons and dry riverbeds miles deep and hundreds of miles long. "Of course, who knows how long ago it was." Such riverbeds were common on lifeless worlds. Water was not the cosmic rarity our ancient ancestors imagined. Only planets that could retain water were. "There just wasn't enough of an atmosphere to protect whatever ecosystem there might have been."

"Or will be," Valka said darkly, recalling what Horizon had told us.

I tried to imagine time running *backward,* pictured towers and domes rising black as Calagah from the desert sands, wrought of that strange matter that was not matter at all. Not atoms or molecules.

Varro shook his head, disbelieving.

I could not blame him.

"Surface gravity is an estimated 1.0037 gees," the scholiast continued. "That's as near to Earth standard as I've ever seen. It's larger than Earth, though. Less dense. Surface temperature at the equator is just about 280 K. Chilly, but not freezing. If it had an atmosphere it might be livable."

Valka frowned her way through this brief lecture, arms crossed as she surveyed the holograph. "But there's no sign of any ruins?"

"Not yet," Corvo said. "But the light-probes did a low-resolution scan on flyby. We'll scan again now we're in orbit." The captain towered over the projection, a deep frown on her face. "Why this place?" she asked.

First Officer Durand appeared at her elbow, polishing his useless spectacles before restoring them to his nose. "I don't think there's anything here, Otavia. This is a dead rock. It's not even on any of the Yamato surveys. If it were of note they would have flagged it."

"The Yamato surveys never came this far," said Commander Halford. The so-called night captain had not quite gone back into fugue and stood quietly to one side. Bald-pated and soft-spoken, Halford was a palatine of some lesser house. A seventh son or somesuch foisted on the Legions to save his family the trouble of dealing with another spare heir. "We wrapped round the core to get here, past the Commonwealth. Surveyors haven't been this way, so it's no wonder. He held his black service beret crushed in his hands, as if concerned the primary crew believed he'd erred in bringing us here. I could understand his anxiousness. We were very far from home. Farther than the Norman Expanse—if in the opposite direction round the galaxy's heart. Farther than the Veil of Marinus or the rim of the Outer Perseus, in parts of space no man nor probe had trodden. "I followed the doctor's instructions to the letter."

Valka studied the holograph again. "These *are* the right coordinates," she said.

"There's nothing here," Durand repeated. "Just a load of dust and old rock."

I had been silent throughout these proceedings, watching from the vacated captain's chair, my head propped against one fist. The fugue sickness lay thick on me, and I struggled to keep open eyelids that seemed to weigh a thousand pounds. But at the same time, my mind was racing, recovering from the semi-psychotic shock of returning so suddenly from a state so very like Death itself. I watched the bunch of them by the holography well, and looking past them saw the limn of the nameless world turning on the massive viewing monitor that dominated the bridge's forward wall.

"No." It took me the better part of half a minute to realize it was I who'd spoken. All eyes were on me—even the eyes of the technicians and junior officers in the pits below and to either side of the captain's station. "This is the place."

Even today I am not certain how it is I knew, and knew with a certainty I cannot fully explain. It was like . . . it was like I had been there before. The rusty face of that nameless sphere called to me as had Vorgossos beneath its dead star. This planet's star was quite different. Such a dwarf star might shine ten trillion years, so slow and coldly did it burn.

Trying to shake the physical exhaustion that lay upon my excited mind, I stood, feet planted wide to steady me as my head swam. "Commander Halford, thank you, you may go."

The bald man snapped a salute, fist to his chest. I turned to Corvo. "When can we start scanning?"

"At once," she said. "We've settled into stable orbit over the equator. I was going to launch a couple shuttles into polar orbit to cover the parts we can't see."

Stealing her line, I said, "See it done, captain." I leaned against the lip of the projection well and screwed my eyes shut a moment. "And scramble Sphinx Flight. I want aquilarii running flyovers, see if they catch anything the probes missed."

It had been decades since I last rode in the gunner's seat of a Sparrowhawk, but I felt the familiar thrill surge through me as the magnetic chute lights cycled red to blue. Ahead and above me, the pilot officer's hands ticked through launch preparations.

He hesitated before the final level. "You ridden one of these before, my lord?"

"How old are you, soldier?" I asked, head back against the headrest, ready.

I could almost hear the fellow blink. "Twenty-eight standard, lord."

It was all I could do to keep from laughing. "Since before your father was born, lad. Take us out."

It's a strange thing. The largest, fastest ships—ships like the *Tamerlane,* like Titus Hauptmann's *Sieglinde,* or the great Sojourners of the Exalted, ships that outpace passing photons a thousand times over—feel slow. So great is their size and so distant any frame of reference that to travel the black seas of space, even at warp, seems more like standing still. But a lightership, a ship such as the little Sparrowhawk in which we rode?

Acceleration slammed us back into our seats as the magnetic accelerator threw us into the void faster than any bullet.

And we were falling. Falling through naked blackness toward a world like rusted iron. I felt my hands go tight on the armrests, and for a moment my vision blurred with red. The lighter was too small to carry a suppression field generator, and so we bore the full brunt of the inertial tide, rolling down from the dark heavens to the barren waste.

Below us, the planet stretched dead and desolate far as the eye could see. Brown peaks and escarpments reared from red sand, and what little atmosphere yet remained turned the sky a sickly yellow.

"Reminds me of Arae," the soldier said. "Bleak place, lord—if you don't mind my saying."

Our flight had leveled off several miles above the surface, so high we cast no shadow on the world below. "Can you take us lower?"

"Aye."

The pilot was right. The place did look a great deal like Arae, though that world had been white with salt where ancient seas had dried and great wind-tossed pans stretched to the horizons. The sky was what did it. The small and too-close sun made the red deserts redder, but that alien sky declared that this was no country for mankind.

I leaned forward in my seat, looking out from beneath the Sparrowhawk's single long wing as it tacked against the too-thin air, solar cells drinking of the wan light. There silence reigned, for there was no wind to carry the cry of birds or the scream of beasts, nor the lash of thunder or rain. Few places I have been in all the universe were as stark, as desolate, or as beautiful.

Corvo was right, and Durand. There was nothing in the desert.

We did not seek *nothing*.

"Take us lower, man," I said, and though he could not see me I pointed out the cockpit glass to where a mighty canyon yawned off our starboard side. "Let's have a nearer look at that trench."

At a gesture from the pilot, the Sparrowhawk's single wing rotated, coming from horizontal out our left side to near vertical. We tipped forward and plunged, angling down through airs so thin they could hardly be called airs at all. I was glad of our repulsors, for surely the Sparrowhawk's long, lonely wing was useless beneath that airless sky.

Descending, I saw that Varro had been correct. The signs of antique waters showed in the striations of rock walls a mile high to either side, red and white, but the ancient river was long gone. Buttes rose like pillars on gnarled corners of the mighty rift, buttressing the sky.

"Do you see anything?" Valka's voice sounded through the conduction patch behind my ear.

"No," I said. "It's beautiful, though."

We flew on in silence a while, eyes and instruments scanning. High above, I knew, the *Tamerlane* and her shuttles spun and searched. If there was anything to find, we'd find it.

"Do you know what we're looking for, my lord?" the pilot officer asked, glancing back over his shoulder.

I did not answer at once, but sat peering down through the glass blister in which I sat, feet in the holsters of the chair. Cocking my ankles, I swiveled, surveying the lands below. Pedals beneath my feet allowed me to rotate in any direction within the gunner's sphere, holographs overlaid on the glass surface and in empty air around, according me a hazy but complete picture of the space around me. Looking through these at the fellow, I said, "Not exactly. But I'll know it when I see it." I realized this was the characteristic sort of non-answer congruent with my nearly mystical reputation, and I tried again: "There'll be structures of some kind. Black stone. Always black stone." I had not seen or been near a Quiet site since Emesh and Calagah, but I remembered plain enough, and remembered also the innumerable holos and phototypes Valka had shown me time after time. The arches, the angled pillars and inhuman geometries, the strange grace and alien beauty of them, fluted and flowing like water. The round marks, the anaglyphs, each hinting at ideas no human hand had deciphered or human mind understood.

As it always did, such thoughts brought me to ancient Egypt, to hieroglyphs forgotten and undeciphered for millennia, to pyramids more ancient than the white megaliths of the Mericanii.

To gods old when man was young.

What gods were on that nameless world were older still, though yet unborn. For if the flow of time is an illusion—a trick of human light—there is no difference between future and past. Thus that which lies in the remotest future is more ancient than the ancient past, for more aeons are there yet to come in cosmic time than have been. So remote, so deep are the epochs which separate my hand and this page from theirs.

"There are no ruins here, lordship," the man said.

I chewed my tongue and pressed a finger to the contact patch behind my ear to broadcast on all channels. "Sphinx Flight, this is Lord Marlowe with Sphinx Zero-Niner. One hundred hurasams to the man who first catches sight of something down there. Do you copy?"

A string of replies came over the line.

"Copy that, lord!"

"Too bad we couldn't have come here before that island on Colchis, eh boys?"

"Smart money's on us!"

"Up yours, Oh-Four!"

Unseen in the gunner's seat, I smiled. Ordinary men. What a relief humanity is just to be around. Here we were at a desert on the edge of the world, on a planet beyond the edge of human knowledge, and the bastards were joking.

May mankind never change.

I switched back to Valka's channel, tipping my chair forward so that I hung against the restraints nearly parallel to the ground. "See anything up there?"

"The shuttles are still taxiing into their orbits," came her reply. "I have a good feeling about this."

"What makes you say that?" I asked.

Her response crackled slightly—sign of magnetic interference from the planet's surprisingly strong fields. "No one's ever been here. Your Chantry won't have ruined the place."

"They're not . . ."

"Not yours, I know." She cut me off.

I grunted. "We might be too early. If all these ruins are running backward in time, they might not have . . ."

"Risen from the sands?" Valka finished for me. I could see her smiling by the holography well at the captain's station as clearly as if I were standing across from her.

"Careful, Valka," I said where only she and the pilot officer could overhear me, "you're starting to sound like me."

"Imagine the horror."

Though our spirits were high as we searched, we saw nothing. Hours went on filled with nothing but spare remarks and the slow scroll of sere lands beneath us.

"Aristedes is on one of the polar shuttles," Valka reported. "He's reporting some water ice in the caps with the dry, but nothing else interesting.

Varro thinks there might be groundwater or something. Underground seas."

"Like Vorgossos," I said. "Can we do a gravimetric scan?"

"Not from orbit," Valka answered. "Effective range is too short. You think 'tis underground, this thing we're after?"

I shrugged in the harness, by then hanging nearly upside down. "I don't know what we're after." I craned my neck, taking in several more square miles of barren emptiness. "Wish you could see this place."

"I am seeing it," she said. "Believe you me, Marlowe, this is one adventure I'm happy to sit through. I hate lighters."

"I just hoped what we were looking for would be obvious. Like the other sites," I said. Calagah had not been easy to miss: a black facade of stairs and arched colonnades fronting the wall of a seaside ravine, shafts opening through the upland miles inland, a network of tunnels and passages such as ancient Minos might have built.

But we had a whole planet to search, and so I knew I should be patient.

I think I dozed in the saddle, our progress gentler now as we swept the horizon. I dreamt of rain on a world that perhaps had never known it. A torrent fell past me through bottomless skies while winds roared and shook trees whose roots I could not see. I fell with the rain, falling until it seemed I traveled not down but *forward* with the ground rushing beneath me.

I stood upon a gray plain, not rough but paved and smooth. Ahead a black dome rose shallow against the sky, perfectly smooth and surrounded by pillars wider than any tree. A great crowd stood about me—but did not mark me as I passed them by. White hair, white horns, black cloaks, and black armor. Black too their banners snapping in the wind, each painted with the device of a white hand wide upon its face. I saw once more the figure of a creature tall and terrible, silver-crowned, leading a man in chains. Without having to be told I knew that here was the Scourge of Earth. The Prophet. The *Aeta Ba-Aetane.* The *Shiomu.* The Pale King. Syriani Dorayaica.

I drew nearer, horror rising in my heart as I beheld the creature it led on its chain.

Violet eyes met my own.

My own eyes.

It was me.

"This is Sphinx Zero-Five, *Tamerlane.* Think we have something in the mountains at twenty-seven north latitude, eighty-one west."

The comms chatter woke me, and swallowing bile I banished my dreams.

Cielcin beneath an open sky . . .

I did not hear Corvo's response as I came back to my senses. Holographs taken from the other lighter appeared on my gunner's display. A red stone mountain rose from the plains. It was clearly volcanic, for it stood alone, apart from the surrounding mountains at the edge of one of the basins Varro suspected had long ago been seas. It rose for miles above the plain and pierced—I think—the upper limits of that dead world's thin air and so brushed naked space.

More images appeared, showing the plain before the mountain. Not the plain from my dream, for I'd a sudden and terrible sense that the black dome I'd just seen would appear before my eyes.

But it was not to be.

Great round arches of stone rose from red sand, black and nearly circular, marking out a path that ran up the foothills of the mountain from the bed below. There five tongues of stone rose, curling from a knurl of rock like the fingers of some impossibly huge hand.

"Valka, you seeing this?" I enlarged the image, and thought I beheld an opening in the mountainside where the five pillars came together.

A door.

"The arches are nearly like the ones on Ozymandias," she said.

"They're nearly full circles," I said.

"If they are like the ones on Ozymandias, they *are* full circles," she said. "The bases are just buried."

"Did you see the door?" I asked. "Up on the slope?"

Valka sounded almost transfixed. "I'll have Otavia put together a landing party—oh, this is marvelous!" We still had some of the prefabricated units we'd bought for our stay on Thessa, enough to build a reasonable base camp. "We'll need to secure the site. I can't believe 'tis really here."

"You doubted it?" I asked.

"Hadrian." I could tell by her tone that she'd ignored my question.

"Yes, Valka?"

"I hope you know . . . 'twas all worth it."

I opened my mouth to respond to that, but the comm line buzzed with outside chatter. "That hundred sovereigns on the table still, Lord Marlowe?" came the spotter's voice over the comm. It was Sphinx Oh-Five.

"And a bottle of Kandarene!" I called back, riding high on the moment of discovery. "Red or white, soldier?"

The aquilarius replied, "More a red man, sire!"

"A man after my own heart!" To my pilot I said, "How fast can we be there?"

"It's damn near the other side of the planet, my lord. A few hours. Faster, if you don't mind getting knocked around a bit."

I gave the order. "Punch it, Ardi."

The Sparrowhawk's single wing snapped round until it stood perfectly vertical, long and towering over the snubbed fuselage like the crest of some dramatic bird. The primary drive kicked, fusion reactor burning with a fury that punched me back into my seat. We were streaking heavenward once more, moving into a parabolic arc designed to carry us around the world far faster than any suborbital flight.

We'd arrived.

CHAPTER 66

EMPIRE OF SILENCE

PEOPLE BELIEVE IT IS silent in airless places, but it is not so. No word or cry carries on the wind, that much is true. There is no wind to carry them. One cannot hear the crack of guns or the distant roar of thunder—one instead hears the crunch of earth beneath one's feet carried through the suit and the metronomic rasp of one's own breathing. Stay in silence long enough, and one can even start to feel the pump and scrape of blood in one's own veins.

It is enough to drive men mad.

Standing on the rise overlooking the fat cargo shuttle as it descended on four repulsor pods, I heard almost nothing. The deep-throated roar of the drives ought to have been like the cry of a thousand voices, but the thin atmosphere reduced the roar to a whine so high and bloodless I could hardly hear it at all. High above, five of Sphinx Flight still circled, long wings like the sails of ancient mariners plying the sky. The ship I'd arrived in remained on the fields below, wing laid flat to one side. The pilot officer, Ardi, stood near at hand. Both of us wore vacuum suits: he an aquilarius's padded flight suit devoid of the legionnaire's white ceramic armor; me in my customary black, unarmored save for the black helmet and mask that connected to the neck joint. I wore my coat overtop, collar needlessly high.

The both of us cast long shadows on the ground. The structure the huge lifter shuttle was depositing was the last in a rough semi-circular arrangement some thousand feet from the first ring. Other shuttles hunched on the rocks further out. Personnel filtered between them and the new-dropped buildings on their landing peds, looking like a herd of overgrown iron beetles black and glassy white. I saw one figure bound down the ramp and peel away from the group it was with and hurry up the slope toward us. Slow clouds of dust erupted beneath its feet as it drew nearer, and I recognized the distinctive gait and the enthusiasm in it.

I waved.

Valka waved back.

Another jogged after her, like a shadow still in Red Company gear. The Norman officers never had taken to wearing the Imperial white. Spying the bandoleer with its many knives, I knew it was Crim. He overtook Valka at the feet of the first slopes and dogged her the while.

"You haven't gone in, have you?" Valka asked. No preamble. No *hello*.

"I was waiting for you," I said, speaking over the proximity band so all nearby could hear. Though I wore no armor, I retained my sword and shield-belt, and hooked my fingers behind the buckle. "I did take a look at the arches, though."

Valka's helmet was not military issue, and where my suit had a mask fashioned like a human face, Valka's was only an arc of clear alumglass. I saw her eyes widen. "And?"

"It's them, all right," I said, gesturing for her to join me. "See for yourself."

The first arch was easily three hundred feet in diameter, a perfect circle with about a quarter of it buried in the sand. Each successive ring marching upslope looked a little smaller—seven in all—until the gate in the mountain's face was only about a hundred feet high. And thick! Each ring was roughly square in cross-section, its form complicated by a strangely organic molding along the outer edge, highlight panels inscribed with one of the familiar circular anaglyphs.

Valka touched one with trembling fingers. "We need to get remote cameras in here to image everything we can," she said. I could practically hear the gears in her mind turning as she peered through glass at the symbols.

"What does it say?" asked the aquilarius, Ardi. I'd forgotten the man was there.

If the question bothered Valka, she gave no sign. "No one knows."

"No one?" the man asked. "We came here to find all this and no one can read it, even?"

I winced for the fellow's sake, expected Valka to wheel on him. But she turned and—hand still on the arch, answered, " 'Tis incredible, no?"

"Incredible?" The fellow shook his head.

I put a hand on his shoulder. "Ardi, take your ship back up to the *Tamerlane,* tell the captain all's well here. She'll need all the help she can get scouting the system."

The man saluted and hurried off, leaving me with Valka and Crim.

" 'Twas not underfoot," Valka said. "You needn't have dismissed him."

I only shrugged.

Valka pressed her visor to my mask and said, "We found them!" I heard her not only over her suit's communicator, but faintly through the clear aluminum and ceramic between our faces. "Hadrian, we found them."

I held her in my arms beneath the alien arch, pitying Crim now and forgetting him in the moment. "We don't know what we've found, yet," I said.

"I know," Valka said. "If what Horizon said is true . . . if this is their oldest site, or their youngest . . . if 'tis crumbling backward through time, there may not be much to see." I still could not fathom it: a place where entropy ran backward and order was restored—not lost—with time. Standing on the slope of that mountain, I could almost imagine the ruins rising from the dust like a holograph of a burning building played in reverse.

Eager to brighten the mood I'd just dampened, I said, "On the other hand—if this is their oldest settlement—their attentions may be more here than elsewhere." Somehow, it sounded less encouraging out loud. I turned my face to the pale yellow of the sky. Despite the coldness of the day, the red sun was warm against my mask. Almost I felt a sensation of eyes upon me, and I shook myself.

Despite the way the rings all marked the approach to the door beneath its five pillars, there was no path. No stair along the ridgeline. Perhaps it had crumbled away. Perhaps it had yet to appear. Nevertheless, we climbed, passing each of the rings in turn, pausing by each to allow Valka the time to take in each facet, each glyph, until we came under the shadow of the curling pillars and the mouth of the cave.

"We really shouldn't go in, Had," Crim said, one hand on his shield-belt, the other grasping the hilt of one knife. "Get a mapping team in here."

"We will," I said, placing a hand on my own shield catch, ready and waiting. "We just want to take a look around."

The one-time assassin cocked his head behind his faceless helm. "Wasn't your mother a storyteller? Do you not know how famous a set of last words those are?"

"We're not children, Karim," Valka said.

"At least wait and let me radio men from the camp for backup, eh?"

"You're all the backup we need!" I said, smiling behind my expressionless mask.

The Norman shrugged. "If I have to carry your corpses down this mountain, I'm not explaining it to the Emperor."

"This is not the day we die!" I exclaimed, and clapped the fellow on the shoulder.

"Those are famous last words, too."

But they would not be mine. Valka plucked a glowsphere from her belt and twisted it to activate both its light and its repulsor. The thing was Tavrosi, one she had carried with her since Emesh. Old though it was, it shone bright and followed her closely, slaved to the implants in her brain. I wondered for half an instant how it had gotten past Gereon and the Grand Inquisitor—but perhaps the forbidden praxis was in Valka's head and not the sphere at all. Lacking for suit lights, I keyed up my terminal's palm-light and flicked the torch up into my hand.

Shoulder to shoulder, Valka and I pressed into the dark, lights illuminating buttressed walls and arches like the arches outside. These continued a ways, shrinking and narrowing as the atrium pierced the flesh of that great mountain—a hundred feet, then a thousand—until it terminated in a door but large enough for three men to walk abreast.

Three men.

We were three.

The serendipity of this was lost on me at the time, but now I think it a kind of signpost, an indication that our feet were on the proper path. There are versions of the story, no doubt, where I had not sent Ardi away. Who knows what lay down those paths, and through what strange and undiscovered countries of time were borne upon those currents?

At once the path began to diverge, wrapping left and right as if in a mighty circle and rising straight before us along a steep gradient, the floor smooth and polished as mirror glass, shining like obsidian in the gleam of our lamps.

We were human. We climbed.

"We will need to get drones in here," Valka said. " 'Twill save time."

In time, we did precisely that. I recall the way the fanning lasers swept the walls, tracing every ridge and ripple of the stone surface, every arch and buttress, every cranny.

"Calagah would fit in this place half a hundred times or more," Valka said when the scans were done. Cracked and crumbling in places, the great halls and narrow corridors of the complex ran for hundreds of miles, honeycombing and filling the mountain like the byways of some extraterranic anthill. There were no windows, no doors, no rooms that spoke of habitation. There were no artifacts. Not pottery, not cloth, not chip of paint or shard of bone, nothing to indicate that anyone had lived there but the structure itself.

Observing the holograph with her in the close gloom of our suite in the campsite, I said, "It's another bloody labyrinth."

Valka shook her head. She wore one of her customary long shirts and a frown. "It looks like no city I've ever seen," she said. " 'Tis no starport, no way of getting water in here, no lighting . . . just all this damn stone." She leaned back on the low couch beneath the ugly narrow windows. "I talked to a scholiast on Colchis about the stuff, you know?"

"About what?"

"The stuff the ruins are made of." She waved an explanatory hand. "You remember, I told you on Emesh we can't break the stuff?" I didn't. " 'Twas nothing in the library about it, so I asked an archivist. Lawrence, he was. I told him the ruins are made of a substance that isn't atomic at all. That it *felt* like stone but showed nothing on the scans."

Not taking my eyes from the spider-web image of the tunnel map between us, I asked, "What did he say?"

"He said 'twas impossible, that if such a thing were so, they would have record of it."

"The Chantry probably blocked that knowledge, even from the scholiasts," I said. "Easy enough to snuff out or discredit a few renegades like us, I guess."

Valka matched my crooked smile. "I guess. But I like to think the truth is more resilient than that."

"Maybe it is," I said.

The next day, I'd drawn my sword in the hall and pressed the point against the wall. Valka objected, but I moved carefully, eager to remove only the tiniest piece. Valka had said the stone would not be cut, but Valka had never carried highmatter. I pressed.

And met resistance.

Slowly, slowly the point of the sword worked into the strange substance. I marveled at the stress fractures we had seen, imagining the titanic forces required to crack stone even highmatter struggled to cut. Drawing the point back, I cut a sliver from the wall and held it in my palm, grinning.

"We can get it down to camp to study!" Valka said, taking it with trembling fingers. She looked up at me. "I should have brought you along sooner." She held the chip up to her eyes, grinning all the while.

And then—without warning—the chip vanished. She did not drop it. It did not melt or disintegrate. It *vanished* as though it had been switched off.

Valka's face went white, and she made a gesture as if to hurl the thing away, swearing in Panthai. "What the hell happened?"

I ran my gloved hand over the wall where I'd cut, but of the notch I'd made there was no sign. It was as if we'd never acted at all.

"I think I understand," I said slowly, unkindling my blade and plunging us back into sphere-lit gloom. "If Horizon was telling the truth, if these ruins really are moving backward through time, then anything we do to them will be undone." I picked a finger over the precise spot I'd mutilated. The stone was smooth as glass. Kindling my sword once more, I swung. I had to lean my weight behind the exotic metal to cut that alien stone, but cut it did, and no sooner was the cut made then it vanished, the wall restored to its perfect form. "We move forward. They go back." I cut the wall again. The stripe vanished. "The damage I just did is in our past now. Its future."

"Just when I thought I was beginning to understand any of this," Valka said. "Then shouldn't we have seen the cuts you made on the wall before you made them?"

The answer came automatically. "I hadn't made them yet." Again I unkindled my sword and clicked the weapon into my belt. "Remember what Horizon said? About time and space and about things moving *sideways in time*?" I felt reasonably confident that I understood. "There were two pasts—two futures for the ruins—that is. One where I cut the wall, one where I didn't. We change the future every time we act, but the future for these stones is the past—because they're running backward."

Valka was shaking her head. " 'Tis madness, all of this."

"We hadn't arrived until we arrived to make the cut in the wall, and so changed the ruins' future—which is our past."

Valka only shook her head, whether from a lack of understanding or from disbelief I was unsure. "It's the perfect way to protect these sites. Not only do they *not* decay as time passes, but any attempts to meddle with them are useless." Beneath my helmet, I was grinning. "Oh, that is brilliant. The Chantry must know all this!"

"How do you think they're doing it?" Valka mused. "Sending things backward in time. 'Tis meant to be impossible."

I had some elementary schooling in physics. I had never intended to be a magus, even in my pursuit of the scholiasts' tradition. My interests had been cultural: artistic, literary, historical—not scientific. It was possible, by way of special relativity, possible to travel into the future by flying near the speed of light or by coasting too near a supermassive object whose gravity bent space and time about it. But always forward, only forward.

"Something in the material, maybe?" I suggested. "These walls aren't ordinary matter, as you well know. Or maybe . . . maybe the Quiet did something to these sites . . . these entire planets maybe. Made their *forward* in time *back*." I sank to the floor at the base of the hall, looking up through Valka as I thought. The computer god's words came back to me, and I muttered, "Toward what you call the future . . ." I thought of my visions again, the rivers of light branching through higher darkness. I wondered if perhaps my visions were easing my comprehension.

Valka completed the picture for me, her perfect memory recalling something else the machine had said. "Time is only another kind of space."

"Imagine a map," I said, sketching a square in the air. "Beginning of time at one end, end at the other, where the line between them is what happens. But to either side there are other lines. Things that don't happen. Things that *might* happen. And as the universe runs forward, our choices weave those other threads in. Braid it. Most of the threads didn't happen because they can't. Or they can't happen because they didn't happen. I don't know. But there aren't just other futures. There are other presents, other pasts. I think. And because these ruins are moving backward we can see that. Maybe *now* . . . if we could come here yesterday . . . the marks I made on the wall would be there."

Valka watched me through her clear visor, gold eyes narrow. "I'll say it again, Marlowe. 'Tis madness."

We climbed the ramp that first day for I don't know how long, ascending until we came to a round chamber where paths branched to all sides. The chamber was easily as large as a floor of the Great Library, half a mile across or more, and the paths that ran away from us varied in width, such that some were wide as avenues and lined with columns like alien trees where others were too narrow even for a child to pass. What must these creatures look like to inhabit such a space, I wondered? My mind went to thoughts of serpents, of trailing robes and tentacles winding in the dark. Of ghosts and green light and my own reflection moving in the dark, glassy surface of the black stone walls. Of mirrors.

The ruin was large as any city, though it felt larger still, for it switched back and was stacked upon itself level upon level upon dozenth level, filling the mountain. Though we spent years combing over its every byway and avenue, still I am certain I did not walk them all. It was vaster by far than the warrens of Calagah, and though the substance of its construction was the same as on Emesh, the effect in that place was not of dank closeness, but of air and darkness. An enchanted city of the night.

"There are windows!" I remember Valka exclaiming. "I've not seen a window in any of these sites, not in all my years!" The windows stood high on the walls of a great and pillared hall, admitting the crimson sunlight in high-angled beams that tracked across the dusty floor. Aisle upon aisle of pillars marched tilted to either side, some of them cracked by cataclysms yet to come. The ruined city had taken on a curious air to me. No longer funereal and sad, no longer a monument to a vanished people and a glory gone from the world. They were not haunted by the ghosts of ancient kings and emperors, but by phantoms yet to come, phantoms greater and more strange than any that stalked the west bank of the Nile when man was young.

Months passed, and at length we found our way—though the journey took days—to the highest halls. There we found the upper gate and came out upon the highest slopes of the mountain.

The red sun shone in a black and starlit sky. Valka and I went out alone onto the shelf and looked down upon the shield of the volcano stretching dozens of miles out and more than twenty miles down to the rusty plains below. We could just see the camp on the plains below and make out the rings and the pillars like the fingers of some almighty hand beneath us.

"Do you hear that?" Valka asked, surveying the whole of the site from our newfound vantage.

There was nothing to hear. I held my breath a moment, and in the moment that followed the only sound was the faint pulse of blood in my ears.

Nothing.

"Silence," I said, finding in myself an ancient scrap of writing. "The great empire of silence: higher than all stars, deeper than the kingdom of death! It alone is great; all else is small."

Valka had understood the Classical English perfectly, and said nothing. We had been too long together. She understood my moods, and these romantic moments had ceased to try her patience. She only stood beside me, each of us a piece of that silence, small ourselves.

But even the very small can challenge empires, or hold them in their hands.

I broke the silence. "We haven't named this place, you know."

"I'd thought about that," she said.

"You should do it."

"You're the one with all the damned quotations and history!" She jostled me.

Turning, I looked down at her. My mask's entoptics made it almost seem like I wore no helmet at all, images from outside shining in twin cones directly at my eyes. I wanted to kiss her, but layers of ceramic and alumglass intervened. "You should do it," I said again.

Valka pulled away and followed the edge of the precipice a ways, testing her footing with light steps. After a dozen paces or so, she turned back. "Annica," she said. "We'll call it Annica."

"Isn't that the name of those musicians you like?" I asked, pointing at my chest as if to indicate some graphic that was not there. "The ones with the skulls?"

She flashed a wry grin through her visor. "It means *impermanence*."

"Annica . . ." I said again, not meditating overmuch on the meaning of the name Valka had given our new world. "Annica it is."

Significant though any naming seems to me, Valka had moved on. "I'll radio the shuttles. We'll need to set up a second camp here, work the site from both ends. I want to complete the holography model of the city by the end of the week if we can."

I let her go, watched her mount the slope, climbing higher in search of a place the shuttles might put in. Already I could see the line of reflective stakes that would be hammered into the red stone to mark the path to the upper gate. Valka could handle the shuttles. I turned and moved back toward the gate, thinking that I would return to our men in the upper atrium where we'd left them before clambering out.

The noise of rock crunching beneath my heels resonated through my boots, punctuating that eerie silence. I had not known it was possible to miss the wind, or even to miss the whir and constant whine of air compressors and climate control.

But we had been uncertain where else or whether the ruins might emerge on the mountain. Quick flybys by Sphinx Flight had revealed another door here and there, but Valka had wanted to be sure, hence our long climb through the dark past the place where the thin and poison air ran out. Though I have stood upon the topless towers of Forum and looked down upon a bottomless sky, never before had I felt so on top of the world. Not even atop Vorgossos's hightower had I felt so tall, for that narrow strand was a cheap construction of human hands, but the mountain was something else entirely.

A seat of gods—empty, quiet, and clean.

I was alone for one brief instant, and stopped on the threshold to look out once more upon our base camp far below. One hand on the round arch, I lingered, delaying my task. The men would keep another moment.

I should not linger in this account—which I fear is too long already, even for one who has lived so long as I. I would not linger and waste this fine red ink were it not for what happened next.

A wind rose and swept the mountaintop, gathering my long coat in its arms. I pressed myself against the arch, for a moment not processing the miracle I was witnessing.

There was no air.

I called out for Valka, but no answer came.

"My lord?" One of the soldiers stood in the hall behind. "Is everything all right?"

"Did you feel it?" I asked. "The wind?"

The man cocked his head, voice flattened by the suit. "Wind, sire?"

It was happening again.

CHAPTER 67

THE SUMMONS

"DID YOU SEE IT yet?" Captain Corvo's holograph asked me. The captain was still in orbit, Durand, Halford, and Aristedes alongside her, their four ghosts hovering life-size in the camp suite's holography booth.

"You know I have," I said, uncrossing my legs to lean forward.

I sat upon a low stool on the edge of the booth, image transmitted to orbit with the usual second or two of lag. Valka sat behind me—just out of frame—with Prince Alexander not far off. My young charge had spent most of those first three years on Annica in fugue, but we'd taken him out, thinking it wise that he should see the truth. Valka and I led him, wide-eyed, through the ruined city and its strange halls.

That had been before the summons came.

It lay paused before me, Sir Friedrich Oberlin's—now Director Friedrich Oberlin's—image frozen mid-sentence, dossiers and reports projected in the black glass of the console to me and the ghosts of my four officers.

Casualty reports. Star charts. Video footage transmitted via the datasphere sat grid.

The records of the crushing defeat at Marinus.

The Veil had fallen and with it—though the rest would be slow in falling—the entire Imperial presence in the Norman Expanse. The freeholders were on their own, and few dozen colonies. Without Marinus to act as a central hub and critical trade nexus—like Gododdin—the region could not resupply itself. Troops could not be moved from front to front as the Cielcin attacked. Logistics became difficult—perhaps impossible—and most people fail to understand just how many battles and wars are won by logistics.

Castrametation, just as Lorian had said.

"They're ordering us to join the fleet at Berenike," said Bastien

Durand. In a rare twist, the fellow had removed his glasses. He looked young without them. "They're planning an expedition to retake Marinus."

"They'll be a while gathering their forces," I said.

"It'll take the better part of a century to mass the fleet at Berenike," Corvo agreed.

"Seventy-eight years," Durand said. "Oberlin says they mean to launch in ISD 16710."

"I read the dispatch," I said. Berenike was on the road to Marinus, a colonial supply depot and Legion fortress world that had played Marinus's role in Imperial conquest and expansion before Marinus had. All ships making for the freeholds and the inner rim followed that ancient road through Gododdin and the Centaurine provinces, through Berenike, to the Veil and Marinus. It was following that road that had called the Cielcin down upon us centuries ago, for beyond Marinus lay Cressgard—burned now to glass to erase the Cielcin and the holocaust they'd visited upon that once-green world. "Berenike," I repeated. I had been through Berenike before—as I had Gododdin—but I had never set foot there. "How quickly can we get there?"

Durand glanced at Corvo, and the captain answered in her gruff way, "Too slow."

Halford cleared his throat. The night captain was clearly still uncomfortable around the main crew. "We're closer to Berenike than we were to Colchis. Our flight here carried us most of the way around the core, so if we wrap around . . . sixty years at full burn, maybe?"

I raised one eyebrow. It was less time than I'd expected, given the long bar of the galaxy's core lay between us and we would have to sail around. The practical wisdom was that flying through the core was a fool's errand. The stars were too numerous and too close together to fly through at warp.

Not answering at once, I ran my hand over the console, swiping through images of the ruined world. Burned cities glowed like the embers of dying fire from the console screen, crashed starships lay broken and shattered on hilltops.

"Was it Dorayaica?" I asked, changing the subject. Attacking the provincial capital smacked of the Scourge of Earth. The Prophet had been silent since the deep plunge into Imperial territory that cost us the shipyards at Hermonassa, unless one counted Iubalu. I filtered the documents before me as I spoke, finding the reports that the orbital troop storage stations had all been fragged. Hundreds of thousands of soldiers died in fugue without ever knowing it.

Aristedes massaged his shoulder with one hand. "Or one of his generals."

"Its," I corrected. Once, I might have insisted on the masculine in reference to a Cielcin chieftain, but I'd learned my lesson with Aranata. No sooner had Aristedes spoken did my hand scroll across an image of a black banner snapping from the spar of a crashed Cielcin landing craft, the White Hand plain to see upon its surface.

Iedyr Yemani.

Corvo cleared her throat. "What should we do?"

Not looking either at the ghosts before me or the people present behind, I asked, "This message arrived by telegraph?"

I could almost *hear* the confused blinking of my audience's eyes, but did not raise my own from my contemplation of the carnage. It felt somehow wrong to avert my gaze from the horror, felt like I *needed* to see.

"Yes, lord," Halford answered.

I glanced at the night captain and the other officers. "Then they won't be expecting us for some time." The decision made itself, and I clenched my fist against the console top, closing down the reel of images beneath my fingertips. "We have come too far to turn back empty-handed. We are not done here."

"We can't!" Alexander stirred behind me, and I turned to see him closing the gap between us. "Sir Hadrian! You saw the footage, we have to go!"

I fixed the princeling with my firmest stare, and the boy's progress halted as if someone had pinned him in place. Putting Alexander from my mind, I turned back to the holograph. "Signal Forum. Tell them we are en route from Colchis. That will buy us time."

"Colchis?" Otavia echoed.

Aristedes was grinning. The quantum telegraph relied on pairs of entangled particles to achieve instantaneous communication at any distance, relying on relays to transmit messages between endpoints not sharing a matched particle pair. It wasn't possible to divine our location from a telegraph reply. When Switch had summoned Bassander Lin to Vorgossos, he had had to manually reveal our location—a feat made possible only because Brethren had been watching the situation from the planet below and allowed word to get out.

"That should give us the time we need to conclude our affairs here and still make Berenike before we're expected there." I had told no one—not even Valka—of the wind that had swept the mountain's top. I'd kept my silence in part because I knew how ridiculous the story would sound, and because I feared they would believe me. "This is the place, ladies, gentlemen. *This* is the planet."

"The planet for what?" asked Halford.

"I don't know," I said, and sensed something huge and shapeless move beneath those words. "I have no more answers than you do," I said simply. "But I have worked too hard and for too long to get here to leave empty-handed."

"But we could already be too late!" Alexander nearly shouted. He'd overcome my glare and lay a hand on the back of my seat to rotate the console's chair. I planted a foot on the ground to halt my progress.

I did not raise my voice, did not turn to look up at the young prince. "Step away, Alexander. Thank you."

"You're making a mistake."

"So are you," I said, voice gone cold and far away. Focusing my attention on the officers in the booth before me, I asked, "What say you?"

Unsurprisingly, Lorian spoke first, spreading his hands in their silver wire braces. "I'm for it," he said. "I don't see much harm in staying. We could finish here in ten years and still be early."

Halford was nodding, but said nothing. I could hardly blame him. Of all the *Tamerlane*'s officers, he'd had the least contact with me personally and so the least contact with all this difficult business. The Quiet were strange to him—though perhaps not so strange as they were to me, who knew them best of all the company. Better then to stay, well . . . *quiet*.

The greater part of wisdom is in silence.

"I agree with your prince," Durand said, ever the prescriptivist. "Without Marinus, the Veil won't hold. Our people," he put a hand on Otavia's shoulder, "our people are doomed. I've no love for the Empire, but the freeholds can't fight the Cielcin alone." I had never heard the fellow speak so candidly. Bastien Durand was the sort of man who guarded his thoughts like gold, kept his mind in shadows because the shadows were safe. Officious, efficient, the consummate middle manager, he was and had been as effective as he was invisible. So often as I have written this account I have forgotten he was even there. But he looked at me then, and I believe I saw him for the first time. "We have to go, my lord, I beg you. My home on Algernon is not two dozen light-years from Marinus. My family may be long dead by now, but it is my home." He leaned forward in his seat, hands clasped between his knees. Beside him, Otavia Corvo was strangely silent, her eyes downcast. Did she feel the same? She must. This was like Vorgossos again. Like Jinan and Bassander.

"We will go," I said. A brief and terrible flash of relief spiderwebbed across Durand's face. But I was not finished. "We will go when we are done here." A raised a hand to forestall the First Officer's protest. "Bastien." I do not think I had ever called the fellow by his given name. "Bastien, there are things involved in all this I do not understand. You've seen what happened to me. You know people who saw it with their own eyes. With their own *eyes!*" I stood then, in part to underscore my sentiment but in part also to get away from Alexander, who yet loomed behind my chair. "I do not understand it. But I do know that it is happening for a reason. If I can find out what that reason is, then maybe I can make a difference in this damned war. No one has given more to this fight than me. We can avenge Marinus, and if we cannot save your homeworld, then we can avenge it, too." Speaking of vengeance made me think of owl-eyed Cassian Powers, the Avenger of Cressgard, and despite my utter seriousness I felt for a moment that I was half a fool.

Durand's eyes narrowed. "That is cold comfort, my lord."

"I understand your frustrations, Bastien," I said, and sensing that Alexander was about to interject, raised a hand to silence him. Even as I did so, I heard him choke off the words he'd been reaching for. "And yours, Your Highness. But consider what we know. I *died* on the *Demiurge.*"

"That's true?" Alexander asked, voice small.

"It's *true*," I said, glancing to Valka. There was no point hiding it, not anymore. "All of it. And we know the Cielcin understand things about all of this." I gestured at the dark walls of the unit and at the Annican sands beyond. "The Quiet. The Watchers. Leopards, lions, and wolves. They have the tactical advantage over us. Better intelligence. We are *losing,* friends. Vorgossos, Aptucca, that business with Iubalu . . . we may be winning battles, but we are losing the war. We've lost an entire *sector* now, and yes—your freeholds will pay for it. I may not be able to stop that. We may not be able to stop that. But we are *here.* Now. Now!" I slammed my fist against the console, making the images flash back onto its surface and dance. The holographs flickered in their booth. "I do not know what we will find here, but we are here for a reason. I am alive for a reason. I ask you all to have faith. We are this close!" I held my gloved fingers—the false fingers of my mutilated hand—mere microns apart. "Leave me here if you must go then, and come back. But here I remain."

My speech concluded, I stood silent watching the others, chin thrust out. I was commander of this expedition, and counted each of them my friends. But I would not be the first lord or captain to fall to mutiny, or the first man in history to be betrayed.

I might have been another, for in that moment my fate and the fate of my quest—and perhaps even the fate of humanity itself—lay, though I did not quite see it until after the moment passed, in the hands of Otavia Corvo.

May we all be so fortunate.

"Five years," she said. It was not the response an Imperial officer would give, was not obedience. But it was not mutiny either, nor was it the lizard-brained demand of a union mob. Hers was not the demand of some disgruntled subordinate holding a club over her betters, nor the mealy-mouthed request of a sycophant.

It was the offer of an equal. Of a friend.

"Five years," I agreed, and would have shaken her hand if not for the thousands of miles that lay between us. It was perhaps enough time. It was certainly enough to still arrive early at Berenike, early enough perhaps to satisfy the rational Bastien and even impulsive Alexander.

It would have to be.

The call ended shortly thereafter, and I stood still facing the empty holography well.

"We should go now," Alexander said again.

"This is enough from you, Your Highness," I said.

"Hadrian . . ." Valka interjected, speaking for the first time since the call started. She'd been uncharacteristically quiet, and was uncharacteristically defending the prince then, reminding me to check myself.

I did, and took a deep breath. "I must ask you not to challenge me in front of my officers, Alexander," I said, voice level. Only then did I turn. The prince had filled out in his time with us, some of the softness had boiled away, and he seemed more sure of himself.

Too sure.

"But you're making a mistake," he said. "You saw the reports, Sir Hadrian. We just lost the *Veil*. We don't have time for this!" Alexander flailed his arms at the environment pod around us, at the dining space and the low couch, the airlock with its suits hanging in niches, the door to the bedchamber. "You *died*? I thought Halfmortal was just because you'd survived so many battles. But these people really believe it?"

" 'Tis true, Alexander," Valka's voice came from behind, and the prince whirled. "I was there."

The prince spun to face her. "Not you, too. This is ridiculous. There is a war on, we just lost an entire territory, and you're digging in the dirt on the edge of nowhere! Why?" He looked back over his shoulder at me. Gesturing to Valka, he added, "Does she have you on so short a leash?"

I took a step toward the boy, and was pleased to see him recoil. Good. He had not unlearned all wisdom. I almost, *almost* seized him by the environment suit. There was a bracket just above the sternum on the prince's suit for attaching a safety line that would just about make a handle, and in Annica's nearly one-gee gravity I could lift him with one hand.

But again, Valka checked my advance. "We could show him." She'd spoken in Panthai to be sure the prince did not understand.

I shook my head, and answering her in the same tongue, I said, "It's on the *Tamerlane.*"

Valka frowned. " 'Tis in my head, too."

How easy it was to forget.

"Show him."

She did, and for the first time I saw what had been done to me through Valka's eyes.

Advancing to the console, Valka pressed her fingertips against the display. I am uncertain just how her praxis functioned, but there must have been something in her hands as well as her head, for without preamble the booth darkened, and once more I beheld the gardens of Kharn Sagara, the dark trees beneath the bloody sky and the flaming wreck of the *Bahali imnal Akura,* Aranata Otiolo's massive worldship.

And Aranata itself, its hulking form wielding Raine Smythe's sword like a knife, hunched shoulders, one mighty horn sheared away. There I was also, clad in legionary white and barely holding my ground. How small I seemed, like a candle flame against Aranata's night. I raised my sword to parry, and lost my arm instead.

"Hadrian!" Valka's own voice shrieked over the sound system.

"Marlowe!" That was Bassander Lin, voice far off and remote.

Moments I thought had taken centuries passed in seconds.

"Do it," I whispered, clutching the bleeding ruin of my right arm. *"Do it."*

Highmatter flashed. My head tumbled from my shoulders. The body stood a moment thereafter. Toppled. Hit the ground with a strangely hollow clattering.

The image vanished as Valka took her hand away. She shut her eyes, but not before I saw the tears in them.

"This is witchcraft," Alexander said, stepping back. He had not noticed the arms were reversed, that Aranata had taken my right—though I was missing my left. I hoped he would not notice. "Trickery."

" 'Tis not," Valka said. "Ask any of the others."

"It isn't real," he shook his head. "You still think I'm a fool." And with that he turned and strode out the airlock, helmet unfolding from the collar baffle of his suit as he shut the inner door behind him.

Night had fallen. The Annican night was deep, without the noise of bird or beast or even the sound of wind. The only sounds were those of the environment pod's air cyclers running and the noise of Valka's slow breathing from the other room. Sleep had not found me abed, and I'd returned to the holograph console in the far corner of the front room. For a time I'd stood and peered out the round window at the mountain, the pillars, and the rings. I'd watched two of our Sparrowhawk fighters circling overhead, quietly at their patrol. There had been little to see, and by night seeing anything was hard, unless it was the low light of the other camp buildings.

For the dozenth time, I pressed the play button on the holograph.

"The death toll was catastrophic . . ." Sir Friedrich Oberlin said, his holograph's eyes staring through me at something no living man could see. "Four million dead in orbital storage. Surface estimates are higher than seven million and climbing. More than twenty thousand shipmen." Images showed behind Sir Friedrich's head: the destruction of one of the orbital medica that housed hundreds of thousands of soldiers sleeping on ice, a dreadnought larger than the *Tamerlane* blown to pieces, a city turned to molten glass. "We are getting reports of survivors. Certain remote settlements were spared in the attack. The governor-general survived in bunkers beneath the capital. We're arranging for evacuation and relief missions as we speak. The Cielcin are gone. They didn't stay for the usual rape and plunder."

"That's because the orbital troop stations were their target," I said, as much to myself as to Oberlin's ghost. Legion Intelligence knew that full well, in any case, and did not need me to tell them.

The images behind Oberlin showed Cielcin ships like broken circles descending from the sky. Landing craft fell like meteors, smashing buildings as they fell in fiery rain. The capital had been ransacked, a million people taken. From city grid footage I saw them crowded aboard lifter rockets and carried back into space. I remember the looks on their faces. The cold fear, the tears. Something huge and winged flew across the sky, blotting out the sun.

Maybe Alexander and Durand were right. Maybe it was madness to stay. I switched the machine off.

CHAPTER 68

ANNICA

"I THINK WE'VE NEARLY finished this level," Valka said, coming back to join me where I sat near the gravitometer in the center of a round chamber off one of the massive, pillared halls. In Calagah, on Emesh, there had been entire chambers separate from the main network of halls and chambers, spaces sealed off and inaccessible. The gravitometer—a metal tripod twice the height of a man with a pendulum hanging from it—probed for minute fluctuations in the planet's gravity that hinted at empty spaces. We'd set up two dozen of the things throughout the ruins, hoping to discover features of the Quiet site that our initial scan with the mapping drones had failed to detect. "Are you all right?"

It took me the space of several heartbeats to realize that I'd been staring, that I hadn't moved. Behind my suit's expressionless black mask, I might have been sleeping.

"Sorry." I shifted where I sat, more to let her know that I was awake than anything. "I was just thinking about Marinus."

Several months had passed since Oberlin's telegraph and the order to make for Berenike, and a listless quality had descended upon our expedition. Durand and the rest of our Norman contingent—up to and including Otavia—were understandably prickly with me, and I was glad that Alexander had retreated to the *Tamerlane*. Valka had said nothing, and I pushed ahead. "I keep thinking about Simeon the Red—you know the story. The way the crew mutinied and he ended up stranded on the surface . . ."

Sighing, Valka seated herself on the floor beside me, back against the wall. We watched the gravitometer tick a moment in companionate silence. "You think they'd betray us?"

"No," I said, and furiously shook my head.

"Otavia wouldn't do that," Valka said.

"I know." I flexed my right hand beneath the suit glove, feeling the ache and tired stiffness in the bones. "But I wouldn't blame them if they did. They're men without country now. It isn't right. A man should have a people. A home." I sensed Valka disagreed. They weren't high on patriotism where she came from, and even clan allegiances had weakened in time, each become no more than an unfortunate extended family.

But she did not argue. "I suppose if Edda were attacked I'd . . . feel it," she said.

"Do you miss it?" I asked.

"Home?" She glanced at me through her helmet visor. "You know I don't."

"I miss mine . . ." I said, thinking of Tor Gibson.

A hand squeezed my knee through the suit. "Hadrian, you hated it there."

"I did," I said, "but it is home. Whatever else I may be, I am a Marlowe."

Not unkindly, Valka added, "Your father disowned you. The *Tamerlane* is your home—and 'tis home for the Normans all now, too." She rested her helmeted head against my shoulder. "We're your people." What I'd have given for a bottle of wine in that moment and the air to share it in. "I just hope we find something here to make it all worthwhile."

"We will," I said, wrapping an arm around her shoulders.

"Are you playing prophet again?"

The word *prophet* made me think of Iubalu and Syriani Dorayaica.

I hadn't told her about the wind on the mountaintop—the story was simultaneously so fabulous and so trivial I didn't know how to bring it up and be believed. "I've been having dreams again," I said. "First when we arrived . . . when we were scouting the planet. I dozed in the scout ship. Then again maybe half a dozen times . . ." I told her about the black dome, about the pillars spiraling toward it across a plain paved flat. About the Cielcin army standing beneath banners bearing the emblem of a white hand. About Dorayaica. About myself.

"Sometimes, the others are there. Pallino, Elara, Crim, and the rest."

"Not me?"

"Not you."

Valka was silent a long moment, her head still on my shoulder. "I thought you couldn't see the future."

"I can't," I said. "I don't." I shifted, turning to face her. "I mean I don't have any control over what I see. They're dreams."

Valka smiled. "They are just dreams, Hadrian." She laid a reassuring hand on my arm and smiled.

"But you remember my vision? The one on Calagah?" The one I'd received from Brethren—the message the Quiet had forced the daimon to deliver to me—was something else entirely.

"When you were lost for hours inside the ruins and we all thought you'd fallen down some shaft and broken your neck?"

Remembered pain flashed across my face, and I was glad that Valka could not see it through my opaque ceramic mask. "Yes." She had called me a liar that day. An unbelievable barbarian. "These dreams feel the same. I'm not like you, Valka. I can't remember everything, but these dreams . . . They're *so* vivid. They don't fade, just like the Dark." She knew exactly what I meant. "If I concentrate, I can *see* them like they're happening again."

She was nodding slowly, one hand still against my thigh. "What do you think they are?" she asked. "These dreams of yours?"

I'd had a lot of time to think about it. We'd been on Annica for months. I looked away from Valka. "Do you remember what Kharn Sagara said about Akterumu?"

" 'Twas Tanaran," Valka said.

"What?"

" 'Twas Tanaran that spoke of Akterumu," she said. "Not Sagara."

I waved this aside. "I've thought about that word a lot these past several years. Suppose *Akterumu* is *Akumn ba-terun*. The place of the rock. Or the dome, maybe? I don't know. There was a dome in the vision. And the Cielcin were out beneath the sky in broad daylight. They don't do that without good reason. Tanaran spoke about it like it was someplace sacred to the Cielcin. Like the site of some pilgrimage. That's how it felt in the dream. Like a . . . a festival."

"Like one of your triumphs."

Snatches of the propaganda films played in my head.

Demon in White.

White demon. Pale demon. Like the Emperor on his chessboard, Dorayaica and I were matched pieces. White and black.

"Dorayaica's general—Iubalu—talked about a sacrifice. It said Dorayaica had foreseen my death."

" 'Twas trying to frighten you," Valka said, waving a dismissive hand.

"What if it wasn't?" I asked. "What if Syriani Dorayaica is receiving visions from the Quiet, too? The Quiet or . . . something else?" I put my face in my hands. "We need answers, Valka. We need them *now,* before Berenike becomes the next Marinus. Before Edda and Delos and all the human universe burns."

She had no answer for that, and we sat together unspeaking for a long while.

"I told you," she said, and I felt her eyes on me, "a long time ago . . . that I won't let you die." Her fingers squeezed mine. "You can have all the dreams you like. All the visions. 'Twill not matter."

Her confidence—hollow though perhaps it was—made me feel better, and the nightmares seemed a little farther away. As if embarrassed, Valka stood and paced toward the gravitometer.

"What do you think we're looking for?" she asked, not turning back to face me.

Thinking of the wind I'd witnessed when we'd first climbed the mountain and of my reflection moving in the walls of Calagah, I said, "I don't know, but I'll know when I see it."

Valka nodded, but did not speak.

"There *is* something here, Valka," I said. "I can . . . well, not quite feel it. But the dreams are getting worse. More vivid. And the wind . . ."

"Wind?"

I hadn't meant to say it, but I'd put my foot in it, and said, "The first day we climbed the mountain, you went up outside to wave the shuttle in. I went back to get the men. There was a wind."

Valka turned to face me, eyes narrowed with skepticism. "Hadrian, there's no air here."

"I know!" I said, feeling the long shadow of her skepticism. "I know that! I know it sounds mad, I . . ."

She crossed her arms. "I believe you. I just don't know what to say."

I felt myself relax. Valka had not believed me when I told her of my vision at Calagah, and though decades had passed between us since then, still a piece of me had feared her scorn. Somewhat ashamed, I hung my head, forgetting that she could not see my face through the suit mask.

"I wish I knew," I said to her. "I wish things were simpler."

"So do I," she said, and offered me her hand. "But smile . . . 'tis what we wanted, this. No?"

I swept the chamber with my eyes, the two of us alone, heading a small expedition on a strange world. It was all we'd ever talked about, and if it was stolen time—like our time in Thessa and on Colchis generally—then so be it. For most of us, stolen time is all we ever have . . . if we can take it.

"You're right," I said. It was what we'd always talked about. Doing this sort of thing together, arm in arm.

Valka stood over me, eclipsing the light of the glowsphere above the gravitometer's slim shape. "We have nearly four years here, you and I," she said. "We'll figure it out."

Four years is a long time.

Too short.

Made shorter by the deceptively long Annican day, days which passed without regard for the standard calendar or the rhythms of our respective bodies. Alexander did not return from the *Tamerlane,* and though Varro joined us from time to time, more often than not Valka and I were alone in the cyclopean city, charting pillared halls and twisting passages, scanning every canting buttress or ribbed ceiling we could. As in Calagah, nearly every surface was covered in round anaglyphs, some larger than my outstretched arms, some no larger than a human eye, each marked and textured with characters no human mind had read, slithering over the black stone in unfathomable patterns.

And yet we tried.

But Valka had tried for decades—for her whole life after her service in the Tavrosi guard—to translate the speech of those ancient others. She had not succeeded, and where the work of decades had failed her, four years would not avail us.

We knew we toiled in vain, poring over the scans we made of the city in our sleeping pod by night, leaving the drones to their slow, steady work. In time, we had one of the camp buildings moved to the top of the mountain as well, to spare our pilots the trouble of ferrying us day after day from the mountain's base to its highest slopes.

Our first year ended, and in time our second was nearly gone. In time we traced more than five thousand miles of tunnel and hall, mapped hundreds of chambers. The gravitometers revealed still more, and though we did not attempt to bore through the rock between and could not cut the stone as it slid by us into the past from its genesis in the distant future, we added them to Valka's rendering.

"You know," Valka said, leading the way along one of the massive vaults. Pillars rose to one side, each marching at an advancing angle, so that at one end of the chamber they stood vertical and at the far end lay almost flat as the ceiling drooped lower and lower above our heads, its surface damasked with anaglyphs. "I think the sealed sections aren't sealed at all."

"What do you mean?" I kept close behind her, the tripod of one folded gravitometer over one shoulder like a crucifix.

Valka stopped, forcing her slaved glowsphere to circle back and orbit her head like a tiny moon. She paused, sweeping golden eyes along a line of glyphs carved into the surface of the nearest pillar. "If what Horizon said is right—if these ruins *are traveling* backward through time—then they're decaying in reverse, yes?"

"Cave-ins," I said.

"Only 'twas no sign of such in the surrounding rock," Valka said, and resumed her pace toward the low arch at the far end of the hall. I let her go ahead. Despite our long sojourn on Annica, the twists and byways of the ruin remained in part a mystery to me, and I relied on Valka to lead us out again.

I watched the glowsphere chase after her, shadows dancing on the shape of her and on the walls. Our own shadows stretched out behind us, massive phantasms licking at the outer dark. "I suppose they haven't caved in yet."

Ahead, Valka shook her head. "Can you imagine? When they do cave in, the halls will *open up,* and the stone just . . . won't have anywhere to go. It doesn't make sense."

"But it does explain the isolated chambers," I said, remembering the scans of Calagah Valka had showed me long ago. Odd chambers had extended from the tunnel complex there. Little spaces sealed away in the midst of solid rock, left there as if by some cutting glitch as happens sometimes with holographs, displacing one element of the image inside another.

I could hear the ruin-lust in her voice once more. "I wish we had the time to put ourselves in fugue for a century or two!" she said. "Now we know to look for it, we could compare the ruins then to today, see what's *grown!*" Valka reached out both arms as if to encompass the hall. She spun, walking backward so I could see the infectious smile on her beloved face. Holding out one hand, she said, "We could go back to Calagah! I took a rendering of it, too! It must have changed since we were there! 'Tis been . . ." she did the arithmetic in her head, "more than four hundred years."

Hearing the figure aloud, I almost skipped a step. I suppose some part of me had known so many years had gone by since Emesh, but to hear it spoken aloud was another thing.

"We can't go to Emesh," I said stonily, realizing I'd been quiet for the space of a dozen paces. As I spoke we passed beneath the arch and out into a narrow hall that stretched left and right, gently curving in a broad circle.

Valka went right, and I followed. The hall curved ahead and to the left, where I knew it encircled several inner chambers and storied galleries that spiraled upward through the heart of the mountain. "I know we can't," Valka said. "But we should. That Mataro girl is certainly dead and gone. She won't be taking you from me!"

I let this jibe about Anaïs Mataro—about whom I'd not thought in years—drift by unremarked upon. "We might try remapping the lower entrance," I suggested. "It's not been quite two years, but there might be subtle changes."

" 'Tis worth a try," Valka said. "But we're not like to see much change, you know? Maybe none."

She was walking normally again, trailing one hand along the wall. The glowsphere kept close behind, throwing the anaglyphs into relief. The beams of my own suit lamps bobbed as I moved, following Valka's swaying progress. She was just barely visible, a dozen paces or more ahead, right where the bend of the tunnel might hide her from view.

"Maybe we could leave mapping drones here," she said. "Set up a transmitter. Do we have extra telegraph equipment aboard?" It was almost as if I were not there anymore. Valka had entered a proper dialogue with herself. "Of course, 'twould take eons to transmit something the size of these renderings via telegraph . . . but if we have the technology . . ."

One of the cross-spars at the top of the gravitometer caught on the inner wall of the tunnel and *pinged,* and I half-dropped the machine. Valka seemed not to notice, for her monologue did not abate in my ears. She vanished round the bend before me, light retreating with her while I stooped to recover the fallen instrument, pausing to check that the clasps were all in place and nothing was damaged.

Everything looked all right. I checked the delicate pendulum, ensuring the mechanism had stayed snug between two of the tripod's legs. A short scratch marred one gunmetal thigh. I rubbed a finger over it.

"I don't think anything broke," I said, hoisting the tripod over my shoulder once more and securing it against my neck, checking this time that the cross-spars stood vertically. "Valka?"

Only slowly did it dawn on me that she'd been silent for a good dozen seconds. That ought not to be. The short distance she must have traveled was not far enough to cut off our suit radios.

Or her light.

"Valka!" I leaped forward, rounding the corner, picking up speed as I went. "Valka!"

The hallway turned, but no light came. Glyphs sped by, and the gravitometer bounced against my shoulder. I knew the way. There were no side doors, no passages, no branchings for perhaps half a mile before the route ran back to a steep and stairless climb to the upper gate.

The hall was not supposed to straighten, not supposed to run for so long it vanished into a darkness absolute as hell. Even my suit's sonar could not show me the end. The walls converged into infinity.

And Valka was gone. Or I was gone from her.

"Valka!" I called her name again.

No one answered.

There was only quiet.

Quiet . . . and the gentle rush of wind.

CHAPTER 69

THE HIGHEST PLACE

"VALKA?" I CALLED AGAIN. There was nothing wrong with my transmitter. It was the *world* that had changed. The wind blew again, beckoning from the tunnel ahead, pushing at my high collar and the tails of my coat.

Holding the cross-beam, I shouldered the device and trudged on, marking the sensor readouts in the corners of my vision. The temperature had increased by nearly five degrees, warm enough that—had there been air—a man might walk in but a light jacket.

"Valka?"

Still nothing.

I pressed on, walked for what felt like half a mile with no change. The gravitometer was not heavy, but the cross-beam cut into my shoulder. How far had I come? I looked back, but the darkness had closed in behind, and the bend in the hall was lost. My universe was a straight line, a single dimension that seemed to march to infinity, limited only by my light.

What else was there to do?

I walked on, the only sounds the clatter of my boots and the rasp of my breathing.

"Valka!"

Eventually, I ceased to call out. Valka was gone, but gone where? I remembered my encounter in Calagah, the way the door to the vision chamber had opened out of nowhere. Had we crossed some threshold in time, perhaps? Opened some path previously hidden? Or was this something else entirely?

The hall ran for miles, or so it seemed. It did not bend or stray, but held the course straight as any laser, running tangent to the circular hall I'd known. I thought of the branching rivers of light I'd seen and swum, the way they shifted and split, showing a million million possible tomorrows; here dividing, there flowing back into the same channel. The tunnels felt to me like those watery passages, the way they ran and changed.

I trudged on, knowing that I was like a tram upon its rail, for I felt certain that were I to turn back I would come not upon the hall of slanting pillars, but to wherever the path willed. I knew—and cannot say *how* I knew—that either way was forward.

Always forward.

Light ahead.

Light.

The sight of it pulled me forward, and—gravitometer still over one shoulder—I hurried toward it. Ahead an archway loomed, round as all the rest, but mighty, for as I approached the door the close walls and ceiling of the tunnel fell away, and the floor of the corridor became a narrow bridge that ran out straight into clear air, striking out away from the mountain across the open, rusty plains.

It wasn't possible. We'd scanned the site a thousand times. There was no bridge.

Without banister or rail of any kind it was, a mile long or more, but no wider than the hall had been, wide enough that a man standing in its center might reach his hands over the edge to either side, and I was glad of the lack of wind, for at our height a gust was sure to knock me from that span and send me falling nearly a mile to the ground below.

I lingered a moment in the shadow of the archway, eyes tracing the bridge where it ran across the wasteland to where another mountain rose in the distance, mightier even than the mountain which Valka and I had explored for so long. Peering up, I could not see the Sparrowhawks circling on patrol, and switched comm channels. "Sphinx Flight, this is Marlowe. Do you copy?"

Silence.

"Sphinx Flight, this is Marlowe. Are you there?"

No answer came.

"Valka?" I stepped out onto the bridge, knowing as I did so that *none* of it had been there when we'd arrived on Annica. Narrow as it was, the bridge was easily a mile off the ground—far further down the mountain than the level I thought Valka and I had been on—and ran across the uneven desert below, supported curving pillars, each like half a thin and graceful arch.

"Sphinx Flight," I tried again, "this is Marlowe. Have you got visuals on a bridge extending from the . . ." I broke off, checking the sky and the course of the sun, "west side of the mountain?"

Still no answer came. Shouldering my burden, I turned back, afraid of the long walk and fall from the bridge. I went back along the hall, back into darkness where the last of the sunlight failed behind me . . .

. . . and found a wall barring my path.

The too-long hallway was gone, sealed behind black stone.

I turned back.

The sunlight fell cold and colorless about me, red as the red landscape, and so added nothing. Looking back, I saw the arching columns above the lower gate rising black against the natural stone far below.

The campsite was gone.

My chest tightened, blood and adrenaline forced into every extremity with such force it ached. "Valka!" I called out again, toggling channels via my helmet's heads-up display. "Sphinx Flight? *Tamerlane?* Anyone? Can anyone hear me?"

They were gone. Everything was gone. And there was nothing to do but walk.

More mountains stood upon the horizon, crowding in like hunched colossi. I moved out upon the bridge, marveling at the way they had all appeared as if from nowhere. Was I still on Annica?

Lingering near the midway point of that mighty span, I looked round. The mountain that before had shown only a rough landscape of red stone and dust capped with the frost of frozen airs was utterly changed. Mighty terraces stood upon its face. Black-walled and beautiful, crowned with towers like the crumbled teeth of giants.

There were giants, too.

Faces vast as starships watched from the mountainsides. Impassive and expressionless, their flat eyes—carved in black stone—watched me as I went.

I came at last to the new mountain, and climbed. No path was there, nor stairs. Only the ruins of that once and future empire ruinous about me. Black canals split the desert below, high-walled, deep, and dry. I climbed for what seemed like hours. My arms turned to lead and I was forced to use the gravitometer as a kind of staff. The sun did not seem to move, and hung always in the east and high above the mountain I had come from, as though time were standing still.

Onward I climbed, higher and higher, not really knowing why, knowing somehow that up was forward, feeling the soulless pressure of those stone faces watching me. How high I climbed or for how long none can say, for no man before me had made that climb, nor any after.

So high was the summit that from its edge I might turn back and see the curve of the world bend back at the horizon. Upon that lofty height the air was so thin the stars peered out of endless night. There heavens and earth met upon the summit of the world, the highest place.

The highest place.

Brethren's voice sounded in my ear, the memory so sharp and present in my exhaustion I almost expected to find pale hands crawling across frost-rimed stone toward me. I was going mad. My legs screamed with exhaustion from the climb, and I leaned against the gravitometer, thrusting its legs through the rime and deep into the soft earth.

I fell to my knees, exhausted, hungry, utterly spent. I would have been dehydrated were it not for the osmosis plant in the thigh packs recycling my body's wastewater. Had I been days climbing? Or only hours?

For nothing.

There was nothing on the mountain. Not even the wind. I rolled onto my back, longing for my bed in the camp environment pod, for our rooms aboard the *Tamerlane*. For food.

"Valka?" I had been so sure when I climbed that mountain. So sure I was meant to. I had been given no other choice.

Stars wheeled overhead, and I think perhaps I dreamed. The sun—faint and flickering as a dying bulb—hung fixed in the firmament, watchful as a lidless eye. How long had I been without food? Two days? Three?

If I sat up, I could see the faces of the mountains below watching me, blank eyes staring at me and through me and past me. The shadow of the instrument that I'd carried all this way—that had supported me in my final ascent—fell across my face.

Light. Darkness. Silence. Night. Day.

Always forward, I told myself, but did not move. How long had I been lying there? *Get up. Get up!* The voice that sounded in my ear sounded like my father. Like Gibson's. Like my own.

Seek hardship.

Brethren's voice joined them, whispering in my ear, and almost I fancied I heard the tread of white hands slapping on the stone around.

Seek them at the highest place.
At the bottom of the world.

The bottom of the world . . . I tried to sit up and failed. My strength was gone from me.

Get up! It was the same inner voice—the same spirit—that had ordered me to stand before Aranata in my final moments. I tried. Tried and succeeded only in rolling onto my belly, my face in the frost.

I could not stand. So I crawled instead. I could go a little higher. The peak of the mountain was a simple crown of bare stone, its surface thick with frost. I crawled, and then I dragged myself toward the summit of that mountain that had not been there when we arrived. At last, I could go no further, and lay myself upon the mountaintop. I prayed for sleep to come, or Death. Alone or hand in hand. The mountain would be my pyramid, my tomb, and no one would ever find me there.

My last thoughts were of Valka and the *Tamerlane*. Where had they gone? Where had I gone? I saw the faces of the mountains watching me with black eyes and green. Dreaming, I saw them stand and bow their mighty heads in silent vigil. But I blinked and they were gone, and the mountains slept beneath me like the wreck of empires broken upon the sand of Annica's endless desert.

Face in the dirt, I slept and drifted in and out of consciousness often long enough only to drink from the water tube in my mask. To try to stand. And fail.

A faint breeze brushed my coat and rasped in my suit's audio pickups. I think it was the noise that woke me. A breeze again where there was no air. I opened my eyes, beheld the dirt and frost. The vile dust. The bottom of the world.

And there it was, impossible as it is to believe.

There upon the mountaintop on that airless, waterless world, amid frost beneath the gaze of a dim sun, grew a single white flower.

For a moment, I thought I was mad. Then I thought it was the blossom of the Galath tree that I had taken from the Cloud Gardens of the Peronine Palace on Forum. Had it fallen from my coat?

But no. This flower was something new, something growing from the cold and lifeless soil. Reaching out, I touched it with gloved fingers. It was real.

So often we don't see the truth because we won't look low enough, Gibson had said at our parting. I could look no lower than the dirt. And looking, I had found a miracle. The wind picked up again and whirled about the summit. Fingers still touching the impossible flower, I looked up, craning my neck to see.

Hadrian . . .

The word was barely a whisper, a noise carried on that wind that should not be.

Hadrian . . .

I put my hands beneath me, and found—to my surprise—that I'd the strength to find my knees. To stand. Turning back I saw where I left the gravitometer standing by the edge of the mountain and the landscape unrolled beyond. The watchful mountains and the crumbling terraces above the first mountain I had climbed, the bridge and pillars that marked the entrance by our vanished camp.

"I can hear you!" I told the Quiet, and spread my arms. "Here I am!"

CHAPTER 70

THE AGONY

THE WIND ROARED IN answer, scouring the mountaintop with such force that—helmeted as I was—I raised an arm to shield my eyes.

Hadrian.

"You called!" I exclaimed, wheeling about as if I might track the gale with my eyes. "I came!"

Take off your mask.

My hands were moving before I was fully aware of it, and I stopped their progress. I could see the indicators in the bottom left of my suit's entoptics. There was still no air outside my suit's protective shell.

There was nothing. And it was very, very cold.

"If I do that," I said, "I'll die."

Silence.

I had come so far. Too far, in truth, for I was not sure I could survive the journey back. I had bent all my efforts for so many years, fought and killed and served the Empire, all to stand on that mountaintop. Looking round, I saw the faces on the stone mountains encircling us. My eyes searched for the lonely flower, but it was gone. Torn out in the wind? Or had I only imagined it?

Was I going mad?

"What is this place?" I asked.

Silence.

"What do you want from me?" I asked to no avail. "Tell me!"

The silence was deafening. I wheeled on the spot, taking in the crumbling splendor all around me. I swore. There was nothing for it.

I gripped my wrist-terminal with my opposite hand. "Fear is a poison," I told myself, and tried to master the panic in my heart.

Fingers keyed the orders into my terminal, sending warning alarms blaring inside my suit so loud they nearly deafened me. Grinding my teeth, I found the hardswitch behind one ear, exhaling as my helmet seals broke and the mask and helm unfolded like the petals of an iron flower, exposing my face as the material collapsed into my collar.

Nothingness hit me like a freight tram, driving what little air remained from my lungs. I tried to breathe, but there was nothing there. Adrenaline's cold fingers closed about my heart and squeezed. I felt the slap of cold and the steady drum of blood running through my veins. Panic seized me, and I fell, vision going dark.

I must have been centuries falling. Eyes veiled in gray mist, I lost sight of the mountaintop, my only sense of place the double impact of my knees striking stone, chest heaving.

Air.

There was air.

I stayed on hands and knees a long while, staring at the ground. Ages passed before I could see it, and I did not move. When at last I could breathe more easily, I rasped, "Was that . . . some kind of test?" I looked up, and my next words died on my tongue, for the sky had changed. Gone was the black of night and the subtle shimmer of starlight. The same red sun hung miniscule in the sky, but it shone somehow brighter and more warmly, its radiance spread through a pale, white daylight that veiled the face of the stars. "Where are we?"

Behind the stage.

I had almost expected to get no answer. The voice—coming as it seemed from a spot just above my shoulder—startled me, and I scrambled to my feet.

"I don't understand!" I said. "I have so many questions! I've come so far!" Still searching for the source of that soundless voice, I spun round, one hand flitting to my sword. "The mountains! The bridge, the flower! I—" My words died on my tongue.

Standing on the edge of the mountain's top—right where I had ascended and right where the flower had grown—stood a massive finger of stone. Half a hundred feet tall it stood, and perhaps ten across. The marker was black as the stone of the ruins below and covered in the same circular marks, some small as coins, some large as dinner plates. It had not been there before.

Silence ruled the mountaintop once more. No word came, nor shout of wind. I moved toward the marker, hand still on my sword. As I did, the light changed, revealing the massive glyph carved at the top: a single circle bisected by a vertical line. The same symbol I had seen in the hidden chamber of Calagah. Remembering that encounter, I approached with caution and stretched out one gauntleted hand to touch my reflection in the mirror-dark stone.

Nothing happened.

Memory of pain and deep cold moved in me, kindling an idea. I fumbled with my glove's seal and cast the first gauntlet aside. "Take off your mask," I muttered, peeling the second from my other hand. I reached out with my bare hands and touched the surface of the monolith.

Again, nothing happened.

Scowling, I stepped back and turned away. I was so sure I'd been right. Resisting an urge to kick one of the gauntlets aside, I strode to the far edge of the mountains. "I don't know what you want from me." I turned back to glare at the monolith . . . and froze.

My reflection had not stirred. It remained standing square in the face of the black stone, one hand flat against the surface just where I had left it.

I did draw my sword then, but left the blade unkindled.

Green eyes met violet.

"What do you want from me?" I asked, drawing nearer with careful steps. No second reflection appeared behind the green-eyed one. "Why did you bring me back?"

The other Hadrian raised his chin in a gesture I knew all too well. His lips did not move as he answered me.

You are the shortest way.

"What does that mean?" I asked.

Silence.

My reflection watched with flat, green eyes, its hand pressed flat against the surface of the stone.

I understood, and held my hand to its.

Pelagic cold poured through the contact, so deep my bones ached. I gasped, sagged against the wall and slid to my knees once more. But my hand would not be moved. I felt as though stone fingers had closed on mine. Referred pain lanced up my arm and kindled in my brain, setting alight that spot behind my left eye and whiting out my vision.

And all at once I was not on the mountain at all.

I was looking down on it instead, soaring as a bird might above the stone giants and crumbling terraces of the city. My vision began to shimmer, to flicker like the shapes in a child's shadow theater as it spun about the lamp. I beheld other mountaintops, retreating in undulating procession east and west into eternity. I saw myself kneeling at the monolith, or standing, or not there at all. The further away I looked, the more different the mountaintops became, until the monolith was gone and the stone faces and the mountain with it. I saw our Sparrowhawks circling in a distant sky, and the white shapes of our camp pitched on red sands at the edges of infinity.

The pain flared white with the flash of revelation, for I understood.

The breadth of time unrolled beneath me. All the places that *might have been* or *might be* breaking like waves against the ever-moving present. I saw possibilities rise to crash upon the now and fall away as time slipped ever on. Infinite possibilities—but only one was real. Only one occurred; the rest fell into darkness in corners of time that never happened. I knelt in such a corner that very moment, upon that strange mountaintop towering above an Annica that would never be, lost to unrealized potential, to entropy. Suddenly I understood what the voice had meant when it spoke of our being *behind the stage.*

The stone giants, the city, the mountain on which I stood existed in another present. One that had not happened—that could not happen—because the past that informed its reality had not. I had come to a time unreal and unrealized.

Beneath the gaze of my vision naked time rolled like a carpet, like a thin sheet of oil atop an ocean of what might be. Time's wave broke, and infinite *nows* shattered and sank into darkness save that one which we would say occurred. The waters of potential receded, running down toward the future—if *future* it could be called—only to be thrown back upon the present in new form.

I looked back—upward, or so it seemed to me—and watched our galaxy play out in innumerable forms. Focusing, I found I could pick out the threads, the rivers of time tangled in that ocean. I saw our Empire—and nations like our Empire, and others totally strange—spread across its face. I saw a mighty dominion of the machines set their hellish order over the stars in a time that never was, and saw strange flags planted on worlds I might have known by other names. I saw the green hills of Earth and witnessed the white pyramids of the Mericanii fall and rise above the cities of our birth. I saw Felsenburgh's peace and the war he'd built it upon. I saw the Earth burning and the white chariot of Apollo that first carried us to the stars. All the empires of man's birth flickered and died small deaths. Rome and Egypt, China and Britain all passed in instants until the Earth quaked beneath the dominion of dragons in the deeps of time.

And I saw myself. My own life ran like a silver thread from Delos to

Emesh, from Emesh to the *Demiurge,* from the *Demiurge* to the very mountain on which I stood. *Broken,* Jari had said, *and broken again.* At last I understood his meaning, seeing clean fractures where my thread passed from Delos and the Quiet had intervened to force me onto Emesh and where Aranata had taken my head. Jari had spoken of roads, but I saw rivers. Perhaps the truth of what I saw is more than any human mind can comprehend, and these visions are only the animal mind's interpretation of the eldritch truth. Perhaps we humans can perceive that truth only by analogy. Even Jari's posthuman mind had failed.

So I looked forward to see what had driven Jari mad when he saw me.

The Cielcin roared and raged across the galaxy. Planets burned and fell. Billions of lives ended. Blood flowed like water and soaked the stars. I felt the heat and saw the sun-flash of nuclear fire as ships and cities died. I saw men and women corralled and chivvied into shuttles to be taken back to victorious Cielcin warships. I saw the white cities of Forum plunge burning from the sky. All that art and history, all the glory of our age and Empire fell in ashes like snow. Red-haired princes hung on hooks like sides of meat, and I recognized faces I knew. Crude Philip and Ricard. Proud Aurelian. There too were Titania and Vivienne and the Empress who hated me.

And there were Selene and Alexander. Each mounted on hooks beneath their ribs, paraded on tall staffs like banners.

I saw the oceans of Delos boiled away and lightning strike the towers of Devil's Rest. A girl with black hair and violet eyes stood upon the highest walks of the Great Keep and watched the black ships descending, unfurling their banners across the sky as cannons rained fire.

The sister I'd never met, perhaps.

I never learned. For some force drew my eye, pulled it forward—downward—along the trough of time's wave, chasing that bright and silver line toward the manifold unfurling futures. Another world. Another star. I knew the black ship well by then. I had died there, after all. Like a ghost I floated amongst its legion of statues, their metal forms pockmarked and scarred. I passed through its hull and down its aimless corridors, through the garden where I'd lost my life and up an empty shaft along one castellated tower to a place I had not been before. The *Demiurge*'s bridge was a dark place. Red holographs gleamed above console banks, and the holograph plates in the foreground showed the system unrolled beneath us: two fleets converging above a green world, its yellow sun shining out clear across the void. I did not then recognize the sun, nor the planet in its orbit.

Never had I seen two fleets of such size. Such mass and charge. They swarmed across the tactical holograph displays like a constellation of fireflies, filling the skies above the planet. How many of our legions were there arrayed? I could not count them.

I know the number now. They recited it to me at my trial.

One hundred twenty-seven legions.

Three million, one hundred seventy-five thousand men. And that was without counting the various logothetes, the courtiers and nobiles who had sailed with our Radiant Emperor to witness his last and final victory over the barbarian xenobites.

That was without counting the more than two billion people on the planet below.

Without counting the Cielcin.

I felt the deck plates cold beneath my feet for the barest instant, and heard a strange, familiar voice. "Are we ready?" A figure stirred in the captain's chair and leaned into the light. Hadrian Marlowe stood, black cloak settling about his frame. It may seem strange to say, but I had not known myself at first glance. Something about me had changed. Something in the shape of the face, perhaps? In the slant of brow and slope of nose? In the way the pointed jaw set as I moved toward the window.

"Aye sir," said a voice I did not know. I could not see its owner. "But . . . are you certain?"

My other self stopped midway between the chair and the forward holograph display. He turned, locking eyes perhaps with the lieutenant who had questioned him. He *almost* faced me, and I saw him plain. His hair fell almost to his shoulders, and there was something in his face wholly unfamiliar to me.

These thoughts were driven from my mind a moment after, for that other Hadrian's eyes met mine. Coincidence? One corner of his mouth twisted up in that familiar half-smile. "Do what must be done," he said—I said—and turned his back on me. "Fire at will."

The vision broadened, blurred, and skipped ahead. I saw the sun split open like a bloated whale and spew its fire forth. Fleets burned and the planet with it . . . and all those lives.

"No!" I screamed. "No!"

The pain flared once more behind my eyes, and all went white as that murdered sun. Pain lanced also down my arm, but I pulled it away, severing contact with the black stone. I fell back upon the rough stone and clutched my frozen hand to my chest. I half-expected to see my own bloody fingertips still glued to the face of the monument, but the flesh was whole and wholly without blemish.

"I won't do it," I said. "I won't!"

The unheard voice descended on me once again. *This must be.*

"Why?" I lay back against the ground, and when I spoke it was in a smaller, weaker voice than before. "In Earth's name, why?"

We must be.

"You?" I scrabbled back, moving farther away from the monument and the dark vision it had offered me. Both Brethren and Horizon had said the Quiet lived in the future—in a possible future—that they interfered to direct the flow of history unto themselves. "The Cielcin have to die so you might live . . ." I massaged my still-aching hand, flexed the fingers. There was no trauma on the flesh. Only the memory of pain. Only the agony. I was shaking my head. "I won't do it. I won't. I won't be your tool." I tried to stand, but my body remembered its exhaustion, its hunger, and I could not stand. "I will not butcher them."

You have before.

The memory of Nobuta's death washed over me, and I felt the creature's body go limp. Uvanari died again beneath my knife. And Iubalu, and the demon on Arae, followed by the nuclear flash as Ulurani's ship exploded in the skies above Aptucca, a little nova to herald the coming death of Gododdin's sun.

I shook my head more furiously, and drove back the visions.

"Those were different," I said. "Those were all different."

The words played again in my ears, my own voice—my own face—alien to me. *Fire at will. Do what must be done.*

What must be.

This must be. The Quiet insisted.

"Why?" I almost shouted, managing this time to lurch all the way to my knees. "Tell me!"

Listen, came the entity's response, a single word no louder than the rustle of wind through autumn leaves. It faded from my hearing and was gone.

I could not leave the mountain, though I tried. Finding my feet I staggered to the edge of the escarpment. The slope descended so steeply and treacherously that in my exhausted state I knew to attempt the descent was to kill me. I'd staggered back and recovered my gloves, still meaning to try. My helmet seals hissed back into place, and the antiseptic blankness of suit oxygen replaced the gunpowder and iron smell of the Annican air.

I made it perhaps ten feet before I fell. One foot went out from under me, and I slipped off the narrow shelf and fell perhaps thirty yards, coat shredding itself along the near-vertical rock face. Only the suit's gel layer saved me, flash-hardening with the impacts to insulate my joints. Landing on an outcrop below, I struck my head and knew no more.

Bleary eyes opened on the Annican sky, still that burned cream color and not the black of night. The same day? Or another day? I drank from my suit's recycler tube, stomach cramping for want of bread. I coughed, spitting water along the inside of the suit mask—a bad situation, that. Still coughing and without thinking about it, I undid my mask's seals. No alarm sounded this time. And I wiped my face on the torn sleeve of the coat I wore over the environment suit.

It was a long time before I sat up, and longer still before I realized where I was.

The monument loomed like a black finger over me, slightly tilted where it stood on the edge of the mountain peak. I was back on the summit. I had no memory of climbing, but in my state that was no guarantee. I fell back in the dirt.

"On your feet, Your Radiance," came an old, rough voice. "This all you got?"

I shut my eyes. I did not want to see Ghen again.

"I forgive you, you know," said another voice. "I'd probably have done the same thing."

I did not want to see Switch either.

"Fall asleep there, and the birds'll get you, Had."

I did open my eyes then, knowing full well what I'd see.

Cat sat on one low rock, legs crossed beneath her patched, filthy dress. Her thick, matted hair stood all on end, but she smiled through the grime. Ghen stood just behind her, hulking in the maroon fatigues of the Red Company, slit nostril flared. Switch sat nearby. Not the man I'd banished, but the boy I'd sheltered in Colosso, befriended, defended, twice failed. He wore the dinted armor of a fighting pit myrmidon, and sat sharpening his steel gladius.

"There are no birds here," I said.

"Not yet," Cat answered me. "But they comin'. Give it time."

I turned my face away, but when I did I found them in similar positions on my other side, such that I could not escape the sight of them. "You're not real," I said. "You're *them*."

"We are," the three said in unison, confirming what I already knew. They were but faces the Quiet wore, as it had for so long worn Gibson's shape—when I believed him dead. I knew Cat and Ghen were dead, having seen both their bodies. The Gray Rot had taken Cat on Emesh, and The Painted Man had done for Ghen, a victim of devilry and my own bad commanding. Switch was probably dead, unless like Gibson he too had spent the long decades since Vorgossos frozen, but I thought not. Whatever powers govern our universe—and I was starting to have my suspicions— they would not allow two such unlikely coincidences to happen within one human lifetime. No, Switch was dead, burned or buried on some rock—I know not where.

"What does that mean?" I asked. Resigning myself to the Quiet's little torment, I sat up and faced the shades of my dead companions.

"We are without beginning," Switch answered, momentarily setting aside his whetstone.

"Without end," Ghen added.

Cat took up the chorus, saying, "We create ourselves."

We are.

"I won't do it," I said, pulling one aching leg in beneath myself.

"You will." Cat smiled at me sweetly.

"You must," Ghen said.

Still holding his sword against his shoulder, Switch said, "To create is to choose."

Frustrated, I surged to my feet. "Speak plainly!" I roared.

But the phantoms were gone, and I stood alone once more upon the mountaintop, wind blowing through my hair.

Listen!

The Quiet's command rang out like thunder, like the lightning itself.

"I am!" I shouted, and beat my breast with a fist.

But no answer came.

I seated myself on one of the low stones, glaring at the monolith. My reflection did not appear. After several minutes passed, I rose and—tearing the gauntlets once more from my hands—placed my palms flat against the cold monolith.

No visions came, no voice spoke to me.

I howled and sat at the base of the monument like Cid Arthur before the Merlin Tree, my back to the stone. Perhaps I slept, or wandered in that country like sleep which is nearer Death than dreaming. Nothing moved, for there was nothing on all that world save the stone of mountains and graven images. Not even the haunted winds blew.

So absolute a silence I have never known.

We fear silence. I said once that darkness is chaos itself, that in darkness any and all things might arise unseen like the cat from Pandora's evil box. Silence is like that, but more profound. There was darkness before the dawn of time, and silence, too, but silence was the deeper thing, the canvas against which all thought is measured. You have heard stories of men driven mad in quiet rooms by the rushing of their own blood. It is not true. It is not the sound that does it, it is themselves. In silence, they are confronted with their own natures—and with nature itself—and cannot look it in the face. As darkness brings forth the creatures of the night, so silence brings forth the things within our hearts . . . if we will but listen to it.

Night came. And day again after. I emptied my suit's water supply again and knew it could not last forever. Hunger gnawed at me and blurred my vision, and I half-expected another shade to appear with offers of food. None did. I had confronted Ghen, and Cat, and Switch, and though they had not recriminated me, the memory of their faces haunted my delirium. I was not the man I could be, *should* be. I had failed them, and failed the bars I'd set for myself. I had punished Switch for caring, and sent Ghen to his death. I could have saved Cat—maybe—if I'd but torn the ring from its chain on my neck and ordered the Borosevo hospitals to treat her.

I hadn't.

Three times I'd failed.

My vision flickered, pulling at the corners where I could not really look. If you have ever seen a creature stir in the corner of your eye, or seen a figure standing there and, turning, found only an empty door . . . you will know how I felt.

Listen.

I had no strength to argue with that supernatural voice anymore. The flickering did not stop. Shades danced there, and I knew that I had only to turn and face them, face Ghen and Switch, Cat and all the rest.

Was I dying again? My first death had come so suddenly that I'd not experienced the end as such. This death—if death it was—came slower.

Listen.

I turned—not my head, not my eyes—but my sight. Turned and saw the things shimmering there, shimmering as the visions the monolith had presented me. I saw again the crest of the wave of time, the mountaintop repeated over and over to infinity in uncounted iterations. I *was* dying, I saw, and would die in innumerable variations that stretched out to my left, expiring at the foot of that monument, dead upon a mountaintop in a universe that never truly occured. To my right . . . I saw myself stand, and saw the path toward standing, dependent on factors so small and improbable they would almost certainly never occur at all. The faint flicker and burn of chemical energy in my body, the constitution of will, the breaths taken just deeply enough to find the air I needed. I had only to choose the path.

I chose.

I stood, and my vision of the choice blended with the reality.

It was not the future I saw—though I tried—it was the now, the infinite possible nows. With each passing moment I moved to open Pandora's box and knew before I did whether her cat was alive or dead.

To create is to choose, the voice repeated, echoing the words of Switch's shade.

Teetering, I leaned against the monument.

"What is happening?" My voice was barely more than a whisper.

You are beginning to see.

White pain flared again behind my eye, and I slumped back against the black pillar.

I was on my hands and knees on a gray stone floor, tangled hoses and cords beneath me. My exhaustion strangely absent, I rose and looked round. The familiar vaults of the alien cathedral rose above my head, pillars graven in the images of inhuman things winged and webbed, supporting Gothic arches in their tentacled grasp. The music box chimed, doleful and serene in that quiet place. I saw the bassinet a moment after, placed in the chancel where an altar ought to be. Careful not to crush the delicate hoses, I moved toward it as I had twice before, one hand on my sword.

No infant cried on this occasion, nor was there any sound but my feet. On reaching the cradle, I saw why. The *egg* was intact. Larger than any melon it was, a sphere of unblemished white. Braided cables and hoses ran through sockets in its shell, and machines I had not marked before in the rim of the bassinet chimed softly in time with the music as the embryonic god dreamed.

Reaching out one hand, I caressed the shell between its hoses, certain that I stood beside the cradle of the Quiet itself. Not a people, as Valka imagined, but a singular *thing*. Its *we* was the *we* of emperors, the style of a being that spoke for multitudes.

Something roared in the distance, and I looked up. The doors of the great cathedral banged open, but what entered then I never saw, for the vision blurred and stretched, flowing beneath my feet like light smeared across the event horizon of a black hole. Though my feet did not move, I sped straight out of that ancient temple along a ribbon of silver light across uncounted billions of years until I approached the murdered sun from the back side and heard once more my own strange voice whisper those three awful words.

"Fire at will."

My vision turned upward, and I beheld the silver line I'd followed, straight as laser light from one to the other. Other lines ran beside it, winding, broken or bent—each longer than the thread I'd taken from the cradle to that dying star.

And I understood.

You are the shortest way.

For the Quiet to be born, the Cielcin had to die.

"But why?" I asked the darkness, sensing the light beneath.

The Quiet's voice was silent, but I understood why. Our words were too small for it. For it to answer in words was like pouring an ocean into a wine cup.

I tried again. "Why kill the Cielcin?" I hoped the narrower question would help. "They worship you!"

No.

The vision changed.

The hundreds of thousands of worlds of mankind's dominion lay beneath my feet, unrolled like the finest Tavrosi carpet. I saw them each, and saw how small we were against the vastness of the galaxy, smaller still against the vastness of time. I witnessed other empires—and nations which were not empires at all—stretched across the heavens in man's name. In some, machines stood by us shoulder to shoulder, or served us as the ancients dreamed. With my own eyes I saw our extinction play out in a million ways across a thousand epochs. I saw the Earth destroyed ten thousand times before we learned to fly. I saw the Cielcin *consume* us until nothing remained. I watched us swallowed by the Mericanii in times that never were, beheld the final defeat of the God Emperor at Avalon and stood witness as even he was strapped to a table in a pyramid raised above the ruins of Caliburn House, his followers given cancers to multiply their cells and stave off death forever while they dreamed infinite dreams and marked their descent into senile dotage, unable even to die.

Small as we were, we were not alone. Looking out across the stars, I perceived the beginnings of countless peoples beneath alien skies. There were cities, towers, tumbled ruins on a thousand thousand worlds across our galaxy and beyond. Places where no human had walked, places where perhaps no human would ever walk: across the Clouds of Magellan, to distant Andromeda, to Triangulum and beyond. There were empires in the far-off Coma Wall that spread across galaxies as we spread across star systems, ruled by peoples terrible and altogether strange.

And I beheld darker things. Older things. Greater ones.

Beings vast and incomprehensible as mountains moved beneath the outer suns, their antique wills slow and slouching as they bent their power on the stars. I saw hideous peoples on their knees in worship, and I knew. Knew it was not the Quiet the Cielcin praised.

Their horrid shapes moved about the fringes of my vision, dark against dark. I caught only glimpses: eyes huge and faceted as gems, wings malformed and time-eaten, pale limbs and claws yellow and cracked with age. Try as I did to look upon their faces, my mind rebelled, recoiled, and would go no farther. Memories of Brethren stirred in me, its many arms, its bloated form, its massive size so great that to escape its confinement in the waters beneath Kharn's palace was to risk death, crushed by its own titanic weight. Large as it had been, I sensed these *things* were larger still and swam between the stars like cuttlefish. They knew us not, so small were we, and so small the affairs of a single galaxy to them.

But their servants had noticed us.

The Cielcin had.

Pale priests offered sacrifices at their altars of bone. I watched as one slashed its hand and allowed black droplets to fall upon a mound of corpses before a black and open portal. Something pallid and boneless slithered out of the dark, tendrils reaching out like snakes, like the fingers of some unseen hand. A dozen of them reached out and embraced the sacrifice, dragging it wetly back across rough stone.

"The Cielcin think you're one of them," I said. "What are they?"

They were.

It was not a helpful answer. "What do you mean, *were?*"

They came before.

"Before what?" There was no answer. "Are you one of them?" I asked.

They are not a kind.

I pondered the implications of this. Each one unique, a species unto itself.

"Why are you showing me this?"

So that you will understand.

"Understand what?"

The music box chimed faintly in the darkness, and turning toward the faint flowering of light, I saw once more the unholy temple of the egg. This time, I recognized the cyclopean forms of the colossi that decorated the pillars. Time unrolled again, branching futures flickering, exposed by the Quiet's hand to my merely human eyes.

There were only two futures running from the egg. Like the contents of Pandora's box, the *thing* inside the Quiet's egg—the Quiet itself—was either living or dead. Down one passage there was only darkness, such a darkness as had been before creation: the darkness of a universe dead and cold, where all energy was lost. There the Watchers ruled in eternal night and plotted their conquest of every corner of time, until everything that ever was or might have been was lost. Down the other, the egg hatched, and beyond its birth I saw the stars reborn. A new universe. A new kingdom. A second life.

The Cielcin were only another battle in the long war. The only war. Not life against life, man against xenobite, and certainly not the petty wars of man against man—whatever their horrors. Theirs was the final war: light against darkness. Good and evil. Heaven and hell.

"Why me?" I asked the darkness once again.

The vision faded, and a voice I heard from behind me said, "Because we have to show them we are not abstractions. Not ghosts."

I knew that voice, though I had not heard it since I was a boy.

Turning, I saw my father's shade standing amidst the tumbled stones of the mountaintop. He looked just as I remembered: the same jet hair and grim expression, the same pale skin and violet eyes to match my own. His long mane was going gray at the temples, and he wore official robes of red-on-black brocade. A silver ring sat upon each of his fingers, and in his hands was strength. He had said those words to me so long ago, after my near murder on the streets of Meidua.

A ghost then? Or only a memory?

"Get up," he said, and the memory of that once-hated voice moved like poison in me.

It was still agony to stand, but I could still see the breadth of time stretching to either side, could still *choose* my moment, as they had chosen for me when they delivered me from my death on the *Demiurge*, selecting another Hadrian—a potential Hadrian—from one of those failed narratives. They had *traded* the Hadrian who died for another Hadrian. For one still living. For one identical to the man who'd died in all but one respect: I had lost the other arm.

For me.

I laughed. Had they foreseen my battle with Irshan in the arena? Had they arranged that moment, too?

"Lorian was right," I said. I was not the same Hadrian at all, not the man who had died by his own blade beside that lake, though his memories were in me. The Quiet had interfered from above the stage like the gods of ancient Greek theater. They needed a miracle, and so they'd made one. "That bastard."

Lord Alistair raised one eyebrow. Once, that expression would have held fear for me, but that was long ago.

"I'm not a monster," I said, and made a gesture as if to throw something away. "All this . . . I can't pretend to understand it all . . . but I cannot do what you ask."

"You must."

"There has to be another way," I said.

No. My father's lips did not move. Snarling, I turned from him, crossing toward the monument, somehow sure I would see for myself. I pressed both hands against the black surface, willing the cold to come. Nothing did.

"Show me," I whispered.

My vision still shimmered at the edges. The strange second sight I'd been granted was still there, and I turned my sight to look in that direction. The Quiet had changed something in me—or perhaps that power had always been there, lurking just out of sight.

A black dome rose above gray plains, surrounded by spiraling columns. A mighty host stood near at hand, and far above the moon-like shape of a worldship blotted out the sun. Beneath that dark star I saw their black banners snapping in the wind, and recognized the sign of the white hand in among the more traditional banners marked with Cielcin calligraphy.

"*Yaiya-toh! Yaiyah-toh! Yaiyah-toh!*" came the Cielcin chant, and the beating of their spears against the earth was like the sound of thunder. A hundred princes of the Cielcin stood there and awaited the coming of one mightier than the rest. Dorayaica came, crowned in horn and silver and leading me on a chain. I looked older than I had in the last vision, gray-templed like my father, haggard and gaunt. Old though I was, I recognized the face more readily than I had aboard the *Demiurge.*

The vision blurred, and I heard a piercing voice cry out, *"Akterumu! Akterumu!"*

Then we were aboard a Cielcin vessel—the same vessel that had eclipsed the sun, I knew. The Prince of Princes stood upon a platform above a throng of its people, clawed hand spread out. I knelt upon the platform beside it, still chained wrist and throat and ankle. Beneath me marched a sea of human faces, goaded forward by Cielcin wielding spears. I saw Otavia's floating hair among them, and heard Pallino cry out. "Give them hell!" he said.

I was powerless to save them.

The Prophet clapped its hands.

Screaming filled my universe, and it was not until my lungs gave out and choked that I realized the screaming was my own. The vision faded again, flickering gone until I observed only the world around me. That vision was the price I paid for failure, I decided, a future I must not allow to come to pass.

"You have to let me go," I said. "Dorayaica is sailing for Berenike, I saw it! You have to let me go!" Where in all that roil I had seen Berenike I could not say. There was too much, and I struggled to hold it all as though I cupped precious wine in my two hands.

Lord Alistair's shade was still standing there, unmoved by the tears streaming down my face.

"I can save them!" I almost screamed the words, and without my new-found vision guiding me I barely kept my feet. "I have to go back."

There is much you do not know, the unheard voice told me. *If you go now, you will go where we cannot reach you.*

"You have done it before," I said.

Time changes, the Quiet said. *Soon your time will go beyond our sight.*

I pictured the wave of time, and thought I understood. "You can only interact with my . . ." I reached for the right word, ". . . my narrative when your future lies within the realm of possibility. But we're outside that now, and the rules are different."

I took their loud silence for a yes, and shook my head. "I have to go to Berenike. If we can stop Dorayaica there . . . I can save them. I can save your future, too. There is a way. There has to be a way!"

The Quiet's voice did not respond, but my father spoke. "Do you swear to see to its end any course begun?"

Confused, I turned to look at him, for it was not the elder Devil of Meidua's voice, but the Emperor's. It was a piece of the oath I'd sworn when I became a knight. How little the words had meant to me so long ago—how much they mattered then.

"I will," I said, rejecting prophecy and fate.

Father's shade raised one hand, pointing at the monument. "Then go."

Then go.

Approaching the black stone, I rested a hand against it, face inches from the glyphs on its surface.

With my new vision, I perceived that they were not glyphs at all. Perceived that all of Valka's efforts over so many decades—all the efforts of her predecessors across centuries to decipher the alien marks—were for nothing. They were not the symbols of an alien language, but the parts of some vast and incomprehensible machine. The monument, the corridors and arches, all the great halls and byways of the ruined city and the ruins on every world the Quiet had touched were parts of a mechanism that reached upward and down into dimensions that we pawns—who move but forward—cannot see. That was how the tunnels moved, how they were propelled backward in time. That was how I came to this place, this other Annica, this universe that time forgot. The Quiet's tunnels were a machine—or something like a machine—that bridged time, that extended north and south, east and west, upward and down across the infinite realms of possibility.

The round symbols began to *turn,* winding like gears in the face of the dark stone, and *retreated* from me. My hand fell *through* the surface, and I watched in dumb amazement as the glyphs wound *backward,* climbing inward and down step by gradual step, until I was looking not upon a monument, but upon an arch opening on a step that ran down.

Mouth open, I peered around the monument, careful with my new and limited sight to choose only the steps that kept me from falling. The monolith couldn't have been more than a foot thick and stood upon the edge of the mountain, but the path that opened in its face ran straight, out and down into empty air.

I knew what I had to do.

I crossed the threshold, following the stairs down, the glyphs turning all around me, building a corridor for me from the dark matter of the walls. I was dimly aware of my progress, but the way was straight and narrow, and I braced myself against the glassy stone to either side. I did not see the hallway, for all was dark, and in time the light of the mountaintop faded away, leaving me in shadow.

Light appeared in time, shining ahead. A mote at first. Then a spot the size of a steel bit. The hall widened to either side, narrow walls belling outward until I walked beneath rounded archways. The light ahead was daylight, and I saw a glowsphere go floating past above my head.

It was one of ours.

I realized then just where I stood. I was in the entrance hall to the ruined city, a suspicion I confirmed a moment later, reaching the level of the outer gate. The way ran straight and clear before me, running downhill clean to where the white buildings of the camp awaited me. I was back in the living world.

I knew the air was gone, but I lifted my face to the sun, feeling the thin sunlight on my bare skin. The second sight remained to me, faint and far away at the edge of my perceptions, but it was enough, enough to choose to stand, enough to hold the effects of the vacuum at bay, if only for a little while. The future was lost to me, and the past was veiled. I was weaker without the Quiet to hand, but it had vanished, its time remote from ours, lost in the ever-changing wilderness of times yet unreal.

But it was enough, enough to carry my exhausted body downslope toward the camp.

And the army and the shuttles that waited there.

CHAPTER 71

WHISPERS

I RAISED BARE HANDS and waved, signaling the troopers below. Someone would have to see me. I could not call to them, not in vacuum, and I would not don my mask again. Not yet. I wanted them to see my bare face. To see I was not dead. Whole *Ibis*-class landing shuttles squatted beyond the camp, their wings folded up like the points of a half dozen metal crowns. Valka must have called in the cavalry when I disappeared. But how long had I been gone?

It took an effort of will to focus on the cresting wave of time, to hold myself along the narrow and increasingly unlikely line where I managed to stay alive. It was like balancing on a wire where I knew that any surprise, any disturbance would spell disaster. The Quiet had given me the gift of second sight, had opened my consciousness across the wave-space of quantum potential.

They had seen me.

Sparrowhawks wheeled overhead, and I—who had so often stood beneath their screaming flight—was transfixed by the silence of them. I saw a skiff speed forward—a low-slung thing like an ancient longship—men in white armor clinging to its gunwale. Three figures sped ahead of them, each riding chariots so that they seemed to fly, leaning against the handlebars, their feet in the platform stirrups.

I recognized Valka leading them all, Crim and Pallino behind. I knew the former by his bandoleer of throwing knives and the latter by the high crest on his faceless helm.

They pulled up before me, throttling their flight platforms back, repulsors throwing up clouds of dust. I smiled and waved, showing my face and bare hands. The skiff pulled up shortly thereafter, men looking on in wonder. Without my helmet on—I'd lost the bone conduction patch somewhere in my agony on the mountain—I could hear no word that passed between them.

Valka slowed as she ran toward me, as if unsure it was really me. Smiling, I presented my scarred left hand, showing her Aranata's ring and the ivory band I wore in her honor.

She closed the gap between us, and threw her arms about my neck. My vision wavered, focus scattering. I gasped, and with an effort of will mastered myself once more. Long enough. Just long enough to key the button on my suit's arm. I could do nothing for my hands, but the mask closed over my face and I felt cool, sterile air blow across my face.

The jets shattered my concentration, and the Quiet's sight collapsed. Immediately I felt cold seep into my hands. "And they say I am a witch," Valka's voice sounded in my ear. "How in the hell—your hands!" She was surveying me at arm's length as she spoke, and reached down, taking my bare hands in hers.

The suit had tightened around my wrists long ago, maintaining pressure elsewhere, but the flesh of my hands was pockmarked where capillaries had burst.

"Lost my gloves," I managed to say . . . and swooned almost to death.

Medica again. Corrective tape on my fingers. The antiseptic odor of curative balms. Feeding tubes. A saline drip. The *beep beep beep* of vital monitors. Dr. Okoyo's stern countenance. Valka's hand.

I awoke, and was surprised to find that I was in medica no longer. I was in my own bed, staring at the ceiling. My limbs were weak and watery, but moved when I willed them to. I held my hands up. The damaged capillaries had nearly healed. Only faint pink spots remained. Everything ached, though whether that was from the power or from the starvation and exhaustion I'd experienced on the mountain I was unsure.

Nevertheless, I sat up and swung my legs round to the floor.

After everything I had seen, the familiar lines of floor and furniture seemed hellish and unreal. I held my face in my hands, remembering those other faces, those other Hadrians. Thousands upon thousands of them, but two above all: that fey man giving orders on the *Demiurge;* and the old man in chains. Was there no other choice? Kill billions—man and Cielcin alike—or watch everyone I cared for die? The Prophet clapped its hands, the dry snap of them like the slamming of a guillotine. Still seated on the edge of the bed, I tried to turn my sight once more in that *other* direction. Vague images of myself sprawled on the bed in a million aspects flashed across my mind. It took me a moment to realize what was missing. I couldn't see any of the narratives where I slept, could only see what my eyes saw, only sense what my senses knew.

"Hadrian?"

Light fell in the opening door and painted a woman's silhouette and shadow on my world. I let the visions fade, and looked up at Valka.

"Okoyo said you'd be awake about now," she said. "She timed your medication."

"I feel awful," I said, and made to stand.

She caught me and forced me to sit back down. "What happened to you?" she asked.

Suddenly I was the ocean, and she the wine cup. I looked down at my hands, the healing capillaries, the scars that would never fully heal. Trying to find the words, I twisted Aranata's and the Emperor's rings in turn. At last I said, "I . . . met the Quiet."

I could feel the weight of her eyes. "I know."

"You know?"

"Hadrian," she said, "you were gone for forty days."

"I . . . what?" I looked back at her, and saw her again for the first time. Her hair was mussed and unwashed, and there were dark shadows beneath the artificial eyes. "Forty . . . that's not possible." I looked back down at my hands, ticked off the days on my fingers. "I didn't eat."

Valka sank onto the ottoman before an antique leather armchair I'd had bolted to the floor. "The moment you disappeared, I knew," she said. "I waved Otavia and had half a chiliad flown down here to start canvassing the ruins."

"I wasn't in them," I said, massaging the deep scars in my left palm.

"I know that, too," she said. "We'd have found you." Glancing up, I marked just how she'd mirrored my posture, the hands between her knees, shoulders hunched, eyes downcast. "We checked your suit chronometer. It said it was only three days since I lost you."

"Three days . . ." I repeated. That felt right. I remembered the sun setting on the mountaintop at least once. I couldn't recall just how long Annica's days were then. Longer than Earth standard, that was certain. Was it possible the rate of what we call time ran differently between narrative worlds? Or is it rather that time has no rate at all, and that the drift I'd experienced occurred simply because the two Annicas I had visited were separate from one another, as if I were a seaman gone ashore while his crew drifted at anchor by night?

"What happened?" Valka asked again.

"I . . . this is going to sound insane," I said.

Valka laughed. "I just saw you standing without a helmet in vacuum," she said. "Alive. I want the truth, Hadrian. All of it."

I found myself nodding. "I'll tell you," I said. "I'll tell you." I started at the beginning, from the moment she'd disappeared around the bend in the hall. I carried her across the bridge and up the new mountain in the shadow of those watchful faces.

"Were they human faces?" Valka asked.

This ground me to a halt. "I . . . yes." I hadn't even stopped to think about it at the time.

A frown carved itself deep upon her sharp features. "Why would that be?" But she waved herself down. "Later."

We climbed the mountain together, and she was silent through the whole narration. Not challenging me as she once had, not calling me a charlatan or a liar, not thinking I insulted her. How far we'd come. I told her of my visions, of the murdered sun, of the Watchers and the birth of the Quiet, of the end of time itself and of our smallest part in that tapestry. Of Akterumu and of the artificial eclipse of the sun.

Of the Prophet, the Prince of the Princes of Hell. And the slaughter at its feast.

"Was I there?" she asked.

"I . . ." I had to think about it, had to re-examine those awful visions. "No."

I could not read the expression on her face. " 'Twill be all right," she said. " 'Twill only happen if you fail, you think?"

I could only nod.

"Then we should make for Berenike at once," she said.

"You believe me?" I heard the surprise in my voice, and felt shame rise, chasing after it.

Valka was on her feet by then, and closed the distance between us. Fingers lifted my chin. "I saw you die, remember?" She brushed my forehead with dry lips. "How can I deny what I've seen? With *my* eyes?" She tapped one ceramic globe with a fingernail, making me wince. "I'll help you get dressed."

"There's more!" I said, flexing my healing hands. "They aren't a language."

Until that moment, I'd not been sure if I was going to tell her or not. It almost seemed cruel. But I had decided it was far crueler to know and never say.

She'd crossed to the closet, had slid the door back into the wall. "What?"

I smiled up at where she leaned against the frame, racks of clothing and shelves behind her. There was no easy way to say it. "The anaglyphs. They're not part of a language at all. They're part of a machine. The ruins . . . the ruins are empty because they were never filled. They're not cities at all. They're . . ." I laughed weakly. "They're a labyrinth." I waved this dramatic distraction aside. "They're a machine that reaches into higher dimensions. The glyphs are components." I told her about my return through the monolith, how the glyphs had rotated and built a door from the black matter of the stone. "Some of it might even be on the suit cameras."

Valka didn't move. " 'Twas nothing," she said, a flatness in her tone somewhere between anger and disbelief. "Almost nothing. Your feed went dead the moment you walked out on this bridge of yours. It didn't resume until you put your helmet back on. 'Tis like your suit was dead."

"Take off your mask . . ." I muttered.

"What?"

"The Quiet . . ." I said. "It ordered me to take my mask off." My mind went to old stories about gods commanding men to cast aside their garments, their shoes. All the things of the world we'd made to hide our nakedness. All our technology. Our progress.

"You think it was trying to hide the evidence?" Valka asked.

"Perhaps . . ." I was stumbling toward an answer . . . "Perhaps it cannot exist when observed. Like . . . like how light changes when you look at it with instrumentation. Particles and waves." I stood, head swimming, and Valka lurched forward to help steady me. "Maybe that's why it never appeared to me when you were there. It could shut off the suit, but it couldn't—wouldn't shut off your eyes."

Valka was shaking where she held me. Tears? But no. Not Valka. Whether it was fear that moved her or rage, I cannot say. I did not ask. She was not a woman to describe her emotions. She suffered them, and needed only for me to stand there, calm. After a moment, she inhaled sharply. "Right," she said. "What are you going to tell them?"

I could only shrug. "The truth."

I'd found the gentleman's cane I'd carried to the triumph ball in a corner of our closet, and leaned heavily upon it as the bulkhead doors to the bridge cycled open. The metal nib *tapped* too loud against the decking as Valka escorted me over the threshold.

"Commandant's on the bridge!" exclaimed one ensign, as he had a thousand times before.

I was back in the waking world.

All eyes turned to face me, and I was made sharply aware of my disheveled appearance, the unbelted tunic, the long coat—so like the one I'd ruined climbing the mountain—and the cane. Self-conscious, I tucked my scarred left hand into my pocket.

"Should you be out of bed, my lord?" asked Lieutenant Koskinen, hurrying forward.

"I'm fine!" I said, a touch too sharply. I addressed Corvo and Durand. "I have what I came here for. We should chart a course for Berenike at once."

Corvo crossed powerful arms. "What happened?"

Repeating a portion of what I'd said to Valka earlier, I said, "I met the Quiet."

"The Quiet?" Durand said, incredulous. "These alien gods of yours?"

"Yes," I snapped, impatience winning over politic comport.

The first officer half-turned. "You really think you're some kind of prophet?"

No one spoke for a good ten seconds, shocked by the Norman's words. Coming from officious, professional Bastien, even I was surprised. Surprised, and stung by the word *prophet,* thinking once more of Dorayaica. "We have to go to Berenike."

Durand wheeled. "So we came here to learn what we already *knew?*"

"Dorayaica will be there," I said, and that brought a chill over the proceedings, even over Durand's crackling rage. "We have to stop it." In all the futures I had seen, I could not recall seeing the battle at Berenike. Neither victory nor defeat. The visions I'd seen had left me blind in this. I stopped short of telling them about the futures I had seen. About the destruction of the Cielcin, about the *Demiurge,* or about the future where I failed to take that option and lost *everything.* I saw my faces reflected in the dark walls of the bridge, the old man in chains and the long-haired hero calling for blood.

No.

"Dorayaica," Aristedes asked, rising from his seat near the captain's console. "You're sure."

I nodded.

"We're still no better off than we were," Durand said. "We knew a fight was coming. That's why staying here was a mistake."

"But we know when," I said, realizing that I knew and wondering what else had seeped into the dark matter of my brain during my time on the mountain. "I need to get word to Legion Intelligence. I'll send a telegraph as soon as we're underway. They need to summon reinforcements. Every ship that can be spared should chart a course for Berenike."

Durand wasn't finished. "This is what we sailed all the way here for? *Reinforcements?* That's hardly prize-winning strategy, *my lord.*"

"Enough!" I snapped, and extended a hand. I had no time for a second Bassander Lin. "Give me your sidearm, commander."

Bastien Durand twitched.

"What?" Corvo stepped between us. "Hadrian, what are you doing?"

I ignored the captain. "Your sidearm, Commander Durand. Please."

Cautious, the Norman officer removed his spectacles and advanced a step, removing his pistol from its thigh holster. As a bridge officer, he was one of the few personnel aboard the *Tamerlane* permitted to go armed when we were not at battle stations. I had left my sword in my quarters. No matter, a sword was not showy enough for what I had in mind. I took the weapon from him, turned it over in my hand. It was heavier than I expected. Not a phase disruptor or plasma burner, but a short-barreled MAG thrower, a high-acceleration, small-caliber railgun. It wasn't Legion regulation; the pellets it threw were too risky aboard a starship, might break a line or pierce the hull in the wrong place. The one-time mercenary had apparently—for once in his life—ignored the letter of the law to suit his comfort and preference.

It was perfect for my purposes.

I found the safety and disengaged it. "Come here," I said, gesturing to the commander, who had stepped back.

"Hadrian, what are you doing?" Corvo asked again.

"I said, come here, Bastien." As I spoke, I unbuttoned the left side of my tunic to bare my chest. Behind me was only a holograph plate mounted to the bulkhead—I held the muzzle of the weapon to my sternum, and taking Bastien's hand in mine, squeezed his finger over the trigger. Valka screamed and stepped forward.

Neither she nor Corvo had the time to stop me.

The railgun whined and snapped as it fired. The holograph plate behind me shattered as the tungsten rod broke to pieces on the heavy bulkhead, shrapnel flying. Men surged forward to pull Durand off of me, to call for the doctor.

"I'm fine," I said. I released Durand's grip—he dropped the gun and staggered back into the arms of two junior officers, eyes wide, hands shaking. I brushed one hand over my unmarked chest, letting my vision fade. There were any number of alternative spaces where Durand never fired. Any number of Hadrians who were never shot. My consciousness spread with my vision across those infinite parallels, and I had traded one for another even as the bullet ripped through me.

Unharmed.

"Do you believe now?" I asked coldly. I took a step nearer and pounded the cane once against the ground. "Does anyone else have doubts?"

All eyes were wide but for Lorian's. The little man was prodding through the damaged projector plate with a finger, already testing that it was real.

"You really can't be killed," Corvo said.

"I can," I said. It had taken an effort of will to hold that power in my hands. "But not so easily as the rest of you."

Consciousness, I think, is a mechanism we humans have evolved for sorting the threads of time. We do it blindly, and that is enough for most of us, most of the time. I am no different, save that I have learned to *listen*.

To see.

Durand was still standing with his mouth open.

"Do you believe me now?" I asked again.

Mute, he nodded.

"Good," I said, and looked round at the others. "That's settled then. We sail for Berenike at once." Still leaning on my cane, I brushed past Durand and stumped toward the forward holograph viewer where it dominated the wall, playing at being a window. It showed Annica's red-umber disc beneath us. I could just make out the lonely mountain on the horizon, brown and scabrous. The other mountains were nowhere to be seen. "Dorayaica knows about Berenike. It attacked Monmara to shock us into retreat, knowing we would mass there. It but waits for the fruit to ripen. By ordering the retreat to Berenike, Oberlin and the Legions have played right into its hands."

"How do you know all this, lord?" Koskinen asked.

Not taking my eyes from the mountain, I answered him. "I saw it."

A murmur went through the junior officers. I heard the word *Halfmortal* whispered there, and recalled Carax and Sir Friedrich and the image of my trident inscribed over the Imperial sun. Another future flashed before me, where I sat upon the Solar Throne with a white stone upon my brow—the very eggshell shard I wore about my neck even then. I could just see its faint reflection in the wall behind the holograph.

So many potential futures.

So much doubt.

CHAPTER 72

BETWEEN THE HAMMER
AND THE ANVIL

THE SKY ABOVE DEIRA city sparked with the flame of sub-light engines. As I often had in the two years since we'd arrived on Berenike, I found myself looking up, past the gray glass towers of the canyon city and the grim stone walls that rose so high to either side, past the terraces on the western crag and the smooth steel expanse of the Storm Wall to the east, and watched our fleet at their maneuvers.

It was like watching constellations come alive. So high were they that even the mightiest dreadnought was reduced until it appeared as one of the common stars fixed above the city or else tacking planet-like across the skies.

"I never get tired of watching it," Pallino said at my shoulder.

I looked round at the old chiliarch—one of the last pair of myrmidons who remained with me from Emesh. My other guards had maintained a respectful distance when I'd tarried by the rail, their faces peering determinedly ahead.

"Back in basic, on Zigana, the sky was always full of ships. Couldn't even see the stars—course, you never missed them. What's the difference?"

Leaning on the gentleman's cane I'd not abandoned since Annica, I said, "You know the ancients used to believe that night was a curtain? That the stars were pinholes you could see the day through?"

"Don't think I did, Had," he said. An uneasy silence settled between us. He wanted me to get moving. We could not afford to be late. "Damn big curtain," he added, squinting up at the night with his two blue eyes. "There sure is an awful lot of Dark."

"It's the light that matters," I said coolly. "That's where our guns are."

Inhaling sharply and gathering my wits, I turned and strode along the path from our apartments in the lower city—where the gubernatorial palaces stood above the great canal amidst the tower penthouses of the wealthy—to the industrial and mercantile quarters above that sheltered in the shadow of the Storm Wall.

Berenike had begun as a mining colony long ago, when human settlement in the Norman Expanse was young. Despite nearly three thousand years of settlement, the planet had never flowered as Marinus or Monmara had. Mining efforts still dominated its lower latitudes in those few places where the surface was not given over to briny, algae-soaked seas, and it was of note on the galactic stage only as a Legion supply post, having once been the Imperial beachhead in the sector in those times before the conquest of Marinus. Aside from the Legion personnel on station in orbit, fewer than ten million people called Berenike home, and every one of them—absent the few hundred intrepid miners in the windswept colonies—huddled in Deira beneath and behind the Storm Wall.

We had a commanding view of the city from the express lift, slim towers retreating into the chasm depths beneath us. The great city had been built in the shelter of the *Valles Merguli,* the Valley of the Diver, a chasm five miles deep in places and several hundred long.

"People will build fucking anywhere, won't they?" Pallino said.

"It's the storms," I said. So much of Berenike's surface was flat that the coriolis winds—spurred on by moist, tropical airs out of the equatorial regions—could whip themselves into gales ten times more horrific than anything our ancestors had known on Earth. Hightower orbital lifts were out of the question—too much risk of a line snapping or a tower being knocked down. All ground-to-orbit traffic came and went through the massive landing field that covered the plains above the windward edge of the *Valles:* tens of miles of paved prairie stretching almost to the horizon.

We could not see it from our lift, for Deira city was fashioned on many levels. The lower wards ran along terraces that lined either side of the great valley, connected by many bridges and shadowed by many towers. Above these on the windward side, a short, inner wall rose, separating the terraces of the valley from the flat, poor neighborhoods that huddled in the shadow of the Storm Wall, which protected these upper quarters and the valley alike from Berenike's scouring winds.

The Storm Wall.

It was a bulwark against the heavens themselves, a barrier built almost a mile high and perhaps a third as broad. Whole segments had been engineered in orbital facilities out-system and flown across the galaxy at

monstrous cost on behalf of the Wong-Hopper Consortium, who had
founded the original joint-stock colony on the planet.

By rights, it should have been the hundredth marvel of the universe,
but there it was, mouldering above a city on a planet that amounted to a
caravansary and refueling depot on the road to the Norman frontier. When
we had first descended from the *Tamerlane,* I had thought it a feature of the
landscape and not a work of human hands, so mighty was it. Tall and broad
it was, and ran for hundreds of miles along the canyon edge. The space on
the far side of the *Valles Merguli* was hardly worth mentioning: an impassable morass of broken stones and sinkholes given over to swampland and
the native scrubby plant life.

"I know it's the storms," Pallino said, ignoring propriety and the decade of guards at our backs. "But we could have picked another planet."

I shrugged, drummed my fingers against the silver head of the cane.
"The air was good. That's rare."

The Legion headquarters were in the barbican of the Storm Wall, a
many-leveled adjunct to the main structure thrust out on the starport side
of the wall itself. Through horizontal, inhuman windows I could look out
on the flat plane outside the city, the airstrips and steel-reinforced concrete
mounds of hangars between and above the shielded blasting pits where
rockets waited for clearance to launch.

"They won't be far behind us," came the familiar gruff voice from over
my shoulder. "We lost one of our outriders on the way in. I can only hope
our boys managed to destroy the ship's computer before the Cielcin got
hold of it, else they'll know our strength."

"They already know," I said, turning from the window to regard the
man at the head of the conference table.

Titus Hauptmann looked more or less precisely as I'd remembered him:
leonine, gray-haired with mighty sideburns, curling mustache, and bushy
eyebrows, positively carnivorous in his black uniform draped with chains
and silver braid. Like the Emperor amidst his retainers, Hauptmann was
seated at the far end of a ring-shaped conference table, surrounded by his
captains and attachés. The First Strategos raised an eyebrow. "Take a seat,
Lord Marlowe."

Rapping my cane against the floor, I said, "Dorayaica planned this. It's
been watching our troop movements for years. Analyzing our logistics,
dissecting our supply trains, making use of captured technology: shields
and so on. It knew we would fall back here. It chased you."

"Do you mean to be insubordinate, Marlowe? I said *sit down*."

"No sir," I said, and paused just long enough to be ambiguous. Moving to take my seat opposite the First Strategos, I said, "It's just my manner."

"Your manner . . ." Hauptmann snorted. "Your *manner* does not exempt you from observing the proper forms, sir knight."

"I'm quite certain you're right, sir," I said. The Duke of Andernach had long ago ceased to terrify me, but I took my seat, lips pressed primly together as I glanced sidelong at Otavia Corvo, who had not stirred from her seat at my right hand.

Hauptmann shifted in his seat, swept his eyes over the half a hundred officers and officers' holographs that sat in council about the table. "We have at best a few weeks to marshal our defenses. Regardless of whether or not we are to believe Lord Marlowe's doomsaying, it is certainly the case that the fleet which assailed Marinus has followed us rather than linger to sack the planet."

"That alone suggests Lord Marlowe speaks the truth," said another familiar voice from the First Strategos's right. Unlike Hauptmann, Bassander Lin seemed to have aged a thousand years since we'd parted after the Vorgossos affair, though he carried none of it on his face. Rather there was something in his posture, something subtle and hard to pin down, a great weight that bent his spirit even as his back was straight. I almost pitied him. He looked more or less like I remembered, high-cheekboned copper face stony beneath woodsmoke hair, dark eyes narrowed. There was perhaps a touch of silver in the dark mane, but he was every ounce still the young officer I recalled—if not young anymore. "It is uncharacteristic of the Cielcin not to linger. If they come so hard on your heels, Lord Strategos, the enemy must have remained at Marinus just long enough to . . ." his voice faltered with the implication of his words, ". . . to reprovision for the journey here. Smash and grab."

As he spoke, Lin's eyes wandered to me, and he set his jaw. The captain had been with us on the *Demiurge,* had been with me when I died. The experience had changed him—at least changed his attitude toward me. Gone was the antagonism, the posturing and constant tension, the rivalry between us. Holy fear had taken its place, sunk roots like talons into the man, and drained blood and fire away. He had not spoken to me since he arrived on Berenike, had not communicated at all, unless it was to watch me as though I were some manner of ghost.

"They are the hammer," I said darkly. "We are glowing iron."

"Excuse me?" asked one of the captains, a gray-faced woman with short, dark hair who might have been cast from the same mold as the late Raine Smythe.

I did not explain the ancient and primitive art of hammer forging to the assembly, but pressed on. "There is another fleet coming. Possibly it is already here . . . or near here. Waiting. The pursuers are meant to attack us, to divert our attention. Marinus was only the bait, my lords. I suspect you are the prize."

"Explain," Hauptmann said.

Extending a hand palm up, I said, "Lord Hauptmann, you have menaced the Cielcin in these regions for decades. If Dorayaica has been studying us, it certainly knows you. I would be prepared to bet this entire performance has been put on for your benefit."

Hauptmann's face was ash and stone. "What makes you so certain?"

I could hardly tell him I had seen it in a vision. At best, they would think me a charlatan, at worst a pretender to the throne. Carax's medallion seemed to flip, coin-like, before my eyes. It struck the table with the scarred face down. I shook myself, and the vision faded.

"He dreamed it, most like," said the gray-faced woman, evincing small smiles and nervous laughter from a few of those present. I was surprised and vaguely unsettled to find that only half of the officers—give or take—joined in. Evidently the footage and legend of my duel with Irshan had spread even as far as the front in the years since I left Forum.

"Marinus is not a random prize," I said, unruffled. "It was our *capital* in the Veil. Its selection was intentional. Deliberate. We are dealing with the same *scianda* that attacked Hermonassa. These are calculated moves. Not the traditional raids we have dealt with across the Veil for centuries. Hermonassa was in the heart of the Empire, thousands of light-years from the front."

Hermonassa had not been the first core world attacked. There had been random raids carried out throughout the crusade. Cai Shen had been such a one, and I wonder now if that, too, had not been the work of Syriani Dorayaica. An early effort. Cai Shen had been a key uranium source for the Legions and Consortium alike. Had it been *targeted*? Had Dorayaica—or a Cielcin very like the *Shiomu*—found record of the planet in the navigational computer of some captured Imperial vessel?

"They chose Marinus to put us on alert," I said. "They knew—somehow they knew—that you would retreat here. The fleet that attacked Marinus is coming, and then the jaws will close."

Another officer—a legate in black and silver with his white beret on the tabletop before him and a face like an old fox—was nodding along. I was a moment recognizing the emblem with two crossed swords on his lapel. It was the badge of the 437th Centaurine Legion. Raine Smythe's Legion. "I can't speak on the subject of Sir Hadrian's visions, but he speaks sense. Why leave Marinus to recover?"

Titus Hauptmann crossed his arms, displaying the ornately sculpted vambraces he wore. "You weren't there, Leonid. Marinus will not *recover*. The place was damn near devastated. The Pale left because there was nothing left."

A scholiast several places down the table cleared her throat. "But it is most unlike the Cielcin to waste resources, Lord Strategos. The first siege at Cressgard took years. The Cielcin were still chasing people out of caves in the mountains when Cassian Powers arrived five years in."

"There is nothing left of Marinus to waste, counselor!" Hauptmann said. "You saw the footage." Memories of blasted cities and of plains turned to glass impressed upon my mind. I remembered the black crater burned into the face of the planet Rustam so long ago, like a black eye. Doubtless Marinus was worse.

"How long is the average Cielcin invasion, exactly?" asked Captain Corvo.

The scholiast shut her eyes, mind ticking through a series of mnemonics to find her answer. "In cases where we have been unable to mount an effective defense? Between three and eight years."

Legate Leonid Bartosz interjected. "The assault on Marinus lasted three days."

The scholiast spread her hands, bronze badges on her green legionary uniform glittering. "With respect, strategos, it is highly unlikely the Cielcin could strip a planet as settled as Marinus of *all* resources in a mere three days."

"And they withdrew first?" I asked, already knowing the answer.

Titus Hauptmann's face grew dark, confirming what I already knew. It was all but impossible to trace a ship through warp. All it took was a stop and a change of trajectory to ensure the subtle distortion and the infinitesimal heat of the ship's drive glow would be lost to even the most watchful eyes. The attackers had not fled Marinus at all, only staged a strategic retreat to mark the humans' own flight to rendezvous with the rest of the fleet on Berenike. They'd lit a fire on Marinus, and like moths we'd come rushing to meet it.

"If you're right," the gray-faced woman said, "we ought to have detected their approach by now."

Corvo pursed her lips. "That would depend on how far out they are and how long they've been there." She was right, but her words conjured images of spiders lurking in their webs, and I imagined Cielcin vessels lying in cold ambush for eons, the Pale xenobites gnawing bones in their dark tunnels, awaiting their coming feast.

"You're proposing that this second fleet of yours has been lying in wait for years—for more than a decade—somewhere beyond the Berenike heliopause?"

"Out beyond your sensor net," Corvo said. "They wouldn't look like any more than a cluster of asteroids unless you got too close."

Taking Corvo's words like a baton in a race, Hauptmann turned to me and asked, "I don't suppose these visions of yours have given you any useful intelligence, Lord Marlowe? The location of this secret fleet, perhaps? How well equipped are they? What are their numbers?"

So dry was the First Strategos's delivery that I could not quite tell if he was being insincere. Feeling the eyes of the gathered captains on me once more, I replied in kind. "Forgive me," I answered him, "I do not have visions. I only guess at strategy."

"Strategy." Hauptmann frowned beneath his thick mustache, disappointment evident in his leonine face. He reminded me of the late Sir William Crossflane. "Forgive *me,* I am not in the habit of acting on guesswork."

"Nevertheless," I said, "that is what I offer." Had I spoken truly, spoken of Annica and the Quiet, I would have been even less believed. For a moment, I considered giving the captains a sign, performing for them some miracle as I had for doubting Durand. But to do so here would be to expose myself to the Imperium, to open myself up to investigation and perhaps to *study.* I did not think the Inquisition would be gentle with me. Not a second time.

"My lord, if I may?" asked Bassander Lin, resting one vambraced arm against the black glass tabletop. Hauptmann signaled for the junior man to speak, and Lin pressed on, "Guesswork or not, what Lord Marlowe suggests strikes me as credible. We should call for reinforcements. Whatever else is true, this Dorayaica's grasp of strategy has proved a world apart from the other Cielcin clans. It was his badge we saw on Marinus."

I watched Bassander with quiet surprise. It had been one thing to find his antagonism washed away, but to win outright support? That was something else entirely.

Another of the legionary captains cleared his throat. "Have there been any disappearances among ships leaving the system in the past several years? Mining convoys? ODF patrols?"

All eyes turned toward the System Commandant, a reedy, older woman named Bancroft with a face caught in a permanent frown. She had been silent through much of the proceedings. Director of the Berenike Orbital Defense Force she might have been, but she was in the presence of seven legates and a strategos of the Imperial Legions—and not just any strategos, the *First* Strategos of all the Centaurine Legions, a man who answered only to the Imperial Council and to the Emperor himself. Next to such worthies, she was little more than a plebeian village eolderman brought before a planetary lord.

"None that I know of . . ." she said, shifting in her seat. "No more than usual, I mean. Maybe one or two to fuel containment leaks in the past decade. Nothing . . . nothing fraught."

Hauptmann's eyes narrowed. "Fraught . . ." he said. "Incident reports were made, I assume?"

Bancroft stammered, trying to articulate a response. "I . . . I . . . well, yes, I—"

"You will have those reports brought to us immediately, Commandant. Thank you." He snapped his fingers, dismissing the system's chief military officer as though she were a common cupbearer.

She went, and in her wake Hauptmann's eyes surveyed us gathered officers, orbs like chips of flint. "It seems there may be something to Sir Hadrian's *clairvoyance,* after all." Hollow laughter accompanied the strategos's words.

Bassander Lin did not join in.

"What a waste of time," Otavia said when we were alone with Pallino and our guards on the platform awaiting the tram to return us across the industrial district and down into the *Valles Merguli.* "It's a miracle, really, that your Empire can respond to any threat, much less conquer anyone else. You know?"

I could only grunt in agreement. I had lost my stomach for state meetings when I was a boy. More and more I found myself agreeing with my father: it was better for the landed palatine houses to rule directly than rely on the vast Imperial state. The feudal lords were individuals, and individually responsible to their peoples and for their territories. Better an individual than an apparatus. I thanked heaven we were not a republic, with so many competing interests given voice and power, each strangling each until blood ran in the streets. Nothing would be done about the Cielcin, not until they knocked the topless towers of the Eternal City from the sky. Or civil war and subtle politicking made us an empire again.

"It gets done because soldiers do it," Pallino said.

"It was soldiers we just listened to talking in circles for three hours," Corvo replied.

"Them's officers, ma'am," he said. "Different species."

I could just see the tops of the highest towers in the lower district rising above the lip of the canyon, rooftops crowned with gardens bright with swaying trees. Above, the day-gray sky still sparked and flickered with fusion flame where the mighty fleet moved, changing orbits, getting out of one another's way. "Careful, Pallino. You're a chiliarch now."

"And a fighting man through and through. But the captains? If those naval lads weren't born with the silver spoon in their mouths, someone gave them one." He paused, and I didn't have to turn to know the man was shaking his head. "Different fucking species, I say. They'll make the call, but it's us who'll fight and die. Us that'll win the victory. And what do we get for our trouble? Frozen."

"You're very gloomy today," Corvo said.

"I'm always gloomy before a fight," he said. "And Elara's on the *Tamerlane*. Always needed a woman before a fight, and she's the only one for me."

"At least Hauptmann's putting the call out for reinforcements . . ." I said.

"Marlowe!"

I turned at the sound of the familiar voice, and looking back along the tram platform, past the odd clusters of soldiers and other personnel waiting beneath the iron-and-glass vaults of the tram station, saw Bassander Lin advancing, his black officer's greatcoat slung over his shoulders like a cape. I flipped my own cape clear of my shoulder and tucked the cane beneath my arm. When Bassander was within ten paces, I said, "Lin."

The line of fire did not redraw between us, though something stretched in its place. Not animosity, but the memory of animosity, awkward and antiseptic. His oiled hair had slipped, long strands stuck to the shaved sides of his head. I guessed he'd been running.

"You remember Pallino and Captain Corvo?" I said.

The Mandari bowed stiffly. "Hello." He advanced on me, eyes held to bare slits, and a piece of me wondered for a moment if he would strike me, though I could not have a named a precise reason why I might have deserved such a thing.

He offered a hand instead, not as he had aboard the *Schiavona* when we'd first set sail for Forum to report to the Emperor and his Council, not as a suppliant eager to touch the robes of some saint or holy man, but as the plebeians do, one man to another. I could just see the faint white bracelet of scar protruding from his sleeve where the hand had been reattached to the wrist.

I took the offered hand and shook it.

"It is true you stopped highmatter with your bare hands?" Lin asked, glancing at the hand he'd shaken and at the glove on my left. Was that it? Had he come seeking after another miracle?

Eyes closed, I drew back. "The bones in my left arm are adamant, remember? Sagara gave them to me in return for his—and her—lives."

Lin nodded. "I'd forgotten." Then, "Who was it?"

The Empress, I wanted to say. *And the Minister of War.* But news of Bourbon's death had reached us on Colchis, and it was better to say nothing. For Crim's sake and my own.

"I don't know," I told him. "But I've been exiled to the front, it seems." My attentions flickered to Otavia and Pallino, and beyond them to the tram sliding sleekly into sight on its magnetic rail. "What do you think Hauptmann will do?"

Lin answered directly. "If Bancroft's reports indicate anything suspicious . . . divide the fleet. If they mean to take us by surprise, we must do likewise. He'll leave a token force here in orbit, withdraw the bulk of his forces out-system, and do to the Cielcin what you think they mean to do to us."

"You know," I said as the tram pulled silent into the station, "I was having the very same thought."

Lin took a sharp step backward, clearing space on the platform for my guards. "I'm glad you're here, Marlowe."

Returning his chilly salute, I said, "And I you, Lin."

CHAPTER 73

BERENIKE

THE NIGHT HELD NO moon, and the stars shone like the drives of starships, not remote but terribly present, pressing against the roof of the world. Some of them were ships, of course. Destroyers and frigates, rapid attack interceptors and courier ships, shuttles and lightercraft and remote-pilot drones, battleships and capital ships, dreadnoughts and the super-dreadnought *Sieglinde* reigning over all, so vast I could make out the shape of her locked in the sky above Deira.

I sketched their fire in white charcoal against the heavy black paper of my folio, setting their lights above the night-lit ramparts of the Storm Wall above, gleaming white and faintly golden. The page opposite showed the mightiest of the massive bridges that spanned the valley high above, homes and shops hanging from its sides and from below its track like the turrets of an inverted castle.

The ships above were sailing.

Sailing away.

Bancroft's reports had confirmed my suspicions.

Only two ships had disappeared in-system in the last decade, less than the standard attrition rate among cargo haulers and the like. Such ships ran for centuries without maintenance, their various owners scraping by, content to spot-weld and patch their leaky vessels. Failure was inevitable. Entropy would wait—but it could not wait forever.

But for two ships to be destroyed within a million miles of one another inside as many months? Two data points may not indicate a trend, but we could hardly afford to ignore them. Scouts dispatched to the region had found no sign of the enemy, but that was no surprise. It was not difficult to imagine a Cielcin migratory cluster coming out of warp in a system's Oort Cloud, masquerading as common asteroids, cutting all thrust and riding their momentum in a steady orbit around the sun. Waiting for their moment and a sign.

"The *Sieglinde* will withdraw with the bulk of the fleet to point-three light-years out-system and above the ecliptic, and there await the rest of the fleet," First Strategos Hauptmann had said, standing somehow at the head of the round table, a holograph display modeling the strategic withdrawal in the space before us. "I will remain here and coordinate planetary defense from Ondu Station. Legate Corran." And here he turned to a hard-faced woman of nearly Jaddian complexion, who cocked an eyebrow at her name. "You will have command of the *Sieglinde* and the rest of the fleet. Bartosz, you and the 437th will command the defense on the ground alongside Lord Marlowe's company. Marlowe will act as your lieutenant."

Bartosz, I thought, looking at the fox-like Sir Leonid. He had been Raine Smythe's commander. The 437th. That meant Bassander Lin again. I studied the holographs, marked the location of Ondu Station in synchronous orbit directly above Deira, a great cylinder encircled by spires and mighty wards to which were docked the dozen or so light destroyers of the Orbital Defense Fleet. And around it the knife-blade shapes of Hauptmann's fleet gathered, an array of several dozen vessels ranging from less than a mile in length to the almost forty-mile-long behemoth that was the *Sieglinde*.

"Why move the *Sieglinde* out-system?" one of the captains asked.

"Because they will notice it is gone," Hauptmann answered. "If this Pale prince is as discerning as Lord Marlowe seems to believe, he imagines that I have decided to sacrifice Berenike and the Veil entire. It might make him overconfident, particularly given this second fleet he may have at his disposal. He may believe he has us in his jaws, ladies and gentlemen. Little does he know we will have him in ours."

Commandant Bancroft cleared her throat. "We should expect them to focus their efforts on the city. They'll guess we're coordinating the defense from here." As she spoke, she found her feet and moved to stand beside the First Strategos. "We expect any ground assault to come across the landing field toward the Storm Wall, which will of course be their primary target." Her display showed a rendering of the Storm Wall with Deira behind and beneath it, the landing field unrolled and almost perfectly level, save where it was broken by the hangar domes and the round maws of blasting pits.

Otavia couldn't help herself, and with crossed arms raised her voice. "Won't they just hit the city from behind? Land on the far side of the canyon or in Deira proper?"

"They will," Bancroft agreed, "but the Storm Wall will be their primary target. The city bunkers are all beneath it. That's where our people will be when they attack."

By way of explanation, one of the ODF junior officers said, "Tomorrow morning we'll give orders to evacuate the city into those bunkers best we can. The Consortium has already ordered its people to the outland mining camps."

"The Cielcin will hit those, too," Bassander said darkly.

"Perhaps," Hauptmann replied, "but perhaps not all of them. And in any event, it will mean fewer mouths if we're forced to dig in here for a protracted siege."

The junior ODF man continued, "There's room enough in the bunkers and the underground starport terminals to house the city population. They'll be safe enough down there from orbital bombardment."

"You mean to sacrifice the city?" I asked, shifting forward in my seat opposite Titus Hauptmann.

The commandant looked down at her boots, afraid perhaps that I was about to embarrass her as Hauptmann had days earlier. "If it means saving the people, yes."

I liked Bancroft. "Very good."

"The city is not as defensible as the Wall at any rate," Hauptmann's scholiast advised.

"The Cielcin may attempt a landing in it all the same," I said, gesturing at the holograph. "Particularly if there's a storm, the wind on the city side will be much less. Even on the far side of the canyon . . ."

A third junior ODF officer spoke up. "The far side is ill-suited to landing, my lord, and worse still for troop deployment. The marshes . . ."

Hauptmann sliced through the growing disorder with a clean precision my father would have admired, not shouting, but raising his voice just a hair, just enough to remind the seated, squabbling officers that *he* was the man in charge. "Sir Hadrian is quite correct. If there is to be an attack from the air it will come on the inside of the Storm Wall. Tor Jeanne, how many of *Javelin-9s* do we still have in storage?"

"On the *Sieglinde?* Eighty-seven, sir," the scholiast answered. "Perhaps some three hundred distributed throughout the fleet."

"Three hundred . . ." Hauptmann's mustache frowned once more as he contemplated the *Javelin* missile batteries. "I'll want them strung along the ramparts at the valley's edge. Plasma howitzers for support where necessary."

I saw the wisdom in this plain enough. The inner wall was situated nearly midway between the Storm Wall and the far edge of the *Valles Merguli*. It commanded angles of attack over both the valley itself and its far side as well as over the industrial quarters between its ramparts and the superhuman rise of the Storm Wall, and its battlements were tall enough not to be overshadowed by the surrounding spires and foundry stacks. Deira was not an ancient city by the standards of the Imperium—perhaps three millennia from its founding—but it was yet the product of another age, its walls and towers cyclopean in their antique grandeur, so mighty that we men were but ants beside them, and might have seemed pitiful were it not that we had built such marvels ourselves. More often than not, the clouds themselves pooled against the outer side of the Storm Wall, running down in gray fog or streaming up and cut to ribbons against the points of the Wall's crown like silver knives.

In the coming weeks I ranged all over the city with Corvo or Aristedes in tow. The little commander had various notions for how the defense of the city should be carried out, and wasted no time sharing these.

I had to commend Bancroft and the governor-general, for never before had I seen so orderly an evacuation of citizens. Local prefects and the soldiers of the ODF emptied one district after another, moving people day by day into the bunkers beneath the Storm Wall and the industrial quarters, accessed through heavy vault doors and tunnels in the terraces of the city along the valley's side. In little less than a fortnight, the city was all but emptied, its only occupants the odd utility workers and the prefects who dragged barricades across roads and bridges and who drove armored groundcars through tight corridors where the buildings stood dark and close.

Our best calculations told us we had only a matter of weeks before the Cielcin arrived, and the silence over Deira city thickened like a sauce, like the fog that dominated the airfield each time I trekked out through the tram tunnels and underground taxiways that honeycombed the landing field beneath the tarmac and stood upon the grid. Beyond the paved miles the prairie stretched forever, and far off I saw the gray hulks of the nuclear plants that powered the massive city, safe across the empty distance. Looking back into the white shadows of the Storm Wall, I spied other hulks.

The colossi waited against the wall, hunched on their massive legs: two and four and six.

Like men, some were, if men were a hundred feet tall. Still others resembled mighty beetles, or moved with the hunched indignity of a bulldog tall as any house of lords. Each was a mobile barracks, a mobile artillery unit. If the Cielcin did mean to assail the Storm Wall from the airfield, they would face our giants of steel.

So mighty a host had we assembled in our defense!

I prayed it would be enough.

"Hauptmann is putting us in the trenches," I said, meaning the city itself. "He's convinced the first assault will aim to terrify, which means berserkers in the streets." I turned my gaze from Corvo to Aristedes, to Varro, Valka, and Durand. Crim and Pallino each sat in the far corner of the room, arms crossed, eyes hard and clear among the other chiliarchs. It was not the first time we'd all gathered before a battle, and I prayed that it would not be the last. Udax and Barda had joined us, for I'd given the order that every man and woman on the *Tamerlane* should be decanted from their icy slumber and brought up to speed on the situation.

The Irchtani watched in solemn silence, listening with heads cocked like curious ravens. Even Prince Alexander was present, having abandoned his white royal garments for a Legion uniform devoid of insignia or rank—as if any man with hair so red needed either.

"I want all our people except the Sixth Cohort deployed to the city with me," I said. "I will take command on the ground. Otavia, you will take the ship and reinforce Hauptmann's fleet in orbit protecting Ondu Station and the approaches down to the city."

Otavia made a face. "And you?"

"I'll be in the city," I said. "I'm no use in a space battle."

The captain's frown deepened considerably. "I don't like this throwing yourself at the enemy thing you've taken a liking to. It's not prudent. You should stay in the command center with Bartosz."

"Not prudent?" I said, chafing against Corvo's perfectly reasonable counsel. "I can't abandon the men. Besides, I want Aristedes in the comm center," I said coolly. "He has a better head for strategy."

"Lord Marlowe prefers tactics," Lorian offered the congregation, smiling his pointed smile. His face darkened beneath his lank, white hair almost at once. "You've . . . spoken to Bartosz and Hauptmann about me?"

"About you what?" I ceased pacing in an arc up and down the landing field conference chamber. Distracted momentarily by the convoy of personnel on chariots streaking across the tarmac from one of the outer hangar domes back toward the line of colossi at the wall. "Ah." I had forgotten. "I told Bartosz the commander would be joining him to coordinate our part of the ground defense. If he or Hauptmann gives you trouble, fall back on your rank and do your duty." *Demons above and below,* I thought. If Hauptmann had thought me insubordinate, I shuddered to think what he would think of Aristedes—and him an intus, no less. "They won't stop you doing your job, and any fool with eyes to see knows you're good at it."

A low *quarking* sound came from the Irchtani corner, and Kithuun-Barda said, "What of us, Devil Man?"

The Irchtani were fresh from the ice, and seeing the xenobites standing there in their vest-like uniform jackets, talons curled against their breasts, threw into sharp relief just how much time had passed since last I'd seen them. I had been in Gabriel's Archive when their time—alone and as a people—to roost on Thessa had come. I had seen neither Udax nor Kithuun-Barda since Forum; since before Selene; before the knife-missile; before Breathnach and Bourbon; before Philip, Ricard, and Irshan; before Colchis, Gibson, and Horizon. Before Annica and the Quiet. The Irchtani seemed to belong to another world, another Hadrian.

I shook myself. "The First Strategos has installed anti-air artillery along the inner wall overlooking the city." I paused, unsure how best to articulate what needed saying. "The fighting is bound to be thick there, *kithuun,* but those missile emplacements and the guns around them are a crucial line of defense. Your men will make a great difference there, but the Cielcin will come for them."

"Let them try, *bashanda,*" Udax said, punching his open palm with one scaled fist. "We are the fighting Irchtani! We defeated their metal monster, you and me! We will do it again."

I hoped the xenobite was right. Whatever else was true, we would be in the thick of the fighting. "Most of Hauptmann's legionaries are keeping to space," I said. Hauptmann planned to take the fight to the Cielcin in orbit, to capture or destroy their ships, for which he needed all the men he could get. A less experienced commander might have been offended at being relegated to groundwork, but I knew better. We were not the rearguard, but a critical element of the defense. Perhaps the critical element. "Let him win the glory, if that's what he wants. Let him add another standard to his collection. Our duty is to protect the people."

Valka was smiling as I spoke and caught my gaze. I returned the expression. "We'll play this close and defensively. Kithuun-Barda, as I say, I want you and your people manning the inner wall. I'll want cohorts three,

four, and five in the industrial quarter defending the approaches to the
Storm Wall with the ODF ground troops. Bartosz is taking the landing
field."

"If they attack at all like the rest of Pale," Lorian said, shifting in his
seat to draw the attention of those around him, "they'll hit us hard and fast.
Hard drop troops from orbit, get them into the city past our guns. They
won't know to hit the Storm Wall yet, they'll go for the city."

"What are you saying?" I asked, and ceased pacing to look at the little
man with his ghost-pale eyes.

Commander Aristedes's smile was all teeth. "Hold the guns until after
they land in the valley. Then close the lid."

"Fire on the city, you mean?" Durand sounded aghast. He had not been
at the meeting with Hauptmann and Bancroft.

"It's empty!" Lorian snapped back. "Why not? Why not do to them
what that Iubalu creature did to us? Draw them in. Let them overextend
themselves." He clambered to his feet and toward the holograph table that
stood between me and the others. "Keep the Irchtani on the inner wall,
but put our men in the city in the approach tunnels to the bunkers where
they'll be safe. Here and here . . . and here." He pointed with those ghoul-
ish fingers of his. The Cielcin will hit the city and start *hunting*—only they
won't find anyone. Draw them in," he said once more, "then close the lid."

I was nodding along quite before I realized it. "Very good," I said.
"Then we'll be prepared to fall back through the bunkers to the Storm
Wall if we lose the city, and re-seal the gates behind us." I glanced at
Corvo and Durand. "Can you speak to Bancroft? We need to make sure
the tunnels are cleared from the lower gates up through to the fortress
proper. I want her refugees out of the way."

"We'll want to mine the lower gates," Pallino said, raising his chin and
his voice from the back. "Last thing we need's the Pale fucking us in the
ass if we have to retreat."

I nodded. We had the beginnings of a plan.

CHAPTER 74

PHYLACTERIES

LIGHTNING CHEWED AT THE horizon, illuminating the distant nuclear plants beneath their pillars of white steam. I was made acutely aware of the *volume* of the air, the height of the clouds above and about me, their weight and charge. I surveyed the land below with new eyes, saw the landing field unfold in countless variations, witnessed countless permutations of the lightning falter across infinite permutations of cloud, watched by infinite versions of me, each so alike that not even I fully understood the differences.

"I thought you'd be up here."

I hadn't seen Valka's approach, but whatever vision I have is limited to those things my senses are aware of, and though I could—if I concentrated—perceive the infinite possible *now*, it was only the little infinity bounded by my senses. On the mountain I had seen with the eyes of the Quiet, seen *everything,* seen beyond the boundaries of my mortal self, beyond the walls of reason and of sleep to realms and narratives so improbable that they were little different than dreams. And perhaps they were.

"I didn't hear you come up," I said, turning.

She looked as she always did, wry smile in place beneath golden eyes and wild, red-black hair. To fight the gusting winds so high atop the Storm Wall, she'd donned her customary short leather jacket, its wine red complimenting the charcoal shirt with its pattern of skulls and the Tavrosi script that confirmed I'd been right. *Annica* was the name of those musicians she liked so much.

"I didn't want you to!" She almost laughed. "Are you all right?"

"Calm before the storm!" I called back—for she was perhaps twenty paces from me. Inclining my head to the lighting, I added, "Literally, in this case." We had weathered our fair share of storms since coming to

Deira, though from the city itself they were no great spectacle. Atop the Storm Wall, winds might reach an excess of six hundred miles per hour, spurred to great speeds by all that open space—and that was without the updrafts from where the winds crashed against the pale ramparts of that mighty edifice of metal and stone.

" 'Tis," she agreed, coming to stand beside me. " 'Tis so still."

"It always is before a battle," I said, "as if the whole world were holding its breath." Off on the horizon, the lightning flashed again, though again the thunder was too remote to be heard. My vision faded away, and I was once more a man wholly present. I drew my cape tight around myself. "Otavia's returned to orbit."

Valka leaned against the parapet, peering down at the colossi four thousand feet below. From our height, the enormous machines appeared almost like ordinary beetles. Above, red lights flared against the higher levels of cloud as ships in orbit fired their engines. "I saw her off," she said. "Will it work?"

I looked round at her, baffled by the question. "I don't know," I said, leaning on the rail. "I really can't see the future, Valka." I'd tried to explain it to her half a hundred times since Annica, before and after the freeze.

"But you *did*," she said. "You said you saw the Pale attack this place."

"On the mountain," I said. "But I wasn't alone then." I took her hands in mine, glad that here the wind and open air would wash my words away. I looked over her shoulder. In the distance, I saw soldiers hurrying about, busying themselves with gun emplacements set upon the wall. Technicians swarmed over the massive shield projector turrets that studded the wall every quarter mile, silvered domes shimmering. I spied also my own guards, faceless Red Company men armed and armored who maintained their quiet distance.

I was never *really* alone.

"But they *are* coming?" she said.

"Yes."

"Another battle." Valka shook her head.

"Perhaps the final battle," I said, recalling my visions. There were so many futures, so many places in time. Had I seen valleys in the great landscape of possibility where the war ended at Berenike? Or were those possibilities only dreams? I knew I must avoid the futures I had seen, that was enough. "We can stop Dorayaica here," I said. "It's the biggest threat. With it gone, the other clans might surrender or . . . run back into the Dark whence they came." No sooner had I opened my mouth than the memory of what lurked in that darkness flashed like the lightnings in my mind. The hideous wings; the writhing, shapeless masses.

"What is it?" Valka asked.

"Nothing," I said, and held one hand to her face. I tried to smile, though I fear the expression was strained. "Ask me again sometime." She pressed against my hand, stepped closer in an uncharacteristically warm public display. I put my other arm around her, mindful—though she was not—of the people all around us.

Valka did not move for a long time, but after a moment she said, "I feel like I've been slipping into your shadow, Hadrian." I did not let her go. I let her talk. "I've studied the Quiet for years. Decades. And I was wrong. Wrong about . . . about everything. 'Twere not an ancient people, 'twere not a people at all, even their *philukun* language was no language at all! And here you are . . . an Imperial fucking *palatine* . . ." Her voice trailed off in frustration, lost in the folds of my cape. "I failed at everything I ever set out to do. After the guard . . . I wanted to be a scientist. But I couldn't even do that right."

I held her tightly and did not speak.

"Decades," she said. "Blood of my fathers, *decades,* Hadrian! Decades I worked on those inscriptions. For nothing."

"Not for nothing!" I said, unable to keep silent any longer. "We figured it out."

She thumped me in the shoulder with an open hand. *"You* figured it out." I could feel her gaze on me and looked down. There were tears in the false eyes. "I should hate you for that. I worked for so long . . . so long. And you . . . it wasn't even a language . . ."

"You had no way of knowing that," I said.

"I told you about Sadal Suud, did I not?" Her words were barely above a whisper. "This was long before I met you. There was this Chantry priest there who kept one of the Cavaraad in chains. I was on the caravan, going to see the Marching Towers. I waited until dark and freed it. I thought 'twould run free, but . . . but it attacked the workers. I guess it wanted revenge . . . I just . . . wanted it to stop hurting." She was shaking by then, and I held her firm in my arms, my own expression grim. I had never seen her come apart like this, unravel like one of the famed carpets of her home. "Why can't I do anything right?" I held her tighter, unsure what to say. Through my embrace she managed to say, "It killed a child. The drover's boy. Stomped him to death. Because of me. Because I'm so . . . *nago.*"

"You're not stupid," I said.

"Yes I am," she said, fallen back into her mother tongue. "All that work wasted."

"It's not finished!" I said, one hand in her hair. "We're not finished, you and I! There's so much we don't understand." I turned her face back up to mine. I would not brush away her tears. "I need you, Valka. I can't do this alone."

Her expression was unreadable despite the tears. Fury mingled there with loathing—not of me, but of herself—and pity danced between them, but there was more. A tightness and . . . was that fear? I could not say. Was she afraid? Of what? Of me?

"Why did you come up here?" I asked at last, and suddenly I was afraid. Not to leave me, surely? Not there and then! Not like this! A lump formed in my stomach, hard and poisonous. I choked it down. Not like this. Where would she go? Where could she? The planet was under martial law.

"I . . ." She stepped away, inhaling sharply through her nose to clear it. "'Tis unimportant. It can wait."

"Valka . . ." I took a step back toward her, but she held up a hand.

"Don't *Valka* me." She shook her head and looked away again. "I want to do one thing right." I realized then what the expression on her face was. Not fear. *Nerves.* My stomach almost fell out of me there on the wall-walk. Lightning flashed again, followed by the dry, sucking rattle of wind as the storm approached, still tens of miles distant. "I know I'm not what you . . . what you expected," she said, hands in the pockets of her coat. "I'm not *Lady Marlowe.* I never will be."

The ivory ring on my gloved hand branded me a liar, and for the first time since that fateful day in the Colosso I was glad of the glove. "You don't have to be. If I'd wanted a wife, I'd have had one. Anaïs or Selene . . ." There had been others. I had been so long a knight and the Emperor's favorite—and so long at court. Had I been more susceptible to the charms of women—which is to say *had I been the sort of man willing to take advantage of women*—I might have had whichever I'd wanted.

I wanted her.

More than a hundred years together by then, and it wasn't enough. I still wanted her. Always her. Only her.

But she was shaking her head. "I know 'tis what you want, but I can't. 'Tis not me. We don't . . . don't marry in Tavros. I just . . . can't. I'm not your Lady Marlowe."

"I don't want you to be," I said again, still terrified at the thought of where this conversation was going and glad the nearest technicians were dozens of yards away. It would not do for Hadrian Halfmortal to come apart where men could see. I confess I tried reaching for my newfound sight, but in my distressed state my mind would not focus the mechanism of my new sense.

But Valka stayed firm. "Yes, you do," she said. "And I'm sorry."

"I'm sorry, too," I said. I did not mean to pressure her, to lay any burden on her she would not bear. We'd had all of marriage a palatine could ask, and more—for we loved one another. Only family—perhaps the greatest part of marriage—remained barred to us, locked behind doors neither Valka nor the High College would open. But what we had? "Valka, I would not trade any of our time together. You don't have to apologize to me."

Turning back to the rail, I looked out for miles across the landing field below. White vapors rose from one of the distant blasting pits like the exhalations of an ancient dragon. Another supply rocket destined for the fleet above. Lightning flashed again, and the fire of distant rocketry in the airless vaults beyond the roof of the world cast its angry shadows on the clouds.

"I'm sorry about the Quiet," I said. My revelation on the mountain had taken her struggle from her, reduced her as my death aboard the *Demiurge* had reduced Bassander. Would she become another worshiper? Another of my shadows? I could scarce imagine anything more horrible, unless it was that she should leave me. "I still don't understand everything that's happened to me—or why it's happening to *me*." My hands curled into fists against the rail. "The Quiet said I was *the shortest way* between now and its future, but it is *trillions* of years to its future. All of this . . ." I waved a hand at the field beneath us. "All of it's just a little piece of something so much bigger. Something I don't understand. I need your help."

Once more I felt the weight of my visions crushing me. All of time and space, of times that never were or never could be. The Watchers and the Quiet and the war between them, carried out across time and space from the first spasm to the final gasp. How small I felt, how meager my actions seemed, and how inconsequential. How tiny were all the actions of man against that blank and uncaring universe?

How could any of it matter? How could any of us?

I know better now. The universe has no center, they say . . . and yet the universe is infinite. Is not then every point the center of the universe, surrounded on all sides by infinite space? Copernicus was as wrong as he was right. The Earth of old was as much the center of the universe as the sun

she circled. So too were Mars, and Jupiter beyond. So too Delos and
Emesh, Vorgossos and Annica.

Berenike and Gododdin.

Every place is the center of the universe. Everything matters.

Every one of our actions, every decision, every sacrifice.

Nothing is without meaning, because nothing is without consequence.

And that was so much worse, so much heavier a burden to bear, though
I carry it as I carried Valka's instrument up the mountain.

"Hadrian?" Valka's voice broke on me, and I shook myself. "Are you
all right?"

"I can't do this alone," I said. "Please don't go."

She started, eyes narrowing as she looked up at me. "What?"

"I thought . . ." I could not get the words out.

"You thought I wanted to leave?" She looked almost wounded. "Where
would I go?" The floor seemed to have disappeared beneath me, and I was
plunging through the Storm Wall's many hundred levels toward the planet's core. But she caught me, reaching up to brush dark hair from my face.
"You're the only mystery I have left."

She kissed me then, not long or deeply, but enough.

Valka rummaged in the pocket of her coat. "I wanted to give you
something, seeing as we might not be long for this world. Again."

She held her palm up for my inspection. Nestled in it was a disc of some
bright metal—platinum, perhaps, or rhodium—a little larger than a silver
kaspum and slightly convex, with a crease along the center. The nervous
tension returned to Valka's face, and for a second I feared she might jerk
her hand away.

It was heavier than I expected, like a slice of meteor iron, and turning
it over I saw the sharp Tavrosi runes carved there. I did not recognize the
symbols at first, but realized Valka had etched the letters H and M atop one
another on one half, the letters V and O superimposed on the other.

"It comes apart here," she said, and pressed two small buttons on either
end with her nails.

The object sprang apart in my hands, as if some magnet had been undone. She took the half with my initials on it and—holding it palm up
herself—said, "We don't marry in Tavros."

"I know."

She hushed me. " 'Tis a phylactery . . . *my* phylactery."

I almost dropped it.

It was a sample of her genetic material, a crystallized blood sample and a digital copy laser-etched in quartz. A piece of her, preserved forever. "At home we . . . give them to one another. When one of us amasses enough social credit to . . . to have a child."

"But . . . we can't," I said, and had to shut my eyes to stop the tears from welling up. "I'm palatine. The High College . . ."

Valka spoke over me, "I know we can't. I still don't . . . don't want that anyway. But I thought . . . well . . ." She held the other half up, showing my initials etched on its face. "Among the clans, 'tis forbidden to exchange them, back and forth. I thought . . . I thought it a fitting compromise." And with that she closed my fingers over her phylactery. "A symbol."

"A symbol!" I almost laughed, and stooped once more to kiss her, fingers tight about the metal sliver she had given me. That piece of her heart. And as we kissed upon the Storm Wall above the fields of Berenike and the *Valles Merguli,* a wind came out of the west and gathered my cape in its fingers. It took our hair—raven and wine-dark—and braided it together. At length we broke apart, and taking Valka by the hand I led her down from the Storm Wall, where we came together never again in this life.

CHAPTER 75

THE NOISE OF THUNDER

ARMORED ALL IN BLACK with Valka's phylactery secure beside the Quiet's eggshell on its chain, I peered from the shadow of the arch at the unquiet sky. Behind me, the tunnel loomed three times the height of a man. Pallino stood fast nearby with Oro and Doran and the men of our First Cohort, each masked and suited and pressed into the vestibule of the tunnel network like ants in the tracks of their hive.

"See anything?" came the bright, beloved voice.

Valka moved to stand beside me. She looked strange in the crimson ceramic and black tunic of an officer. She had no insignia, wore no cape. She looked wholly unlike herself, though she had been a soldier once.

"Not yet."

"We'll hear 'em 'fore we see 'em, doctor!" Pallino said, leaning on his lance. "Tearing up the sky." Far off, the thunder rolled, threatening another of the constant storms. A piece of me wished I'd taken Corvo up on her advice and stayed in the command center in the Storm Wall with Leonid Bartosz and young Aristedes, but I am no great commander, not a Pyrrhus or a Wellington, and certainly no Hannibal.

I was right where I should have been; I only hated that I was blind.

Speaking into my terminal patch, I said, "How are things above, Aristedes?"

A single xenobite craft had emerged from warp near the edge of the system, just beyond the heliopause. We had detected the flash of radiation as its warp bubble collapsed, but before Hauptmann could scramble lighters in response or launch missiles across the interplanetary desert the vessel was gone.

But it had lingered long enough, a few hours. Plenty of time to sweep the system, to know our strength and numbers and the distribution of our powers. Dark as space is, there is nowhere in its folds to hide.

"No sign," the intus said. "Hauptmann's taken the fleet to full alert. Shields up. Says he'll hold them in orbit best he can."

Eyes raking over Valka and the others in the tunnel behind, I said, "He'll fail. They'll hit us hard and hit us fast. If I'm right . . . if the main force of the enemy is waiting in ambush . . ."

Lorian finished the thought for me. "Then the purpose of this first wave will be to divide our attention."

"To make us panic. They'll hit the city. Not the Wall. They'll want to pillage."

" 'Twill give them a chance to frighten us," Valka said darkly, eyes glowing in the dim.

Looking back, I saw the ranks of faceless men stretching back in the gloom. There must have been a couple hundred of us in that tunnel, with the rest of the men lurking in similar access ways along the terraces on the wall-ward side of Deira city. I gestured to Oro and Doran and another centurion who had come up from his place. "Back to your units, all of you. It won't be long now."

They went, and the thunder greeted them as they left the shelter of our cave. I followed them, peering with naked eyes up at the clouds. I could not see the sky, and Berenike's wan white sun lay hid beyond the Storm Wall.

"Keep me informed," I said over the link.

Lorian answered, and I could hear the lazy salute reflected in his tone. "Of course."

Looking down, I saw bridges and towers rising below, and birds flying, roosting in trees that flowered in the valley all the way down to the level of the fat, brown river that ran away south toward shallow seas.

"Lord Marlowe?"

I had wandered almost to the rail overlooking the lower terraces, a good dozen paces from the tunnel mouth, and I was surprised to find the common soldier standing there, a woman by her size and by the lightness of her voice. I know it seems odd to say—and perhaps it is only a trick of the memory—but I had thought it was Carax of Aramis for a moment before I turned, and no woman at all.

"Yes?" I asked.

"Is it the day, lord?" she asked, shifting her weight unsteadily.

I did not take her meaning. "What day?"

"The men say you are the Chosen. The Son of Earth come again," she said, and kneeling set her lance at my feet. "They say you will reveal yourself in battle here and drive the Scourge back into the Dark."

The old vision of myself enthroned with Selene at my feet blossomed before my eyes once more, and I fancied the arch of the tunnel behind the girl was the Arch of Titus itself and heard Selene's words.

The first steps.

I did not move. The other soldiers had come forward, crowding past Pallino and Valka in their officers' red. I sensed them listening through their helmet pickups, and felt the weight of so many eyes.

What could I say? To deny her was to rob her of hope and of belief in me in this hour when it was needed most. I looked to Valka, but there were no answers in her face—and nothing whatsoever in Pallino's.

"Take off your mask," I said, words springing to me unbidden. The Quiet's words.

Somewhere in the distance below, a bird cried.

The young lady saluted and—holding her fist to her breast—keyed the release on her helmet. It unfolded like a paper sculpture, revealing a plain, blunt-featured face, but one without the weathered statue appearance I have so often marked in members of the plebeian caste. Her eyes shone bright, blue as any palatine's beneath the rubberized coif, which she pulled back to reveal short, bronze hair.

"What is your name, soldier?"

"Renna, lord."

"Renna. A good name." I held her gaze a moment and looked to the others. I was trapped. "I do not long for the throne!" I said, unsure whether or not I spoke in front of cameras or only to the men and women there gathered. "I do not want power, but peace." The men shifted, leaning on their lances and against the walls of the tunnel. I wished that all my Company might have been present, but the few centuries I had would do. "I sense fear in you! Be not afraid. The men, the women and children—the people of this world—in the caverns behind you are afraid! Take heart! Have courage for their sakes!" Pausing, I gathered myself for fear that my tongue would run too fast and far ahead of me. I am not a pious man—but piety was called for. "You ask when the Earth will return and Her Chosen with her! I do not know! But I know this: this is not the day! This is not the hour!" I almost added, *I am not the man!* But prudence and the look in Renna's bright eyes stayed my tongue.

She believed, and would fight *because* she believed.

"It is *our* hour!" I said, "Our fight! For them!" And here I pointed at the caves behind their heads. "Some of you will have heard stories about me. Some of you were there and know that they are true! I do not deny them. But this is not *my* hour! It is ours! *We* must stand together with the men of our Legions against what is to come!"

Looking down upon the woman kneeling at my feet, I said, "Will you fight with me, Renna? Not for prophecy, but for the people of this world?"

The soldier bowed her head. "I will, lord."

"They cannot hear you, girl!" I said. "Will you fight with me?"

"I said 'I will, lord!'" she nearly shouted.

"Will you all fight with me?" I called, and raised my good right hand.

"Aye!" the men cried out, and the thunder of their voices rang in answer to the thunder of the heavens above. And more than thunder, for in that instant the bottoms of the clouds flashed red and white with the light of fires blazing in the void beyond the circles of that far-flung world.

Aristedes's high voice crackled over the suit link, disrupted by the cosmic radiation that moved behind the new visible light. "Contact! Cielcin fleet emerged from warp in high orbit. They're closing on the fleet."

Frustrated still by my blindness, I asked, "Worldship?"

"No, my lord. Looks like . . . twenty . . . twenty-two ships? A dozen medium-size attack cruisers, Class-3, perhaps Class-4. Bigger ships look to be about Class-8. They've engaged the fleet!"

Too well I knew the vessels Lorian described. Cielcin starships—the truly big ones, at any rate—were not built in factories. They did not come off assembly lines, were not built to standard technical specifications. Each was unique, and categorized by us not according to any factory model, but by sheer mass. I pictured them emerging round the limn of Berenike to attack our fleet and our orbital platform behind its Royse field curtains: knuckled, shapeless things like bits of bone or the severed fingers of some massive, skeletal hand.

"We have incoming!" Lorian said. "The Class-8s dropped siege towers, they're heading our way."

I made to push past Renna. I had to order everyone back into the tunnel mouth to withstand the shelling that was to come, but the young soldier seized my hand.

I looked down at her, ready to say some harsh word and send her running to her place. She seized more tightly, and almost I feared to feel a poisoned needle embedded in her palm. But this was no assassin. "Are you the Chosen?"

So shocked was I by the fervency of her question that I answered without thought. "We are all chosen for something," I said, and laid my free hand on her shoulder. Coming to my senses I added, "On your feet, Renna. Into the tunnels! Everyone back!"

No sooner had I gotten the words out when the whole sky erupted with white light and the hellish scream of atmospheric entry. I lingered on the threshold, peering back at the sky. Great pillars of fire raked across the heavens, slicing through the morn. The air vibrated as if the clouds were the surface of some immeasurable drum. Screeching metal answered, and turning I watched a flight of Sparrowhawks tack their single wing-sails and wheel to intercept, missiles blazing like flying sparks.

One of the pillars of fire exploded, and another, black clouds erupting to mark the places where our missiles felled them. But the horde kept coming, and I saw one clip the wing of a Sparrohawk and smash it out of the sky.

The Cielcin horde fell like a heavy rain, ships like dark towers a hundred feet high. As I watched, the blue flame of retro-rockets flared and slowed their descent. Slowed . . . but did not stop. The armored base of the nearest siege tower smashed through a white arch and the outer wall of a block of townhouses. The earth shook again and again as if beneath the impetus of some mighty hammer, and the whole of the *Valles Merguli* rang to the sound of its blows. Looking out from our place on the ramparts, my men and I beheld a changed city. Black towers stood amid clouds of dust and the smoke of new-set fires.

Too late, the raid sirens began their unholy wail: a high, keening, and ceaseless drone that caught on the towers and terraces of the city and echoed off the pale walls.

"Target the towers!" I said, and pressed back into the tunnel with my men to await the coming firestorm.

In the brief moment before Lorian's response, I heard the frightened whispering of one of the soldiers at my back. "Bless us with the sword of your courage, O Fortitude . . ."

"Targets acquired," came the tactical officer's reply.

From the relative safety of the tunnel mouth, I had an excellent seat for the violence. I saw Lorian's Javelin missiles rain down from the wall above us with fire nearly equal to the fire that had brought the towers. The tower nearest us—the one that smashed the arch and the townhouses up the street to our right—exploded in a torrent of flame so great I felt the shockwave and the fading heat half a mile distant. I was grateful to my body armor for dampening the sound.

But other towers resisted, and it was not until afterward that I realized how the unshielded vessels had stood up to Lorian's artillery.

A faint haze wrapped itself around the towers, colorless and vaguely oily. Not the fractal shimmering of a shield curtain. From my distant vantage, it seemed almost to writhe and twist about the Cielcin towers, a disturbance that put me in mind of the way magnetism warped iron filings into mighty coils, of eels contorting. Of serpents.

"Snakes!" the cry snapped over the line.

"Nahute," Valka said, peering out past me. Her inhuman eyes, I knew, could magnify her vision, resolving details over distances no human eye could fathom. "Thousands of them."

The snake-like drones had emerged from ports high in the landing towers. They set to orbiting about them, weaving themselves into a dense screen that insulated the towers against attack.

"I've never seen them do that before," Pallino said.

Lorian interjected, voice high and tight from the command center. "They only delay the inevitable." Another salvo fired from on high, missiles arcing at their targets. But there were hundreds of the evil drones, thousands, and I'll wager it took more than two or three to block the incoming missiles.

Above, the flight of Sparrowhawks circled back, all guns blazing.

I was glad the city had been emptied, was doubly glad when I saw more drones stream out of the siege towers and fly out across the city, threading their evil way through the streets, drill-bit mouths whining as they quested for meat. They would latch onto any source of heat or movement they could find and bore their way to the center of mass. I pitied the stray dogs, the birds and other creatures that remained in Deira, and knew the gutters would run red with the blood the *nahute* left behind.

"Bless us with the sword of your courage, O Fortitude . . ."

"I've never seen them do anything like this," Pallino said again, as if for emphasis.

High above it all the sirens played, the scream filling the air from river to terrace to cloud and back. Lighters streaked overhead, firing on the next wave of towers falling from the sky like slow meteors. The smoking wreckage of alien drop towers and broken lighters rained and smote the pale towers of the city, or else kindled the groves and gardens that grew on narrow ledges or upon the roofs of mighty buildings.

Hell had come to Berenike, seeped down from the stars and set the city to burning. How fortunate that the starport and so much of that ancient city had been built below ground. Those ancient builders—eager to shelter from Berenike's coriolis storms—had inadvertently saved so many million souls.

So long as we could hold the gates, that was.

"Movement on the towers!" came one centurion's words. An indicator flashed the man's location and call sign in the corner of my helm's entoptic vision—two levels down and three miles south. Our troopers were spread thin: five thousand men distributed in clusters no greater than the hundred men who stood at my back were stretched along the two-dozen mile length of the emptied city.

"Ramps deployed below Eighty-Seventh Street!"

"Hatches opening!"

"Contact, contact!"

The muted sound of gunfire played across the common channel, louder and more present than the ethereal keening of the raid siren. Without having to consult other men's entoptic feeds through my helmet, I knew the Cielcin had emerged, marching out from their dark towers beneath the swarming murmurations of their evil machines.

From my vantage point, I could make out the violet muzzle flash of plasma discharge in the streets above and below.

"Won't someone kill that fucking siren?" Pallino half-shouted, voice amplified by his suit speakers.

I wanted to scream. What good was I, standing there above it all, waiting for the *nahute* or their Pale masters to find us? I should have been on the terraces above, fighting with the Irchtani and Hauptmann's fusiliers, or in the streets below locking blades alongside the men of my own Red Company.

A horrific buzzing rose beneath the siren's wail, high and deep at once and grinding, and as I watched, the cloud of *nahute* spreading out upon the city about us rose, sweeping up to where the artillery stood on the lip separating the industrial quarter from the lower districts in the valley itself, directed there by some unseen hand—a Cielcin ground commander, no doubt watching from the shielded safety of one of the siege towers. I reminded myself that these were more than killing machines. They were reconnaissance. The Cielcin were mapping the city as surely as we mapped their vessels when we managed to land a boarding party.

"I noticed," Aristedes said dryly when I pointed this out.

"Can we stop them?" I asked.

"Not unless you want to detonate an atomic in the upper atmosphere."

I did not, as it happened.

"Then we'll have to shoot them," I said.

Lorian made no reply.

There must have been half a hundred siege towers looming over the city by that point, each surrounded by an undulating cloud of *nahute* drones.

"We should close the gate," Valka said, words barely audible over the siren. "If those drones get into the hypogeum, 'twill mean bloodshed."

"There are inner doors sealed," I objected. "And we may need that gate open to retreat through if the time comes."

A body fell from the terrace above and smacked wetly on the stones.

A Cielcin body. I recognized the organic design of the armor, the rubbery material recalling the shapes of the bone and fascia beneath, the pale hair braided and tied with strips of black cloth. Ichor black as ink pooled beneath it where it lay, and I did not doubt that it was dead. Its mask was turned toward me, a thing of pale ceramic, white as its broken sword and whiter than the silver-chalk complexion of its exposed lower jaw, thin lips and translucent teeth wet and black. The mask accentuated the rise and curl of horns, made the xenobite's face somehow more pointed and angular.

And between the eyes like slits in burnished black was the symbol of a Pale hand. Clawed. Six-fingered. Grasping.

Shielded and with Pallino cursing after me, I took a few halting steps forward, sword unkindled in my hands. Its was the first body I'd seen in all that violence—though it would not be the last.

"Dorayaica . . ." I said, letting the creature's limp head fall.

One of my guards fired his plasma burner: a tight, double burst. Two *nahute* struck the ground not five paces from where I knelt. Their smoldering wreckage twitched spasmodically on the paving stones and went dead. I half-expected to see a dozen more of the evil things descending from the crowd, but there was for the moment no sign.

"*Yukajjimn! Uiddaa! Uiddaa!*"

Though I had known the xenobites had come, to hear their words so plain beneath the light of day was a quiet horror, for creatures of the night such as they have no place in the sun. And yet there they were, rendered more horrifying by the daylight than any concealing darkness might have done. There must have been two dozen of them, garbed in the same organic-looking armor, black rubber and ceramic beneath short capes blacker still and decorated with swirling patterns of the *Udaritanu,* the circular writing that aped the marks of the Quiet's monuments, a kind of blasphemous appropriation. Pale white were their horned masks and white the true horns of their crests that rose like diabolic crowns from their brows.

All this I processed in the space of an instant, for a moment thereafter the flash of two dozen *nahute* filled the air between us. Plasma fire answered. I kindled my sword and stepped forward, sensing Pallino and one of the others—Renna, perhaps?—close behind. I slashed one of the *nahute* neatly in half and closed on the enemy . . . and stopped, remembering the force at my back, hidden from the Cielcin by the angle of the street and the tunnel mouth. I smiled, plasma and xenobite weapons flashing about me, and drew back a step.

The Cielcin came on, and beneath the masks they wore to shield their eyes I saw the bare-toothed snarl that was a smile for their kind. My helm's impassive human face offered them no reply, no indication of the trap *they* had walked into. Thus concealed, I allowed myself a satisfied grimace, teeth clenched and ready.

"On my mark, turn and run," I said.

"Eh?" Pallino sounded scandalized.

"Just past the opening to the tunnel," I said, flinching as one of the *nahute* battered against my shield.

Understanding filled the chiliarch's loud *Ooh* and the comm channel— muffled by our suits and unheard by the Cielcin—shook with the rough sound of the old soldier's laughter. "Well, why not?" He relayed an order to his men in the tunnel. "Ready."

"Now!"

I turned and—spurring Valka ahead of me—pressed back along the high street, past the round arch of the tunnel and the iron-barred gates that had kept the citizens out of the hypogeum in peacetime. Hooting and screeching, the Cielcin followed, and the shadows of their pale swords chased us along the stone. Passing the gate, we turned, and I sliced another of the *nahute* out of the sky. Its pieces bounced away. One went over the railing to the terraces below. The five guardsmen who'd left the tunnel with me to investigate the corpse turned and fired past them, but their shots went wide. One round struck the beast I felt certain was their commander, distinguished by its nearly eight-foot height and ceramic brooch that held its cape in place: fashioned in the shape of a skeletal white hand.

The commander leered as the plasma round *washed off* it. I saw the brief glimmer of a shield curtain and turned back myself to face the creature.

That was when our men opened fire.

Plasma fire and MAG rounds tore from the mouth of the tunnel and turned the unshielded *scahari* to mounds of meat and smoking armor. But the commander was not alone in being shielded. Five stood alongside it, laughing and defiant. They saw our numbers in the hall and knew they must die, but would die in glory and battle and take as many of us as they could back to hell with them.

"Svassa!" I said. *Surrender!*

The commander looked at me, teeth bared. Long ago, on Emesh, the Ichakta Uvanari had surrendered to us because its will was broken. It was surrounded, its people injured, its ship lost beyond recall. Its had not been a combat expedition, but an exploratory one. They had not thought to find humanity on Tamnikano—on Emesh. The Battle of Emesh had been no proper battle, and the Cielcin we'd faced there were no true soldiers.

These were.

Still leering, the commander peeled its *nahute* from its belt and hurled it at me.

I sliced the weapon from the air and closed the space between us in five long strides, sword rising in a diagonal cut. The commander must not have known highmatter, for it raised its sword to parry. My blade clove through the xenobite's zircon sword and through rubber and armor and flesh. Black blood spattered the stone at my feet as the creature fell in twain. Pallino and Valka and the soldier Renna all moved forward to stand with me against the others.

The Battle for Berenike had begun at last.

CHAPTER 76

THE GIANT

"FALL BACK!" ONE CENTURION cried.

I watched from the rail as one unit pulled back across one of the arching bridges that spanned the river a thousand feet below. The Cielcin followed on, *nahute* swarming about them like a plague of locusts, tearing at the defenders.

The bridge exploded an instant after. Chunks of mortar and white stone flew in every direction. Red flame, black smoke, the tangled shrapnel of bodies torn asunder. In the middle distance, one of the Cielcin siege towers erupted in a cloud of fire that tore the crumbling walls about it apart and set the trees on the terrace to burning.

Sparrowhawks screamed above, circling over the city, tangling with the black darts of Cielcin fliers that had come down with the towers. If I stood by the rail and looked up along the terraced wall of the *Valles,* I could see the square ramparts that lined the edge of the valley and the winged shapes of Irchtani wheeling overhead, their *zitraa* flashing in the sun. Beyond them, the sky glowed red and violent white as weapons fire discharged in the void about Ondu Station.

The sirens wailed above it all, a ceaseless, flat droning in the ears. The noise gave the tableau a sense of unreality as I watched, a part of and yet apart from the violence. Gunshots sounded on the level above us, and I heard the thump and rattle of armored feet. Briefly I caught a glimpse of white armor and red tabards on the terrace above, the cough and shout of plasma fire as the men fired over their shoulders. A school of *nahute* swam on the airs after them, writhing, churning, hungry for flesh. There must have been three dozen of them.

"Here!" I cried, waving my hands. "Here!"

One of the soldiers spied me as they rounded the bend beyond—and to my horror I saw that they were all peltasts. Unshielded. There were seven of them, the remnants of some larger unit. Where their decurions were I could not guess. Spying me, they changed plan and half-threw themselves down the steps, the evil drones grinding at their heels.

"Lord Marlowe!" one cried.

"Back!" I shouted, pushing the man past me. "Valka!"

The last in line of the peltasts stumbled on the uneven flagstone steps that led to the thoroughfare and staggered a moment against the rail. It was one moment too long. Three of the *nahute* overtook him, snarling heads catching on the rubberized polymers of his suit underlayment, tearing as they burrowed. The man's screams were piercing even with the sirens' blast. Blood sheeted over white ceramic.

He was dead before I got to him.

The *nahute* emerged a moment later, wet and dripping. I destroyed them before they could fully emerge and shake off the blood and torn flesh. Half a dozen more locked onto me and charged, rebounded as they struck my shield curtain. It would take their primitive machine brains a moment to work out the shield's weakness, but in that space of time they were within the reach of my sword. Highmatter shone blue about me, and the serpent machines fell in pieces.

But there were too many. Behind me, my guard opened fire, and I heard screaming as one of the alien drones found its way through the man's defenses. Try as I might to attract the worst of them, the *nahute* kept coming. I felt the teeth of one grind against one armored thigh, piercing my shield by accident. One hand flailed reflexively and snapped the thing away, but it was too late. The diamond-bit teeth had caught on my armor and began to turn. I flipped my sword round and slashed at it, hewing the metallic snake just behind its jaw. Grasping what remained, I tugged it loose and cast its ruin upon the stones at my feet.

There were always more. The air about churned and buzzed with the thrum of their primitive repulsors, so loud and so close that even the wailing siren was dimmed.

And then they stopped, and full dozens fell lifeless to the street about me.

Turning, I saw Valka standing with hand outstretched and head cocked to one side. She gave me a satisfied little nod and tapped her temple. I could not see her face through the featureless red of the visor, but I knew her tight smile was firmly in place.

"What would you do without me?" she asked.

Something huge and dark fell on her from above. Man-shaped and more than man-high, white hands grasping. Valka yelled as the thing crushed her beneath it. A moment later, a half dozen more of the *scahari* warriors fell from the street above. Another of my guardsmen fell with a scimitar in his throat. I didn't hesitate, but threw myself toward Valka's attacker and opened it from hips to shoulder blade with a rising flicker of my moonlight blade.

Valka seized my hand and I helped her to her feet.

"You were saying?"

Pallino fired a round from his lance that felled another of the attackers, and Renna and another soldier did for another. Valka drew her sidearm, the antique plasma repeater, and unloaded three rounds in the back of a third. The remaining Cielcin tried to flee, to break off and regroup—but it was too late. Another decade of troops poured forth from the shadow of the tunnel mouth and claimed them.

In the eerie stillness that followed, some of the others picked over the bodies, relieving them of knives and scimitars and other artifacts worth saving.

"Where do you come from?" Pallino asked the survivors.

One man, a triaster, answered, "Up a ways." The man turned his head from the chiliarch, not seeing him or else afraid to see.

It was not a substantial answer, not an informative one. "Name and rank, out with it!"

The fellow just turned away, glancing back at his fellow dead on the stairs. Pallino slapped him with the butt of his lance. "Eyes up, soldier!"

The man seemed to come back to himself. "Kuhn, sir. Four-Beta two-two. Triaster."

"Fourth Cohort . . ." Pallino said. "This your first?"

"Sir, no sir."

"Then stop acting like it," Pallino's words came flat. "The hell happened?"

"Demons!" one of the others said. "Giants, sir!"

Giants. Behind my mask I shut my eyes, gathered what scattered pieces of myself I could to ask, "Were they chimeras?"

The men of the Fourth Cohort had not fought aboard Iubalu's ship, nor had any of them plumbed the depths of the fortress at Arae.

"Chi . . . what?" The legionnaire struggled with the antique word.

"Machines," I said. "Metal."

Triaster Kuhn only bobbed his head. I imagined his face green, lips compressed behind the dull white helm.

Giants. The word conjured memories of Iubalu's looming bulk, its white arms and swords, its fingers like scalpel blades. Bastard creation of Cielcin blood and Extrasolarian praxis, hateful and accursed.

"Giants . . ." I said, and pointing to the tunnel, I said, "Triaster, take your men to the rear. You're no use to anyone as you are." I brushed past the fellow, stepping over the bodies of the Cielcin as carefully as I could, white cape gathered in one fist, blade unkindled in the other. "We need to see what's going on out there," I said to Pallino. "Send two decades."

Pallino chose two of his decurions. With Siran gone, the chiliarch had not appointed a new prime centurion to replace her, and the duty fell to two officers who had been with us since before Aptucca. I watched them go: the glint of red fires on armor the color of bone, the way the decurions' crests swayed as they ran. Still I felt useless waiting and watching. Weak. I tried to reach for my vision of the endless present, but try as I might to look in those directions no mortal eye was meant to see, I could not find it. I could not focus, and my frustration only further alienated me from the *sight.*

Cannon fire filled the air from the inner wall above as the wreckage of towers fell like rain. Off in the distance, another of the towers erupted in white flame, and a cheer went up through the comm line.

But it was not to last.

"More ships incoming!" Lorian's words came like evil prophecy falling from on high, and accompanying them came the roar of entry and the scream of retro-rockets as Cielcin siege towers crashed against the shores of our world.

"Keep firing!" I said, watching another of the towers explode as it slowed in its final descent.

A horrible flash filled the air. Not the red glow of weapons fire like lightning beyond the clouds, but something orange and horribly *present,* and a dozen things happened at once.

The sirens died, and all the lights of the city of Deira from the highest terrace to the river far below. An instant later the earth groaned and shook as with spasm, and I staggered against the rail. Shouts and cursing filled the common band, mingled with cries of despair. The city was *dead.* I knew before I asked Lorian what had happened.

"They hit the nuclear generator," came the intus's words. "City's switching to emergency power."

"Geothermal?" I asked, thinking of the tunnels and the old mines that ran beneath the Storm Wall.

"Yes."

With the raid sirens gone, there was nothing to deaden the noise of fighting, the screams of men and Cielcin, the crack and roar of fires and of weapons. It was almost quiet, and the sudden clearness of the air lent an eerie sense of stillness to all that passed above and below and about us, as if we were all a part of some frieze carved on a Chantry wall.

"We're well outside the exclusion zone," Lorian said. I hadn't thought that far ahead. The power plant had been built nearly forty miles from the Storm Wall, far enough to keep the people safe from radiation. "The wind could be a problem." The blast must have carried radioactive material higher than the level of wall.

"Let's pray not."

A horrible sound arose from the depths of that fading city. High and piercing, vibrating clearer and colder than the noise of any human throat. I felt my blood run cold. There was no sound like it in all the human universe, for its makers were far from human. That terrible sound had once issued from deep caverns beneath alien suns where the forefathers of the forefathers of the Cielcin had scrambled in the ceaseless dark. It was the sound of black caverns, of volcanic tubes and grottoes filled with blind things that splashed and paddled in forsaken pools. It was the noise of creatures that spilled blood and sacrificed to nameless things in darkness deeper still.

"Lorian!" I said, voice tense even in my own hearing. "Lorian, open fire!"

The commander did not reply. Not with words. The Javelin missiles rained down the city and broke against the shoals of *nahute* defending the towers. Another of the siege towers blew apart, blasting shrapnel five hundred feet into the sky.

Snatches of comms chatter clipped over one another on the general comm, bits of shouted intel overlapping as I tried to make sense of the shape of the fighting on my suit's display.

"Half a dozen towers in the industrial quarter—"

"—lost the whole eighth decade."

"Man down! Man down!"

"Stick to your target! Remember the simulations!"

"—the size of them!"

"Came in too fast, I—"

And then I heard the fateful words, the words that told me my hours of waiting by the sidelines must end: "They're climbing the inner wall!"

I switched lines. "Kithuun-Barda!"

The Irchtani commander's voice croaked in my ear. "Lord?"

"Don't let the Cielcin take those guns!"

"We see them!" he said. "They're climbing with their bare hands! These are not Cielcin."

"They're chimeras," I said. "Udax and I killed one in our last battle."

"There are many more than one," the *kithuun* answered.

I clenched my jaw. "I'm coming to you."

Pallino, who had heard that much at least from where he stood beside me, said, "You should stay here, Had! Let me go."

"No!" I shouted. "We've waited long enough. The lower city's overrun. If we lose those guns we'll have them knocking on the Storm Wall gates in half an hour. We're going."

The old myrmidon paused a moment, the Pallino who was my officer warring with the man who was my friend. "Right then," he said at last. "Decades eight, nine, ten: hold the gate and be prepared to pull back if you're overwhelmed! All the rest: with me!"

The base of the wall was not far: up the way the retreating soldiers had come and along a short path beneath the shuttered fronts of shops and eateries to where the banks of public lifts stood. We encountered no resistance as we hurried along. The bulk of the fighting was further north along the valley, near the center where the city was widest and the shadow of the largest bridge fell across the ravine.

The Irchtani screeched above us. As we rounded the corner, I beheld a great swath of the striated rock rising above the domes of the low, concrete buildings built along the lip of the terrace above us. The lift tubes—built into that mighty edifice—rose perhaps five hundred feet above our heads to the battlement-crowned heights of Deira's inner wall. The flash of plasma cannons and the roar of the Javelins played from those battlements, and I saw Irchtani auxiliaries leaping from the merlons and wheeling in the air, shooting and sweeping the swirling *nahute* from the sky with their long cutlasses.

And I saw *them,* not darkly clad but armored as Iubalu had been in plate of shimmering white, their jointed limbs and spade-like hands sinking deep into the stone of the rock face and into mortar where masonry began. Kuhn had been right to name them giants, for even at a distance I knew them to be more than twice the height of a man—perhaps three times. Like were they in design to Iubalu, and yet unlike, for though their size was greater, they lacked the second set of arms and elongated, feline torso, having instead too-long legs bent backward like a goat's.

I despaired, recalling how difficult the battle against Iubalu had been, for there were two—no, three—dozen of the hateful things climbing the terraces above. They did not move quickly, though they climbed faster than any man, horrid hands climbing hand-over-hand with the inexorable precision of clockwork, closing in on the missile batteries that lined the canyon's lip between the city's upper and lower quarters. The hand that had fashioned them I knew too well, having encountered their laboratory beneath the mountain fortress of Arae.

Here was the black product of an alliance between mankind and the Empire's two greatest enemies. The once-human magi who called themselves MINOS had accepted the Faustian bargain Raine Smythe and I had refused on the *Demiurge;* they had sold themselves and their services to the Cielcin.

To Syriani Dorayaica.

And for what? For power? For knowledge—like Faust himself? Or out of simple resentment? Hatred of the Sollan Empire?

"Shoot them down!" I shouted.

The men about me aimed lances and plasma burners and fired.

The shots struck home, and the Cielcin demons *kept climbing.*

"Bastards are wearing shields," Pallino said. "Hold your fire!"

"Up to the walls!" I said, and signaling the Irchtani *kithuun,* I added, "Barda, don't let those *things* up there!"

With the funiculars and the freight lifts all disabled and the city power gone, access to the higher levels was possible only by a series of winding stairs that switched back and forth across the face of the mighty cliff. These were reserved for the poorest citizens of Deira in peacetime, those unwilling or unable to pay the single-kaspum lift toll, but that day—I thought—the stair would command a toll steeper still.

I was halfway to the base of the stair when I heard it again: that guttural, metallic *roar,* more like the noise of a jet engine than the scream of any throat and yet at once terribly animal in its wetness and evident malice.

For there was laughter in the sound.

Turning my head, I did not know what it was I'd expected to find, but *nothing* could have prepared me for the horror that was to come. Smoke filled the streets beside us, and the opening to the largest of these was framed by a round arch that supported a bank of apartments.

A *hand* appeared from the smoke. A white, six-fingered hand felt around and gripped the bottom of the arch. Then an arm emerged and a pointed elbow followed by the fingers of another hand that gripped the far corner of the apartment block. The world was momentarily silent, and I stood transfixed, stunned to realize that each hand was the size of fully grown man.

For a moment, I thought that the worst of my visions had come real, that here was one of the Watchers dragging itself from the Stygian black of dreams. The way it pulled its incredible bulk through the avenue put me in mind of some terrible infant clawing its way from the birth canal with taloned fingers, and the masonry crunched in its grasp. But this was not one of the nightmare *things* I had witnessed in my visions, but a terror of ceramic and steel.

A metal face appeared, and the terrible impression I had had of an infant only intensified, for it was bulbous and swollen, its huge machine eyes glowing like dying coals. It screamed again, jaws mighty enough to snap a man in two, and, with titanic effort, dragged its broad torso forward, shoulders scraping the sides of the avenue and cracking the archway.

And then it stood, and *kept* standing. Twenty feet tall it was, twenty-five. Thirty! A hulking monstrosity in black and white, clear cousin in design to the lesser giants that climbed the wall above, but greater than any I had seen. Greater than Iubalu, greater than the living failures I had encountered in the experiment tanks of Arae. Great almost as the smallest of our colossi.

I knew then with certainty that here was another of the *Vayadan,* the holy slaves that gathered round the person of the Prince of Princes, and facing it there in the square before the wall and the ascent, there was but one thing I could do.

"Run!" I pushed Renna past me, and four others after her, and turning spurred my men toward the stair.

Answering some command, perhaps, or heeding only the call to violence in its blood, one of the lesser demons on the wall above let go. It fell more than two hundred feet and struck the stones on all fours. The hindmost decade of our little force peeled off and spread out along the perimeter at the base of the stairs, for to keep tight formation against such a foe was to court death swift and hard.

Flagstones rose to meet me as I climbed, and my suit's positive pressure helped to force hyper-oxygenated air into my lungs. Still, my breath came hard, and I spurred Valka on ahead of me, steadying her with a hand.

The beast below bellowed and swept its arms through the roof of the nearest building, dislodging the sniper that had nested there and sending the man's mangled body careering over the heads of those fighting in the square below. Heedless of the men about it as a boy is to the insects beneath his feet, the demon advanced toward the wall, its shield and heavy armor drinking the fire forced upon it like sweet rain.

I climbed faster, hearing the metal crash behind. I knew the demon had killed our decade and was climbing the stair, limbs punching through men as it crawled after our heels.

Boom.

The hollow reverberation of a grenade blast sounded, and looking back I saw the metal monster reel and stagger back, momentarily disoriented, its armor cracked. Someone had tossed a mine at it, slow throw bypassing the shield as the device's electromagnet clamped it to the ferrous endoskeleton beneath the white zircon of its armor.

But the steel limbs twitched, and though black ichor ran from the ruin of its jaw, it came, heedless to its own injuries as the undead SOMs that had served the Painted Man in the Arslan tea house. Smoking, staggering, the horrid creature stood.

The giant in the square bellowed again. A flaring flight of missiles flowered from its shoulder and studded the masonry about us, blowing stone pillars and fascia apart. A rain of splinters fell about us, rattling against my armor.

"We're going to die here," Pallino's voice snarled in my ear. "There's no way we're making the top."

" 'Twas a mistake!" Valka put in, unhelpful.

Of the seventy that had left the safety of the tunnel mouth, perhaps forty remained.

"Climb!" I ordered them all. It was no mistake. The wall had to be defended. It was only that it might be impossible.

Unless . . .

"Barda!" I rasped, sheltering with Valka behind the pillar on the landing as the blast of another magnetic mine sounded behind us. "Barda, we're pinned down on the stair!"

I did not hear the Irchtani *kithuun*'s reply, for the *vayadan*-general below chose that moment to scream again.

This time another scream answered it, free and high and wild on the winds, and for a moment—despite the horror and dire moment in which we all stood—I was a boy again, and running on the wall-walks of Devil's Rest playing Simeon the Red.

Gray- and green-feathered shapes fell from the sky, pulling knots of *nahute* in their wake. Plasma fire peppered the stair behind us, and turning I beheld the spread of mighty wings and felt the wind buffet me.

There must have been three hundred of them.

How they had come so fast I could not say, but there they were, and a moment after clawed feet with talons long as daggers gripped my shoulders and my feet *left* the ground.

One of the Irchtani had me in its claws, and with each beat of its wings we rose higher, leaving that doomed stair and the Cielcin behind.

"You are heavy, Devil Man!" came the familiar voice, and I recognized Udax.

"That is twice now I owe you my life!" I said.

"Which puts you in my debt!" the centurion replied.

Despite the *nahute* and the enemy fire still thick around us, I laughed. "Just so!"

Another of the xenobites carried Valka ahead of me, and there were Pallino and Renna. Another explosion rocked the stairs behind, and I saw the ruined demon fall back at last in splinters. The magi of MINOS had done their work well, for the inhuman *things* were built to withstand far more than any man or Cielcin could bear.

One soldier leaped from the rail, and a diving Irchtani caught him by his ankle mere feet from the ground. Another stood on the precipice, hand outstretched. I thrust out my hand. "Take it!" I cried. "Jump, you fool!"

The man did not jump, for in that moment the ancient stair—which had stood since the founding of Deira when the settlers had carved their strange metropolis out of the *Valles Merguli*—cracked and broke as last. I can still imagine that I felt his hand brush mine as he fell, and cursed myself. My vision might have saved him, if I could have but reached it in the chaos.

I do not know his name, did not see his face in those last moments.

I had a lingering image of the crumbling stair as we flew up and away: the lower levels of masonry rotting with flame and rocked by weapons fire. One of the Irchtani above us was struck by a missile launched by the horrific titan below and fell with his human charge—but not Udax.

We flew.

CHAPTER 77

UPON THE RAMPARTS

UDAX DROPPED ME AMONG my men. Human hands seized me, but the closeness of them and the adrenaline still toxic in my blood drove me to panic, and I tore my mask from my face. Only with the helmet removed did I recognize the green star of medical technicians, and waved them back.

"I'm not hurt!" I said, then more forcibly, "I'm fine! Damn your eyes, get back!"

"What the hell was that?" Valka asked, still helmeted not far off.

Udax answered her. "It is coming."

On my feet once more, I answered her. "That," I rubbed my face with my hands, "that . . . was one of the chimeras MINOS built for Dorayaica."

"But 'tis so much . . . so much bigger than the others."

"One of a number," I muttered, repeating the words Iubalu had said to me. "One of six."

"What?"

"Are you all right, Had?" Pallino cut in, tilting his head behind his red-and-black chiliarch's visor.

I pushed the medtechs away from me. "I'm fine, damn it! It's their commander. Like the one we killed on that ship." I gestured to Udax.

The Irchtani hopped from one foot to the other. "It is different," he said. "We cannot kill it like the last."

"Perhaps not," I said.

The Irchtani had brought us to a command post atop the inner wall, and there we'd won a brief respite. The square-lined black mass of a Javelin missile battery hunched not far off, and the space about held armored crates of weapons and explosives. Hauptmann's men—legionnaires and naval technicians alike—moved about with cold precision, doing all they could to manage the fight below and about them.

"Who has command here?" I asked, and struck by a notion, said, "Belay that! Aristedes!"

"Still here," came the intus's reply.

"Where are those lighters? We need air support. There's a . . . *thing* in the square at the base of the wall. A giant Cielcin chimera, must be thirty feet high!"

Aristedes's response was hesitant. "There are still men in the plaza."

"Then get them out!" I ordered him, half-running to the parapet to look down. The behemoth was still there, watching from the arch while its lieutenants and their troopers battled our men on the plaza five hundred feet below.

"Target the hybrids!" I said to the gunnery officer at hand. "Now!"

Below, our men were breaking, running in accordance with Lorian's orders, pulling back into the city, where at least they might thin out the herd of pursuing Cielcin even as the machines focused on the wall. I could not shake the feeling that the day had slipped from me. Cursing, I wheeled, and saw here and there hoplites with shoulder-mounted grenade launchers standing at the edge of the parapet, each steadied by one or two of his compatriots. They fired down on the enemy, but to no avail.

One of them leaped bodily onto the walls, one spade hand punching through the throat of a grenadier and hurling his body into the next man behind him. We could not fire the missiles at it, not at such close range, not with our men about.

The air roared with the noise of engines, and three Sparrowhawk lighters tore the sky above us, machine guns opening fire on the face of the wall beneath us, but even as they strafed the escarpment, three more of the metal monsters leaped onto the battlements. One of the javelin emplacements erupted in a nimbus of scarlet flame, and I was glad at least that with the stair destroyed the main body of the Cielcin host below would have to trek nearly a mile to reach the next one. But there were Cielcin in the upper district, and it was against them that most of Hauptmann's ground troops were dedicated.

"We're going to lose the city," Valka said, speaking over our private channel through the bone conduction patch behind my ear.

Turning to look at her, I found her surprisingly far away. Without the helmet it was easy to forget the comms apparatus. I offered her a sad smile, and mouthed the words, "Not yet."

She shook her head.

The Sparrowhawks screamed by again, and I drew back from the parapet and donned my helmet once more. The false-color imagery cut the haze and smoke, and the suit's recycled air, while stale and antiseptic, smelled less of blood and ash and burning bodies. The square below erupted in florets of red and white, and the air shook as I leaped down the short stair from the turret to the wall. Another of the chimeras had gained the battlements and stood with one clawed foot planted on the decorative merlon and the other clamped around the face of a newly dead soldier. Seeing it, I swore.

"Ti-saem gi!" I cried out, and kindled my sword. "Here! Here!"

The chimera turned its head. A blank arc of metal covered all its face but its jaws, just like Iubalu. But it was smaller than that other monstrosity, and had only the one sword in its grasp. Sighting me and guessing me for an officer by my strange costume and gleaming weapon, it crouched low and came forward, moving like some species of ape. The blade it held was longer than even the longest claymore made for human hands. Almost contemptuously, it swept the weapon through two men within reach. The ceramic blade notched their armor, but it was the force of the blow that carried them over the parapet and dropped them screaming five hundred feet to the burning plaza below.

"Lord Marlowe." It was Aristedes. I did not answer him. "Their fleet is peeling off the attack in orbit, diverting to the ground. You have incoming."

I ignored him. My mind crouched in that same place our ancestors so often found themselves when faced with the standing cobra. I knew full well how fast the creatures could move. For a moment—a brief moment—my vision flickered and I saw the parallel instances of my opponent and the battlement on which we stood, saw the subtle variations in movement and force. The different outcomes. Some piece of my focus had clicked into place, and I was clear as mountain water.

The xenobite struck . . .

. . . and fell in two pieces.

I had seen the angle of its attack and stepped inside it, aiming my sword along a hair-fine fault in the adamant plate and shearing the chimera in half with a rising cut. I was so stunned, my unnatural vision shattered as half the creature tumbled over the parapet.

I'd felled the beast with a single blow.

An almighty cheer went up from the defenders, and I almost laughed aloud. Something in the state of alert focus that the coming threat had placed on me jogged my mind to the right attitude, and the vision shifted into place.

Emboldened by my little miracle, the men fought with vigor renewed . . . or might have done, were it not that elation turned to dread the moment after, for even as the ruin of my enemy smote the earth, the sky turned all to fire and thickened with smoke and light.

An armada descended. Dozens of siege towers and shuttles and lighter craft quitting the battle above screamed out of space with a vengeance. Too many, far more than had appeared in our scans of the first attack group. Their second fleet had arrived. And behind? Behind the gray skies were made white with the flash of annihilation to shame the very sun.

Annihilation.

For a moment, neither man nor Cielcin moved, and all was still in Deira but the flames.

Then the chilling alien cry rose up again, and a voice deep as the waters of Vorgossos spoke from below in the tongue of men. "Your fleet is gone."

Peering down from the battlements, I saw the thirty-foot monstrosity standing there, its bulbous head and glowing metal eyes sweeping along the line of the battlement, and knew that deep voice was its own.

Not to be persuaded by the enemy, I radioed the command center. "Report."

It was not Aristedes who answered me, but the grim voice of Leonid Bartosz. "They came out of nowhere. The Cielcin got a . . . got one of their ships inside Ondu Station defenses. Blew their own reactor."

Cold iron seized my heart. "And the fleet?"

"Reeling. Mostly destroyed."

"Hauptmann clustered them too close," Lorian said. "Set off a chain annihilation."

"The *Tamerlane*?" I could hardly manage the words. Corvo, Durand, Crim, Ilex, Elara, Okoyo, and all the rest . . . they could not be gone. I had an inkling then of how Aranata Otiolo must have felt standing in the garden while its whole world burned. "Is there word from Corvo?"

The intus answered, "If there is, comms won't get through until the radiation dissipates."

No word, then. I held my breath in the strange stillness of the wall, eyes pressed momentarily shut as I tried and failed to master myself. The horror was too much. Was that a tear on my face? I clenched my jaw, and as

Aranata had sworn vengeance, I swore I would tear every remaining ship from the sky with my bare hands if I had to.

The sky!

The Cielcin fleet had quit the field and cleared it for their suicidal attack on our own, and their arrival on Berenike carved black channels of smoking cloud across the heavens. Blue-white flared the sparks of retro-rockets slowing their descent, and the noise of them put the thunder to shame. Our Sparrowhawks rose in answer, and the flash of their guns and of the javelins on the wall below turned many a vessel into a fine mist and rain of shrapnel in the upper airs. Lightning flashed from the encroaching storm clouds, and far along the wall I saw two more of the demons of Arae make the ramparts and fall among my men.

I am not certain if a hell awaits the unjust hereafter, but I know there are hells in this life.

"*Velenammaa totajun!*" came a bass rumble from the realms below. "Take them! Take them all!"

Looking out, I saw the giant had left the shadow of the arch. Like the smaller chimeras, it moved ape-like across the plaza below, moving on hands and knees with a noise like mighty hammers pounding.

"*Paqqaa omandiun ija ba-totajun!*"

"Message from Corvo!" Lorian said. "She's alive!"

Relief blossomed in me even as I watched that hideous giant reach the foot of the wall. "Patch her through!" I almost shouted, fear and fury warring with relief to find the Norman captain still alive.

Her voice floated in a moment after, pressed flat and oddly hollow in my ears. "Hadrian . . ." No rank, no *Marlowe*.

"What the hell happened?"

Fire rained on the giant below as once more the Sparrowhawks wheeled. A massive siege tower smashed the ramparts a mile south of our position and almost instantly *scahari* screamed from its holds. The tower exploded a moment after, destroyed by the Javelin emplacement it had landed within a thousand feet of.

"Their second fleet just . . . *appeared*. Must have come out of warp on the far side of the planet, else we'd have seen them sooner. Surveillance grid's in shambles." I could hear the strain in her voice, the numbing shock ebbing as awareness of loss drained in. "Their first fleet scattered, made an opening. They sacrificed a frigate, flew it clean through Hauptmann's cordon and slowed up inside the station's shields."

I swore. Ondu Station had contained huge reserves of antihydrogen for refueling warp drives, and the resulting annihilation had cascaded, bypassing shield after shield in its unholy fury until no ship left was left within range. Mere chance had saved Corvo and the *Tamerlane*.

"We got lucky, but I'd wager there aren't more than a dozen of us left up here," she said. "What should we do?"

"How long until the rest of the fleet returns?" I asked.

"Three days," Lorian answered. "Any closer and the Cielcin might have detected them, realized they weren't really gone."

Three days. "We can't hold for three days," I said. We would not hold out three hours. "Especially not with that second fleet."

"They hit us from both ends," Corvo said. "Tore the defense fleet apart. They must have . . . a thousand ships? Fifteen hundred?"

"Is there any sign of the worldship?"

"No, nothing."

I clenched my jaw. If there had been it might have been possible to launch a bombing run on it with all available ships, force the Cielcin to panic, but unlike Ulurani and Aranata and all the other princes I had known, this Dorayaica had held its worldship in abeyance, safe from harm.

A luxury it could afford with a fleet of its size.

The Cielcin had boxed us in nicely. We were trapped on Berenike with their army at the gates and no relief coming for days. Plenty of time for the giant and its forces to crack the Storm Wall like an egg and suck the life from its heart. When the rest of the Cielcin fleet arrived—if more were indeed coming, as I feared—we would all be neatly counted and packed aboard their siege towers for return to the alien Dark. And worse . . . whatever else happened, the Cielcin had already achieved what I guessed was their aim.

Titus Hauptmann was dead.

The stodgy old officer had held the front for more than a century, and if the attack on Marinus was a trap set to catch the old hunter it had succeeded. Perhaps our single greatest asset in the Veil and Expanse was lost. But there had been no way to know how fast this fleet of Dorayaica's was. It was an incredible thing, a dozen times larger than any fleet of the Pale heretofore encountered by man.

Recalling my vision of strange kingdoms and empires stretched across the farther stars, the immeasurable scope of them all . . . I shivered and swore, "Black planet . . ."

Present necessity brought me back from those distant shoals. Bartosz's voice sliced through my black mood. "Marlowe, pull your men back into the tunnels."

A hollow formed in the pit of my stomach. "Abandon the city?"

"The city is lost," he said, sounding light-years away. "Abandon the wall!"

"We can't, sir," I said. "Not without abandoning the Javelins to the enemy!"

The line was dead.

"Aristedes?" I said. "Marlowe to Aristedes."

"Still here."

"What happened?"

Lorian paused a moment, and I imagined him peering over the lip of his console in the command center. I could almost feel the slow track of his watchful eyes as he said, "The legate *quit* the field, sir."

"What do you mean he quit the field?" I clambered back into the command post, brushing past Valka and Pallino on the stair. "Where did he go?"

"He just . . . *left,* lord," Lorian said, uncharacteristically formal.

I swore. "You're in command there, then."

The wall rocked beneath me, and I lurched against an open crate of energy lances. A huge iron *hand* wrapped fingers around the merlon nearest me, crushing stone beneath its weight, and a moment later a single massive red eye peered over the ramparts.

Pallino shot it.

Shield flicker fading, the giant pulled itself higher until its whole head loomed before me. The face was large as a passenger shuttle, like a huge moon rising above the wall. I could see the aperture in one massive eye tighten and focus.

"You." Its voice was like the sea in storm. *"Tuka okun-se belu wo."*

I am proud to say I did not falter, but locked eyes with the creature some fifty feet away.

Valka and Pallino stayed behind me. No one fired their weapon—no one seemed to move. Surprising even myself, I took a step forward. *"Marossa okun-kih!"* I said. *Name yourself.*

The giant laughed. "You are the one who liberated poor Iubalu? You are so small." One fist wide as I was tall clenched and crushed the battlement between its fingers, sending up clouds of dust.

"You know me?" I asked, speaking the alien tongue. I wondered at its use of the word *liberated.* I had killed Iubalu—with Udax and Siran's help— but then, perhaps death was liberation to the Pale.

"Your image is known."

"Tuka okun-se belu ba-Iedyr Yemani ne?" I asked.

The giant's metal eyes narrowed in that smooth white face. It opened its fist, showcasing the giant imitation of a Cielcin hand the MINOS engineers had forged. "One of six," it said.

"Six," I said, casting about. "Six, six." I raised my human hand. "Five now."

The beast hissed, but made no move against me. "I am Bahudde. *Vayadan ba-Shiomu.*"

Just as I had thought.

"You must surrender," the giant said. "You cannot win. *Tuka uelacyr ba-vakun-kih celaj'jyr.*"

I struggled with the words a moment. The grammar was ungainly, arcane, the pronunciation somehow more stressed and inhuman than I was used to, but I got it in the end.

Your time has ended.

"Our *time*?" I asked, mind racing of its own accord to the bright thread of narrative time I had seen weaving its way through the tapestry of infinite possibility. The word *time, uelacyr,* took on a special meaning, sharp and filled with an almost religious power. "That is not for you to decide." As I spoke, I tapped the emergency beacon on my wrist-terminal, as I had in the alleyways of Meidua so long ago. The signal would carry to the command center in the Storm Wall.

To Lorian Aristedes.

"He will scratch you out," the *vayadan* said. "Carve you off the face of every world you have infested. Crack the bones. And suck the marrow dry." The beast spoke Galstani, its voice projecting from speakers hidden on its back so loud that all could hear. Around us, more and more of the siege craft were landing, black towers rising amidst dust and smoke and the ruins of the valley city below.

"You will try," I said, and looked past the monster to the specks in the eastern distance over the scrub land beyond the far side of the rift valley.

Bahudde seemed to notice my staring. "Do you look for the sun, *yukajji?* It is going down. It is setting on your kind."

The beast was not wrong; the sun had since vanished behind the mighty bulwark of the Storm Wall, and gray shadows hung upon the city, made grayer by the smoke of the almighty burning.

"They say the suns never set on our Empire," I said, focusing on its hideous smooth face once more. "There is always light somewhere." I kindled my sword, highmatter flowing like water, blue light flowering in the gloom. Bravely—madly—I rushed forward.

A high and whining squeal escaped the behemoth, and it raised its arms to strike me.

An explosion struck the behemoth full in face, and it reeled back. Its shield had taken the worst of the impact, and it caught the parapet with its other hand, digging huge feet into the stone face.

Lorian had struck just in time. The tall-masted craft sliced the air overhead with a sound like tearing metal as it circled back and fired again. The shock of the blast threw me back, slamming me into a heavy weapons crate.

Hands seized me. Valka's. Pallino's.

"We have to go now!" the chiliarch shouted over the din and the ringing in my ears.

He had no cornicen to sound the retreat, and so the task fell to Lorian Aristedes, whose dry, palatine accents calmly ordered every legionnaire left standing in Deira to fall back to the tunnels. With the nearest stair destroyed, we had a half-mile run along the wall-walk above lift lobbies and urban utilities stations.

Shooting as we went, I saw the flash of missiles firing, rapid now and less precise as Lorian burned through the last of our assets before they could fall into the hands of the enemy. Siege towers went up in flames, and whole shoals of the questing *nahute* died defending others. Cielcin airships burned and plummeted from the sky, and our Sparrowhawks died with them. I passed the broken bodies of men and Irchtani lying on the wall.

Bahudde did not appear, and yet I was certain the lighters had not killed him. Killing Iubalu had taken a measure of doing, and Iubalu was only a little bigger than an ordinary Cielcin.

At last we made the stairs, and cut our way down. I soon found myself leading from the front, sword tearing.

"The Cielcin are taking up position over the city," Aristedes said. "Should I order the fleet in?"

I had forgotten about the fleet. I rested a moment in the shadow of a line of townhouses, panting as I waved my column of soldiers past me, following Pallino and Renna toward the arch and the gated tunnel that led to the safety of the old mines.

"How many are left?" I asked.

"Not enough. Thirteen ships."

But Corvo and the *Tamerlane* were alive. That was not nothing. "And Bassander Lin?"

"He's alive," came Aristedes's reply.

The soldiers were nearly all past me. I wanted to be in the rearguard, to be the last of our people over that threshold and leave no man behind. Valka had gone on with Pallino, and behind I heard the raw battle cry of the Pale. The sound of *nahute* buzzing filled the airs, and slowly I started to run, following the loping soldiers as each followed the man in front of him.

We hadn't far to go.

"Order them away," I said, answering quickly—though whether it was impulse or inspiration only time could tell.

Time.

"Are you sure, Hadrian?" The commander's brittle, battlefield demeanor blinked a moment.

"Damn it, Lorian!" I hurried on, keeping pace with the end of our retreating train. "Have them link up with the relief force. I won't risk the *Tamerlane* or Lin's or any of them. They won't last long against that fleet. We'll last longer here."

The good commander replied, "What makes you say that?"

"Because they want to eat us," I said. "They sacrificed one meal on Marinus. They won't waste a second."

I spoke sense, and Lorian knew it. Perhaps the little man resented admitting defeat, perhaps it was frustration with Hauptmann and Bartosz. The former had made a critical error cordoning his ships so tight together. Shields were not proof against matter-antimatter reactions—that was elementary warcraft. How Hauptmann might have overlooked it, there was no telling, but overlooked it he had. And all it had cost him was *everything,* leaving us to pay his debts. And Bartosz?

I had words for Leonid Bartosz.

A stone arch above the entrance to a backyard exploded onto the street before me, and a white-armored creature appeared, cousin to the one I'd slain on the wall-walk, flanked by four *scahari* in white masks blazoned with the sigil of the White Hand in black outline. I slew one of them before even the chimera knew I was upon them, and the rearguard fell on one of the others, relying on the bayonets of their energy lances to kill the shielded foe.

The metal creature swung its huge sword. I ducked and heard a clear *pang* as the zircon blade caught on an iron lamppost. I was not as fortunate in this encounter as I'd been with the last, and striking the creature's armored thigh with my sword, I found adamant proof against highmatter.

Blood hammered in my ears, thick with adrenaline, and the vision would not come. Eyes stretched wide beneath their mask, I struck again. The zircon blade came whistling, and I parried and cut the blade in two. Plasma fire from my men peppered the creature's hide, and it snarled and punched one man in the chest with a clawed foot so hard his ceramic armor shattered and he went flying straight back into the storefront behind, dead of blunt trauma.

Seeing my chance, I lunged at the exposed leg joint, blade slipping beneath armor plating to notch the common metal there. The beast whined, and fingers hard as iron and long as snakes seized me by the head. I felt the plates in the armor bending, flexing at the joints. My entoptic vision sparked and fizzed, and I felt that surely at any moment the helmet would crack and that would be the end of Hadrian Marlowe. I hewed at the metal arm with my sword, but to no avail. The beast lifted me bodily from the earth and squeezed tighter. I could hear its machine-aided breathing low and deep and steady.

It released me. I landed on my knees—nearly putting my sword through my bowels in the process—and looking up I beheld a strange sight. The giant chimera wobbled as if drunk and slipped on its injured leg, crashing through the window of a clothier to land on hands and knees. It wheeled about, but its movements were muddy, dumb. And then the most incredible thing of all happened.

The faceplate that concealed black eyes and nose-slits and the seam where flesh was sewn into metal *opened* like the lid of a great, white eye and bared the face and brain to my blade.

Gasping, I did not waste time. I raised my sword.

The thing fell dead, and I looked round, not astonished but relieved to find Valka standing there, hand outstretched. She'd worked her witchcraft on the creature's human-manufactured circuitry.

" 'Tis two now you owe me!" she said.

The tunnel arch loomed through the smoke ahead, and to my astonishment I found our detachment of men still holding the threshold. The survivors hurried through, and I caught the shoulder of the decurion Pallino had left holding the gate.

"Give me the detonator!" I said, referring to the mines we'd set in the tunnel mouth before the battle had begun.

This is not defeat, I told myself. *We planned for this.*

I pushed the decurion along, intending to be the last in the tunnel. Men were fighting on the thoroughfare outside. I could hear their cries and the shout of plasma fire. I advanced to the level of the inner gate, clutching the detonator—a capped cylinder about the size of a fountain pen—in my false-boned hand. There I turned, and shouted orders for the rearguard to fall back.

They did, retreating in that shuffling way armed men have while maintaining fire.

Cielcin came fast behind, shadows advancing up the hall.

"Oyumn saryr suja wo!" I said, ordering them to halt.

The figures stopped and laughed behind their masks.

"Run away, little rat!" their leader barked. "Run and hide! We will catch you, drag you out of your little holes, and strip you to the bone!"

I signaled that the decurion should close the bulkhead.

One of the others nudged its master in the arm. "Why don't we have some fun with it first, Goraba? The *yukajimn* are sweetest when they fight back."

"Quiet, worm!" the leader said, shoving its underling aside. "We kill them and take them to the *vayadan.*"

"Not today, I think!" I heard the fellow turn the key and the warning lights flared. *"Sim udantha!"*

The bulkhead began rolling shut, three feet of solid steel. An alarm sounded, ordering all hands clear as the great gear-teeth rolled into place. The Cielcin all rushed forward, but too late.

I thumbed the detonator the moment after, and felt the blast like distant thunder.

CHAPTER 78

OF RATS AND FALCONS

"EXPLAIN YOURSELF!" I SAID, wrapping my hands about the lapels of the vulpine legate. Earth and Emperor, I was strong! The older officer came clear out of his seat, eyes vacant and detached from my face. He said nothing, and I shook him, heedless of the man's rank and command. "We needed you. Your men needed you!"

Bartosz's gray eyes slid farther away with each passing instant.

"Titus is dead," came the reply, so distant. "He's dead. The fleet is lost. We're all lost. They're at the gates. It is hopeless."

The legate's chair rolled away and toppled with a crash as I pushed him back against the wall. "They are not *inside*. This was always a possibility."

Bartosz's eyes flicked to mine for the barest instant. "You saw what they did. The size of that fleet! We never imagined—never imagined *anything* like it."

"*Our* fleet is coming," I said. "Hauptmann summoned ships from across the whole sector." As I am now, I understand Leonid's black mood, that crippling despair, for it exists in every man. I would feel it myself, and more sharply, before the end.

The officer almost laughed. "It won't be enough. They have fifteen hundred ships!"

"Most of them small, rapid attack craft. Unshielded."

"It won't matter. We will all die here."

His back against the wall, I lifted Leonid bodily from the floor, muscles straining at the effort in Berenike's somewhat heavy gravity. "We are *alive*," I hissed.

Those gray eyes found me at last, wide and empty. "Not for long," he said again. "Titus is dead." Disgusted, I dropped the man and turned for the door without intending to say another word. But the legate was not finished. "Go!" he sneered, word stretching on the air. "Go and die as you please. I shall die here, and die a man and not a *rat*."

"A rat?" I turned back, fully intending to hand the bastard a knife myself. *Yukajjimn*. Vermin. "If that is what we are, so be it. I will not give up hope."

"Hope!" Leonid said. "There is no hope!" He slumped to the floor, back against the smooth wall of the conference chamber. In a small voice, he said, "They say you are a prophet, Marlowe, but you're blind if you can't see this is the end."

End. The word plucked a lonely note in me. Bahudde's words echoed after it. *Your time is ended*. I had seen those ends, had I not? Played out in infinite forms across the limitless tapestry of time? Thus I knew no thing was determined, decided. Done.

"Nothing is ended," I said, recalling my vision of the end of time, of the egg that was itself a new beginning. "Nothing ever ends."

Leonid shook his head, lips curling. "You're a fool," he said. "You will die a fool."

"I will die a man!" The sound of my voice rang in the hollow hall and almost rattled the plate windows with their vision of the landing field and the Cielcin ships swarming over it. Not even Death was an ending. Not for me. Not for Leonid either, not that day at least. His death awaited him on another battlefield, about a different star. I took my hand off the knife. "Which is more than any man can say of you."

In the hallway, I seized a centurion of the Red Company and two men. "The legate intends to kill himself for his dishonor. You are *not* to permit him to do so."

"But sir!" one of the men said. He was a junior Legion officer, one of Bartosz's own men.

"He is to be placed in fugue for his own protection. You are to disregard any order he gives you, or by Earth and Emperor, I will send you out the front gates alone. Am I clear?" I turned to face the fellow squarely.

He balked. "Yes, my lord. At once."

Tired eyes greeted me in the command center as the door cycled shut.

"Lord Marlowe." Aristedes looked up from his console, gesturing to cut off the report he was hearing from one junior officer.

Advancing to stand just inside the circle of the tactical console, I said, "How are our defenses holding?" I made no mention of the legate.

"They're trying to clear some of the tunnels on the city side, but they're holding back the full brunt of their assault. Like they're waiting for something." Lorian indicated the wall of security panels behind him, image after image showcasing the Storm Wall's defenses and the city and airfield outside.

I shifted to stand beside him, peering at the wall and at the console table in turn. Lorian's display showed a topographic map of the city and the Storm Wall, critical systems and troop deployments mapped. "Waiting for what?"

"Your guess is good as mine." The intus shoved lank white hair from his bony face. "Shields should hold indefinitely. They're drawing power direct from the planet's core. We should be safe so long as our concrete defenses hold." He pointed to various points on his map as he spoke, indicating the collapsed tunnels and the main gates.

"I thought you said they won't shell us from orbit anyhow," said a familiar voice from the corner of the room. Prince Alexander was seated there, trying to stay out of the way. He held his chin in one hand, looking for all the world like some bored monarch listening to the concerns of his subjects. I was surprised how calm he looked—I'd expected some behavior cousin to that of the panicked legate.

I inclined my head. "Very good." Fixing my attention back on Lorian, I said, "They'll want to take us intact. We are a valuable resource, after all."

"They'll start digging," Valka said. She'd removed her helmet and the elastic coif, and sweat caked her hair. I had never seen her so tired, so bloodless and ragged-looking. "They must have used sonar or gravitometers and found the tunnels. They'll know that's where the people went."

The prince sat back in his seat, arms crossed. "They must be hungry."

Put so plainly, that part of the reality of our position chilled the command center, and the aides and junior officers all were still.

I broke the stillness with a question, rapping the console with my unscarred hand. "Corvo and the fleet are gone?"

Aristedes sank back into his chair, massaging one knee that seemed to pain him. He found his cane—more out of reflex than necessity—and answered, "Yes. All gone." I could see the wreckage of Ondu Station and Hauptmann's proud defensive fleet smoldering in the upper atmosphere, mingling with the threatening clouds. "We need to buy enough time to guard against their return. Three days."

"Assuming the fleet returned the moment you signaled the attack," Alexander said.

"They did," Lorian answered.

I let them bicker a moment, brushing past a trio of young officers who stood looking on to stand at the low, broad-framed window. The command center was situated high up in the Storm Wall. While holograph plates on the back wall showed a false view of Deira and the *Valles Merguli*, the room's true windows looked out on the starport, where at a distance in rough formation waited the spindle-shadows of Cielcin siege towers—a hundred of them at least. About them swarmed a great tumult as the xenobites hurried about inhuman business. From the way they ran I guessed they knew a storm was coming.

"Storm's coming," I said. "Probably tonight. Whatever attempt they'll make, they'll make it from the city side. Unless they dig into those blast pits." I gestured at the starport landing craters out the window and turned back.

The intus was nodding, massaging his jaw with one delicately braced hand. "The pits are hardened against rocketry. They couldn't be more fortified." He had a point, and it was one that ought to have occurred to me. As if noting my embarrassment, he added, "But they may still try it."

"We have men in the underground terminals," the prince said, stirring in his seat.

A junior officer piped up, "And in the maintenance tunnels, aye."

Lorian waved his hand, silver glittering. It was, I thought, an astonishingly casual gesture with which to dismiss the words of an Imperial prince, but for once Alexander raised no objections. "And each unit with artillery-grade plasma howitzers dug in by the bulkheads leading in from the pits. No, gentlemen, ladies. No. They'll make their assault through the gates on the city side, assuming they can't excavate the tunnels. We need to consider our options."

It was inevitable that someone would object, and so no one was surprised when that objection came, voiced by a Legion navy captain who had remained with Bartosz rather than fly out with the fleet, a sallow woman with a face like spoiled milk. I didn't know her. "Who exactly put you in charge, mutant?"

Lorian's pale, watery eyes flicked to me. I signaled the affirmative, and a positively lupine grin flowered on the young officer's face. "Ask the legate."

Sensing my cue, I stepped forward. "Lord Bartosz is under arrest at present."

"Arrest!" The captain's hand twitched toward her sidearm. "Sedition!" Her underlings all tensed.

"Peace, soldier!" I made to stand between her and Lorian. "The legate was planning suicide. The loss of Lord Hauptmann and the fleet took him hard." As I spoke, it occurred to me that this woman's ship was likely among those killed in the orbital engagement—that she had lost people. In a smaller, kinder, voice, I added, "He is being placed in cryonic suspension for his own safety. I am in command here, and you *will* obey Commander Aristedes. Am I clear?"

She did not answer, and so I redoubled my efforts, turning instead to the entire assembly of officers, technicians, and aides. "Am I clear?" I pressed forward, advancing on the patrician woman like a shadow.

"Yes, my lord," she said, and bowed her head.

"Very good." I turned sharply away, the entire matter forgotten.

The chamber was silent for the span of a half dozen heartbeats. Lorian broke it, tapping his cane against the metal floor. "The gates are heavily fortified," he said, indicating the angled approaches to the Storm Wall's city gates, each dominated by a huge thrust of whitewashed concrete and steel fleshed with slitted windows, gun emplacements, and the silvered dishes of static field projectors made to short out the Royse shields of anything that passed beneath their watchful eye. Each was dominated by a massive plasma turret—more flamethrower than firearm—capable of flooding the entire wedge-shaped space with matter hot as the surface of Berenike's sun. "They tried a push on the gate here, above White Street, during the initial offensive, but we burned them pretty bad. Possibly that's part of why they're waiting. That and the storm." I could see Lorian's mind working, ticking over fact after fact. The man should have been a scholiast; he had a mind like an ancient computer, all switches and wires.

"Surely they could find a way in if they wanted," Valka said, sinking into an abandoned seat near the dull wall.

Alexander's frown was audible before I saw his face. "You think they're waiting on something more?" He looked round at us. "Not numbers! They must know . . ."

Between Hauptmann and Bartosz's men and the survivors of the Red Company, we were fewer than eighty thousand. Eighty thousand against untold millions of the Pale. We had superlative defenses, superior technology, but the numbers? Even if we were to arm every man and woman of fighting age in the bunkers below, we would still be overmatched. Outnumbered one hundred to one. And at any rate to send so many peasants—untested and untrained—into the web of the Pale was more liability than asset, for the chaos of their panic would surely spell our undoing.

"We could bomb the city."

I am no longer certain who it was made the suggestion, except that I know it was not myself. Perhaps here was the conclusion of Lorian's frantic considerations, or a piece of Alexander's casual disregard. Maybe it was only a suggestion floated by one of the odd captains or by Valka herself. It wasn't me, nor was it Commandant Bancroft, who had returned from an inspection of the Wall's defenses while Lorian still deliberated.

We could bomb the city.

Bancroft stood silent, her face utterly drained of blood.

"You said it yourself in council," I said, trying to sound conciliatory.

Bancroft shook her head, but still said nothing.

"I am sorry," I added.

"This is our home, my lord," she said, wiping at her eyes. "I never thought it would come to this." She did not beg, only stated the simple fact.

To my astonishment, it was Valka who answered her. "Look around you. You have no homes."

Win or die, the people of Berenike could not remain on their world. Berenike had but one city, and its infrastructure was gone. Its people would be refugees, resettled or frozen and placed in colonial stores—a difficulty to be solved some other day. With the power plant compromised, it would not be long before the urban farms began dying, the water systems ruined, and offworld trade would all but cease, for to venture to worlds the Cielcin knew the location of was to incur disaster. It was rare but not unheard of to find that where one *itani* had come, others followed. Even if resettlement were not to be made mandatory, there would be thousands willing to sell themselves into serfdom or outright slavery for relocation to some garden world of the Outer Perseus.

In a sense, Bahudde had been right. Our time on this world was ended. We had expanded too far, brushed against the borders of infinity.

Infinity had pushed back.

"We still have our lighter craft." Lorian laid his cane across his knees, knuckles white on the shaft. "But Sparrowhawks are no good, too light."

Bancroft hesitated only a moment, as if steeling herself for the inevitable. In a voice thin and airless she said, "There's a fleet of old Falcon-IIs at the ODF base in Iselia."

"Iselia?" Valka asked.

"Coastal town, about a hundred miles south," Bancroft answered. "Down where the Mergo empties into the sea."

Alexander frowned. "But have they been hit?"

Bancroft snapped her fingers at a pair of comms officers, who went about the business of answering the prince's question.

"Falcon-IIs?" Lorian was frowning. "I didn't know those still flew."

"We get what the Legions cast off," the commandant said with a shrug. "They'll get the job done."

The intus's demonic smile returned. "Plasma or chemical explosives?"

"Plasma," Bancroft answered.

The comms officer butted in. "Iselia command's still there."

All eyes shifted to me, and I turned to look at the good commander who sat—legs dangling—in the console seat as though it were the Solar Throne.

Lorian Aristedes wasted no time, but drew himself up and—in a passable impersonation of Otavia Corvo—said, "See it done."

From the south they came, and the burning followed. Indistinguishable at first from the thunder, the blue fire of their drives shone like lightning against the clouds. The Falcons came in low, carving a phalanx through the air and up the valley, rushing up the coast to the shelter of the Storm Wall in those regions where its height was not yet the full mile.

Then the Cielcin answered, firing missiles of strange design. From Lorian's still-functioning surveillance equipment, we could just make out the shapes of Pale warriors scrambling to get under cover of Deira's many terraces, to shelter beneath domes and in narrow streets or in the relative safety of their siege tower vessels. To my astonishment, great clouds of *nahute* rose to greet the falling bombs, and many of the plasma charges erupted in the air, violet blossoms filling the sky above Deira like fireworks at Summerfair.

No one spoke, unless it was the junior officers coordinating with the Falcon team aquilarii. Not Valka, not Alexander, not even I had words as the city burned and Falcons fell and burned themselves in the smoking ruins of the once-great city.

I remember the hunched shape of Lorian Aristedes, red-lit from beneath by the glow of the console table, still and uncharacteristically silent.

One might have thought him a statue, a gargoyle such as decorated Devil's Rest and the cathedrals of old Europe, wide-eyed and watchful. He didn't move, didn't blink, but drew one knee to his chin in the high seat that was too big for him and stirred only to give some order or relay some news.

And when the dust settled and the smoke was washed away by the wind, Deira was in ruins, a slagheap of blasted stone and twisted iron snarling from the Valley of the Diver like so many rotten teeth. The shattered shapes of siege towers smoldered amidst that ruin, and nothing moved.

Across the landing field on the other side of the Storm Wall, the remaining host of the Pale waited, crouched in their vessels like a forest of angry knives. We had stung them, but ours was a passing victory. Storm clouds rushed in, and the wrack of winds came on with all the thunder and lightning they portended. Rain began to fall, waves beating against the panes of the Storm Wall's narrow windows, and even through the steel and reinforced concrete of that cyclopean fastness one could hear the whine and howl of the storm winds.

The true battle still lay ahead.

CHAPTER 79

THE DISMAL NIGHT

THE STORM RAGED ON, and no word or shot came from the enemy across that endless-seeming no man's land. The survivors of the fighting in the city were tended to, and I surrendered my damaged armor to Bancroft's engineers for repair, pausing only to wash the sweat and stink of smoke away in the officers' barracks adjoining the command center.

The nights on Berenike were long, each more than fifteen standard hours. Two stood between us and the return of our nine legions on the third day. How foolish our plan to divide our forces seemed by the moonless dark of that dismal night, though it was perhaps our salvation. Had those legions stood arrayed against that alien horde in the first exchange, I think they too would have fallen.

What I would have given to see again as I had seen on the Quiet's mountain! To know the consequences of each choice before it was made! But as I have said time and again . . . I am no prophet. Whatever change the eldritch Quiet made in me, it was not to instill the gift of foresight.

"What do you think they're doing?"

I had heard the prince approach, recognized the almost tinny sound of his bootheels ringing on the concrete. I did not turn, but folded the black-paged folio and peered once more out through the window I'd been sitting in. Rain lashed the round pane, and I could just make out the pits on the airfield below, lit by red landing lights beneath the wire frames of starship mooring towers.

"Holding their breath," I said at last, addressing Alexander's pale reflection in the glass. The young nobile had aged decades in the last week. Even reflected, there were shadows beneath the Imperial green eyes, and a sunkenness to his features that spoke of a man of three hundred, not thirty. "They but wait for an opening."

The prince took a few steps nearer, image growing before me. "They say the storm will break sometime mid-morning."

"Then that is how long we have left," I said. Presently the lightning flashed, revealing the dark towers and improbable shapes of Cielcin landing craft hunched at the extremity of the field.

"I suppose they've no experience with storms where they come from," the prince said.

"Or weather of any kind," I replied. "It is a pity the storm won't hold until reinforcements arrive."

Alexander drew nearly level with where I sat, and I became aware of the shape of him hovering at my shoulder. Still I did not turn. I wished he were gone, or else still frozen aboard the *Tamerlane*. Our confrontation on Annica had been too painful a sequel in our ongoing comedy of errors. It would have been better, far better, to be quit of him. But Corvo and Aristedes alike had thought him safer in the Storm Wall and the bunkers beneath Deira than on the ship in battle above.

They'd been proven right.

"Did you find them?" he asked. I could feel his eyes burning the back of my head.

Still not turning, I asked him, "Find what?"

"They said you found them," Alexander said. "Your xenobites."

I shut my eyes against the royal reflection. Someone had told the prince about Annica, about my little stunt with Bastien and the handgun, I could sense it in the tension on the air. The boy had come to see a miracle. But I would not provide one.

"The Quiet," I said. "Yes. I found it."

"It?" The confusion in Alexander's voice was thick enough to cut.

"It's not a people," I said in answer. "We were wrong."

The prince made a small noise of understanding, and I heard him shift nearer. Opening my eyes, I found his pale reflection looking down on me, framed against the night and the storm in the round window.

"What happened?"

"It sent me here," I said. "It showed me the Cielcin fleet. The attack. That's why we split our defenses."

Alexander's voice tightened. "And got Hauptmann and the rest killed."

"Hauptmann did that himself," I said, turning at last. Alexander was just outside arm's reach, hands shoved into his pockets to disguise the fact that they were clenched into fists. "He thought the station defenses would hold, wanted to maximize the strength of our secondary fleet to match whatever they had coming." I swallowed, leaned forward with hands between my knees. "It was a bad plan."

"We could die here," the prince said, soberly. He took a step around me, moved closer to the window. "Did you really die? Fighting that Cielcin, I mean." That asked, he fixed all his attention on me, searching for the real answer in my face.

I shrugged. "Believe what you will."

I could not tell Alexander what had happened on Annica, should not have showed him Pallino's recording. I was close to what the God Emperor had been. Chosen—not by Mother Earth—but by the Quiet. Chosen to play my part in their incomprehensible scheme where kings and emperors—even the God Emperor of old—are pawns.

It wouldn't matter. The Chantry, the Empress, the Old Lions all believed me some would-be usurper. I could deny it with every breath—deny it with my final breath—and they would not believe. I had denied I was anything like the God Emperor, and here I was cast in his mold. All the efforts of the Imperium to duplicate old William had come to naught, and I—a lesser cousin of the least line—found myself heir to all his legendary power.

"Is that it?" Alexander almost sneered. *"Believe what I will?"*

Looking at my face in the dark glass, I saw the familiar vision once again: the Emperor Hadrian seated—white-robed and crowned—upon the Solar Throne with Selene at his feet.

I did not want it.

I did not want Alexander to think I wanted it.

Unable to bear the quiet, Alexander said, "You were supposed to be this great hero. But you're a fraud. It's all . . . stories, isn't it? When that assassin tried to kill you . . . they said it was the Earth that saved you, but your bones were replaced with adamant. You said it yourself. It's all tricks like that! You're a fraud!" He broke off, and for a moment I thought he'd decided that he'd gone too far. "What did you find?"

"I told you," I said, coolly. "We found the Quiet, and it sent us here."

Alexander barked a hollow laugh. "The Quiet. I don't believe it. I don't."

"You were with us when we met the machine," I said. "Horizon."

Anticipating where this bit of conversation was leading, the prince said, "You think I would trust the word of a machine?" He shook his head, stepping back. "You say this . . . *Quiet* thing spoke to you. You act like you have visions. But you don't."

I couldn't stop myself. "You really are an idiot, aren't you?" I asked, standing and advancing on the younger man. "You think this is about you? All this?" I gestured at the room about us, at the ruined city and the lurking force outside. "You think it was all for your benefit? Gododdin? Nemavand? The coliseum? Colchis and Annica? You think this has all been some play for your attentions? You think I'm trying to trick you?" I was standing mere inches from the prince by then. "Why would anyone go to such trouble just to impress *you?*"

Alexander twitched and drew back. "Mother said you're after power. That you want my sister and a seat on the council."

"Do you think I want these things?" I said. "You have traveled with me now for *years,* boy. Do you *really* think I want these things?" I could see uncertainty playing at the corner of the prince's eyes. I had only to push a little further. "Do you really think I am the sort of man who wants power?"

The prince hesitated, stammering, "I . . . I . . ."

"You don't know me at all," I said. "I told you what I was after. I told you my dream: understanding, and a peaceful galaxy to seek it in. And to save everyone on this planet if I can. I do not want the Empire. I did not want any of this. We do not get to choose our circumstances or our trials. We can only choose how to respond to them."

Alexander remained silent for a long moment, longer than I'd thought him capable of, truth be told. Then he asked a question I had been asked already a hundred hundred times. "Whom do you serve?"

The Emperor had last asked that question of me. I hadn't had a good answer for him. *Humanity,* I'd said. Or the idea of humanity. I could not tell this red prince I served the Quiet, though perhaps that was true—at least insofar as our purposes seemed aligned.

"The truth," I said, and added, "the good."

The prince sneered, "What in Earth's name does that mean?"

"I don't know," I said, coolly defiant.

Alexander turned away, disgusted. He made it three paces before I said, "But I know protecting our people is good, whatever else may be."

The Aventine prince whirled in a flurry of white cloth. "Mother was right about you," he said. "You're dangerous."

"I am no threat to your house," I said, "whatever your mother may believe."

"If you are what they say you are," the prince said, "prove it."

Hooking thumbs through the loops of my shield-belt, I raised my chin. "What do they say I am, Alexander?"

The boy almost spat. "As if you don't know! The Chosen! The God Emperor reborn."

Even to deny that charge was to confirm it in the mind of the young prince. How could I answer? How could I possibly give Alexander an answer he would accept?

I couldn't.

I could only tell the truth.

"I don't know what any of that means," I said. "I'm only me." The prince's scowl deepened, precisely as I knew and feared it would. Taking one careful step forward, I said, "What do you want of me, Alexander?"

The prince chewed his tongue. "Kneel."

"I'm sorry?" I looked round. We were alone in the gallery. Had he really come here with no guards? Were they waiting in the hall outside?

"Kneel." Alexander's voice was tight with angst, eyes smoldering.

It was foolishness, a hollow exercise of power performed to salve the boy's wounded ego. But it cost nothing, meant nothing, to kneel. My knee bent easily, and I knelt before Alexander as I had before his Imperial father. Not out of obedience, not for principle or for love of the person before me. But for peace.

Alexander slapped me.

The force of the blow turned my head, but did not stagger me. I kept my cheek turned away. "You are *my* servant! Mine!" the prince gasped. Turning only my eyes, I saw his hands were shaking. "You are a knight of the Empire. *My Empire.* My family's Empire! We built it. Not you."

"Cling to your rights, Your Highness," I spoke softly, still not turning to face the prince, "and you may find you cannot hold onto them." It was a threat, and I ought never to have spoken it. A cold anger burned in me, clear and free, almost serene. Alexander raised his hand once more to strike me. Vision splintering, I *chose.*

The prince struck my cheek in just the right way—in just the way I had chosen. The prince gasped and cursed, cradled his newly broken finger.

"Careful," I said, fixing the prince with my coldest glare. Let him guess it was me. Let him know.

The prince's eyes widened, though if he guessed at my powers there was no sign. Embarrassment flowered visibly, flushing up his neck as he stumbled backward, still grasping the injured hand.

"Never forget what you are," he said.

For once, I let someone else have the final word. If we came out of this battle alive, I would have no choice but to put the young prince on ice until he could be returned to Forum.

I was alone again.

But there is alone and *alone*.

"You heard all that, I gather?" I asked, speaking to the shadows.

Valka appeared from behind one of the room's large columns. She'd been listening for some time. I'd picked up the familiar smoke-and-sandalwood smell of her perfume. She must have entered by some door other than the hall, else surely Alexander or the guards I felt sure had accompanied him would have seen her.

There were moments where she truly earned her reputation for witch-craft.

"I did," she said, and seated herself in the window seat where I had been sitting when Alexander arrived, her back to the night and the storm. "He is a problem."

"He is," I agreed, and was shocked to find sadness in my tone. "Would it were not so."

" 'Tis too late for such, I think," she said, and glanced over her shoulder, exposing the glass-edged sharpness of her profile.

Moving to join her, I said, "I know." I did not sit, but stood over her, watching her watch the darkness. What her inhuman eyes saw there I could only guess, unless it was what little the lightnings revealed. Another bolt flashed then, and I saw a forest of alien spires like black teeth in gray gums, ships and weapons alike.

"You don't really think they're waiting for the storm to break, do you?" Valka asked.

Still she did not turn. "No," I said. "They're certainly not waiting for the dawn. I'm sure they'd much rather attack at night." I looked over her head through the glass as if I could somehow see. The smoke of the ruined nuclear plant was lost in the darkness, and the rain had extinguished the flames. But I could feel the weight of the army there and the malice like the pressure of so many thousand eyes. "They're waiting for something else," I said.

"For what?" she asked, and turned her face to me.

"I wish I knew," I said.

"Don't you?"

"Not you too," I replied, and it was a struggle to keep the exasperation from my voice. "I can't see the future."

Valka made a face. "I know that," she almost snapped, voice sharp, "but you must have some idea."

I shrugged. "Reinforcements?" I said. "But what reinforcements do they need? We're hopelessly outmatched. We've no ships. The Wall's shields will hold unless they get inside, which they *will* do. It won't even be hard. Even with our fortifications, we don't have the men to hold the entire wall. Not for long."

"Then we should attack," she said. "Send out the colossi."

"The colossi? Maybe," I said. Lorian had weighed that option hours before, but the storm had made their deployment untenable. Not until the winds died down.

"We cannot do nothing," she said. Valka seized my wrist and looked up at me imploring. *"Do something."* I blinked. What did she expect of me? One of the miracles I barely understood?

"I can't," I said. "I'm not ready. I don't understand enough."

"Do something," she said again. She stood, taking my gloved hand in both of hers. Something clicked in me, like a key turning. Valka was not imploring. She never implored, never begged. Her word was a command.

I did not kneel. She did not ask it of me.

I pressed my forehead to hers, and said, "As you will, then."

CHAPTER 80

BLACK SUN

AS WE HAD LONG believed, Berenike had been watched keenly and closely by intelligences alien to ours, if just as mortal. In the freezing Dark, where the light of the white sun faded at the system's edge, there had lurked for years unknown and unseen a terrible menace of which the black fleet at anchor above our world was but a vanguard. Just how long it had waited there and spun its evil web, I dare not guess. But spun it had, and we were caught in its net.

With our fleet more than decimated, its survivors fled, and the planet's satellite grid in shambles, our first indication that it had stirred from its deeping haunt in the dark at system's edge—our first indication that it existed at all—was the tides. All over Berenike, from the highland lakes to the south's vast shallow seas, the waters rose and spasmed. Rivers flooded their banks, seas retreated and exposed beds untouched by sunlight for thousands of years. The world quaked, and dust fell from the roof above our heads.

But that was only the beginning.

I hurried from the conference chamber where I'd been overseeing a part of our defense and climbed toward the command center, taking the steps three at a time.

Day had come to Berenike, and the gray and trailing clouds were passing, breaking upon the battlements of the Storm Wall. Pale sunlight fell on the landing field, illuminating the Boschian horror of the tableau. The Cielcin ships did not belong, as if the depths of the sea had come to land, or else the artifacts of some distant age had crashed against the shores of our present.

The ships did not belong.

"What's going on?" I demanded. "Have they moved?"

Lorian Aristedes—who from his stooped posture and hooded eyes seemed not to have slept in eons—answered me. "They haven't moved. They're still in their towers, *waiting*."

I pushed past a pair of junior logothetes, advancing toward the false windows that showed the vista beyond and below the wall. Lorian was right, the Cielcin hadn't moved. Their fleet of landing craft still stood like a forest of alien trees along the rim of the landing field, black and implacable, unmoved by the wind. Turning, I spared a glance for the ruined city behind, smoke rising to lick the sky.

Above it all, the white sun rode high and silent, light untouched by the burning of our world, touching all. Though I beheld only an image of that morning sun, the pristine beauty of it smote my heart. There was still light, higher and brighter than any evil or act of man could deface. Though hell had come to Berenike, our world was not yet ended.

The ground shook beneath us, and I gripped the edge of the holograph plate. A rush of voices filled the room at my back as consoles began to chime.

"Movement on the field below!" cried one of the men.

I rounded from the sun and the burning city and turned back toward the landing field.

A solitary figure approached from the arrayed vessels, striding out into the emptiness between siege towers and wall. It was not Bahudde—though that the *vayadan*-general lived I had no doubt. It was a single Cielcin clad in ceremonial white, its cloak and robes snapping and pushing in the hollow airs. Clouds stood overhead, and a colorless light fell through them, muting all the world beneath that distant sun to blacks and whites and dull grays.

"Enhance," I said, moving to stand before the false window.

The image grew, tracked a moment until I beheld the figure plain as though it stood a dozen yards away. Dust and smoke burned about it, threading the fingers of its crown of thorns. One of its two primary prongs curled back and inward, the other straight and tall, giving it a curiously lopsided appearance. Bands of pale gold encircled the horns, hung with chains and gemstones black as night. It wore no mask, only a pair of ornamented goggles with slits over the eyes that gleamed dully red even over the camera feed.

In one clawed hand it clutched the ceremonial spear, tiny silver bells and chimes tied to cords beneath the headpiece. Here then was a *coteliho*, a kind of herald and cornicen come to announce the doom of its master: the

Scourge of Earth. Here then was the mouth of Syriani Dorayaica, the Prophet, the Prince of Princes, the great enemy of man.

Some ceremonial number of steps having been taken, the herald stopped and thrust its staff toward the heavens. The fetish rattled, and I saw the familiar broken circle symbol—like two curling horns—flash atop the spear. And between those curling prongs of metal, wrought of the same iridium by vile and detailed craftsmanship, was the open-fingered sculpture of a six-fingered hand.

The *coteliho* offered no words, for where it stood in no man's land neither its own people nor we could hope to hear its speech or the chiming of its bells. But I saw its fanged jaws part and hinge forward as I had first seen Prince Aranata do so long before.

We could not hear its scream, but we heard the screams that joined with it. All at once that mighty host of the Pale lifted up one voice and shook the very clouds. And from atop each of the hundred-and-more of their dark towers a snapping banner unfurled, not black but a deep, startling blue, each displaying the clawed White Hand that had been the last sight of so many million men across the galaxy. I felt certain then that the heart of every man who held the Storm Wall must break with terror, and the mettle in them melt, for I knew that at that very moment our last defenders each looked out from the fortifications with ashes where their hearts should be. And if they did not break then, surely they broke the moment after, for all in time there arose an evil chanting from the earth below in time to the stamping of feet.

"Velnun! Velnun! Velnun!"

"The hell are they doing?" Pallino asked, keeping his voice low where he stood beside me. The chant was like a distant thunder heard through the walls, barely discernible. But I knew what they chanted by the shape of the herald's mouth on the holograph plate.

"Velnun! Velnun! Velnun wo!"

"What are they saying?" Aristedes asked, half-rising from his seat.

In a dry voice, I answered him. "He comes."

The herald raised its staff toward the Storm Wall once more, and once more the vast army of the Pale shrieked from the shadows of their landing craft. And then something terrible happened, something I could not have predicted.

Night fell in mid-morning, as though some god-like hand had blotted out the sun.

Men gasped and panicked cries sounded on our comms. On the field below, the Cielcin roared again.

"What happened?" an officer asked aloud, terror evident in her tone. I imagined what Leonid Bartosz might say, had he still been among the waking.

"The sun!" came the voice of one of the techs. "Look what they've done to the sun!"

"Black planet, what is it?"

"It must be massive!"

Horror waited and watched in the Dark beyond the stars, and in its time had come to that smoldering city of man. Just how vast it was, no man could say—for no man had seen its black face and lived to tell of it. I alone of all men yet living have stood upon its surface and trod its evil halls. I had seen Cielcin worldships before, fought in warrens carved out in the hollow bowels of an asteroid, but this! This was something on a scale I could scarce imagine. A moon had appeared in Berenike's sky, and the sudden shock of its presence had shaken the shallow seas and set the whole world to shuddering.

"I've seen smaller planets!" Lorian whispered.

That we had no sign of its coming until it blocked the sun was a sign of just how devastated our sensor network was. It should not have existed at all—for surely something so massive could not sail between the stars— yet there it was! I knew it not then, but for the first time I looked with my own eyes upon that greatest citadel of the enemy.

Fortress of iron. Palace of bone. Castle of ice and torment.

Dharan-Tun.

How many soldiers waited aboard or how many slaves toiled in its depths I cannot guess, nor could I wonder in that black instant in what age or place or by what hands it was forged. I could only stand slack-jawed in mingled awe and horror at the sight and the pale limn of the sun shining about its edge.

A small voice murmured, "I guess we know what they were waiting for," and it was a full five seconds before I realized the voice was my own.

Marshaling my wits, I rounded on the officers in the room at my back. "Shoot the herald!" I said, speaking from impulse. The officers around me all hesitated, swaying as if stunned. "Are you deaf?" I howled. "Fire on that Pale!"

A moment after, something coughed through the Storm Wall's

superstructure, and a line of smoke and fire blazed across no man's land and struck that solitary figure. Not a plasma shot, not a bullet. A missile. A rosette flowered on the tarmac, a dull and angry red. Inky smoke pulled away from the smooth plain, revealing cracked concrete and scorch marks.

I nodded to myself, satisfied.

A piercing wail sounded from the Cielcin host arrayed against us, and as I watched bright flashes filled the heavens above. A moment later sirens sounded on several consoles.

"Direct hit on the wall shields above Whitechapel Gate!" one of the technicians shouted.

Lorian kicked his chair sideways and craned his neck to peer at the young lady. "What did they hit us with?"

"Don't know, sir!" she said. "Vaporized on the shield curtain. Some kind of slug."

The little man hissed through his teeth. "Bastards are throwing rocks at us."

"They won't throw anything too big," Bancroft said. "They know we're shielded." The commandant had been strangely silent for some time, shocked I think into a species of defeatist catatonia not unlike the demon that had gripped poor Bartosz.

Commander Aristedes snarled, "Right, then. We'll be playing this one bloody damn close to the chest. There's nothing we can do about that worldship."

"Even if the fleet returns there's nothing we can do about that worldship," dared one junior man.

For a moment, I considered ordering the man from the command center. *Rage is blindness,* I told myself, and paused a moment to master my breathing. "This is *not* the end," I said, speaking just loud enough to be heard. "Do you hear me? This is *not* the end! I have not given my life to this fight once already to die cowering here like a worm beneath a rock!"

The silence that followed was punctuated only by the distant howling of the Cielcin at their landing field. For an instant, no one in the command center moved or made a sound.

Then it happened again.

"Halfmortal," one man whispered.

"Halfmortal." Another.

I cut across the whispers, halted them in their tracks. "Do you want to die?" I rounded on the lot of them, cape swirling about me as I turned. "Do you?" I waited them out, waited for them all to realize the question was not rhetorical. These were officers, technicians of the ODF, not fighters. These were soldiers like Valka had been: men and women enlisting with little expectation of violence. Until recently, Berenike had been a minor transit hub on the road to the frontier. They had not expected to be fighting for their lives against the largest host the Cielcin had ever brought to the field. They had expected to live their short, plebeian lives before trouble came to their shores—if it ever came.

"Fuck no!" Pallino said. Bless him.

"Do you want to die? I said!" I nearly shouted, taking two steps into the room.

"No!" came the choral response.

"Of course not!" I said. "Our fleet will be here in two days! Our angels of retribution! Two days!" I held my fingers up—the first and last in the old warding gesture against evil. "We can survive for two days."

Then the voice of one man was lifted up from the rear of the dim command center. "Are the stories they tell of you true, lord?" I never saw his face. "Did you really die?"

I was about to deny it again, to say that no, that story was simply foolishness.

But Pallino spoke. "Aye, it's true. All of it."

The silence rushed in again and filled the low chamber. The gruff chiliarch had lit a spark in the men about us, an electric tension. In those times when he was silent, all was dark. Something had changed. Looking left and right with my strange vision across that crashing wave of time, I saw the answer I should give—or thought I should give—and gave it.

"I will die again if I must."

Snatches of the uproar about me filtered through, voices tumbling, rising and falling over and under one another as men stood and turned and swore.

"That's impossible!"

"He's mad!"

"—expects us to believe that . . ."

"Halfmortal! Halfmortal!"

"It's true? It can't be true . . ."

And yet beneath the words and loud doubt the tension lingered, wound up as a spring. Belief, of a kind. Hope. "Enough!" I shouted. "We have work to do. Prepare for battle!"

The instant the words escaped my lips, a peal of thunder shook the station, and a signal flared. "They fired on our shields again!" one of the technicians said.

"Bastards'll have to attack the wall overland if they want in here," Pallino said.

"Let them come," Lorian said coolly. "The wall's fortifications will hold. And there's still the colossi."

Commandant Bancroft cleared her throat. "Do we have eyes on that . . . that mothership?"

One of the ODF men answered her. "No ma'am. Orbital Defense grid is gone."

Looking out the false windows, I saw streaks of red and pale gold illuminating the artificially darkened sky and knew it to be the wreckage of our fleet. *One of those stars is Titus Hauptmann,* I remember thinking. The proud lion of the Veil was no more, and it was left to the devil to avenge him.

The false night flared red with the glare of fire, and looking up I saw a red streak falling from the sky. Not the shriek of weapons and wicked flash of impact, but the blaze and heavy burn of descent engines fighting the inexorable tide of gravity. For a moment, the brightness overpowered the holograph plate's adjustments and the whole thing whited out. The earth trembled as something far more massive than the siege towers struck the tarmac with the weight of a mountain landing.

It *was* a siege tower, but that was not all it was. The behemoth stood on three bowed legs, each a pylon a hundred feet high and bent like the leg of some leaping insect. I recognized it at once, had seen such engines used in battle against our starships to devastating effect.

Though it was more massive than the siege towers, its central spire was not filled with *scahari* fighters, but was dominated by a single shaft whose magnetic coils—more than thirty feet in diameter—were designed to accelerate a rod of meteor iron to titanic speeds over a remarkably short distance.

It was a ram.

Cielcin engineers had wrought the evil thing to clamp onto the hulls of starships and crack them open. It had been one way to bypass our shields. I had never seen the things deployed on land before, and yet a moment after the first another landed with a crash and the low growl of descent rockets. Then a third.

"Concentrate fire on those siege engines!" Lorian shouted.

Red light flashed in the false darkness, and the nearest of the rams burst into flames and fell. I felt a thrill of success rush through me. "What are they trying to do?" I asked. "They can't hope to use them on the wall . . ."

"They won't get close . . ." Lorian said.

It turned out they didn't have to.

Thunder cracked the sky, but the thunder was false as the night. It was the sound of the ram hammering. Hammering against the ground. The tarmac buckled, and the steel beams beneath it bent and cracked as the hammer fell again, opening a yawning gash in the surface. The ram exploded in the following instant—too late.

Lights flashed on consoles and alarms filled the command center. In a panicked voice, one of the ODF men said, "They've breached Terminal G!"

In a full, deep voice I'd not known him capable of, Lorian Aristedes shouted, "Pull yourself together, man. Are there people in that terminal?"

"Some of the refugees," said an older woman in ODF grays who had not quite lost her head.

"Soldiers?"

"Captain Lin's men are nearest," said a round-faced tactical officer, one of Lorian's staff. "Guarding the tramway between us and the starport terminals."

"Get them out there!" Lorian said. "And order the refugees back before the Pale get their troopers in. Seal what inner doors you can." He pointed his cane at one of the junior officers. "You. See it done." The man leaped to obey. Lorian hunched in his seat. "We are going to lose people now."

I let those words hang on the air like smoke, and fancied I looked *through* them down on the ruin before us. Arms crossed, I looked down upon the field, upon the smoldering rams and black forces of the Prophet arrayed behind. Swarms of *nahute* flew like clouds over the heads of the enemy, visible at this distance only as a kind of flashing shadow, dark against the dark of the eclipted air.

"We have to send in the colossi," I said. "And whatever air support we can muster."

"Can they fly that side of the Storm Wall?" asked Pallino, speaking for every man in the room.

Looking square at Lorian, I answered him, "We can't afford for them not to."

The intus nodded and gave the order. "What about the terminal?"

"Leave the terminal to me."

CHAPTER 81

THE LABYRINTH AGAIN

DARKNESS AGAIN, BUT NOT the darkest I have known.

The tramway stank, and the red shine of emergency lights above revealed the sure footprint of humanity. Trash plastered the ceramic tiles: food wrappers, sanitary napkins, bottles, and bits of abandoned clothing. I lingered a moment over a plebeian child's toy, a plastic doll dressed like a Sollan legionnaire in faceless helm and red tunic, white mask and armor scuffed and soiled. Its owner must have dropped it when the overflow of refugees had been pushed down the tunnels to the starport from the safety of the Storm Wall fortress.

"Movement ahead!" Pallino shouted, snapping his lance to attention.

" 'Tis one of ours!" Valka said, gently pressing the weapon down.

My own men moved past, forming ranks. The Cielcin could not have reached us so far from the starport—more than three miles of tunnel separated the Storm Wall's hypogeum from the terminal complex—but it never hurt to be careful.

A single trooper emerged from the gloom, armor rattling as he ran. He stopped five paces from my foremost guards. "Lord Marlowe!" He snapped a salute. "Captain Lin sent me to escort you. He's gone on ahead to the starport."

"And the refugees?" I wasted no time. They'd only been sent to the starport in the first place because the fortress was already well past capacity. The Deira bunkers had been designed in an age when Deira's population was a mere four million and projected to double in the coming years. Now it was ten, and space beneath Berenike's last fortress was cramped and close. It would not be long before water would need rationing, and less time before the stink would be enough to kill.

The scout saluted again when he saw me. "On their way, sir."

The tunnel shook, dust falling in little rivulets from the ceiling panels overhead.

Boom. Then again, *boom.*

The colossi were moving, massive feet striking the roof overhead like the slow beat of a drum. "We have to move," I told the scout.

"This way."

In reading accounts or taking in holographs of the battle, you will have a very different perspective than I. Military historians and the amateur enthusiasts who fancy themselves tacticians look at battles in terms of blocks and arrows. Chess pieces, of a sort. In reviewing the situation on Berenike, they will see the line of colossi arrayed on the tarmac above, the line of Cielcin opposite it. They will note the aircraft on both sides and squint at the tangled warrens of the starport and tram tunnels beneath the surface. They will cluck about the errors Hauptmann made, and Bartosz, and Lorian. They will criticize *me,* saying I should have remained in the command center.

They are brave, sitting in their chairs centuries removed from the horrors of war, in ages that will never know the Cielcin because of me. But such worthies have one advantage over me, indeed over the lowest pig-boy-turned-soldier under me: they can see it all. The battle in space, the city, the Storm Wall, the tarmac torn between two mighty hosts, even my tunnels. They can see it all with the eyes of a god—albeit one blinkered and foolish as all men are. With all the time academic comfort can afford, they can see the labyrinth unrolled before their eyes and see clear the path to its center while we pieces in the labyrinth are blind. I do not know the Battle of Berenike as they do. I know only the labyrinth, the strange other world of war that I have spoken of time and time again.

Unwashed faces turned toward us as we entered the starport. The breached terminal was still ahead, and even in the gloom I could see the whites of these refugees' eyes. I felt their silence; the scared, hopeful way they watched me. Waiting for a sign.

Bassander Lin came running forward, his helmet removed, face flushed. Behind, men crouched behind hard field projectors and around columns near the heavy doors from the starport atrium to the terminal halls.

"You're just in time!" he said. "They're inside!"

"Where?"

Lin ignored the question. "You have to get these people out of here!" he said, indicating the refugees pressed against either wall of the atrium and massed on the too-few benches. Some sat on bags, others on the floor. Bassander's men stood by them with stunners drawn, as though they were criminals and not the lowborn desperate for their lives.

"Is everyone out of the terminal?" I asked, pushing past Pallino.

The captain shook his head. "Everyone we could. There was no time."

Valka swore violently in Panthai. Familiar visions of the Cielcin piling stunned humans onto sledges blossomed in my mind, and Lorian's dire pronouncement echoed in my ears. *We are going to lose people now.* It had struck me as a funny thing to say at the time. We had already lost people fighting in the streets, had lost an entire fleet and orbital defense platform. We had been losing people for days. He'd meant civilians, but the word choice stuck with me. What were soldiers then, if not people?

"Valka?" I put a hand on her arm.

Despite the mask covering her face, I felt the flash in those golden eyes. "No. Pick someone else."

"But . . ."

"No, Hadrian. I'm not going."

Chewing my tongue a moment, I turned to Pallino. "Where's Oro?"

"I'll do it!" It took me a moment to recognize the voice. Turning, I saw the unmarked legionnaire press forward. Only then did I recognize her. "I can do it, lord," she said.

I glanced at Pallino. The chiliarch cocked his head, though whether in dismissal or approval was anybody's guess. I did not ask for clarification, but turned to the legionnaire. Cowardice or bravery? I didn't know that, either, and chose to assume bravery. "Very good, Renna."

"Protect the people, you said," Renna said. She had survived the battle in the city and had stuck with me through it all. I could hardly contain my surprise.

"I did."

The roof shook above us again, and I clapped the soldier on the shoulder. "Go then! Quickly!"

Renna turned, and to my almost astonishment shouted orders to the other legionnaires in her unit. "We need to get these people out of here. Let's move!"

Slow dust fell on all assembled, and I turned from Renna as she set about herding the survivors back toward the tramway. Gunshots sounded down a side corridor, and the words *"Snakes! Snakes!"* sounded in my ear. "Snakes in the access tunnels!"

Snakes meant *nahute*. Whirling, I brushed past Bassander for the side door whence the noise had come. *Nahute* meant the Pale themselves could not be far behind.

Pallino roared in my ear, voice amplified by the general band and by the speakers in his breastplate. "Don't let one of them in!"

"Can we seal off the tunnels?" Valka asked.

I did not hear Bassander Lin's answer, for distant thunder roared from the direction I guessed the fleet of alien landing craft stood on the tarmac above. Our lighter wing had come around again, Sparrowhawks or Falcon-IIs striking at the grounded ships and the net of serpentine drones that defended them.

Up above, the colossi marched forward, and the tramp of their mighty feet was like the mountains moving. Great piles of steel two and three hundred feet high marched on legs mighty as the trunks of trees. Guns blazed, and above their fire Lorian Aristedes sat cold and saturnine in his command chair like Kharn Sagara on his throne, tapping his cane against the edge of the console. The Cielcin were moving as we moved beneath them, spilling forward like an oily tide loosed from a sluice gate. They reached the wreckage of their ram and spilled underground like ants swarming.

"You have company," Lorian said.

By then I'd reached the side door and saw the faint smoke rising from the wreckage of a dozen *nahute* lying blasted on the floor. Sword in hand, I pressed forward, my men about me.

We'd come to it at last: the desperate hour.

The fortress breached, our people besieged.

There are endings, Reader, and there in the dark of the ruined starport there were *many* endings. Pale faces shone in the dark at the end of that hall, lit by the ruddy light, their swords like fingers of bone, silver serpents writhing in their fists.

I raised my sword in answer, in salute.

They threw their *nahute* and charged in. Plasma fire and the high-pitched chime of energy lances sounded about me, and some of the Cielcin fell, but their fellows paid no heed. They are not men, and thought little of climbing over their brethren and broodmates to get at us. One leaped at me, sword drawn back to strike. I thrust out with my blade, point catching the leaping xenobite below the ribs and rising, opening it to the shoulder through one of its two hearts.

Its bulk fell against me, and I shoved it aside, staggering a moment against the wall. Awareness filled me of the closeness of those walls in the maintenance tunnel, of the low height of the ceiling and the plumbing that ran along it. So narrow a space, so narrow the eye of that needle through which my survival—and the survival of human life on Berenike—must thread.

The high whine of energy lances sounded and two more of the xenobites fell. Shoving myself from the wall, I slashed at one of the *nahute* as it sped by, cutting it to ribbons. I moved forward, taking the impact of another serpentine drone on my shield. Coming at us straight down a hall, the Pale were at a disadvantage, for these at least wore no shields, and I pressed through to the far end, where to my astonishment I found the hallway empty. There was the other side of the gate Bassander's men were working to fortify with shield projectors and armed men. The Cielcin had not yet assailed it. The dozen dead in the hall behind were only the vanguard. Scouts.

I relayed this to Bassander and said, "We have to seal the breach, same as the tunnels in the city."

"We need explosives!" Valka put in.

"I'll send a team," the Mandari captain said. He did not argue or shout orders at me. This new Bassander was strange.

"Good," I said, "and close that maintenance hall behind us, but be ready to open it if we need to come back."

Bassander's team was three decades of legionnaires headed by a first-grade decurion with the double horizontal stripe on the left cheek of his faceplate above an upside-down triangle that marked him as explosives certified. His entire decade carried the same triangle marker on the left sides of their helms and hard packs on their backs. Units like theirs had mined the access ways from the *Valles Merguli* into the tunnels beneath the Storm Wall.

"It's not far," said the decurion, indicating the overhead signs that marked the way to the various starport terminals. "This way."

We crossed the hall without resistance, moving up a short flight of steps toward a curving hall that led to another tram platform. The earth groaned once more beneath the tramp of the colossi overhead and the impetus of that evil moon. We splashed forward into thin puddles where a burst water main spilled across the floor, ruining carpets and carrying refuse from the thousands that had been cramped into this space mere minutes before.

"Up ahead!" Pallino pointed with his bayonet.

I'd seen them, too.

There were people ahead, running toward us, carrying packs or children or nothing but themselves. Men and women who had been on the wrong side of the main gate when Bassander closed it. I ordered my men against one wall, letting the crowds swarm past. There were still hundreds of them. Thousands. Too many.

"Get behind us!" I called out, voice boosted by the speakers in my suit. "Back toward the Storm Wall." I hoped that they would make it, and pressed past. In the distance, I heard a man yell, then shriek. It was no sound a human throat ought to make, high and piercing, like a pig skewered on the hunt. The sound died almost as quickly as it had begun.

Shoving a big man out of my way, I skirted the throng, shouting for them to hurry back all the while. I was glad of my helmet and the suit's air cyclers, for surely the air of that close space was hot with the fetid damp of breathing, stuffy and claustrophobic.

"Out of the way!" I cried.

Pallino joined me. "Everyone to the right! Move! Move!" He lowered his truncheon toward the oncomers, and the sight of the muzzle and the white spike of the bayonet gave them pause. They crushed right, making a channel through which we could pass. Following Pallino and a trias of hoplites, I surged forward.

More screams rose to greet us, desperate and frenzied and punctuated by cruel, cold laughter. Beneath it all, the buzzing sound of the drones feeding echoed up the hall. Here the stragglers scrambled on, hurrying past us in their desperation to be away. I prayed the Cielcin did not find a way around the retreating throng, lest we were sending them to their deaths. The tiles in the chamber beyond the hall were smeared with blood, walls spattered where the drones had drilled their way through unprotected civilians. I stepped over the husk of a woman, fighting the temptation to duck as two *nahute* hissed overhead. Pallino had told me long ago that proper Sollan officers don't duck.

In the open, a shot will find you crouching as easily as standing, he'd said. *Plus the men don't like it.* That had always stuck with me. *The men don't like it.*

Another of the drones pinged off my shield as I hurried forward.

The Cielcin emerged from the dimness, white masks and horns

seeming to float above bodies black in the gloom. I remember little of the chamber, the emergency lighting full and red against the shuttered stalls and service counters, the tiles slick beneath my feet. Shots flew past me, striking drones and warriors alike. Here and there, stolen shields flashed in answer. Writing now, I can hardly believe them the same species that surrendered to me on Emesh. The difference between a beaten Cielcin like Uvanari and this *horde* of the Pale King was like night and day.

"Forward!" I cried, and raised my sword to parry a blow from one of the Pale. The sword broke on mine, blade clattering to the floor. I turned, and struck the head off the demon, shoving its body to the ground. The terminal could not be far, for the force of the enemy ahead was beyond counting. They must have climbed down through the shattered roof.

The roof.

The whole chamber rang like a bell, and I had visions of a metal foot large as an armored tank striking the tarmac and the metal reinforcements beneath it. On the field above, Lorian's artillery had engaged the enemy. Colossi and lighter wings alike charged forward against the siege towers and ground troops marching beneath the banner of the white hand. There was a door ahead, low and wide enough that ten men might walk abreast. Through it I saw the hulking white shapes I'd feared. The chimeras had come. The Demons of Arae. A dozen at least, with untold hundreds of *scahari* warriors about them, screamers hot for blood.

"At least that giant isn't here," Pallino said, voice flat.

"Yet," I said darkly, and glanced at Valka. "Can you do something about those hybrids?"

I could almost hear her savage grin. "Give me a moment."

The whole chamber shook again, and I heard something my brain did not at once understand. A squealing, a heavy metal groan like the creaking of timbers in an antique sailing vessel. How I heard it at all over the noise of the fighting I cannot say, nor explain the sense of dread that flooded me even before my conscious mind realized what was coming.

The ceiling broke, metal arches buckling, bending beneath a weight greater than any their designers had predicted. And then it came crashing down: a foot and metal thigh six times the height of a man, broader than the broadest tree. It crashed into the center of the terminal platform, crushing men and Cielcin alike beneath it. The soldiers drew back, carving a space around the foot of the downed colossus. I had a brief impression of movement, as if the hulking machine were a shark covered in lesser fish or a wolf swarmed by mice. There were black shapes clinging to handholds on the surface, and with a shock I realized the Pale were *clinging* to it, had climbed the legs to the platforms about the body of the walking machine to fight the gunners and grenadiers on the catwalks there.

The wind rushed in, whistling through fingers of torn metal and broken tarmac, and for an instant both armies stood still. Dust settled. Smoke rose. Above our heads, the black sky peered in, and high in those heavens I beheld the limn of that occulted sun and the dark outline of the worldship peering down at us like the pupil of some immeasurably vast eye. And looking up I knew that we had failed. I'd failed. We might have sealed one breach, but two?

Cielcin warriors leaped from the platforms above, landing cat-like amongst my men. Still more crawled headfirst along the leg of the damaged colossus, moving like crabs toward us, gripping the machine's carapace with fingers and toes. Even as I watched, a shot tagged one of the beasts between the shoulder blades. It fell thirty feet and struck the terminal floor.

"We're never going to close the breach now!" Pallino's voice rang in my ear.

"I know!" I said.

"And we can't stay here either!"

"I *know!*" I said more forcefully.

The sound of thunder rolled in the distance, though whether it was true thunder or the sound of the Falcons was anybody's guess. I cut down a passing *nahute,* drawing back with two men behind a pillar. The great foot of the colossus was moving, was still drawing power from its reactor, still trying to rise from the pit it had fallen into.

Frantic fingers changed comms channels. "Lin!" I waited for the Mandari captain's reply before asking, "Are the survivors secure?"

"Not all of them. We're pushing them back along the tunnels as we speak."

They'll never make it, I thought, screwing my eyes shut. "Can you seal the tramway behind them?"

"We were going to hold the gate," he said.

"Damn the gate!" I said, "I need you *here*. One of the colossi broke through the roof—we're pinned down!" One of the chimeras chose that moment to scream, its horrid battle cry scraping at the vaulted ceiling above our heads.

Lin did not answer at once. "But . . ."

"That's an *order,* captain!" I did not wait for any argument. I killed the line. When we had parted, the Mandari captain had been my superior. Now I was a Knight Victorian, and even had it not been for Bassander's odd change in attitude toward me, that change in rank was enough to guarantee his obedience. Bassander was a soldier through and through, an officer of the most classic kind.

Shots rang down from above, and looking I saw a knot of grenadiers crouched on the hip of the colossus above, each secured by tethers of whiskered carbon. One of the chimeras launched itself toward them, not slowing at all as it hauled itself upward. One of the incendiary rounds broke on the creature's shields, and the men tried to retreat. Iron hands seized the foremost of the fire team and tore one leg off at the hip. Blood issued from the torn stump, and the chimera beat the man in the face with his own thigh before tossing the torn limb aside.

His head followed, followed by another man. There was nothing I could do from my vantage point on the ground. The chimera crawled back and forth over the metal leg, moving from soldier to shrinking soldier. Until one man unclipped himself from his line and half ran, half tumbled from his place on the sloping surface of the machine and threw his arms around the neck of the alien warrior. The surprise weight knocked the chimera clean off the colossus, and man and xenobite fell back toward the terminal floor.

Somewhere in between, the both of them erupted in scarlet flame. The soldier must have detonated one of the charges in his bandoleer, sacrificing himself to take out the enemy.

He was braver than I ever was. Braver . . . or more foolish. Or perhaps they are the same thing.

Beside me, Valka swore in Panthai. I glanced at her. I thought we'd been separated in the fighting. "Are you all right?"

She only nodded.

"Stay by me," I said, and put a hand on her arm.

"We can't stay here," she said.

Breathing a bit ragged, I replied, "Lin's coming."

I could practically feel her eyes widening. "But the people . . ."

"He sent them back down the tramway. He's going to mine the tunnel entrance."

" 'Twon't hold them back for long," she said. "They should never have been out here."

"There's not enough room in the bunkers," I said. "There's still not enough room." The tram tunnels were the last resort, the last refuge for the thousands that would fit nowhere else.

The pressure of her unseen eyes vanished, and she turned her head away. "What about us?"

"Over the top," I said, and pointed with my sword at the slant of the giant's leg where it descended into the chamber.

Valka looked at me. "You're mad."

"We can't stay here."

"We can lead them deeper into the tunnels," she said.

That gave me pause. "Do you think we can get up under their fleet?"

She thought about this for an instant. "Maybe we can get close."

"Lorian!" I changed comms channels again. When the intus's voice came in over the comm, I asked him the question again.

"That's out past the edge of the starport," he said, and my heart sank, visions of the earth opening to swallow that forest of dark towers crumbling in my mind's eye. "But . . ."

"But what?" I glanced sharply at Valka.

Aristedes's reply came haltingly as he studied the relevant schematics. "There's a tunnel. Tramway maybe. Looks like it runs out to those perimeter towers." I knew the ones he meant, the little mushroom-like structures that stood at intervals along the uttermost edge of the starport landing field where the port authority had its stations.

"Good enough," I said.

"I can mark it for you," Lorian said, meaning on the suit's display.

"Do it," I said.

Valka cut in. "Sapping one tunnel won't destroy the whole landing fleet."

"Do you have a better idea?"

She was silent.

"Lorian," I asked, "are there still rockets in any of the blast pits?"

CHAPTER 82

THE DEPTHS BELOW

ON THE FIELD ABOVE, the battle raged. The colossi—hemmed in by the sinkhole that had swallowed one of their number—retreated and took up a defensive position nearer the Storm Wall itself. They could not risk losing another of the goliath machines. I imagined Lorian grinding his teeth at his display, cursing himself for a fool. It was easy to picture the fellow as a kind of impatient spider, ordering the colossi back to within the protective cordon of the wall and its guns.

The Cielcin, I later learned, had not followed them, finding the Storm Wall's shields and guns—with their overlapping fields of fire—wholly impenetrable to attack on an open field. Even the *nahute* kept their distance, or followed their masters down the twin breaches in the tarmac to the terminal halls below.

The black fortress of *Dharan-Tun* hung above all, the corona of the blackened sun white around its edge. I saw it again before ducking into a side passage after Valka, though at our great distance I little guessed at the dark towers and channels that ran across its surface. The forests of steam-work pipes and oceans of frozen air, the grub farms near the surface where slaves—human and Pale alike—toiled beneath the whip. Nor could I guess at the number of those slaves, nor the torments they endured. And yet they all were there, hidden in the shadow of that eclipse. And there too watched and waited the owner of that White Hand, surveying its triumph.

Syriani Dorayaica.

Valka's shouting brought me back to myself, and I followed her and Bassander Lin into the side passage. The Mandari captain had come forward with nigh on a thousand men—leaving the collapsed tramways behind them. It was cruel sealing so many people in such cramped quarters.

Cruel and desperate, but desperation was not so bad as desertion, as leaving them to die.

We could not hope to win the battle in the fight in the terminal—there were too many. But Bassander's men had turned the tide for the moment, along with the grenadiers on the flank of the colossus above.

The empty hall echoed to the sounds of our feet, one of the hundreds of similar tunnels the dock workers and starport custodial staff used in maintaining the complex. We hurried on, three men abreast, following the map Lorian had given us.

We had not far to go.

Fifty men had followed us into the tunnel, led by Bassander, Valka, and myself. Pallino had stayed behind with Oro and Doran to command the force in the terminal proper. A silver thread projected on the hall by my suit's entoptics led the way, around blind corners and down narrower passages toward the place Lorian had marked for us.

Somewhere up ahead was a cargo ship, the *Kupari,* whose fuel cells— along with a single remote-detonated plasma grenade—would be precisely the thing we needed. It was not the closest ship to the terminal, not by half . . . but it *was* the closest to the lonely tramway that ran through the undeveloped portion of the landing field toward the port authority watchtowers. The inner bulkhead was open as we approached, and the outer hatch opened on a wheel-lock.

The wind rushed in, whistling over the titanium and the ceramic outer shell. Beyond, white tiles greeted us, dust-streaked and burned black. The *Kupari* stood above us, a silver finger burned black itself in places, surface ionized and corroded. It looked in every way like one of the rockets of utmost antiquity, red-finned and ice-cauled where the fuel cells were kept cold, their contents held under extraordinary pressure. The cells themselves formed a girdle near the base of the lifter, near the aftermarket repulsor nacelles her owner had welded on to offset some of the payload. She had dozens of them, each about eight feet long and about a cubit in diameter.

"How many do we need?" Lin asked. The cells contained a chemical accelerant that assisted with the primary drive—a primitive, hydrogen-oxygen burning rocket. The *Kupari* was no interstellar craft, was little more than a surface-to-space freighter, one that would park itself in the hold of some large ship and ride along to its next stop. It was as elementary as rocketry got, riding explosives to the stars.

It was exactly what we needed.

"Four or five should do," Lorian answered when I repeated the question.

One of the soldiers chipped in, "There should be a float pallet around the bay somewhere, sirs . . ."

"Can we carry them?" Valka asked.

"If we put four or six men on each," Bassander said, "but that doesn't leave much for defense if it comes to fighting."

Pushing past him, I shouted orders at three of the men who'd followed us into the pit, eyes wandering among the gantries and fuel arms attached to the fuselage of the glorified missile in whose shadow we stood. I could not see the sun or the great vessel that blocked it, but so deep in the well of that pit I could see the stars, bright and clear and pure through the lazy coils of cloud.

Turning back to Bassander Lin and to Valka, I said, "Then we had best hope it does not come to fighting." The thought of a stray shot or sword blow flooding the cramped quarters with chemical accelerant was not a happy one. "Quickly now!" But I had found what I was looking for, and moved toward it. A spout ran along the inside of the pit, shielded from the main shaft behind the inner curve of the artificial crater. The ladder ran up it for more than fifty feet to where the nose cone and upper sections of the *Kupari* rose above the landing field. It was not a short climb, but we had a moment. Ignoring the chastisement of Valka and my guards at my back, I mounted the first rungs. I knew I could not stand on the surface without risking the attention of the Pale, but I could peer out at the world above.

I reached the top and raised my eyes above the lip of the crater, bracing myself against the far side of the shaft where a carved foothold waited, trying not to think about the fall beneath me. There was the black sun high in the sky above, and there the dark forest of siege towers at one margin of my world. I could not see the blasted nuclear plant so near the ground, nor spy the perimeter towers behind that thicket of evil spires. But I saw the Cielcin plain enough, massing in the shadows of their ships. I hoped I was far off enough not to be a target for the *nahute* that moved like shoals of fish in the air above them.

Turning my head to look through fields of smoke and smoldering fires, I beheld the burning wreckage of the downed colossus. The fallen colossus—four-legged and with a body like a saucer—lay shattered and burning. Its weight hadn't broken the vaults of the terminals below. Its fall had. Looking past it to the wall, I could just make out the other platforms standing at attention. Bipeds, tripods, quadrupeds—and the hexapods largest of all. Our iron guardians. I knew plenty of strategoi and logothetes in the Defense Ministry who argued the massive war machines were impractical. Foolhardy. Expensive and impossible to maintain. But one could not deny: they were breathtaking.

The mightiest of these stood easily three hundred feet high, dwarfing the men and smaller tanks that clustered about its legs. Red lights glinted in the narrow slit about its equator from which its drivers watched, weapons at the ready. The Cielcin had given up trying to engage those mighty war machines, seemed clustered instead about the spots where the tarmac had been breached about the smoldering wreckage of the colossus and the alien ram.

The Cielcin had set up a line of cannons along the right flank of their army. Bristling, spiny things of the same darkly organic design as their armor, ribbed and corded as muscle tissue. As I watched, they fired, thunder slapping the air. One of our Falcons fell, transformed into a tumbling ball of flame. And above that, upon the uttermost crown of the Storm Wall, barely noticeable against the blackness, I saw the winged shapes of our Irchtani beating the air.

Something nearer at hand caught my eye. The glint of light on white metal, on ceramic, on bone. And there it was, huge and hideous and very much alive. The *vayadan*-general Bahudde emerged from the midst of its army. Even at this distance, it looked the worse for wear: armor dinted, the linkages of one arm exposed, the light of one red eye put out. But the creature's brain and coiled spine were yet intact, safe in some jar in its chest. I bared my teeth involuntarily.

The beast strode out past the foremost ranks of its men, arms raised. Above it, the clouds parted in fire as another siege tower—this one larger than the rest—smashed down from the heavens. Its engines blazed to slow its descent, filling the air with the noise of fire. Our lighters were nowhere to be seen—had the xenobites' cannons done for them? And what was in the massive dropship?

"Hadrian!"

I must have lingered longer than I thought, and slid quickly back down the ladder, ducking back into the scorched landing pit.

"See anything?" Valka asked.

"That giant's still alive."

"Fuck me!" One of the men swore. "The one from the city?" Bassander cleared his throat, but the fellow didn't seem to get the message. "The one that looks like a fucking *baby*?"

"Language, soldier," the captain said, acid in his words.

Facing the vulgar soldier, I said, "The same. They've called down another tower—bigger than the rest."

"Dorayaica?" Bassander asked.

I shrugged. "Could be, but it looked more like a cargo rocket. Like they've brought the heavy artillery."

"Fuck me with a lance!" the soldier swore, turning away.

"Order!" Bassander clipped the fellow with the butt of his lance, hard but not hard enough to do any real harm. "Pull yourselves together. We have work to do."

There was no float pallet to be found, and in the end, it took a half dozen men apiece to lift and carry the big fuel cells. It was slow going, for the cells were heavy and the halls just wide enough to accommodate the men and their load.

"It's not far," Bassander said for what felt like the dozenth time. Somewhere ahead was a tram platform and tunnel that ran directly beneath the enemy army. "With any luck, there'll be a tram in the platform."

As he spoke, I had visions of loading the fuel cells aboard a train and sending that unmanned down the tunnel. *Lorian Aristedes, you've done it again.*

The Cielcin it seemed had not penetrated so far back into the complex from the holes torn in the tarmac, or else they'd not found their way into the maintenance passages as yet. If Lorian's maps were correct, we would remain in access corridors until we hit the concourse, and then it was another five hundred feet or so to the tramway platform. That would be the point of maximum danger.

Tap.

Was it my imagination? Or had I heard something coming behind?

Near the rear of the line, I turned, looking back into emergency-lit gloom. Nothing but red darkness greeted me. Cautious, I slid my sword from its holster, fingers ready on the trigger.

"What is it?" Valka asked.

I shook my head, nodded for her to move on ahead of me.

We kept moving, progress slowed by the weight of the canisters. Sounds from the fighting still played over the comm, and Pallino's voice overrode the din. "You all best hurry up, Had. We won't hold long here."

"Get them air support, damn it!" I growled at Lorian, ears pricking for the sound again.

Tap-tap.

Memories of the way Iubalu had hounded us in the bowels of its ship came back to me, and I moved a little faster, butting up against the rear of our column. It took a measure of self-control to slow my pace, to allow space to form again between us. I was certainly not imagining things. Something had found us in the dark. I tried to call on my new vision, but could see only the hall about me and our small caravan playing out around me, refracted across countless variations of the same slow passage.

Tap. Tap-tap.

A low grinding like the noise of chainsaws sputtering to life roared up not twenty paces behind. The number of possible presents—possible hallways—fractured in my new awareness, little infinities spawning larger ones. I saw them in my vision before I saw them with my eyes, before I turned my head. The *nahute* had been slithering along the ceiling, invisible along the piping and the ductwork there. Five of them leaped at once, and at once I turned, vision bright and clear. Highmatter kindled in my fist, and taking hold of the vision I stepped from one instance of our hallway to the next, to a place in possible time where my blade sliced clean through all five of the metal drones. Some unconscious part of me, I think, had recognized the danger before my waking mind and imported that danger to my vision, clarifying it. The torn devices tumbled in pieces around me, and I stood a moment open-mouthed, shocked that it had worked.

So shocked that the vision broke and I was left standing there amazed when the snakes' owner leaped from the darkness. The *scahari* moved like an ape, bounding forward on hands and feet. I had a momentary impression of black claws and glassy teeth before it struck me full in the chest with its horned crest. I hurtled backward with it on top of me, claws sinking into my suit's environment layer. I felt bruises flower and blood well between the fibers even as the gel layer hardened to protect my flesh.

But for once in all my life, I'd managed to *keep* my sword. Any ordinary blade would have been useless slapping an armored opponent in the back, but Sir Olorin's sword was anything but ordinary. Despite the creature's weight on my chest and arm, I could still bend my wrist, still push the blade effortlessly down into the flesh of the creature atop me. Black blood flowed, and the beast sagged against me.

I threw it off and—rolling over—made to scrabble to my feet.

Clawed hands seized me, slashing my white cape. Only on my knees, I fell, sword punching a hole in the concrete floor. A shot rang out, and dead weight collapsed on me once more. Rough hands seized mine and hauled me to my feet, pulling me clear of the enemy.

"Run!" I cried out, waving my hand.

The men carrying the payloads began to trot, moving in time with a chant begun by one of the triasters to keep them from jostling the dangerous accelerant. Bassander took the lead, his own sword—the sword he'd taken from Admiral Whent on Pharos—lighting the way like a beacon.

It wasn't fast enough.

Tearing my mangled cape from my shoulders, I turned and faced the other Pale who had come. Four of them stood there masked and armored. Their leader had only one eye in its mask. The other side bore the image of the Hand.

"Go on!" I called to the guards behind me. "Protect the others."

"But!" Valka said, and I sensed her take a step nearer.

"They'll need you if any of those metal monsters catch up!" I said, and waved her back.

I do not dare write down Valka's curse.

"Noyn jitat," I said under my breath, knowing I would not hear the end of it if we escaped Berenike alive.

Having seemingly learned their lesson from the two Pale dead at my feet, the others kept their distance, shrinking from the advance of my moonlight blade. They clustered behind their leader, who I felt certain must be shielded. Step by careful half-step, I pressed forward. They drew back. They had no *nahute,* no firearms, would not risk their own lives on explosives in so confined a space.

"Tuka . . . devil *ne?"* their leader asked, struggling with the terminal consonant on the human word *devil.*

"I am," I said, standing straighter.

The commander drew back, breath hissing past glass teeth. *"Numeu ti-Shiomu, yukajji!"* it said. *You belong to the Prophet, vermin.*

"If your master wants me," I said, trying not to be fazed by this grim pronouncement, *"marerra o-tajun civaqari eza velenamuri ti-koun!"*

Tell it to come and take me!

That said, I took three great halting steps forward, blade raised and pointed at the enemy, ready to strike. Then the most incredible thing happened: the Cielcin turned and ran. Perhaps they realized they were outmatched. Perhaps there was no way they might take me alive. Perhaps they meant to lead me into a trap and hoped I'd charge after them. Acting fast,

I drew my plasma burner and fired left-handed. The violet arc lanced out. Too late.

They were gone.

I found the others on the tram platform. Bassander only nodded when I emerged from the darkness and the rearguard put up their guns at the sight of me. Valka sniffed and turned her head.

"Are you hurt?" she asked stonily, still caring.

"They ran," I said. "Didn't like their chances against a shielded man with this." I waved the unkindled sword.

The Tavrosi woman made a clicking sound with her tongue.

"There's no tram," said the vulgar soldier from earlier.

Bassander jumped down from the platform to the rails below. "Then we carry them."

The soldier was not alone in swearing.

"Pass the payload off where you can. Fresh arms. Double time!" And to Lin's credit he stowed his own blade and helped a brawny decurion muscle the first of the canisters onto the tracks. "Marlowe, guard the tunnel mouth." *There* was a flash of the old Lin. The heat of the moment had driven his holy terror of me from his mind a moment, and he added, "We'd know if they'd breached the tunnel at the other end, right?"

"It would be on our sensors," Lorian confirmed when I relayed the question. "Hurry, Pallino's men are getting it hard."

"If this doesn't distract them," I told the good commander, "I don't know what will."

In a matter of moments, Bassander's men traded the canisters down to their fresher comrades on the tracks below—save where a few of the hardier volunteers kept going. The Mandari captain and his men vanished into the darkness, and we had only the slow rattle of their armor to keep us company on the platform. There were little more than a dozen of us, and we were alone in the eye of the storm.

"This is all too easy," Valka said.

"You call this easy?" I asked, unable to keep the pain from my voice. I knew what she meant, but my encounter with the Cielcin in the hall was still with me, and my blood was cold as the sounds of Pallino's men fighting rang constant in my ear.

"Bastards got behind us!"

"Fall back! Fall back!"

I kept waiting to hear the two messages I feared to hear most of all: that Pallino was dead, or that the Cielcin had gotten into the tram tunnels between the starport and the Storm Wall. I felt that one or both was inevitable, and that one or both must come soon. I kept reviewing the starport map in the corner of my vision. If we went by the main concourse, we could rejoin Pallino in minutes.

"The fuckers are breaking off!" came one voice. "They're pulling back."

"Hit 'em hard!"

I glanced at Valka, brows contracting beneath the mask. "Pallino." I pressed fingers to reseat the bone conduction patch behind my ear. "What's going on?"

"Not sure, Had! They're pulling back deeper into the terminals."

"Into the terminals?" I asked. "Toward us?"

"Might be! Might be they just got enough down here now they're spreading out. It's thick as hell here!"

Fingers still on the patch beneath the undersuit, I said, "We're almost there. Just need a little more time."

"Damn it!" the chiliarch replied. "Damn it. Had, I think they found the tunnels."

My blood—already cold—froze over. Bassander had left a small rear-guard detachment with the refugees when he mined the tramway tunnels, and a few hoplites with hard shields and a plasma howitzer or two could hold a narrow way against a horde, but not forever. I had visions of the Cielcin and their *nahute* chewing their way down those tunnels like lightning down a wire and clenched my jaw. I thought of the soldier, Renna. She was going to die.

"We have to get them out of there," I said. And there was still the matter of Bahudde's siege tower to consider. What had the *vayadan*-general called down from its master's dark fortress?

Valka massaged her neck. "We can't do anything for them. The Storm Wall is full. There's nowhere to go. We have to hope this," she nodded at the tramway and Bassander's makeshift bomb, "will distract them."

"We need to hit them hard," I said.

"How?" she demanded.

I cast about for an answer, circling where I stood, but there was nothing. Growling, I looked back along the tramway. "Lin, tell me you're almost done."

"Nearly there!" came the Mandari captain's groaning reply. It sounded as though he was carrying one of the fuel cells himself. "This had better work."

Silently, I agreed with him, and seized Valka's hand. She did not pull away, not even when the sounds of hurrying feet slapped the concourse in the dark ahead, back the way we had come. I took a half-step forward, ordering the small knot of exhausted men around us to form a cordon, hoplites in front.

"Done!" Bassander's voice crackled in my ears. "On our way back."

A full squad of Cielcin appeared, running hunched and bow-legged, clearly hunting.

"*Yukajjimn!*" one said, jostling its brother. Whatever had made the Pale in the tunnel retreat had no effect on these. The Cielcin fanned out, circling our little knot. Bassander would be back in moments. How long should it take for his men to run back? Five minutes? Six? Less, if all they needed was to be within firing distance.

I let go of Valka's hand, raised my sword.

"Run, little worms!" one of the xenobites said. "Run and hide!" Its brethren all laughed.

"*Veih ioman!*" I called back. "No more!"

I felt strangely naked without my cape, but drew myself up to my full height all the same, the better to stand as near to eye-to-eye with the enemy as was possible. The Pale leaped from either side, fast as cavalry. There must have been thirty of them, more than twice the number of men who'd remained on the platform. I heard a cry as one of ours went down, crushed beneath the bulk of two inhuman berserkers. Pressing forward, I sliced clear through one of the attackers, sinking into a low guard, blade thrust straight out.

"Stick close!" I said to Valka, throwing an arm between her and the Pale. Plasma arcs burned around me, violet cutting the air and boiling it even through the insulating layers of my suit. The Cielcin retreated, losing four or five of their number in the brief conflagration. Behind me, I heard the tinny sound of a spent heat sink clattering to the floor.

"Your time is almost up! Not long! Not long now!" one of the xenobites said, teeth gnashing beneath the lip of its mask. "*Velnuri mnu.*"

But the lull in combat lasted only so long as it took the Cielcin to half-encircle us again. Again they leaped, pincering from either side. Again I rushed forward, hewing at their weakened center, trying not to think about the noise one of our men had made as the creatures felled him.

There must have been just over twenty of them remaining. There were perhaps ten of us. Flames smoldered on padded benches, and the cherry-red glow of plasma scoring arced on the walls.

Not long indeed.

Valka went down beside me. Something had caught her ankle, and whirling I found one of the berserkers crawling across the floor, dragging a leg that left a black smear on the tile floor. Even as I turned, Valka kicked it mightily in the face, knocking its mask off. I had a brief impression of round, hollow eyes beneath the smooth ridge of brow. Before I could get to her, Valka got the muzzle of her antique repeater between her and that face. Fired.

Then it was left to me to haul her out from beneath the monster.

Fire rained about us, and I turned my head in time to see a squad of men returning up the hall, Bassander Lin at their head, firing his lance, bayonet flashing dully in the red gloom. They made the platform in seconds.

"We need to move quickly!" Bassander said, already brushing past. The Cielcin lay dead and dying about us, bodies mingled with the bodies of our own fallen men. The captain stepped blithely over human and inhuman alike, lingering only to wave to the survivors—leading from the front. "This way!"

We had to put distance between ourselves and the blast, had to close distance with Pallino's survivors, because the minute our makeshift bomb went off, there was no telling what the xenobites would do.

Then came the call I feared most that bloody day.

"They're in the tunnels!" said one.

"Must have cleared the rubble!" said another.

I swore an oath to make even Valka blush. "Bassander!"

"Not yet!"

I was glad at least I could not hear the screams. How many had Lorian packed back into the Storm Wall? How many were left squeezed into that tunnel, close as fugue-sleepers? Ten thousand? Twenty? There had been hundreds of thousands in the starport when the attack began, and the tunnels beneath the Storm Wall were already well past capacity, and Lorian's efforts to save everyone could as well damn them to a slow death safe in the bunkers. Too little air, too little water, too much heat. They might hold 'til the fleet came, but if they failed? Starvation, pestilence, and thirst would claim us all.

"Now!" The captain produced a detonator wand. He drew to a stop, the better to ensure he made no mistakes. He flicked the cap up, and his thumb down.

Thunder. White heat burned even so far down the hall. I felt the wave rush over us, saw the distant glow of fire. And then?

There was another explosion, deeper, darker than the first. Lorian hooted in my ear, and I guessed the plan had worked. On the surface above, the earth split, heaving two of the siege towers skyward as the vaults below erupted. One rocket crashed quiescent to the earth below, the other buckled and burst as it fell, erupting in a nimbus of fire that consumed the other downed vessel and the hundreds of *scahari* about them.

As above, so below.

As Hauptmann's fleet had been the victim of a runaway matter-antimatter cascade, so the destruction of those two siege towers fanned out, breaching fuel containment in three more of the ships around. In moments, a full third of the Cielcin landing craft were reduced to burning slag, and thousands of the creatures nearest were swallowed in the firestorm.

Underground, I knew nothing of this.

Underground, I knew only the strange hollering of the Pale as they got the message. Something in the air twanged, and the tenor shifted as the enemy reeled, confused. We'd struck them a mighty blow. Thus we returned to the chamber where the colossus had broken through. Its leg had shifted, splayed out so that it made a shallow incline from floor to earth above. There the survivors of Pallino's unit clustered in the midst of that hall, pressed into knots about the foot of the fallen colossus.

Bassander and I fell into step beside one another, each of us cutting a swath through the enemy. Swords that once had clashed with one another rang then side by side, and the enemy fell back, parting before the onslaught of those unstoppable blades.

"Took you long enough!" Pallino shouted, sounding the whistle that made his men shift ranks, rotating fresh men to the front.

"We ran into some trouble!" I shot back. "Is this all there is?" I gestured at the knot of men about him, mingled hoplites and peltasts standing— each bracing the man in front of him—in a box formation against the wall and the ruined machine.

The chiliarch shook his head. "I sent Oro and three hundred men after them into the tunnels, and there are some that got cut off nearer Terminal G, where the first breach is." He pointed. I pulled Valka through the defensive lines, ducking a blow from one Cielcin screamer as we went. The creature fell a moment after, struck down by the hoplites at the front of the line. "We can't stay here!"

"We can't abandon the refugees!" I shouted back, clambering onto the lip of the machine beside.

Pallino seized me by the shoulders. "We're no good to them dead. We need to *move*." He pointed up the leg of the colossus and out onto the surface.

"Over the top?" I asked, echoing the words Valka had said were madness.

"Over the top."

CHAPTER 83

NO MAN'S LAND

I REACHED THE LIP of the tarmac just behind the first wave, scrambling hand over foot to clear the titan's leg and allow the men behind to clamber up. Below, I could see the last rank of hoplites holding their ground against the horde below. Still a knot of the grenadiers held forth upon the hip of their downed colossus, keeping the space about them clear enough for us to establish a beachhead on the surface.

"Back to the wall?" Valka asked, sticking close to my side, gun drawn. She fired past me.

"Yes!" I said, trying not to think about all we left behind in the tunnels below. Still, I knew Pallino was right, knew we needed to stay alive, to fight. Wind tore around us, and looking up once more I saw the shape of clouds boiling across the sky. Soon even the black sun would be obscured. Looking past the ranks of the enemy, I saw the ruin of their fleet. Angry flames burned orange against the sky, and even half a mile off bright cinders floated on the breeze before my eyes. And there—ahead and apart from the main body of the enemy—stood the massive landing tower I had seen.

Speaking as much to Lorian and the command center as to Valka and the men about me, I said, "We're going to lose everyone in those tram tunnels unless we can draw the enemy out. Can you open the rear of the tunnel?"

I could almost hear Lorian shaking his head. "The minute I do that, they'll stampede one another and all the people inside."

"Tell them to clear a space!"

"There is no space to clear, Hadrian!" the intus shouted. "The hypogeum is packed to bursting already."

"Open the bloody gates, Lorian!"

The commander wasted no time. "If I do that, Hadrian, people will die!"

"If you don't do it people will die, damn it!"

"I can't do it," Lorian said. "I can't jeopardize the lives of everyone in this facility for the sake of a few more."

"Damn your eyes, Aristedes! Do as I say!"

A hand touched my arm, and I started.

It was Valka. Her grip tightened on my arm. "He's right."

I tore my arm away. "Do as you will!" A dull concussion sounded near at hand, making me flinch. One of the grenadiers still taut on his line on the hip joint above us fired again, sending a pair of Cielcin sailing through the air. Whirling, I opened my mouth to give Aristedes a new set of orders . . . and stopped dead.

Doom.

Doom-doom.

A sepulchral drumming filled the air, deep sound echoing across that vast, empty plain. The Cielcin answered the sound, whooping and calling out on the wind in words not even I could understand.

"What's going on?"

Clearly, some sign or command had been given, though what it portended was any man's guess. The drumming continued, and all the while my men climbed from the depths below, pulled onto the plain beneath the shadow of the fallen colossus's saucer-like body.

Doom.

Doom-doom.

The drumming grew louder, amplified by the addition of the Cielcin's stamping feet, and one hundred thousand alien voices lifted up in chanting: *"Te! Teke! Te! Teke! Teke! Teke!"*

It didn't make any sense. *Teke* meant *jar* in the Cielcin tongue, but that was nonsense.

Unless it was some other language entirely. Like the *yaiya-toh* I had heard the Pale speak before, here was an invocation in a language wholly strange to me.

"What are they saying?" asked one of the soldiers. "Lord Marlowe?"

I could only shake my head. "I don't know."

We had an answer—of a kind—in the form of the sky falling. The great shoals of *nahute* still wove their nets above the siege towers and the burning wreck of the same. All at once great ribbons of them sped forward, soaring like the fingers of an almighty hand across the plain, so distant they seemed almost slow.

"Run!" Bassander Lin exclaimed, pointing his sword back toward the Wall and the safety of the colossi.

"Aristedes, we need reinforcements! Air support!" I cried, leaping to follow the Mandari. Lin ran ahead, sword upraised like a banner, and a thousand men ran after.

The commander's voice was tight. "There aren't many lighters left."

"Send them!" I shouted.

Lorian signaled the affirmative before adding, "If you can draw those drones in nearer to the colossi, they'll cover you."

"Yes, thank you." I ground my teeth, each pounding step hammering though me as I ran. "I was already doing that."

Doom.

Doom-doom.

They were already firing. Rounds flew over our heads, chewing through the metallic swarm that hounded us across that vast, flat no man's land. It was farther than it looked, a mile or more. But the colossi were marching once again, spurred by necessity. Their massive feet shook the earth, their every gun blazing. I kept seeing visions of that metal tide overtaking us, grinding us to paste with its jaws. And through it all that evil chant pursued us: *"Teke! Teke! Teke!"*

The colossi marched toward us. I could spy the men upon their crabbed parapets, gunners and grenadiers safe behind the shimmer of their shields. Looking back, I saw the Cielcin in pursuit, running after us through the flames. Then a hellion screech filled the air. Relief! Four lonely Sparrowhawks shrieked down over the Storm Wall, their single wings laid flat and sharp as swords. They fired, and fountains of dust and stone peppered the space behind as they shot through the slow-descending ribbons of *nahute*. Drones fell like flies. Valka flagged beside me, and I spurred her on. "Not far! Not far now!"

In ages to come, the armchair generals and amateur doctors of war would write about mad Marlowe's run across the fields of Deira, about his ill-considered defense of the men and women in the tunnels of the starport—and how he failed them. They have written little of the bomb that had claimed fully a third of the Cielcin landing fleet, I note, and less of Aristedes, whose decision not to open the gates perhaps saved thousands of lives. Our sortie had saved no one, but it had struck one hell of a blow against the enemy.

Alien cannons fired. One of the Sparrowhawks fell and smote the tarmac between our party and the coming tide of the Cielcin host. On an open plain, the xenobites moved faster than any human being could run. They were like cavalry, and though the fire of our guns tore at them, still they came, heedless for their individual lives as ants are heedless but to the needs of their colony. They were like an army of the dead and damned, and did not retreat.

They were not human.

Reaching the shadow of the nearest colossus—one of the mighty hexapods—I stopped and turned. Behind us, the *nahute* fell burning like a heavy rain, torn to shreds by the thunder of our artillery. It wasn't enough. They fell on us like a wave breaking. Men screamed and fell writhing where they were not shielded. But the line of colossi kept marching, moving past us, their legs like the trunks of almighty trees. Standing clear of the others, I spun my sword like a dervish, slicing through the serpentine machines. Their severed hulks crashed about me, or fell from the sky above. One man stumbled past me, and I had a horrible vision of him trying to pull one of the snakes from his side where it had burrowed into the meat of him.

He was not alone.

The Cielcin were almost on us, white swords flashing in the light of the flames behind.

One of the armored chimeras leaped ahead and above the rest and was blown to pieces by the colossi's guns. The air cleared a moment around me, and I drew my sword across my face and back to guard, ready for the next—perhaps final—effort, glad at least that Valka was by my side, if heartsick that she was there at all.

Then the air opened up with a cry fierce and piercing and higher than Pale laughter. Warm air buffeted me, filled with the sound of wings.

The Irchtani had come.

Green feathers and gray filled the space above me, and looking back I saw their phalanx like a single pair of mighty wings spread back from the line of colossi to the Wall. Udax and Barda and the rest cut low beneath the *nahute* and the artillery fire, their *zitraa* long and sharper than their claws, sharp almost as monofilament, as highmatter. The *nahute* dove amongst them, and many of our winged allies fell.

Still more flew, and the flashing of their sabers and the shout of their arms drove the Pale back, and for a moment we stood firm and marshaled our defenses. "Get back in formation!" Pallino shouted on the common band. "Form ranks, you bloody fools!" In the distance, another of the Cielcin towers erupted in flames. The smaller colossus had closed the gap across the open field and opened fire. I could see Cielcin clinging to its legs, trying to climb upward to reach the access hatches on the upper levels.

Screaming through the air, the few remaining Sparrowhawks circled back, making a run for the huge, solitary landing tower that had arrived last of all. It crouched apart from the main body of the Pale army, nearer the Wall and far off to one side. They dropped in low, carving a trench in the air, guns blazing as they flew straight toward it. I saw the tell-tale flash of a Royse shield as their bullets glanced off. My heart sank. The Cielcin had not shielded any of their vessels save this. Why?

A moment later, the whole empty landscape between the lighters and the alien landing craft glowed a chalky, granular red. It lasted only an instant. A second or two, no more. By the time I realized what it was, it was gone.

It was a targeting laser. The weapon came an instant after, a pillar of light and fire a thousand times brighter than the sun, so bright my suit's entoptics blacked out to save my vision. There was no sound, only the blast wave of heat as the orbital laser scorched the tarmac and burned our ships from the sky. The light returned as the beam faded, and I saw the red streak of molten rock where the weapon had scratched a channel on the tarmac.

The swarms of *nahute* had thinned, and—reeling—I staggered from the shadow of the great machine above me. As I watched, the great siege tower opened, disgorging its precious cargo. The machine within shuddered and advanced on mighty treads, pistons like exposed bone working as it moved. The ghastly thing must have been three hundred feet across and more than twice that high, a horror of dark metal and glass. A Cielcin colossus to match our own. The nearest of our colossi opened fire on it, but the impact broke against a shield curtain. More of our stolen praxis.

With inexorable slowness it advanced, rolling across no man's land for the gray-white fastness of the Storm Wall.

"What the hell is that?" asked one of the men.

What exactly it was did not matter. That it was bent on the Wall told me all I needed to know: that it was a weapon. A ram or bombard meant to crack our fortress open despite our shield and despite the men who defended it.

"We have to stop it!" I said, seizing Lin by the shoulder.

"How?" he demanded. "You saw that orbital laser!"

I clenched my teeth. A Royse shield could stop energy weapons, but a weapon of that magnitude? The personal shields we wore would overload and fry us in an instant if we tried to charge the siege engine. We'd never make it.

Lin appeared to be thinking the same thing. "We can't approach on foot."

"The colossi?" Valka said, gesturing at the saucer section above our heads.

"Too slow," Lorian chipped in. He'd been listening, evidently. "Their shields won't hold."

I cut into the sudden silence, "The Wall's shield draws energy from the planet's core."

"And from the emergency reactors in the lower level," Lorian said. "But the inclusion zone only extends about fifty feet from the wall."

One could practically hear Lin's frown through his helmet. "Fifty feet does not give us a great deal of space to work with." He shook his head.

"What about the Irchtani?" I asked, remembering the way Udax and his people had carried us away from the ruined stair in the midst of the city. "If we can get above the crawler, they can't risk using that orbital gun without attacking their own assets."

"*If* we can get above them," Lin countered. "What's to stop them shooting you out of the sky the minute you get close?"

Lorian's voice overrode the comm. "We'll make it look like a retreat."

The colossi firing was our cue. All at once, the mighty war machines advanced, pressing forward toward the remainder of the Cielcin landing towers where they stood—a fleet of rockets—camped at the far edge of the field. All but two of the tripods, which Lorian turned about and ordered after the huge crawler that even then rolled its slow way toward the wall. Pallino once more remained behind to marshal our forces on the ground, orchestrating a steady retreat toward the wall while Lin, Valka, and I—along with a detachment of some thirty men—hurried across no man's land in the general direction of the Wall.

Looking back over my shoulder, I saw the colossi marching to engage the enemy, sweeping the perimeter of the field to avoid the pitfalls that had claimed the other. They were like a forest of columns walking, and the fire of their guns fell like red hail upon the enemy. The clouds of *nahute* contracted, shimmering in the scant light of the eclipse.

It was almost beautiful.

"Kithuun-Barda, where are you?" I spoke into my helmet's pickups, feet pounding the pavement as we ran.

"Nearly there!" came the croaked reply.

Shadows moved on the ground before my feet, and looking up I saw the whole phalanx of the Irchtani moving, filling the sky with their wings. There were yet hundreds of them, and to a man they'd disengaged with the enemy and were flying back toward the Wall. On we ran, and with every step I expected to see the crimson shine of the targeting laser and feel the cold white flash of light come down and end it all.

It never did.

Ahead, the Cielcin crawler rose, black and hideous against the pale stone of the Storm Wall in the distance. All the hallmarks of Cielcin design were on it. It had the look of some fetid organ, all gnarled organic lines and asymmetries, surface fibrous and textured like tissue. From this angle, I could see no armature, no muzzle, no maw.

"Do you think it's some kind of plasma bore?" Lin asked, voice ragged as he ran.

Thinking of the way our boarding craft cut aboard enemy starships, I said, "I don't know."

An explosion sounded behind us, and looking back once more I saw a fury of red flame. One of the colossi was burning. I saw Cielcin fighters leaping from the upper platform, their cloaks afire. A moment later the mighty tripod toppled, crushing men and xenobites alike beneath its bulk.

Then talons gripped me, and looking up I saw the shape of a black-winged Irchtani stretch wide and pulse. My stomach lurched, and once more I was lifted from the earth, feet dangling uselessly as the bird lifted me with huge wings. How the Irchtani could fly at all I'd no idea. In full kit, I must have weighed twice so much as he.

Yet fly he did.

I did not know him, but he bore me up and his brothers after him carried Valka and Lin and our men. We rose and joined the phalanx of the Irchtani as they winged toward the Wall, climbing high and ever higher. I shut my eyes, certain that at any moment the red flash would claim us. But if the dark powers in space above marked our progress, they did not respond.

Lorian was right. They thought we were just retreating. All we needed to do was get close enough to the crawler before the Cielcin could respond. I opened my eyes again. From above, the tarmac really did look flat, like some artist's unfinished rendering of a world. The Storm Wall rose ahead, pale face lined with channels that deflected the coriolis winds up and over the ramparts. The crawler was alone, separated from the main body of the Cielcin army by about half a mile of open, flat space. Cannon fire stitched the air around us, and once my guide's *zitraa* flashed and sliced a stray *nahute* in half. The blow jounced me, but the auxiliary held me in his talons and glided lower with the strike.

Red light flashed behind, and I turned in time to see the horrid beam of white energy blaze and crack the air. I felt the heat wave rush over me and yelled as my guardian dove, speeding forward and down like an arrow loosed from god.

"Hold on, *bashanda!*" he said. I gripped his ankles tight, murmuring an aphorism against fear, but no scholiast's wisdom could quell the mad hammering of my heart. We were almost in free fall then, the two of us and several of those around. I thought I saw Valka in—was that Udax's grasp? But when I turned my head to see, they had moved. One of the anti-air cannons the xenobites had brought caught one of our fellows, blowing human and Irchtani apart. They died together and plummeted. Once more the red laser painted its target, and I saw our shadows far below. But my guide opened his wings and slowed our descent—heedless of the raw shout in my throat as we lurched upward and away, out of the pillar of fire that blazed from the black star above.

We circled lower, and for a moment all I could smell was ozone from the laser's wild ionization. The earth smoldered below, angry and red. Once more, I shut my eyes. We lurched, plunging again.

"We lost two in that last one," came Lin's voice.

"We're almost there!" said one of the Irchtani. Was that Barda?

Against my better judgment, I opened my eyes. We were nearly there. The crawler moved beneath us, a few hundred feet ahead and below. I could see Cielcin moving on the parapets of the craft, pointing and turning weapons toward us. A shot burst against my shield, and my guide twitched, pulling back.

We dropped fifty feet, falling nearly straight down as the Irchtani holding me tucked his wings. Shots flashed above us, caught an unshielded peltast where he hung in the talons of another Irchtani. The dead man fell, and his guardian peeled away.

"Let me drop!" I said, slapping the Irchtani on one scaled ankle. About a hundred feet separated me from the deck. Far, but not so far that my suit's gel layer could not take the impact. I hoped. "Let me drop!"

"Are you certain?" the bird man carrying me asked.

I released his ankles, eyed the platform beneath me. Floating there on his wings, I felt a momentary serenity sweep over me. I was apart from the violence, above it—if only so long as no shots sounded my way. The Wall stretched ahead and above, and below the plain of the landing field unrolled to the forest of burning towers and beyond beneath skies that threatened storm.

"Go!" I said, and reached. Ever the faithful soldier, my guide released me, talons unclicking like part of some jeweled mechanism. Countless Hadrians fell across countless threads of possibility. So many of them died, or broke their legs, or missed the platform entirely. But those tragedies spun off and vanished down spiralling corridors of time that never were.

I did not die, but hit the deck boots first, knees bent.

"Black planet!" one of the men above swore. "Did you all see that?"

A Cielcin marksman looked on, momentarily stunned. But the sword that flashed in my grip reminded it where it was and what was happening, and it leaped back. The shot from its reverse-engineered rifle snapped against my shield, and it thrust the blade-end of the weapon at my eyes. I parried, highmatter parting steel without resistance or sound. I punched out with the blade and put the point clean through my enemy's chest. It sagged against the rail, and I looked up in time to see another of the fusiliers spin round and train its weapon on me. A white shape fell out of the sky above, and the Cielcin vanished behind it. One of the legionnaires had joined me. And another. Another. The Irchtani circled close, firing one-handed with their long-barreled pistols, falling as they did and flapping back skyward until we fought in the midst of a swirling vortex of green and black feathers.

There was Udax, claws planted on the level above the catwalk where I stood fighting another of the Pale! And there was Valka, firing from amidst a trias of men on the level below. And there Bassander and Kithuun-Barda side by side, the Mandari's highmatter sword flashing blue in the dark day.

"There has to be a hatch somewhere!" I cried, slicing clean through another of the inhuman berserkers. "We have to get inside." There was no telling what might await us within the alien war machine, but the Wall was growing ever nearer, and we hadn't much time. In the distance, white light flashed, and looking out I saw the orbital laser slam down upon the crabbed back of one colossus, its beam warped and deflected by the platform's Royse shield. The weapons platform survived, but I knew its shields could not withstand another blast from *Dharan-Tun's* orbital laser. Pallino's men had engaged the Cielcin surrounding the anti-air guns on the left flank. How small they all seemed, a patch of white shifting against an ocean of Dark!

We had to move quickly. For all I knew the inside of the crawler would prove another kind of labyrinth, another honeycomb of endless tunnels and blind turns. There wasn't time. I dove out of the way of another enemy fusilier, pressing myself against the rail. Another of our legionnaires landed *behind* it, armor rattling, and fired. The Cielcin fell into me, and I shoved it to the ground.

"Find the way in!" I shouted.

Away on the horizon, the orbital laser flashed again, striking the shielded colossi. The enemy's anti-air cannons lay burning upon the field, and Pallino's men encircled one limb of the Cielcin army. *Nahute* whipped past me so fast my shield deflected them, and the decking beneath my feet rattled and shook as I clambered down a stair that seemed nearly a ladder.

"Found a hatch, sir!" came the sound of one of the soldiers. "In back!"

I was near the rear, but half a hundred feet of catwalk lay between me and the corner. Fifty feet. And three Cielcin. Shielded, sword in hand, I pressed forward. The first of them held its *nahute* like a whip, swinging it in slow arcs. I paused. Wielded thus, the drone was even more dangerous, for it moved slow enough that my shield was no good. The Cielcin snapped it toward my face, forcing me to fade. On the second swing, I was ready, and cut the braided metal *thing* in two. Its owner lashed out with one clawed fist, clouting me on the side of the head. I staggered, but managed to raise my sword in time to catch my attacker in the ribs. Shoving it to one side, I advanced, cutting my way through the next xenobite with almost contemptuous ease. The third threw its *nahute* at me, and ducking I cut it in two, the still-spinning head tumbling away over the side to strike the pavement three hundred feet below.

When I reached the rear of the crawler, I had a clear view of our colossi stretched across the horizon. I had a clear view of the flash, too. The Cielcin's orbital laser struck again, swift and silent. This time it overwhelmed one colossi's shield. For a moment, I saw the outline of the thing *through* the scatter of that impossibly bright beam as vision returned to my suit's entoptics. Saw it crumble to dust. When the light faded and my suit showed me the world as it truly was, there was nothing left. Uncounted tons of metal and an unknown count of men were gone, transformed to atoms and a smoldering pile of molten metal.

"Lorian!" I rasped, and leaned on the rail with my free hand. "Get those men out of there!" I did not wait for a reply, but met the men who had found the hatch. Bassander Lin appeared as I drew near, and after a brief inspection during which we failed to ascertain the mechanism for opening that alien door, the two of us worked together in cutting our way through. The heavy metal resisted, but the highmatter was sharp enough, and the door fell inward with a bang.

Darkness greeted us, darkness and the sense that we were running out of time.

CHAPTER 84

THE CRAWLER

BASSANDER WENT AHEAD WITH two hoplites. I followed, keeping Valka in front of me so I knew where she was at all times. Behind came several others, Udax and the bird who had carried me among them. Still more remained on the platforms outside, fighting to clear them. The thin light of the false night shone in, illuminating halls like the inside of huge intestines wrought of metal and dark stone. As with so many of the Cielcin constructs I have seen, that machine must once have been some hollowed asteroid converted to foul purpose by the Pale. The walls sweat on either side, and our little party drew close together.

"This isn't any kind of plasma bore," I said, looking at the walls. Machinery ran along the inner wall and along the ceiling above, rippling pipes and lengths of conduit. Dials and blinking indicators shone there, though what they portended I could not guess.

Valka lingered by one of these, head cocked. "Pressure gauges?" she asked, prodding one with a finger.

"Hydraulics?" I asked. "They don't mean to cut through the wall with *water,* surely?" It was so primitive.

"Could be," she said. "This thing . . . 'tis big enough to carry a reservoir."

A shot sounded ahead, and something sparked against the wall. It sounded like a nerve disruptor. That shouldn't be. The Cielcin did not use nerve disruptors. They did not *have* them. One of the men beside Bassander raised his lance to fire back, but the captain threw an arm out to stop him. "No beams. There's no telling what you'd hit."

"It went around the bend," Valka said. Her eyes were better than ours.

"We'll split up," Lin said. "I'll take five and go after our friend. Marlowe, you take the bridge."

I gripped one of the conduits on the wall to steady myself. The shaking I'd felt on the decks outside was more pronounced within. The whole thing reminded me of nothing so much as the uranium mining crawlers on whose backs my family made their fortune.

"We stay together," I said, not willing to have a repeat of the tragedy on Iubalu's ship. "I'll not have any of us getting lost in here. Forget them." The whole crawler shook again as sounds of fighting from the outside filtered through the walls.

I wished we had mapping drones.

"That's Barda," Udax said, shoulders hunched, head cocked as it listened to the Irchtani unit's channel. "They're trying to disable the wheels."

"There must be something like a lift in here," Valka said. "We need to get to the bottom."

"Won't the bridge be high?" Lin asked.

"You're thinking like a human," I said in answer.

No lift, but we did find the ladder not long after, bracketed to the outer wall. Two hoplites went first, securing the space below. We followed this level around. Like the level above, it described a U-shape or semi-circle, floors enclosing some larger space—possibly the very reservoir Valka guessed would be there. We moved swiftly, but with caution, so that when two *scahari* fighters leaped at us from an outer room, they fell quickly. The light from our suit lamps blazed in that dim place, walls so black they were almost green.

"Something's wrong," Lin said when we had descended to a third level. "This place should be teeming with soldiers."

Memory of our first push to board Iubalu's ship played over and over in my mind, and I found myself watching the walls, expecting false panels to fold back and reveal black-suited foes. None did.

"We know we're not alone in here," I said dryly, shifting my unkindled sword in my hand. I'd had enough of crawling round in tunnels to last a lifetime.

The next level down we found what we'd been searching for: a hatch on the inner wall. The crawler had been built like one of those antique nesting dolls, with the encircling halls, hull, and outer fortifications wrapped around a nucleus that doubtless housed the thing's engines and whatever nasty surprise it held for the Storm Wall and the men and women inside it. This too opened on a wheel-lock, one which took three men to turn. It swung inward, admitting a rush of cool, damp air. The chamber inside stank of ozone and spent gunpowder, electonics and burning stone.

I should not have smelled it through my suit, but the seals had taken damage somewhere in all the fighting.

The room stretched the full space of the crawler, levels of catwalks rising in a dense tangle beneath braided cables and bits of machinery bracketed to the convex dome of the ceiling.

Reservoir indeed.

Along the far wall—which was the front of the crawler—I could see a red-lit line of windows, and through them the horned shapes of Cielcin at work operating the great machine. How strange it was, seeing them at a task so mundane, so *human*. Beneath those windows was a flat expanse of wall that I guessed must be some kind of ramp or outer doors. And dead ahead? The snarling cylinder of a mining drill a hundred feet in diameter stood bracketed to floor and ceiling and hung in the air between like the egg sac of some evil iron spider.

A drill. They meant to drill through the Storm Wall.

Stepping out onto the catwalk near the end of the mining rig, I almost laughed. It was easy to forget how primitive the Pale were, how antiquely industrial. But it was no laughing matter. Primitive or no, it would breach the Wall if we did not stop it.

A disruptor bolt struck my shield.

"That is far enough, my lord!"

I froze.

The voice was high and nasal—and unmistakably *human*.

Looking up, I saw a man standing on a higher catwalk, looking down on us. He was hairless, and pale almost as a Cielcin, but he was human all the same. He had no horns, and though his eyes were black even at this distance, they were the ordinary eyes of mankind. He had a nose, too: hooked and wicked above thin and pallid lips. Human indeed. Still, there was something *wrong* about him, as though the god who crafted him had blurred his initial sketch. Everything seemed a little too short, too thin. In a certain light, he might have reminded me of Aristedes. As it was, he only reminded me of an overlarge and emaciated infant, still wet from the birthing vat.

A rush of understanding overtook me, and I said, "You're with MINOS, aren't you?" The Extrasolarian company had designed the chimeras for Prince Syriani. It made sense one of their representatives would be present. It explained the Prophet's willingness and ability to adapt human technologies—like the captured body shields—to its efforts. It had allies.

The man made no expression. "I serve the Prince of Princes." He took a step to one side, surveying the crowd behind me. "I saw you. At Arae. It's Lord Marlowe, is it not?"

I thought back to that battle, to the room of dead men we'd found. The bodies the MINOS workers had left behind when they broadcast their minds into space. "Who are you to ask for my name?"

"I am called Urbaine. You met my colleague, Doctor Severine."

"Severine?" Had that been the name of the doctor on Arae?

"You don't remember?" Urbaine asked. "She nearly killed you. Or . . . our creations nearly did. No matter." He turned his back, looking up at the orb behind him. "It was good of you to come in person. The *Shiomu* will be so pleased. He has looked forward to this meeting for quite some time."

Bassander Lin fired, but his shot broke on the doctor's shield. Urbaine did not even notice. Remembering my previous encounter with one of the doctors of MINOS, I switched off my suit's communications completely and signaled for the others to do the same. Urbaine was an Extrasolarian. There would be machines in his head—like Valka—that could access and control our suits if the villain had a mind. Bassander flashed a hand sign, ordering triases of men along the perimeter catwalks in a search of a stair.

Pushing the familiar horror at the thought the Cielcin wanted *me* aside, I said, "You should surrender."

"Surrender? When victory is at hand?" The Extrasolarian turned to look back at me. "Your theatrics are as redundant as your heroics, my lord. All this violence, all this sacrifice . . . and for what? You cannot win. Against what is coming *no one can*." He sounded almost like Bartosz, if Bartosz had been triumphant and not teetering on the last abyss of despair.

"What is coming?" I asked.

Urbaine laughed, a high, quiet sound. "You think you are fighting a *war?*" he said. "You are fighting the end. Your end. There are powers in play you do not understand."

"The Watchers, do you mean?" I said, and felt a thrill as the man took a step back, stunned.

"So you have some knowledge." The doctor smiled, though I think he only hid his surprise. "But knowledge is not power, and even if it was there is no power that can avail against *Them*. We have flourished for twenty thousand years because They had not deigned to notice us. They have noticed now."

I matched his smile.

"Enough talk, doctor," came a voice deep as the sea.

What I had taken for part of the machinery shifted, stooped, and became Bahudde. The metal giant loomed out of the dark above, its lone remaining eye red as dying coals.

"Are we in position?" the Extrasolarian asked.

"Nearly." The crawler shook again. Bahudde looked toward the ceiling. "The *yukajjimn* and their slaves mean to halt our advance." I thought that a remarkably bland statement, and wondered if the giant was slow, or if the heavy abstraction MINOS had visited upon its body had warped its mind and made it dumb.

"Eilatono de wo!" Urbaine laughed again. "Let them try! Kill them, general!"

Enough of this, I thought. Before the giant could so much as move, I raised my voice and spoke one short, simple command. "Now, Udax!"

The winged centurion understood me all too well. Udax spread his wings and vaulted into the air, moving faster than the lumbering Bahudde could track. He alighted on the rail above Doctor Urbaine, his cutlass shining in one taloned hand. The *zitraa* flashed, freeing the Extrasolarian scientist's head from his shoulders. The headless body stood there a moment as mine had once done, teetered, and fell.

In the instant that followed, Bahudde slammed one man-sized fist down through the catwalk. Udax would have fallen into the giant's grasp had the centurion not leaped away, winging to the level above and nearer the massive drill. Urbaine's headless body slid down the ramp and tumbled to the floor fifty feet below.

"Run!" I shouted, spurring Valka on ahead of me. "We have to get above it!"

Our little unit scattered. The few other Irchtani leaped into the air, following the lead of their centurion. Bassander and his men scattered to either side while Valka and I led a small knot of men straight forward. The crawler shook beneath the assault from outside, making us stumble. "Move!" I shouted, praying the metal monster was not on our heels. I had barely survived my battle with Iubalu, had barely survived my first brush with this member of the Iedyr Yemani. If we were to survive this one, we were going to have to be clever.

A man screamed, and I knew Bahudde had seized its first victim. Shots rained down from the Irchtani in the gantry above, peppering the catwalks and the armored goliath below. Bahudde roared, the horrific sound of it scraping at the walls and the inverse dome of the reservoir above our heads.

The giant did not dare use its missiles in that enclosed space, could not risk harm to its siege engine. It was an advantage—small though it was.

"Can we destroy the drill?" I asked. I had half a mind to shoot the tank above, but refrained on the off chance the Cielcin planned to cool the drill with something other than water.

Valka shook her head. "Maybe! Or maybe Barda can destroy the wheels!"

We were running out of time, for we were surely within half a mile of the Wall.

A stair rose ahead of us and left. Valka leaped onto its lower rungs just ahead of me, pulling herself up toward the level Urbaine had occupied. We were nearly above the rear of the giant's arms by then, and the red light of the bridge rose in front of us. Glancing back, I saw Bahudde with one of our men in its huge fingers. As I watched, the *vayadan*-general slapped the man against the wall. He went limp as a boned fish. Dead, unconscious, paralyzed—none could say. The giant tossed the soldier aside and ripped the catwalk we'd just crossed out with a contemptuous swipe of its hand. The size of those arms! Each must have been three times the height of a man and big around as wine barrels.

It swept the room with its solitary red eye. The damaged linkages in its one shoulder spat sparks into the air as it pointed up at me. *"Okun-kih!"* it said. "You damaged me!"

A single shot rang out and broke against my shield. Too late, I threw an arm across my face.

"Hadrian!" Valka called from the level above. "Come on!"

I turned to follow. "To the bridge!" I cried. "We have to stop them!" If we could get inside, we could stop the crawler in its tracks, stop the drill and the Cielcin effort to breach the Wall. They might still win a way inside—push through the tunnels in the starport, or overwhelm the defenses on the city side—but if all we did was buy time for the fleet to arrive, it would be worth it. "Go!"

I was halfway up the stairs when the ground vanished beneath me. The catwalk below and the flowing metal of the steps fell away. Valka screamed, and I seized the rail with my left hand. The stair swung, half-pulled free from the structure above. I saw Valka above me. She fired past me at the giant far below. I cast about for some handhold. There was nothing. The level above was out of reach. The staircase clanged as another of the bolts released. I knew I had seconds. There! I leaped out through open air, back toward the drill and the catwalk that ran alongside it for maintenance. The rail caught me about the midsection, and I groaned.

"Hadrian!" Valka cried again. Her voice could not have sounded farther away.

Before I could mount the rail and regain my feet, the catwalk was torn from beneath me. How far I fell was any man's guess. Sixty feet? Seventy? I landed on my shoulder, suit's gel layer cushioning my fall. I lay there stunned, stars dancing across the inside of my mask.

Before I could rise—before I could even see straight—iron fingers each big around as the arms of a full-grown man seized about my waist. The lonely red eye descended like a falling star, its twin guttering in the gloom beside it.

"Is this . . . all there is?" the deep voice asked. "No fight? No . . . resistance?" The *vayadan*-general lifted me bodily from the floor, fingers clamping tighter. "I expected *more*."

My arms were still free, and I pounded on the huge hand with my fists and tried to pry the first finger loose. It was useless. I was trapped. Hysteric, my mind raced to the memory of that legionnaire doll I'd seen on the floor of the tramway, for I was as powerless in the giant's grip as any toy in the hand of its child. I balled up my fists in impotent fury and realized incredibly—*impossibly*—that my sword was still in my hand.

Against all odds . . . *I hadn't dropped it.*

I would have laughed, but the breath had fled my lungs.

"The prince will thank me for this," Bahudde said, speaking its native tongue. Steel fingers tightened, and I felt my suit straining to protect the flesh within. "I will deliver you to him myself."

Teeth clenched, I squeezed the hilt of Olorin's sword. The blade appeared, flashing in the dim. I hewed at Bahudde's wrist with all my strength. No good. The creature's hand was adamant, and the highmatter would not bite. Sparks hissed from the damaged linkages in the chimera's shoulder. I struck again, and the adamant jarred my hand. I almost lost my grip, and winced as Bahudde's hand tightened further still.

"*Iubalu-kih rakunyu ba-okun biqari,*" it said, voice deep as the Dark of space. *Iubalu was not yours to kill.* "She belonged to the prince." My vision grayed about the edge, and the beating of my heart was ragged in my ears. My limbs felt heavy. Heavy and uncharacteristically warm. "I should kill you," Bahudde rumbled, ignoring the impact of weapons fire from the Irchtani and Bassander's men. Where was Bassander? Where was Valka?

The grayness in my eyes went to black, and I sensed that deeper Dark beneath, howling up to greet me.

I was going to die again.

The pressure vanished, and air and blood rushed back, driving back that final darkness. "But you belong to the prince. Just like me." It squeezed again, grip shifted higher, and I felt my ribs groan, threatening to form those greenstick fractures that heralded the final breaks. My vision blurred again, and I screamed out all the air in me, praying that my suit would save me from the bone-crushing weight.

It would be easy to let go, to let everything go.

So easy to die. Again.

A white blur fell from on high and struck the giant, clinging to its neck like the apes I'd read about in storybooks as a boy. I saw a flash of blue.

The weight of iron fingers vanished, and I was falling again.

Something heavy crashed to the earth beneath me as I landed, the wind all knocked out of me. My suit worked to force air back into my lungs. My vision cleared steadily. Bahudde's fingers curled loose around me, the palm—large almost as I was tall—beneath me. Wheezing, I looked up and understood. Bassander Lin stood upon the shoulder of the giant above me, his highmatter sword in hand, its point buried deep in the linkages of the chimera's damaged shoulder.

He had cut off the giant's arm.

For a single, beautiful moment he stood like a conqueror atop the statue of a deposed tyrant. Then he was gone, leaping away before Bahudde could seize him with its one remaining hand. He dove wildly through the air, careening toward the floor without any net or hope of salvation—and was caught by two Irchtani who bore him safely to ground.

I might have cheered.

Still breathing hard, I tried to sit up. Where was my sword? I'd lost it at last in the fall. It must have rolled away. I twisted round, trying to locate it on the floor.

But the *vayadan* had not forgotten about me.

Even severed, the machine body of the giant obeyed its animal brain.

The iron fist slammed shut once more, trapping me in its grip. I groaned, tried once more to wrestle free while the chimera went after Bassander and his men. I had one arm still free, and cast about for my weapon. There! The deck plates were uneven, ridged and folded like the insides of a living thing, and my sword had rolled against one of these. It took every ounce of effort to strain toward it with my free hand. The fingertips just scraped the pommel, and I groaned.

No good.

I dug my heels into the floor and pushed, trying to scrape the huge hand and the severed arm across the floor, but it must have weighed more than a ton. I wasn't going anywhere.

Unless . . .

Relaxing, I shut my eyes and tried to master my breathing, to call to mind a number of Tor Gibson's old aphorisms against fear and panic, to reach that quiet place where my mind could see with eyes unclouded. Surely there was a way, a place in time where some errant bump or motion of the ship slid the weapon into my waiting fingers. I could just see it, I only had to reach out and *choose.*

Bahudde's massive, clawed foot smashed the ground not three yards from my head. The vision shattered. Above me, the giant tore another catwalk from the gantry above, tumbling three men to their doom. Abandoning my previous plan, I strained once more, willing myself to stretch just that little bit more. Then something impossible happened.

I squirmed free.

The hideous strength of the giant's hand just *disappeared.* I seized my blade and stumbled to my feet, wheeling to face the severed limb with highmatter kindling in my fist. The fingers twitched. Spasmed. Went still. Red lights along hatches on the inside of the wrist went dead.

" 'Tis well I was not left on the *Tamerlane,* mm?" came a cutting voice from on high. I looked up. Valka was leaning against the rail of one of the highest catwalks, peering down at me.

I raised my sword in salute.

" 'Tis thrice now I've saved you," she said, calling down since my suit's communications were still closed.

"Yes, yes." I shook myself. *"Noyn jitat."*

At the other end of the hold, Bahudde snatched one of the Irchtani from the air and slammed it headfirst into the wall, denting steel and spattering dark blood across the metal.

"Are you all right?" Valka asked.

I'd taken a few steps toward the general, meaning to rejoin the fight.

"I've had worse." I stopped sharp. "What about the bridge?"

I could practically hear her eyes narrow. "You're welcome."

Half a dozen retorts flew to my lips, but I bit them all back. She'd come back for me, just as I would have done. I opened my mouth to respond—though whether it would have been in thanks or a smart riposte I never learned.

Valka *screamed.*

No shout of surprise this, no shocked curse. Hers was the sound of deepest, purest agony, a sound older than human reason, an animal's terror and pain. Cold fingers seized my heart as surely as Bahudde's had. Looking up, I saw her arch backward and fall convulsing on the catwalk above, limbs tearing, scrabbling at rails and floor.

"Valka!"

Where was the nearest ladder? I looked round, the drill, the giant, the war itself forgotten in that instant. Nothing mattered. Nothing but her. I started running.

"That will teach you to meddle!" came a high, nasal voice, ringing off the walls. "Rob the prince of his prize, will you? Oh no-no no-no no . . ."

I froze where I stood.

It was the voice of Doctor Urbaine.

The Extrasolarian had survived.

At once I understood what was happening. Valka had opened her mind to comms channels to use her praxis on Bahudde—to save me—thinking the MINOS doctor dead. In doing so, she had only exposed herself to the predations of the doctor himself.

Even as I stood there reeling, a silent alarm began. Red lights flashed about the chamber, and the hatchway at the fore began to open, revealing the white face of the Storm Wall not two thousand feet away.

But I had other things to occupy me. Valka was still screaming, still writhing a hundred feet above my head. One of the men nearest her seized her arms, trying to still her.

Where had the doctor's body fallen? There was the catwalk he'd been standing on when Udax struck him down, fallen like a ramp to the floor. Ignoring the giant and the fight raging around us, I hurried toward it, ducking round the struts that supported the massive body of the drill.

"Time is short, general!" Urbaine was shouting. *"Biqqa totajun!* Kill them and have done!"

Above our heads the huge drill began turning slowly in its housing, the titanic bit extending, sliding forward toward the open front of the crawler platform. The Wall was closing in.

I saw the doctor's body then, one arm broken beneath the narrow chest. Metal bones protruded from the ruined neck, and with growing horror I realized that Doctor Urbaine was no man at all. He was a SOM. I knew then what I had already suspected, knew what I must find.

"*Biqqa totajun, vayadan-do!*" Urbaine shrieked. "I cannot hold her!"

Hearing that, I could not help but grin savagely behind my helmet. Whatever the doctor was doing to Valka, she was still fighting. Her screaming rebounded off the reservoir dome above, and I shoved a packing crate aside and found it.

The Extrasolarian's head lay against the heavy base of some alien mining implement. He was upside-down, and so I had a clear view of the severed neck and the machine lights blinking in it, the torn wires beside torn arteries and the silver shine of bone. Udax must have sheared clear between the vertebrae, and I marveled at the skill and chance of that blow.

Aiming the point of my sword directly above the doctor's eye, I said, "Let her go."

Urbaine leered up at me, mouth open. The lips did not move as he said, "It is too late. The ram has touched the wall!"

"Not yet!" I looked up at the drill telescoping fifty feet above my head. We still had a thousand feet or more of empty tarmac separating us from the Wall.

"There's nothing you can do," came the voice from the severed head at my feet. Snarling, I stooped and seized the creature by the ear, holding it sideways with my blade whispering just below it. "Even if you stop this wave," Urbaine's jaw hung slack, "we are only the vanguard. I said your heroics were redundant. Succeed, and the Prince will but land his fleet."

Beneath my mask, I bared my teeth. The doctor was right.

"It is inevitable," he said smoothly. "You would do as well to fight *entropy*."

On the walk above, Valka screamed again.

I crushed his ear in my fist. "Let her go." Urbaine's leer only widened, wrinkles forming at the corners of his eyes. Blood dripped from the ruin of his neck. "Let her go, damn you!"

"*Never,*" he said.

I let him go. The head fell and met the edge of my sword. Highmatter cut without resistance and sliced the head in two. I brought it down on the cranium for good measure and stamped on the pieces. My hand was halfway to my much-neglected sidearm before I realized . . . the screaming had stopped.

An explosion rocked the chamber the moment after, and turning I saw the giant reel and crash into the wall. One of its ankles was smoking, tossing sparks. Someone had gotten a grenade wedged in a flange of its armor and blown the adamantine plates apart. In retaliation, the giant pointed its remaining arm at a trias of men on the ground. Flares fired from the wrist, followed by the silent whistle of darts. Evidently the giant had recalled it had some weapons it could fire without damaging the crawler at large.

I saw Bassander Lin running on an upper balcony, location betrayed by the gleam of his sword. The Irchtani flitted about him, firing down at the giant. Even as I watched, Bahudde shot one of them full of holes, and he tumbled from domed ceiling to ridged floor in instants. The whole crawler rattled, and high above those of Valka's little team not watching over her quiescent form were still trying to cut their way onto the bridge, but the doors were of titanium, or of some alloy of it that would not easily burn.

"Valka?" I opened my suit's communications. "Valka, are you all right?" I was close to tears. Close to shouting. "Valka, it's Hadrian. Are you all right?"

No answer came. Aside from Valka, no one on the crawler had their comms open for fear of Urbaine's sorcery, and no signal could penetrate the crawler's metal shell. There was nothing but *silence*.

I found a ladder and started to climb, heedless of the drill and the giant and the battle around me. Damn the Wall, damn the war, damn it all if she was not all right. I skirted a torn spot in one catwalk. The crawler shook again beneath my feet, and a horrific grinding filled all the air. Without warning, the entire crawler tipped and fell to one side, shifting everything not secured on the floor below. I gripped the rail to steady myself, unsure of what had happened for just a moment . . . until I realized.

The crawler had stopped.

It was Barda, I realized, Barda and the Irchtani wing that had carried us to the crawler in the first place. They had remained outside, keeping the enemy soldiers distracted. They must have succeeded in destroying one set of the mighty treads that pulled the impossibly huge vehicle forward.

"Earth!" came the expected cry from ragged throats above and below me. "Earth! Earth!"

I did not join them, but found a way up to that highest level and went to my knees beside Valka, tearing at the hard switch on my neck that released and collapsed my black helm.

"Valka!" I cradled her head in my hands, numb fingers fumbling for the catch on her own armor. The helmet hinged open, folding back to reveal her face. Never had I seen her so pale and lifeless. The elastic coif beneath the helmet was sticky with sweat. "Can you hear me?" I whispered. "No no no, don't be dead."

"Sir . . ." One of the legionnaires stepped in. I realized I'd been saying all this aloud.

"Don't touch me!" I snarled, and the man backed away.

"Quiet, *anaryan*," she said, lips barely moving.

Gold eyes fluttered open, and the hand I held tightened.

A strangled sound, half-laughter and half-sob, escaped me.

"Are you all right?" I asked.

I felt her arm spasm. She shook her head. "Hadrian?"

"It's me," I said.

Her eyes could not seem to find focus. My own vision blurred with tears. One of her eyes drifted, the pupil contracting, dilating randomly, giving her a deranged appearance. I felt a leaden weight forming in the pit of my stomach.

" 'Tis something in my head," she said.

The weight only grew heavier. I know little of machines, knew less then. "Can we fix it?"

A tremor ran through her. "Maybe. I think. Not here." She clenched her teeth. "I can stand." Before I could stop her, she was moving. I rose with her, and caught her when one of her legs convulsed and went out from under her. I tried not to think about the fighting below, about what the men around us thought of the *witch* at my side and the price she had paid for her magic. One arm hung limp at her side, and the hand that still held mine opened and closed spasmodically. Her whole body shook. "I can't control my hands . . ." she said.

"Demons above and below . . ." I breathed. "What did he do to you?"

"Virus," she said, as if that explained anything. "What happened?"

"We stopped them," I said. "Barda and his men took out the wheels."

Beneath us, Bahudde pounded another of our men to death beneath his feet.

"Not yet," Valka said, looking down at it with her one still-functioning eye. I followed her gaze to the metal giant below. As I watched, she whispered in my ear, and for a moment I did not recognize the words, for it took me a moment to realize she was speaking the tongue of the enemy. *"Weme uja,"* she said. *But I'll die.*

Looking round, I raised inquiring eyebrows at her. "What?"

Her lips moved, and breathlessly she spoke, another voice answering the first. "There is no other way, *ushan belu.*"

Ushan belu. Beloved. Prized one.

"I have failed you, master," she murmured, and I realized she was speaking for the giant crouched below. Turning, I saw Bahudde crouched in the rear of the hold, arm across its face, shielding itself from the Irchtani and Bassander's men. Somehow, some part of Valka's mind—of the machines that dwelled within her mind—had reached out and touched the mind of the *vayadan.*

Her damaged eye twitched, pupil expanding more than any ordinary human's should. The other voice answered, pulling Valka's vocal chords high and tight. "For which you must pay. You must light the fire."

Valka was silent a long moment, and I thought that whatever fey connection there was between her and the great chimera had broken. But she spoke again, still in that high and breathless way. "For thus were you made."

Silence again for a great moment. Silence, then, "Your will *is,* Aeta ba-Aetane, and I obey it."

Even as Valka spoke, the giant in the hold below stood, great arm sweeping aside four Irchtani as easily as though they were a flock of sparrows. It shambled forward, slowed by its damaged ankle. Shots fired by Bassander and his men nipped at its heels, but still the chimera seemed not to heed them and it limped forward with the inexorable gravity of a funeral march.

Aeta ba-Aetane.

Prince of Princes.

The other voice that Valka's praxis had channeled was no less than the Scourge of Earth itself. Syriani Dorayaica. And the Prophet had given its deadly orders.

"Destroy it!" I shouted. "Bassander, take it down!" As if the soldiers needed any encouragement. Deep in the heart of the metal giant there was doubtless an energy source great enough to put a hole in the Storm Wall, a grain of antimatter, or a microfusion reactor no larger than a wine barrel.

It would be enough.

A horrid premonition gripped me. With the drill compromised, the crawler would be of no use to that dark power above, and though Dorayaica desired me for a captive I little imagined that desire would outweigh the benefits of removing the only threat on the field to his general's last, suicidal mission.

"Lin! Udax!" I shouted at the Irchtani below. "Don't let the chimera off the crawler!" Turning to the men about me, I said, "We have to move." Not slowing, I scooped Valka up in my arms, held her tight to stop her spasming, and made for the stairs. Below Bahudde struggled with a knot of men near the ramp. The drill still turned uselessly above as we hurried down the uneven alien steps. Twice I nearly fell, nearly crushed the injured Valka beneath me. We reached the ground level even as the giant flattened another of our men beneath its fist.

Blood dripped from iron fingers, and Bahudde's deep voice filled the hold. "Why won't you *die?*"

Still carrying Valka, we retreated down the ramp, gunfire and the flash of grenades halting the advance of the limping chimera. Bahudde opened fire, letting forth a rain of heavy darts that peppered the tarmac about our feet. One of them slammed through the breastplate of an unshielded peltast and left a hole big around as my thumb. He lumbered on a moment, blood rushing down over his white armor before he fell. Turning back, I saw Barda's troopers wheeling over the black tower of the crawler like vultures above the carcass of some stranded whale. And there was Bahudde, framed by the door of the ramp, the snarling teeth of the drill above its head.

Even absent an arm and limping on one damaged leg, the giant was terrifying. Its white carapace shone sickly in the thin light of the occulted sun, and the flame of its lone remaining eye was like the sun going down in wrath. As it advanced down the ramp, one clawed foot opened and released a mangled shape that once had been a man.

It was not alone. Two dozen of the Cielcin came with it, the pilots and their guards. Dorayaica had surprised me, not calling down its weapon on the ruined crawler. I ground my teeth. This was about to get harder.

Lin retreated ahead of the enemy, his men about him. Udax and his Irchtani flew between us and closed ranks. Unsteadily, I set Valka on her feet. She sagged against me, whole body still shaking.

"You two." I gestured toward two of the Irchtani who alighted around us. "Carry Doctor Onderra back to the Wall."

Before they could hop forward to take her, Valka seized me with one half-working arm. "Don't you dare," she said. "You need me."

"You can't even stand!"

Her eyes—unfocused—drifted to a point over my shoulder, back toward the wreck of the crawler and the monster emerging from it. "I don't need to stand," she said. "I can still fight."

I had no mask then to hide my tears. "I can't lose you," I said.

"You won't," she answered, fingers twitching against my cheek. "Not ever." She leaned forward and in the sight of men and xenobites alike pressed her lips to mine. "Go!" She pushed me away and stumbled, hissing with the pain as one of the Irchtani caught her. "I am with you to the . . . to the end," she said. "Finish this."

CHAPTER 85

THE WINGED CENTURION

THE SHADOW OF THE crawler loomed before me, crooked and burned from where Barda's men had crippled it. The Pale giant looked almost small before it, one clawed hand at the ready, dragging its mangled foot. Bassander's men kept firing on it, and the Irchtani swooped above, raining fire on Bahudde's shield. The shot I expected to fall from the heavens never came. The giant, our men, and the crawler were all too close together.

Sword in hand and unhelmed, I strode back across the tarmac, Udax and Barda both at my side. "Still not much we can do about that armor," I said.

"We can take its other eye," Udax snarled, beak snapping.

"See it done," I said, little knowing what I asked.

Taking his cue, Udax let out a piercing, savage cry and spread wide his vast wings. The centurion leaped into the air, his kinsman after him, pinions beating about my head. For a moment, Hadrian Marlowe stood alone in no man's land, no company but the wind. Valka remained behind with the rearguard, Bassander ahead in the van.

For an instant, it was almost peaceful. The smoky wind blew across my face, carrying on it the stench of war and stink of burning.

Shots flashed against Bahudde's shield but left no mark. I was doubly certain now that the power generator the chimera carried was powerful enough to run a small starship, for rarely have I seen a Royse shield so resilient. It advanced almost as if Bassander were not there, slouching toward Deira and the Storm Wall with clockwork certainty.

"Explosives, damn you! Use explosives!" I heard Bassander cry.

In the instant that followed, the starburst flash of a grenade filled the air, the noise of it bruising eardrums. The giant stumbled, one mighty knee crashing to the tarmac. But twisted as the minds of the Extrasolarian designers doubtless were, their craft was true. Bahudde brought its fist down like a hammer and pulped a legionnaire who had come too close and used the hand to push itself to its feet. A spray of missiles filled the air from the giant's shoulder. A dozen Irchtani fell mangled from the sky; still more vanished in a constellation of orange flame. Through it all flew Udax and his team, cutting tight spirals through the air. In the false night, the silver of the swords flashed like stars. I saw the centurion duck beneath a feral swipe of the general's arm, his actions according Bassander and his men on the ground a chance to draw back.

The Mandari captain drew close to me. "We need to buy Valka time," I said. "She has some sort of plan."

"Is she all right?" the captain asked. He had heard her screaming, too.

I only shook my head. I dared not answer, for to answer was to acknowledge that the answer was *no*. "We have to keep it from the Wall," I said. "It has orders to overload its own power cells!"

"How do you know that?" Bassander looked at me, and I could imagine the look on the face beneath that faceless mask.

"Valka," I said in answer. "How much time can you give us?"

The captain studied the earth for a short moment. "A few minutes. No more."

"It will have to be enough," I said. Remembering myself, I added, "You saved my life."

A piece of the old Lin asserted itself. "We have work to do!" Then he raised Whent's sword and ordered his men forward. There was something admirable in the stolid, simple directness with which he did all things. His enemy stood thirty feet high, weighed several tons, and even crippled was more lethal than a platoon.

But Bassander Lin did not hesitate, nor could I.

I pressed in his wake, following at a jog. A lope. A dead run.

We ran together, and the flashing of our swords in that darkness was like the coming of lightning to a desert with the threat of rain. The general's *scahari* fell before our blades, for no weapon or armor of Cielcin make could withstand the bite of highmatter.

Above our heads, Udax and the Irchtani wheeled, drawing the ire of the general. Bahudde's massive hand caught one of the birds in its fingers and crushed the auxiliary as a man might crack a walnut. The giant's huge feet crashed around us, and another of the birds wheeled overhead and struck a grenade to the general's side. The explosion made Bahudde stumble, and it roared something incomprehensible in its native tongue. Bassander hewed at the damaged foot—but to no avail.

Ignoring him, the giant took one uneven step away, tracking a duo of Irchtani as they swooped about it. They all had sheathed their cutlasses and aimed their plasma burners at Bahudde, peppering its shield with fire. The light and heat clouded the chimera's vision, flooded its sensors and overwhelmed them on infrared and visual light alike.

I parried a blow from one of the crawler pilots and sliced the Cielcin in two. One of the others' *nahute* snapped at me, teeth latching onto the flanged plates in my left shoulder. I cut away and peeled the dying head from my shoulder, glad that only the armor layer was damaged, not the undersuit or the flesh beneath.

"I think 'tis working," came Valka's voice in one ear. I forced down the welter of emotion that came with the weak sound of that voice and flinched as a foot vast as the bole of some ancient tree cracked the pavement not two yards from where I stood. There was a crack in the adamant plate on the calf above the shattered ankle, a hairline break where some flaw in the long-chain molecules of the armor had broken through. I pushed my sword through it, the liquid metal flowing, compressing through the gap. Something sparked, and Bahudde twitched and pulled the leg away, nearly tearing the sword from my grasp.

The great machine rested its weight gingerly upon the damaged limb, surveying the small force arrayed between it and its suicidal goal. It kicked the nearest of our men out of its way, toe hitting with the force of a freight train. The man was dead before he hit the ground.

In rushed Bassander Lin, sword held high, a magnetic grenade clutched in his off hand. The captain slapped the explosive to the giant's calf near where I'd cut and made to leap away.

He was only a little luckier than the last man.

The same leg lanced out and caught Bassander beneath the ribs, striking him with enough force to lift him bodily from the tarmac. He sailed less far than the last man, but hit the tarmac and tumbled, sword flying from his hands. His grenade exploded an instant later, obscuring the enemy's limb from view. The wind carried black smoke away, and a moment after I saw what the captain had bought with his sacrifice.

Nothing at all.

"Lin!" I shouted, but there was no time to see if the captain was dead or alive. Another of the Irchtani struck the pavement at my feet. Dropped there. I looked up, and saw Bahudde's horribly neotenous face peering down at me, one-eyed and teething.

"We cannot be stopped," it said. "You will stand before the Prophet, devil! Just as he has foreseen. Kill me, and our fleet will still land. You will fall. If not today, then the next, or the next, or the next!" It took one limping step toward me, joints whining, and spoke the last words I ever wished to hear from one of its kind. *"Oyade ni."*

This must be.

Choking back unholy terror, I drew myself up to my full height and called back. "If I stand before your master," I said, "it will be to give it your head, and to tell it how you *failed.*"

Brute fury overcame all thought, and Bahudde howled and pulled back its enormous fist to strike me down.

A curious calm stole over me, a serenity empty as the wind. It was a serenity I'd felt only once before, in the instant before Aranata struck me down. I stood there, sans hope, sans fear, sans fury, sans . . . everything. Everything but that deep quiet of the soul that is in all men if we but listen.

I raised my left hand to guard my face, making a bar of my forearm.

The man-high fist struck me a moment after, a vicious hook powerful enough to smash stone to powder.

I didn't flinch.

I stood unmoving as the hills, knees bent, wind rising about us.

Bahudde recoiled and broke the stunned silence. *"Veih!"* it said. "No, it's . . . it's not possible!"

Not likely, I thought, vision fading with that inhuman serenity and focus.

Into the shocked stillness there came a scream, and a dark shape plunged out of the heavens above. Looking straight up, I saw a phalanx of the Irchtani fall out of the darkened sky like a bolt of lighting, wings tucked, claws extended. And their point came Udax, the tip of his *zitraa* extended like a lance. The others fired their plasma burners, filling the air with light and heat enough to blind the giant.

Udax flew on.

Bahudde roared, and the noise of it shook the Wall from its foundations to the white pennons snapping upon the battlements of its uttermost crown. And when the light had faded and the smoke rose to the blackened sky I saw our winged centurion standing with its claws clamped tight to the giant's face, and its sword?

The razor-pointed *zitraa* quivered, buried to the hilt in the sputtering red ruin of Bahudde's last remaining eye.

The *vayadan* swayed, and I felt certain that it would topple and fall dead. I cheered and raised my sword to heaven.

We had won.

The Irchtani crowed about me, voices raised in a piercing cry that was both scream and song of victory.

But Bahudde did not topple or fall dead. It held still for only an instant, swaying like a tree in the wind, for it was no living thing, and though Udax had struck true, there was no brain behind that shattered red eye. No life to take. Bahudde reached up with its lone remaining hand and seized Udax where he stood upon its face. The blind general did not hesitate, but clenched its fist and crushed Udax between its fingers.

Once more, the giant roared, and there was fury and triumph both in the sound.

It dropped the ruin of Udax's body at its feet and crushed the centurion beneath its claws.

All that remained of Udax of Judecca was a red smear on the pavement. That, and a few brown feathers still dancing on the air. Eyes wide with sorrow and rage, I watched that redness spread.

Red blood, I thought. *So like the red of man.*

We are men, Udax had said to me once. *Not things.*

So he was. So he had been. Human or not, he died a man.

The Irchtani whirled into a frenzy and screamed with vengeance for their fallen comrade. They flew at Bahudde, who—though blind—fought back with tooth and claw and what weapons remained to him.

I ran, lest I be crushed beneath its feet. "Valka!" I spoke into the collar baffle of my suit. "If you're going to do something, now would be the time!"

Blinded, the giant stomped and cracked the pavement, shaking the world with the thunder of its fury. I kept running, moving back toward the Wall at an angle that carried me still away from Valka. The soldiers with me, fearing to share in either Udax's or Bassander's fate.

"*Jakaku totajun kizaa wo!*" Bahudde shrieked. The same threat it had made to me on the inner wall of the city. "He will scratch you all out!"

I turned.

Bahudde was running, stumbling blind over the field. Not straight at the wall, but toward it. Its furnace heart still burned, I knew, with fire enough to shatter our Wall. Perhaps the eyes of its master in *Dharan-Tun* above directed it.

"Shoot it down!" I screamed. "Lorian! Shoot it down!"

But we had no lighters, no missiles, and the plasma cannons on the Wall were too few and too short-ranged to avail us.

"Destroy it!"

The Irchtani still flocked about Bahudde, firing where they could. I realized the plasma cannons on the Wall were useless anyhow. Useless as the burners the auxiliaries carried against something so shielded and so well engineered.

It was over, after all.

It had all been for nothing.

Hauptmann's death. The loss of the fleet. The division of our forces. The destruction of the city, the deaths in the starport tunnels. Udax's sacrifice. My quest to Annica. What Urbaine had done to Valka.

All of it for *nothing.*

Nothing.

One of the giant's knees buckled without warning, and it fell, crashing into the pavement like a mountain falling on the plains.

And I heard a voice—a small, bright voice stretched taut with pain—whisper in my ear.

"I have you, you bastard!" Valka spat.

A thrill went through me, and as I stood there—formerly helpless—I watched as the *Vayadan*-General Bahudde of the Iedyr Yemani fell to hands and knees, its titanic form gouging the earth with its convulsions. Too many times, I have seen the bodies of dead men burned to cinder in bombed-out cities in the wake of a Cielcin attack. As men burn, their muscles shorten, cords tightening until the body is crabbed and crouched low like a boxer. The titan folded in on itself the same way, metal body and artificial voice groaning as legs buckled and neck bent and the remaining arm curled tight.

I looked back across the great emptiness of no man's land and saw her. She had fallen beside an Irchtani who crouched to aid her. Her legs were all a tangle, but her back was straight, and she was so far off I could not see her palsied movements or the fever in her eyes. She raised a hand and pointed. Something behind me hissed, and turning I saw the giant's chest cavity open and reveal what remained inside.

Of Iubalu nothing of the flesh remained save the brain and the smile. Of Bahudde there was little more. No face, but the black matter of its brain floated in azure fluid, still connected to the coiled spinal nerve in its glossy sheath—the whole thing shot through with needles and glass wires finer than any hair. There were no heart or lungs to speak of, but three dried fruit-looking organs I took for kidneys hung in suspension, doubtless to clean the blood they supplied to the scant remaining tissue.

"You think this is victory?" The voice that issued from the chassis's internal speakers was thin and airy, nasal almost as Urbaine's voice. "He will . . . be the end of all of you."

I approached the giant, facing the open cavity and the ruins of the creature inside.

I had only one question. "Why?"

Bahudde did not move. It did not answer.

"Why?" I asked again. *Detu marerra o-koun wo!*

"So that he . . . can become *like Them*."

For the thousandth time that day, my blood ran cold. "The Watchers?"

But the lights on the general's chassis were gone. Whether by some art of Valka's or by its own hand I was not sure, but Bahudde was dead. All was quiet but the wind and the burning of the crawler and the distant thunder of the greater battle away by the Cielcin landing fleet.

Lifting my right hand, I kindled my sword again, meaning to *scratch out* what remained of our enemy. To avenge Udax. But the Irchtani were watching. I let my hand fall and turned away. Gesturing sharply at the ground, I said, "It's all yours."

Huge wings filled the air, and the day was filled with the noise of birds.

CHAPTER 86

THE SCOURGE OF EARTH

THE GENERAL'S DEATH SENT shockwaves through the Cielcin vanguard on the ground. Without any clear leader, their command fragmented as groups turned on one another, commanders who had been equally subordinate to the *vayadan* each refusing to follow the other. Pallino told me later that he saw groups of the Pale tear at one another even as our soldiers cut into their ranks, slaughtering as they were slaughtered by man and Cielcin alike. Thus it was he made a wedge of his smaller force and cleaved through the enemy ranks and set fire to their fleet of black ships.

I feared for them. Nearly two miles of open landing field separated them from the Wall. With nothing left to lose, the Cielcin might open fire on the army from orbit at any moment. There was nothing we could do to save them, not cornered and defanged as we were.

Some of their commanders retreated. I saw their rockets streak heavenward from my place beside Bahudde's corpse, believing them the first sign of some new devilry from the black fleet above. For I knew that whatever else had happened—it was only their vanguard that had failed. Out in the Dark beyond the top of the sky the enemy waited. Their black fortress still blocked out the sun. Above us even still was arrayed the greatest fleet of the Pale that mortal man had ever seen. We had cut another finger off the White Hand, but in the dark halls of *Dharan-Tun*, the Prophet watched us all with academic malice.

And our fleet was still more than a day away . . . it would never reach us in time.

Dorayaica had won, and knew it. It had but to reach out its hand and take us, and there was nothing any son of Earth could do to stop it.

The gates of the Storm Wall loomed dead ahead. With not a one of the enemy within a mile of our position, I ordered Lorian to open them. "Get the wounded through!" I said, waving the others on. A knot of men staggered past, some carrying men on their backs or over their shoulders between them. Still more carried men prostrate and lifted them above their heads and bore them like the bodies of conquering heroes passed off hand to hand. Two of the Irchtani carried Valka on interlaced wings. I had walked beside, hurrying our bruised and bloody little convoy back to our doomed fortress to await the final blow of the hammer.

Last of all, eight men carried the unconscious and broken body of Bassander Lin upon their shoulders. His suit had hardened completely, but the triaster trained in field medicine told us his back and ribs were shattered. How he had survived none could say, and yet there was a pulse.

The gates—huge panels of green bronze decorated with relief images of the Exodus from Old Earth—ground steadily open. I drew aside to let the others pass, lingering long enough to shout orders at the men inside that Valka and Lin should be seen to at once. The surgeons might do for Lin, but the hurt on Valka was deeper than anything a medic of the Imperium could heal.

She drew level with me, limping between her Irchtani supporters. Her shoulders shook, and her head lolled to one side, the left eye still sputtering, pupil dilating and contracting as it darted left and right. She looked mad, as mad as any of the beggars I have seen broken on Chantry steps.

"Go on," I said to them. "I'm right behind."

"You aren't coming?" She looked at me confused.

"I want to make sure everyone gets inside," I replied. "I'll be right there." I seized her hand, but her fingers would not close. They fluttered against the back of my hand, weak as sparrow wings. I held her there, not wanting to let go. "Can we fix this?"

Her good eye fixed on me, head hanging like dead weight on her neck. "Probably," she said. "At home, maybe. On Edda. In Tavros. Maybe . . ." Her words trailed off, and she shut her eyes. "I don't know what he did to me."

The line moved around us, men limping back to the safety of the Wall. In the distance, I could see the smoke of the burning fleet rising, red-lit from below.

When next she spoke, it was in Panthai, so the others would not understand. "Maybe you were right. Maybe I shouldn't have come here."

I twitched, eyes pulled back to her face. For an instant, it was as if

Urbaine's curse had never happened. She looked like herself, head hung low, eyes hooded, red-black hair matted to her scalp. "Don't say that." I squeezed her hand and did not let go when the tremors started. "We'd all be dead if not for you."

Switching back to Galstani, she whispered, "We might still die."

"We might," I said. "But not today."

"Not today," she snorted. "Tomorrow."

She pulled free of the Irchtani minding her and slumped into my arms, laying her full weight on me. I held her, and pressed her cheek to mine. "Tomorrow," I agreed. "Tomorrow may be all the time we need."

Haltingly, she wrapped one arm around my neck. Her whole body shook. How light she seemed, insubstantial as the paper lanterns lit at funerals. Almost I feared to let her go, afraid that she—like the lanterns—would fall into the sky. She was so unlike herself, so frail and fading, as though it were a memory of Valka I held and not Valka herself.

"Put me on . . . on ice," she said. "I don't know if 'twill get worse." My grip only tightened, and she said on, "Just until you can . . . can get me home . . ."

I was nodding, swallowing hard. "Tell Lorian I ordered it." Pulling back, I pressed my forehead to hers, screwed my eyes shut. "I'm sorry, Valka. I'm so sorry."

"I'm not," she said. "I saved you." She kissed me again, and half-stepping away, she staggered back into the arms of the Irchtani. "Take me," she said to them, a measure of her former command creeping into her tone. I watched her go, supported by the two xenobite auxiliaries, half-carried, half-stumbling. I blinked back tears and—once more screwing my eyes shut—turned to walk back along the line. I would be the last of our little force back behind Deira's walls.

"Hadrian!" she called after me, and turning I saw her looking back over her shoulder. I stopped walking. "I love you!"

The tears welled up again, and I sucked in my breath to still them, Gibson's antique remonstrances echoing in my mind, urging my heart to stillness. It would not still. In all our long years, I could count the number of times Valka had said those words to me upon my fingers. Not because she did not feel them, but because she was who she was, and who she was was guarded.

Letting all the air out of me, I called back the only answer that fit. "You're not wrong!"

Her smile was the last I saw of her as she vanished beneath the mighty arch, and it lifted my heart. She vanished within the fortress, the line grown short behind her, men and Irchtani filing in.

"So few . . ." croaked a voice from behind.

Kithuun-Barda had landed beside me. He was right. A thousand of his people had flown out from Gododdin to face the Pale. Less than half that number remained.

"Another victory like this," I said, "and we're finished."

The inhuman chiliarch made a low chirruping nose and tucked its beak against its armored breast, gripped its crossed bandoleers with its talons.

"They died bravely," I said, placing a hand on the old bird's shoulder.

"They *died*," Barda said. "So many young ones gone before their nesting."

"Dead," I said, "is not gone." Sensing the creature's eyes on me, I added, "Death is not the end, *kithuun*. Nothing ends." The elder had nothing to say to that, and together we watched the line pass on. Bahudde's words danced inside my skull and seemed to caper and rub unseen hands there. *Your time has ended.*

Urbaine's word joined them: *You are fighting the end. Your end.*

I prayed they were both wrong.

"I'm sorry," I said. "I know that's cold comfort." I looked down at the tribesman and smiled my broken Marlowe smile. "Udax saved my life."

Barda croaked loudly, making me think of nothing so much as an overlarge parrot. "Udax owed you his life. This he repaid."

"And your tribe has paid hundreds of times," I said. "Your people will be honored throughout the Empire, you have my word." Not knowing if I had the power or the right to make such promises, I added, "You should be made full subjects of the throne."

The elder said nothing, but watched the line go by. When at last the hindmost had passed us and passed on toward the gate, the *kithuun* leaped away, flapping to join its men without another word. Alone then, I glanced back toward the wreck of the fleet and the fighting. Pallino's men would follow soon. Thunder rolled, and lightning cracked the far horizon, lighting the blackened sky.

A ghastly white light bathed the landscape, a great questing beam scouring all the space from the Wall to the burning fleet. Fearing some weapon like the orbital laser, I flung an arm across my eyes and ducked my head in expectation of the final blast.

No blast came.

The beam dimmed, became a faint glow that illuminated the gray expanse of the field and the white rims of blasting pits and set the whole of the Storm Wall to shining as though it were wrought all of moonstone.

"Lord Marlowe, get back to the Wall!" came Lorian's whisper in my ear.

He didn't have to tell me twice. I turned and ran. It wasn't three hundred feet to the bronze-fronted gates, and less than that to the edge of the shield's inclusion zone. I ran, pteruges snapping at my knees.

I did not make it even halfway.

"Surrender!"

The word fell like a blow and smote all of Berenike, so loud was it and incredible. The ground shook and dust ran like rain down the surface of the Wall above me. I froze, realizing only haltingly that the word had been spoken in the tongue of men.

Again, that word filled the vaults of air and shook the world with its winding.

"Surrender!"

The light on the Storm Wall flickered with movement like the reflection of a white garment in dark glass.

"Hadrian," Lorian asked, all formal protocol forgotten, "are you seeing this?"

Something moved in the corner of my vision, and I spun round, hand sliding toward my sword. But that same hand fell away in futility and in horror when I saw what awaited above the plains of Deira.

It was a giant to dwarf the mightiest of our colossi, an image of terror and majesty to dwarf even the high parapet of the Storm Wall, so tall the points of its iron crown were lost in the roiling clouds. It was a holograph miles high, a luminous shadow cast upon the plains from the evil fortress above. Ghost-blue it was and insubstantial. I saw the clouds through it, and so faint was it in outline and so uncertain its resolution that its feet were altogether lost. Above, legs vast as towers and clad in enameled armor rose for hundreds of feet to the too-narrow torso and shoulders, above which rose the long neck and hideous smooth face of the dark lord of the abyss itself crowned in silver and iron.

Eyes like twin pits surveyed the land below, and a sucking dread moved in me, for it was a face I'd seen before, the same sepulchral visage I had witnessed in dreams and in visions of times unrealized. The Prince of Princes and Prophet of the Cielcin, anointed of the Watchers who dream beneath the stars. *Aeta ba-Aetane* and *Shiomu*. The Scourge of Earth. The *thing* that would be king.

Syriani Dorayaica.

"Surrender!" the thunderhead image spoke, seeming to crouch over the Wall and the city behind it. I was an ant at its feet, wholly unseen.

Lorian spoke up. "My lord, they're *hailing* us."

"Can you put me through?" I asked.

"I . . . yes, my lord."

"It's trying to impress us," I said. "It wants us to cower."

The commander's voice came tight over the line. "We can't surrender." I heard the rest of Lorian's thought without him having to say it. *They'll kill us anyway.* Both Aristedes and myself were silent a long moment, and he added, "We can't negotiate with the Pale."

I barked a hollow laugh, standing just inside the shadow of the gate, the better to see the awful specter and remain unseen. *That* was the truth, and one I'd paid dearly to learn. "I know they're going to kill us," I said. "Put me through."

"My lord," Lorian said, "it would be better to leave it. We are as safe here as we can be. We might be able to stall and await the fleet."

"All the more reason to keep it talking," I said. "It doesn't know they're coming."

A moment's silence, then Aristedes said, "Audio only. You're on."

I did not speak at once, but stood there, unmoving beneath twin statues of Ever-Fleeting Time carved to either side of the great door. The two-faced statues peered in and out, one youthful, one aged, watching all approaches to the gates of the city. The wounded still massed within, the atrium crowded with men and Irchtani and medical staff bearing the sign of the green star. Of Lin and Valka there was no sign. I sensed eyes on me: the eyes of men and bird men and of the nurses in white caps. I sensed too the hollow gaze of the holographed giant outside, though it had not fixed upon me.

Still unseen by the enemy, I stepped into the center of the arch and watched the ghostly titan looming above, crown higher than the crown of many mountains. Looking past the blue-white image to the false moon occluding the sun, I raised my voice. "I have been waiting a long time for this moment," I said.

The giant cocked its head, eyes contracting behind lids and nictitating membranes. "Your voice . . ." It spoke in perfect Galstani, voice cold and high as the clouds that wreathed its head. "I have studied you for years, kinsman. Well met at last."

"Kinsman?" I took a step back, uncomprehending.

"We are the same, Lord Marlowe." I could just see the shape of glassy teeth projected in the ship-sized face above. "You conquered Otiolo. We are brothers, you and I. *Aetamn*."

"*Aetamn*," I echoed. *Both Aeta.*

The Prophet bared its teeth in a monstrous smile. "You killed Aranata. By our laws, you are *Aeta. Aeta ba-Yukajjimn*."

The King of Vermin, I translated. "The Rat King." I had nothing to say to that.

"But a king nonetheless," the Scourge of Earth replied. "And you slew Ulurani as well, I hear. You are doing my work for me." The conqueror drew itself up, and though its image stretched more than five thousand feet into the sky, I wondered if it was not smaller than Aranata had been, narrower in the shoulder. But the sharp edge of command cracked in its voice, and it spoke the tongues of men with a polish I'd not thought to find in such a creature. "But your reign is done. You will surrender yourself and come to me."

"And if I refuse?"

"You must not refuse," Syriani Dorayaica said.

"Why me?"

"Because you belong to *it*," the Prophet answered. "It is an abomination. You are an abomination. You call it *Quiet,* but it is no such thing. Its *word* has been heard across the stars, its challenge to the very *gods*." I was silent, not knowing what to say to this pronouncement. Syriani knew of the Quiet. Of course it did. Had not Iubalu said it had spoken with the Watchers themselves? That it had visions, same as me? "You know of what I speak, kinsman," it said.

The wailing of an infant sounded in my ears, and the image of the egg and the cathedral beneath the dark emptiness of the sky. The war. The one war. Had the Prophet seen what I'd seen? Its armies marching across the stars, burning planet after planet? Had it seen the *Demiurge* and heard me speak those terrible words? Had it seen me in chains beneath the black dome above the sea of lofty pillars?

"And if I surrender, you'll spare the rest of my people on this world?" I drew back as I spoke, deeper into the shadows of the arch between the twin icons of Time. "You'll guarantee their safe conduct offworld?"

"Hadrian, no!" I heard Lorian shout. I silenced his line with a gesture on my terminal.

"Safe . . . conduct," the Cielcin prince repeated. I wondered if it struggled with the concept of negotiation as Aranata had. There was something in Syriani's eyes—even in holograph—that chilled me. A depth of wisdom and antiquity, an antique malice that reminded me more of Kharn Sagara than it did any prince of the Pale. "One life for millions. You value yourself too highly."

"Those are my terms," I said. "And you will return any prisoners you have captured this day to us."

The Prophet laughed, a high, braying sound that thrust daggers of ice between the discs of my spine. "This I will not do! You are in little position to be making demands."

"I have cut off two of your fingers!" I said. "I will take the whole hand if you try me."

"With what men?" the Prince of Princes asked, laughing still. "Your force is broken. My *vanguard* was sufficient to take your city from you. Your fleet is no more. The beast, Hauptmann, is dead. You have nothing."

A pang went through me. So, it knew about Hauptmann. But I marshaled myself, and looking up at the mile-high giant hovering over the plain, I answered it. "We have *millions.*"

"Cattle!" the titan sneered in its turn. "Not fighters."

"But they will fight," I said. "We will not be the first men to endure you." As I spoke, it occurred to me that it was precisely for our habit of digging in for sieges that the Pale called us *vermin.* Rats. True warriors would meet them in the field, in the black of space, and not hide beneath thousands of tons of stone.

This time Syriani did not laugh. The giant apparition shifted, one taloned finger pointing down at the line of the Wall with supernatural derision. "Surrender yourself to me, and I will withdraw from this system, but I will not relinquish the prizes we took in the city. My soldiers must feed." I pressed my tongue against the roof of my mouth and did not reply, tried not to think about the people in the tunnels we had failed. "That is my offer, kinsman. Do with it as you will." The cloud-bound giant turned as if to walk away and vanish into the coming storm.

"Wait!" I cried, and stepped out from the arch. Still unseen by the giant and by the Cielcin who watched from above, I said, "What assurance can you give that you will honor this bargain?"

The Prince of Princes clasped ringed and taloned hands behind its back. Silver chains hung from its horns and the iron tines of its crown and twinkled in its braided, chalk-white hair. It peered back over one black-robed shoulder. "You doubt me?" It turned away, raised one hand. "I shall allow your men on the field to return to your fortress *unharmed.*"

Against my will, my eyes closed with relief. The fate of Pallino and the men in the field had hung heavy on my mind ever since I returned to the fortress. I had a choice to make. Accept the prince's terms, sacrifice myself, and save every man and woman on Berenike—or refuse, and fight to the last. It was not really a choice. I thought back to my visions. Had I stood alone in chains before the black dome? Or had my men stood with me? It seemed I remembered both visions. By agreeing to the prince's terms, was I placing myself on the path that led to that end?

Or . . .

"Lorian, how long before the fleet is projected to return?" I asked, switching the lines with a twist of my terminal controls.

The answer came faster than I thought possible. "Anywhere between twenty-seven and thirty-one hours. Hadrian, I know what you're thinking. Just refuse, we can hold another day, don't—"

I killed the call a second time and shut my eyes again, thinking. There was a chance, narrow though it was, a chance that we would not have to suffer another day of fighting at all. I could not trust Dorayaica or any of the Cielcin to keep its word, but to keep its word for a day? To allow Pallino and the men back into the Wall and to hold their fire just long enough for Otavia and the whole of the Imperial fleet to converge on Berenike with fire and sword? I had risked my life for less. I had only to make the choice.

To create is to choose, that was what the Quiet said.

I chose.

"Very well," I said. "I will surrender myself at this time tomorrow." Days on Berenike stretched for nearly forty hours. It was more than enough time to give the fleet time to appear.

"You will surrender yourself *now,*" the prince said, still not turning back to face me.

"No," I said. "I must set my affairs in order." I looked up at the giant towering among the clouds. "You've won, Your Highness." If the prince expected me to grovel or throw myself upon its mercy, I did not quite disappoint it. "I ask you only for this small mercy. *Ndaktu.*"

"*Ndaktu.*" The prince's shoulders hunched. It was a formal plea for mercy, the sort of plea a slave might make of its master, as Uvanari had once made to me.

"You have until the sun rises above your Wall tomorrow," it said. And with that, the Scourge of Earth vanished, its titanic phantasm vanishing in a swirling of gray cloud and grayer dust. In its wake came quiet and the sound of wind. In the heavens far above, the dark shadow of *Dharan-Tun* slid off the face of the sun, and pale sunlight fell once more upon the world of men. I watched the fortress go; black and mottled white it fell across the sky like an evil moon. Not gone. Only biding its time.

Beneath the black towers of smoke from the wreck of burning ships, I saw the white shapes of men returning home alive. Alone then but for the wounded men behind me, I staggered a few steps out from the bronze gate and the arch and sank to my knees on the pavement. Not caring who saw, I wept.

CHAPTER 87

NO SWORD CAN CUT

"MY LORD, THIS IS a mistake."

"I have to do it," I said, looking down at the little man before me. Lorian Aristedes hadn't slept since before the attack began, and the strain of some stimulant was in his eyes. He leaned heavily on his cane, and I wondered just how much more weight those narrow and fragile shoulders could bear. He might have to bear *all,* I realized, or break trying. I had no right to place the load on him, and he had no right to refuse. "The fleet will make it here in time."

Lorian's fevered eyes narrowed. "They might not."

"You're mad, Had," Pallino said. We were alone in the lift, the three of us, descending from the command center back toward the atrium-turned-hospital near the lower gate. The old soldier had returned just after sundown the previous night—the last son of Earth to quit the field. He'd brought up the rear of the line, the arm of a wounded legionnaire wrapped around his shoulders. The girl had taken a shot to the knee and had to hop along with her commanding officer's help. Seeing her, I thought of Renna. The peasant girl had probably died fighting in the tram tunnels. I hoped she had, for the alternative was that she had been taken alive by Dorayaica's soldiers and was even now interned in the labor camps of *Dharan-Tun.*

Cattle, Dorayaica had said of his captives. *Yukajjimn.*

Rats.

"You're only learning this now, old man?" I tried to smile. I failed.

"They should have been here already," Lorian said. Twenty-eight hours had passed since the Prophet made its appearance. We were well into the window Lorian had given me, but the fleet had not appeared.

I placed a hand on the smaller man's shoulder. "They'll be here," I said. "They have to be."

We descended in silence after that for several levels, the lights of floors strobing by. To my surprise, Pallino reached out and punched the control that stopped the lift descending. We ground to a halt.

I looked at the old man—though he was old no longer. His short, dark hair stuck out at rough angles, and a skein of silver surgical scars shone like wire though the leathery skin of his face. He was not the same man who had climbed out of the fighting pits with me on Emesh, but the eyes were the same. It was only that there were two of them now.

"Let me go with you," he said.

Unbidden, a smile tore at my lips. Pallino and Elara were all I had left of Had the myrmidon, now that Siran was gone. With Valka—and I supposed Bassander Lin—they were all I had left of Emesh. And so when Pallino spoke it was almost as though I were Had the myrmidon again and not Sir Hadrian, not Halfmortal, not Demon in White. It felt right.

"Had?" he asked. I hadn't spoken. "You're not going alone."

Sparing a glance for Lorian, who hung his head, I said, "You'd go with me to the Cielcin? To the end?"

"If you asked me to," he said, and held my gaze without blinking. "You bought me this second life. I may as well pay for it."

Thinking of Udax, I said, "I've had enough of people repaying their debts to me. You should live like Siran. If the fleet doesn't come . . . if they take me, you run." I looked at Lorian. "Both of you. You've fought enough."

"Fight's not done," Pallino said.

"What about Elara?" I asked. "You'd leave her behind?"

The old soldier didn't blink. "That's rich coming from you, lad. Doctor Onderra's on ice."

"Valka will understand," I said, but winced inwardly. The old bastard was right.

"No, she won't," he retorted. "She'll kill you."

At once I found I could look at neither Pallino nor Lorian. "She won't have to. I'll be dead."

"I'd hope so for your sake when she finds out what you've done," Pallino said. Lorian made a face, but kept uncharacteristically silent. He ducked his head, fingers drumming on the shaft of his cane.

"The fleet will make it," I said. "And you're not coming with me."

"You don't get a bloody say, lad," Pallino said. "I'm not letting you go alone." He held my gaze, unblinking.

Unspeaking, I reached out and punched the button that resumed our descent. I did not break eye contact with the other man, but watched for some tic, some tell, some fault line in his convictions. There was none.

The doors hissed open a moment after, and I stepped into the crowded hall. Men languished on cots or on pallets on the ground. This near the gates, the men were all soldiers, survivors of the previous day's battle and those members of the rearguard who had remained to defend the Wall. Faces turned toward us as we stepped into the hall. Men sat straighter, some stood to salute. A murmuration of voices followed us.

"That's him?"

"The devil?"

"Marlowe?"

"He's shorter than I expected."

"Quiet!"

"Is he going?"

"It can't be! It's some kind of trick!"

I let them talk, and stepped carefully between pallets, careful not to put my boot on anything any man called his bed. The path was narrow, and wound down the hall toward the space where the ceiling opened up and the tiled floor of the atrium ran past the customs houses to the outer gates. The whole space was filled with soldiers. Sitting, standing—most of them reclining on the floor, awaiting the alarm blast and the news that battle had come.

"If you go," Lorian whispered, "they'll lose hope."

"If I go," I said back, "they might not need it."

"Even if the fleet comes," Lorian stopped walking and planted his cane between his feet, "the minute you're in their hands, you're dead."

I kept walking, Pallino close behind. I did not look back. "Haven't you heard? I can't be killed." I said the words loud enough that the men about me froze and fell deadly silent. I had said the thing jovially, conjuring up the old gladiatorial bravado. Lorian wasn't wrong. Whatever I was, whatever I meant to the soldiers, my loss would be a blow. Moving slowly, I passed beneath the arches of the customs gates and past the arches that led down toward the tram platforms that led out to the starport terminals and the tunnels where the spillover refugees had been taken by the enemy. The men ahead were all on their feet, all armored, all armed. They parted ranks as we approached.

"Has it moved?" I asked one of the wardens, an older man whose dark face reminded me so much of the soldier Carax.

"No, lord. It's just . . . watching."

The Prophet's giant apparition had returned not half an hour before and demanded I surrender myself. Ever since, the specter had floated more than a mile high above the city and the Wall, surveying all there was to survey with eyes like pools of ink. It had not spoken again, had not stirred.

"Shall I open the gate, sir?" the warden asked.

Fear is a poison, I told myself, and squared myself to the door. "Do it," I said.

A chink of sunlight appeared between the mighty doors. The relief-cast bronzes slid apart, admitting the curling wind. The day outside was fair— all hints of the storm promised yesterday were gone. Empty promises. Lacking the white cape, I had donned my old familiar greatcoat over the black armor. I pulled its collar up about my ears. It was now or never.

"Guards." I raised my chin. "Do not let the chiliarch through those doors."

"What?" Pallino surged forward, but a half dozen men converged to block his way. I heard Pallino cuff one of them and winced internally.

Pallino growled. "Had, you son of a bitch!"

I looked back. "Give my love to Elara," I said, and shifting my gaze to Lorian, I added, "If this doesn't work, you get these people home." Pallino struck one of the men holding him and nearly broke free, but three more piled on. It took nine men to restrain him properly.

The good commander flashed a salute, and for once in his life there was no air of casual mockery in the gesture.

I started walking, and passed the icons of Time and so exited the city of men.

It took a moment to resolve the ghastly image of Syriani Dorayaica against that pale and sunlit sky, but it was there, if less substantial than the clouds above.

"Any time now, Corvo," I muttered, looking out on the ruin of the last day's battle. The crawler stood not far off, still smoking, and Bahudde's mutilated form beside it. The smoke of the burning fleet and the blasted power plant still tainted the sky, but they were far off, and did not trouble my universe. The noon-high sun cast no shadows on the earth, and so I had no company whatever as I marched out across the wastes of no man's land.

It was so quiet, so still. It was almost peaceful.

"How small you are," Dorayaica said. Looking up, I saw the massive holograph smile, and even as it did once more the dark fastness of

Dharan-Tun washed across the sun. The Prince of Princes had timed its orbit almost perfectly. The day turned gray around us. Grayer. Then black. A second eclipse, dark as the last but infinitely more lonely. The mountain-high holograph's smile turned only more intense in the blackness.

I offered no reply. Every silence prolonged affairs, and every prolongation brought Corvo and the whole of the fleet nearer. I decided I had gone far enough, and stopped.

Silence.

I had not slept, and stood there in an exhaustion close to dreaming. With my second sight I saw the rivers of time, the other presents playing about me. We all stood waiting under that darkling sky. Every Hadrian that could be, that could come from that moment.

"Have you nothing to say?" The phantasm's voice shook the air.

I spread my arms and spoke over the same band as the day before. "Here I am."

"Alone?" Dorayaica asked.

"That was the agreement!" I said, arms still raised. "Send your shuttle. You have what you want."

More starkly visible by the light of its eclipse, the giant holograph stooped, crouching as the real Prophet crouched upon the projection plate in its ship. It loomed over me, face large as a city block, eyes deep and fathomless as hell. "I do." There briefly it flashed its glassy teeth.

Syriani Dorayaica stood.

"And I have your word?" I asked. "You will spare the people of this world? Grant them safe conduct back to our land?"

"My word," the giant agreed. "Yes. They will be spared. They will deliver my message to your *Aeta ba-Aetane ba-Yukajjimn,* your *Emperor.*"

I raised my chin, defied the giant and asked—though I knew the answer— "What message?"

When Dorayaica spoke, it was not to me. It spoke to the Wall, to the millions of people in it and under it. To Lorian Aristedes, to Commandant Bancroft, the governor-general, and every clerk and logothete of the Imperial government on Berenike—to every soldier and peasant, too—and to Alexander, a prince of the realm. "That Hadrian Marlowe has fallen. That I broke him on the field of battle. And that he can—in fact—be killed."

That—more than anything—reassured me that the creature meant what it said. We had not made a deal at all, had not bargained. The survival of the others was no concession granted me as an equal, for among the

Cielcin there are no equals. It was only part of the great prince's plan. I was
to be carried away, dragged to hell above in the sight of millions.

A *triumph.*

How long had it been watching us? Learning our ways? The *Shiomu*
knew our tongue as if it had been born to it, and knew our minds. I
thought of the rage in Pallino's eyes. The desperation. The fever and exhaustion in Lorian's. As we had paraded Iubalu through the streets and
over the sky-bridges of the Eternal City, so I had been paraded across no
man's land—would be paraded to the alien stars to die some wretched and
lonely death. There would be no body to burn in state, no organs for the
canopic jars. No symbol to rally about. It would be as if Hadrian Marlowe
had never existed at all. I looked along the cresting wave of time, saw that
infinity of myself peering back. All of it—all of us—*gone.*

Only there was no ship. No shuttle. No black tower crashing upon our
shores from the ocean of stars above. No chariot of fire.

Only emptiness. Only quiet. Only the stage the enemy had set for its
little show.

A vague sense of uneasiness began to creep over me, and I looked up
into the face of the giant floating in the firmament above. Dorayaica's
moon of a face grinned down at me, teeth seeming black in the pale blue
of the projection. "I expected better of you, *kinsman.*" It straightened, jew-
els flashing in its crown and on the bands wrapped about its horns. It
laughed low and quiet in its throat. "I am so disappointed. *This* bested two
of my fellow princes? Slew two of my generals? This?" It looked round,
and I guessed that just as Syriani Dorayaica performed for the millions
behind the Wall at my back, it addressed an audience of its own kind as
well. "This is the White Devil? The one they call Halfmortal? I am Syriani, Blood of Elu! Blessed of Miudanar! The one the *yukajjimn* call the
Scourge of Earth! Prince of Princes! Master of the Thirteen Tribes of Eue!
And you, you are *nothing!*"

Light blossomed all around me, red and granular. Too late, I realized
my mistake. I had become too fixed upon my vision, upon the dome and
the forest of black pillars, upon the image of myself paraded in chains. The
Cielcin in the tunnels had said *I belonged to the Prophet.* Bahudde had promised to bring me before its master. I had imagined that I was to be taken
offworld, to be brought to that evil place before the dome. I thought—
what had I thought? That Syriani would sacrifice me to its dark gods, to
the Watchers, the way I had seen bodies sacrificed in my visions atop the
mountain?

But Syriani intended none of these things. If its men had their orders to take me alive, it was only that I might be killed publicly. Violently. In full sight of man and Cielcin alike. I had thought it would send an escort—thought I had time.

I was wrong.

I shut my eyes, turned my face down against the laser flash I knew was coming.

For anyone else, it was the end.

But I had one move left on the board. Only one.

But it was a remarkably good move.

It had, after all, worked astonishingly well on Durand.

The air around stank of ozone, of burning stone. The atmosphere crackled as with the tang that preceded lightning, and I felt as if I stood in the door of a kiln. There had been no sound, no sound at all. Only white heat, red hot. I died—or might have died. I died a thousand times, but for every universe, every narrative where the laser struck me down, there was another where it failed. Strands of possibility indistinguishable from our own. I had but to reach out and *choose*—and *create* the world I wanted. And just as Durand's bullet had passed through me, so too the laser fell by, burning all around . . .

. . . save me.

The tarmac all about me boiled and glowed with molten heat that rose in terrible waves. Undaunted, unburnt, I stepped forward, still clinging to the vision of those other worlds, selecting with each step—as I had on Annica—from those unlikely quantum states that kept me miraculously intact.

Stepping out from the burning circle and the column of white smoke, I raised my arms in defiance of the god-like apparition that recoiled in the air above.

"You should have sent an army!" I said, speaking for all the world to hear. The prince's trap was almost perfect. Almost.

It had not known what gift the Quiet had given me. For all Syriani knew and might have known of the Quiet and of the dark gods who dream behind the stars, it had not known enough. It *should* have sent an army. For all its pomp and circumstance, all its carefully staged theatrics and drama, Syriani had chosen the one weapon I knew I could escape.

The giant's eyes widened with horror. "How?"

"You said it yourself," I said, unable to help myself. "I'm an abomination."

Certain the prince would fire again at any moment, I shut my eyes and tried to focus. My awareness of the infinite potential stretch of time widened again, consciousness spanning countless narrative moments, ready to choose.

"Our offer stands, *kinsman!*" I spat the final word, still holding my eyes shut and focus tight in my hands. "If you want me, come and take me!"

The fleet had not come, after all. Opening my eyes, I turned and began walking back. I had only to walk straight across the lone and level earth, the Prophet's *triumph* turning to ashes around me . . . and the Devil victorious.

Right on cue, the targeting laser painted the landscape red around me. I reached, selected the narrative, the probability state.

I shut my eyes and kept walking. White light—brighter than anything I'd known, brighter than all I would know but once—still bled through my eyes. There came the smell of ozone, the stench of burning stone. The air about me once more thrummed with the tang of static lightning.

I did not stop.

And there! A brighter light boiled across the sky, and looking back I saw white light and crimson fill the heavens like the novae of a million dying stars. They flashed across the void like summer lightning and struck the face of that evil moon, and the ghastly phantasm faltered, flickered, and died.

Syriani Dorayaica vanished, its holograph crashing apart like an image upon a broken windowpane. Turning back to watch, I saw a fireball blaze in the night, and knew that somewhere a ship had been destroyed. I smiled, and raised my hand to the heavens even as *Dharan-Tun* slid once more from the face of our sun.

The fleet had come at last—so late, but not too late to save us. Otavia and the *Tamerlane* had returned with Corran and the *Sieglinde* and nine legions of the sun! And not alone. Every ship of the sector followed on, all those who had come late and rallied at Hauptmann's rendezvous point in the Dark beyond the system's edge.

We'd won.

Heavy bronze doors ground open ahead of me. My shadow—cast by the newly liberated sun—led the way. There are silences and *silences*, Reader, and they are not the same. So many times I had heard the empty silence of space, or the deep quiet of the wild. They are empty silences. This silence was full. Thousands of faces looked at me from the atrium ahead. There was Lorian, and there Pallino and the warden of the gate. And there was Barda among the Irchtani, their beady eyes and beaked faces mingled with the wide-eyed stares of men. And every one of them was silent.

Crowds that size are never silent.

Or never silent long.

"He's alive . . ."

"Did you see?"

"We all saw, Iorath!"

"Alive? But how?"

"That shot should have blown him to atoms . . ."

"Alive! Alive?"

"Let me at him!" came the familiar voice, full of relief and raw anger. "I'll knock his teeth in!" I could not help but smile. Pallino had broken free and came racing out the gateway toward me. I raised my hands, a sign both of greeting and surrender. The big myrmidon seized me by the lapels and shook me. "You absolute whoreson!" he screamed, mere inches from my face. "You fucking lunatic! What the hell was that?" He did not let go.

Placing my hands on both his wrists, I forced him to release me. "If you'd come with me, Pallino, you'd be dead."

"And they say Valka's the fucking witch, man. Black Earth!" He drew back, shaking his head. "Black fucking Earth . . . did you know it was going to do that?"

I could not look the man in the eyes. "No. No, I didn't. I didn't want you throwing your life away." Looking past him, I saw Lorian standing beneath the sculpted image of Time. "What's happening up there?"

The little man kept a finger on the patch behind his ear to ensure good conduction. "Their worldship just jumped to warp. You must have really rattled them with that stunt of yours." An evil-looking smile cut across the intus's bony face. "We did it."

"And not a moment too soon," Pallino said.

Thinking of the two shots that should have killed me, I said, "They could have come sooner."

"Lord Marlowe!" one of the soldiers cried, coming forward. "Is it true?" The fellow came only a little forward, but stopped at the gates and fell to his knees like a man in temple. "Are you the Chosen?"

It was the same question Renna had asked me when the battle began. The question doubtless on the lips of every man and woman in the hall.

"Is he the Chosen?"

"The Chosen?"

"The Son of Earth!"

"The God Emperor reborn!

"The Chosen! The Chosen One is here!"

My answer did not even matter. Everyone last one of them had *seen,* had witnessed the confrontation on the plain. No answer of mine could make a difference. No answer at all. I had lost control of my dream. I was Chosen because they believed me to be, whatever the truth may be. That was what the Chantry would say, what they would tell the Emperor.

I could not hide anymore.

As if summoned by that thought I looked up to the concourse overlooking the customs stations and saw red hair among the peasant taupe and brown. Alexander caught my eye and held it. There was nothing in his face but cold fear and suspicion. I hung my head, wishing I could be anywhere else, while all around me ten thousand voices rang against the filigreed vaults:

"The Son of Earth! The Son of Earth! The Son of Earth has come!"

There are endings, Reader, and this is one: a victory . . . and a defeat. A victory because we turned back the Scourge of Earth and its army. A defeat because no victory—no change—comes without loss. A defeat because so many thousands lay dead in the city of Deira and in the skies above it and beneath its Wall. A defeat because thousands more were taken to serve and fodder the Pale armies of the enemy. And a defeat because it cost me my secrecy. As I stood in the shadow of that cyclopean gate, I knew . . .

. . . there was no going back. My feet were on the path, though whether that path led to a black dome or a day of fire I could not say, and so stood by beneath the hateful gaze of a *human* prince while his people cheered and called me a living god.

If what I have done disturbs you, Reader, I do not blame you. If you would read no further, I understand. You have the luxury of foresight. You know where this ends.

I shall go on alone.

THE MEIDUA RED COMPANY

FOLLOWING HIS INDUCTION INTO the ranks of the Royal Knights Victorian, Hadrian Marlowe's Red Company entered the service of His Radiance, William XXIII. They served the throne for decades at more than half a dozen battles, including Arae, Cellas, Thagura, Oxiana, and—most famously—at Aptucca, where Hadrian Marlowe slew the Cielcin Prince Ulurani. At its height, the Red Company numbered nearly 100,000 men, mostly plebeian soldiers kept in cryonic fugue aboard the *ISV Tamerlane*, an Eriel-class battleship. Marlowe's Red Company is peculiar among companies in the Imperial service, in that its upper echelons were composed primarily of Norman foederati personally loyal to Hadrian himself and not Imperial loyalists, though this changed somewhat with the passage of time.

Here follows a list of those members of the Red Company mentioned in this third volume of Lord Marlowe's account:

LORD HADRIAN ANAXANDER MARLOWE, Royal Knight Victorian, Lord Commandant of the Red Company, Hero of Aptucca. The Halfmortal, the Sun Eater, Starbreaker, Palekiller, Deathless. Notorious genocide responsible for the death of the entire Cielcin species.

—His paramour, **VALKA ONDERRA VHAD EDDA,** a Tavrosi demarchist and xenologist interested in the Quiet phenomenon. Scientific advisor to the Red Company.

—His myrmidons, friends and former coliseum fighters from Emesh:

—**PALLINO OF TRIESTE,** chiliarch and Hadrian's bound armsman. A veteran of the Cielcin Wars, raised to the patrician class. Originally lost his eye in the Battle of Argissa.

—His paramour, **ELARA OF EMESH,** quartermaster for the *ISV Tamerlane* and Hadrian's bound armsman. Raised to the patrician class.

—**SIRAN OF EMESH,** first centurion and Hadrian's bound armsman. Raised to the patrician class.

OTAVIA CORVO, captain of the *ISV Tamerlane*, former Norman mercenary recruited during the Pharos Affair. Possibly a homunculus.

—Her First Officer, **BASTIEN DURAND,** commander, former Norman mercenary from Algernon recruited during the Pharos Affair.

—Her officers:

—**RODERICK HALFORD,** commander, the so-called night captain, in charge of running the *Tamerlane* while the rest of the crew rested in cryonic fugue, the seventh son of a minor palatine lord.

—**LORIAN ARISTEDES,** commander and tactical officer for the *ISV Tamerlane*. The bastard son of the Grand Duke of Patmos and one of his knights, a palatine intus plagued by idiosyncratic pain and connective tissue disorders.

—**KARIM GARONE,** called **CRIM,** lieutenant commander and Security Officer for the *ISV Tamerlane*, former Norman mercenary recruited during the Pharos affair.

—His paramour, **ILEX,** lieutenant commander, ship's engineer. A dryad homunculus recruited on Monmara.

—**FELIX KOSKINEN,** lieutenant and ship's helmsman. A young palatine officer.

—**ADRIC WHITE,** lieutenant and ship's navigator. A young palatine officer.

—**JULIANA PHERRINE,** lieutenant and ship's communications officer. A young palatine officer.

—**LUANA OKOYO,** lieutenant commander and ship's chief medical officer. Former Norman mercenary recruited during the Pharos affair.

—**TOR VARRO,** Chalcenterite scholiast and scientific advisor.

Certain junior officers:

—**PETROS OF PALLIOCH, CALLISTA OF ALTRIFAE,** and **DASCALU VOIVANEU,** lesser chiliarchs, the latter of Durantine origin.

—**CADE, DORAN,** and **ORO,** centurions under the command of Pallino of Trieste.

—**CASDON,** a lieutenant in the security department on the *Tamerlane*.

—**MALAG,** Siran's optio and second-in-command.

Certain enlisted men:

—**BARO, BREDA, TENNER, GAERT,** and **VIDAN,** soldiers under the command of Pallino of Trieste.

—**RENNA,** a soldier under the command of Pallino of Trieste.

—**ARDI,** an aquilarius.

—**MARTIN,** a batman in service to Hadrian Marlowe on the *Tamerlane*.

The Irchtani Auxiliary Unit:

BARDA, kithuun and chiliarch of the unit, an older Irchtani.

—His first centurion, **UDAX,** a brash young warrior.

—His compatriots, **GAARAN, IVAR,** and **LUEN.**

—His subordinate, **MORAG.**

THE AVENTINE DYNASTY & THE ETERNAL CITY

The planet Forum is an oddity: a gas giant, the presence of enormous, membranous creatures called pseudocnidae in the lower atmosphere has led to an enormous amount of nitrogen and carbon dioxide in the upper atmosphere. In time, terraforming efforts have made the planet's air breathable.

Construction on the Eternal City began early in the sixth millennium under the direction of Emperor Raphael IV while the Empire—and Avalon in particular—was still recovering from the devastation caused by Boniface Grael's brutal interregnum. The City itself comprises several thousand floating barges, each held up by repulsors and monstrous balloons that float atop the denser air at the bottom of the habitable layer of Forum's atmosphere. There is no place like it in all the universe. Each successive Emperor has added to its splendor until it sprawls across thousands of miles of open sky, all shielded by a series of cloth sails and Royse shields that protect it from the high-altitude winds. Nearly thirty billion people—nobiles, soldiers, servants, and court functionaries—call the city home, including the bulk of the Imperial family and the Emperor himself (with the rest remaining at the old capital on Avalon or else spread throughout the Imperium).

Here follows a list of those members of the Imperial Aventine House mentioned in this third volume of Lord Marlowe's account:

His Imperial Radiance, the **EMPEROR WILLIAM THE TWENTY-THIRD OF THE HOUSE AVENT;** Firstborn Son of the Earth; Guardian of the Solar System; King of Avalon; Lord Sovereign of the Kingdom of Windsor-in-Exile; Prince Imperator of the Arms of Orion, of Sagittarius, of Perseus, and Centaurus; Magnarch of Orion; Conqueror of Norma; Grand Stratego of the Legions of the Sun; Supreme Lord of the Cities of Forum; North Star of the Constellations of the Blood Palatine; Defender of the Children of Men; and Servant of the Servants of Earth.

—His wife, **EMPRESS MARIA AGRIPPINA AVENT,** Princess of Avalon, Archduchess of Shakespeare, and Mother of Light.

—Her friend, **LADY SIBYLLA,** a Jaddian *eali* noblewoman.

—Their children:

—**AURELIAN,** Crown Prince and firstborn child.

—**IRENE,** second-born child.

—**FAUSTINUS,** thirteenth-born child. Famously said to resemble Hadrian Marlowe.

—**MATTHIAS,** thirty-fourth-born child.

—**RICARD ANCHISES,** forty-seventh-born child.

—**PHILIP,** fifty-second-born child, a notorious gambler and womanizer.

—His servant, **IRSHAN,** a Jaddian Swordsmaster of the Fifth Circle, in the service of PRINCE PHILIP AVENT, formerly the *sulshawar* protector of the Jaddian PRINCE CONSTANS DU OLANTE.

—**ELEANOR,** seventy-seventh-born child.

—**ELARA,** seventy-eighth-born child.

—**SELENE,** ninety-ninth-born child, potentially betrothed to Hadrian Marlowe.

—Her handmaids, **CYNTHIA, KIRIA,** and **BAYARA.**

—**ALEXANDER,** one-hundred-seventh-born child and squire to Sir Hadrian Marlowe.

—**TITANIA,** one-hundred-eighteenth-born child.

—**VIVIENNE,** one-hundred-twenty-sixth-born child.

—His ancestor, {**KING WILLIAM VII WINDSOR**}, called **WILLIAM THE ADVENT,** the God Emperor, Emperor of Avalon and Eden, Last King of the United Kingdom of Great Britain, King-in-Avalon, and Lord Sovereign of the Kingdom of Windsor-in-Exile. The first Sollan Emperor, deified by the Chantry.

—His predecessor and mother, {**TITANIA AUGUSTA III**}, whose reign first brought humanity into contact with the Cielcin. Fondly remembered for her hawkish response to the crisis.

The Imperial Council:

—**PRINCE HECTOR AVENT,** Supreme Chancellor of the Imperial Council, Prince of Aeolus, a brother of the EMPEROR.

—**SYLVA,** the Chancellor's secretary.

—**LORD AUGUSTIN BOURBON,** Minister of War and member of the Lion Party. Son of the disgraced {PRINCE PHILIPPE BOURBON}, who attempted to usurp the rights of his late brother, {PRINCE LOUIS LIV}.

   —**SIR LORCAN BREATHNACH,** patrician, Director of the Legion Intelligence Office.

      —**SIR FRIEDRICH OBERLIN,** a junior functionary in the Legion Intelligence Office and possible member of the Halfmortal mystery cult.

      —**SIR GRAY RINEHART,** a logothete in the Legion Intelligence Office.

      —His cousin, **PRINCE CHARLES LIV BOURBON,** Lord of Verehaut, King of France, Duke of Anjou, Lion of Earth.

—**LORD ALLANDER PEAKE,** Minister of Justice, a member of the Lion Party.

—**LORD PETER HABSBURG,** Minister of Works, a member of the Lion Party.

—**LADY LEDA ASCANIA,** Minister of Public Enlightenment, a member of the Lion Party.

—**LORD HAREN BULSARA,** Director of the Colonial Office, a member of the Lion Party.

—**LADY MIANA HARTNELL,** Minister of Welfare.

—**LORD NOLAN CORDWAINER,** Minister of Revenue.

—**LORD CASSIAN POWERS,** Special Advisor on the Cielcin Question and Baron of Ashbless. The so-called Avenger of Cressgard, formerly a strategos in the Legions who led humanity to their first victory against the Cielcin in the Second Battle of Cressgard. A member of the Lion Party.

—His Holy Wisdom, **VERGILIAN XIII,** Synarch of the Holy Terran Chantry, First-Among-Equals of the Synod and the Choir, Grand Prior of Forum, Metropolitan High Priest of the Eternal City, and Speaker for the Vanished Earth.

Unnamed members of the Council:

—The **LORD MINISTER OF RITES**.

—The **DIRECTOR OF THE HOME OFFICE,** a member of the Lion Party.

Also in the Eternal City:

The **GRAND INQUISITOR,** a chief investigator of the Holy Office in Forum system.

—Her subordinate, **GEREON,** an Inquisitor.

PRINCE MARIUS HOHENZOLLERN, Lord of Swabian Prime, King of the Germans, King of Prussia and Brandenburg. A member of the Lion Party.

—His wife, **PRINCESS WILHELMINA HOHENZOLLERN.**

CARAX OF ARAMIS, a common legionnaire, veteran of the Battles of Aptucca and Hermonassa.

—His superior officer, {**PETER THAILLES**}, decurion, killed in the Battle of Hermonassa.

LORD ANDREW CURZON, a minor lord of House Curzon of Dhaka.

MANN, FEDER, CAMBIAS, CARRICO, MASSA, and **GANNON,** military officers and members of the War Ministry's offices on Forum.

ON GODODDIN

The planet Gododdin has been of strategic importance to the Sollan Empire's Colonial Office since humanity first began expanding into the Centaurus Arm of the galaxy. The Gododdin system lies midway between the Sagittarius and Centaurus Arms, in the midst of the great Sullen Gulf—an island on the otherwise decades-long route through empty space to the nearest settled system, making it an important trade hub and military base.

For this reason, it has remained under direct control of the Sollan Emperor, who appoints a governor-general to oversee the territory. It is famous for the role it played in the Cielcin Wars, where it was the site of Emperor William XXIII's last stand against the combined forces of the alien invaders—and the site of Hadrian Marlowe's great and terrible victory.

Here follows a list of those persons appearing on Gododdin in this third volume of Lord Marlowe's account:

LORD NICHOLAS AVENT, Governor-General of Gododdin, a cousin of the Emperor.

SIR AMALRIC OSMAN, Lord Castellan of Fort Din, supreme commander of the legionary forces in the Gododdin system.

—His Officers:

—**RUAN INSEN,** Strategos, Commandant of an orbital hospital and deployment station.

—**MAHENDRA VERUS,** Captain of the *ISV Mintaka.*

—**CORNELIUS ELDAN,** Captain of the *ISV Pride of Zama.*

—**WEN ADINA,** Captain of the *ISV Cyrusene.*

—**MAGNUS YANEK,** Captain of the *ISV Androzani.*

LODGE, a prisoner.

ON COLCHIS

Colchis is the primary moon of the planet SAG-8813D, colloquially known as Atlas. Human settlement on Colchis goes back to the fifth millennium ISD, following the Hundred Year Terror, in which House Avent was removed from the throne by Boniface the Pretender. In the wake of that civil war, the newly reinstated Emperor Gabriel II ordered the Imperial Archives moved from Avalon to the newly minted colony of Colchis, then a remote military outpost. Ever since, it has been the site of the Imperial Great Library and maintained by the scholiasts. Despite this crucial function, the rest of Colchis has remained relatively undeveloped, its human settlements scattered wildly across the planet's many little islands. Large-scale settlement of the moon is forbidden by Imperial decree, and those not living in the Library and in the capital city of Aea are mostly descended from those few settlers whose presence on Colchis predated the construction of the Library.

Here follows a list of those persons appearing on Colchis in this third volume of Lord Marlowe's account:

TOR ARRIAN, formerly **LORD MARCUS AVENT,** a cousin of the Emperor. Primate of Nov Belgaer athenaeum and master of the Imperial Library.

—His daughter, **SISTER EKATERIN,** an intus and palatine bastard. Serves as the primate's secretary.

TOR GIBSON OF SYRACUSE, an archivist. Former tutor to House Marlowe of Delos and something of a father figure to Hadrian. Banished from Delos for abetting Hadrian's escape from his father.

—**SISTER CARINA,** a junior archivist.

BROTHER VAN, a novice training to be a scholiast.

TOR IMLARROS, a scholiast specializing in engineering tasked with the maintenance of the gates.

{**TOR ARAMINI**}, ancient architect of the Great Library, the brother of Emperor Gabriel II.

LEM, a fisherman. The eolderman of the village of Racha.

HORIZON, a Mericanii artificial intelligence.

ON BERENIKE

The planet Berenike was first colonized by the Sollan Empire in ISD 13112 with the assistance of the Wong-Hopper Consortium. A tectonically dead world dominated by flatlands and shallow, algae-rich seas, the planet was an important mining colony and transit hub during the early phases of Sollan expansion into the Veil of Marinus, as well as a base of Legion operations during the wars of annexation between the empire and various freeholder territories. Due to its lack of mountains, enormous coriolis storms whip up around the equatorial regions, with winds reaching an excess of two hundred miles per hour quite regularly, forcing the planet's settlements to be either underground or—in the case of Deira, the planet's only major city—built into the planet's largest canyon, the *Valles Merguli*. The so-called Valley of the Diver follows the track of the Mergo River from its headwaters down to the sea.

Berenike was never given over to a nobile house and remains a holding of the Solar Throne, and as such is ruled by a governor-general appointed by the Imperial Council. It fell from prominence after the conquest of Marinus shifted Imperial focus in the region, but remains a well-trafficked port on the route from the inner empire to the frontier.

LORD TITUS HAUPTMANN, Duke of Andernach and First Strategos of the Legions of Centaurus.

—His counselor, **TOR JEANNE,** a scholiast.

—**LEONID BARTOSZ,** Legate of the 437th Centaurine Legion.

—**BASSANDER LIN,** a captain of the 437th Legion and former Commandant of the Red Company.

—**CORRAN,** another Legion legate.

BANCROFT, Commandant of the Berenike Orbital Defense Force.

THE CIELCIN AND THEIR ALLIES

Se Vattayu, the homeworld of the Cielcin, has never been found. The Pale are a nomadic race, long since having abandoned any attempts to settle other worlds. Preferring instead to live in migratory clusters of starships that move from system to system in their constant forage for meat and resources, they have never stopped for long. Each fleet is its own nation bound together by blood and absolute subservience to their clan chiefs, the Aeta. For centuries, these countless tribes have assailed human space and the Sollan Empire in particular, pillaging without plan.

The Aeta Syriani Dorayaica was different. A keen student of human culture and strategy, the Aeta altered the face of the Cielcin Wars by making a series of calculated strategic attacks: crippling military production and fuel refineries, attacking supply lines, and making forays far deeper into Imperial space than any Cielcin clan previously. Imperial intelligence suggests the Aeta has gone to war with the other xenobite clans, and that it intends to make itself a king.

Here follows a list of those Cielcin mentioned in this third volume of Lord Marlowe's account:

SYRIANI DORAYAICA, the Prophet of the Cielcin and Prince of Princes. Shiomu. Aeta-ba-Aetane. Blood of Elu. Blessed of Miudanar. Master of the Thirteen Tribes of Eue. Called the Scourge of Earth by the humans. A Cielcin conqueror responsible for the lion's share of all Cielcin attacks on human and imperial space in the last several centuries, considered the greatest threat to the Empire.

—Its generals, the **IEDYR YEMANI:**

    —**IUBALU,** the Four-Handed. One of Syriani's vayadan, its servant and concubine, converted into a half-machine chimera with the aid of MINOS. Commander of the fleet at the Battle of the Beast.

    —**BAHUDDE,** the Giant. One of Syriani's vayadan, its servant and concubine. Converted into a half-machine chimera with the aid of MINOS. Commander of the vanguard at the Battle of Berenike.

    —**GORABA,** a common soldier.

—Its human allies:

    —**URBAINE,** a MINOS scientist.

    —**SEVERINE,** a MINOS scientist whom Hadrian Marlowe encountered on Arae.

KOLERITAN and **HASURUMN,** the chieftain princes of two other clans.

{ARANATA OTIOLO}, former Aeta of the Otiolo clan, killed by Hadrian Marlowe at the battle aboard the *Demiurge*.

—Its child, **{NOBUTA OTIOLO}**, killed by Hadrian Marlowe at the battle aboard the *Demiurge*.

—Its servants:

—**{CASANTORA TANARAN IAKATO}**, a baetan, priest-historian of its clan.

—**{ITANA UVANARI AYATOMN}**, ichakta, captain of the ill-fated Cielcin expedition to Emesh.

{VENATIMN ULURANI}, former Aeta of the Ulurani clan, killed by Hadrian Marlowe in single combat at the Battle of Aptucca, allowing a nearly bloodless human victory.

{ELU}, a mythical figure. According to legend, the Cielcin High King who first brought its tribe into space.

THE WIDER WORLD

Many persons appearing or referenced in this volume do not belong to any of the groups referenced above. These have been divided by location where possible, including the planets Vorgossos and Delos, the Principalities of Jadd, and the Kingdom of Latarra.

Here follows a list of all those persons mentioned in this third volume of Lord Marlowe's account not tied to the above locations:

KHARN SAGARA, called the UNDYING, King of Vorgossos. Presumably the same Kharn Sagara from ancient legend, making him more than fifteen thousand years old. Last seen divided into two bodies.

—His children: **{SUZUHA}** and **{REN}**, both clones. Dead; the mind and personality of Kharn Sagara has possessed both of their bodies.

—**BRETHREN,** a Mericanii artificial intelligence composed of human tissue confined to the underground sea beneath Vorgossos.

—**CALVERT,** Exalted magus in charge of the cloning program and body farms of Vorgossos.

—His servant, **YUME,** a golem or android.

LORD ALISTAIR DIOMEDES FRIEDRICH MARLOWE, Archon of Meidua Prefecture and Lord of Devil's Rest, former Lord Executor of Delos System, and Butcher of Linon. Hadrian's father.

—His wife, **LADY LILIANA KEPHALOS-MARLOWE,** a celebrated librettist and filmmaker.

—Their other children:

—**CRISPIN ORESTES MARLOWE,** presumptive heir to Devil's Rest.

—**SABINE DORYSSA MARLOWE,** a daughter born to replace Hadrian after his exile.

—His castellan, **SIR FELIX MARTYN,** Commander of the House Guard and Master-at-Arms in charge of instructing the Marlowe children.

—His counselor, **TOR ALCUIN,** a scholiast.

SIR OLORIN MILTA, a Jaddian Maeskolos of the Ninth Circle and the *sulshawar* protector of LADY KALIMA DI SAYYIPH.

—His lieutenant, **JINAN AZHAR,** Hadrian Marlowe's former lover.

CALEN HARENDOTES, the so-called MONARCH of Latarra, an Extrasolarian warlord gathering power in the Veil of Marinus.

EDOUARD ALBÉ, an Imperial intelligence officer.

INDEX OF WORLDS

HEREIN IS APPENDED A list of all those worlds mentioned in this third volume of Lord Marlowe's account. The purpose of this list is simply to remind the reader which world is which. Detailed astrographic and geological documents—as well as economic and historical texts—may be found elsewhere in the library. What information I have provided is all that is necessary to understand Lord Marlowe's text.

—Tor Paulos of Nov Belgaer

Algernon   A Norman freehold world located very close to Marinus.

Annica   An airless world orbiting a red dwarf somewhere on the far side of the galactic core, apparently connected to the Quiet.

Aptucca   An Imperial colony in the Veil of Marinus in the Norma Arm, site of the defeat of the Cielcin Prince Ulurani in single combat by Hadrian Marlowe.

Arae   Site of a battle in the Cielcin Wars where Hadrian Marlowe discovered evidence of an alliance between the Cielcin and Extrasolarian humans.

Aramis   An Imperial agricultural colony in Sagittarius. Its star is dim, so it uses orbital mirrors to intensify the sunlight and make the planet livable.

Arcturus   A red giant star near to Old Earth. With no planets, it is nevertheless the home of the Wong-Hopper Consortium's core space habitats and is their base of operation.

Argissa   Site of an early battle in the Cielcin Wars, an Imperial colony in the Veil of Marinus.

Ashbless   A minor colony in the Centaurine provinces most famous as the birthplace of Sir Cassian Powers.

Atlanta   An ancient Mericanii colony.

Avalon   One of the original human colonies, site of heavy European colonization by generation ark. Birthplace of the Sollan Empire.

Baltimore   An ancient Mericanii colony.

Bargovrin   An Imperial colony in the Centaurine provinces, site of a brutal defeat of humanity by the Cielcin in the Crusades.

Belusha   The most famous of the Imperial prison planets, the last destination of many political prisoners. A dismal, cold world.

Berenike   A former trading hub and mining colony on the Centaurine frontier on the border with the Veil of Marinus, site of a major battle in the Cielcin Wars.

Cai Shen   An ethnically Mandari world in the Imperium, famed for its Bashang Temple. It was ruled by House Min Chen up until ISD 16130, when it was destroyed by the Cielcin.

Car-Tannae   An Imperial colony on the outer rim of the galaxy in the Perseus Arm. Its gladiators are famous for fighting with nets and spears.

Caritas   The home of the New Vatican and central world of the Museum Catholic Church, windy and twilit.

Cellas   Site of a major battle during the Cielcin Wars.

Centaurus Arm The innermost and farthest of the four arms of the galaxy colonized by the Sollan Empire, north of Sagittarius, Orion, and Perseus. Most Centaurine provinces are clustered near the heart of the galaxy, just south of the Veil of Marinus and the galactic core.

Colchis	The first Imperial colony in the Centaurus Arm, named for the garden at the end of the world, a moon of the gas giant Atlas. Never an important colony (it was eclipsed quickly by its neighbors), it is known for the massive scholiast athenaeum of Nov Belgaer.
Cressgard	A lost Imperial colony in the Veil of Marinus, site of the first contact with the Cielcin at the Battle of Cressgard in ISD 15792.
Delos	Birthplace of Hadrian Marlowe and seat of the Duchy of House Kephalos in the Spur of Orion, a temperate world with wan sunlight, famed for its uranium deposits, which made it extremely wealthy.
Denver	An ancient Mericanii colony.
Dharan-Tun	A Cielcin worldship larger than some moons, the seat of Prince Syriani Dorayaica.
Dion Station	An Imperial refueling outpost on the route from Gododdin across the gap between the Sagittarius and Centaurus Arms of the galaxy.
Edda	An arid, windy world in the Demarchy known for its canyons, sinkholes, and subterranean oceans. Its people are primarily ethnic Nordei and Travatskr.
Emesh	A watery world in the Veil of Marinus, seat of House Mataro. Home of the coloni Umandh and the subterranean ruins at Calagah. Originally a Norman colony.
Forum	The capital of the Sollan Empire. A gas giant with a breathable atmosphere in whose cloud belt are several flying palace cities that serve as the administrative hub of the Imperium.
Gododdin	A system between the Centaurus and Sagittarius Arms of the galaxy, famously destroyed by Hadrian Marlowe during the final battle in the Crusade.
Hermonassa	An Imperial world in the Sagittarine provinces, the site of a major Red Star Foundries Legion shipyard. Destroyed by Syriani Dorayaica in the Cielcin Wars.
Jadd	The planet of fire, sacred capital of the Jaddian Principalities, on whose soil none shall tread without the express permission of the High Prince.
Judecca	A frigid, mountainous world in the Sagittarius Arm. Famously the site of the Temple of Athten Var and birthplace of the Irchtani species. Site of Simeon the Red's struggle against the mutineers, a famous story.
Kandar	An extremely wealthy agricultural world in the inner Empire, frequently considered the definitive source for luxury products, especially wine and genuine livestock. Seat of House Markarian.
Lasaia	An Imperial colony in the Orion provinces, the site of a major Red Star Foundries Legion shipyard, like Hermonassa.
Lassira	An old Imperial world in the Orion provinces, the seat of one branch of House Curzon.
Latarra	A former Norman Freehold in the Veil conquered by the Monarch, Calen Harendotes, an Extrasolarian warlord.

Luin	A planet famous for its xenobitic forests, considered something of a fantasy land. Known for the phasma vigrandi, a species of floating organism that glows like faerie lights.
Marinus	The first Norman Freehold seized by the Imperium and amongst their first colonies in the Expanse. The Imperial capital in the Veil of Marinus.
Mars	One of Old Earth's sister planets and the site of the first major offworld colonial efforts during the Exodus but before the Peregrinations.
Monmara	A water world and a Norman freehold, known for the cheap mass production of starships.
Nagapur	A trading hub on the old core-roads from the Orion provinces out toward Centaurus and the Veil.
Nagramma	A Norman freehold settled primarily by Cid Arthurian religious refugees.
Nemavand	An Imperial colony in Rammanu Province on the Centaurine frontier.
Norman Expanse	See VEIL OF MARINUS. The terms are used interchangeably, though the Veil moniker is more common in the Empire, while the Normans refer to it as the Expanse.
Old Earth	Birthplace of the human species. A nuclear ruin and victim of environmental collapse, she is protected by the Chantry Wardens and none may walk there.
Olympia	An ancient Mericanii colony.
Orion Arm	The first arm of the galaxy settled by humankind, site of Old Earth. North of Perseus, but south of Sagittarius and Centaurus. Comprises the core of the Sollan Empire, including Forum and Delos.
Orlando	An ancient Mericanii colony.
Oxiana	The site of a minor battle in the Cielcin Wars.
Ozymandias	Old Imperial colony in the Sagittarius Arm, arid. Known for being home to the extinct Arch-Builders, and for the massive stone arches they purportedly left behind.
Pagus Minor	One of the Sollan Empire's prison planets.
Patmos	A planet and grand duchy in the Orion provinces, famously the birthplace of Hadrian Marlowe's friend, Lorian Aristedes.
Perfugium	A colonial distribution center in the Centaurine provinces, the home of billions of sleeping human colonists. The site of a major battle in the Cielcin Wars.
Perseus Arm	The outermost of the four settled arms of the galaxy, comprising most of the outer rim territories. Variously settled by the Sollan Empire, the Principalities of Jadd, the Durantine Republic, and various freeholder colonies and smaller states not annexed or allied with a greater power.
Pharos	A Norman freehold ruled for a time by Marius Whent, an ex-Imperial legate defeated by Hadrian Marlowe during his time as a mercenary.

Ramannu An Imperial colony on the Centaurine frontier, right on the border with the Veil of Marinus.

Renaissance One of the most populous worlds in the Empire, located in the Spur of Orion. A cultural center almost entirely covered by urban development. Formerly a Mericanii colony called Yellowstone, located in the Epsilon Eridani system.

Rubicon An Imperial planet bearing the signs of an extinct xenobite civilization.

Rustam An Imperial colony in the Norman Expanse, site of a minor engagement with the Cielcin that culminated in the destruction of its capital city.

Sadal Suud A wild world in the Spur of Orion, kept mostly untrammeled. Home to the Cavaraad Giants, a huge species of xenobite, as well as to the Marching Towers, one of the Ninety-Nine Wonders of the Universe. Ruled by House Rodolfo.

Sagittarius Arm The second arm of the galaxy colonized by humanity, north of Orion but south of Centaurus. Comprises the core of the Sollan Empire—along with Orion—but the Lothrian Commonwealth constitutes a large portion of its western frontier.

Senuessa A Sagittarine world, site of the Battle of Senuessa, one of the bloodiest in the entirety of the Cielcin Wars.

Shakespeare A planet and archduchy in the Orion provinces held by the Aventine House.

Sinara Site of a battle during the Cielcin Wars.

Teukros A desert world in the Imperium, notably the site of the scholiasts' athenaeum at Nov Senber.

Thagura Site of a major battle in the Cielcin Wars.

Utah An ancient Mericanii colony.

Veil of Marinus The region of space at the base of the Norma Arm of the galaxy where it joins the galactic core. Formerly a colonial expansion region dominated by the Sollan Empire and Norman Freeholders, it is also the site of most Cielcin incursions into human space.

Vorgossos A mythical Extrasolarian world orbiting a brown dwarf, said to be a mecca for the black market genetics trade. Formerly a hideout for the Exalted, presided over now by a warlord known as the Undying.

LEXICON

HEREIN IS INCLUDED AN index of those terms appearing in this third volume of Lord Marlowe's manuscript which are not easily translated into the Classical English or which bear a specific cultural or technical definition. For a more complete explanation of the methodology I employed in devising these coinages in translating from the Galstani in which the original was written, please refer to the appendices in volume one of this translation.

—Tor Paulos of Nov Belgaer

adamant   Any of the various long-chain carbon materials used for starship hulls and body armor.

adorator   A member of any antique religious cult maintained by the Empire and tolerated by the Chantry.

Aeta   A Cielcin prince-chieftain. Appears to have ownership rights over its subjects and their property.

Aeta Ba-Aetane   The Cielcin Prince of Princes. A rare title reserved for those Aeta who conquer and subordinate another Aeta without killing it.

akaranta   The dominant Cielcin sexual role.

androgyn   A homunculus exhibiting either neither or both male and female sex characteristics.

annuid   In the scholiast order, a practitioner who has sworn him or herself to the order for a standard year.

apatheia   The emotionless state pursued by the scholiasts to facilitate their computation function. Has roots in classical Stoicism.

aquilarius   A fighter pilot.

Arch-Builders   Extinct species of coloni xenobite native to the planet Ozymandias. So called for the massive structures built above the plains of their home.

Archprior   Within the Chantry clergy, a senior prior, usually one entrenched in the Chantry bureaucracy.

armsman   Any individual—usually patrician—sworn to serve the person of a palatine lord or his/her house in perpetuity.

auctor   An office appointed by the Emperor to serve as his proxy, to speak with his voice and authority in matters where the Emperor cannot be present.

auxilia   A soldier or unit of soldiers—usually volunteered—attached to the Legions without being a formal part of the Legion structure. Often, auxiliary units are non-citizens looking to obtain citizenship.

azhdarch   A xenobite predator common in the Colosso, like a lizard with a long neck open from top to bottom in a fanged mouth.

baetan   In Cielcin culture, a sort of priest-historian of the scianda.

bastille   Any Chantry judicial and penal center, usually attached to a temple sanctum.

bromos   A protein-rich strain of engineered hyper-oat that serves as the basis for ration bars and as protein base for artificial meat production.

castellan   The chief military officer on a nobile estate, tasked with the defense of the castle and holdings. Usually a knight.

cathar   A surgeon-torturer employed by the Holy Terran Chantry.

centennid   In scholiast life, any member of the order who has sworn him or herself to service for one hundred years. Often a monastic.

centurion   A rank in the Imperial Legions, commands a CENTURY.

century   In the Imperial Legions, a unit comprising ten decades (100 men).

Chalcenterite   A fraternal order of the scholiasts, noted for their asceticism.

Chantry   The Holy Terran Chantry, state religion of the Empire. Functions as the judicial arm of the state, especially where the use of forbidden technology is involved.

chiliad   In the Imperial Legions, a unit comprising ten centuries (1000 men).

chiliarch   A rank in the Imperial Legions, commands a CHILIAD.

chimera   Any genetically altered or artificially created animal, usually by blending the genetic code of two or more animals.

Choir   The CHANTRY's clandestine research and intelligence division.

Cielcin   Spacefaring alien species. Humanoid and carnivorous.

cohort   In the Imperial Legions, a unit comprising six chiliads (6000 men).

Colosso   A series of sporting events held in a coliseum involving professional gladiators, slave myrmidons, animals, races, and more.

colossus   Any huge mobile artillery unit, especially those designed to walk on legs. May be several hundred feet tall.

consortation   One of the TWELVE ABOMINATIONS. Conversing with or having similar contact with artificial intelligence, even unknowingly.

Consortium   The Wong-Hopper Consortium. The largest of the Mandari interstellar corporations, specializing in terraforming technologies.

constellation   Among the palatine, a super-group of interrelated families, usually possessed of certain signifying features and traits.

cornicen   In the Legions, a soldier tasked with playing the horn or trumpet at parades.

coteliho   In Cielcin culture, roughly equivalent to a Lord's herald or majordomo.

cryoburn   Burns incurred as a side effect of improper cryonic freezing.

cubiculum   A chamber where persons are kept in cryonic fugue, usually aboard a starship.

daimon   An artificial intelligence. Sometimes erroneously applied to non-intelligent computer systems.

datanet   The loose association of all planetary dataspheres connected by quantum telegraphs and inter-space satellite relays.

datasphere   Any planetary data network. In the Empire, access is strictly restricted to the patrician and palatine caste.

decade   In the Imperial Legions, a unit of ten soldiers comprising three groups of three and their decurion.

decurion — A rank in the Imperial Legions, commands a DECADE.

Demarchy of Tavros — A small interstellar polity found in the Wisp. Radically open to technology, the people vote on all measures using neural lace implants.

demoniac — A person who has incorporated machines into their body, particularly with the intent of altering their cognitive processes.

dispholide — A rare hemotoxic poison, likely of Chantry design and manufacture, that disables the coagulation process and dissolves collagen and even bone at an astonishing rate, effectively liquefying the victim.

Druaja — A board game, sometimes called labyrinth chess.

dryad — Any of a species of green-skinned homunculi capable of photosynthesis, designed for work in outer space.

duplication — One of the TWELVE ABOMINATIONS. The copying of an individual's genetics, likeness, personality, or memories through cloning or related practices.

Durantine Republic — An interstellar republic of some three thousand worlds. Pays tribute to the Empire.

Eali — The Jaddian ruling caste, product of intense eugenic development. Practically superhuman.

Emperor — The supreme ruler of the Sollan Empire, considered a god and the reincarnation of his/her predecessor. Holds absolute power.

energy-lance — A bladed spear with a high-energy laser built into the shaft. Used as formal weapons by guards, especially in the Imperium.

entoptics — Augmented reality device where images are projected directly onto the retina.

eolderman — The elected head of a plebeian community. Typically seen in more rural regions on Imperial planets.

Eudoran — Any of the spacefaring bands claiming descent from the failed colony on Europa in Old Earth's system. An ethnic group known for their interstellar wanderings.

Exalted — A faction among the Extrasolarians noted for their extreme cybernetic augmentations.

Excubitor — The innermost circle of the Emperor's guard, comprising 108 of the finest knights and fighters in the Empire.

Exodus — The expansionist period following the environmental collapse of Earth. The Peregrinations from Old Earth System before the Foundation War.

Expeditionary Corps — Branch of the Imperial Legions tasked with exploring the galaxy and with laying the groundwork for colonization.

Extrasolarian — Any of the barbarians living outside Imperial control, often possessing illegal praxis.

extraterranic — In terraforming and ecology, refers to any organism not of Old Earth extraction. Extraterrestrial.

Foundation War — The war between the early Empire and the Mericanii, in which the Mericanii were destroyed and the Sollan Empire founded.

Galstani — The common language of the Sollan Empire, descended from Classical English, with heavy Hindi and Franco-Germanic influences.

glowsphere — A spherical, bright light source floating on Royse repulsors, battery- or chemically powered.

God Emperor — The first Sollan Emperor, William I, who defeated the Mericanii. It is believed his return will usher in a new Golden Age for the Empire.

golem — A mechanical being fashioned in the shape of a man, containing no organic parts.

High College — Imperial political office tasked with reviewing palatine requests for children and with overseeing the pregnancies of same. Prevents mutations.

highmatter — A form of exotic matter produced by alchemists. Used to make the swords of Imperial knights, which can cut almost anything.

hightower — An elevator designed to lift cargo from the surface of a planet to orbit and vice versa.

homunculus — Any artificial human or near-human, especially those grown for a task, or for aesthetic purposes.

hoplite — A shielded foot soldier. Heavy infantry.

hoplon — An antique-style round shield, used in the Colosso.

hurasam — Gilded coin used among the Imperial peasant classes, worth their mark-weight in gold. Print notes for various denominations exist.

hypogeum — The underground maintenance complex beneath a coliseum. More generally, any underground complex.

ice — In computing, software designed to monitor traffic in and out of a system and to prevent access based on perceived threat.

ichakta — A Cielcin title, referring to the captain of a ship.

Iedyr Yemani — The six *vayadan*-generals sworn in fanatic servitude to Syriani Dorayaica. The so-called White Hand.

ietumna — The submissive Cielcin sexual role.

Imperium — See SOLLAN EMPIRE.

indoctrination — The process by which a person is treated with specially tailored RNA packets to learn and absorb new information and skills quickly.

infestation — In Chantry religious law, the state in which a computer system may contain elements of artificial intelligence or the precursors to same, often leading to POSSESSION.

inmane — An offensive slur meaning that someone is less than human. Literally *impure*.

Inquisition   The judicial branch of the Imperial Chantry, primarily concerned with the use of illegal technologies.

Inquisitor   A Chantry official tasked with conducting judicial investigations and overseeing the torture of criminals.

intus   A palatine born outside the oversight of the High College, usually possessing several physical or psychological defects; a bastard.

Irchtani   Species of coloni xenobite native to the planet Judecca. Bird-like with massive wings. Considered an exemplar of coloni assimilation.

kaspum   Silver-plated coin used among the Imperial peasant classes. Twelve kaspums make one gold hurasam. Print notes for various denominations exist.

kithuun   In Irchtani culture, a tribal chieftain or military commander.

knife-missile   A kind of drone, little more than a remote-controlled flying knife. A favorite of assassins.

knight   Sollan military honor conferred by the nobility for services rendered; usually includes a small fief. May carry highmatter weapons.

legate   A rank in the Imperial Legions, commands an entire Legion.

Legions   The military branch of the Sollan Empire, loyal directly to the Emperor and Imperial house, comprising naval and ground forces.

Legion Intelligence Office   The Empire's military intelligence, espionage, and foreign intervention agency.

legionnaire   Any soldier in the Imperial Legions, especially the common foot soldier.

lictor   A bodyguard for a nobile or other dignitary. Usually a knight.

light-probe   Any of a class of very small, ultralight reconnaissance devices propelled by shipboard laser to nearly the speed of light.

lighter   Any starship small enough to make landfall on a planet.

Lions   An unofficial political party in the Sollan Empire, comprising the more conservative royalist houses.

logothete   A minister in any of the governmental agencies of any palatine house, used colloquially of any civil servant.

Lothrian Commonwealth   The second largest human polity in the galaxy, a totalitarian collectivist state. Longtime antagonist of the Empire.

Maeskolos   One of the legendary Swordmasters of Jadd, drawn exclusively from the eali caste. Credited with superhuman speed and skill.

Magnarch   The chief Imperial Viceroy in each arm of the galaxy: Orion, Sagittarius, Perseus, and Centaurus. Essentially co-Emperors.

Makers   A pantheon of gods worshiped by the Cielcin, possibly the same as the WATCHERS.

mamluk	Any homunculus slave-soldier of the Jaddian Principalities.
Mandari	An ethnic group semi-detached from Imperial society, most commonly found staffing the massive interstellar trading corporations.
mandyas	Traditional garment of the Maeskoloi. Half a robe with one flowing sleeve worn over the left shoulder, cinched at the waist.
Martian Guard	The Emperor's palace guard, an elite corp of soldiers raised from the population on Earth's nearest neighbor, Mars.
medica	A hospital, typically aboard a starship.
megathere	A massive, three-eyed amphibious predator native to the planet Epidamnus.
Mericanii	The ancient first interstellar colonists. A hyper-advanced technologic civilization run by artificial intelligences. Destroyed by the Empire.
Messer/Madam	Polite address in the Empire, used of anyone without formal title.
Museum Catholic Church	An adorator cult centered on the planet Caritas, believed to have existed since the Golden Age of Earth and protected on reservations by Imperial decree.
myrmidon	In the Colosso, any contract or slave fighter not a professionally trained gladiator.
nahute	A Cielcin weapon. Resembles a flying metal snake. Seeks out targets and drills into them.
natalist	A specialist practiced in the art of growing and gene-crafting living organisms, human or otherwise.
nobile	Blanket term referring to any member of the palatine and patrician castes in the Sollan Empire.
Nordei	The principle language of the Demarchy. A patois of Nordic and Thai with some Slavic influences.
Norman Expanse	The frontier of human settlement in the Norma Arm of the Milky Way, near to the galactic core.
novice	A student initiated into the rites and curricula of the scholiasts with the intention of becoming one.
nuncius	In Imperial society, an announcer or herald.
Orbital Defense Force	The fleet maintained by any palatine lord for the defense of his or her planet or system.
outcaste	In Imperial society, any former member of the palatine or patrician castes stripped of their station. May also refer to similar persons in Jadd.
palatine	The Imperial aristocracy, descended from those free humans who opposed the Mericanii. Genetically enhanced, they may live for several centuries.
Pale	The Cielcin. Slang, considered offensive by xenophiles.

panegyrist	A Chantry priest tasked with performing the call to prayer at sundown.
Panthai	A Tavrosi language descended from the Thai, Lao, and Khmer-speaking peoples who settled the Wisp alongside the Nordei.
patrician	Any plebeian or plutocrat awarded with genetic augmentations at the behest of the palatine caste as a reward for services rendered.
Peregrination	Any of the historical evacuations from Earth's system for the extrasolar colonies.
phase disruptor	A sort of firearm that attacks the nervous system. Can stun on lower settings.
phylactery	A device for storing the genetic and epigenetic information of an individual for the purposes of artificial reproduction.
plasma burner	A firearm which uses a strong loop of magnetic force to project an arc of super-heated plasma across short to moderate distances.
plebeian	The Imperial peasantry, descended from unaltered human stock seeded on the oldest colony ships. Forbidden to use high technology.
poine	A structured, small-scale war carried out between imperial palatine houses. Subject to the scrutiny of the Inquisition.
possession	One of the TWELVE ABOMINATIONS. The state in which an individual or computer system is under the sway of an artificial intelligence.
praxis	High technology, usually of the sort forbidden by Chantry law.
primate	The highest administrative office of a scholiasts' athenaeum, akin to a university chancellor.
profanation	One of the TWELVE ABOMINATIONS. The mingling of human flesh with machine implants or prostheses, especially in cases where such modifications transcend ordinary human function.
Protocols	The strict guidelines outlining the behaviors of the Chantry's INQUISITION in carrying out an investigation.
Quiet	The hypothetical first civilization in the galaxy, allegedly responsible for several ancient sites, including those on Emesh, Judecca, Sadal Suud, and Ozymandias.
repulsor	A device which makes use of the Royse Effect to allow objects to float without disturbing the air or environment.
satrap	A planetary governor in the Principalities of Jadd, subordinate to one of the regional Princes.
scahari	In Cielcin culture, the warrior caste.
scholiast	Any member of the monastic order of researchers, academics, and theoreticians tracing their origins to the Mericanii scientists captured at the end of the Foundation War.
scianda	*Pl. sciandane.* A Cielcin migratory fleet, comprising several *itanimn* and presided over by a single Aeta.

sirrah	An honorific used to refer to one's social inferiors, usually males.
Sojourner	Any of a class of massive Extrasolarian starship, often hundreds of miles long, especially those crewed by the EXALTED.
Sollan Empire	The largest and oldest single polity in human-controlled space, comprising some half a billion habitable planets
SOM	The lobotomized shell of a human being animated by machines, used for slave labor and as soldiers by the Extrasolarians.
strategos	An admiral in the Imperial Legions, responsible for the command of an entire fleet, comprising several legions.
Stricture	The formal rules governing the lifestyle and behavior of those members of the scholiast order as outlined in *The Book of the Mind* and the rest of Imore's writings.
sulshawar	In Jaddian culture, a warrior who serves as bodyguard to a prince, satrap, or other important personage. May also represent that person in legal duels. Comparable to a lictor.
Summerfair	A common midsummer holiday celebrated throughout the Imperium. Its date varies from world to world, depending on the local calendar.
suppression field	A Royse Effect field designed to simulate gravity.
Synarch	The highest ecclesiastic office of the Imperial Chantry. Their most important function is the coronation of new Emperors.
Tavrosi	Any of the languages from the Demarchy of Tavros. Typically refers to Nordei.
terranic	In terraforming and ecology, refers to any organism of Old Earth extraction. Not extraterrestrial.
trias	A unit of three legionnaires, usually two peltasts and one hoplite.
triaster	The commander of a trias, usually a shielded hoplite.
Twelve Abominations	The twelve most grievous sins according to the Chantry. Legal privileges do not apply in such cases.
Udaritanu	A complex, non-linear writing system used by the Cielcin.
Umandh	A coloni species native to the planet Emesh. Amphibious and tripedal, they have an intelligence comparable to that of dolphins.
vayadan	In Cielcin culture, the bound mates and bodyguards of an Aeta.
verrox	A powerful pseudoamphetamine derived from the leaves of the verroca plant. It is taken by ingesting the leaves, which are usually candied.
Victorian Knights	An order of Imperial knights bound in service to the person of the Emperor and the Aventine House directly, not to the Imperial Office.
Watchers	According to this account, a species or collection of powerful xenobites, possibly worshiped as gods by the Cielcin and other alien races.

worldship   Any of the massive Cielcin vessels—some as large as moons—which make up the core of their fleets.

Writ of Nativity   A formal petition—or grant of said petition—enabling a palatine lord of the Sollan Empire to produce a child under the auspices of the High College.

xenobite   Any life form not originating in terranic or human stock, especially those life forms which are considered intelligent; an alien.

zitraa   The traditional weapon of an Irchtani warrior. A thin, curved cutlass approximately seven feet long.